Robert Asprin's

∂MYTH∞ ADVENTURES

VOLUME ONE

Meisha Merlin Publishing, Inc.
Atlanta, GA

This book is printed on an acid-free and buffered paper that meets the NISO standard ANSI/NISO Z39.48-1992, Permanence of Paper for Publications and Documents in Libraries and Archives.

Published by Meisha Merlin Publishing, Inc.
PO Box 7
Decatur, GA   30031

Editing by Stephen Pagel
Interior layout by Lynn Swetz
Cover art and interior illustrations by Phil Foglio
Cover design by Kevin Murphy

ISBN: Hard Cover   1-59222-110-6
ISBN: Soft Cover   1-59222-111-4

First MM Publishing edition: July 2006

Printed in Canada
0 9 8 7 6 5 4 3 2 1

TABLE OF CONTENTS

LOOK FOR THESE TITLES IN VOLUME TWO

M.Y.T.H. Inc. Link

Myth-Nomers and Im-Pervections

M.Y.T.H. Inc. In Action

Sweet Myth-tery of Life

Myth-ion Improbable

Something M.Y.T.H. Inc.

Another Fine Myth

I.

"There are things on heaven and earth, Horatio, Man was not meant to know."
HAMLET

ONE OF THE *few redeeming facets of instructors,* I thought, *is that occasionally they can be fooled. It was true when my Mother taught me to read, it was true when my Father tried to teach me to be a farmer, and it's true now when I'm learning magik.*

"You haven't been practicing!" Garkin's harsh admonishment interrupted my musings.

"I have too!" I protested. "It's just a difficult exercise."

As if in response, the feather I was levitating began to tremble and wobble in midair.

"You aren't concentrating!" he accused.

"It's the wind," I argued. I wanted to add "from your loud mouth," but didn't dare. Early in our lessons Garkin had demonstrated his lack of appreciation for cheeky apprentices.

"The wind," he sneered, mimicking my voice. "Like this, dolt!"

My mental contact with the object of my concentration was interrupted as the feather darted suddenly toward the ceiling. It jarred to a halt as if it had become embedded in something, though it was still a foot from the wooden beams, then slowly rotated to a horizontal plane. Just as slowly it rotated on its axis, then swapped ends and began to glide around an invisible circle like a leaf caught in an eddy.

I risked a glance at Garkin. He was draped over his chair, feet dangling, his entire attention apparently devoted to devouring a leg of roast lizard-bird. A bird I had snared, I might add. Concentration indeed!

He looked up suddenly and our eyes met. It was too late to look away so I simply looked back at him.

"Hungry?" His grease-flecked salt-and-pepper beard was suddenly framing a wolfish grin. "Then show me how much you've been practicing."

It took me a heartbeat to realize what he meant; then I looked up desperately. The feather was tumbling floorward, a bare shoulder-height from landing. Forcing the sudden tension from my body, I reached out with my mind...gently...form a pillow...don't knock it away...

The feather halted a scant two hand-spans from the floor.

I heard Garkin's low chuckle, but didn't allow it to break my concentration. I hadn't let the feather touch the floor for three years and it wasn't going to touch now.

Slowly I raised it until it floated at eye level. Wrapping my mind around it, I rotated it on its axis, then enticed it to swap ends. As I led it through the exercise, its movement was not as smooth or sure as when Garkin set his mind to the task, but it did move unerringly in its assigned course.

Although I had not been practicing with the feather, I *had* been practicing. When Garkin was not about or was preoccupied with his own studies, I devoted most of my time to levitating pieces of metal keys, to be specific. Each type of levitation had its own inherent problems. Metal was hard to work with because it was an inert material. The feather, having once been part of a living thing, was more responsive...too responsive. To lift metal took effort; to maneuver a feather required subtlety. Of the two, I preferred to work with metal. I could see a more direct application of that skill in my chosen profession.

"Good enough, lad. Now put it back in the book."

I smiled to myself. This part I had practiced, not because of its potential applications, but because it was fun.

The book was lying open on the end of the workbench. I brought the feather down in a long lazy spiral, allowing it to pass lightly across the pages of the book and up in a swooping arc, stopped it, and brought it back. As it approached the book the second time, I disengaged part of my mind to dart ahead to the book. As the feather crossed the pages, the book snapped shut like the jaws of a hungry predator, trapping the missile within its grasp.

"Hmmmm..." intoned Garkin, "a trifle showy, but effective."

"Just a little something I worked up when I was practicing," I said casually, reaching out with my mind for the other lizard-bird leg. Instead of floating gracefully to my waiting hand, however, it remained on the wooden platter as if it had taken root.

"Not so fast, my little sneak-thief. So you've been practicing, eh?" He stroked his beard thoughtfully with the half-gnawed bone in his hand.

"Certainly. Didn't it show?" It occurred to me that Garkin is not as easy to fool as it sometimes seems.

"In that case, I'd like to see you light your candle. It should be easy if you have been practicing as much as you claim."

"I have no objections to trying, but, as you have said yourself so many times, some lessons come easier than others."

Although I sounded confident, my spirits sank as the large candle came floating to the work table in response to Garkin's summons. In four years of trying I was yet to be successful at this particular exercise. If Garkin was going to keep me from food until I was successful, I could go hungry for a long time.

"Say, uh, Garkin, it occurs to me I could probably concentrate better on a full stomach."

"It occurs to me that you're stalling."

"Couldn't I…"

"Now, Skeeve."

There was no swaying him once he used my proper name. That much I had learned over the years. Lad, Thief, Idiot, Turnip-Head, though derogatory, as long as he used one of these, his mind was still open. Once he reverted to using my proper name, it was hopeless. It is indeed a sorry state when the sound of your own name becomes a knell of doom.

Well, if there was no way around it, I'd just have to give it my best shot. For this there could be no half-effort or feigned concentration. I would have to use every ounce of my strength and skill to summon the power.

I studied the candle with a detached mind, momentarily blanking the effort ahead from my consciousness. The room, the cluttered workbench, Garkin, even my own hunger faded from view as I focused on the candle, though I had long since memorized its every feature.

It was stout, nearly six inches across to stabilize its ten-inch height. I had carved numerous mystic symbols into its surface, copied painstakingly from Garkin's books at his direction, though many of them were partially obliterated by hardened rivulets of wax. The candle had burned many long hours to light my studies, but it had always been lit from a taper from the cooking fire and not from my efforts.

Negative thought. Stop it.

I will light the candle this time. I will light it because there is no reason I should not.

Consciously deepening my breathing, I began to gather the power. My world narrowed further until all I was aware of was the curled, blackened wick of the candle.

I am Skeeve. My Father has a farmer's bond with the earth. My Mother was an educated woman. My teacher is a master magician. I am Skeeve. I will light this candle.

I could feel myself beginning to grow warm as the energies began to build within me. I focused the heat on the wick.

Like my Father, I tap the strength of the earth. The knowledge my Mother gave me is like a lens, enabling me to focus what I have gained. The wisdom of my teacher directs my efforts to those points of the universe most likely to yield to my will. I am Skeeve.

The candle remained unlit. There was sweat on my forehead now, and I was beginning to tremble with the effort. No, that was wrong; I should not tense. Relax. Don't try to force it. Tension hinders the flow. Let the energies pass freely; serve as a passive conductor. I forced myself to relax, consciously letting the muscles in my face and shoulders go slack as I redoubled my efforts.

The flow was noticeably more intense now. I could almost see the energy streaming from me to my target. I stretched out a finger which focused the energies even more. The candle remained unlit.

I couldn't do it. Negative thought. Stop it. I am Skeeve. I will light the candle. My father...No. Negative thought. Do not rely on others for your strength. I will light the candle because I am Skeeve.

I was rewarded by a sudden surge of energy at the thought. I pursued it, growing heady with power. *I am Skeeve. I am stronger than any of them. I escaped my father's attempts to chain me to a plow as he had my brother. My mother died from her idealism, but I used her teachings to survive. My teacher is a gullible fool who took a thief for an apprentice. I have beaten them all. I am Skeeve. I will light the candle.*

I was floating now. I realized how my abilities dwarfed those around me. Whether the candle lit or not was inconsequential. *I am Skeeve. I am powerful.*

Almost contemptuously I reached out with my mind and touched the wick. A small bright ember appeared in answer to my will.

Startled, I sat up and blinked at the candle. As I did, the ember disappeared, leaving a small white plume of smoke to mark its departure. I realized too late that I had broken concentration.

"Excellent, Lad!"

Garkin was suddenly beside me pounding my shoulder enthusiastically. How long he had been there I neither knew nor cared.

"It went out," I said plaintively.

"Never you mind that. You lit it. You have the confidence now. Next time it will be easy. By the stars, we'll make a magician of you yet. Here, you must be hungry."

I barely got my hand up in time to intercept the remaining lizard-bird leg before it smacked into my face. It was cold.

"I don't mind admitting I was beginning to despair, lad. What made that lesson so hard? Has it occurred to you you could use that spell to give you extra light when you're picking a lock or even to start a fire to serve as a diversion?"

"I thought about it, but extra light could draw unwanted attention. As for starting a diversion, I'd be afraid of hurting someone. I don't want to hurt anyone, just..."

I stopped, realizing what I was saying. Too late. A heavy cuff from Garkin sent me sprawling off my stool.

"I thought so! You're still planning to be a thief. You want to use my magiks to steal!"

He was towering in his rage, but for once I stood my ground.

"What of it?" I snarled. "It beats starving. What's so good about being a magician, anyway? I mean, your life style here gives me so much to look forward to."

I gestured at the cluttered room that was the entirety of the hut.

"Listen to the wolfling complain," Garkin sneered. "It was good enough for you when the winter drove you out of the woods to steal. 'It beats sleeping under a bush,' you said."

"And it still does. That's why I'm still here. But I'm not going to spend the rest of my life here. Hiding in a little hut in the woods is not my idea of a future. You were living on roots and berries until I came along and started trapping meat for the fire. Maybe that's your idea of a wonderful life, Garkin, but it's not mine!"

We glared at each other for several long moments. Now that my anger was vented, I was more than a little afraid. While I had not had extensive experience in the field, I suspected that sneering at magicians was not the best way to ensure a long and healthy future.

Surprisingly enough, it was Garkin who gave ground first. He suddenly dropped his gaze and bowed his head, giving me a rare view of the unkempt mass of hair atop his head.

"Perhaps you're right, Skeeve," his voice was strangely soft. "Perhaps I have been showing you all the work of magik, but not the rewards. I constantly forget how suppressed magik is in these lands."

He raised his eyes to meet mine again, and I shivered at the impact. They were not angry, but deep within them burned a glow I had never seen before.

"Know you now, Skeeve, that all lands are not like this one, nor was I always as you see me now. In lands where magik is recognized instead of feared as it is here, it is respected and commissioned by those in power. There, a skillful magician who keeps his wits about him can reap a hundred times the wealth you aspire to as a thief, and such power that…"

He broke off suddenly and shook his head as if to clear it. When he opened his eyes again, the glow I had seen burning earlier had died to an ember.

"But you aren't to be impressed by words, are you, lad? Come, I'll show you a little demonstration of some of the power you may one day wield—if you practice your lessons, that is."

The joviality in his voice was forced. I nodded my agreement in answer to that burning gaze. Truth to tell, I needed no demonstration. His soft, brief oration had awed me far more than any angry tirade or demonstration, but I did not wish to contradict him at this time.

I don't believe he actually noticed my response. He was already striding into the large pentagram permanently inscribed in the floor of the hut. As he walked, he gestured absentmindedly and the charred copper brazier scuttled forth from its place in the corner to meet him at the center of the pentagram.

I had time to reflect that perhaps it was that brazier that had first drawn me to Garkin. I remembered the first time I peered through the window of his hut seeking to identify and place objects of value for a later theft. I had seen Garkin as I have seen him so often since, pacing restlessly up and down the room, his nose buried in a book. It was a surprising enough sight as it was, for reading is not a common pastime in this area, but what captured my attention was the brazier. It hobbled about the room, following Garkin like an impatient puppy that was a little too polite to jump up on its master to get his attention. Then Garkin had looked up from his book, stared thoughtfully at his workbench; then, with a nod of decision, gestured. A small pot of unidentified content rose from the clutter and floated to his waiting hand. He caught it, referred to his book again, and poured out a dollop without looking up. Quick as a cat, the brazier scrambled under his hand and caught the dollop before it reached the floor. That had been my introduction to magik.

Something wrenched my attention back to the present. What was it? I checked Garkin's progress. No, he was still at work, half-hidden by a floating cloud of vials and jars, mumbling as he occasionally plucked one from the air and added a bit of its contents to the brazier. Whatever he was working on, it promised to be spectacular.

Then I heard it again, a muffled step outside the hut. But that was impossible! Garkin always set the…I began to search my memory. I could not recall Garkin setting the protective wards before he started to work. Ridiculous. Caution was the first and most important thing Garkin hammered into me, and part of caution was always setting wards before you started working. He couldn't have forgotten…but he had been rather intense and distracted.

I was still trying to decide if I should attempt to interrupt Garkin's work when he suddenly stepped back from the brazier. He fixed me with his gaze, and my warning died in my throat. This was not the time to impose reality on the situation. The glow was back in his eyes, stronger than before.

"Even demonstrations should give a lesson," he intoned. "Control, Skeeve. Control is the mainstay of magik. Power without control is a disaster. That is why you practice with a feather though you are able to move much larger and heavier objects. Control. Even your meager powers would be dangerous unless controlled, and I will not teach you more until you have learned that control."

He carefully stepped out of the pentagram.

"To demonstrate the value of control, I will now summon forth a demon, a being from another world. He is powerful, cruel, and vicious, and would kill us both if given the chance. Yet, despite this, we need not fear him, because he will be controlled. He will be unable to harm us or anything else in this world as long as he is contained within that pentagram. Now watch, Skeeve. Watch and learn."

So saying, he turned once more to the brazier. He spread his hands, and as he did, the five candles at the points of the pentagram sprang to life, and the lines of the pentagram began to glow with an eerie blue light. Silence reigned for several minutes, then he began to chant in a low mumble. A thread of smoke appeared from the brazier, but instead of rising to the ceiling, it poured onto the floor and began to form a small cloud that seethed and pulsed. Garkin's chanting was louder now, and the cloud grew and darkened. The brazier was almost obscured from view, but there...in the depths of the cloud...something was taking shape.

"Isstvan sends his greetings, Garkin!"

I nearly jumped out of my skin at the words. They came from inside the hut, but not inside the pentagram! I whirled toward their source. A figure was standing just inside the door, blinding in a glowing gold cloak. For a mad moment I thought it was the demon answering Garkin's summons. Then I saw the crossbow. It was a man, alright, but the crossbow, cocked and loaded in his hand, did little for my peace of mind.

Garkin did not even turn to look.

"Not now, you fool!" he snarled.

"It has been a long hunt, Garkin," the man continued as if he hadn't heard. "You've hidden yourself well, but did you really hope to escape..."

"You dare!?!" Garkin spun from his work, towering in his rage.

The man saw Garkin's face now, saw the eyes, and his face contorted in a grotesque mask of fear. Reflexively, he loosed the bolt from his crossbow, but too late. I did not see what Garkin did, things were happening too fast, but the man suddenly disappeared in a sheet of flame. He shrieked in agony and fell to the floor. The flame disappeared as suddenly as it had come, leaving only the smoldering corpse as evidence it had existed at all.

I remained rooted to the spot for several moments before I could move or even speak.

"Garkin," I said at last, "I...Garkin!"

Garkin's form was a crumpled lump on the floor. I was at his side in one bound, but I was far too late. The crossbow bolt protruded with silent finality from his chest. Garkin had given me my last lesson.

As I stooped to touch his body, I noticed something that froze my blood in its veins. Half-hidden by his form was the extinguished candle from the north point of the pentagram. The lines were no longer glowing blue. The protective spell was gone.

With agonizing effort, I raised my head and found myself gazing into a pair of yellow eyes, flecked with gold, that were not of this world.

II.

"Things are not always as they seem."
MANDRAKE

ONCE, IN THE woods, I found myself face to face with a snake-cat. On another occasion, I encountered a spider-bear. Now, faced with a demon, I decided to pattern my behavior after that which had saved me in the aforementioned situations. I froze. At least, in hindsight, I like to think it was a deliberate, calculated act.

The demon curled its lips back, revealing a double row of needle-sharp teeth.

I considered changing my chosen course of action; I considered fainting.

The demon ran a purple tongue over his lips and began to slowly extend a taloned hand toward me. That did it! I went backward, not in a graceful catlike bound, but scrabbling on all fours. It's surprising how fast you can move that way when properly inspired. I managed to build up a substantial head of steam before I crashed head-first into the wall.

"Gaahh…" I said. It may not seem like much, but at the time it was the calmest expression of pain and terror I could think of.

At my outburst, the demon seemed to choke. Several ragged shouts erupted, then he began to laugh. It wasn't a low, menacing laugh, but the wholehearted enthusiastic laughter of someone who has just seen something hysterically funny.

I found it both disquieting and annoying. Annoying because I had a growing suspicion I was the source of his amusement; disquieting because…well…he was a demon and demons are…

"Cold, vicious, and bloodthirsty," the demon gasped as if he had read my thoughts. "You really bought the whole line, didn't you, kid?"

"I beg your pardon?" I said because I couldn't think of anything else to say.

"Something wrong with your ears? I said 'cold, vicious…'"

"I heard you. I meant what did you mean."

"What I meant was that you were scared stiff, by a few well chosen words from my esteemed colleague, I'll wager." He jerked a thumb at Garkin's body. "Sorry for the dramatics. I felt a touch of comic relief was necessary to lighten an otherwise tragic moment."

"Comic relief?"

"Well, actually, I couldn't pass up the opportunity. You should have seen your face."

He chuckled to himself as he strode out of the pentagram and began a leisurely inspection of the premises.

"So this is Garkin's new place, huh? What a dump. Who would have thought he'd come to this?"

To say I was perplexed would be an understatement. I wasn't sure how a demon should act, but it wasn't like this.

I could have bolted for the door, but I didn't seem to be in immediate danger. Either this strange being meant me no harm, or he was confident of his ability to stop me even if I tried to flee. For the sake of my nervous system, I decided to assume the former.

The demon continued to inspect the hut, while I inspected him. He was humanoid; that is, he had two arms, two legs, and a head. He was short but powerfully built, a bit broader across the shoulders than a man, and heavily muscled, but he wasn't human. I mean, you don't see many hairless humans with dark green scales covering their body and pointed ears lying flat against their head.

I decided to risk a question.

"Ah, excuse me."

"Yeah, kid?"

"Um, you are a demon, aren't you?"

"Huh? Oh, yeah, I guess you could say I am."

"Well, if you don't mind my asking, why don't you act like a demon?"

The demon shot me a disgusted look, then turned his head heavenward in a gesture of martyrdom.

"Everybody's a critic. Tell ya what, kid, would you be happier if I tore your throat out with my teeth?"

"Well, no, but..."

"For that matter, who are you, anyway? Are you an innocent bystander, or did you come with the assassin?"

"I'm with him," I hastened to reply, pointing a shaky finger at Garkin's body. That bit about tearing my throat out had me on edge again. "Or at least I was. Garkin. The one who summoned... him!...I'm...I was his student."

"No kiddin'? Garkin's apprentice?" He began advancing toward me, reaching out a hand, "Pleased ta…what's wrong?"

As he moved toward me, I had started backing away from him. I tried to do it casually, but he had noticed.

"Well…it's…you *are* a demon."

"Yeah. So?"

"Um…well, demons are supposed to be…"

"Hey, relax, kid. I don't bite. Look, I'm an old buddy of Garkin's."

"I thought you said you were a demon?"

"That's right. I'm from another dimension. A dimension traveler, or demon for short. Get it?"

"What's a dimension?"

The demon scowled.

"Are you sure you're Garkin's apprentice? I mean, he hasn't told you anything at all about dimensions?"

"No," I answered. "I mean, yes, I'm his apprentice, but he never said anything about the demon-suns."

"That's dimensions," he corrected. "Well, a dimension is another world, actually one of several worlds, existing simultaneously with this one, but on different planes. Follow me?"

"No," I admitted.

"Well, just accept that I'm from another world. Now, in that world, I'm a magician just like Garkin. We had an exchange program going where we could summon each other across the barrier to impress our respective apprentices."

"I thought you said you were a demon," I said suspiciously.

"I am! Look, kid. In my world, you'd be a demon, but at the current moment I'm in yours, so I'm a demon."

"I thought you said you were a magician."

"I don't believe this!" The demon made his angry appeal to the heavens. "I'm standing here arguing with some twerp of an apprentice…Look, kid."

He fixed me with his gaze again.

"Let me try it this way. Are you going to shake my hand, or am I going to rip your heart out?"

Since he put it that way…I mean, for a minute there, when he lost his temper and started shouting, he sounded just like Garkin. It gave credibility to his claim of friendship with my ex-teacher. I took his extended hand and shook it cautiously.

"I'm...My name is Skeeve."

His grip was cold, but firm. So firm in fact that I found it impossible to reclaim my hand as rapidly as I would have liked.

"Pleased ta meetcha, kid. I'm Aahz."

"Oz?"

"No relation."

"No relation to what?" I asked, but he was examining the room again.

"Well, there's certainly nothing here to arouse the greedy side of his fellow beings. Early primitive, enduring, but not particularly sought after."

"We like it," I said, rather stiffly. Now that I was over being scared, I didn't like the sneer in his voice. The hut wasn't much and I certainly wasn't overly fond of it, but I resented his criticism.

"Don't get your back up, kid." Aahz said easily. "I'm looking for a motive, that's all."

"Motive?"

"A reason for someone to off old Garkin. I'm not big on vengeance, but he was a drinking buddy of mine and it's got my curiosity up."

He broke off his inspection of the room to address me directly.

"How about you, kid? Can you think of anything? Any milk-maids he's seduced or farmers he's cheated? You've got an interest in this too, you know. You might be the next target."

"But the guy who did it is dead." I gestured to the charred lump by the door. "Doesn't that finish it?"

"Wake up, kid. Didn't you see the gold cloak? That was a professional assassin. Somebody hired him, and that somebody would hire another one."

A chill ran down my spine. I hadn't really thought of that. I began to search my memory for a clue.

"Well...he said Isstvan sent him."

"What's an Isstvan?"

"I don't...wait a minute. What do you mean, I might be the next target?"

"Neat, huh?" Aahz was holding up the gold cloak. "Lined, and completely reversible. Always wondered how come no one noticed them until they were ready to pounce."

"Aahz..."

"Hmmm? Oh, didn't mean to scare you. It's just if someone's declared open season on magicians in general or Garkin specifically, you might have some...Hello, what's this?"

"What's what?" I asked, trying to get a look at what he had found.

"This," he said, holding his prize aloft. "It seems I'm not the only demon about."

It was a head, apparently the assassin's. It was badly charred, with bone showing in several places. My natural revulsion at the sight was compounded by several obvious features. The chin and ears of the head were unnaturally pointed, and there were two short, blunt, horns protruding from the forehead.

"A devil!" I exclaimed in horror.

"A what? Oh, a Deveel. No, it's not from Deva, it's from Imper. An Imp. Didn't Garkin teach you anything?"

"Come again?" I asked, but Aahz was busy scowling at the head.

"The question is, who would be crass enough to hire an Imp as an assassin? The only one I can think of is Isstvan, but that's impossible."

"But that's who did it. Don't you remember? I told you..."

"I thought you said 'Isstvan,'"

"I did! Wait a minute. What did you say?"

"I said Isstvan. Can't you tell the difference?"

"No," I admitted.

"Hmmm...must be too subtle for the human ear to detect. Oh, well. No matter. This changes everything. If Isstvan is up to his old tricks there's no time to lose. Hey! Wait a minute. What's this?"

"It's a crossbow," I observed.

"With heat-seeking armor piercing quarrels? Is that the norm in this world?"

"Heat-seeking..."

"Never mind, kid. I didn't think so. Well, that tears it. I'd better check this out quick."

He began to stride into the pentagram. I suddenly realized he was preparing to leave.

"Hey! Wait a minute! What's going on?"

"It would take too long to explain, kid. Maybe I'll see you again sometime."

"But you said I might be a target!"

"Yeah, well, that's the way it crumbles. Tell ya what. Start running and maybe they won't find you until it's over."

My head was awhirl. Things were happening far too fast for clear thought. I still didn't know what or who the demon was or if I should trust him, but I did know one thing. He was the nearest thing to an ally I had in a situation where I was clearly outclassed.

"Couldn't you help me?"

"No time. I've got to move."

"Couldn't I come with you?"

"You'd just get in the way, maybe even get me killed."

"But without you, I'll be killed!"

I was getting desperate, but Aahz was unimpressed.

"Probably not. Tell ya what, kid. I've really got to get going, but just to show you I think you'll survive, I'll show you a little trick you might use sometime. You see all this crud Garkin used to bring me across the barrier? Well, it's not necessary. Watch close and I'll show you how we do it when our apprentices aren't watching."

I wanted to shout, to make him stop and listen to me, but he had already started. He spread his arms at shoulder height, looked heavenward, took a deep breath, then clapped his hands.

Nothing happened.

III.

"The only thing more reliable than magik is one's friends!"
MACBETH

AAHZ SCOWLED AND repeated the gesture, a bit quicker this time, The scene remained unchanged.

I decided something was wrong.

"Is something wrong?" I asked politely.

"You'd better believe there's something wrong," Aahz snarled. "It's not working."

"Are you sure you're doing it right?"

"Yes, I'm sure I'm doing it right, just like I've been sure the last fifty times I did it!"

He was starting to sound annoyed.

"Can you…"

"Look, kid, If I knew what was wrong, I'd have fixed it already. Now, just shut up and let me think!"

He sank down to sit cross-legged in the center of the pentagram where he began sketching vague patterns in the floor as he mumbled darkly to himself, I wasn't sure if he was trying some alternate incantation or was simply thinking hard, but decided it would be unwise to ask. Instead, I used the time to organize my scrambled thoughts.

I still wasn't sure if Aahz was a threat to me or if he was my only possible salvation from a greater threat. I mean, by this time I was pretty sure he was kidding about ripping my heart out, but that's the sort of thing one wants to be *very* sure of. One thing I had learned for certain: there was more to this magik stuff than floating feathers around.

"That's got to be it!"

Aahz was on his feet again, glaring at Garkin's body.

"That ill-begotten son of a wombat!"

"What's a wombat?" I asked, then immediately wished I hadn't. The mental image that sprang into my mind was so horrifying I was sure I didn't want details. I needn't have worried. Aahz was not about to take time to answer me.

"Well, it's a pretty crummy joke. That's all I have to say."

"Um…What are you talking about, Aahz?"

"I'm talking about Garkin! He did this to me. If I thought it would go this far, I would have turned him into a goat-fish when I had the chance."

"Aahz…I still don't…"

I stopped. He had ceased his ranting and was looking at me. I shrank back reflexively before I recognized the snarl as his smile. I liked it better when he was raving.

"I'm sorry, Skeeve," he purred. "I guess I haven't been very clear."

I was growing more uneasy by the minute. I wasn't used to having people, much less demons, being nice to me.

"Um…That's okay. I was just wondering…"

"You see, the situation is this. Garkin and I have been…playing little jokes on each other for some time now. It started one time when we were drinking and he stiffed me with the bill. Well, the next time I summoned him, I brought him in over a lake and he had to do his demon act armpit deep in water. He got even by…well, I won't bore you with details, but we've gotten in the habit of putting each other in awkward or embarrassing situations. It's really very childish, but quite harmless. But this time…" Aahz's eyes started to narrow, "But this time the old frog-kisser's gone too…I mean, it seems to have gotten a little out of hand. Don't you agree?"

He bared his fangs at me again in a smile. I wanted very badly to agree with him, but I didn't have the foggiest idea what he was talking about.

"You still haven't told me what's wrong."

"What's wrong is that stinking slime-monger took away my powers!" he roared, forgetting his composure. "I'm blocked! I can't do a flaming thing unless he removes his stupid prankish spell, and he can't 'cause he's dead! *Now* do you understand me, fly-bait?"

I made up my mind. Savior or not, I'd rather he went back where he came from.

"Well, if there was anything I could do…"

"There is, Skeeve, my boy." Aahz was suddenly all purrs and teeth again. "All you have to do is fire up the old cauldron or whatever and remove this spell. Then we can each go our separate ways and…"

"I can't do that."

"Okay, kid," his smile was a little more forced. "I'll stick around until you're on your feet. I mean, what are friends for?"

"That's not it."

"What do you want? Blood?" Aahz was no longer smiling. "If you're trying to hold me up, I'll..."

"You don't understand!" I interrupted desperately. "I can't do it because I can't do it! I don't know how!"

That stopped him.

"Hmm. That could be a problem. Well, tell you what. Instead of pulling the spell here, what say you just pop me back to my own dimension and I'll get someone there to take it off."

"I can't do that either. Remember, I told you I'd never even heard of..."

"Well, what can you do?!"

"I can levitate objects...well, small objects."

"And..." he encouraged.

"And...um...I can light a candle."

"Light a candle?"

"Well...almost."

Aahz sank heavily into a chair and hid his face in his hands for several minutes. I waited for him to think of something.

"Kid, have you got anything in this dump to drink?" he asked finally.

"I'll get you some water."

"I said something to drink, not something to wash in!"

"Oh. Yessir!"

I hastened to bring him a goblet of wine from the small keg Garkin kept, hoping he wouldn't notice the vessel wasn't particularly clean.

"What will this do? Will it help you get your powers back?"

"No. But it might make me feel a little better." He tossed the wine down in one swallow, and studied the goblet disdainfully. "Is this the biggest container you've got?"

I cast about the room desperately, but Aahz was way ahead of me.

He rose, strode into the pentagram, and picked up the brazier. I knew from past experience it was deceptively heavy, but he carried it to the keg as if it were weightless. Not bothering to empty out Garkin's concoction, he filled it to the brim and took a deep draught.

"Aah! That's better." he sighed.

I felt a little queasy.

"Well, kid," he said, sweeping me with an appraising stare, "it looks like we're stuck with each other. The set-up isn't ideal, but it's what we've got. Time to bite the bullet and play the cards we're dealt. You do know what cards are, don't you?"

"Of course," I said, slightly wounded.

"Good."

"What's a bullet?"

Aahz closed his eyes as if struggling against some inner turmoil.

"Kid," he said at last, "there's a good chance this partnership is going to drive one of us crazy. I would guess it will be me unless you can knock off the dum-dum questions every other sentence."

"But I can't understand half of what you're saying."

"Hmm. Tell ya what. Try to save up the questions and ask me all at one time once a day. Okay?"

"I'll try."

"Right. Now here's the situation as I see it. If Isstvan is hiring Imps for assassins…"

"What's an Imp?"

"Kid, will you give me a break?"

"I'm sorry, Aahz. Keep going."

"Right. Well…umm…It's happening!" he made his appeal to the heavens. "I can't remember what I was saying!"

"Imps," I prompted.

"Oh! Right. Well, if he's hiring Imps and arming them with non-spec weapons, it can only mean he's up to his old tricks. Now since I don't have my powers, I can't get out of here to sound the alarm. That's where you come in, kid…Kid?"

He was looking at me expectantly. I found I could contain my misery no longer.

"I'm sorry, Aahz," I said in a small, pitiful voice I hardly recognized as my own. "I don't understand a single thing you've said."

I suddenly realized I was about to cry, and turned away hurriedly so he wouldn't see. I sat there, with tears trickling down my cheeks, alternately fighting the urge to wipe them away and wondering why I was concerned over whether or not a demon saw me crying. I don't know how long I stayed that way, but I was brought back to reality by a gentle hand on my shoulder. A cold, gentle hand.

"Hey, kid. Don't beat on yourself," Aahz's voice was surprisingly sympathetic. "It's not your fault if Garkin was tight with his secrets. Nobody expects you to have learned something you were never taught, so there's no reason you should expect it either."

"I just feel so stupid," I said, not turning. "I'm not used to feeling stupid."

"You aren't stupid, kid. That much I know. Garkin wouldn't have taken you for an apprentice if you were stupid. If anybody here's stupid, it's me. I got so carried away with the situation, I forgot myself and tried talking to an apprentice as if he were a full blown magician. Now *that's* stupid."

I still couldn't bring myself to respond.

"Heck, kid." He gave my shoulder a gentle shake. "Right now you can do more magik than I can."

"But you know more."

"But I can't use it. You know, kid, that gives me an idea. With old Garkin dead there, you're kind of cut off. What say you sign on as my apprentice for a while? We'll take it from the top with me teaching you as if you were a new student who didn't know a thing. We'll take it step by step from the beginning. What da ya say?"

In spite of my gloom I felt my spirits lift. Like he said, I'm not stupid. I could recognize a golden opportunity when I saw one.

"Gee, that sounds great, Aahz."

"Then it's a deal?"

"It's a deal," I answered and stuck out my hand.

"What's that?" he snarled. "Isn't my word good enough for you?"

"But you said…"

"That's right. You're my apprentice now, and I don't go around shaking apprentices' hands."

I withdrew my hand. It occurred to me this alliance might not be all roses and song.

"Now as I was saying, here's what we've got to do about the current situation…"

"But I haven't had any lessons yet!"

"That's right. Here's your first lesson. When a crisis shapes up, you don't waste energy wishing for information or skills you haven't got. You dig in and handle it as best you can with what you've got. Now shut up while I fill you in on the situation… apprentice."

I shut up and listened. He studied me for a moment, then gave a small, satisfied nod, took another gulp from the brazier and began.

"Now, you have a vague idea about other dimensions because I told you about them earlier. You also have first-hand experience that magicians can open passages in the barriers between those dimensions. Well, different magicians use that power in different ways. Some of them, like Garkin, only use it to impress the yokels: summon a demon, visions of other worlds, that kind of schtick. But there are others whose motives are not so pure."

He paused to take another gulp of wine. Surprisingly, I felt no urge to interrupt with questions.

"Technology in different dimensions has progressed at different rates, as has magik. Some magicians use this to their own advantage. They aren't showmen; they're smugglers, buying and selling technology across the barriers for profit and power. Most of the inventors in any dimension are actually closet magicians."

I must have frowned without realizing it, but Aahz noted it and acknowledged it with a wink and a smirk.

"I know what you're thinking, Skeeve. It all sounds a little dishonest and unscrupulous. Actually, they're a fairly ethical bunch. There's a set of unwritten rules called the Smugglers' Code they adhere to pretty closely."

"Smugglers' Code?" I asked, forgetting myself for a moment. Aahz didn't seem to mind this time.

"It's like the Mercenaries' Code, but less violent and more profitable. Anyway, as an example, one item in that code states you cannot bring an 'invention' into a dimension that is too far in advance of that dimension's technology, like bringing guided missiles into a longbow culture or lasers into a flint-and-powder era."

I kept my silence with great difficulty.

"As I've said, most magicians adhere to the code fairly closely, but once in a while a bad one crops up. That brings us to Isstvan."

I got a sudden chill at the sound of that name. Maybe there *was* something different in the way Aahz pronounced it.

"Some say Isstvan isn't playing with a full deck. I think he's been playing with his wand too much. But whatever the reason, somewhere he's gotten it into his head he wants to rule the dimensions, all of them. He's tried it before, but we got wind of it in time and a bunch of us teamed up to teach him a lesson in manners. As a matter of fact, that's when I first met Garkin there."

He gestured with the brazier and slopped a bit of wine on the floor. I began to doubt his sobriety, but his voice seemed steady enough as he continued.

"I thought he had given the thing up after his last drubbing. We even gave him a few souvenirs to be sure he didn't forget. Then this thing pops up. If he's hiring cross-dimension help and arming them with advanced-technology weapons, he's probably trying to do it again."

"Do what?"

"I just told you. Take over the dimensions."

"I know, but how? I mean, how does what he does in this dimension help him rule the others?"

"Oh, that. Well, each dimension has a certain amount of power that can be channeled or converted into magik. Different dimensions have different amounts, and each dimension's power is divided up or shared by the magicians of that dimension. If he can succeed in controlling or killing the other magicians in this dimension, he can use its entire magical energy to attack another dimension. If he succeeds in winning there, he has the power from two dimensions to attack a third, and so on. As you can see, the longer he keeps his plot moving, the stronger he gets and the harder he'll be to stop."

"I understand now," I said, genuinely pleased and enthusiastic.

"Good. Then you understand why we've got to stop him."

I stopped being pleased and enthusiastic.

"We? You mean us? You and me?"

"I know it's not much of a force, kid, but like I said, it's all we've got."

"I think I'd like a little of that wine now."

"None of that, kid. You're in training now. You're going to need all the practice time you can get if we're going to stop Isstvan. Bankers or not, he's no slouch when it comes to magik."

"Aahz," I said slowly, not looking up. "Tell me the truth. Do you think there's a chance you can teach me enough magik that we'll have a chance of stopping him?"

"Of course, kid. I wouldn't even try if we didn't have a chance. Trust me."

I wasn't convinced, and from the sound of his voice, neither was he.

IV.

"Careful planning is the key to safe and swift travel."
ULYSSES

"HMMM…WELL, IT'S not a tailored jump-suit, but it will have to do."

We had been trying to outfit Aahz in a set of clothes, and he was surveying the results in a small dark mirror we had found, turning it this way and that to catch his reflection piecemeal.

"Maybe if we could find some other color than this terrible brown."

"That's all we've got."

"Are you sure?"

"Positive, I have two shirts, both brown. You're wearing one, and I'm wearing the other,"

"Hmmm…" he said, studying me carefully. "Maybe I would look better in the lighter brown. Oh, well, we can argue that out later."

I was curious about his attention to his appearance. I mean, he couldn't be planning on meeting anyone. The sight of a green, scaly demon would upset most of the locals no matter what he was wearing. For the time being, however, I deemed it wisest to keep quiet and humor him in his efforts.

Actually, the clothes fit him fairly well. The shirt was a bit short in the sleeves due to the length of his arms, but not too because I was taller than him, which made up for most of the difference. We had had to cut off some of the trouser legs to cover for his shorter legs, but they, like the body of the shirt, were not too tight. I had made the clothes myself originally, and they tended to be a bit baggy, or at least they were on me. Tailoring is not my forté.

He was also wearing Garkin's boots, which fitted him surprisingly well. I had raised minor protest at this, until he pointed out that Garkin had no further use for them but we did. Pragmatism, he called it. Situational ethics. He said it would come in handy if I was serious about becoming a magician.

"Hey, kid!" Aahz's voice interrupted my thoughts. He seemed to be occupied rummaging through the various chests and cupboards of the hut. "Don't you have anything here in the way of weapons?"

"Weapons?"

"Yeah, you know, the things that killed old Garkin there, Swords, knives, bows, stuff like that."

"I know what they are, I just wasn't expecting you to be interested in them, that's all."

"Why not?"

"Well...I thought you said you were a magician."

"We aren't going to go through that again, are we, kid? Besides, what's that got to do with weapons?"

"It's just that I've never known a magician who used weapons other than his powers."

"Really? How many magicians have you known?"

"One," I admitted.

"Terrific. Look, kid, if old Garkin didn't want to use weapons, that's his problem. Me, I want some. If you'll notice, Garkin is dead."

It was hard to argue with logic like that.

"Besides," he continued, "do you really want to take on Isstvan and his pack with nothing but your magik and my agility going for us?"

"I'll help you look."

We went to work rummaging for weapons, but, aside from the crossbow that had killed Garkin, we didn't find much. One of the chests yielded a sword with a jewel-encrusted handle, and we discovered two knives, one white-handled and one black-handled, on Garkin's workbench. Aside from those, there was nothing that even remotely resembled a fighting utensil in the hut. Aahz was not overjoyed.

"I don't believe this. A sword with a cruddy blade, bad balance, and phony jewels in the handle and two knives that haven't been sharpened since they were made. Anybody who keeps weapons like this should be skewered."

"He was."

"True enough. Well, if that's all we've got, that's what we'll have to use."

He slung the sword on his hip and tucked the white-handled knife into his belt. I thought he would give me the other knife, but instead he stooped down and secured it in his boot.

"Don't I get one?"

"Can you use it?"

"Well..."

He resumed his task. I had a small knife I used to skin small game tucked under my shirt. Even to my inexperienced eye it was of better quality than the two Aahz had just appropriated. I decided not to bring it to his attention.

"Okay, kid. Where did the old man keep his money?"

I showed him. One of the stones in the fireplace was loose and there was a small leather pouch hidden behind it. He peered at the coins suspiciously as they poured into his palm.

"Check me on this, kid. Copper and silver aren't worth much in this dimension, right?"

"Well, silver's sorta valuable, but it's not worth as much as gold."

"Then what's with this chicken-feed? Where's the real money?"

"We never really had much."

"Come off it...I haven't met a magician yet who didn't have a bundle socked away. Just because he never spent any of it doesn't mean he doesn't have it. Now think. Haven't you ever seen anything around that was gold or had gems?"

"Well, there are a few items, but they're protected by curses."

"Kid, think for a minute. If you were a doddering old wreck who couldn't fight your way out of a paper bag, how would you protect your treasures?"

"I don't know."

"Terrific. I'll explain while we gather it up."

In short order we had a modest heap of loot on the table, most of it items I had long held in awe. There was a gold statue of a man with the head of a lion, the Three Pearls of Kraul, a gold pendant in the shape of the sun with three of its rays missing, and a ring with a large jewel we took from Garkin's hand. Aahz held up the sun pendant.

"Now this is an example of what I mean. I suppose there's a story about what happened to the missing three rays?"

"Well," I began, "there was a lost tribe that worshipped a huge snake-toad..."

"Skip it. It's an old dodge. What you do is take your gold to a craftsman and have him fashion it into something with a lot of small out-juttings like fingers or arms..." He held up the pendant. "...rays of sun. It gives you the best of two worlds.

"First, you have something mystical and supernatural; add a ghost story and no one will dare to touch it. Second, it has the advantage that if you need a little ready cash, you just break off a ray or an arm and sell it for the value of the gold. Instead of losing value, the price of the remaining item increases because of its mystical history, the strange circumstances under which it was torn asunder purely fictional, of course."

Strangely enough, I was not surprised. I was beginning to wonder if anything Garkin had told me was true.

"Then none of these things have any real magical powers or curses?"

"Now, I didn't say that. Occasionally, you stumble across a real item, but they're usually few and far between."

"But how can you tell the real thing from a fake?"

"I take it that Garkin didn't teach you to see auras. Well, that figures. Probably was afraid you'd take his treasure and run. Okay, kid. Time for your first lesson. Have you ever day-dreamed? You know, just stared at something and let your mind wander?"

I nodded.

"Okay, here's what I want you to do. Scoot down in your chair until your head is almost level with the table. That's right. Comfortable? Fine. Now I want you to look across the table at the wall. Don't focus on it, just stare at it and let your mind wander."

I did as he said. It was hard not focusing on a specific point, so I set my mind to wandering. What to think about? Well, what was I thinking about when the candle almost lit. Oh yes. *I am Skeeve. I am powerful and my power is growing daily.* I smiled to myself. With the demon's aid, I would soon become a knowledgeable sorcerer. And that would just be the start. After that...

"Hey!" I said, sitting upright.

"What did you see?"

"It was...well, nothing, I guess."

"Don't give me a hard time, kid. What did you see?"

"Well, for a second there I thought I saw sort of a red glow around the ring, but when I looked at it squarely, it disappeared."

"The ring, eh? It figures. Well, that's it. The rest of the stuff should be okay."

He scraped the rest of the loot into a sack, leaving the ring on the table.

"What was it?"

"What? Oh, what you saw? That was an aura. Most people have them. Some places do, but it's a sure test to check if an item is truly magical. I'd be willing to bet that the ring is what old Garkin used to fry the assassin."

"Aren't we going to take it with us?"

"Do you know how to control it?"

"Well…no."

"Neither do I. The last thing we need is to carry around a ring that shoots fire. Particularly if we don't know how to activate it. Leave it. Maybe the others will find it and turn it on themselves."

He tucked the sack into his waistband.

"What others?" I prompted.

"Hmmm? Oh, the other assassins."

"What other assassins?" I was trying to be calm, but I was slipping.

"That's right. This is the first time you've tangled with them, isn't it? I would have thought Garkin…"

"Aahz, could you just tell me?"

"Oh! Sure, kid. Assassins never work alone. That's why they never miss. They work in groups of two to eight. There's probably a backup team around somewhere. Realizing Isstvan's respect for Garkin, I'd guess he wouldn't send fewer than six out on an assignment like this. Maybe even two teams."

"You mean all this time you've been fooling around with clothes and swords, there've been more assassins on the way?"

"Relax, kid. That's the backup team. They'll be waiting a ways off and won't move until tomorrow at the earliest. It's professional courtesy. They want to give this bozo room to maneuver. Besides, it's tradition that the assassin who actually does the deed gets first pick of any random booty lying around before the others show up to take even shares. Everyone does it, but it's considered polite to not notice some of the loot has been pocketed before the official split."

"How do you know so much about assassins, Aahz?"

"Went with one for a while…lovely lass, but she couldn't keep her mouth shut, even in bed. Sometimes I wonder if any profession really guards its secrets as closely as they claim."

"What happened?"

"With what?"

"With your assassin?"

"None of your business, kid." Aahz was suddenly brusque again. "We've got work to do."

"What are we going to do?"

"Well, first we bury the Imp. Maybe it'll throw the others off our trail. With any luck, they'll think he grabbed all the loot and disappeared. It wouldn't be the first time."

"No, I mean after that. We're getting ready to travel, but where are we going?"

"Kid, sometimes you worry me. That isn't even magic. It's common-sense military action. First, we find Isstvan. Second, we appraise his strength. Third, we make our plans, and fourth, we execute them, and hopefully him."

"Um…Aahz, could we back up to one for a minute? Where are we going to find Isstvan?"

That stopped him.

"Don't you know where he is?"

"I never even heard his name before today."

We sat in silence staring at each other for a long time.

V.

*"Only constant and conscientious practice in the
Martial Arts will ensure a long and happy life."*
                                              B. LEE

"I THINK I'VE got it figured out, kid."

As Aahz spoke, he paused in honing his sword to inspect the
edge. Ever since our trek began he had seized every opportunity to
work on his weapons. Even when we simply paused to rest by a
stream he busied himself working their edges or adjusting their balance. I felt I had learned more about weapons in the last week just
watching him tinker than I had in my entire previous life.

"Figured what out?"

"Why people in this world are trained in weapons or magik, but
not both."

"How's that?"

"Well, two reasons I can see just offhand. First off, it's a matter
of conditioning. Reflexes. You'll react the way you're trained. If you've
been trained with weapons, you'll react to crisis with a weapon. If
you're trained in magik, you'll react with magik. The problem is, if
you're trained both ways, you'll hesitate, trying to make up your
mind which to use, and probably get clobbered in the process. So to
keep things simple, Garkin only trained you in magik. It's probably
all he had been trained in himself."

I thought about it.

"That makes sense. What's the other reason?"

He grinned at me.

"Learning curve. If what you told me about life expectancy in this
world is even vaguely accurate, and if you're any example of how fast
people in this world learn, you only have time to learn one or the other."

"I think I prefer the first explanation."

He chortled to himself and went back to sharpening his sword.

Once, his needling would have bothered me, but now I took it
in stride. It seemed to be his habit to be critical of everything in our
world, and of me in particular. After a week of constant exposure
to him, the only time I would worry is if he stopped complaining.

Actually I was quite pleased with my progress in magik. Under Aahz's tutelage, my powers were growing daily. One of the most valuable lessons I had learned was to draw strength directly from the earth. It was a matter of envisioning energy as a tangible force, like water, and drawing new energy up one leg and into my mind while releasing exhausted energy down the other leg and back into the earth. Already, I could completely recharge myself even after a hard day's walking just by standing motionless with my eyes closed for several minutes and effecting this energy exchange. Aahz, as always, was unimpressed. According to him, I should have been able to do the energy exchange while we were walking, but I didn't let his grumbling dampen my enthusiasm. I was learning, and at a faster pace than I had dreamed possible.

"Hey, kid. Fetch me a piece of wood, will you?"

I smiled to myself and looked around. About ten feet away was a small branch of deadwood about two feet long. I leisurely stretched out a finger and it took flight, floating gently across the clearing to hover in the air in front of Aahz.

"Not bad, kid," he acknowledged. Then his sword flashed out, cutting the branch into two pieces which dropped to the ground. He picked up one of the pieces and inspected the cut.

"Hmmm...there may be hope for this sword yet. Why did you let them fall?"

This last was directed at me.

"I don't know. I guess you startled me when you swung the sword."

"Oh, really?"

Suddenly he threw the stick at me. I yelped and tried to duck out of the way, but it bounced painfully off my shoulder.

"Hey! What was that for?"

"Call it an object lesson. You know you can control the stick because you just did it when you fetched it for me. So why did you duck out of the way? Why not just stop it with your magik?"

"I guess it never occurred to me. You didn't give me much time to think."

"Okay, so think! This time you know it's coming."

He picked up the second piece of wood and waited, grinning evilly, which, with pointed teeth, is easy. I ignored him, letting my mind settle; then I nodded that I was ready.

The stick struck me squarely in the chest.

"Ow!!" I commented.

"And there, my young friend, is the difference between the classroom and field. Classroom is fine to let you know that things can be done and that you can do them, but in actual practice you will never be allowed the luxury of leisurely gathering your power, and seldom will you have a stationary target."

"Say, uh, Aahz. If you're really trying to build up my self-confidence, how come you always cut my legs out from under me every time I start thinking I'm getting someplace?"

He stood up, sheathing his sword.

"Self-confidence is a wonderful thing, kid, but not if it isn't justified. Someday we'll be staking one or both of our lives on your abilities, and it won't do us any good if you've been kidding yourself along. Now let's get down to work!"

"Um...have we got the time?"

"Relax, kid. Imps are tenacious, but they travel slow."

Our strategy upon leaving the hut had been simple. Lacking a specific direction for our search, we would trace the force lines of the world until we either found Isstvan or located another magician who would be able to steer us to him.

One might ask what force lines are. I did. Force lines, as Aahz explained them, are those paths of a world along which its energies flow most freely. In many ways, they are not unlike magnetic lines.

One might ask what magnetic lines are. I did. I will not quote Aahz's answer to that, but it was not information.

Anyway, force lines are a magician's ally and his enemy. Those who would tap the energies of those lines usually set up residence on or near one of those lines. This makes it easier for the magicians to draw upon the energies. It also makes it easier for their enemies to find them.

It was Aahz's theory that searching the force lines was how Garkin was located. It was therefore logical that we should be able to find Isstvan the same way.

Of course, I knew nothing of force lines or how to follow them, at least until Aahz taught me. It was not a difficult technique, which was fortunate, as I had my hands full trying to absorb all the other lessons Aahz was deluging me with.

One simply closes one's eyes and relaxes, trying to envision a two-pointed spear in glowing yellows and reds suspended in midair. The intensity of the glow indicates the nearness to a force line; the direction of the points shows the flow of energies. Rather like the needle of a compass. Whatever that is.

Once we had determined that Garkin had set up shop directly on a force line, as Aahz had suspected, and established direction of the flow of energies, we had another problem. Which way did we follow it?

The decision was doubly important as, if Aahz was correct, there would be a team of Imp assassins waiting in one direction, very probably in the direction we wanted to go.

We solved the problem by traveling one day's journey perpendicular to the force line, then for two days parallel to the line in our chosen direction, then returning to the line before continuing our journey. We hoped this would bypass the assassins entirely.

It worked, and it didn't.

It worked in that we didn't walk into an ambush. It didn't work in that now it seemed they were on our trail, though whether they were actually tracking us or merely following the force line back to Isstvan was unknown.

"I keep telling you, kid," Aahz insisted, "It's a good sign. It means we've chosen the right direction, and that we'll reach Isstvan ahead of his assassins' report."

"What if we're heading in the wrong direction?" I argued. "What if they're really following us? How long do we travel in this direction before we give up and admit it?"

"How long do you figure it will take for you to learn enough magik to stand up to a pack of Imp assassins armed with off-dimension weapons?"

"Let's get to work," I said firmly.

He looked around, and pointed to a gnarled fruit tree strewn round with windfalls across the clearing.

"Okay. Here's what I want you to do. Stare at the sky or contemplate your navel or something. Then when I give the word, use your power to grab one of those fruits and toss it to me."

I don't know how many hours we spent on that drill. It's more difficult than it sounds, mustering one's powers from a standing start. Just when I thought I had it down pat, Aahz switched tactics. He would engage in a conversation, deliberately leading me on, then interrupt me in mid-sentence with his signal. Needless to say, I failed miserably.

"Relax, kid. Look, try it this way. Instead of mustering your power from scratch each time, create a small space inside yourself and store

up some energy there. Just habitually keep that reserve squirreled away
and ready to cover for you while you get set to level your big guns."

"What's a gun?"

"Never mind. Just build that reserve and we'll try it again."

With this extra bit of advice at my disposal the drill went noticeably better. Finally Aahz broke off the practice session and put me to
work helping him with his knife practice. Actually I rather enjoyed this
task. It entailed my using my powers to levitate one of the fruits and
send it flying around the clearing until Aahz pegged a knife into it. As
an extra touch of finesse, I would then extract the knife and float it
back to him for another try. The exercise was monotonous, but I
never tired of it. It seemed almost supernatural the way the shimmering, somersaulting sliver of steel would dart out to intercept the fruit
as Aahz practiced first overhand, then underhand, now backhand.

"Stop it, Skeeve!"

Aahz's shout jolted me out of my reverie. Without thinking, I
reached out with my mind and…and the knife stopped in midair! I
blinked, but held it there, floating a foot from the fruit which also
hung suspended in place.

"Hel-lo! That's the stuff, Skeeve! Now *there's* something to have
confidence in!"

"I did it!" I said, disbelieving my own eyes.

"You sure did! That little piece of magik will save your life
someday."

Out of habit, I floated the knife back to him. He plucked it
from the air and started to tuck it in his belt, then halted, cocking his
head to one side.

"In the nick of time, too. Someone's coming."

"How can you tell?"

"Nothing special. My hearing's a bit better than yours is all. Don't
panic. It isn't the Imps. Hoofed beast from the sound of it. No wild
animal moves in that straight a line, or that obviously."

"What did you mean, 'in the nick of time?' Aren't we going to hide?"

"Not this time." He grinned at me. "You're developing fast. It's
about time you learned a new spell. We have a few days before
whoever it is gets here."

"Days?"

Aahz was adapting rapidly to our dimension, but units of time
still gave him trouble.

"Run through those time measurements again," he grumbled.

"In seconds, minutes, hours…"

"Minutes! We've got a few minutes."

"Minutes! I can't learn a new spell in a few minutes!"

"Sure you can. This one's easy. All you've got to do is disguise my features to look like a man."

"How do I do that?"

"The same way you do everything else, with your mind. First, close your eyes…close 'em…okay, now picture another face…"

All I could think of was Garkin, so I pictured the two faces side by side.

"Now move the new face over mine…and melt away or build up the necessary features. Like clay…just keep that in the back of your mind and open your eyes."

I looked, and was disappointed.

"It didn't work!"

"Sure it did."

He was looking in the dark mirror which he had fished from his belt pouch.

"But you haven't changed!"

"Yes I did. You can't see it because you cast the spell. It's an illusion, and since your mind knows the truth, it isn't fooled, but anyone else will be. Garkin, huh? Well, it'll do for now."

His identification of the new face took me aback.

"You can really see Garkin's face?"

"Sure, want to look?"

He offered the mirror and grinned. It was a bad joke. One of the first things we discovered about his dubious status in this world was that while he could see himself in mirrors, nobody from our world could. At least, I couldn't.

I could now hear the sounds of the rider coming.

"Aahz, are you sure…"

"Trust me, kid. There's nothing to worry about."

I was worried. The rider was in view now. He was a tall, muscular man with the look of a warrior about him. This was reinforced by the massive war unicorn he was riding, laden with weapons and armor.

"Hey, Aahz. Shouldn't we…"

"Relax, kid. Watch this."

He stepped forward, raising his arm.

"Hello, Stranger! How far to the next town?"

The man veered his mount toward us. He half raised his arm in greeting, then suddenly stiffened. Heaving forward, he squinted at Aahz, then drew back in terror.

"By the Gods! A demon!"

VI.

*"Attention to detail is the watchword for gleaning
information from an unsuspecting witness."*
INSP. CLOUSEAU

THE WARRIOR'S TERROR did not immobilize him long. In fact,
it didn't immobilize him at all! No sooner did he make his discovery
than he took action. Strangely enough, that action was to lean back in
his saddle and begin rummaging frantically through one of his saddle-
bags, a precarious position at best.

Apparently I was not the only one to notice the instability of his
pose. Aahz sprang forward with a yell, waving his arms in the
unicorn's face. Being a reasonable creature, the unicorn reared and
bolted, dumping the warrior on his head.

"By the Gods!" he bellowed, trying to untangle himself from the
ungraceful heap of arms and weapons. "I've killed men for less!"

I decided that, if his threat was to be avoided, I should take a
personal hand in the matter. Reaching out with my mind, I seized a
fist-sized rock and propelled it forcefully against his unhelmeted brow.
The man went down like a pole-axed steer.

For a long moment Aahz and I considered the fallen man, catching
our breath.

"'Relax, Skeeve! This'll be easy, Skeeve! Trust me, Skeeve.' Boy,
Aahz, when you miss a call you don't do it small, do you?"

"Shut up, kid!"

He was rummaging through his pouch again.

"I don't want to shut up. I want to know what happened to the
'foolproof' spell you taught me."

"I was kind of wondering that myself." He had produced the
mirror again and was peering into it. "Tell you what, kid. Check his
aura and watch for anything unusual."

"'Shut up, kid! Check his aura, kid!' You'd think I was some
kind of...Hey!"

"What is it?"

"His aura! It's a sort of a reddish yellow, except there's a blue
patch on his chest."

"I thought so!!" Aahz was across the clearing in a bound, crouching at the fallen man like a beast of prey.

"Look at this!!"

On a thong around the man's neck was a crude silver charm depicting a salamander with one eye in the center of its forehead.

"What is it?"

"I'm not sure, but I've got a hunch. Now play along with me on this. I want you to remove the shape warp spell."

"What spell?"

"C'mon, kid, wake up! The spell that's changing my face."

"That's what I mean. What spell?"

"Now look, kid! Don't give me a lot of back talk. Just do it! He'll be waking up soon."

With a sigh I shut my eyes and set about the seemingly pointless task. It was easier this time, imagining Garkin's face, then melting away the features until Aahz's face was leering at me in my mind's eye. I opened my eyes and looked at Aahz. He looked like Aahz. Terrific.

"Now what?"

As if in answer, the warrior groaned and sat up. He shook his head as if to clear it and opened his eyes. His gaze fell on Aahz, whereupon he blinked, looked again, and reached for his sword, only to find it missing. Also missing were his dagger and hand-axe. Apparently Aahz had not been idle while I was removing the spell.

Aahz spoke first.

"Relax, stranger. Things are not as they seem."

The man sprang to his feet and struck a fighting stance, fists clenched.

"Beware, demon!" he intoned hollowly. "I am not without defenses!"

"Oh yeah? Name three. But like I say, relax. First of all, I'm not a demon."

"Know you, demon, that this charm enables me to look through any spells and see you as you really are."

So that was it! My confidence in my powers came back with a rush.

"Friend, though you may not believe me, the sight of that talisman fills me with joy, for it enables me to prove what I am about to tell you."

"Do not waste your lies on me. Your disguise is penetrated! You are a demon!"

"Right. Could you do me one little favor?" Aahz leisurely sat cross-legged on the ground. "Could you take the charm off for a minute?"

"Take it off?" For a moment the man was puzzled, but he quickly rallied his forces. "Nay, demon. You seek to trick me into removing my charm that you might kill me!"

"Look, dummy. If we wanted to kill you we could have done it while you were knocked out cold!"

For the first time, the man seemed doubtful.

"That is, indeed, a fact."

"Then could you humor me for a moment and take the charm off?"

The warrior hesitated, then slowly removed the charm. He looked hard at Aahz and scowled.

"That's strange. You still look like a demon!"

"Correct, now let me ask you a question. Am I correct in assuming from your words you have some knowledge of demons?"

"I have been a demon hunter for over fifteen years now," he declared proudly.

"Oh, yeah?" For a minute I was afraid Aahz was going to blow the whole gambit, but he got himself back under control and continued.

"Then tell me, friend. In your long experience with demons, have you ever met one who looked like a demon?"

"Of course not! They always use their magik to disguise themselves."

Fat lot he knew about demons!

"Then that should prove my point!"

"What point?"

I thought for a moment Aahz was going to take him by the shoulders and shake him. It occurred to me that perhaps Aahz's subtleties were lost on this world.

"Let me try, Aahz. Look, sir. What he's trying to say is that if he were a demon he wouldn't look like a demon, but he does so he isn't."

"Oh!" said the man with sudden understanding.

"Now you've lost *me*," grumbled Aahz.

"But if you aren't a demon, why do you look like one?"

"Ahh..." Aahz sighed, "therein lies the story. You see, I'm accursed!"

"Accursed?"

"Yes. You see, I am a demon hunter like yourself. A rather successful one, actually. Established quite a name for myself in the field."

"I never heard of you," grumbled the man.

"Well, we've never heard of you either," I chimed in.

"You don't even know my name!"

"Oh, I'm sorry." I remembered my manners. "I'm Skeeve, and this...demon hunter is Aahz."

"Pleased to meet you. I am known as Quigley."

"If I could continue…"

"Sorry, Aahz."

"As I was saying, I had achieved a certain renown among the demons due to my unprecedented success. At times it was rather bothersome, as when it was learned I was coming, most demons would either flee the territory or kill themselves."

"Does he always brag this much?"

"He's just getting started."

"Anyway…one day I was closing with a demon, a particularly ugly brute, when he startled me by addressing me by name, 'Aahz!' says he, 'before you strike, you should know your career is at an end!' Of course I laughed at him, for I had slain demons more fierce than he, sometimes in pairs. 'Laugh if you will,' he boomed, 'but a conclave of demons empowered me to deal with you. Whether you kill me or not, you are doomed to suffer the same end you have visited on so many of us.' I killed him of course, assuming he was bluffing, but my life has not been the same ever since."

"Why not?"

"Because of the curse! When I returned to my horse, my faithful squire here took one look at me and fainted dead away."

"I did no such thing! I mean…it was the heat."

"Of course, Skeeve." Aahz winked slyly at Quigley.

"At any rate, I soon discovered, to my horror, that the demon had worked a spell on me before he expired, causing me to take on the appearance of a demon to all who beheld me."

"Fiendish. Clever, but fiendish."

"You see the subtlety of their plan! That I, fiercest of demon hunters, am now hunted in turn by my fellow humans. I am forced to hide like an animal with only my son here for companionship."

"I thought you said he was your squire."

"That, too. Oh, the irony of it all."

"Gee, that's tough. I wish I could do something to help."

"Maybe you can," Aahz smiled winningly.

Quigley recoiled. I found it reassuring that someone else shared my reaction to Aahz's smile.

"Um…how? I mean, I'm just a demon hunter."

"Precisely how you might be of assistance. You see, at the moment we happen to have several demons following us. It occurs to me we might be of mutual service to each other. We can provide you with targets, and you in turn can rid us of a bloody nuisance."

"They're bloody?" Quigley was horrified.

"Just an expression. Well, what do you say? Is it a deal?"

"I dunno. I'm already on a mission and I don't usually take on a new job until the last one's complete. The misinformed might think I was quitting or had been scared off or something. That sort of thing is bad for the reputation."

"It'd be no trouble at all," Aahz persisted. "It's not like you'll have to go out of your way. Just wait right here and they'll be along."

"Why are they following you, anyway?"

"A vile magician sent them after us after I was foolish enough to seek his aid. The curse, you know."

"Of course…wait a minute, Was that magician's name Garkin by any chance?"

"As a matter of fact it was. Why? Do you know him?"

"Why, he's my mission! That's the man I'm going to kill."

"Why?" I interrupted. "Garkin's no demon."

"But he consorts with demons, lad." Aahz scowled warningly at me. "That's enough for any demon hunter. Right, Quigley?"

"Right. Remember that, lad."

I nodded vigorously at him, feeling suddenly very nervous about this whole encounter.

"Where did you hear about Garkin anyway, Quigley?" Aahz asked casually.

"Strangely enough, from an innkeeper…Isstvan, I think he said his name was…a bit strange, but a sincere enough fellow. About three weeks ride back…but we were talking about your problem. Why did he send demons after you?"

"Well, as I said, I sought him out to try to get him to remove my curse. What I did not realize was that he was actually in league with demons himself. He had heard of me, and flatly refused me aid. What is more, after we left he set some of his demons on our trail."

"I see. How many of them did you say there were?"

"Just two." Aahz assured him. "We've caught glimpses of them occasionally."

"Very well," concluded Quigley. "I'll do it. I'll assist you in your battle."

"That's fine except for one thing. We won't be here."

"Why not? I should think that as a demon hunter you'd welcome the chance once the odds were even."

"If I were here there would be no fight," Aahz stated grandly. "As I have said, I have a certain reputation among demons. If they saw me here they would simply flee."

"I frankly find that hard to believe," commented Quigley. I was inclined to agree with him, but kept my silence.

"Well, I must admit their fear of my charmed sword has a bit to do with their reluctance to do battle."

"Charmed sword?"

"Yes." Aahz patted the sword at his side. "This weapon once belonged to the famous demon hunter Alfans De Clario."

"Never heard of him."

"Never heard of him? Are you sure you're a demon hunter? Why, the man killed over two hundred demons with this sword. They say it is charmed such that whomever wields it cannot be killed by a demon."

"How did he die?"

"Knifed by an exotic dancer. Terrible."

"Yes, they're nasty that way. But about the sword, does it work?"

"It works as well as any sword, a little point-heavy, maybe, but…"

"No. I mean the charm. Does it work?"

"I can testify that I haven't been killed by a demon since I started using it."

"And demons actually recognize it and flee from its owner?"

"Exactly. Of course, I haven't had occasion to use it for years. Been too busy trying to get this curse removed. Sometimes I've thought about selling it, but if I ever get back into business it would be a big help in…um…reestablishing my reputation."

I suddenly realized what Aahz was up to. Quigley rose to the bait like a hungry pike-turtle.

"Hmm…" he said. "Tell you what. Just to give a hand to a fellow demon hunter who's down on his luck, I'll take it off your hands for five gold pieces."

"Five gold pieces! You must be joking. I paid three hundred for it. I couldn't possibly let it go for less than two hundred."

"Oh, well, that counts me out. I only have about fifty gold pieces on me."

"Fifty?"

"Yes, I never travel with more than…"

"But then again, times have been hard, and seeing as how you would be using it to do battle against the fiends who put the curse on me…Yes, I think I could let you have it for fifty gold pieces."

"But that's all the money I have."

"Yes, but what good is a fat purse if you're torn asunder by a demon?"

"True enough. Let me see it."

He took the blade and hefted, giving it a few experimental swings.

"Crummy balance." He grimaced.

"You gt used to it."

"Lousy steel," he declared, squinting at the blade.

"Nice edge on it, though."

"Well, my trainer always told me 'If you take care of your sword, it will take care of you!'"

"We must have had the same trainer."

The two of them smiled at each other. I felt slightly ill.

"Still, I dunno. Fifty pieces of gold is a lot."

"Just look at those stones in the handle."

"I did. They're fake."

"Aha! They're made to look fake. It hides their value."

"Sure did a nice job. What kind of stones are they?"

"Blarney stones."

"Blarney stones?"

"Yes. They're said to ensure your popularity with the ladies, if you know what I mean."

"But fifty gold pieces is all the money I have."

"Tell you what. Make it forty-five gold pieces and throw in your sword."

"My sword?"

"Of course. This beauty will take care of you, and your sword will keep my squire and me from being defenseless in this heathen land."

"Hmm. That seems fair enough. Yes, I believe you have made a deal, my friend."

They shook hands ceremoniously and began effecting the trade. I seized the opportunity to interrupt.

"Gee, it's a shame we have to part so soon."

"Why so soon?" The warrior was puzzled.

"No need to rush off," Aahz assured him, giving me a solid elbow in the ribs.

"But Aahz, we wanted to travel more before sundown and Quigley has to prepare for battle."

"What preparations?" asked Quigley.

"Your unicorn," I continued doggedly. "Don't you want to catch your unicorn?"

"My unicorn! All of my armor is on that animal!"

"Surely it won't wander far..." Aahz growled.

"There are bandits about who would like nothing better than to get their hands on a good war unicorn." Quigley heaved himself to his feet. "And I want him at my side to help me fight the demons. Yes, I must be off. I thank you for your assistance, my friends. Safe journey until we meet again."

With a vague wave of his hand, he disappeared into the woods whistling for his mount.

"Now what was all that about?" Aahz exploded angrily.

"What, Aahz?"

"The big rush to get rid of him. As gullible as he was, I could have traded him out of his pants or anything else vaguely valuable he might have had on him. I specifically wanted to get my hands on that charm."

"Basically I wanted to see him on his way before he caught on to the flaw in your little tale."

"What, the son-squire slip? He wouldn't have..."

"No, the other thing."

"What other thing?" I sighed.

"Look, he saw through your disguise because that pendant lets him see through spells, right?"

"Right, and I explained it away saying I was the victim of a demon's curse..."

"...that changed your appearance with a spell. But if he could see through spells, he should be able to see through that spell to see you as a normal man. Right?"

"Hmm...Maybe we'd better be on our way now that we know where Isstvan is."

But I was unwilling to let my little triumph go so easily.

"Tell me, Aahz. What would you do if we encountered a demon hunter as smart as me?"

"That's easy." He smiled, patting the crossbow. "I'd kill him. Think about it."

I did.

VII.

"Is there anything in the universe more beautiful and protective than the simple complexity of a spider's web?"
CHARLOTTE

I CLOSED MY eyes for concentration. This was more difficult than drawing energies from the force line directly into my body. I pointed a finger for focus at a spot some five yards distant from me.

The idea of drawing energies from a distant location and controlling them would have seemed impossible to me, until Aahz pointed out it was the same as the candle lighting exercise I had already mastered. Now it did not seem impossible, merely difficult.

Confidently, I narrowed my concentration, and in my mind's eye saw a gleaming blue light appear at the designated point. Without breaking my concentration, I moved my finger overhead in a slow arc. The light followed the lead, etching a glowing blue trail in the air behind it. As it touched the ground again, or where I sensed the ground to be, I moved my finger again, moving the light into the second arc of the protective pentagram.

It occurred to me that what I was doing was not unlike forming the normal flat pentagram Garkin had used at the hut. The only difference being that instead of being inscribed on the floor, this was etched overhead with its points dipping downward to touch the earth. It was more an umbrella than a border.

The other major difference, I thought as I completed the task, was that *I* was doing it. Me. Skeeve. What I had once watched with awe, I was now performing as routine.

I touched the light down in its original place, completing the pentagram. Quietly pleased, I stood for a moment, eyes closed. Studying the glowing blue lines etched in my mind's eye.

"Terrific, kid," came Aahz's voice. "Now what say you damp it down a bit before we draw every peasant and demon hunter in the country."

Surprised, I opened my eyes.

The pentagram was still there! Not imagined in my mind, but actually glowing overhead. Its cold blue light gave an eerie illumination to the scene that negated the warmth of our little campfire.

"Sorry, Aahz." I quickly eased my control on the energy and watched as the lines of the pentagram faded to invisibility. They were still there. I could feel their presence in the night air above me. Now, however, they could not be seen with normal vision.

More for the joy of it than out of any lack of confidence, I closed my eyes again and looked at them. They glowed there in shimmering beauty, a cooler, reassuring presence to counter the impatience of the red-gold glow of the force-line spear pointing doggedly toward tomorrow's path.

"Sit down, kid, and finish your lizard-bird."

We were out of the forest proper now, but despite the presence of the nearby road, game was still plentiful and fell ready victim to my snares. Aahz still refused to join me in the meals, insisting alcohol was the only thing in this dimension worth consuming, but I dined frequently and royally.

"You know, kid," he said, looking up from his endless sword-sharpening. "You're really coming along pretty well with your studies."

"What do you mean?" I mumbled through a bone, hoping he would elaborate.

"You're a lot more confident with your magik. You'd better watch your controls, though. You had enough energy in that pentagram to fry anything that bumped against it."

"I guess I'm still a bit worried about the assassins."

"Relax, kid. It's been three days since we set 'em up in that ambush of Quigley's. Even if he didn't stop 'em, they'll never catch up with us now."

"Did I really summon up that much power?" I urged, eager for praise.

"Unless you're actually engaged in magical battle, wards are used as a warning signal only. If you put too much energy into them it can have two potentially bad side effects. First, you can draw unnecessary attention to yourself by jarring or burning an innocent bystander who blunders into it. Second, if it actually reaches a magical opponent, it probably won't stop him; just alert him that he has a potentially dangerous foe in the area."

"I thought it was a good thing if I could summon up lots of power."

"Look, kid. This isn't a game. You're tapping into some very powerful forces here. The idea is to strengthen your control, not see

how much you can liberate. If you get too careless with experimenting, you could end up helpless when the actual crunch comes."

"Oh," I said, unconvinced.

"Really, kid. You've got to learn this. Let me try an example.
Suppose for a minute you're a soldier assigned to guard a pass. Your
superiors put you on the post and give you a stack of ten-pound
rocks. All you have to do is watch to see if anyone comes, and if
someone does, drop a rock on his head. Are you with me so far?"

"I guess so."

"Fine. Now it's a long, boring duty, and you have lots of time to
think. You're very proud of your muscles, and decide it's a bit insult-
ing that you were only given ten-pound rocks. Twenty-pound rocks
would be more effective, and you think you could handle them as
easily as the ten-pound variety. Logical?"

I nodded vaguely, still not sure what he was driving at.

"Just to prove the point to yourself, you heft a twenty-pound
rock, and, sure enough, you can handle it. Then it occurs to you if you
can handle a twenty-pounder, you should be able to handle a forty-
pounder, or even a fifty-pounder. So you try. Then it happens."

He was getting so worked up I felt no need to respond.

"You drop it on your foot, or you pull a muscle, or you keel
over from heat exhaustion, or any one of a hundred other things.
Then where are you?"

He leveled an accusing finger at me.

"The enemy strolls through the pass you're supposed to be guarding and you can't even lift the original ten pound rock to stop them.
All because you indulged in needless testing of idiotic muscle power!"

I was impressed, and gave the matter serious thought before
replying.

"I see what you're saying, Aahz, but there's one flaw in your
example. The keyword is 'needless.' Now in my case, it's not a matter of having a stack of ten pound rocks that would do the job. I
have a handful of gravel. I'm trying to scrounge around for a rock
big enough to do some damage."

"True enough," Aahz retorted, "but the fact remains if you over-
extend yourself you won't be able to use what you already have.
Even gravel can be effective if used at the right time. Don't under-
rate what you've got or what you're doing. Right now you're keeping the finder spear going, maintaining the wards, and keeping my

disguise intact. That's a lot for someone of your abilities to be doing simultaneously. If something happened right now, which would you drop first?"

"Um…"

"Too late! We're already dead. You won't have time to ponder energy problems. That's why you always have to hold some back to deal with immediate situations while you rally your energies from other activities. Now do you see?"

"I think so, Aahz," I said haltingly. "I'm a bit tired."

"Well, think about it. It's important. In the meantime get some sleep and try to store up your energies. Incidentally, let the finder spear go for now. You can summon it up again in the morning. Right now, it's just a needless drain."

"Okay, Aahz. How about your disguise?"

"Hmm…better keep that. It'll be good practice for you to maintain both that and the wards in your sleep. Speaking of which…"

"Right, Aahz."

I drew my acquired assassin's cloak about me for warmth and curled up. Despite his gruff manner, Aahz was insistent that I get enough sleep as well as food.

Sleep did not come easily, however. I found I was still a bit wound up over casting the wards.

"Aahz?"

"Yeah, kid?"

"How would you say my powers right now stack up against the devils?"

"What devils?"

"The assassins that were following us."

"I keep telling you, kid. Those weren't Deveels, those were Imps."

"What's the difference?"

"I told you before. Imps are from Imper, and Deveels…"

"…are from Deva," I finished for him. "But what does that mean? I mean, are their powers different or something?"

"You'd better believe it, kid." Aahz snorted. "Deveels are some of the meanest characters you'd ever not want to tangle with. They're some of the most feared and respected characters in the dimensions."

"Are they warriors? Mercenaries?"

Aahz shook his head.

"Worse!" he answered. "They're merchants."

"Merchants?"

"Don't sneer, kid. Maybe merchants is too sedate a phrase to describe them. Traders Supreme is more like it."

"Tell me more, Aahz."

"Well, history was never my forte, but as near as I can tell, at one time the entire dimension of Deva faced economic ruin. The lands suffered a plague that affected the elements. Fish could not live in the oceans, plants could not grow in the soil. Those plants that did grow were twisted and changed and poisoned the animals. The dimension was no longer able to support the life of its citizenry."

I lay, staring up at the stars as Aahz continued his tale.

"Dimension travel, once a frivolous pastime, now became the key to survival. Many left Deva, migrating singly or in groups to other dimensions. The tales of their barren, miserable homeland served as a prototype for many religious groups' concept of an afterworld for evil souls."

"The ones who stayed, however, decided to use the power of dimension travel in a different way. They established themselves as traders, traveling the dimensions buying and selling wonders. What is common in one dimension is frequently rare in another. As the practice grew, they became rich and powerful…also the shrewdest hagglers in all the dimensions. Their techniques for driving a hard bargain have been passed down from generation to generation and polished until now they are without equal. They are scattered through the dimensions, returning to Deva only occasionally to visit the Bazaar."

"The Bazaar?" I prompted.

"No one can travel extensively in all the dimensions in one lifetime. The Bazaar on Deva is the place the Deveels meet to trade with each other. An off-dimension visitor there will be sore pressed to not lose o'er much, much less hold his own. It's said if you make a deal with a Deveel, you'd be wise to count your fingers afterward…then your arms and legs, then your relatives…"

"I get the picture. Now how about the Imps?"

"The Imps." Aahz said the word as if it tasted bad. "The Imps are inferior to the Deveels in every way."

"How so?"

"They're cheap imitations. Their dimension, Imper, lies close to
Deva, and the Deveels bargain with them so often they're almost
bankrupt from the irresistible 'fair deals." To hold their own, they've
taken to aping the Deveels, attempting to peddle wonders through
the dimensions. To the uneducated, they may seem clever and powerful; in fact, occasionally they try to pass themselves off as Deveels.
Compared to the masters, however, they're bungling incompetents."

He trailed off into silence. I pondered his words, and they
prompted another question.

"Say, Aahz?"

"Hmm? Yeah, kid?"

"What dimension do you come from?"

"Perv."

"Does that make you a Pervert?"

"No. That makes me a Pervect. Now shut up!"

I assumed he wanted me to go to sleep, and maintained silence
for several minutes. There was just one more question I had to ask,
however, if I was going to get any sleep at all.

"Aahz?"

"Keep it down, kid."

"What dimension is this?"

"Hmmm? This is Klah, kid. Now for the last time, shut up."

"What does that make me, Aahz?"

There was no answer.

"Aahz?"

I rolled over to look at him, He was staring out into the darkness and listening intently.

"What is it?"

"I think we've got company, kid."

As if in response to his words, I felt a tremor in the wards as
something came through.

I bounded to my feet as two figures appeared at the edge of
the firelight. The light was dimming, but was sufficient to reveal the
fact that both figures were wearing the hooded cloaks of assassins,
and the gold side was out!

VIII.

"In times of crisis, it is of utmost importance not to lose one's head."
M. ANTOINETTE

THE FOUR OF us stood in frozen tableau for several moments studying each other. My mind was racing, but could not focus on a definite course of action. I decided to follow Aahz's lead and simply stood regarding the two figures coolly, trying to ignore the two crossbows leveled steadily at us.

Finally, one of our visitors broke the silence.

"Well, Throckwoddle? Aren't you going to invite your friends to sit down?"

Surprisingly, this was addressed to me!

"Ummm…" I said.

"Yes, Throckwoddle," Aahz drawled, turning to me. "And aren't you going to introduce me to your colleagues?"

"Um…" I repeated.

"Perhaps he doesn't remember us," the second figure injected sarcastically.

"Nonsense," responded the first with equal sarcasm. "His two oldest friends? Brockhurst and Higgens? How could he possibly not remember our names? Just because he forgot to share the loot doesn't mean he'd forget our names. Be fair, Higgens."

"Frankly, Brockhurst," responded the other. "I'd rather he remembered the loot and forgot our names."

Their words were stuffy and casual, but the crossbows never wavered.

I was beginning to get the picture. Apparently these were the two Imps Aahz had assured me couldn't overtake us. Fortunately, it seemed they thought I was the Imp who had killed Garkin…at least, I thought it was fortunate.

"Gentlemen," Aahz exclaimed, stepping forward. "Let me say what a great pleasure it is to…"

He stopped as Brockhurst's crossbow leapt to his shoulder in one smooth move.

"I'm not sure who you are," he intoned. "But I'd advise you to stay out of this. This is a private matter between the three of us."

"Brockhurst," interrupted Higgens. "It occurs to me we may be being a bit hasty in our actions."

"Thank you, Higgens," I said, greatly relieved.

"Now that we've established contact," he continued, favoring me with an icy glare, "I feel we should perhaps secure our traveling companion before we continue this...discussion."

"I suppose you're right, Higgens," Brockhurst admitted grudgingly. "Be a good fellow and fetch him along while I watch these two."

"I feel that would be ill-advised on two counts. First, I refuse to approach that beast alone, and second, that would leave you alone facing two-to-one odds, if you get my point."

"Quite. Well, what do you suggest?"

"That we both fetch our traveling companion and return without delay."

"And what is to keep these two from making a hasty departure?"

"The fact that we'll be watching them from somewhere in the darkness with crossbows. I believe that should be sufficient to discourage them from making any...ah...movements which might be subject to misinterpretation."

"Very well," Brockhurst yielded grudgingly. "Throck-woddle, I would strongly suggest you not attempt to avoid us further. While I don't believe we could be any more upset with you than we already are, running away might actually succeed in provoking us further."

With that, the two figures faded back into the darkness.

"What are we going to do, Aahz?" I whispered frantically.

He seemed not to hear me.

"Imps!" he chortled, rubbing his hands together gleefully. "What a stroke of luck!"

"Aahz! They're going to kill me!"

"Hm? Relax, kid. Like I said, Imps are gullible. If they were really thinking, they would have shot us down without talking. I haven't met an Imp yet I couldn't talk circles around."

He cocked his head, listening.

"They're coming back now. Just follow my lead. Oh yes...I almost forgot. Drop the disguise on my features when I give you the cue."

"But you said they couldn't catch…"

I broke off as the two Imps reappeared. They were leading a war unicorn between them. The hoods of the cloaks were back now, revealing their features. I was moderately surprised to see they looked human, seedy perhaps, but human nonetheless. Then I saw Quigley.

He was sitting woodenly astride the unicorn, lurching back and forth with the beast's stride. His eyes were staring fixedly straight ahead and his right arm was raised as if in salutation. The light of the fire reflected off his face as if it were glass, and I realized with horror he was no longer alive, but a statue of some unidentified substance.

Any confidence I might have gained from Aahz's assurances left me in a rush. Gullible or not, the Imps played for keeps, and any mistake we made would, in all likelihood, be our last.

"Who's that?" Aahz asked, interrupting my thoughts.

I realized I had been dangerously close to showing a betraying sign of recognition of the statue.

"There will be time for that later, if indeed there is a later," said Higgens, grimly dropping the unicorn's reins and raising his crossbow.

"Yes," echoed Brockhurst, imitating Higgen's move with his own weapon. "First there is the matter of an explanation to be settled. Throckwoddle?"

"Gentlemen, gentlemen," said Aahz soothingly, stepping between me and the crossbows. "Before you proceed I must insist on introducing myself properly. If you will but allow me a moment while I remove my disguise."

The sight of the two weapons had rattled me so badly I almost missed my cue. Fortunately, I managed to gather my scattered senses and closed my eyes, shakily executing the change features spell to convert Aahz back to his normal dubious appearance.

I'm not sure what reaction I had expected from the Imps at the transformation, but the one I got surpassed any possible expectations.

"By the Gods below!" gasped Brockhurst.

"A Pervert!" gasped Higgens.

"That's Per*vect!*" smiled Aahz, showing all his pointed teeth. "And don't ever forget it, friend Imps."

"Yessir!" they chorused in unison.

They were both standing in slack-jawed amazement, cross-bows dangling forgotten in their hands. From their terrified reactions, I began to suspect that, despite all his bragging, Aahz had perhaps not told me everything about his dimension or the reputation of its inhabitants.

Aahz ignored their stares and plopped down again at his place by the fire.

"Now that that's established, why don't you put away those silly crossbows and sit down so we can chat like civilized folk, eh?"

He gestured impatiently and they hastened to comply. I also resumed a sitting position, not wishing to be the only one left standing.

"But...what are...why are you here...sir...if you don't mind my asking?" Brockhurst finally managed to get the whole question out.

However incompetent he might be as a demon, he sure knew how to grovel.

"Ah!" smiled Aahz. "Therein lies a story."

I settled back. This could take a while.

"I was summoned across the dimensions barrier by one Garkin, a magician I have never cared much for. It seems he was expecting some trouble from a rival and was eager to enlist my aid for the upcoming fracas. Now, as I said before, I had never been fond of Garkin and was not particularly wild about joining him. He began growing unpleasant in his insistence to the point that I considered swaying from my normal easy-going nature to take action against him, when who should appear but Throckwoddle here who did me the favor of putting a quarrel into the old slime-stirrer."

Aahz acknowledged me with an airy wave. I tried to look modest.

"Naturally, we fell to chatting afterward, and he mentioned he was in the employment of one Isstvan and that his action against Garkin had been part of an assignment."

"You answered questions about an assignment?" Higgens turned to me aghast.

"Yes I did," I snarled at him. "Wouldn't you, considering the circumstances?"

"Oh, yes...of course." He darted a nervous glance at Aahz and lapsed into respectful silence again.

"Anyway," Aahz continued, "it occurred to me that I owed this fellow Isstvan a favor for ridding me of a nagging nuisance, so I suggested I accompany Throckwoddle back to his employer that I might offer him my services, on a limited basis, of course."

"You could have waited for us." Brockhurst glowered at me.

"Well...I wanted...you see...I..."

"I insisted," Aahz smiled. "You see, my time is quite valuable and I had no desire to waste it waiting around."

"Oh," said Brockhurst.

Higgens was not so easily swayed.

"You could have left us a message," he muttered.

"We did," Aahz replied. "My ring, in full view on the table. I see you found it."

He pointed an accusing finger at Brockhurst. I noticed for the first time the Imp was wearing Garkin's ring.

"This ring?" Brockhurst started. "Is it yours? I thought it was part of Garkin's loot that had been overlooked."

"Yes, it's mine." Aahz bared his teeth. "I'm surprised you didn't recognize it. But now that we're united, you will, of course, return it."

"Certainly!" the Imp fumbled in his haste to remove the ring.

"Careful there," Aahz cautioned. "You do know how to operate it, don't you? It can be dangerous in ignorant hands."

"Of course I know how to operate it," Brockhurst replied in an injured tone. "You press against the ring with the fingers on either side of it. I saw one like it at the Bazaar on Deva once."

He tossed the ring to Aahz who caught it neatly and slipped it on his finger. Fortunately, it fit. I made a mental note to ask Aahz to let me try using the ring sometime, now that we knew how it worked.

"Now that I've explained about me, how about answering my question," Aahz said, leveling a finger at the Quigley statue. "Who is that?"

"We aren't sure ourselves," Higgens admitted.

"It's all quite puzzling, really," Brockhurst added.

"Would you care to elaborate on that?" Aahz prompted.

"Well, it happened about three days back, We were following your trail to...um...with hopes of reuniting our group. Suddenly this warrior gallops out of the brush ahead of us and bars our path. It was as if he knew we were coming and was waiting for us. 'Isstvan was right!' he shouts, 'This region does abound with demons!'"

"Isstvan?" I said, doing my best to look puzzled.

"That's what he said. It surprised us, too. I mean, here we are working for Isstvan, and we're set upon by a man claiming to be sent by the same employer. Anyway, then he says, 'Behold the instroment of your doom!' and draws a sword."

"What kind of sword was it?" Aahz asked innocently.

"Nothing special. Actually little substandard from all we could see. Well, it put us in a predicament. We had to defend ourselves, but were afraid to harm him on the off-chance he really was working for Isstvan."

"What did you do?" I asked.

"Frankly, we said 'to heck with it' and took the easy way out. Higgens here bounced one of his stone balls off the guy's forehead and froze him in place. We've been dragging him along ever since. We figure we'll dump him in Isstvan's lap and let him sort it out."

"A wise solution," commented Aahz.

They inclined their heads graciously at the compliment.

"One question I'd like to ask," I interjected. "How were you able to overtake us, encumbered as you were?"

"Well, it was no small problem. We had little hope of overtaking you as it was, and with our new burden, it appeared it would be impossible," Brockhurst began.

"We were naturally quite eager to…ah…join you, so we resorted to desperate measures," Higgens continued. "We took a side trip to Twixt and sought the aid of the Deveel there. It cost us a pretty penny, but he finally agreed to teleport our group to the trail ahead of you, allowing us to make our desired contact."

"Deveel? What Deveel?" Aahz interrupted.

"Frumple. The Deveel at Twixt. The one who…"

Brockhurst broke off suddenly, his eyes narrowing suspiciously. He shot a dark glance at Higgens, who was casually reaching for his crossbow.

"I'm surprised Throckwoddle hasn't mentioned Frumple to you," Higgens purred. "After all, he's the one who told us about him."

IX.

*"To function efficiently, any group of people or
employees must have faith in their leader."*
CAPT. BLIGH (ret.)

"YES, THROCKWODDLE." IF anything, Aahz's voice was even more menacing than the Imps. "Why didn't you tell me about the Deveel?"

"It...ah...must have slipped my mind," I mumbled.

With a massive exertion of self control, I shot my most withering glare at the Imps, forcing myself to ignore the menace of the crossbows. I was rewarded by seeing them actually look guilty and avoid my gaze.

"Slipped your mind! More likely you were trying to hold back a bit of information from me," Aahz said accusingly. "Well, now that it's out, let's have the rest of it. What about this Deveel?"

"Ask Brockhurst," I grumbled. "He seems to be eager to talk about it."

"Well, Brockhurst?" Aahz turned to him.

The Imp gave me an apologetic shrug as he started.

"Well, I guess I've already told you most of it. There's a Deveel, Frumple, in residence in Twixt. He goes under the cover of Abdul the Rug Merchant, but he actually maintains a thriving trade in the usual Deva manner, buying and selling across the dimensions."

"What's he doing in Klah?" Aahz interrupted. "I mean, there's not much business here. Isn't it a little slow for a Deveel's taste?"

"Well, Throckwoddle said..." Brockhurst broke off and shot me a look.

"Go on, tell him." I tried to sound resigned.

"Well," the Imp continued, "rumor has it that he was exiled from Deva and is in hiding here, ashamed to show his face in a major dimension."

"Barred from Deva? Why? What did he do?"

I was glad Aahz asked. It would have sounded strange coming from me.

"Throckwoddle wouldn't tell us. Said Frumple was sensitive on the subject and we shouldn't bring it up."

"Well, Throckwoddle?" Aahz turned to me.

I was so caught up in the story it took me a few beats before I remembered that I really didn't know.

"Um...I can't tell you." I said.

"What?" Aahz scowled.

I began to wonder how much he was caught up in the story and had lost track of the realities of the situation.

"I learned his secret by accident and hold it as a personal confidence," I said haughtily. "During our travels these last few days, I've learned some rather interesting items about you and hold them in the same esteem. I trust you will respect my silence on the matter of Frumple as I expect others to respect my silence about those matters pertaining to you."

"Okay, okay. You've made your point." Aahz conceded.

"Say...um...Throckwoddle," Higgens interrupted. "I would suggest we all shed our disguises like our friend Perver...um, Pervect here has. No sense in using up our energies keeping up false faces among friends."

His tone was casual, but he sounded suspicious. I noticed he had not taken his hand off his crossbow.

"Why?" argued Brockhurst. "I prefer to keep my disguise on at all times when in another dimension. Lessens the chance of forgetting to put it on at a crucial moment."

"I think Higgens is right," Aahz stated before I could support Brockhurst. "I for one like to see the true faces of the people I'm talking to."

"Well," grumbled Brockhurst, "if everyone is going to insist."

He closed his eyes in concentration, and his features began to shimmer and melt.

I didn't watch the whole process. My mind was racing desperately back to Garkin's hut, when Aahz held up the charred face of the assassin. I hastily envisioned my own face next to it and began working, making certain obvious modifications to its appearance to repair the fire damage.

When I was done, I snuck a peek out of one eye. The other two had changed already. My attention was immediately drawn to their complexion. Theirs was a pinkish red, while mine wasn't. I hastily re-closed my eye and made the adjustment.

Satisfied now, I opened my eyes and looked about me. The other two Imps now showed the apparently characteristic pointed ears and chins. Aahz looked like Aahz. The situation had completely reversed since the Imps had arrived. Instead of being normal surrounded by three disguised demons, I was now surrounded by three demons while I was disguised. Terrific.

"Ahh. That's better," chortled Aahz.

"You know, Throckwoddle," Higgens said, cocking a head at me. For a moment there in the firelight you looked different. In fact…"

"Come, come, gentlemen," Aahz interrupted. "We have serious matters to discuss. Does Isstvan know about Frumple's existence?"

"I don't believe so," answered Brockhurst. "If he did, he would have either enlisted him or had him assassinated."

"Good," exclaimed Aahz. "He could very well be the key to our plot."

"What plot?" I asked.

"Our plot against Isstvan, of course."

"What?" exclaimed Higgens, completely distracted from me now. "Are you insane?"

"No," retorted Aahz. "But Isstvan is. I mean, think! Has he been acting particularly stable?"

"No," admitted Brockhurst. "But then neither has any other magician I've met, present company included."

"Besides," Higgens interrupted, "I thought you were on your way to help him."

"That's before I heard your story," Aahz pointed out. "I'm not particularly eager to work for a magician who pits his own employees against each other."

"When did he do that?" Higgens asked.

Aahz made an exasperated gesture.

"Think, gentlemen! Have you forgotten our stony-faced friend there?" He jerked a thumb at the figure on the unicorn. "If you recall your tale correctly, his words seemed to imply he had been sent by Isstvan to intercept you."

"That's right," said Brockhurst. "So?"

"What do you mean, 'So?'" Aahz exploded. "That's it! Isstvan sent him to kill you. Either he was trying to cut his overhead by assassinating his assassins before payday, or he's so unstable mentally he's lashing out blindly at everyone, including his own allies. Either way he doesn't sound like the most benevolent of employers."

"You know, I believe he has a point there," I observed, determined to be of some assistance in this deception.

"But if that's true, what are we to do?" asked Higgens.

"Well, I don't have a firm plan of action," Aahz admitted. "But I have some general ideas that might help."

"Such as?" prompted Brockhurst.

"You go back to Isstvan. Say nothing at all of your suspicions. If you do, he might consider you dangerous and move against you immediately. What's more, refuse any new assignments. Find some pretext to stay as close to him as possible. Learn all about his habits and weaknesses, but don't do anything until we get there."

"Where are you going?" asked Higgens.

"We are going to have a little chat with Frumple. If we're going to move against Isstvan, the support of a Deveel could be invaluable."

"And probably unobtainable," grumbled Brockhurst. "I've never known a Deveel yet to take sides in a fight. They prefer being in a position to sell to both sides."

"What do you mean 'we?'" asked Higgens. "Isn't Throckwoddle coming with us?"

"No. I've developed a fondness for his company. Besides, if he doesn't agree to help us, it would come in handy to have an assassin close by. Frumple's too powerful to run the risk of leaving him unallied to help Isstvan."

As Aahz was speaking, Brockhurst casually leaned back out of his line of vision and silently mouthed the word "Pervert" at Higgens. Higgens quietly nodded his agreement, and they both shot me sympathetic glances.

"Well, what do you think?" Aahz asked in conclusion.

"Hmm...what do we do with him?" Higgins indicated the Quigley statue with a jerk of his head.

"We'll take him with us," I chimed in hastily.

"Of course!" agreed Aahz, shooting me a black look. "If you two took him back to Isstvan, he might guess you suspected his treachery."

"Besides," I added, "maybe we can revive him and convince him to join us in our battle."

"I suppose you'll be wanting the antidote then." Higgins sighed, fishing a small vial from inside his cloak and tossing it to me. "Just sprinkle a little on him and he'll return to normal in a few minutes.

Watch yourself, though. There's something strange about him. He seemed to be able to see right through our disguises."

"Where's the sword you were talking about?" Aahz asked.

"It's in his pack. Believe me, it's junk. The only reason we brought it along was that he seemed to put so much stock in it. It'll be curious to find out what he thought it was when we revive him."

"Well, I believe that just about covers everything," Brockhurst sighed. "I suggest we get some sleep and start on our respective journeys first thing in the morning."

"I suggest you start on your journey now," Aahz said pointedly.

"Now?" Brockhurst exclaimed.

"But it's the middle of the night," Higgens pointed out.

"Might I remind you gentlemen that the longer you are away from Isstvan, the greater the chances are he'll send another assassin after you?"

"He's right, you know," I said thoughtfully.

"I suppose so," grumbled Higgens.

"Well," said Brockhurst, rising to his feet, "I guess we'll be on our way then as soon as we divide Garkin's loot."

"On the contrary," stated Aahz. "Not only do we not divide the loot, I would suggest you give us whatever funds you have at your disposal."

"What?" they chorused, their crossbows instantly in their hands again.

"Think, gentlemen," Aahz said soothingly. "We'd be trying to bargain with a Deveel for his support. As you yourselves have pointed out, they are notoriously unreasonable in their prices. I would hate to think we might fail in our negotiations for a lack of funds."

There was a pregnant silence as the Imps sought to find a hole in his logic.

"Oh, very well," Brockhurst conceded at last, lowering his crossbow and reaching for his purse.

"I still don't think it will do any good," Higgens grumbled, imitating Brockhurst's move. "You probably couldn't buy off a Deveel if you had the Gnomes themselves backing you."

They passed the purses over to Aahz, who hefted them judiciously before tucking them into his own waistband.

"Trust me, gentlemen." Aahz smiled. "We Pervects have methods of persuasion that are effective even on Deveels."

The Imps shuddered at this and began edging away.

"Well...umm...I guess we'll see you later," Higgens mumbled. "Watch yourself, Throckwoddle."

"Yes," added Brockhurst. "And be sure when you're done, the Deveel is either with us or dead."

I tried to think of something to say in return, but before anything occurred to me they were gone.

Aahz cocked an eyebrow at me and I held up a restraining hand until I felt them pass through the wards. I signaled him with a nod.

"They've gone," I said.

"Beautiful!" exclaimed Aahz gleefully. "Didn't I tell you they were gullible?"

For once I had to admit he was right.

"Well, get some sleep now, kid. Like I said before, tomorrow's going to be a busy day, and all of a sudden it looks like it's going to be even busier."

I complied, but one question kept nagging at me.

"Aahz?"

"Yeah, kid."

"What dimension do the Gnomes come from?"

"Zoorik," he answered.

On that note, I went to sleep.

X.

"Man shall never reach his full capacity while chained to the earth. We must take wing and conquer the heavens."
ICARUS

"ARE YOU SURE we're up to handling a Deveel, Aahz?" I was aware I had asked the question countless times in the last few days, but I still needed reassurance.

"Will you relax, kid?" Aahz growled. "I was right about the Imps, wasn't I?"

"I suppose so," I admitted hesitantly.

I didn't want to tell Aahz, but I wasn't that happy with the Imp incident. It had been a little too close for my peace of mind. Since the meeting, I had been having recurring nightmares involving Imps and crossbows.

"Look at it this way, kid. With any luck this Frumple character will be able to restore my powers. That'd take you off the hotseat."

"I guess so," I said without enthusiasm.

He had raised this point several times since learning about Frumple. Each time he did, it gave me the same feeling of discomfort.

"Something bothering you, kid?" Aahz asked, cocking his head at me.

"Well…it's…Aahz, if you do get your powers back, will you still want me as an apprentice?"

"Is that what's been eating at you?" he seemed genuinely surprised. "Of course I'll still want you. What kind of a magician do you think I am? I don't choose my apprentices lightly."

"You wouldn't feel I was a burden?"

"Maybe at first, but not now. You were in on the start of this Isstvan thing, you've earned the right to be in on the end of it."

Truth to tell, I wasn't all that eager to be there when Aahz confronted Isstvan, but that seemed to be the price I would have to pay if I was going to continue my association with Aahz.

"Um…Aahz?"

"Yeah, kid?"

"Just one more question?"

"Promise?"

"How's that?"

"Nothing. What's the question, kid."

"If you get your powers back, and I'm still your apprentice, which dimension will we live in?"

"Hmm. To be honest, kid, I hadn't really given it much thought. Tell ya what, we'll burn that bridge when we come to it, okay?"

"Okay, Aahz."

I tried to get my mind off the question. Maybe Aahz was right. No sense worrying about the problem until we knew for sure it existed. Maybe he wouldn't get his powers back. Maybe I'd get to be the one to fight Isstvan after all. Terrific.

"Hey! Watch the beast, kid!"

Aahz's voice broke my train of thought. We were leading the war unicorn between us, and the beast chose this moment to act up.

It nickered and half-reared, then planted its feet and tossed its head.

"Steady…ow!"

Aahz extended a hand trying to seize its bridle and received a solid rap on the forearm from the unicorn's horn for his trouble.

"Easy, Buttercup," I said soothingly. "There's a good boy."

The beast responded to my coaxings, first by settling down, pawing the ground nervously, then finally by rubbing his muzzle against me.

Though definitely a friendly gesture, this is not the safest thing to have a unicorn do to you. I ducked nimbly under his swinging horn and cast about me quickly. Snatching an orange flower from a nearby bush, I fed it to him at an arm's length. He accepted the offering and began to munch it contentedly.

"I don't think that beast likes demons," Aahz grumbled sullenly, rubbing his bruised arm.

"It stands to reason," I retorted. "I mean, he was a demon hunter's mount, you know."

"Seems to take readily enough to you, though," Aahz observed. "Are you sure you're not a virgin?"

"Certainly not," I replied in my most injured tone.

Actually I was, but I would rather have been fed to vampire-slugs than admit it to Aahz.

"Speaking of demon hunters, you'd better check on our friend there," Aahz suggested. "It could get a bit grisly if an arm or something broke off before we got around to restoring him."

I hastened to comply. We had rigged a drag litter for the Quigley-statue to avoid having to load and unload him each night, not to mention escaping the chore of saddling and unsaddling the war unicorn. The bulk of the gear and armor was sharing the drag-litter with the Quigley-statue, a fact which seemed to make the unicorn immensely happy. Apparently it was far easier to drag all that weight than to carry it on one's back.

"He seems to be okay, Aahz," I reported.

"Good," he sneered. "I'd hate to think of anything happening to him, accidental-like."

Aahz was still not happy with our traveling companions. He had only grudgingly given in to my logic for bringing them along as opposed to leaving them behind. I had argued that they could be of potential assistance in dealing with the Deveel, or at least when we had our final showdown with Isstvan.

In actuality, that wasn't my reasoning at all. I felt a bit guilty about having set Quigley up to get clobbered by the Imps and didn't want to see any harm befall him because of it.

"It would make traveling a lot easier if we restored him," I suggested hopefully.

"Forget it, kid."

"But Aahz…"

"I said, forget it! In case you've forgotten, that particular gentleman's major pastime seems to consist of seeking out and killing demons. Now I'm aware my winning personality may have duped you into overlooking the fact, but I am a demon. As such, I am not about to accept a living, breathing, and, most importantly, functioning demon hunter as a traveling companion."

"We fooled him before!" I argued.

"Not on a permanent basis. Besides, when would you practice your magik if he was restored? Until we meet with the Deveel, you're still our best bet against Isstvan."

I wished he would stop mentioning that. It made me incredibly uncomfortable when he did. Besides, I couldn't think of a good argument to it.

"I guess you're right, Aahz," I admitted.

"You'd better believe I'm right. Incidentally, since we seem to be stopped anyway, this is as good a time as any for your next lesson."

My spirits lifted. Besides my natural eagerness to extend my magical abilities, Aahz's offer contained an implied statement that he was pleased with my progress so far in earlier lessons.

"Okay, Aahz," I said, looping the unicorn's reins around a nearby bush. "I'm ready."

"Good," smiled Aahz, rubbing his hands together. "Today we're going to teach you to fly."

My spirits fell again.

"Fly?" I asked.

"That's what I said, kid. Fly. Exciting, isn't it?"

"Why?"

"Whadya mean, why? Ever since we first cast jealous eyes on the creatures of the air we've wanted to fly. Now you're getting a chance to learn. That's why it's exciting!"

"I meant, why should I want to learn to fly?"

"Well...because everybody wants to fly."

"I don't," I said emphatically.

"Why not?"

"I'm afraid of heights, for one thing," I answered.

"That isn't enough reason to not learn," Aahz scowled.

"Well, I haven't heard any reasons yet as to why I should." I scowled back at him.

"Look, kid," Aahz began coaxingly, "it isn't so much flying as floating on air."

"The distinction escapes me," I said dryly.

"Okay, kid, Let me put it to you this way. You're my apprentice, right?"

"Right," I agreed suspiciously.

"Well, I'm not going to have an apprentice that can't fly! Get me!?" he roared.

"All right, Aahz. How does it work?" I knew when I was beaten.

"That's better. Actually it doesn't involve anything you don't already know. You know how to levitate objects, right?"

I nodded slowly, puzzled.

"Well, all flying is is levitating yourself."

"How's that again?"

"Instead of standing firm on the ground and lifting an object, you push against the ground with your will and lift yourself."

"But if I'm not touching the ground, where do I draw my power from?"

"From the air! C'mon, kid, you're a magician, not an elemental."

"What's an elemental?"

"Forget it. What I meant was you aren't bound to any of the four elements, you're a magician. You control them, or at least influence them and draw your power from them. When you're flying, all you have to do is draw your power from the air instead of the ground."

"If you say so, Aahz," I said doubtfully.

"Okay, first locate a force line."

"But we left it when we started off to see the Deveel," I argued.

"Kid, there are lots of force lines. Just because we left one of the ground force lines doesn't mean we're completely out of touch. Check for a force line in the air."

"In the air?"

"Believe me, kid. Check."

I sighed and closed my eyes. Turning my face skyward, I tried to picture the two-headed spear. At first I couldn't do it, then realized with a start I was seeing a spear, but a different spear. It wasn't as bright as the last spear had been, but glowed softly with icy blues and whites.

"I think I've got one, Aahz!" I gasped.

"It's blue and white, right?" Aahz sneered sarcastically.

"Yes, but it's not as bright as the last one."

"It's probably farther away. Oh well, it's close enough for you to draw energy from. Give it a try, kid. Hook into that force line and push the ground away. Slowly now."

I did as I was instructed, reaching out with my mind to tap the energies of that icy vision. The surge of power I felt was unlike any I had experienced before. Whereas before, when I summoned the power, I felt warm and swollen with energy, this time I felt cool and relaxed. The power flow actually made me feel lighter.

"Push away, kid," came Aahz's voice. "Gently!"

Lazily I touched the ground with my mind, only casually aware of the curious sensation of not physically feeling anything with my feet.

"Open your eyes, kid! Adjust your trim."

Aahz's voice came to me from a strange location this time. Surprised, my eyes popped open.

I was floating some ten feet above the ground at an angle that was rapidly drifting toward a horizontal position. I was flying!

The ground came at me in a rush. I had one moment of dazed puzzlement before it slammed into me with jarring reality.

I lay there for a moment forcing air back into my lungs and wondering if I had broken anything.

"Are you okay, kid?" Aahz was suddenly looming over me. "What happened, anyway?"

"I…I was flying!" I forced the words at last.

"Yeah, so? Oh, I get it. You were so surprised you forgot to maintain the energy flow, right?"

I nodded, unable to speak.

"Of all the dumb…look, kid, when I tell you you're going to fly, believe it!"

"But…"

"Don't 'but' me! Either you believe in me as a teacher or you don't! There's no buts about it!"

"I'm sorry, Aahz." I was getting my breath back again.

"Ahh…didn't mean to jump on you like that, kid, but you half scared me to death with that fall. You've got to understand we're starting to get into some pretty powerful magik now. You've got to expect the magik to work. A surprise-break like that last one with the wrong thing could get you killed. Or me, for that matter."

"I'll try to remember, Aahz. Shall I try it again?"

"Just take it easy for a few minutes, kid. Flying can take a lot out of you, even without the fall."

I closed my eyes and waited for my head to stop whirling.

"Aahz?" I said finally.

"Yeah, kid?"

"Tell me about Perv."

"What about it?"

"It just occurred to me, those Imps seemed scared to death when they realized you were a Pervect. What kind of a reputation does your dimension have?"

"Well," he began, "Perv is a self-sufficient, stand-offish dimension. We may not have the best fighters, but they're close enough that other dimension travelers give them lots of room. Technology and magik exist side by side and are intertwined with each other. All in all it makes a pretty powerful little package."

"But why should anyone be afraid of that?"

"As I said, Perv has a lot going for it. One of the side effects of success is an abundance of hangers-on. There was a time when we were close to being swamped with refugees and immigrants from other dimensions. When they got to be too much of a nuisance, we put a stop to it."

"How?" I pushed.

"First, we took the non-contributing outsiders and ran 'em out. Then, for an added measure of insurance, we encouraged the circulation of rumors of certain anti-social attitudes of Pervects toward those from other dimensions."

"What kind of rumors?"

"Oh, the usual. That we eat our enemies, torture folks for amusement and have sexual practices that are considered dubious by any dimension's standards. Folks aren't sure how much is truth and how much is exaggeration, but they're none to eager to find out first hand."

"How much of it is true, Aahz?" I asked propping myself up on one elbow.

He grinned evilly at me.

"Enough to keep 'em honest."

I was going to ask what it took to be considered a contributing immigrant, but decided to let it pass for a while.

XI.

"One of the joys of travel is visiting new towns and meeting new people."
G. KHAN

"AH! WHAT A shining example of civilization!" chortled Aahz exuberantly as he peered about him, delighted as a child on his first outing.

We were sauntering casually down one of the lesser-used streets of Twixt. Garbage and beggars were strewn casually about while beady rodent eyes, human and inhuman, studied us from the darkened doors and windows. It was a cluster of buildings crouched around an army outpost which was manned more from habit than necessity. The soldiers we occasionally encountered had degenerated enough from the crisp, recruiting poster model that it was frequently difficult to tell which seemed more menacing and unsavory, the guards or the obviously criminal types they were watching.

"If you ask me, it looks more like mankind at its worst!" I mumbled darkly.

"That's what I said, a shining example of civilization!"

There wasn't much I could say to that, not feeling like getting baited into another one of Aahz's philosophical lectures.

"Aahz, is it my imagination or are people staring at us?"

"Relax, kid. In a town like this the citizens will always instinctively size up a stranger. They're trying to guess if we're victims or victimizers. Our job is to make sure they think we're in the second category."

To illustrate his point he suddenly whirled and crouched like a cat, glaring back down the street with a hand on his sword hilt.

There was sudden movement at the windows and doorways as roughly a dozen half-seen forms melted back into the darkness.

One figure didn't move. A trollop leaning on a window-sill, her arms folded to display her ill-covered breasts, smiled invitingly at him. He smiled and waved. She ran an insolent tongue tip slowly around her lips and winked broadly.

"Um…Aahz?"

"Yeah, kid?" he replied, without taking his eyes from the girl.

"I hate to interrupt, but you're supposed to be a doddering old man, remember?"

Aahz was still disguised as Garkin, a fact which seemed to have momentarily slipped his mind.

"Hmm? Oh, yeah. I guess you're right, kid. It doesn't seem to bother anybody else though. Maybe they're used to feisty old men in this town."

"Well, could you at least stop going for your sword? That's supposed to be our surprise weapon."

Aahz was wearing the assassin's cloak now, which he quickly pulled forward again to hide his sword.

"Will you get off my back, kid? Like I said, nobody seems to be paying any attention."

"Nobody?" I jerked my head pointedly toward the girl in the window.

"Her? She's not paying any more attention to us than she is anyone else on the street."

"Really?"

"Well, if she is, it's more because of you than because of me."

"Me? C'mon, Aahz."

"Don't forget, kid, you're a pretty impressive person now."

I blinked. That hadn't occurred to me. I had forgotten I was disguised as Quigley now.

We had hidden the demon hunter just outside of town…well, actually we buried him. I had been shocked by the suggestion at first, but as Aahz pointed out, the statue didn't need any air, and it was the only surefire way we had of ensuring he wouldn't be found by anyone else.

Even the war unicorn following us, now fully saddled and armored, did not help me keep my new identity in mind. We had been traveling together too long now.

I suppose I should have gotten some satisfaction from the fact I could now maintain not only one, but two disguises without consciously thinking about it. I didn't. I found it unnerving that I had to remember other people were seeing me differently than I was seeing myself.

I shot a glance as the trollop. As our eyes met, her smile broadened noticeably. She displayed her increased enthusiasm by leaning further out of the window until I began to worry about her falling out…of the window or her dress.

"What did I tell you, kid!" Aahz slapped me enthusiastically on the shoulder and winked lewdly.

"I'd rather she was attracted to me for me as I really am," I grumbled darkly.

"The price of success, kid," Aahz responded philosophically. "Well, no matter. We're here on business, remember?"

"Right," I said firmly.

I turned to continue our progress, and succeeded only in whacking Aahz soundly in the leg with my sword.

"Hey! Watch it, kid!"

It seemed there was more to this sword-carrying than met the casual eye.

"Sorry, Aahz," I apologized. "This thing's a bit point-heavy."

"Yeah? How would you know?" my comrade retorted.

"Well…you said…"

"I said? That won't do it, kid. What's point-heavy for me may not be point-heavy for you. Weapon balance is a personal thing."

"Well…I guess I'm just not used to wearing a sword," I admitted.

"It's easy. Just forget you're wearing it. Think of it as part of you."

"I did. That's when I hit you."

"Hmm…we'll go into it more later."

Out of the corner of my eye, I could still see the trollop. She clapped her hands in silent applause and blew me a kiss. I suddenly realized she thought I had deliberately hit Aahz, a premeditated act to quell a rival. What's more, she approved of the gesture.

I looked at her again, more closely this time. Maybe later I would give Aahz the slip for a while and…

"We've got to find Frumple." Aahz's voice interrupted my wandering thoughts.

"Hmm…? Oh. How, Aahz?"

"Through quick and cunning. Watch this, kid."

So saying, he shot a quick glance up and down the street. A pack of three urchins had just rounded the corner, busily engaged in a game of keep-away with one of the group's hat.

"Hey!" Aahz hailed them. "Where can I find the shop of Abdul the Rug Dealer?"

"Two streets up and five to the left," they called back, pointing the direction.

"See, kid? That wasn't hard."

"Terrific," I responded, unimpressed.

"Now what's wrong, kid?"

"I thought we were trying to avoid unnecessary attention."

"Don't worry, kid."

"Don't worry!? We're on our way to meet a Deveel on a supposedly secret mission, and you seem to be determined to make
sure everybody we see notices us and knows where we're going."

"Look, kid, how does a person normally act when they come
into a new town?"

"I don't know," I admitted. "I haven't been in that many towns."

"Well, let me sketch it out for you. They want to be noticed.
They carry on and make lots of noise. They stare at the women and
wave at people they've never seen before."

"But that's what we've been doing."

"Right! Now do you understand?"

"No."

Aahz heaved an exasperated sigh.

"C'mon, kid. Think a minute, even if it hurts. We're acting like
anyone else would walking into a strange town, so nobody will look
at us twice. They won't pay any more attention to us than they would
any other newcomer. Now if we followed your suggestion and
came skulking into town, not talking to anyone or looking at anything, and tried real hard not to be noticed, then everyone and his
kid brother would zero in on us trying to figure out what we were
up to. Now do you understand?"

"I...I think so."

"Good...cause there's our target."

I blinked and looked in the direction of his pointing finger.
There, squatting between a blacksmith's forge and a leather-worker's
displays, was the shop. As I said, I was new to city life, but I would
have recognized it as a rug merchant's shop even if it was not adorned
with a large sign proclaiming it such. The entire front of the shop
was lavishly decorated with colorful geometric patterns apparently
meant to emulate the patterns of the rugs inside. I guess it was intended to look rich and prosperous. I found it unforgivably gaudy.

I had been so engrossed in our conversation, I had momentarily
forgotten our mission. With the shop now confronting us at close
range, however, my nervousness came back in a rush.

"What are we going to do, Aahz?"

"Well, first of all, I think I'm going to get a drink."

"A drink?"

"Right. If you think I'm going to match wits with a Deveel on an empty stomach, you've got another think coming."

"A *drink?*" I repeated, but Aahz was gone, striding purposefully toward a nearby tavern. There was little for me to do but follow, leading the unicorn.

The tavern was a dingy affair, even to my rustic eye. A faded awning sullenly provided shade for a small cluster of scarred wooden tables. Flies buzzed around a cat sleeping on one of the tables…at least I like to assume it was asleep.

As I tied the unicorn to one of the awning supports, I could hear Aahz bellowing at the innkeep for two of his largest flagons of wine. I sighed, beginning to despair that Aahz would never fully adapt to his old-man disguise. The innkeep did not seem to notice any irregularity between Aahz's appearance and his drinking habits, however. It occurred to me that Aahz might be right in his theories of how to go unnoticed. City people seemed to be accustomed to loud, rude individuals of any age.

"Sit down, kid," Aahz commanded. "You're making me nervous hovering around like that."

"I thought we were going to talk with the Deveel," I grumbled, sinking into a chair.

"Relax, kid. A few minutes one way or the other won't make that much difference. Besides, look!"

A young, well-dressed couple was entering the rug shop.

"See? We couldn't have done any business anyway. At least not until they left. The kind of talk we're going to have can't be done in front of witnesses. Ahh!"

The innkeeper had arrived, clinking the two flagons of wine down on the table in a lack-luster manner.

"About time!" Aahz commented seizing a flagon in each hand and immediately draining one. "Aren't you going to have anything, kid?"

A toss of his head and the second flagon was gone.

"While my friend here makes up his mind, bring me two more…and make them a decent size this time, even if you have to use a bucket!"

The innkeep retreated, visibly shaken. I wasn't. I had already witnessed Aahz's capacity for alcohol, astounding in an era noted for heavy drinkers. What did vex me a bit was that the man had departed without taking my order.

I did eventually get my flagon of wine, only to find my stomach was too nervous to readily accept it. As a result, I wound up sipping it slowly. Not so Aahz. He continued to belt them down at an alarming rate. For quite some time he drank. In fact, we sat for nearly an hour, and there was still no sign of the couple who had entered the shop.

Finally, even Aahz began to grow impatient.

"I wonder what's taking them so long," he grumbled.

"Maybe they're having trouble making up their mind," I suggested.

"C'mon, kid. The shop's not that big. He can't have too large a selection."

He downed the last of his wine and stood up.

"We've waited long enough," he declared. "Let's get this show on the road."

"But what about the couple?" I reminded him.

"We'll just have to inspire them to conclude their business with a bit more speed."

That had a vaguely ominous ring to it, and Aahz's toothy grin was additional evidence that something unpleasant was about to happen.

I was about to try to dissuade him, but he started across the street with a purposeful stride that left me standing alone.

I hurried to catch up with him, leaving the unicorn behind in my haste. Even so, I was unable to overtake him before he had entered the shop.

I plunged after him, fearing the worst. I needn't have worried. Except for the proprietor, the shop was empty. There was no sign of the couple anywhere.

XII.

"First impressions are of major importance in business matters."
J. PIERPONT FINCH

"MAY I HELP you, gentlemen?"

The proprietor's rich robes did not successfully hide his thinness. I am not particularly muscular...as Skeeve, that is...but I had the impression that if I struck this man, he wouldn't bruise, he'd shatter. I mean, I've seen skinny men before, but he seemed to be a skeleton with a too-small skin stretched over the bones.

"We'd like to talk with Abdul," Aahz said loftily.

"I am he, and he is I," recited the proprietor. "You see before you Abdul, a mere shadow of a man, pushed to the brink of starvation by his clever customers."

"You seem to be doing all right for yourself," I murmured, looking about me.

The shop was well-stocked, and even my untraveled eye could readily detect the undeniable signs of wealth about. The rugs were delicately woven in soft fabrics unfamiliar to me, and gold and silver shone from the depths of their designs. Obviously these rugs were intended for the wealthy, and it seemed doubtful their current owner would be suffering from a lack of comfort.

"Ahh. Therein lies the tale of my foolishness," cried the proprietor wringing his hands. "In my blind confidence, I sank my entire holdings into my inventory. As a result, I starve in the midst of plenty. My customers know this and rob me in my vulnerable times. I lose money on every sale, but a man must eat."

"Actually," Aahz interrupted, "we're looking for something in a deep shag wall-to-wall carpet."

"What's that?...I mean, do not confuse poor Abdul so, my humble business..."

"Come off it, Abdul...or should I say Frumple." Aahz grinned his widest grin. "We know who you are and what you are. We're here to do a little business."

At his words, the proprietor moved with a swiftness I would not have suspected him capable of. He was at the door in a bound, throwing a bolt and lowering a curtain which seemed to be of a substance even more strange than that of his rugs.

"Where'd you learn your manners?" he snarled back over his shoulder in a voice quite unlike the one used by the whiny proprietor. "I've got to live in this town, you know."

"Sorry," Aahz said, but he didn't sound at all apologetic.

"Well, watch it next time you come barging in and start throwing my name around. People here are not particularly tolerant of strange beings or happenings."

He seemed to be merely grumbling to himself, so I seized the opportunity to whisper to Aahz.

"Psst. Aahz. What's a wall-to-wall..."

"Later, kid."

"You!" The proprietor seemed to see me for the first time. "You're the statue! I didn't recognize you moving."

"Well...I..."

"I should have known," he raved on. "Deal with Imps and you invite trouble. Next thing you know, every..."

He broke off suddenly and eyed us suspiciously. His hand disappeared into the folds and emerged with a clear crystal. He held it up and looked through it like an eye glass, scrutinizing us each in turn.

"I should have known," he spat. "Would you be so kind as to remove your disguises? I like to know who I'm doing business with."

I glanced at Aahz who nodded in agreement.

Closing my eyes, I began to effect the change back to our normal appearance. I had enough time to wonder if Frumple would wonder about my transformation, if he realized I was actually a different person than the statue he had seen earlier. I needn't have worried.

"A Pervert!" Frumple managed to make the word sound slimy.

"That's Pervect if you want to do business with us," Aahz corrected.

"It's Pervert until I see the color of your money," Frumple sneered back.

I was suddenly aware he was studying me carefully.

"Say, you wouldn't by any chance be an Imp named Throckwoddle, would you?"

"Me? No! I...I'm..."

But he was already squinting at me through the crystal again.

"Hmph," he grunted, tucking his viewer back in his robe. "I guess you're okay. I'd love to get my hands on that Throckwoddle, though. He's been awfully free spreading my name around lately."

"Say, Frumple," Aahz interjected. "You aren't the only one who likes to see who he's doing business with, you know."

"Hm? Oh! Very well, if you insist."

I expected him to close his eyes and go to work, but instead he dipped a hand into his robe again. This time he produced what looked like a small hand mirror with some sort of a dial on the back. Peering into the mirror, he began to gently turn the dial with his fingers.

The result was immediate and startling. Not merely his face, but his whole body began to change, filling out, and taking on a definite reddish hue. As I watched, his brows thickened and grew closer together, his beard line crept us his face as if it were alive, and his eyes narrowed cruelly. Almost as an afterthought, I noted that his feet were now shiny cloven hooves and the tip of a pointed tail appeared at the bottom hem of his robe.

In an impressively short period of time, he had transformed into a…well, a devil!

Despite all my preparations, I felt the prickle of superstitious fear as he put away the mirror and turned to us again.

"Are you happy now?" he grumbled at Aahz.

"It's a start," Aahz conceded.

"Enough banter," Frumple was suddenly animated again. "What brings a Pervert to Klah? Slumming? And where does the kid fit in?"

"He's my apprentice," Aahz informed him.

"Really?" Frumple swept me with a sympathetic gaze. "Are things really that tough, kid? Maybe we could work something out."

"He's quite happy with the situation," interrupted Aahz. "Now let's get to our problem."

"You want me to cure the kid's insanity?"

"Huh? No. C'mon, Frumple. We came here on business. Let's declare a truce for a while, okay?"

"If you insist. It'll seem strange, though; Perverts and Deveels have never really gotten along."

"That's Pervects!"

"See what I mean?"

"Aahz!" I interrupted. "Could you just tell him?"

"Hmm? Oh. Right, kid. Look, Frumple. We've got a problem we were hoping you could help us with. You see, I've lost my powers."

"What?!" exploded Frumple. "You came here without the magical ability to protect yourself against being followed? That tears it. I spend seven years building a comfortable front here, and some idiot comes along and…"

"Look, Frumple. We told you the kid here's my apprentice. He knows more than enough to cover us."

"A half-trained apprentice! He's trusting my life and security to a half-trained apprentice!"

"You seem to be overlooking the fact we're already here. If anything was going to happen it would have happened already."

"Every minute you two are here you're threatening my existence."

"Which is all the more reason for you to deal with our problem immediately and stop this pointless breast-beating!"

The two of them glared at each other for a few moments, while I tried to be very quiet and unnoticeable. Frumple did not seem to be the right choice for someone to pin our hopes on.

"Oh, all right!" Frumple grumbled at last. "Since I probably won't be rid of you any other way."

He strode to the wall and produced what looked like a length of rope from behind one of the rugs.

"That's more like it," Aahz said triumphantly.

"Sit down and shut up," ordered our host.

Aahz did as he was bid, and Frumple proceeded to circle him. As he moved, the Deveel held the rope first this way, then that, sometimes looped in a circle, other times hanging limp. All the while he stared intently at the ceiling as if reading a message written there in fine print.

I didn't have the faintest idea what he was doing, but it was strangely enjoyable to watch someone order Aahz about and get away with it.

"Hmm…" the Deveel said at last. "Yes, I think we can say that your powers are definitely gone."

"Terrific!" Aahz growled. "Look, Frumple. We didn't come all this way to be told something we already knew. You Deveels are supposed to be able to do anything. Well, do something!"

"It's not that easy, Pervert!" Frumple snapped back. "I need information. How did you lose your powers, anyway?"

"I don't know for sure," Aahz admitted. "I was summoned to Klah by a magician, and when I arrived they were gone."

"A magician? Which one?"

"Garkin."

"Garkin? He's a mean one to cross. Why don't you just get him to restore your powers instead of getting me involved?"

"Because he's dead. Is that reason enough for you?"

"Hmm...that makes it difficult."

"Are you saying you can't do anything?" Aahz sneered. "I should have known. I always thought the reputation of the Deveels was overrated.

"Look, Pervert! Do you want my help or not? I didn't say I couldn't do anything, just that it would be difficult."

"That's more like it," Aahz chortled. "Let's get started."

"Not so fast," interrupted Frumple. "I didn't say I *would* help you, just that I *could*."

"I see," sneered Aahz. "Here it comes, kid. The price tag. I told you they were shake-down artists."

"Actually," the Deveel said dryly, "I was thinking of the time factor. It would take a while for me to make my preparations, and I believe I've made my feelings quite clear about you staying here longer than is absolutely necessary."

"In that case," smiled Aahz, "I suggest you get started. I believe I've made my feelings quite clear that we intend to stay here until the cure is effected."

"In that case," the Deveel smiled back at him, "I believe you raised the matter of cost. How much do you have with you?"

"Well, we have..." I began.

"That strikes me as being unimportant," Aahz glared warningly at me. "Suppose you tell us how much you feel is a fair price for your services."

Frumple graced him with one withering glare before sinking thoughtfully into his calculations.

"Hmm...material cost is up...and of course, there's my time...and you *did* call without an appointment...let's say it would cost you, just as a rough estimate, mind you, oh, in the neighborhood of...Say!"

He suddenly brightened and smiled at us.

"Maybe you'd be willing to work this as a trade. I cure you, and you do me a little favor."

"What kind of a favor?" Aahz asked suspiciously.

For once I was in complete agreement with him. Something in Frumple's voice did not inspire confidence.

"A small thing, really," the Deveel purred. "Sort of a decoy mission."

"We'd rather pay cash," I asserted firmly.

"Shut up, kid," Aahz advised. "What kind of a decoy mission, Frumple?"

"You may have noticed the young couple who entered my shop ahead of you. You did! Good. Then you have doubtless noticed they are not on the premises currently."

"How did they leave?" I asked curiously.

"I'll get to that in a moment," Frumple smiled. "Anyway, theirs is an interesting—if common—story. I'll spare you the details, but they're young lovers kept apart by their families. In their desperation, they turned to me for assistance. I obliged them by sending them to another dimension where they can be happy, free of their respective families intervention."

"For a fee, of course," Aahz commented dryly.

"Of course," Frumple smiled.

"C'mon, Aahz," I chided. "It sounds like a decent thing to do, even if he was paid for it."

"Quite so!" beamed the Deveel. "You're quite perceptive for one so young. Anyway, my generosity has left me in a rather precarious position. As you have no doubt noticed, I am quite concerned with my image in this town. There is a chance that that image may be threatened if the couple's relatives succeed in tracking them to my shop and no farther."

"That must have been some fee," Aahz mumbled.

"Now my proposition is this: in exchange for my assistance, I would ask that you two disguise yourselves as that couple and lay a false trail away from my shop."

"How much of a false trail?" I asked.

"Oh, it needn't be anything elaborate. Just be seen leaving town by enough townspeople to ensure that attention will be drawn away from my shop. Once out of sight of town, you can change to any disguise you like and return here. By that time, my preparations for your cure should be complete. Well, what do you say? Is it a deal?"

XIII.

*"The secret to winning the support of large
groups of people is positive thinking."*
N. BONAPARTE

"PEOPLE ARE STARING at us, Aahz."

"Relax, kid. They're supposed to be staring at us."

To illustrate his point, he nodded and waved to a knot of glowering locals. They didn't wave back.

"I don't see why I have to be the girl," I grumbled.

"We went through that before, kid. You walk more like a girl than I do."

"That's what you and Frumple decided. I don't think I walk like a girl at all!"

"Well, let's say I walk less like a girl than you do."

It was hard to argue with logic like that, so I changed subjects.

"Couldn't we at least travel by less-populated streets?" I asked.

"Why?" countered Aahz.

"Well, I'm not too wild about having a lot of people seeing me when I'm masquerading as a girl."

"C'mon, kid. The whole idea is that no one would recognize you. Besides, you don't know anybody in this town. Why should you care what they think of you?"

"I just don't like it, that's all," I grumbled.

"Not good enough," Aahz asserted firmly. "Being seen is part of our deal with Frumple. If you had any objections you should have said so before we closed the negotiations."

"I never got a chance," I pointed out. "But since the subject's come up, I do have a few questions."

"Such as?"

"Such as what are we doing?"

"Weren't you paying attention, kid? We're laying a false trail for…"

"I know that," I interrupted. "What I mean is, why are we doing what we're doing? Why are we doing Frumple a favor instead of just paying his price?"

"You wouldn't ask that if you'd ever dealt with a Devcel before," Aahz snortcd. "Their prices are sky-high, especially in a case like ours when they know the customer is desperate. Just be thankful we got such a good deal."

"That's what I mean, Aahz. Are we sure we've gotten a good deal?"

"What do you mean?"

"Well, from what I've been told, if you think you've gotten a good deal from a Deveel, it usually means you've overlooked something."

"Of course you speak from a wide range of experience," Aahz sneered sarcastically. "Who told you so much about dealing with Deveels?"

"You did," I said pointedly.

"Hmmm. You're right, kid. Maybe I have been a little hasty."

Normally I would have been ecstatic over having Aahz admit I was right. Somehow, however, in the current situation, it only made me feel that much more uncomfortable.

"So what are we going to do?" I asked.

"Well, normally I deal honestly unless I think I'm being doublecrossed. This time, however, you've raised sufficient doubt in my mind that I think we should bend the rules a little."

"Situational ethics again?"

"Right!"

"So what do we do?"

"Start looking for a relatively private place where we can dump these disguises without being noticed."

I began scanning the streets and alleys ahead of us. My uneasiness was growing into panic, and it lent intensity to my search.

"I wish we had our weapons along," I muttered.

"Listen to him," Aahz jeered. "It wasn't that long ago you were telling me all about how magicians don't need weapons. C'mon, kid. What would you do with a weapon if you had one?"

"If you want to get specific," I said dryly, "I was wishing you had a weapon."

"Oh! Good point. Say...ah...kid? Are you still looking for a private place?"

"Yeah, I've got a couple possibles spotted."

"Well forget it. Start looking for something wide open with a lot of exits."

"Why the change in strategy?" I asked.

"Take a look over your shoulder...casual-like."

I did as I was told, though it was not as casual as it might have been. It turned out my acting ability was the least of our worries.

There was a crowd of people following us. They glared at us darkly and muttered to themselves. I wanted very badly to believe we were not the focus of their attention, but it was obvious that was not the case. They were clearly following us, and gathering members as they went.

"We're being followed, Aahz!" I whispered.

"Hey, kid. I pointed them out to you, remember?"

"But why are they following us? What do they want?"

"Well, I don't know for sure, of course, but I'd guess it has something to do with our disguises."

I snuck another glance at the crowd. The interest in us did not seem to be lessening at all. If anything, the crowd was even bigger and looked even angrier. Terrific.

"Say, Aahz?" I whispered.

"Yeah, kid?"

"If they're after us because of our disguises, why don't we just change back?"

"Bad plan, kid. I'd rather run the risk of them having some kind of grudge against the people we're impersonating then face up to the consequences if they found out we were magicians."

"So what do we do?"

"We keep walking and hope we run into a patrol of soldiers that can offer us some protection."

A fist-sized rock thudded into the street ahead of us, presumably thrown by one of the people following us.

"...or..." Aahz revised hastily, "we can stop right now and find out what this is all about."

"We could run," I suggested hopefully, but Aahz was already acting on his earlier suggestion.

He stopped abruptly and spun on his heel to face the crowd.

"What is the meaning of this?" he roared at the advancing multitude.

The crowd lurched to a halt at the direct address, those in the rear colliding with those in front who had already stopped. They seemed a bit taken aback by Aahz's action and milled about without direction.

I was pleasantly surprised at the success of my companion's maneuver, but Aahz was never one to leave well enough alone.

"Well?" he demanded, advancing on them. "I'm waiting for an explanation."

For a moment the crowd gave ground before his approach. Then an angry voice rang out from somewhere in the back.

"We want to know about our money!"

That opened the door.

"Yeah! What about our money?!"

The cry was taken up by several other voices, and the crowd began to growl and move forward again.

Aahz stood his ground and held up a hand commanding silence.

"What about your money?" he demanded haughtily.

"Oh, no, you don't," came a particularly menacing voice. "You aren't going to talk your way out of it this time!"

A massive bald man brandishing a butcher's cleaver shouldered his way through the crowd to confront Aahz.

"My good man," Aahz sniffed. "If you're implying..."

"I'm implying nothing!" The man growled. "I'm saying it flat out. You and that trollop of yours are crooks!"

"Now, aren't you being just a bit hasty in..."

"Hasty!" the man bellowed. "Hasty! Mister, we've already been too patient with you. We should have run you out of town when you first showed up with your phony anti-demon charms. That's right, I said phony! Some of us knew it from the start. Anyone with a little education knows there's no such things as demons."

For a moment I was tempted to let Aahz's disguise drop. Then I looked at the crowd again and decided against it. It wasn't a group to joke with.

"Now, some folks bought the charms because they were gullible, some as a gag, some of us because...well, because everyone else was buying them. But we all bought them, just like we bought your story that they had to be individually made and you needed the money in advance."

"That was all explained at the time," Aahz protested.

"Sure it was. You're great at explanations. You explained it just like you explained away those two times we caught you trying to leave town."

"Well...we...uh," Aahz began.

"Actually," I interrupted, "we were only..."

"Well, we've had enough of your explanations. That's what we told you three days ago when we gave you two days to either come up with the charms or give us our money back."

"But these things take time..."

"You've used up that excuse. Your time was up yesterday. Now do we get our money, or..."

"Certainly, certainly," Aahz raised his hands soothingly. "Just give me a moment to speak with my colleague."

He smiled at the crowd as he took me by the arm and drew me away.

"What are we going to do, Aahz?"

"Now we run," he said calmly.

"Huh?" I asked intelligently.

I was talking to thin air. Aahz was already legging it speedily down the street.

I may be slow at times, but I'm not that slow. In a flash I was hot on his heels.

Unfortunately, the crowd figured out what Aahz was up to about the same time I did. With a howl they were after us.

Surprisingly, I overtook Aahz. Either he was holding back so I could catch up, or I was more scared than I thought, which is impossible.

"Now what?" I panted.

"Shut up and keep running, kid," Aahz barked, ducking around a knot of people.

"They're gaining on us," I pointed out.

Actually, the group we had just passed had joined the pursuit, but it had the same effect as if the crowd was gaining.

"Will you knock it off and help me look?" Aahz growled.

"Sure. What are we looking for?"

"A couple dressed roughly like us," he replied.

"What do we do if we see them?"

"Simple," Aahz replied. "We plow into them full tilt, you swap our features for theirs, and we let the mob tear them apart."

"That doesn't sound right somehow," I said doubtfully.

"Kid, remember what I told you about situational ethics?"

"Yeah."

"Well, this is one of those situations."

I was convinced, though not so much by Aahz's logic as by the rock that narrowly missed my head. I don't know how the crowd managed to keep its speed and still pick up things to throw, but it did.

I began watching for a couple dressed like us. It's harder than it sounds when you're at a dead run with a mob at your heels.

Unfortunately, there was no one in sight who came close to fitting the bill. Whoever it was we were impersonating seemed to be fairly unique in their dress.

"I wish I had a weapon with me," Aahz complained.

"We've already gone through that," I called back. "And besides, what would you do if you had one? The only thing we've got that might stop them is the fire ring."

"Hey! I'd forgotten about that," Aahz gasped. "I've still got it on."

"So what?" I asked. "We can't use it."

"Oh, yeah? Why not?"

"Because then they'd know we're magicians."

"That won't make any difference if they're dead."

Situational ethics or not, my stomach turned at the thought of killing that many people.

"Wait, Aahz!" I shouted.

"Watch this, kid." He grinned and pointed his hand at them. Nothing happened.

XIV.

"A little help at the right time is better than a lot of help at the wrong time."
TEVYE

"C'MON, AAHZ!" I shouted desperately, overturning a fruit stand in the path of the crowd.

Now that it seemed my fellow humans were safe from Aahz, my concern returned to making sure he was safe from them.

"I don't believe it!" Aahz shouted, as he darted past.

"What?" I called, sprinting after him.

"In one day I believed both a Deveel and an Imp. Tell you what, kid. If we get out of this, I give you my permission to kick me hard. Right in the rump, twice."

"It's a deal!" I panted.

This running was starting to tax my stamina. Unfortunately, the crowd didn't seem tired at all. That was enough to keep me running.

"Look, kid!" Aahz was pointing excitedly. "We're saved."

I followed his finger. A uniformed patrol was marching...well, sauntering down the street ahead of us.

"It's about time," I grumbled, but I was relieved nonetheless.

The crowd saw the soldiers, too. Their cries increased in volume as they redoubled their efforts to reach us.

"C'mon, kid! Step on it!" Aahz called. "We're not safe yet."

"Step on what?" I asked, passing him.

Our approach to the patrol was noisy enough that by the time we got there, the soldiers had all stopped moving and were watching the chase. One of them, a bit less unkempt than the others, had shouldered his way to the front of the group and stood sneering at us with folded arms. From his manners, I guessed he was an officer. There was no other explanation for the others allowing him to act the way he was.

I skidded to a stop in front of him.

"We're being chased!" I panted.

"Really?" he smiled.

"Let me handle this, kid," Aahz mumbled, brushing me aside. "Are you the officer in charge, sir?"

"I am," the man replied.

"Well, it seems that these…citizens," he pointed disdainfully at our pursuers, "intend us bodily harm. A blatant disregard for your authority…sir!"

The mob was some ten feet distant and stood glaring alternately at us and the soldiers. I was gratified to observe that at least some of them were breathing hard.

"I suppose you're right," the officer yawned. "We should take a hand in this."

"Watch this, kid," Aahz whispered, nudging me in the ribs as the officer stepped forward to address the crowd.

"All right. You all know it is against the law for citizens to inflict injuries on each other," he began.

The crowd began to grumble darkly, but the officer waved them into silence as he continued.

"I know, I know. We don't like it either. If it were up to us we'd let you settle your own differences and spend our time drinking. But it's not up to us. We have to follow the laws the same way you do, and the laws say only the military can judge and punish the citizenry."

"See?" I whispered. "There are some advantages to civilization."

"Shut up, kid," Aahz hissed back.

"So even though I know you'd love to beat these two to a bloody pulp, we can't let you do it. They must be hanged in accordance with the law!"

"What?"

I'm not sure if I said it, or Aahz, or if we cried out in unison. Whichever it was, it was nearly drowned out in the enthusiastic roar of the crowd.

A soldier seized my wrists and twisted them painfully behind my back. Looking about, I saw the same thing had happened to Aahz. Needless to say, this was not the support we had been hoping for.

"What did you expect?" the officer sneered at us. "If you wanted help from the military, you shouldn't have included us on your list of customers. If we had had our way, we would have strung you up a week ago. The only reason we held back was that these yokels had given you extra time and we were afraid of a riot if we tried anything."

Our wrists were secured by thongs now. We were slowly being herded toward a lone tree in front of one of the open-air restaurants.

"Has anyone got some rope?" the officer called to the crowd.

Just our luck, somebody did. It was passed rapidly to the officer, who began ceremoniously tying nooses.

"Psst! kid!" Aahz whispered.

"What now?" I mumbled bitterly.

My faith in Aahz's advice was at an all time low.

"When they go to hang you, fly!"

"What?"

Despite myself, I was seized with new hope.

"C'mon, kid. Wake up! Fly. Like I taught you on the trail."

"They'd just shoot me down."

"Not fly away, dummy. Just fly. Hover at the end of the rope and twitch. They'll think you're hanging."

I thought about it...hard. It might work, but...I noticed they were tossing the nooses over a lower limb of the tree.

"Aahz! I can't do it. I can't levitate us both. I'm not that good yet."

"Not both of us, kid. Just you. Don't worry about me."

"But...Aahz..."

"Keep my disguise up, though. If they figure out I'm a demon they'll burn the bodies...both of us."

"But...Aahz..."

We were out of time. Rough hands shoved us forward and started fitting the nooses over our heads.

I realized with a start I had no time to think about Aahz. I'd need all my concentration to save myself, if there was even time for that!

I closed my eyes and sought desperately for a force line in the air. There was one there...faint, but there. I began to focus on it.

The noose tightened around my neck and I felt my feet leave the ground. I felt panic rising in me and forced it down.

Actually it was better this way. They should feel weight on the rope as they raised me. I concentrated on the force line again...focus...draw the energies...redirect them.

I felt a slight loosening of the noose. Remembering Aahz's lectures on control, I held the energies right there and tried an experimental breath. I could get air! Not much, it was true, but enough to survive.

What else did I have to do? Oh yes, I had to twitch. I thought how a squirrel-badger acted when caught in a snare.

I kicked my legs slightly and tried an experimental tremor. It had the overall effect of tightening the noose. I decided to try another tactic. I let my head loll to one side and extended my tongue out of the corner of my mouth.

It worked. There was a sudden increase in the volume of the catcalls from the crowd to reward my efforts.

I held that pose.

My tongue was rapidly drying out, but I forced my mind away from it. To avoid involuntarily swallowing, I tried to think of other things.

Poor Aahz. For all his gruff criticism and claims of not caring for anyone else but himself, his last act had been to think of my welfare. I promised myself that when I got down from here…

What would happen when I got down from here? What do they do with bodies in this town? Do they bury them? It occurred to me it might be better to hang than be buried alive.

"The law says they're supposed to hang there until they rot!"

The officer's voice seemed to answer my thoughts and brought my mind back to the present.

"Well, they aren't hanging in front of the law's restaurant!" came an angry voice in response.

"Tell you what. We'll come back at sundown and cut them down."

"Sundown? Do you realize how much money I could lose before sundown? Nobody wants to eat at a place where a corpse dangles its toes in his soup. I've already lost most of the lunch rush!"

"Hmm…It occurs to me that if the day's business means that much to you, you should be willing to share a little of the profit."

"So that's the way it is, is it? Oh, very well. Here…for your troubles."

There was the sound of coins being counted out.

"That isn't very much. I have to share with my men, you know."

"You drive a hard bargain! I didn't know bandits had officers."

More coins were counted, accompanied by the officer's chuckle. It occurred to me that instead of studying magik, I should be devoting my time to bribes and graft. It seemed to work better.

"Men!" the officer called. "Cut this carrion down and haul it out of town. Leave it at the city limits as a warning to anyone else who would seek to cheat the citizens of Twixt."

"You're too considerate." The restaurant owner's voice was edged with sarcasm.

"Think nothing of it, citizen," the officer sneered.

I barely remembered to stop flying before they cut the rope. I bit my tongue as I slammed into the ground, and risked sneaking it back into my mouth. No one noticed.

Unseen hands grabbed me under the armpits and by the ankles, and the journey began to the city limits.

Now that I knew I wasn't going to be buried, my thoughts returned to my future.

First, I would have to do something to Frumple. What, I wasn't sure, but something. I owed Aahz that much. Maybe I could restore Quigley and enlist his aid. He was supposed to be a demon hunter. He was probably better equipped to handle a Deveel than I was. Then again, remembering Quigley, that might not be a valid assumption.

Then there was Isstvan. What was I going to do about him? I wasn't sure I could beat him with Aahz's help. Without it, I wouldn't stand a chance.

"This should be far enough. Shall we hang them again?"

I froze at the suggestion. Fortunately the voice at my feet had different ideas.

"Why bother? I haven't seen an officer yet who'd move a hundred paces from a bar. Let's just dump 'em here."

There was a general chorus of assent, and the next minute I was flying through the air again. I tried to relax for the impact, but the ground knocked the wind out of me again.

If I was going to continue my efforts to master flying, I'd have to devote more time to the art of forced landings.

I lay there motionless. I couldn't hear the soldiers any more, but I didn't want to run the risk of sitting up and betraying the fact I wasn't dead.

"Are you going to lay there all day or are you going to help me get untied?"

My eyes flew open involuntarily. Aahz was sitting there grinning down at me.

There was only one sensible thing to do, and I did it. I fainted.

XV.

*"Anyone who uses the phrase 'easy as taking candy from
a baby' has never tried taking candy from a baby,"*
R. HOOD

"CAN WE MOVE now?" I asked.

"Not yet, kid. Wait until the lights have been out for a full day."

"You mean a full hour."

"Whatever. Now shut up and keep watching."

We were waiting in the dead-end alley across the street from Frumple's shop. Even though we were supposedly secure in our new disguises, I was uneasy being back in the same town where I had been hung. It's a hard feeling to describe to someone who hasn't experienced it. Then too, it was strange being with Aahz after I had gotten used to the idea of him being dead.

Apparently the neck muscles of a Pervect are considerably stronger than those of a human. Aahz had simply tensed those muscles and they provided sufficient support to keep the noose from cutting off his air supply.

As a point of information, Aahz had further informed me that his scales provided better armor than most chain-mail or plate armor available in this dimension. I had heard once that demons could only be destroyed by specially constructed weapons or by burning. It seemed the old legend may have actually had some root in fact.

"Okay, kid," Aahz whispered. "I guess we've waited long enough."

He eased himself out of the alley and led me in a long circle around the shop, stopping again only when we had returned to our original spot by the alley.

"Well, what do you think, kid?"

"Don't know. What were we looking for?"

"Tell me again about how you planned to be a thief," Aahz sighed. "Look, kid. We're looking over a target. Right?"

"Right," I replied, glad to be able to agree with something.

"Okay, how many ways in and out of that shop did you see?"

"Just one. The one across the street there."

"Right. Now how do you figure we're going to get into the shop?"

"I don't know," I said honestly.

"C'mon, kid. If there's only one way in…"

"You mean we're just going to walk in the front door?"

"Why not? We can see from here the door's open."

"Well…if you say so, Aahz. I just thought it would be harder than that."

"Whoa! Nobody said it was going to be easy. Just because the door's open doesn't mean the door's open."

"I didn't quite get that, Aahz."

"Think, kid. We're after a Deveel, right? He's got access to all kinds of magic and gimmicks. Now what say you close your eyes and take another look at that door."

I did as I was told. Immediately the image of a glowing cage sprang into my mind, a cage that completely enclosed the shop.

"He's got some kind of ward up, Aahz," I informed my partner. It occurred to me that a few short weeks ago I would have held such a structure in awe. Now, I accepted it as relatively normal, just another obstacle to be overcome.

"Describe it to me," Aahz hissed.

"Well…it's bright…whitish purple…there's a series of bars and crossbars forming squares about a handspan across…"

"Is it just over the door, or all over the shop?"

"All over the shop. The top's covered, and the bars run right into the ground."

"Hmm, well, we'll just have to go through it. Listen up, kid. Time for a quick lesson."

I opened my eyes and looked at the shop again. The building looked as innocent as it had when we first circled it. It bothered me that I couldn't sense the cage's presence the way I could our own wards.

"What is it, Aahz?" I asked uneasily.

"Hmm? Oh, it's a ward, kind of like the ones we use, but a lot nastier."

"Nastier, how?"

"Well the kind of ward I taught you to build are an early warning system and not much else. From the sounds of it, the stuff Frumple is using will do considerably more. Not only will it kill you, it'll knock you into pieces smaller than dust. It's called disintegration."

"And we're going to go through it?" I asked, incredulously.

"After you've had a quick lesson. Now, remember your feather drills? How you'd wrap your mind around the feather for control?"

"Yeah," I said, puzzled.

"Well, I want you to do the same thing, but without the feather. Pretend you're holding something that isn't there. Form the energies into a tube."

"Then what?"

"Then you insert the tube into one of the squares in the cage and expand it."

"That's all?"

"That's it. C'mon now. Give it a try."

I closed my eyes and reached out with my mind. Choosing a square in the center of the open doorway, I inserted my mental tube and began to expand it. As it touched the bars forming the square, I experienced a tingle and a physical pressure as if I had encountered a tangible object.

"Easy, kid," Aahz said softly. "We just want to bend the bars a bit, not break them."

I expanded the tube. The bars gave way slowly, until they met with the next set. Then I experienced another tingle and additional pressure.

"Remember, kid. Once we're inside, take your time. Wait for your eyes to adjust to the dark. We don't want to tip Frumple off by stumbling around and knocking things over."

I was having to strain now. The tube had reached another set of bars now, making it a total of twelve bars I was forcing outward.

"Have you got it yet?" Aahz's whisper sounded anxious.

"Just a second...Yes!"

The tube was now big enough for us to crawl through.

"Are you sure?"

"Yes."

"Okay. Lead the way, kid. I'll be right behind you."

Strangely enough, I felt none of my usual doubts as I strode boldly across the street to the shop. Apparently my confidence in my abilities was growing, for I didn't even hesitate as I began to crawl through the tube. The only bad moment I had was when I suddenly realized I was crawling on thin air about a foot off the ground. Apparently I had set the tube a little too high, but no matter. It held! Next time I would know better.

I eased myself out of the end of the tube and stood in the shop's interior. I could hear the soft sounds of Aahz's passage behind me as I waited for my eyes to adjust to the dark.

"Ease away from the door, kid," came Aahz's whispered advice in my ear as he stood behind me. "You're standing in a patch of moonlight. And you can collapse the tube now."

Properly notified, I shifted away from the moonlight. I was pleased to note, however, that releasing the tube did not make a significant difference in my mental energies. I was progressing to where I could do more difficult feats with less energy than when I started. I was actually starting to feel like a magician.

I heard a slight noise behind me and craned my neck to look. Aahz was quietly drawing the curtains over the door.

I smiled grimly to myself. Good! We don't want witnesses.

My eyes were nearly adjusted now. I could make out shapes and shadows in the darkness. There was a dark lump in the corner that breathed heavily. Frumple!

I felt a hand on my shoulder. Aahz pointed out a lamp on a table and held up four fingers.

I nodded and started counting slowly to four. As I reached the final number, I focused a quick flash of energy at the lamp, and its wick burst into flame, lighting the shop's interior.

Aahz was kneeling beside Frumple, knife in hand. Apparently he had succeeded in finding at least some of our weapons in the dark.

Frumple sat up blinking, then froze in place. Aahz had the point of his knife hovering a hairsbreadth from the Deveel's throat.

"Hello, Frumple," he smiled. "Remember us?"

"You!" gasped the Deveel. "You're supposed to be dead!"

"Dead?" Aahz purred. "How could any harm befall us with our old pal Frumple helping us blend with the citizenry?"

"Gentlemen!" our victim squealed. "There seems to have been a mistake!"

"That's right," I commented. "And you made it."

"You don't understand!" Frumple persisted, "I was surprised and horrified when I heard about your deaths."

"Yeah, we weren't too happy about it ourselves."

"Later, kid. Look, Frumple. Right now we have both the ability and the motive to kill you. Right?"

"But I..."

"Right?"

Aahz moved the knife until the point indented the skin on Frumple's throat.

"Right!" the Deveel whispered.

"Okay, then." Aahz withdrew the knife and tucked it back in his waistband. "Now let's talk business."

"I...I don't understand," Frumple stammered, rubbing his throat with one hand as if to assure himself that it was still there.

"What it means," Aahz explained, "is that we want your help more than we want revenge. Don't relax too much, though. The choice wasn't that easy."

"I...I see. Well, what can I do for you?"

"C'mon, Frumple. You can honor our original deal. You've got to admit we've laid one heck of a false trail for your two fugitives. Now it's your turn. Just restore my powers and we'll be on our way."

The Deveel blanched, or at least he turned from red to pink.

"I can't do that!" he exclaimed.

"What?"

The knife appeared in Aahz's hand again as if by magik. "Now look, you double-dealing refugee. Either you restore my powers or..."

"You don't understand," Frumple pleaded. "I don't mean I won't restore your powers. I mean I can't. I don't know what's wrong with you or how to counter it. That's why I set you up with the mob. I was afraid if I told you before, you wouldn't believe me. I've spent too much time establishing myself here to risk being exposed by an unsatisfied customer. I'm sorry, I really am, and I know you'll probably kill me, but I can't help you!"

XVI.

*"Just because something doesn't do what you
planned it to do doesn't mean it's useless."*
T. EDISON

"HMMM," AAHZ SAID thoughtfully. "So you're powerless to restore my powers?"

"Does that mean we can kill him after all?" I asked eagerly. I had
been hopeful of having Aahz's powers restored, but in lieu of that,
I was still a bit upset over having been hung.

"You're a rather vicious child," Frumple looked at me specula-
tively. "What's a Pervect doing traveling with a Klahd, anyway?"

"Who's a clod?" I bristled.

"Easy, kid," Aahz said soothingly. "Nothing personal. Everyone
who's native to this dimension is a Klahd. Klah…Klahds…get it?"

"Well, I don't like the sound of it," I grumbled.

"Relax, kid. What's in a name, anyway?"

"Then it doesn't really matter to you if people call you a Pervect
or a Pervert?"

"Watch your mouth, kid. Things are going bad enough without
you getting cheeky."

"Gentlemen, gentlemen," Frumple interrupted. "If you're going to fight would you mind going outside? I mean, this is my shop."

"Can we kill him now, Aahz?"

"Ease up, kid. Just because he can't restore my powers doesn't
mean he's totally useless. I'm sure that he'll be more than happy to
help us, particularly after he failed to pay up on our last deal. Right,
Frumple?"

"Oh, definitely. Anything I can do to make up for the inconvenience I've caused you."

"Inconvenience?" I asked incredulously.

"Steady, kid. Well, Frumple, you could start by returning the
stuff we left here when we went off on your little mission."

"Of course. I'll get it for you."

The Deveel started to rise, only to find Aahz's knife threatening
him again.

"Don't trouble yourself, Frumple, old boy," Aahz smiled. "Just point out where they are and we'll fetch them ourselves…and keep you hands where I can see them."

"The…your things are over there…in the big chest against the wall," Frumple's eyes never left the knife as he spoke.

"Check it out, kid."

I did and, surprisingly, the items were exactly where the Deveel said they would be. There was, however, an intriguing collection of other strange items in the chest also.

"Hey, Aahz!" I called. "Take a look at this!"

"Sure, kid."

He backed across the shop to join me. As he did, he flipped the knife into what I now recognized as a throwing grip. Apparently Frumple recognized it too, because he stayed frozen in position.

"Well, what have we here?" Aahz chortled.

"Gentlemen," the Deveel called plaintively. "I could probably help you better if I knew what you needed."

"True enough," Aahz responded, reclaiming his weapons.

"Frumple, it occurs to me we haven't been completely open with you. That will have to be corrected if we're going to be allies."

"Wait a minute, Aahz," I interrupted. "What makes you think we can trust him after he's tried so hard to get us killed?"

"Simple, kid. He tried to get us killed to protect himself, right?"

"Well…"

"So once we explain it's in his own self-interest to help us, he should be completely trustworthy."

"Really?" I sneered.

"Well, as trustworthy as any Deveel can be," Aahz admitted.

"I resent the implications of that, Pervert!" Frumple exclaimed. "If you want any help, you'd better…"

Aahz's knife flashed through the air and thunked into the wall scant inches from the Deveel's head. "Shut up and listen, Frumple!" he snarled. "And that's Per*vect!*"

"What's in a name, Aahz?" I asked innocently.

"Shut up, kid. Okay, Frumple, does the name Isstvan mean anything to you?"

"No. Should it?"

"It should if you want to stay alive. He's a madman magician who's trying to take over the dimensions, starting with this one."

"Why should that concern me?" Frumple frowned. "We Deveels trade with anyone who can pay the price. We don't concern ourselves with analyzing politics or mental stability. If we only dealt with sane beings, it would cut our business by a third…maybe more."

"Well, you'd better concern yourself this time. Maybe you didn't hear me. Isstvan is starting with this dimension. He's out to get a monopoly on Klah's energies to use on other dimensions. To do that, he's out to kill anyone else in this dimension who knows how to tap those energies. He's not big on sharing."

"Hmmm. Interesting theory, but where's the proof—I mean, who's he supposed to have killed?"

"Garkin, for one," I said, dryly.

"That's right," Aahz snarled. "You're so eager to know why the two of us are traveling together. Well, Skeeve here was Garkin's apprentice until Isstvan sent his assassins to wipe out the competition."

"Assassins?"

"That's right. You saw two of them, those Imps you teleported about a week back." Aahz flourished the assassin's cloak we had acquired.

"Where did you think we got this? In a rummage sale?"

"Hmmm," Frumple commented thoughtfully.

"And he's arming them with tech weapons. Take a look at this crossbow quarrel."

Aahz lobbed one of the missiles to the Deveel who caught it deftly and examined it closely.

"Hmmm. I didn't notice that before. It's a good camouflage job, but totally unethical."

"Now do you see why enlisting your aid takes priority over the pleasure of slitting your lying throat?"

"I see what you mean," Frumple replied without rancor. "It's most convincing. But what can I do?"

"You tell us. You Deveels are supposed to have wonders for every occasion. What have you got that would give us an edge over a madman who knows his magik?"

Frumple thought for several minutes. Then shrugged. "I can't think of a thing just offhand. I haven't been stocking weapons lately. Not much call for them in this dimension."

"Terrific," I said. "Can we kill him now, Aahz?"

"Say, could you put a muzzle on him?" Frumple said. "What's your gripe anyway, Skeeve?"

"I don't take well to being hung," I snarled.

"Really? Well, you'll get used to it if you keep practicing magik. It's being burned that's really a pain."

"Wait a minute, Frumple," Aahz interrupted. "You're acting awfully casual about hanging for someone who was so surprised to see us alive."

"I was. I underestimated your apprentice's mastery of the energies. If I had thought you could escape, I would have thought of something else. I was trying to get you killed, after all."

"He doesn't sound particularly trustworthy," I observed.

"You will notice, my young friend, that I stated my intentions in the past tense. Now that we share a common goal, you'll find me much easier to deal with."

"Which brings us back to our original question," Aahz asserted. "What can you do for us, Frumple?"

"I really don't know," the Deveel admitted. "Unless…I know! I can send you to the Bazaar!"

"The Bazaar?" I asked.

"The Bazaar on Deva! If you can't find what you need there, it doesn't exist. Why didn't I think of that before? That's the answer!"

He was on his feet now, moving toward us.

"I know you're in a hurry, so I'll get you started…"

"Not so fast, Frumple."

Aahz had his sword out menacing the Deveel.

"We want a guarantee this is a round trip you're sending us on."

"I…I don't understand."

"Simple. You tried to get rid of us once. It occurs to me you might be tempted to send us off to some backwater dimension with no way to get back."

"But I give you my word that…"

"We don't want your word," Aahz grinned. "We want your *presence*."

"What?"

"Where we go, you go. You're coming with us, just to be extra sure we get back."

"I can't do that!" Frumple seemed honestly terrified. "I've been banned from Deva! You don't know what they'd do to me if I went back."

"That's too bad. We want a guaranteed return before we budge, and that's you!"

"Wait a minute! I think I've got the answer!"

The Deveel began frantically rummaging through chests. I watched, fascinated, as an astounding array of strange objects emerged as he searched.

"Here it is!" he cried at last, holding his prize aloft.

It appeared to be a metal rod, about eight inches long and two inches in diameter. It had strange markings on its sides, and a button on the end.

"A D-Hopper!" Aahz exclaimed. "I haven't seen one of those in years."

Frumple tossed it to him.

"There you go. Is that guarantee enough?"

"What is it, Aahz?" I asked, craning my neck to see.

He seized the ends of the rod and twisted in opposite directions. Apparently it was constructed of at least two parts, because the symbols began to slide around the rod in opposite directions.

"Depending on where you want to go, you align different symbols. Then you just push the button and…"

"Wait a minute!" Frumple cried. "We haven't settled on a price for that yet!"

"Price?" I asked.

"Yeah, price! Those things don't grow on trees, you know."

"If you will recall," Aahz murmured, "you still owe us from our last deal."

"True enough," Frumple agreed. "But as you yourself pointed out, those D-Hoppers are rare. A real collector's item. It's only fair that our contract be renegotiated at a slightly higher fee."

"Frumple, we're in too much of a hurry to argue," Aahz announced. "I'll say once what we're willing to relinquish over and above our original deal and you can take it or leave it. Fair enough?"

"What did you have in mind?" Frumple asked, rubbing his hands together eagerly.

"Your life."

"My…Oh! I see. Yes, that…um…should be an acceptable price."

"I'm surprised at you, Frumple," I chimed in. "Letting a collector's item go that cheap."

"C'mon, kid." Aahz was adjusting the settings on the D-Hop-per. "Let's get moving."

"Just a second, Aahz. I want to get my sword."

"Leave it. We can pick it up on the way back."

"Say, Aahz, how long does it take to travel between dimensions any…"

The walls of Frumple's hut suddenly dissolved in a kaleido-scope of color.

"Not long, kid. In fact, we're there."

And we were.

XVII.

"The wonders of the ages assembled for your edification,
education, and enjoyment—for a price."
P. T. BARNUM

WHILE I KNEW my home dimension wasn't particularly colorful,
I never really considered it drab...until I first set eyes on the Bazaar
at Deva.

Even though both Aahz and Frumple, and even the Imps, had
referred to this phenomenon, I had never actually sat back and tried
to envision it. It was just as well. Anything I could have fantasized
would have been dwarfed by the real thing.

The Bazaar seemed to stretch endlessly in all directions as far
as the eye could see. Tents and lean-tos of all designs and colors
were gathered in irregular clumps that shoved against each other
for more room.

There were thousands of Deveels everywhere of every age and
description. Tall Deveels, fat Deveels, lame Deveels, bald Deveels,
all moved about until the populace gave the appearance of being
one seething mass with multiple heads and tails. There were other
beings scattered through the crowd. Some of them looked like nightmares come to life; others I didn't recognize as being alive until they
moved, but they all made noise.

The noise! Twixt had seemed noisy to me after my secluded life
with Garkin, but the clamor that assailed my ears now defied all
description. There were shrieks and dull explosions and strange bur-
bling noises emanating from the depths of the booths around us,
competing with the constant din of barter. It seemed no one spoke
below a shout. Whether weeping piteously, barking in anger, or displaying bored indifference, all bartering was to be done at the top
of your lungs.

"Welcome to Deva, kid," Aahz gestured expansively. "What do
you think?"

"It's loud," I observed.

"What?"

"I said, it's loud!" I shouted.

"Oh, well. It's a bit livelier than your average Farmer's Market or Fisherman's Wharf, but there are noisier places to be."

I was about to respond when a passerby careened into me. He, or she, had eyes spaced all around his head and fur-covered tentacles instead of arms.

"Wzklp!" it said, waving a tentacle as it continued on its way.

"Aahz!"

"Yeah, kid?"

"It just occurred to me. What language do they speak on Deva?"

"Hmm? Oh! Don't worry about it, kid. They speak all languages here. No Deveel that's been hatched would let a sale get away just because they couldn't speak the right tongue. Just drop a few sentences on 'em in Klahdish and they'll adapt fast enough."

"Okay, Aahz. Now that we're here, where do we go first?"

There was no answer. I tore my eyes away from the Bazaar and glanced at my partner. He was standing motionless, sniffing the air.

"Aahz?"

"Hey kid, do you smell that?" he asked eagerly.

I sniffed the air.

"Yeah!" I gagged. "What died?"

"C'mon, kid. Follow me."

He plunged off into the crowd, leaving me little choice but to trail after him. Hands plucked at our sleeves as we passed, and various Deveels leaned out of their stalls and tents to call to us as we passed, but Aahz didn't slacken his pace. I couldn't get a clear look at any of the displays. Keeping up with Aahz demanded most of my concentration. One tent, however, did catch my eye.

"Look, Aahz!" I cried.

"What?"

"It's raining in that tent!"

As if in answer to my words, a boom of thunder and a crackle of lightning erupted from the display.

"Yeah. So?" Aahz dismissed it with a glance.

"What are they selling, rain?"

"Nah. Weather control devices. They're scattered through the whole Bazaar instead of hanging together in one section. Something about the devices interfering with each other."

"Are all the displays that spectacular?"

"That isn't spectacular, kid. They used to do tornados until the other booths complained and they had to limit their demonstrations to the tame stuff. Now hurry up!"

"Where are we going anyway, Aahz? And what is that smell?"

The repulsive aroma was growing noticeably stronger.

"That," proclaimed Aahz, coming to a halt in front of a dome-shaped tent, "is the smell of Pervish cooking!"

"Food? We came all this way so you could have a *meal?*"

"First things first, kid. I haven't had a decent meal since Garkin called me out of the middle of a party and stranded me in your idiot dimension."

"But we're supposed to be looking for something to use against Isstvan."

"Relax, kid. I haggle better on a full stomach. Just wait here. I won't be long."

"Wait here? Can't I go in with you?"

"I don't think you'd like it, kid. To anyone who wasn't born on Perv, the food looks even worse than it smells."

I found that hard to believe, but pursued the argument gamely.

"I'm not all that weak-stomached, you know. When I was living in the woods, I ate some pretty weird things myself."

"I'll tell ya, kid, the main problem with Pervish food is keeping the goo from crawling out of the bowl while you're eating it."

"I'll wait here."

"Good. Like I say, I won't be long. You can watch the dragons until I get back."

"Dragons?" I said, but he had already disappeared through the tent flap.

I turned slowly and looked at the display behind me.

Dragons!

There was an enormous stall stocked with dragons not fifteen feet from where I was standing. Most of the beasts were tethered at the back wall which kept me from seeing them as we approached, but upon direct viewing there was no doubt they were dragons.

Curiosity made me drift over to join the small crowd in front of the stall. The stench was overwhelming, but after a whiff of Pervish cooking, it seemed almost pleasant.

I had never seen a dragon before, but the specimens in the stall lived up to the expectations of my daydreams. They were huge,

easily ten or fifteen feet high at the shoulder and a full thirty feet long.
Their necks were long and serpentine, and their clawed feet dug
great gouges in the ground as they shifted their weight nervously.

I was surprised to see how many varieties there were. It had never
occurred to me that there might be more than one type of dragon, but
here was living proof to the contrary. Besides the green dragons I had
always envisioned, there were red, black, gold and blue dragons. There
was even one that was mauve. Some were winged and some weren't.
Some had wide, massive jaws and others had narrow snouts. Some had
eyes that were squinting and slanted, while others had huge moonlike
eyes that never seemed to blink. They had two things in common,
however: they were all big and they all looked thoroughly nasty.

My attention was drawn to the Deveel running the operation.
He was the biggest Deveel I had ever seen, fully eight feet tall with
arms like trees. It was difficult to say which was more fearsome in
appearance, the dragons or their keeper.

He brought one of the red dragons to the center of the stall and
released it with a flourish. The beast raised its head and surveyed the
crowd with seething yellow eyes. The crowd fell back a few steps
before that gaze. I seriously considered leaving.

The Deveel shouted a few words at the crowd in gibberish I couldn't
understand, then picked up a sword from the rack by the wall.

Fast as a cat, the dragon arched his neck and spat a stream of
fire at its keeper. By some miracle, the flame parted as it hit the
Deveel and passed harmlessly on either side of him.

The keeper smiled and turned to shout a few more words at his
audience. As he did, the dragon lept at him with murderous intent.
The Deveel dove to the ground and rolled out from under the
attack as the beast landed with an impact that shook the tent. The
dragon whirled, but the keeper was on his feet again, holding aloft a
pendant before the beast's eyes.

I didn't understand his move, but apparently the dragon did,
for it cowered back on its haunches. The Deveel pointed forcefully
and it slunk back to its place at the back of the stall.

A small ripple of applause rippled through the crowd. Apparently they were impressed with the ferocity of the dragon's attack.
Me, I was impressed by the pendant.

The keeper acknowledged the applause and launched into another
spiel of gibberish, this time punctuated by gestures and exclamations.

I decided it was about time for me to go.

"Gleep!"

There was a tug at my sleeve.

I looked around. There, behind me, was a small dragon! Well, he was about four feet high and ten feet long, but after looking at the other dragons, he seemed small. He was green with big blue eyes and what appeared to be a drooping white mustache.

For a split second I felt panicky, but that rapidly gave way to curiosity. He didn't look dangerous. He seemed quite content just standing there chewing on...

My sleeve! The beast was eating a piece of my sleeve! I looked down and confirmed that part of my shirt was indeed missing.

"Gleep," said the dragon again, stretching his neck out for another mouthful.

"Go away!" I said, and cuffed him before I realized what I was doing.

"Gleep?" it said, puzzled.

I started to edge away. I was unsure of what to do if he cut loose with a blast of fire and therefore eager to avoid it.

"Gleep," it said, shuffling after me.

"Gazabkp!" roared a voice behind me.

I spun and found myself looking at a hairy stomach. I followed it up, way up, and saw the dragonkeeper's face looming over me.

"I'm sorry," I apologized readily. "I don't speak your language."

"Oh. A Klahd!" The Deveel boomed. "Well, the statement still stands. Pay up!"

"Pay up for what?"

"For the dragon! What do you think, we're giving away samples?"

"Gleep!" said the dragon, pressing his head against my leg.

"There seems to be some mistake," I said hastily.

"I'll say there is," the Deveel scowled. "And you're making it. We don't take kindly to shoplifters on Deva!"

"Gleep!" said the dragon.

Things were rapidly getting out of hand. If I ever needed Aahz's help or advice, it was now. I shot a desperate glance toward the tent he was in, hoping beyond hope to see him emerge.

He wasn't there. In fact, the tent wasn't there. It was gone, vanished into thin air, and so had Aahz.

XVIII.

*"No matter what the product or service might be,
you can find it somewhere else cheaper!"*
E. SCROOGE

"WHERE DID THAT tent go?" I demanded desperately.

"What tent?" The keeper blinked, looming behind me.

"That tent," I exclaimed, pointing at the now vacant space.

The Deveel frowned craning his neck, which, at his height, gave him considerable visibility.

"There isn't any tent there," he announced with finality.

"I know! That's the point!"

"Hey! Quit trying to change the subject!" The keeper growled, poking me in the chest with an unbelievably large finger. "Are you going to pay for the dragon or not?"

I looked around for support, but no one was watching. Apparently disputes such as this were common on Deva.

"I told you there's been a mistake! I don't want your dragon."

"Gleep!" said the dragon, cocking his head at me.

"Don't give me that!" the keeper boomed. "If you didn't want him, why did you feed him?"

"I didn't feed him! He ate a piece of my sleeve!"

"Gleep!" said the dragon, making another unsuccessful pass at my shirt.

"So you admit he got food from you?"

"Well...in a manner of speaking...yeah! So what?" I was getting tired of being shouted at.

"So pay up! He's no good to me anymore."

I surveyed the dragon. He didn't seem to be any the worse for having eaten the shirt.

"What's wrong with him? He looks all right to me."

"Gleep!" said the dragon, and sidled up to me again.

"Oh! He's fine," the keeper sneered. "Except now he's attached. An attached dragon isn't any good except to the person or thing he's attached to."

"Well, who's he attached to?"

"Don't get smart with me! He's attached to you! Has been ever since you fed him."

"Well, feed him again and unattach him! I have pressing matters elsewhere,"

"Just like that, huh?" the Deveel said skeptically, towering to new heights. "You know very well it doesn't work that way. Once a dragon's attached, it's attached forever. That's why they're so valuable."

"Forever?" I asked.

"Well…until one of you dies. But any fool knows not to feed a dragon unless they want it attached to them. The idiot beasts are too impressionable, especially the young ones like this."

I looked at the dragon again. He was very young. His wings were just beginning to bud, which I took as a sign of immaturity, and his fangs were needle-sharp instead of worn to rounded points like his brethren in the stall. Still, there was strength in the muscles rippling beneath those scales…Yes, I decided, I'd back my dragon in a fight against any…

"Gleep!" said the dragon, licking both ends of his mustache simultaneously with his forked tongue.

That brought me to my senses. A dragon? What did I want with a dragon?

"Well," I said haughtily, "I guess I'm not just any fool, then. If I had known the consequences of allowing him to eat my sleeve, I would have…"

"Look, sonny!" the Deveel snarled, poking my chest again. "If you think you're going to…"

Something inside me snapped. I knocked his hand away with a fury that surprised me.

"The name isn't 'Sonny,'" I hissed in a low voice I didn't recognize as my own. "It's Skeeve! Now lower your voice when you're talking to me and keep your dirty finger to yourself!"

I was shaking, though whether from rage or from fear I couldn't tell. I had spent my entire burst of emotion in that outburst, and now found myself wondering if I would survive the aftermath.

Surprisingly, the keeper gave ground a few steps at my tirade, and was now studying me with new puzzlement. I felt a pressure at the back of my legs and risked a glance. The dragon was now crouched behind me, craning his neck to peer around my waist at the keeper.

"I'm sorry." The keeper was suddenly humble and fawning. "I didn't recognize you at first. You said your name was...?"

"Skeeve." I prompted haughtily.

"Skeeve." He frowned thoughtfully. "Strange. I don't remember that name."

I wasn't sure who or what he thought I was, but if I had learned one thing traveling with Aahz, it was to recognize and seize an advantage when I saw one.

"The secrecy surrounding my identity should be a clue in itself, if you know what I mean," I murmured, giving him my best conspiratorial wink.

"Of course," he responded. "I should have realized immediately..."

"No matter," I yawned. "Now then, about the dragon..."

"Yes. Forgive me for losing my temper, but you can see my predicament."

It seemed strange having someone that immense simpering at me, but I rose to the occasion.

"Well, I'm sure we can work something out," I smiled.

As I spoke, a thought flashed through my head. Aahz had all our money! I didn't have a single item of any value on me except...

I reached into my pocket, forcing myself to make the move casual. It was still there! The charm I had taken from Quigley's statue-body that allowed the wearer to see through spells. I had taken it when Aahz wasn't looking and had kept it hidden in case it might be useful in some crisis. Well, this definitely looked like a crisis!

"Here!" I said, tossing the charm to him. "I believe this should settle our accounts."

He caught it deftly and gave it a fast, squinting appraisal.

"This?" he said. "You want to purchase a hatchling dragon for this?"

I had no idea of the charm's relative worth, but bluffing had gotten me this far.

"I do not haggle," I said coldly. "That is my first and final offer. If it is not satisfactory, then return the charm and see if you can get a better price for an attached dragon."

"You drive a hard bargain, Skeeve." The Deveel was still polite, but his smile looked like it hurt. "Very well, it's a deal. Shake on it."

He extended his hand.

There was a sudden hissing noise and my vision was obscured. The dragon had arched his neck forward over my head and was confronting the Deveel eye-to-eye. His attitude was suddenly a miniature version of the ferocity I had seen displayed earlier by his larger brethren. I realized with a start that he was defending me!

Apparently the keeper realized it too, for he jerked back his hand as if he had just stuck it in an open fire.

"...if you could call off your dragon long enough for us to close the deal?" he suggested with forced politeness.

I wasn't sure just how I was supposed to do this, but I was willing to give it a try.

"He's okay!" I shouted, thumping the dragon on the side of the neck to get his attention.

"Gleep?" said the dragon, turning his head to peer into my face.

I noticed his breath was bad enough to kill an insect in flight.

"It's okay," I repeated, edging out from under his neck.

Since I was already moving, I stepped forward and shook the keeper's hand. He responded absently, never taking his eyes from the dragon.

"Say," I said. "Confidentially, I'm rather new to the dragon game. What does he eat...besides shirts, I mean?"

"Oh, a little of this and a little of that. They're omnivorous, so they *can* eat anything, but they're picky eaters. Just let him alone and he'll choose his own diet...old clothes, selected leaves, house pets."

"Terrific!" I mumbled.

"Well, if you'll excuse me I've got other customers to talk to."

"Just a minute! Don't I get one of those pendants like you used to control the big dragons?"

"Hmm? What for?"

"Well...to control my dragon."

"Those are to control unattached dragons. You don't need one for one that's attached to you and it wouldn't work on a dragon that's attached to someone else."

"Oh," I said, with a wisdom I didn't feel.

"If you want one, though, I have a cousin who has a stall that sells them. It's about three rows up and two rows over. It might be a good investment for you. Could save wear and tear on your dragon if you come up against an unattached dragon. It'd give junior there a better chance of growing up."

"That brings up another question," I said. "How long does it take?"

"Not long. It's just three rows up and…"

"No. I mean how long until my dragon reaches maturity?"

"Oh, not more than four or five centuries."

"Gleep!"

I'm not sure if the dragon said that or I did.

XIX.

*"By persevering over all obstacles and distractions, one may
unfailingly arrive at his chosen goal or destination."*
C. COLUMBUS

"C'MON, GLEEP," I said.

"Gleep," my dragon responded, falling in behind me.

Now that I was the not-so-proud owner of a permanently immature dragon, I was more eager than ever to find Aahz. At the moment, I was alone in a strange dimension, penniless, and now I had a dragon tagging after me. The only way things could be worse would be if the situation became permanent, which could happen if Aahz decided to return to Klah without me.

The place previously occupied by the Pervish restaurant tent was definitely empty, even on close examination, so I decided to ask the Deveel running the neighboring booth.

"Um…excuse me, sir."

I decided I was going to be polite as possible for the duration of my stay on Deva. The last thing I needed was another dispute with a Deveel. It seemed, however, in this situation I needn't have worried.

"No excuses are necessary, young sahr." The proprietor smiled eagerly, displaying an impressive number of teeth.

"You are interested in purchasing a stick?"

"A stick?"

"Of course!" the Deveel gestured grandly around his stall. "The finest sticks in all the dimensions."

"Aah…thanks, but we have plenty of sticks in my home dimension."

"Not like these sticks, young sahr. You are from Klah, are you not?"

"Yes, why?"

"I can guarantee you, there are no such sticks as these in all of Klah. They come from a dimension only I have access to and I have not sold them in Klah or to anyone who was going there."

Despite myself, my curiosity was piqued. I looked again at the sticks lining the walls of the stall. They looked like ordinary sticks such as could be found anywhere.

"What do they do?" I asked cautiously.

"Aah! Different ones do different things. Some control animals, others control plants. A few very rare ones allow you to summon an army of warriors from the stones themselves. Some of the most powerful magicians of any dimension wield staffs of the same wood as these sticks, but for most people's purposes the smaller model will suffice."

"Gleep!" said the dragon, sniffing at one of the sticks.

"Leave it alone!" I barked, shoving his head away from the display.

All I needed was to have my dragon eat up the entire stock of one of these super-merchants.

"May I inquire, is that your dragon, young sahr?"

"Well...sort of."

"In that case, you might find a particular use for a stick most magicians wouldn't."

"What's that?"

"You could use it to beat your dragon."

"Gleep!" said the dragon, looking at me with his big blue eyes.

"Actually, I'm not really interested in a stick."

I thought I'd better get to my original purpose before this conversation got out of hand.

"Ridiculous, young sahr. Everybody should have a stick."

"The reason I stopped here in the first place is I wondered if you knew what happened to that tent."

"What tent, young sahr?"

I had a vague feeling of having had this conversation before.

"The tent that was right there next to your stall."

"The Pervish restaurant?!" The Deveel's voice was tinged with horror.

"Gleep," said the dragon.

"Why would you seek such place, young sahr? You seem well-bred and educated."

"I had a friend who was inside the tent when it vanished."

"You have a Pervert for a friend?" His voice had lost it's friendly tone.

"Well actually...um...it's a long story."

"I can tell you this much, punk. It didn't disappear, it moved on," the Deveel snarled, without the accent or politeness he had displayed earlier.

"Moved on?"

"Yeah. It's a new ordinance we passed. All places serving Pervish food have to migrate. They cannot be established permanently, or even temporarily, at any point in the Bazaar."

"Why?" I asked.

"Have you ever smelled Pervish food? It's enough to make a scavenger nauseous. Would you want to man a stall down- wind of that for a whole day? In this heat?"

"I see what you mean," I admitted.

"Either they moved or the Bazaar did, and we have them out-numbered."

"But what exactly do you mean, move?"

"The tents! All that's involved is a simple spell or two, Either they constantly move at a slow pace, or they stay in one place for a short period and then scuttle off to a new location, but they all move."

"How does anyone find one, then, if they keep moving around?"

"That's easy, just follow your nose."

I sniffed the air experimentally. Sure enough, the unmistakable odor was still lingering in the air.

"Gleep!" the dragon had imitated my action and was now rubbing his nose with one paw.

"Well, thank you...for...your..."

I was talking to thin air. The Deveel was at the other end of the stall, baring his teeth at another customer. It occurred to me that the citizens of Deva were not particularly concerned with social pleasantries beyond those necessary to transact a sale.

I set out to follow the smell of the Pervish restaurant with the dragon faithfully trailing along behind. Despite my growing desire to reunite with Aahz, my pace was considerably slower than that Aahz had set when we first arrived. I was completely mesmerized by this strange Bazaar and wanted to see as much of it as I could.

Upon more leisurely examination, there did seem to be a vague order to the Bazaar. The various stalls and booths were generally grouped by type of merchandise. This appeared to be more from circumstance than by plan. Apparently, if one Deveel set up a display, say, of invisible cloaks, in no time at all he had a pack of competitors in residence around him, each vying to top the other for quality of goods or prices. Most of the confused babble of voices were disputes between the merchants over the location of their respective stalls or the space occupied by the same.

The smell grew stronger as I wandered through an area specializing in exotic and magical jewelry, which I resisted the temptation to examine more closely. The temptation was even stronger as I traversed an area which featured weaponry. It occurred to me that I might find a weapon here we could use against Isstvan, but the smell of the Pervish food was even stronger now, and I steeled myself to finish my search. We could look for a weapon after I found Aahz. From the intensity of the stench, I was sure we would find our objective soon.

"C'mon, Gleep," I encouraged.

The dragon was hanging back now and didn't respond except to speed his pace a bit.

I expectantly rounded one last corner and came to an abrupt halt. I had found the source of the odor.

I was looking at the back of a large display of some alien livestock. There was a large pile of some moist green and yellow substance in front of me. As I watched, a young Deveel emerged from the display holding a shovel filled with the same substance. He glanced at me quizzically as he heaved the load onto the pile and returned to the display.

A dung heap! I had been following the smell of a dung heap!

"Gleep!" said the dragon, looking at me quizzically.

He seemed to be asking me what we were going to do next. That was a good question.

I stood contemplating my next move. Probably the best chance would be to retrace our step back to the stick seller and try again.

"Spare a girl a little time, handsome?"

I whirled around. A girl was standing there, a girl unlike any I had ever seen before. She was Klahdish in appearance and could have passed for another of my dimension except for her complexion and hair. Her skin was a marvelous golden-olive hue, and her head was crowned with a mane of light green hair that shimmered in the sun. She was a little taller than me and incredibly curvaceous, her generous figure straining against the confines of her clothes.

"...or have you really got a thing about dung heaps?" she concluded.

She had almond cat-eyes that danced with mischief as she talked.

"Um…are you talking to me?" I stammered.

"Of course I'm talking to you," she purred, coming close to me and twining her arms around my neck. "I'm certainly not talking to your dragon. I mean, he's cute and all, but my tastes don't run in those directions."

"Gleep!" said the dragon.

I felt my body temperature soar. The touch of her arms caused a tingling sensation which seemed to wreak havoc on my metabolism.

"Um…actually I'm looking for a friend," I blurted.

"Well, you've found one," she murmured, moving her body against me.

"Aah…I…um." Suddenly I was having trouble concentrating. "What is it you want?"

"Hmm," she said thoughtfully, "Even though it's not my normal time, I think I'd like to tell your fortune…free."

"Oh?" I said, surprised.

This was the first time since I reached the Bazaar that anyone had offered me anything for free. I didn't know if I should be happy or suspicious.

"You're going to have a fight," she whispered in my ear. "A big one."

"What?" I exclaimed. "When? With who?"

"Easy, handsome," she warned, tightening her grip around my neck. "When is in a very few minutes. With who is the rat pack over my shoulder…don't look right at them!"

Her final sharp warning checked my reflexive glance. Moving more cautiously, I snuck a peek out of the corner of my eye.

Lounging against a shop wall, watching us closely, were a dozen or so of the ugliest, nastiest-looking characters I have ever seen.

"Them? I mean, all of them?" I asked.

"Uh-huh!" she confirmed, snuggling into my chest.

"Why?" I demanded.

"I probably shouldn't tell you this," she smiled, "but because of me."

Only her firm grip on me kept me from dislodging her with a shove.

"You? What about you?"

"Well, they're an awfully greedy bunch. One way or another, they're going to make some money from this encounter. Normally, you'd give the money to me and I'd cut them in for a share. In the unlikely event that doesn't work, they'll pretend to be defending my honor and beat it out of you."

"But you don't understand! I don't have any money."

"I know that. That's why you're going to get into a fight, see?"

"If you knew I didn't have any money, why did you…"

"Oh, I didn't know when I first stopped you. I found out just now when I searched you."

"Searched me?"

"Oh, come on, handsome. There's more ways to search a person than with your hands." She winked knowingly at me.

"Well, can't you tell them I don't have any money?"

"They wouldn't believe me. The only way they'd be convinced is searching you themselves."

"I'd be willing to let them if that's what it takes to convince them."

"I don't think you would," she smiled, stroking my face with her hand. "One of the things they'll look for is if you swallowed your money."

"Oh!" I said, "I see what you mean. But I can't fight them. I don't have any weapons."

"You have that little knife under your shirt at the small of your back," she pointed out.

I had forgotten about my skinning knife. I started to believe in her no-hands frisking technique.

"But I've never been in a fight before."

"Well, I think you're about to learn."

"Say, why are you telling me all this, anyway?" I asked.

"I don't know," she shrugged. "I like your act. That's why I singled you out in the first place. Then again, I feel a little guilty about having gotten you into this."

"Will you help me?"

"I don't feel that guilty, handsome," she smiled. "But there is one more thing I can do for you."

She started to pull me toward her.

"Wait a minute," I protested. "Won't that…"

"Relax, handsome," she purred. "You're about to get pounded for offending my honor. You might as well get a little of the sweet along with the bitter."

Before I could protest further, she kissed me. Long and warm and sweet, she kissed me.

I had never been kissed by anyone except my mother. This was different! The fight, the dragon, Aahz, everything faded from my mind. I was lost in the wonder of that moment.

"Hey!"

A rough hand fell on my shoulder and pulled us apart.

"Is this shrimp bothering you, lady?"

The person on the other end of that hand was no taller than I was, but he was twice as broad and had short, twisted tusks protruding from his mouth. His cronies had fanned out behind him, effectively boxing me in against the dung-heap.

I looked at the girl. She shrugged and backed away.

It looked like I was going to have to fight all of them. Me and the dragon. Terrific.

I remembered my skinning knife. It wasn't much, but it was all I had. As casually as I could, I reached behind me and tugged at my shirt, trying to pull it up so I could get at the knife.

The knife promptly fell down inside my pants.

The wrecking crew started forward.

XX.

"With the proper consideration in choice of allies,
victory can be guaranteed in any conflict."
                                        B. ARNOLD

"GET 'EM, GLEEP!" I barked.

The dragon bounded into action, a move which I think surprised me more than it did my assailants.

It leaped between me and the advancing rat-pack and crouched there, hissing menacingly. His tail gave a mighty lash which neatly swept the legs out from under two of the flanking members of the party. Somehow, he seemed much bigger when he was mad.

"Watch out! He's got a dragon!" the leader called.

"Thanks for the warning," one of the fallen men growled, struggling to regain his feet.

"I've got him!" came a voice from my left.

I turned just in time to see a foot-long dagger flashing through the air at the dragon's neck. *My* dragon!

Suddenly I was back at the practice sessions. My mind darted out and grabbed at the knife. It jerked to a halt in mid-air and hovered there.

"Nice move, handsome!" the girl called. "Hey! The shrimp's a magician!" The pack fell back a few steps.

"That's right!" I barked. "Skeeve's the name, magik's the game. What kind of clod did you think you were dealing with?"

With that, I brought the dagger down, swooping it back and forth through their formation. I was mad now. One of these louts had tried to kill my dragon!

"A dozen of you isn't enough!" I shouted. "Go back and get some friends...if you have any!"

I cast about desperately for something else to throw. My eyes fell on the dung-heap. I smiled to myself despite my anger. Why not?

In a moment I had great gobs of dung hurtling through the air at my assailants. My accuracy wasn't the best, but it was good enough as the outraged howls testified.

"Levitation!" the leader bawled. "Quanto! Stop him!"

"Right, boss!"

One of the plug-uglies waved in affirmation and started rummaging through his belt pouch.

He had made a mistake identifying himself. I didn't know what he was about to come up with, but I was sure I didn't want to wait and find out.

"Stop him, Gleep!" I ordered, pointing to the victim.

The dragon raised his head and fixed his gaze on the fumbling brigand. With a sound that might have been a roar if he were older, he shot a stream of flame and charged.

It wasn't much of a stream of flame, and it missed to boot, but it was enough to get the brigand's attention. He looked up to see a mountain of dragon flesh bearing down on him and panicked. Without pausing to call to his comrades, he spun and ran off screaming with the dragon in hot pursuit.

"Okay, shrimp! Let's see you stop this!"

I jerked my attention back to the leader. He was standing now, confidently holding aloft a stick. Yesterday it wouldn't have fazed me, but knowing what I did now, I froze. I didn't know what model it was, but apparently the leader was confident its powers would surpass my own.

He grinned evilly and slowly began to level the stick at me.

I tried desperately to think of a defense, but couldn't. I didn't even know what I was supposed to be defending against!

Suddenly, something flashed across my line of vision and the stick was gone.

I blinked and looked again. The stick was lying on the ground, split by a throwing knife. A black-handled throwing knife.

"Any trouble here, Master Skeeve?" a voice boomed.

I spun toward the source of the voice. Aahz was standing there, cocked crossbow leveled at the pack. He was grinning broadly, which I have mentioned before is not that comforting to anyone who doesn't know him.

"A Pervert!" the leader gasped.

"What?" Aahz swung the crossbow toward him.

"I mean a Pervect!" the leader amended hastily.

"That's better. How about it, Skeeve? You want 'em dead or running?"

I looked at the rat pack. Without breaking their frozen tableau, they pleaded with me with their eyes.

"Um...running, I think," I said thoughtfully. "They smell bad enough alive. Dead they might give the Bazaar a bad name."

"You heard him," Aahz growled. "Move!"

They disappeared like they had melted into the ground.

"Aahz!"

The girl came flying forward to throw her arms around him.

"Tanda!" Aahz exclaimed, lowering the crossbow. "Are you mixed up with that pack?"

"Are you kidding? I'm the bait!" she winked bawdily.

"Little low-class for you, isn't it?"

"Aah...it's a living."

"Why'd you leave the Assassins?"

"Got tired of paying union dues."

"Um...harrumph..." I interrupted.

"Hmm?" Aahz looked around. "Oh! Sorry, kid. Say, have you two met?"

"Sort of," the girl acknowledged. "We...say, is this the friend you were looking for, handsome?"

"Handsome?" Aahz wrinkled his nose.

"Well, yes," I admitted. "We got separated back by the..."

"Handsome?" Aahz repeated.

"Oh, hush!" the girl commanded, slapping his stomach playfully. "I like him. He's got style."

"Actually, I don't believe we've met formally," I said, giving my most winning smile. "My name is Skeeve."

"Well, la-de-dah!" Aahz grumbled.

"Ignore him. I'm Tananda, but call me Tanda."

"Love to," I leered.

"If you two are quite through..." Aahz interrupted. "I have a couple questions..."

"Gleep!" said the dragon, prancing up to our assemblage.

"What's that?" Aahz demanded.

"It's a dragon," I said helpfully. Tanda giggled rudely.

"I know that," Aahz barked. "I mean what is he doing here?"

Suddenly I was hesitant to supply the whole story. "There are lots of dragons at the Bazaar, Aahz," I mumbled, not looking at him. "In fact, there's a stall just down the way that..."

"What is that dragon doing here?"

"Gleep!" said the dragon, rubbing his head against my chest.

"Um...he's mine," I admitted.

"Yours?" Aahz bellowed. "I told you to *look* at the dragons, not *buy* one!"

"But Aahz..."

"What are we going to do with a dragon?"

"I got a good deal on him," I chimed hopefully.

"What did you say, kid?"

"I said I got a good deal..."

"From a Deveel?"

"Oh. I see what you mean."

"C'mon. Let's have it. What were the terms of this fantastic deal?"

"Well...I...that is..."

"Out with it!"

"I traded Quigley's pendant for him."

"Quigley's pendant? The one that sees through spells? You traded a good magical pendant for a half-grown dragon?"

"Oh, give him a break, Aahz," Tanda interrupted "What do you expect letting him wander off alone that way? You're lucky he didn't get stuck with half the tourist crud on Deva! Where were you all this time, anyway?"

"Well...I was...um..."

"Don't tell me," she said, holding up a hand, "If I know you, you were either chasing a girl or stuffing your face, right?"

"She's got you there, Aahz," I commented.

"Shut up, kid."

"...so don't get down on Skeeve here. Compared to what could have happened to him, he didn't do half bad. How did you find us, anyway?"

"I listened for the sounds of a fight and followed it," Aahz admitted.

"See! You were expecting him to get into trouble. Might I point out he was doing just fine before you barged in? He and his dragon had those thugs treed all by themselves. He's pretty handy with that magik, you know."

"I know," Aahz responded proudly. "I taught him."

"Gee, thanks, Aahz."

"Shut up, kid."

"Gleep," said the dragon, craning his neck around to look at Aahz upside down.

"A dragon, huh?" Aahz said, studying the dragon more thoughtfully.

"He might help us against Isstvan," I suggested hopefully.

"Isstvan?" Tanda asked quizzically.

"Yeah," Aahz replied. "You remember him, don't you? Well, he's up to his old tricks, this time in Klah."

"So that's what's going on, huh? Well, what are we going to do about it?"

"We?" I asked surprised.

"Sure," she smiled. "This racket is a bit low-class, like Aahz says. I might as well tag along with you two for a while…if you don't mind, that is."

"Terrific!" I said, and meant it for a change.

"Not so fast, Tanda," Aahz cautioned. "There are a few details you haven't been filled in on yet."

"Such as?"

"Such as I've lost my powers."

"No fooling? Gee, that's tough."

"That means we'll be relying on the kid here to give us cover in the magik department."

"All the more reason for me to come along. I've picked up a few tricks myself."

"I know," Aahz leered.

"Not like that," she said, punching him in the side. "I mean magik tricks."

"Even so, it's not going to be easy."

"C'mon, Aahz," Tanda chided. "Are you trying to say it wouldn't be helpful having a trained Assassin on your side?"

"Well…it could give us a *bit* of an advantage," Aahz admitted.

"Good! Then it's settled. What do we do first?"

"There're some stalls just around the corner that carry weapons," I suggested. "We could…"

"Relax, kid. I've already taken care of that."

"You have?" I asked, surprised.

"Yeah. I found just what we need over in the practical jokes section. I was just looking for you before we headed back."

"Then we're ready to go?" Tanda asked.

"Yep," Aahz nodded, fishing the D-Hopper out of his shirt.

"What about my dragon?"

"What about him?"

"Are we going to take him with us?"

"Of course we're going to take him with us! We don't leave anything of value behind…"

"Gleep!" said the dragon.

"…and he must be valuable to someone!" Aahz finished, glaring at the dragon.

He pressed the button on the D-Hopper. The Bazaar wavered and faded…and we were back in Frumple's shop…sort of.

"Interesting place you've got here," Tanda commented dryly. "Did you do the decor?"

All that was left of Frumple's shop was a burnt-out shell.

XXI.

*"One must deal openly and fairly with one's forces
if maximum effectiveness is to be achieved."*
D. VADER

"WHAT HAPPENED?" I demanded of Aahz.

"Hey, kid. I was on Deva, too. Remember?"

"Um...hey, guys. I hate to interrupt," Tanda interrupted, "but shouldn't something be done about disguises?"

She was right. Being on Deva had made me forget the mundane necessities of our existence. I ignored Aahz's sarcastic reply and set to work.

Aahz returned to his now traditional Garkin disguise. Tanda was fine once I changed her complexion and the color of her hair. After a bit of thought, I disguised Gleep as the war unicorn. It was a bit risky, but it would do as long as he kept his mouth shut. Me, I left as myself. I mean, what the heck. Tanda liked my looks the way they were.

Fortunately, the sun wasn't up yet, so there weren't any people about to witness the transformation.

"Say, handsome," Tanda commented, observing the results of my work, "you're a pretty handy guy to have around."

"His name's Skeeve," Aahz grumbled.

"Whatever," Tanda murmured. "He's got style."

She snuggled up to me.

"Gleep!" said the dragon, pressing his head against my other side.

I was starting to feel awfully popular.

"If you can spare a few minutes, kid," Aahz commented dryly, "we *do* have a mission, remember?"

"That's right," I said, forcing my attention away from Tanda's advances. "What do you think happened to Frumple?"

"Either the citizens of Twixt got wise to him, or he's off to tell Isstvan we're coming, would be my two guesses."

"Who's Frumple?" Tanda asked.

"Hmm? Oh, he's the resident Deveel," Aahz said. "He's the one who helped us get to the Bazaar."

"...at sword point," I added sarcastically.

"What's a Deveel doing here?"

"All we know is that rumor has it he was barred from Deva," I told her.

"Hmm…sounds like a bit of a nasty character."

"Well, he won't win any popularity contests."

"It occurs to me," Aahz interrupted, "that if either of my two guesses are correct, we'd best be on our way. Time seems to be running out."

"Right," agreed Tanda. "Which way is Isstvan?"

"First, we've got to pick up Quigley," I inserted.

"Why?" asked Aahz. "Oh, I suppose you're right, kid. We're going to need all the help we can muster."

"Who's Quigley?" Tanda asked.

"Later, Tanda," Aahz insisted. "First help us see if there's anything here worth salvaging."

Unfortunately, there wasn't. In fact, there weren't even the charred remains of anything left for our discovery. Even the garish sword I had left behind seemed to have vanished.

"That settles it," Aahz commented grimly as we completed our search. "He's on his way to Isstvan."

"The natives might have taken the sword after they burned the place," I suggested hopefully.

"No way, kid. Even yokels like these wouldn't bother with a crummy sword like that."

"It was that bad?" Tanda asked.

"It was that bad," Aahz assured her firmly.

"If it was that worthless, why would Frumple take it with him?" I asked.

"For the same reason we've been lugging it around," Aahz said pointedly. "There's always some sucker to unload it on for a profit. Remember Quigley?"

"Who's Quigley?" Tanda insisted.

"Well," sighed Aahz, "at the moment he's a statue, but in duller times he's a demon hunter."

"Swell," she commented sarcastically. "Just what we need."

"Wait until you meet him," Aahz rolled his eyes and sighed. "Oh well, let's go."

Our departure from Twixt was blissfully uneventful. On the road, we rehearsed our story until, by the time we finally dug up

Quigley and sprinkled him with the restoring powder, we were ready
to present a united front.

"Really? Turned to stone, you say?" he said, brushing the dirt
from his clothes.

"Yes," Aahz assured him. "They were looting your body when
we launched our counterattack. It's lucky for you we decided to
come back and fight at your side."

"And they took my magik sword and my amulet?"

I felt a little uneasy on those subjects, but Aahz never batted an eye.

"That's right, the blackguards!" he snarled. "We tried to stop
them, but they eluded us."

"Well, at least they didn't get my war unicorn," muttered the
demon-hunter.

"Um..." I said, bracing myself for my part in this charade.
"We've got some bad news about that, too."

"Bad news?" Quigley frowned, "I don't understand. I can see
the beast with my own eyes and he seems fit enough."

"Oh, he's fine physically," Aahz reassured him, "but before they
disappeared, the demons put a spell on him."

"A spell?"

"Yes," I said. "Now he...um...well...he thinks he's a dragon."

"A dragon?" Quigley exclaimed.

"Gleep!" said the dragon.

"And that's not all," Aahz continued. "The beast was so wild at
first that only through the continued efforts of my squire here were
we able to gentle him at all. Frankly, I was for putting the poor
animal out of its misery, but he insisted he could tame it and you see
before you the results of his patient teachings."

"That's wonderful!" exclaimed Quigley.

"No. That's terrible," corrected Aahz. "You see, in the process,
your animal has formed a strong attachment for my squire...stronger,
I fear, than his attachment for you."

"Hah! Ridiculous," Quigley proclaimed. "But I do feel I owe
you an additional debt of gratitude, lad. If there's ever anything I
can..."

He began to advance on me with his hand extended. In a flash,
Gleep was between us, head down and hissing.

Quigley froze, his eyes bulging with surprise.

"Stop that!" I ordered, cuffing the dragon.

"Gleep!" said the dragon, slinking back to his place behind me.

"See what I mean?" Aahz said pointedly.

"Hmm…" Quigley mumbled thoughtfully. "That's strange, he never defended me that way."

"I guess we'll just have to buy him from you," I said eagerly.

"Buy him?" Quigley turned his attention to me again.

Aahz tried to catch my eye, shaking his head emphatically, but I ignored him.

"That's right," I continued. "He's no good to you this way, and since we're sort of to blame for what happened to him…"

"Think nothing of it, lad." Quigley drew himself up proudly. "I give him to you as a gift. After all, if it weren't for you he'd be dead anyway, and so would I, for that matter."

"But I…"

"No! I will hear nothing more." The demon hunter held up a restraining hand. "The matter is closed. Treat him well, lad. He's a good animal."

"Terrific," muttered Aahz.

"Gleep," said the dragon.

I felt miserable. It had occurred to me that our plans involved taking shameless advantage of Quigley's gullibility. As he was my only fellow Klahd in this adventure, I had wanted to force Aahz into giving him some money under the guise of buying the "war unicorn." It would have salved my conscience a bit, but Quigley's generosity and sense of fair play had ruined my plan. Now I felt worse than before.

"Actually, Quigley," Aahz smiled, "If there's anyone you should thank, it should be Tananda here. If it were not for her, we would be in dire straits indeed."

"It's about time," mumbled Tanda, obviously unimpressed with Aahz's rhetoric.

"Charmed, milady," Quigley smiled, taking her hand to kiss.

"She's a witch," added Aahz casually.

"A witch?" Quigley dropped her hand as if it had bitten him.

"That's right, sugar," Tanda smiled, batting her eyes at him.

"Perhaps I should explain," Aahz interrupted mercifully. "Tananda here has certain powers she has consented to use in support of our war on demons. You already noticed I have regained my normal appearance?"

Another blatant lie. Aahz was currently disguised as Garkin.

"Yes," the demon hunter admitted hesitantly.

"Tananda's work," Aahz confided. "Just as it was her powers that restored you after you had been turned to stone."

"Hmmm…" Quigley said, looking at Tanda again.

"Really, you must realize, Quigley, that when one fights demons, sometimes it is helpful to employ a demon's weapons," Aahz admonished gently.

"Tananda here can be a powerful ally…and, frankly, I find your attitude toward her deplorable and ungrateful."

"Forgive me, milady," Quigley sighed, stepping up to her again. "I did not mean to offend you. It's just that…well…I've had some bad experiences with those who associate with demons."

"Think nothing of it, sugar," said Tanda the demon, taking his hand. "And call me Tanda."

While they were occupied with each other, I seized the opportunity and snagged Aahz's arm.

"Hm? What is it, kid?"

"Give him back his sword!" I hissed.

"What? No way, kid. By my count he's still got five pieces of gold left. I'll sell it to him."

"But he gave us his unicorn."

"He gave us a dragon…*your* dragon! I fail to see anything benevolent in that."

"Look, Aahz. Either you give him that sword or you can work you own magik! Get me?"

"Talk about ingratitude! Look kid, if you…"

"Aahz!" Tanda's voice interrupted our dispute. "Come help me convince Quigley to join our mission."

"Would that I could, milady," Quigley sighed, "but I would be of little help. This late misfortune has left me afoot, weaponless, and penniless."

"Actually," Aahz chimed, "you still have five…"

I interrupted him with an elbow in his ribs.

"What was that, Aahz?" Quigley asked.

"Aah…my…um…squire and I were just discussing that and we have reached a decision. So…um…so fine a warrior should not be left so destitute, so…um…we…"

"We've decided to give you back your sword," I announced proudly.

"Really?" Quigley's face lit up.

"I didn't know you had it in you, Aahz," Tanda smiled sweetly.

"I say, this is comradeship indeed!" Quigley was obviously beside himself with joy. "How can I ever repay you?"

"By never mentioning this to anyone," Aahz growled.

"How's that again?"

"I said don't mention it," Aahz amended. "It's the least we can do."

"Believe him," I smiled.

"Now I will gladly assist you on your mission," Quigley answered. "Why, with a weapon and good comrades, what more could a warrior ask for?"

"Money," Aahz said bluntly.

"Oh Aahz." Tanda punched him a little too hard for it to be playful. "You're such a kidder."

"Don't you want to know what the mission is?" I asked Quigley.

"Oh, yes, I suppose you're right, lad. Forgive me. I was carried away by my enthusiasm."

"Tell him, Skeeve," prompted Tanda.

"Actually," I said, with a sudden flash of diplomacy, "Aahz explains it much better than I do."

"It's really quite simple," mumbled Aahz, still sulking a bit. "We're going after Isstvan."

"Isstvan?" Quigley looked puzzled. "The harmless old innkeeper?"

"Harmless? Harmless, did you say?" Aahz took the bait. "Quigley, as one demon-hunter to another, you've got a lot to learn."

"I do all right for myself."

"Sure you do. That's why you got turned to stone, remember?"

"I got turned to stone because I put my faith in a magik-sword that…"

Things were back to normal.

"Gentlemen, gentlemen," I interrupted. "We were talking about the upcoming mission."

"Right, kid. As I was saying, Quigley, that harmless old innkeeper is working so closely with demons I wouldn't be surprised to learn he was one himself."

"Impossible!" scoffed Quigley. "Why, the man sent me out hunting for demons."

"Ahh!" smiled Aahz. "Therein lies the story."

I caught Tanda's eyes and winked. She smiled back at me and nodded. This might take a while, but as of now Quigley was in the bag!

XXII.

"This is another fine myth you've gotten me into!"
LOR L. AND HAR D.

THERE WAS SOMETHING there in the shadows. I could sense its presence more than see it. It was dark and serpentine…and it was watching me.

I was alone. I didn't know where the others had gone, but I knew they were counting on me.

"Who's there?" I called.

The voice that came back to me out of the darkness echoed hollowly.

"I am Isstvan, Skeeve. I've been waiting for you."

"You know who I am?" I asked, surprised.

"I know all about you and your friends. I've known all along what you're trying to do."

I tried to set wards about me, but I couldn't find a force line. I tried to run, but I was rooted to the spot.

"See how my powers dwarf yours? And you expected to challenge me."

I tried to fight back a wave of despair.

"Wait until the others come," I cried defiantly.

"They already have," the voice boomed. "Look!"

Two objects came rolling at me out of the darkness. I saw with horror that they were heads—Tanda's and Quigley's!

I felt ill, but clung to a shred of hope. There was still no sign of Aahz. If he was still at large, we might…

"Don't look to your Pervert for help," the voice answered my thoughts. "I've dealt with him too."

Aahz appeared, sheathed in fire. He staggered and fell, writhing on the ground as the flames consumed his body.

"Now it's just you and me, Skeeve!" the voice echoed. "You and me."

"I'll go!" I shouted desperately. "You've won. Just let me go."

The darkness was moving closer.

"It's too late. I'm coming for you Skeeve…Skeeve…"

"Skeeve!"

Something was shaking my shoulder. I bolted upright, blinking my eyes as the world swam back into focus.

The camp was asleep. Aahz was kneeling beside me, the glow from the campfire's dying embers revealing the concerned expression on his face.

"Wake up, kid! If you keep thrashing around, you'll end up in the fire,"

"It's Isstvan!" I explained desperately. "He knows all about us."

"What?"

"I was talking to him. He came into my dream!"

"Hmmm…sounds more like a plain old nightmare," Aahz proclaimed. "I warned you not to let Tanda season the food."

"Are you sure?" I said doubtfully.

"Positive," Aahz insisted. "If Isstvan knew we were coming, he'd hit us with something a lot more powerful than making faces at you in a dream."

I guess that was supposed to reassure me. It didn't. All it did was remind me I was thoroughly outclassed in the upcoming campaign.

"Aahz, can't you tell me anything about Isstvan? What he looks like, for instance?"

"Not a chance, kid," Aahz grinned at me.

"Why not?"

"Because we won't both see him the same way, or at least we wouldn't describe him the same way. If I describe him to you, one of two things will happen when you first see him. If he looks scarier to you than I've described him, you'll freeze. If he looks more harmless than I've described him, you'll relax. Either way, it'll slow your reactions and give him the first move. There's no point in gaining the element of surprise if we aren't going to use it."

"Well," I persisted. "Couldn't you at least tell me about his powers? What can he do?"

"For one thing, it would take too long. Just assume that if you can imagine it, he can do it."

"What's the other?" I asked.

"The other what?"

"You said 'for one thing.' That implies you have at least one other reason."

"Hmm," Aahz pondered. "Well, I'm not sure you'll understand, but to a certain degree what he can do, I mean the whole list, is irrelevant."

"Why?"

"Because we're taking the initiative. That puts him in a reactive instead of an active role."

"You're right," I said thoughtfully. "I don't understand."

"Look kid, if we just sat here and waited for him, he could take his time and choose exactly what he wanted to do and when he wanted to do it. That's an active role and lets him play with his entire list of powers. Right?"

"I guess so."

"But we aren't doing that. We're carrying the attack to him. That should limit him as to what he can do. There are only a certain number of responses he can successfully use to each of our gambits, and he'll have to use them because he can't afford to ignore the attack. Most of all, we'll rob him of time. Instead of making a leisurely choice about what to do next, he'll have to choose fast. That mean's he'll go with the option he's surest of, the one he does best."

I considered this for a few moments. It sort of made sense.

"Just one question, Aahz," I asked finally.

"What's that, kid?"

"What if you've guessed wrong?"

"Then we drop back ten and punt," he answered lightly.

"What's a..."

"Then we try something else," he amended hastily.

"Like what?"

"Can't tell yet," Aahz shrugged. "Too many variables. We're going with my best guess right now. Beyond that we'll just have to wait and see."

We sat staring into the dying fire for a few minutes, each lost in our own thoughts.

"Say, Aahz?" I said at last.

"Yea, kid?"

"Do you think we'll reach Isstvan before Frumple does?"

"Relax, kid. Frumple's probably drinking wine and pinching bottoms in some other dimension by now."

"But you said..."

"I've had time to think about it since then. The only reason a Deveel does anything is for a profit or out of fear. As far as his sticking his head into this brawl goes, I figure the fear will outweigh the profit. Trying to sell information to a madman is risky at best. My bet is he's lying low until the dust settles."

I reminded myself again of my faith in Aahz's expertise in such matters. It occurred to me, however, there was an awful lot of guesswork in our planning.

"Um, Aahz? Wouldn't it be a little safer if we had invested in a couple of those jazzy weapons back in Deva?"

"We don't need them," he replied firmly. "Besides, they're susceptible to Gremlins. I'd rather go into a fight with a crude but reliable weapon than pin my hopes on a contraption that's liable to malfunction when you need it most."

"Where are Gremlins from?" I asked.

"What?"

"Gremlins. You said…"

"Oh, that. It's just a figure of speech. There are no such things as Gremlins."

I was only listening with half an ear. I suddenly realized that, while I could see Quigley's sleeping form, there was no sign of Tanda or Gleep.

"Where's…um…where's Gleep?" I asked abruptly.

Aahz grinned at me.

"Gleep is standing watch…and just in case you're interested, so's Tanda."

I was vaguely annoyed he had seen through me so easily, but was determined not to show it.

"When is…um…are they coming back?"

"Relax, kid. I told Tanda to leave you alone tonight. You need the sleep for tomorrow."

He jerked his head pointedly toward the assassin's robe I had been using for a pillow. I grudgingly resumed my horizontal position.

"Did I wake you up, Aahz?" I asked apologetically. "With the nightmare, I mean."

"Naw. I was still up. Just making a few last minute preparations for tomorrow."

"Oh," I said drowsily.

"Say, uh, kid?"

"Yes, Aahz?"

"We probably won't have much time to talk tomorrow when Quigley's awake, so while we've got a few minutes alone I want to say, however it goes tomorrow...well...it's been nice working with you, kid."

"Gee, Aahz..." I said, starting to sit up.

A rough hand interrupted me and pushed me back down.

"Sleep!" Aahz commanded, but there was a gentle note lurking in his gruff tone.

XXIII.

"Since prehistoric man, no battle has ever gone as planned."
D. GRAEME

WE CROUCHED IN a grove of small trees on a knoll overlooking the inn, studying our target. The inn was as Quigley had described it, an isolated two-story building with an attached stable squatting by a road overgrown with weeds. If Isstvan was relying on transients to support his business, he was in trouble, except we knew he was doing no such thing. He was mustering his strength to take over the dimensions, and the isolated inn was a perfect base for him to work from.

"Are you *sure* there are no wards?" Aahz whispered.

He addressed his question to Tanda. She in turn shot me a glance. I gave a small nod of my head.

"Positive," she whispered back.

It was all part of our plan. As far as Quigley was concerned, Tanda was the only one of our group that had any supernatural powers.

"Good," said the demon-hunter. "Demon powers make me uneasy. The less we have to deal with, the better I like it."

"Don't get your hopes up," Aahz commented, not taking his eyes from the inn. "They're there all right. The easier it is to get in, the harder it'll be to get out…and they're making it awfully easy for us to get in."

"I don't like it," said Tanda firmly.

"Neither do I," admitted Aahz. "But things aren't going to get any better, so let's get started. You might as well get into disguise now."

"Right, Aahz," she said.

Neither of them looked at me. In fact Aahz stared directly at Tanda. This kept Quigley's attention on her also, though I must admit it helped that she began to writhe and gyrate wildly. Unobserved, I shut my eyes and got to work.

I was getting pretty good at this disguise game, which was fortunate because I was going to be sorely tested today. With a few masterful strokes, I converted Tanda's lovely features into the dubious face of the Imp Higgens...or, rather, Higgens' human disguise. This done, I opened my eyes again.

Tanda was still gyrating. It was a pleasant enough sight that I was tempted to prolong it, but we had work to do. I cleared my throat and Tanda acknowledged the signal by stopping.

"How do I look?" she asked proudly.

"Terrific!" I exclaimed with no trace of modesty.

Aahz shot me a dirty look.

"It's uncanny!" Quigley marveled. "How do you do that?"

"Professional secret." Tanda winked at him.

"Off with you!" Aahz commanded. "And you too, Skeeve."

"But Aahz, couldn't I..."

"No you can't. We've discussed it before. This mission's far to dangerous for a lad of your inexperience."

"Oh, all right, Aahz," I said, crestfallen.

"Cheer up, lad," Quigley told me. "Your day will come. If we fail, the mission falls to you."

"I suppose so. Well, good luck..."

I turned to Tanda, but she was already gone, vanished as if the ground had swallowed her up.

"I say!" cxclaimed Quigley. "She does move quietly, doesn't she?"

"I told you she could handle herself," Aahz said proudly. "Now it's your turn, Skeeve."

"Right, Aahz!"

I turned to the dragon.

"Stay here, Gleep. I'll be back soon, and until then you do what Aahz says. Understand?"

"Gleep?" said the dragon, cocking his head.

For a minute I thought he was going to ruin everything but then he turned and slunk to Aahz's side and stood there regarding me with mournful blue eyes.

Everything was ready.

"Well, goodbye. Good luck!" I called, and trudged slowly back over the knoll, hopefully a picture of abject misery.

Once out of sight, however, I turned and began to sprint as fast as I could in a wide circle around the inn.

On the surface, our plan was quite simple. Aahz and Quigley were to give Tanda enough time to circle around the inn and enter it over the stable roof. Then they would boldly enter the front door. Supposedly this would create a diversion, allowing Tanda to attack Isstvan magically from the rear. I was to wait safely on the knoll until the affair was settled.

In actuality, our plan was a bit more complex. Unbeknownst to Quigley, I was also supposed to circle the inn and find a covert entrance. Then, at the appropriate moment, Tanda and I were to create a magical diversion, allowing Aahz to use the secret weapon he had acquired on Deva.

A gully blocked my path. I took to the air without hesitation and flew over it. I had to be in position in time, or Aahz would have no magical support at all.

Actually magik was quite easy here. The inn was sitting squarely on an intersection of two ground force lines, while a force line in the air passed directly overhead. Whatever happened in the upcoming battle of magik, we wouldn't suffer for a lack of energy.

I wished I knew more about Aahz's secret weapon. He had been doggedly mysterious about it, and neither Tanda nor I had been able to pry any information out of him. He had said it had to be used at close range. He had said it couldn't be used while Isstvan was watching him. He had said it was our only hope to beat Isstvan. He had said it was supposed to be a surprise.

Terrific!

Maybe when all this was over I would find a mentor who didn't have a sense of humor.

I slowed my pace. I was coming to the back of the inn now. The brush had grown right up to the wall, which made my approach easy.

I paused and checked for wards again.

Nothing.

Trying to force Aahz's "easy in, hard out" prophecy from my mind, I scanned the upper windows. None of them were open, so I chose the nearest one and levitated to it. Hovering there, I cautiously pushed, then pulled at the frame.

Locked!

Hurriedly, I pulled myself along the wall with my hands to the next window.

Also locked.

It occurred to me it would be ironic if, after all our magikal preparations, we were stopped by something as mundane as a locked window.

To my relief, the next window yielded to my pressure, and in a moment I was standing inside the inn, trying to get my heartbeat under control.

The room I was in was furnished, but vacant. Judging from the dust on the bed, it had been vacant for some time.

I wondered for a moment where demons slept, if they slept at all, then forced the question from my mind. Time was running out and I wasn't in position yet.

I darted silently across the room and tried the door. Unlocked!

Getting down on my hands and knees, I eased the door open and crawled through, pushing it shut behind me.

After studying the inn's interior so often in Quigley's dirt sketches, it seemed strange to actually be here. I was on the long side of an L-shaped mezzanine which gave access to the upper story rooms. Peering through the bars of the railing that lined the mezzanine, I could look down into the inn proper.

There were three people currently occupying a table below. I recognized the disguised features of Higgens and Brockhurst as two of them. The third was sitting hunched with his back to me, and I couldn't make out his face.

I was debating shifting to another position to get a better view when a fourth figure entered bearing an enormous tray with a huge jug of wine on it as well as an assortment of dirty flagons.

"This round's on the house, boys!" the figure chortled merrily. "Have one on old Isstvan."

Isstvan! *That* was Isstvan?

The waddling figure below did not seem to display any of the menacing features I had expected in a would-be ruler of the dimensions.

Quickly I checked him for a magical aura. There was none. It wasn't a disguise. He really looked like that. I studied him carefully.

He was tall, but his stoutness kept his height from being imposing. He had long white hair and a longer white beard which nearly covered his chest with its fullness. His bright eyes were set in a face that seemed to be permanently smiling, and his nose and cheeks were flushed, though whether from drink or laughter I couldn't tell.

This was the dark figure of evil I had been dreading all these weeks? He looked like exactly what Quigley said he was…a harmless old innkeeper.

A movement at the far end of the mezzanine caught my eye. Tanda! She was crouched behind the railing like I was, on the other side of the stairs, and at first I thought I had just seen the movement of her easing into position. Then she looked my way and cautiously waved her hand again, and I realized she was signaling for my attention.

I waved an acknowledgement, which she must have seen, for she stopped signaling and changed to another set of actions. Glancing furtively at the figures below to be sure she wasn't observed, she began a strange pantomime.

First she made several repeated gestures around her forehead, then pointed urgently behind her.

I didn't understand, and shook my head to convey this.

She repeated the gestures more emphatically, and this time I realized she was actually pointing down and behind her. The stables! Something about the stables. But what about the stables?

I considered her first gesture again. She appeared to be stabbing herself in the forehead. Something had hit her in the stables? She had killed something in the stables?

I shook my head again. She bared her teeth at me in frustration.

"Innkeep!"

I jumped a foot at the bellow.

Aahz and Quigley had just walked through the door. Whatever Tanda was trying to tell me would just have to wait. Our attack had begun.

"Two flagons of your best wine…and send someone to see to my unicorn."

Aahz was doing all the talking, of course. It had been agreed that he would take the lead in the conversation. Quigley hadn't been too happy about that, but in the end had consented to speaking only when absolutely necessary.

Their entrance had had surprisingly little impact on the assemblage below. In fact, Isstvan was the only one to even look in their direction.

"Come in. Come in, gentlemen," he smiled, spreading his arms wide in welcome. "We've been expecting you!"

"You have?" blurted Quigley, echoing my thoughts.

"Of course, of course. You shouldn't try to fool old Isstvan." He shook a finger at them in mock sternness. "Word was just brought to us by…oh, I'm sorry. I haven't introduced you to my new purchasing agent yet."

"We've met," came the voice of the hunched figure as he turned to face them.

Frumple!

That's what Tanda had been trying to tell me! The war-unicorn, Quigley's unicorn, was down in the stable. For all our speed, Frumple had gotten here ahead of us.

"Who are you?" asked Quigley, peering at the Deveel.

For some reason this seemed to set Isstvan off into peals of laughter from his eyes. "We are going to have such fun this afternoon!"

He gestured absently and the inn door slammed shut. There was a sudden ripple of dull clunks behind me, and I realized the room doors were locking themselves. We were sealed in. All of us.

"I don't believe I've had such a good time since I made love to my week-dead sister."

Isstvan's voice was still jovial, but it struck an icy note of fear within me. I realized that not only was he a powerful magician, he was quite insane.

XXIV.

"Ya gotta be subtle!"
M. HAMMER

THERE WAS A TENSE, expectant silence as the foursome leaned forward to study their captives. It was as if two songbirds had tried to edge through a crowd of vultures to steal a snack only to find they were the intended meal.

I knelt, watching in frozen horror, fully expecting to witness the immediate demise of my two allies.

"Since Frumple's already announced us," Aahz said smoothly, "I guess there's no need to maintain this disguise."

The confident tone of his voice steadied my shattered nerve. We were in it now, and win or lose we'd just have to keep going.

Quickly, I shut my eyes and removed Aahz's Garkin-disguise.

"Aahz!" cried Isstvan in delight. "I should have known it was you."

"He's the one who…" Brockhurst began.

"Do you two know each other?" Frumple asked, ignoring the Imp.

"Know each other?" Isstvan chortled. "We're old enemies. He and a couple other scalawags nearly destroyed me the last time we met."

"Well it's our turn now, right Isstvan?" smiled Higgens, leisurely reaching for his crossbow.

"Now, now!" said Isstvan, picking the Imp up by his head and shaking him gently. "Mustn't rush things."

"Seems to me," Aahz sneered, "that you're having trouble finding decent allies, Isstvan."

"Oh, Aahz," Isstvan laughed. "Still the sharp tongue, eh?"

"Imps?" Aahz's voice was scornful. "C'mon, Isstvan. Even you can do better than that."

Isstvan sighed and dropped Higgens back in his chair.

"Well, one does what one can. Inflation, you know."

He shook his head sadly, then brightened again.

"Oh you don't know how glad I am to see you, Aahz. I thought I was going to have to wait until we conquered Perv before I got my revenge, and here you just walk in. Now don't you dare pop off before we've settled our score."

"I told you before," Frumple interrupted. "He's lost his powers."

"Powers. Hmph! He never had any powers," Quigley chimed in, baited from his frightened silence at the insult of having been ignored.

"Well, who do we have here?" Isstvan smiled looking at Quigley for the first time. "Have we met?"

"Say Isstvan," interrupted Aahz. "Mind if I have some of that wine? No reason to be barbaric about this."

"Certainly, Aahz." Isstvan waved him forward. "Help yourself."

It was eerie listening to the conversation: apparently civilized and friendly, it had a cat-and-mouse undercurrent which belied the casual tones.

"Watch him!" Frumple hissed, glaring at Aahz.

"Oh, Frumple! You are *such* a wart," Isstvan scolded. "Why, you're the one who assured me that he had lost his powers."

"Well, I think he makes sense," Brockhurst grumbled, rising and backing away as Aahz approached the table. "If you don't mind, Isstvan, I'll watch from over here."

He sat on the bottom steps of the flight of stairs heading up to the mezzanine where Tanda and I were hidden. His tone was conversational, but it was clear he was only waiting for Isstvan's signal to loose him on the helpless pair.

"Oh, you Imps are worse than the Deveels!" Isstvan scowled.

"That's a given," Frumple commented dryly.

"Now look, Frumple..." Higgens began angrily.

"As to who *this* figure is," Frumple pointed to Quigley, ignoring the Imps. "That is Garkin's apprentice. He's the one who's been handling the magik for our Pervert since he lost his powers."

"Really?" asked Isstvan eagerly. "Can you do the cups and balls trick? I love the cups and balls trick."

"I don't understand," mumbled Quigley vacantly, backing away from the assemblage.

Well, if we were ever going to have a diversion, it would have to be now. Closing my eyes, I changed Quigley's features. The obvious choice for his disguise was...me!

"See," said Frumple pointing proudly. "I told you so."

"Throckwoddle!" exclaimed the two Imps simultaneously.

"What?" said Frumple, narrowing his eyes suspiciously.

I was ready for them. As the exclamations rose, I changed Quigley again. This time, I gave him Throckwoddle's features.

"Why, it *is* Throckwoddle," cried Isstvan. "Oh, that's funny."

"Wait a minute!" Brockhurst hissed. "How could you be Throckwoddle when we turned you into a statue before we caught up with Throckwoddle?"

This set Isstvan off into even greater peals of laughter. "Stop," he called, breathless. "Oh, stop! Oh! My ribs hurt! Aahz, you've outdone yourself this time."

"It's nothing really," Aahz acknowledged modestly.

"There's something wrong here," Frumple declared. He plunged a hand deep into his robe, never taking his eyes from Quigley. Almost too late I realized what he was doing. He was going for his crystal, the one that let him detect disguises. As the glittering bauble emerged, I swung into action.

A simple levitation, a small flick with my mind, and the crystal popped out of Frumple's grasp and plopped into the wine jug.

"Framitz!" Frumple swore, starting to fish for his possession.

"Get your hands out of the wine, Frumple!" Aahz chided, slapping his wrist. "You'll get your toy when we finish the jug!"

As if to illustrate his point, he hefted the jug and began refilling the flagons around the table.

"Enough of this insanity!" Quigley exploded.

I winced at the use of the word "insanity," but Isstvan didn't seem to mind. He merely leaned forward to watch Quigley.

"I am neither Skeeve nor Throckwoddle," Quigley continued, "I am Quigley, demon-hunter extraordinaire! Let any dispute who dare, and man or demon I'll show him who I am!"

This proved too much for Isstvan, who actually collapsed in laughter.

"Oh, he's funny, Aahz," he gasped. "Where did you find this funny man?"

"You sent him to me, remember?" Aahz prompted.

"Why, so I did, so I did," Isstvan mused, and even this fact he seemed to find hysterically funny.

The others were not so amused.

"So you're a demon-hunter, eh?" Frumple snarled. "What's your gripe, anyway?"

"The offenses of demons are too numerous to list," Quigley retorted haughtily.

"We aren't going anywhere for a while," Brockhurst chimed in from the stairs. "And neither are you. List us a few of these offenses."

"Well…" began Quigley, "you stole my magik pendant and my magik sword…"

"We don't know anything about a magik pendant." Higgens bristled. "And we gave your so-called magik sword to…"

"What else do demons do?" Frumple interrupted, apparently none too eager to have the discussion turn to swords.

"Well…you bewitched my war unicorn into thinking he's a dragon!" Quigley challenged.

"Your war unicorn is currently tethered in the stable," Higgens stated flatly. "Frumple brought him in."

"My unicorn is tethered outside the door!" Quigley insisted "And he thinks he's a dragon!"

"Your unicorn is tethered in the stable." Higgens barked back. "And we think you're a fruitcake!"

"Gentlemen, gentlemen," Isstvan managed to hold up his hands despite his laughter. "All this is quite amusing, but…well, will you look at that!"

This last was said in such a tone of wonder that the attention of everyone in the room was immediately drawn to the spot he was looking at.

Suspended in mid-air, not two hand-spans from Isstvan's head, was a small red dart with gold and black fletchings.

"An assassin's dart!" Isstvan marveled, gently plucking the missile from where it was hovering. "Now who would be naughty enough to try to poison me from behind?"

His eyes slowly moved to Brockhurst sitting casually on the stairs.

Brockhurst suddenly realized he was the object of everyone's attention. His eyes widened in fright.

"No! I…Wait! Isstvan!" He half-rose holding out a hand as if to ward off a blow. "I didn't…No! Don't. Glaag!"

This last was said as his hands suddenly flew to his throat and began choking him violently.

"Glaak…eak…urk…"

He fell back on the stairs and began rolling frantically back and forth.

"Isstvan." Higgens began hesitantly. "Normally I wouldn't interfere, but don't you think you should hear what he has to say, first?"

"But I'm not doing anything," Isstvan blinked with hurt innocence.

My eyes flashed to the other end of the mezzanine. Tanda was
crouched there, her eyes closed. She seemed to be choking an invisible
person on the floor in front of her. With dawning realization, I began
to appreciate more and more the subtleties of a trained assassin.

"You aren't doing anything?" Higgens shrilled, "Well, then do
something! He's dying!"

I thought for a moment that the ludicrous statement would set
Isstvan to laughing again, but not this time.

"Oh," he sighed. "This is all so confusing. Yes, I guess you're right."

He clicked his fingers and Brockhurst stopped thrashing about
and began breathing again in long ragged breaths.

"Here, old boy," said Aahz. "Have some wine."

He offered Brockhurst a brimming flagon which the Imp began
to gulp gratefully.

"Aahz," Isstvan said sternly. "I don't think you've been honest with us."

"Me?" Aahz asked innocently.

"Even you couldn't have caused this much havoc without assistance. Now where is it coming from?"

He closed his eyes and turned his face toward the ceiling for a
moment.

"Aah!" he suddenly proclaimed. "Here it is."

There was a squawk from the other end of the mezzanine and
Tanda was suddenly lifted into view by unseen hands.

"Higgens!" exclaimed Isstvan, "Another one! Well, well, the day
is full of surprises."

Tanda held her silence as she was floated down to a chair on a
level with the others.

"Now, let's see." Isstvan mumbled to himself. "Have we missed
anybody?"

I felt the sudden pressure of invisible forces and realized I was
next. I tried desperately to think of a disguise, but the only thing that
came to mind was Gleep...so I tried it.

"A dragon!" cried Brockhurst as I popped into view.

"Gleep!" I said, rolling my eyes desperately.

"Oh now that's too much," Isstvan pouted. "I want to see who
I'm dealing with."

He gave a vacant wave of his hand, and the disguises disappeared…
all of them. I was me, Quigley was Quigley, Tanda was Tanda, the
Imps were Imps, and the Deveel was a Deveel. Aahz, of course,
was Aahz. Apparently a moratorium had been declared on disguises,
by a majority of one: Isstvan.

I came floating down to join the others, but my entrance was
generally ignored in the other proceedings.

"Tanda!" Isstvan cried enthusiastically. "Well, well. This *is* a
reunion, isn't it?"

"Bark at the moon, Isstvan," Tanda snarled defiantly.

Quigley was looking at everyone else with such speed I thought
his head would fall off.

"I don't understand!" he whimpered plaintively.

"Shut up, Quigley," Aahz growled. "We'll explain later."

"That's assuming there *is* a later," Frumple sneered.

I tended to agree with Frumple. The atmosphere in the room
no longer had even the semblance of joviality. It was over. We had
lost. We were all exposed and captured, and Isstvan was as strong as
ever. Whatever Aahz's secret weapon was, it apparently hadn't worked.

"Well, I'm afraid all good things must come to an end," Isstvan
sighed, draining his flagon. "Now I'm afraid I'll have to dispose
of you."

He sounded genuinely sad, but somehow I couldn't muster any
sympathy for his plight.

"Just one question before we begin, Aahz," he asked in surprisingly sane tones.

"What's that?" Aahz responded.

"Why did you do it? I mean, with as feeble a team as this, how
could you possibly hope to beat me?"

Isstvan sounded genuinely sincere.

"Well, Isstvan," Aahz drawled, "that's a matter of opinion."

"What's that supposed to mean?" Isstvan asked suspiciously.

"I don't 'hope' we can beat you," Aahz smiled. "I *know* we can."

"Really?" Isstvan chuckled, "And upon what are you basing
your logic."

"Why, I'm basing it on the fact that we've already won," Aahz
blinked innocently. "It's all over, Isstvan, whether you realize it or not."

XXV.

"Just because you've beaten a sorcerer doesn't mean you've beaten a sorcerer."
TOTH-AAMON

"AAHZ," ISSTVAN SAID sternly, "there comes a time when even your humor wears a little thin."

"I'm not kidding, Isstvan," Aahz assured him. "You've lost your powers. Go ahead, try something. Anything!"

Isstvan hesitated. He closed his eyes.

Nothing happened.

"You see?" Aahz shrugged. "You've lost your powers. All of them. And don't look to your associates for help. They're all in the same boat."

"You mean we've really won?" I blurted out, the full impact of what was transpiring finally starting to sink in.

"That's right, kid."

Aahz suddenly leaned forward and clapped Frumple on the shoulder.

"Congratulations, Frumple," he exclaimed. "I've got to admit, I didn't think you could do it."

"What?" blinked the Deveel.

"I'm just glad this squares our debt with you," Aahz continued without pause. "You won't try to back out on it now, will you?"

"Frumple!" Isstvan's voice was dark with menace. "Did you do this to us?"

"I...I..." Frumple stammered.

"Go ahead, Frumple. Gloat!" Aahz encouraged. "He can't do anything to you now. Besides, you can teleport out of here anytime you want."

"No, he can't!" snarled Higgens, and his arm flashed forward.

I caught a glimpse of a small ball flying through the air before it exploded against Frumple's forehead in a cloud of purple dust.

"But..." began Frumple, but it was too late.

In mid-gesture his limbs became rigid and his face froze. We had another statue on our hands.

"Good move, Higgens," applauded Aahz.

"If it wouldn't be too much trouble, Aahz," interrupted Isstvan. "Could you explain what's going on here?"

"Aah!" said Aahz, "therein lies a story."

"This sounds familiar," Quigley mumbled.

I poked him in the ribs with my elbow. We weren't out of this yet.

"It seems that Frumple learned about your plans from Throckwoddle. Apparently he was afraid that if you succeeded in taking over the dimensions, you would implement price controls, thereby putting him out of business as a merchant. You know how those Deveels are."

The Imps snorted. Isstvan nodded thoughtfully.

"Anyway, he decided to try to stop you. To accomplish this, he blackmailed the four of us into assisting him. We were to create a diversion while he effected the actual attack."

"Well, what did he do?" prompted Higgens.

"He drugged the wine!" explained Aahz. "Don't you remember?"

"When?" asked Brockhurst.

"When he dropped that phony crystal into the jug, remember?"

"But he drank from the jug, too!" exclaimed Higgens.

"That's right, but he had taken an antidote in advance," Aahz finished with a flourish.

"So we're stuck here!" Brockhurst spat in disgust.

"You know, Aahz," Isstvan said slowly. "It occurs to me that even if everything happened exactly as you described it, you and your friends here played a fairly large part in the plot."

"You're right, Isstvan," Aahz admitted, "but I'm prepared to offer you a bargain."

"What kind of a bargain?" Isstvan asked suspiciously.

"It's in two parts. First, to clear Tanda and myself from having opposed you in your last bid for power, I can offer transportation for you and your allies out of this dimension."

"Hmm…" said Isstvan. "And the second part?"

"For the second part, I can give you the ultimate vengeance to visit on Frumple here. In exchange, I want your promise you'll bear no grudge against the four of us for our part in today's misfortune."

"Pardon for four in exchange for vengeance on one?" Isstvan grunted. "That doesn't sound like much of a deal."

"I think you're overlooking something, Isstvan," Aahz cautioned.

"What's that?"

"You've lost your powers. That makes it four of us against three of you."

"Look at your four," Brockhurst sneered. "A woman, a half-trained apprentice, a broken down demon-hunter and a Pervert."

"Broken-down?" Quigley scowled.

"Easy, Quigley…and you too, Tanda," Aahz ordered. "Your three are nothing to brag about either, Brockhurst. Two Imps who've lost their powers and a fat madman."

Surprisingly, this seemed to revive Isstvan's humor. The Imps were not amused.

"Now look, Aahz," Higgens began, "if you want a fight…"

"You miss the point entirely, gentlemen," Aahz said soothingly. "I'm trying to *avoid* a fight. I'm merely trying to point out that if this comes to a fight, you'll lose."

"Not necessarily," Brockhurst bristled.

"Inescapably," Aahz insisted. "Look, if we fight and we win, you lose. On the other hand, if we fight and we lose, you lose."

"How do you figure that?" Higgens asked suspiciously.

"Simple!" said Aahz smugly, "If you kill us, you'll have lost your only way to get out of this dimension. You'll be stuck forever on Klah. By my figuring, that's losing."

"We're in agreement there," Brockhurst mumbled.

"Oh, stop this bickering!" Isstvan interrupted with a chuckle. "Aahz is right as usual. He may have lost a couple of fights, both magical and physical, but I've never heard of anyone out-arguing him."

"Then it's a deal?" Aahz asked.

"It's a deal!" Isstvan said firmly. "As if we had any choice in the matter."

They shook hands ceremoniously.

I noticed that the Imps were whispering together and shooting dark glances in our direction. I wondered if a deal with Isstvan was binding on the Imps. I wondered if a handshake was legally binding in a situation such as this. But most of all, I wondered what Aahz had up his sleeve this time.

"Well, Aahz?" Isstvan asked. "Where is this escape clause you promised?"

"Right here!" Aahz said, fishing a familiar object from inside his shirt and tossing it to Isstvan.

"A D-Hopper!" Isstvan cried with delight. "I haven't seen one of these since…"

"What is it?" Higgens interrupted.

Isstvan scowled at him.

"It's our ticket off this dimension," he exclaimed grudgingly.

"How does it work?" Brockhurst asked suspiciously.

"Trust me, gentlemen." Isstvan's distasteful expression gave lie to the joviality of his words. "It works."

He turned to Aahz again. "Imps!" he mumbled to himself.

"You hired 'em." Aahz commented, unsympathetically.

"So I did. Well, what is this diabolical vengeance you have in mind for Frumple?"

"That's easy," smiled Aahz. "Use the D-Hopper and take him back to Deva."

"Why Deva?" Isstvan asked.

"Because he's been banned from Deva," Higgens answered, the light dawning.

"…and the Deveels are unequaled at meting out punishment to those who break their laws," Brockhurst finished with an evil smile.

"Why was Frumple banned from Deva?" Tanda whispered to me.

"I don't know," I confided. "Maybe he gave a refund or something."

"I don't believe it," she snorted, "I mean, he *is* a Deveel."

"Aahz," Isstvan smiled, regarding the D-Hopper, "I've always admired your sense of humor. It's even nastier than mine."

"What do you expect from a Pervert?" snorted Brockhurst.

"Watch your mouth, Imp," I snarled.

He was starting to get on my nerves.

"Then it's settled!" Isstvan chortled, clapping his hands together gleefully. "Brockhurst! Higgens! Come gather around Frumple here. We're off to Deva."

"Right now?" asked Brockhurst.

"With…things here so unsettled?" Higgens added, glancing at us again.

"Oh, we won't be long," Isstvan assured them. "There's nothing here we can't come back and pick up later."

"That's true," admitted Brockhurst, staring at me thoughtfully.

"Umm…Isstvan?"

It was Quigley.

"Are you addressing me?" Isstvan asked with mock formality.

"Yes." Quigley looked uncomfortable. "Am I to understand you are all about to depart for some place completely populated with demons?"

"That is correct," Isstvan nodded.

"Could...that is...would you mind if I accompanied you?"

"What?" I exclaimed, genuinely startled. "Why?"

"Well..." Quigley said hesitantly, "if there is one thing I have learned this day, it's that I really know very little about demons."

"Hear, hear!" mumbled Aahz.

"I am undecided as to whether or not to continue in my chosen profession," Quigley continued, "but in any case it behooves me to learn more about demons. What better place could there be for such study than in a land completely populated with demons?"

"Why should we burden ourselves with a demon-hunter, of all things?" Brockhurst appealed to Isstvan.

"Maybe we could teach him a few things about demons," Higgens suggested in an overly innocent voice, giving his partner a covert poke in the side.

"What? Hmm...You know, you're right, Higgens." Brockhurst was suddenly smiling again.

"Good!" exclaimed Isstvan. "We'll make a party of it."

"In that case," purred Tanda, "you won't mind if I tag along, too."

"What?" exclaimed Brockhurst.

"Why?" challenged Higgens.

"To help, of course," she smiled. "I want to be there when you teach Quigley about demons. Maybe I can help him learn."

"Wonderful, wonderful," Isstvan beamed, overriding the Imps objections. "The more the merrier. Aahz? Skeeve? Will you be joining us?"

"Not this time, thanks," Aahz replied before I could open my mouth. "The kid here and I have a few things to go over that won't wait."

"Like what?" I asked.

"Shut up, kid," Aahz hissed, then smiled again at the group. "You all run along. We'll be here when you come back."

"We'll be looking forward to it." Brockhurst smiled grimly.

"G'bye, Aahz, Skeeve!" Tanda waved. "I'll look for you next time around."

"But Tanda..." I began.

"Don't worry, lad." Quigley assured me. "I'll make sure nothing happens to her."

Behind him, Tanda shot me a bawdy wink.

"Aahz!" Isstvan chuckled. "I do enjoy your company. We must work together more often."

He adjusted the settings on the D-Hopper and prepared to trigger it.

"Good-bye, Isstvan." Aahz smiled and waved. "Remember me!"

There was a rippling in the air and they were gone. All of them.

"Aahz!" I said urgently. "Did you see how those Imps looked at us?"

"Hmm? Oh. Yeah, kid. I told you they were vicious little creatures."

"But what are we going to do when they get back?"

"Don't worry about it, kid."

"Don't worry about it!" I shrieked. "We've got to..."

"...because they aren't coming back." Aahz finished.

That stopped me.

"But...when they get done on Deva..."

"That's the joke, kid," Aahz grinned at me. "They aren't going to Deva."

XXVI.

"A woman, like a good piece of music, should have a solid end."
F. SCHUBERT

"THEY AREN'T GOING to Deva?"

I was having a rough time dealing with the concept.

"That's right, kid," Aahz said, pouring himself some more wine.

"But Isstvan set the D-Hopper himself."

"Yeah!" Aahz grinned smugly. "But last night I made one extra preparation for this sortie. I changed the markings on the dials."

"Then where are they going?"

"Beats me!" Aahz shrugged, taking a deep draught of the wine. "But I'm betting it'll take 'em a long time to find their way back. There are a lot of settings on a D-Hopper."

"But what about Tanda and Quigley?"

"Tanda can take care of Quigley," Aahz assured me. "Besides, she has the powers to pull them out anytime she wants."

"She does?"

"Sure. But she'll probably have a few laughs just tagging along for a while. Can't say as I blame her. I'd love to see Quigley deal with a few dimensions myself."

He took another generous gulp of the wine.

"Aahz!" I cried in sudden realization. "The wine!"

"What about it? Oh. don't worry kid," he smiled. "I've already lost my powers, remember? Besides, you don't think I'd drug my own wine, do you?"

"*You* drugged the wine?"

"Yeah. That was my secret weapon. You didn't really believe all that bunk about Frumple, did you?"

"Ahh...of course not," I said, offended.

Actually, even though I knew Frumple hadn't done it, I had completely lost track of actually who *had* done what, and to whom.

"Here, kid." Aahz handed me his flagon and picked up the jug. "Have some yourself. You did pretty good this afternoon."

I took the flagon, but somehow couldn't bring myself to drink any.

"What did you put in the wine, anyway?" I asked.

"Joke powder," Aahz replied. "As near as I can tell, it's the same stuff Garkin used on me. You can put it in a drink, sprinkle it over food, or burn it and have your victim inhale the smoke."

I had a sudden flash recollection of the brazier billowing smoke as Aahz materialized.

"What does it do?"

"Weren't you paying attention, kid?" Aahz cocked his head at me. "It takes away your powers."

"Permanently?"

"Of course not!" Aahz scoffed. "Only for a century."

"What's the antidote?"

"There isn't one...at least, I couldn't get the stall-proprietor to admit to having one. Maybe when you get a little better with the magik, we'll go back to Deva and beat an answer out of him."

I thought for a few minutes. That seemed to answer all my questions...except one.

"Say...um, Aahz?"

"Yeah, kid?"

"What do we do now?"

"About what?" Aahz asked.

"I mean, what do we do? We've been spending all the time since we met getting ready to fight Isstvan. Well, it's over. Now what do we do?"

"What *you* do, apprentice," Aahz said sternly, "is devote your time to your magik. You've still got a long way to go before you're even close to Master status. As for me...well, I guess most of my time will be spent teaching you."

He poured a little more wine down his throat.

"Actually, we're in pretty good shape," he stated. "We've got a magik crystal courtesy of Frumple...and that crummy sword if we search his gear."

"And a malfunctioning fire-ring," I prompted.

"Um..." said Aahz. "Actually. I...ahh...well, I gave the ring to Tanda,"

"Gave?" I asked. "You gave something away?"

Aahz shrugged.

"I'm a soft touch. Ask anybody."

"Hmm..." I said.

"We've, um, also got a war-unicorn if we want to go anywhere," Aahz hastened on, "and that stupid dragon of yours."

"Gleep isn't stupid!" I insisted hotly.

"Okay, okay," Aahz amended, "…your intelligent, personable dragon."

"That's better," I mumbled.

"Even though it beats me why we'd want to go anyplace," Aahz commented, looking around him. "This place seems sound enough. You'd have some good force lines to play with, and the wine-cellar will be well stocked, if I know Isstvan. We could do lots worse for a base of operations."

Another question occurred to me.

"Say, Aahz?"

"Yeah, kid?"

"A few minutes ago you said you wanted to see Quigley when he visited other dimensions…and you seem to have a weak spot for Tanda…"

"Yeah?" Aahz growled. "So?"

"So why didn't you go along with them? You didn't have to get stranded in this dimension."

"Isstvan's a fruitcake," Aahz declared pointedly, "and I don't like Imps. You think I'd like having them for traveling companions?"

"But you said Tanda could travel the dimensions by herself. Couldn't you and she have…"

"All right, all right," interrupted Aahz. "You want me to say it? I stayed here because of you."

"Why?"

"Because you're not up to traveling the dimensions yet. Not until you…"

"I mean, why stay with me at all?"

"Why? Because you're my apprentice! That's why." Aahz seemed genuinely angry. "We made a deal, remember? You help me against Isstvan and I teach you magik. Well, you did your part, and now I'm going to do mine. I'm going to teach you magik if it kills you…or me, which is more probable!"

"Yes, Aahz," I agreed hastily.

"Besides," he mumbled taking another drink. "I like you."

"Excuse me?" I said. "I didn't quite hear that."

"Then pay attention!" Aahz barked. "I said drink your wine, and give some to that stupid dragon of yours. I will allow you one…count it, *one*…night of celebration. Then, bright and early tomorrow, we start working in earnest."

"Yes, Aahz," I said obediently.

"And kid," Aahz grinned, "don't worry about it being boring. We don't have to go looking for adventure. In our professions it usually comes looking for us."

I had an ugly feeling he was right.

Myth Conceptions

I.

"Life is a series of rude awakenings."
R. V. WINKLE

OF ALL THE various unpleasant ways to be aroused from a sound sleep, one of the worst is the noise of a dragon and an unicorn playing tag.

I pried one eye open and blearily tried to focus on the room. A chair toppled noisily to the floor, convincing me the blurred images my mind was receiving were due, at least in part, to the irregular vibrations coming from the floor and walls. One without my vast storehouse of knowledge—hard won and painfully endured—might be inclined to blame the pandemonium on an earthquake. I didn't. The logic behind this conclusion was simple. Earthquakes were extremely uncommon in this area. A dragon and a unicorn playing tag weren't.

It was starting out as an ordinary day...that is, ordinary if you're a junior magician apprenticed to a demon.

If I had been able to predict the future with any degree of accuracy and thus, foreseen the events to come, I probably would have stayed in bed. I mean, fighting has never been my forte, and the idea of taking on a whole army...but I'm getting ahead of myself.

The thud that aroused me shook the building, accompanied by the crash of various dirty dishes shattering on the floor. The second was even more spectacular.

I considered doing something. I considered going back to sleep. Then I remembered my mentor's condition when he had gone to bed the night before.

That woke me up fast. The only thing nastier than a demon from Perv is a demon from Perv with a hangover.

I was on my feet and headed for the door in a flash. (My agility was a tribute to my fear rather than any inborn talent.) Wrenching the door open, I thrust my head outside and surveyed the terrain. The grounds outside the inn seemed normal. The weeds were totally out of hand, more than chest-high in places. Something would have to be done about them some day, but my mentor didn't seem to mind their riotous growth, and since I was the logical candidate to cut them if I raised the point, I decided once again to keep silent on the subject.

Instead, I studied the various flattened patches and newly torn paths in the overgrowth, trying to determine the location or at least the direction of my quarries' movement. I had almost convinced myself that the silence was at least semi-permanent and it would be all right to go back to sleep, when the ground began to tremble again. I sighed and shakily drew myself up to my full height, what there was of it, and prepared to meet the onslaught.

The unicorn was the first into view, great clumps of dirt flying from beneath his hooves as he ducked around the corner of the inn on my right.

"Buttercup!" I shouted in my most authoritative tone.

A split second later I had to jump back into the shelter of the doorway to avoid being trampled by the speeding beast. Though a bit miffed at his disobedience, I didn't really blame him. He had a dragon chasing him, and dragons are not notoriously agile when it comes to quick stops.

As if acting on a cue from my thoughts, the dragon burst into view. To be accurate, he didn't really burst, he thudded, shaking the inn as he rebounded off the corner. As I said, dragons are not notoriously agile.

"Gleep!" I shouted. "Stop it this instant!"

He responded by taking an affectionate swipe at me with his tail as he bounded past. Fortunately for me, the gesture went wide of its mark, impacting the inn with another jarring *thud* instead.

So much for my best authoritative tone. If our two faithful charges were any more obedient, I'd be lucky to escape with my life. Still, I had to stop them. Whoever came up with the immortal quote about waking sleeping dragons had obviously never had to contend with a sleeping demon.

I studied the two of them chasing each other through the weeds for a few moments, then decided to handle this the easy way. Closing my eyes, I envisioned both of them, the dragon and the unicorn. Then I superimposed the image of the dragon over that of the unicorn, fleshed it out with a few strokes of my mental paint brush, then opened my eyes.

To my eyes, the scene was the same, a dragon and a unicorn confronting each other in a field of weeds. But, of course, I had cast the spell, so, naturally, I wouldn't be taken in. Its true effect could be read in Gleep's reaction.

He cocked his head and peered at Buttercup, first from this angle, then that, stretching his long, serpentine neck to its limits. Then he swiveled his head until he was looking backward and repeated the process, scanning the surrounding weeds. Then he looked at Buttercup again.

To his eyes, his playmate had suddenly disappeared, to be replaced by another dragon. It was all very confusing, and he wanted his playmate back.

In my pet's defense, when I speak of his lack of agility, both physically and mentally, I don't mean to imply he is either clumsy or stupid. He's young, which also accounts for his mere ten-foot length and half-formed wings. I fully expect—when he matures, in another four or five hundred years—that he will be very deft and wise, which is more than I can say for myself. In the unlikely event I should live that long, all I'll be is old.

"Gleep?"

The dragon was looking at me now. Having stretched his limited mental abilities to their utmost, he was turning to me to correct the situation or at least provide an explanation. As the perpetrator of the situation causing his distress, I felt horribly guilty. For a moment, I wavered on the brink of restoring Buttercup's normal appearance.

"If you're quite sure you're making enough noise..."

I winced at the deep, sarcastic tones booming close behind me. All my efforts were for naught. Aahz was awake.

I assumed my best hang-dog attitude and turned to face him. Needless to say, he looked terrible.

If, perchance, you think a demon covered with green scales already looks terrible, you've never encountered one with a hangover. The normal gold flecks in his yellow eyes were now copper, accented by a throbbing network of orange veins. His lips were drawn back in a painful grimace which exposed even more of his pointed teeth than his frightening, reassuring smile. Looming there, his fists clenched on his hips, he presented a picture terrifying enough to make a spider-bear faint.

I wasn't frightened, however. I had been with Aahz for over a year now and knew his bark was worse than his bite. Then again, he had never bitten me.

"Gee, Aahz," I said digging a small hole with my toe. "You're always telling me if I can't sleep through anything, I'm not really tired."

He ignored the barb, as he so frequently does when I catch him with one of his own quotes. Instead, he squinted over my shoulder at the scene outside.

"Kid," he said. "Tell me you're practicing. Tell me you haven't really scrounged up another stupid dragon to make our lives miserable."

"I'm practicing!" I hastened to reassure him.

To prove the point, I quickly restored Buttercup's normal appearance.

"Gleep!" said Gleep happily, and the two of them were off again.

"Really, Aahz," I said innocently to head off his next caustic remark. "Where would I find another dragon in this dimension?"

"If there was one to be found here on Klah, you'd find it," he snarled. "As I recall, you didn't have that much trouble finding this one the first time I turned my back on you. Apprentices!"

He turned and retreated out of the sunlight into the dim interior of the inn.

"If I recall," I commented, following him, "that was at the Bazaar on Deva. I couldn't get another dragon there because you won't teach me how to travel through the dimensions."

"Get off my case, kid!" he moaned. "We've been over it a thousand times. Dimension traveling is dangerous. Look at me! Stranded without my powers in a back-assward dimension like Klah, where the lifestyle is barbaric and the food is disgusting..."

"You lost your powers because Garkin laced his special-effects cauldron with that joke powder and then got killed before he could give you the antidote," I pointed out.

"Watch out how you talk about your old teacher," Aahz warned. "The old slime-monger was inclined to get carried away with practical jokes once in a while, true. But he was a master magician...and a friend of mine. If he wasn't, I wouldn't have saddled myself with his mouthy apprentice," he finished, giving me a meaningful look.

"I'm sorry, Aahz," I apologized. "It's just that I..."

"Look, kid," he interrupted wearily. "If I had my powers, which I don't, and if you were ready to learn dimension-hopping, which you aren't, we could give it a try. Then, if you miscalculated and dumped us into the wrong dimension, I could get our tails out before anything bad happened. As things stand, trying to teach you dimension-hopping would be more dangerous than playing Russian roulette."

"What's a Russian?" I asked.

The inn shook as Gleep missed the corner turn again.

"When are you going to teach your stupid dragon to play on the other side of the road?" Aahz snarled, craning his neck to glare out a window.

"I'm working on it, Aahz," I insisted soothingly. "Remember, it took me almost a whole year to housebreak him."

"Don't remind me," Aahz grumbled. "If I had my way, we'd…"

He broke off suddenly and cocked his head to one side.

"You'd better disguise that dragon, kid," he announced suddenly. "And get ready to do your 'dubious character' bit. We're about to have a visitor."

I didn't contest the information. We had established long ago that Aahz's hearing was much more acute than mine.

"Right, Aahz," I acknowledged and hurried about my task.

The trouble with using an inn, however abandoned or weatherbeaten it might be, as a base of operations was that occasionally people would stop here seeking food and lodging. Magik was still outlawed in these lands, and the last thing we wanted was witnesses.

II.

"First impressions, being the longest lasting, are of utmost importance."
J. CARTER

AAHZ AND I had acquired the inn under rather dubious circumstances. Specifically, we claimed it as our rightful spoils of war after the two of us (with the assistance of a couple allies, now absent) had routed Isstvan, a maniac magician, and sent him packing into far dimensions along with all his surviving accomplices. The inn had been Isstvan's base of operations. But now it was ours. Who Isstvan had gotten it from, and how, I didn't want to know. Despite Aahz's constant assurances, I lived in dread of encountering the inn's rightful owner.

I couldn't help remembering all this as I waited outside the inn for our visitor. As I said, Aahz has very good hearing. When he tells me he hears something "close by," he frequently forgets to mention that "close by" may be over a mile away.

I have also noted, over the course of our friendship, that his hearing is curiously erratic. He can hear a lizard-bird scratching itself half a mile away, but occasionally seems unable to hear the politest of requests no matter how loudly I shout them at him.

There was still no sign of our rumored visitor. I considered moving back inside the inn, out of the late morning sun, but decided against it. I had carefully arranged the scene for our guest's arrival, and I hated to disrupt it for such a minor thing as personal comfort.

I had used the disguise spell liberally on Buttercup, Gleep and myself. Gleep now looked like a unicorn, a change which did not seem to bother Buttercup in the slightest. Apparently unicorns are less discriminating about their playmates than are dragons. I had made them both considerably more disheveled and unkempt-looking than they actually were. This was necessary to maintain the image set forth by my own appearance.

Aahz and I had decided early in our stay that the best way to handle unwanted guests was not to threaten them or frighten them away, but rather to be so repulsive that they left of their own accord. To this end, I had slowly devised a disguise designed to convince strangers they did not want to be in the same inn with me, no matter how large the inn was or how many other people were there. In this disguise, I would greet wayward travelers as the proprietor of the inn.

Modestly, I will admit the disguise was a screaming success. In fact, that was the specific reaction many visitors had to it. Some screamed, some looked ill, others sketched various religious symbols in the air between themselves and me. None of them elected to spend the night.

When I experimented with various physical defects, Aahz correctly pointed out that many people did not find any single defect revolting. In fact in a dimension such as Klah, most would consider it normal. To guarantee the desired effect, I adopted all of them.

When disguised, I walked with a painful limp, had a hunched back and a deformed hand which was noticeably diseased. What teeth remained were twisted and stained, and the focus of one of my eyes had a tendency to wander about independently of the other. My nose, in fact my entire face, was not symmetrical, and, in a master stroke of my disguise abilities, there appeared to be vicious-looking bugs crawling about my mangy hair and tattered clothes.

The overall effect was horrifying. Even Aahz admitted he found it disquieting, which, realizing what things he's seen in his travels through the dimensions, was high praise indeed.

My thoughts were interrupted as our visitor came into view. He sat ramrod-straight astride a huge, flightless riding bird. He carried no visible weapons, and wore no uniform, but his bearing marked him as a soldier much more than any outer trappings could have. His eyes were wary, constantly darting suspiciously about as he walked his bird up to the inn in slow, deliberate steps. Surprisingly enough, his gaze passed over me several times without registering my presence. Perhaps he didn't realize I was alive.

I didn't like this. The man seemed more hunter than casual traveler. Still, he was here and had to be dealt with. I went into my act.

"Does the noble sahr require a room?"

As I spoke, I moved forward in my practical, rolling gait. In case the subtlety of my disguise escaped him, I allowed a large gob of spittle to escape from the corner of my mouth where it rolled unhindered down to my chin.

For a moment, the man's attention was occupied controlling his mount. Flightless or not, the bird was trying to take to the air.

Apparently my disguise had touched a primal chord in the bird's mind that went back prior to its flightless ancestry.

I waited, head cocked curiously, while the man fought the bird to a fidgety standstill. Finally, he turned his attention to me for a moment. Then he averted his eyes and stared carefully at the sky.

"I come seeking the one known as Skeeve the magician," he told me.

Now it was my turn to jump. To the best of my knowledge, no one knew who and what I was, much less where I was, except for Aahz and me.

"That's me!" I blurted out, forgetting myself and using my real voice.

The man turned horrified eyes on me, and I remembered my appearance.

"That's me master!" I amended hastily. "You wait…I fetch."

I turned and scuttled hastily into the inn. Aahz was waiting inside.

"What is it?" he demanded.

"He's…he wants to talk to Skeeve…to me!" I babbled nervously.

"So?" he asked pointedly. "What are you doing in here? Go outside and talk to the man."

"Looking like this?"

Aahz rolled his eyes at the ceiling in exasperation.

"Who cares what you look like?" he barked. "C'mon, kid. The man's a total stranger!"

"I care!" I declared drawing myself up haughtily. "The man asked for Skeeve the magician, and I think…"

"He what?" Aahz interrupted.

"He asked for Skeeve the magician," I repeated, covertly studying the figure waiting outside. "He looks like a soldier to me," I supplied.

"He looks scared to me," Aahz retorted. "Maybe you should tone down your disguise a bit next time."

"Do you think he's a demon-hunter?" I asked nervously.

Instead of answering my questions Aahz turned abruptly from the window.

"If he wants a magician, we'll give him a magician," he murmured. "Quick, kid, slap the Garkin disguise on me."

As I noted earlier, Garkin was my first magik instructor. An imposing figure with a salt-and-pepper beard, he was one of our favorite and most oft-used disguises. I could do Garkin in my sleep.

"Good enough, kid," Aahz commented, surveying the results of my work. "Now follow close and let me do the talking."

"Like this?" I exclaimed.

"Relax, kid," he reassured me. "For this conversation I'm you. Understand?"

Aahz was already heading out through the door, without waiting for my reply, leaving me little other choice than to follow along behind him.

"Who seeks an audience with the great Skeeve?" Aahz bellowed in a resonant bass voice.

The man shot another nervous glance at me, then drew himself up in stiff formality.

"I come as an emissary from his most noble Majesty, Rodrick the Fifth, King of Possiltum, who..."

"What's Possiltum?" Aahz interrupted.

"I beg your pardon?" the man blinked.

"Possiltum," Aahz repeated. "Where is it?"

"Oh!" the man said with sudden understanding. "It's the kingdom just east of here...other side of the Ember River...you can't miss it."

"Okay," Aahz nodded. "Go on."

The man took a deep breath, then hesitated, frowning.

"...King of Possiltum..." I prompted.

"Oh yes! Thanks," the man shot a quick smile, then another quick stare, then continued, "...King of Possiltum, who sends his respects and greetings to the one known as Skeeve the magician..."

He paused and looked at Aahz expectantly. He was rewarded with a polite nod of the head. Satisfied, the man continued.

"His Majesty extends an invitation to Skeeve the magician to appear before the court of Possiltum that he might be reviewed for his suitability for the position of court magician."

"I don't really feel qualified to pass judgement on the king's suitability as a court magician," Aahz said modestly, eying the man carefully. "Isn't he content just to be king?"

"No, no!" the man corrected hastily. "The king wants to review your suitability."

"Oh!" Aahz said with the appearance of sudden understanding. "That's a different matter entirely. Well, well. An invitation from...who was it again?"

"Rodrick the Fifth," the man announced lifting his head haughtily.

"Well," Aahz said grinning broadly. "I've never been one to refuse a fifth!"

The man blinked and frowned, then glanced at me quizzically.

"You may tell His Majesty," Aahz continued, unaware of our confusion. "I shall be happy to accept his kind invitation. I shall arrive at his court at my earliest convenience."

The man frowned.

"I believe His Majesty requires your immediate presence," he commented darkly.

"Of course," Aahz answered smoothly. "How silly of me. If you will accept our hospitality for the night, I and my assistant here will be most pleased to accompany you in the morning."

I knew a cue when I heard one. I drooled and bared my teeth at the messenger.

The man shot a horrified look in my direction.

"Actually…" he said hastily, "I really must be going. I'll tell His Majesty you'll be following close behind."

"You're sure you wouldn't like to stay?" Aahz asked hopefully.

"Positive!"

The man nearly shouted his reply as he began backing the bird away from us.

"Oh well," Aahz said. "Perhaps we'll catch up with you on the road."

"In that case," the man said turning his bird. "I'll want a head…that is, I'd best be on my way to announce your coming."

I raised my hand to wave good-bye, but he was already moving at a rapid pace, urging his mount to still greater speeds, and ignoring me completely.

"Excellent!" Aahz exclaimed, rubbing his hands together gleefully. "A court magician! What a soft job! And the day started out so miserably."

"If I can interrupt," I interrupted. "There's one minor flaw in your plan."

"Hmm? What's that?"

"I don't want to be a court magician!"

As usual, my protest didn't dampen his enthusiasm at all.

"You didn't want to he a magician, either," he reminded me bluntly. "You wanted to be a thief. Well, here's a good compromise for you. As a court magician, you'll be a civil servant…and civil servants are thieves on a grander scale than you ever dreamed possible!"

III.

"Ninety percent of any business transaction is selling yourself to the client."
X. HOLLANDER

"NOW LET ME see if I've got this right," I said carefully. "You're saying they probably won't hire me on the basis of my abilities?"

I couldn't believe I'd interpreted Aahz's lecture correctly, but he beamed enthusiastically.

"That's right, kid," he approved. "Now you've got it."

"No, I don't," I insisted. "That's the craziest thing I've ever heard!"

Aahz groaned and hid his face in his hand.

It had been like this ever since we left the inn, and three days of a demon groaning is a bit much for anyone to take.

"I'm sorry, Aahz," I said testily. "But I don't believe it. I've taken a lot of things you've told me on faith, but this…this goes against common sense."

"What does common sense have to do with it?" he exploded. "We're talking about a job interview!"

At this outburst, Buttercup snorted and tossed his head, making it necessary for us to duck out of range of his horn.

"Steady, Buttercup!" I admonished soothingly.

Though he still rolled his eyes, the unicorn resumed his stoic plodding, the travois loaded with our equipment dragging along behind him still intact. Despite incidents such as had occurred back at the inn, Buttercup and I got along fairly well, and he usually obeyed me. In contrast, he and Aahz never really hit it off, especially when the latter chose to raise his voice angrily.

"All it takes is a little gentleness," I informed Aahz smugly. "You should try it sometime."

"While you're showing off your dubious rapport with animals," Aahz retorted, "you might call your dragon back. All we need is to have him stirring up the countryside."

I cast a quick glance about. He was right. Gleep had disappeared…again.

"Gleep!" I called. "Come here, fella!"

"Gleep!" came an answering cry.

The bushes off to our left parted and the dragon's head emerged.

"Gleep?" he said cocking his head.

"Come here!" I repeated.

My pet needed no more encouragement. He bounded into the open and trotted to my side.

"I still say we should have left that stupid dragon back at the inn," Aahz grumbled.

I ignored him, checking to be sure the gear, hung saddle-bag fashion over the dragon's back, was still secure. Personally, I felt we were carrying far too much in the way of personal belongings but Aahz had insisted. Gleep tried to nuzzle me affectionately with his head, and I caught a whiff of his breath. For a moment, I wondered if Aahz had been right about leaving the dragon behind.

"What were you saying about job interviews?" I asked, both to change the subject and to hide the fact I was gagging.

"I know it sounds ridiculous, kid," Aahz began with sudden sincerity, "and it is, but a lot of things are ridiculous, particularly in this dimension. That doesn't mean we don't have to deal with them."

That gave me pause to think. To a lot of people, having a demon and a dragon for traveling companions would seem ridiculous. As a matter of fact, if I took time to think it through, it seemed pretty ridiculous to me.

"Okay, Aahz," I said finally. "I can accept the existence of ridiculousness as reality. Now try explaining the court magician thing to me again."

We resumed walking as Aahz organized his thoughts. For a change, Gleep trailed placidly along beside Buttercup instead of taking off on another of his exploratory side trips.

"See if this makes any sense," Aahz said finally. "Court magicians don't do much…magically, at least. They're primarily kept around for show, as a status symbol to demonstrate a court is advanced enough to rate a magician. It's a rare occasion when they're called upon to do anything. If you were a jester, they'd work your tail off, but not as a magician. Remember, most people are skittish about magik, and use it as seldom as possible."

"If that's the case," I said confidently, "I'm qualified. I'll match my ability to do nothing against any magician on Klah."

"No argument there," Aahz observed drily. "But it's not quite that easy. To hold the job takes next to no effort at all. Getting the job can be an uphill struggle."

"Oh!" I said, surprised.

"Now to get the job, you'll have to impress the king and probably his advisors," Aahz continued. "You'll have to impress them with you, not with your abilities."

"How's that again?" I frowned.

"Look, kid. Like I said, a court magician is window-dressing, a showpiece. They'll be looking for someone they want to have hanging around their court, someone who is impressive whether or not he ever does anything. You'll have to exude confidence. Most important, you'll have to look like a magician...or at least, what they think a magician looks like. If you can dress like a magician, talk like a magician, and act like a magician, maybe no one will notice you don't have the abilities of a magician."

"Thanks, Aahz," I grimaced. "You'll really doing wonders toward building my confidence."

"Now don't sulk," Aahz admonished. "You know how to levitate reasonably large objects, you can fly after a fashion, and you've got the disguise spell down pat. You're doing pretty well for a rank novice, but don't kid yourself into believing you're anywhere near full magician status."

He was right, of course, but I was loathe to admit it.

"If I'm such a bumbling incompetent," I said stiffly, "why are we on our way to establish me as a court magician?"

Aahz bared his teeth at me in irritation.

"You aren't listening, kid," he snarled. "Holding the job once you've got it will be a breeze. You can handle that now. The tricky part will be getting you hired. Fortunately, with a few minor modifications and a little coaching, I think we can get you ready for polite society."

"Modifications such as what?" I asked, curious despite myself.

Aahz made a big show of surveying me from head to foot.

"For a start," he said, "there's the way you dress."

"What's wrong with the way I dress?" I countered defensively.

"Nothing at all," he replied innocently. "That is, if you want people to see you as a bumpkin peasant with dung on his boots. Of course, if you want to be a court magician, well that's another story. No respectable magician would be caught dead in an outfit like that."

"But, I *am* a respectable magician!" I argued.

"Really? Respected by who?"

He had me there, so I lapsed into silence.

"That's specifically the reason I had the foresight to bring along a few items from the inn," Aahz continued, indicating Buttercup's burdens with a grand sweep of his hand.

"And here I thought you were just looting the place," I said drily.

"Watch your mouth, kid," he warned. "This is all for your benefit."

"Really? You aren't expecting anything at all out of this deal?"

My sarcasm, as usual, was lost on him.

"Oh, I'll be around," he acknowledged. "Don't worry about that. Publicly, I'll be your apprentice."

"My apprentice?"

This job was suddenly sounding much better.

"Publicly!" Aahz repeated hastily. "Privately, you'll continue your lessons as normal. Remember that before you start getting frisky with your 'apprentice.'"

"Of course, Aahz," I assured him. "Now, what was it you were saying about changing the way I dress?"

He shot me a sidelong glance, apparently suspicious of my sudden enthusiasm.

"...Not that there's anything wrong with me the way I am," I added with a theatrical scowl.

That seemed to ease his doubts.

"Everything's wrong with the way you dress," he growled. "...We're lucky those two Imps left most of their wardrobe behind when we sent 'em packing along with Isstvan."

"Higgens and Brockhurst?"

"Yea, those two," Aahz grinned evilly at the memory. "I'll say one thing for Imps. They may be inferior to Deveels as merchants, but they are snappy dressers."

"I find it hard to believe that all that stuff you bundled along is wardrobe," I observed skeptically.

"Of course it isn't," my mentor moaned. "It's special effects gear."

"Special effects?"

"Don't you remember anything, kid?" Aahz scowled. "I told you all this when we first met. However easy magik is, you can't let it look easy. You need a few hand props, a line of patter…you know, like Garkin had."

Garkin's hut, where I had first been introduced to magik, had been full of candles, vials of strange powers, dusty books…now there was a magician's lair! Of course, I had since discovered that most of what he had was unnecessary for the actual working of magik itself.

I was beginning to see what Aahz meant when he said I'd have to learn to put on a show.

"We've got a lot of stuff we can work into your presentation," Aahz continued. "Isstvan left a lot of his junk behind when he left. Oh, and you might find some familiar items when we unload. I think the Imps helped themselves to some of Garkin's equipment and brought it back to the inn with them."

"Really?" I said, genuinely interested. "Did they get Garkin's brazier? You remember, you used it to drink wine out of when you first arrived."

"That's right! Yeah, I think I saw it in there. Why?"

"No special reason," I replied innocently. "It was always a favorite of mine, that's all."

From watching Garkin back in my early apprentice days, I knew there were secrets to that brazier I was dying to learn. I also knew that, if possible, I wanted to save it as a surprise for Aahz.

"We're going to have to do something about your physical appearance, too," Aahz continued thoughtfully.

"What's…"

"You're too young!" he answered, anticipating my question. "Nobody hires a young magician. They want one who's been around for awhile. If we…"

He broke off suddenly and craned his neck to look around.

"Kid," he said carefully, studying the sky. "Your dragon's gone again."

I did a fast scan. He was right.

"Gleep!" I called. "Here, fella!"

The dragon's head appeared from the depths of a bush behind us. There was something slimy with legs dangling from his mouth, but before I could manage an exact identification, my pet swallowed and the whatzit disappeared.

"Gleep!" he said proudly, licking his lips with his long, forked tongue.

"Stupid dragon," Aahz muttered darkly.

"He's cheap to feed," I countered, playing on Aahz's tight-fisted nature.

As we waited for the dragon to catch up, I had time to reflect that, for once, I felt no moral or ethical qualms about taking part in one of Aahz's schemes. Even if the unsuspecting Rodrick the Fifth was taken in by our charade and hired us, I was confident the king would be getting more than he bargained for.

IV.

"If the proper preparations have been made and the necessary precautions taken, any staged event is guaranteed success."
ETHELRED THE UNREADY

THE CANDLE LIT at the barest flick from my mind.

Delighted, I snuffed it and tried again.

A sidelong glance, a fleeting concentration of my will, and the smoldering wick burst into flame again.

I snuffed the flame and sat smiling at the familiar candle.

This was the first real proof I'd had as to how far my magical powers had developed in the past year. I knew this candle from my years as Garkin's apprentice. In those days, it was my arch-Nemesis. Even focusing all my energies failed to light it then. But now...

I glanced at the wick again, and again it rewarded me with a burst of flame.

I snuffed it and repeated the exercise, my confidence growing as I realized how easily I could now do something I once thought impossible.

"Will you knock it off with the candle!"

I jumped at the sound of Aahz's outburst, nearly upsetting the candle and setting the blanket afire.

"I'm sorry, Aahz," I said, hastily snuffing the candle for the last time. "I just..."

"You're here to audition for Court Magician," he interrupted. "Not for town Christmas tree!"

I considered asking what a Christmas tree was, but decided against it. Aahz seemed uncommonly irritable and nervous, and I was pretty sure that, however I chose to phrase my question, the answer would be both sarcastic and unproductive.

"Stupid candle blinking on and off," Aahz grumbled half to himself. "Attract the attention of every guard in the castle."

"I thought we were *trying* to attract their attention," I pointed out, but Aahz ignored me, peering at the castle through the early morning light.

He didn't have to peer far, as we were camped in the middle of the road just short of the castle's main gates. As I said, I was under the impression our position was specifically chosen to attract attention to ourselves.

We had crept into position in the dead of night, clumsily picking our way among the sleeping buildings clustered about the main gate. Not wishing to show a light, unpacking had been minimal, but even in the dark, I had recognized Garkin's candle.

All of this had to do with something Aahz called a "dramatic entrance." As near as I could tell, all this really meant was that we couldn't do anything the easy way.

Our appearance was also carefully designed for effect, with the aid of the Imps' abandoned wardrobe and my disguise spells.

Aahz was outfitted in my now-traditional "dubious character" disguise. Gleep was standing placidly beside Buttercup disguised as a unicorn, giving us a matched pair. It was my own appearance, however, which had been the main focus of our attentions.

Both Aahz and I had agreed that the Garkin disguise would be unsuitable for this effort. While my own natural appearance was too young, Garkin's would be too old. Since we could pretty much choose the image we wanted, we decided to field a magician in his mid-to-late thirties; young without being youthful, experienced without being old, and powerful but still learning.

To achieve this disguise involved a bit more work than normal, as I did not have an image in mind to superimpose over my own. Instead, I closed my eyes and envisioned myself as I appeared normally, then slowly erased the features until I had a blank face to begin on. Then I set to work with Aahz watching carefully and offering suggestions and modifications.

The first thing I changed was my height, adjusting the image until the new figure stood a head and a half taller than my actual diminutive stature. My hair was next and I changed my strawberry-blond thatch to a more sinister black, at the same time darkening my complexion several shades.

The face gave us the most problem.

"...Elongate the chin a little more," Aahz instructed. "Put on a beard...not that much, stupid! Just a little goatee!...That's better! ...Now lower the sideburns...okay, build up the nose...narrow it... make the eyebrows bushier...no, change 'em back and sink the eyes a little instead...for crying out loud change the eye color! Make 'em brown...okay, now a couple frown wrinkles in the middle of the forehead...Good. That should do it."

I stared at the figure in my mind, burning the image into my memory. It was effective, maybe a bit more sinister than I would have designed if left to my own devices, but Aahz was the expert and I had to trust his judgement. I opened my eyes.

"Terrific, kid!" Aahz beamed. "Now put on that black robe with the gold-and-red trim the Imps left, and you'll cut a figure fit to grace any court."

"Move along there! You're blocking the road!"

The rude order wrenched my thoughts back to the present.

A soldier, resplendent in leather armor and brandishing an evil-looking pike, was angrily approaching our crude encampment. Behind him, the gates stood slightly ajar and I could see the heads of several other soldiers watching us curiously.

Now that the light was improving, I could see the wall better. It wasn't much of a wall, barely ten feet high. That figured. From what we had seen since we crossed the border, it wasn't much of a kingdom, either.

"You deaf or something?" the soldier barked drawing close. "I said, *move along!*"

Aahz scuttled forward and planted himself in the soldier's path.

"Skeeve the magnificent has arrived," he announced. "And he—"

"I don't care who you are!" the soldier snarled, wasting no time placing his pike between himself and the figure addressing him. "You can't—"

He broke off abruptly as his pike leaped from his grasp and floated horizontally in mid-air until it was forming a barricade between him and Aahz.

The occurrence was my doing, a simple feat of levitation. Regardless of our planned gambit, I felt I should take a direct hand in the proceedings before things got completely out of hand.

"I am Skeeve!" I boomed, forcing my voice into a resonant bass. "And that is my assistant you are attempting to threaten with your feeble weapon. We have come in response to an invitation from Rodrick the Fifth, King of Possiltum!"

"That's right, Bosco!" Aahz leered at the soldier. "Now just run along like a good fellow and pass the word we're here...eh?" As I

noted earlier, all this was designed to impress the hell out of the general populace. Apparently the guard hadn't read the script. He did not cower in terror or cringe with fear. If anything, our little act seemed to have the exact opposite affect on him.

"A magician, eh?" he said with a mocking sneer. "For that I've got standing orders. Go around to the back where the others are."

This took us aback...well, at least it took *me* aback. According to our plan, we would end up arguing whether we entered the palace to perform in the king's court, or if the king had to bring his court outside to where we were. Being sent to the back door was not an option we had considered.

"To the back?" Aahz glowered. "You dare to suggest a magician of my master's stature go to the back door like a common servant?"

The soldier didn't budge an inch.

"If it were up to me, I'd 'dare to suggest' a far less pleasant activity for you. As it is, I have my orders. You're to go around to the back like all the others."

"Others?" I asked carefully.

"That's right," the guard sneered. "The king is holding an open air court to deal with all you 'miracle workers.' Every hack charm-peddler for eight kingdoms is in town. Some of 'em have been in line since noon yesterday. Now get around to the back and quit blocking the road!"

With that he turned on his heel and marched back to the gate, leaving his pike hanging in mid-air.

For once, Aahz was as speechless as I was. Apparently I wasn't the only one the king had invited to drop by. Apparently we were in big trouble.

V.

"...Eye of newt, toe of frog..."
Believed to be the first recipe for an explosive
mixture...the forerunner of gunpowder.

"WHAT ARE WE going to do, Aahz?"

With the guard out of earshot, I could revert to my normal voice and speech patterns, though it was still necessary to keep my physical disguise intact.

"That's easy," he responded. "We pack up our things and go around the back. Weren't you listening, kid?"

"But what are we going to do about..."

But Aahz was already at work, rebinding the few items we had unpacked.

"Don't do anything, kid," he warned over his shoulder. "We can't let anyone see you doing menial work. It's bad for the image."

"He said there were other magicians here!" I blurted at last.

"Yeah...So?"

"Well, what are we going to do?"

Aahz scowled.

"I told you once. We're going to pack our things and..."

"What are we going to do about the other magicians?"

"Do? We aren't going to do anything. You aren't up to dueling, you know."

He had finished packing and stepped back to survey his handiwork. Nodding in satisfaction, he turned and shot a glance over my shoulder.

"Do something about the pike, will ya, kid?"

I followed his gaze. The guard's pike was still hanging suspended in mid-air. Even though I hadn't been thinking about it, part of my mind had been keeping it afloat until I decided what to do with it. The question was, what should I do with it?

"Say, Aahz..." I began, but Aahz had already started walking along the wall.

For a moment I was immobilized with indecision. The guard had gone, so I couldn't return his weapon to him. Still, simply letting it drop to the ground seemed somehow anti-climactic.

Unable to think of anything to do which would have the proper dramatic flair, I decided to postpone the decision. For the time being, I let the pike float along behind me as I hurried after Aahz, first giving it additional elevation so it would not be a danger to Gleep and Buttercup.

"Were you expecting other magicians to be here?" I asked, drawing abreast of my mentor.

"Not really," Aahz admitted. "It was a possibility, of course, but I didn't give it a very high probability rating. Still, it's not all that surprising. A job like this is bound to draw competition out of the woodwork."

He didn't seem particularly upset, so I tried to take this new development in stride.

"Okay," I said calmly. "How does this change our plans?"

"It doesn't. Just do your thing like I showed you and everything should come out fine."

"But if the other magicians..."

Aahz stopped short and turned to face me.

"Look, kid," he said seriously. "Just because I keep telling you you've got a long way to go before you're a master magician doesn't mean you're a hack! I wouldn't have encouraged you to show up for this interview if I didn't think you were good enough to land the job."

"Really, Aahz?"

He turned and started walking again.

"Just remember, as dimensions go, Klah isn't noted for its magicians. You're no master, but masters are few and far between. I'm betting that, compared to the competition, you'll look like a real expert."

That made sense. Aahz was quite outspoken in his low opinion of Klah and the Klahds that inhabited it, including me. That last thought made me fish for a bit more reassurance.

"Aahz?"

"Yea, kid?"

"What's your honest appraisal of my chances?"

There was a moment of silence before he answered.

"Kid, you know how you're always complaining that I keep tearing down your confidence?"

"Yea?"

"Well, for both our sakes, don't push too hard for my honest appraisal."

I didn't.

Getting through the back gate proved to be no problem... mostly because there wasn't a back gate. To my surprise and Aahz's disgust, the wall did not extend completely around the palace. As near as I could see, only the front wall was complete. The two side walls were under construction, and the back wall was nonexistent. I should clarify that. My statement that the side walls were under construction was an assumption based on the presence of scaffolding at the end of the walk rather than the observation of any activity going on. If there was any work being performed, it was being done carefully enough not to disturb the weeds which abounded throughout the scaffolding.

I was beginning to have grave doubts about the kingdom I was about to ally myself with.

It was difficult to tell if the court was being convened in a garden, or if this was a courtyard losing its fight with the underbrush which crowded in through the opening where the back wall should have been. Having grown up on a farm, my basic education in plants was that if it wasn't edible and growing in neat rows, it was a weed.

As if in answer to my thoughts, Buttercup took a large mouthful of the nearest clump of growth and began chewing enthusiastically. Gleep sniffed the same bush and turned up his nose at it.

All this I noted only as an aside. My main attention was focused on the court itself.

There was a small, open-sided pavilion set against the wall of the palace, sheltering a seated figure, presumably the king. Standing close beside him on either side were two other men. The crowd, such as it was, was split into two groups. The first was standing in a somewhat orderly line along one side of the garden. I assumed this was the waiting line...or, rather, I hoped it was, as that was the group we joined. The second group was standing in a disorganized mob on the far side of the garden watching the proceedings. Whether these were rejected applicants or merely interested hangers-on, I didn't know.

Suddenly, a young couple in the watching group caught my eye. I hadn't expected to encounter any familiar faces here, but these two I had seen before. Not only had I seen them, Aahz and

I had impersonated them at one point, a charade which had resulted in our being hanged.

"Aahz!" I whispered urgently. "Do you see those two over there?"

"No," Aahz said bluntly, not even turning his head to look.

"But they're the…"

"Forget 'em," he insisted. "Watch the judges. They're the ones we have to impress."

I had to admit that made a certain amount of sense. Grudgingly, I turned my attention to the figures in the pavilion.

The king was surprisingly young, perhaps in his mid-twenties. His hair was a tumble of shoulder-length curls, which, combined with his slight build, almost made him look effeminate. Judging from his posture, either the interviews had been going on for some time, or he had mastered the art of looking totally bored.

The man on his left bent and whispered something urgently in the king's ear and was answered by a vague nod.

This man, only slightly older than the king but balding noticeably, was dressed in a tunic and cloak of drab color and conservative cut. Though relaxed in posture and quiet in bearing, there was a watchful brightness to his eyes that reminded me of a feverish weasel-ant.

There was a stirring of the figure on the king's right which drew my attention in that direction. I had a flash impression of a massive furry lump, then I realized with a start that it was a man. He was tall and broad, his head crowned with thick, black, unkempt curls, his face nearly obscured by a full beard and mustache. This, combined with his heavy fur cloak, gave him an animal appearance which had dominated my first impression. He spoke briefly to the king, then recrossed his arms in a gesture of finality and glared at the other advisor. His cloak opened briefly during his oration, giving me a glimpse of a shirt of glittering mail and a massive, double-headed hand-axe hung on a belt at his waist. Clearly this was not a man to cross. The balding figure seemed unimpressed, matching his rival's glare with one of his own.

There was a sharp nudge in my ribs.

"Did you see that?" Aahz whispered urgently.

"See what?" I asked.

"The king's advisors. A general and a chancellor unless I miss my guess. Did you see the gold medallion on the general?"

"I saw his axe!" I whispered back.

The light in the courtyard suddenly dimmed.

Looking up, I saw a mass of clouds forming overhead, blotting out the sun.

"Weather control," Aahz murmured, half to himself. "Not bad."

Sure enough, the old man in the red cloak currently before the throne gestured wildly and tossed a cloud of purple powder into the air, and a light drizzle began to fall.

My spirits fell along with the rain. Even with Aahz's coaching on presentation, my magik was not this powerful or impressive.

"Aahz..." I whispered urgently.

Instead of responding, he waved me to silence, his eyes riveted on the pavilion.

Following his gaze, I saw the general speaking urgently with the king. The king listened for a moment, then shrugged and said something to the magician.

Whatever he said, the magician didn't like it. Drawing himself up haughtily, he turned to leave, only to be called back by the king. Pointing to the clouds, the king said a few more words and leaned back. The magician hesitated, then shrugged and began gesturing and chanting once more.

"Turned him down," Aahz said smugly.

"Then what's he doing now?"

"Clearing up the rain before the next act goes on," Aahz informed me.

Sure enough, the drizzle was slowing and the clouds beginning to scatter, much to the relief of the audience, who, unlike the king, had no pavilion to protect them from the storm. This further display of the magician's power, however, did little to bolster my sagging confidence.

"Aahz!" I whispered. "He's a better magician than I am."

"Yeah," Aahz responded. "So?"

"So if they turned *him* down, *I* haven't got a chance!"

"Maybe yes, maybe no," came the thoughtful reply. "As near as I can tell, they're looking for something specific. Who knows? Maybe you're it. Remember what I told you: cushy jobs don't always go to the most skillful. In fact, it usually goes the other way."

"Yea," I said trying to sound optimistic, "Maybe I'll get lucky."

"It's going to take more than luck," Aahz corrected me sternly. "Now, what have you learned watching the king's advisors?"

"They don't like each other." I observed immediately.

"Right!" Aahz sounded surprised and pleased. "Now, that means you probably won't be able to please them both. You'll have to play up to one of them…or, better still, insult one—that'll get the other one on your side faster than anything. Now, which one do you want on your side?"

That was easier than his first question.

"The general," I said firmly.

"Wrong! You want the chancellor."

"The chancellor?!" I exclaimed, blurting the words out louder than I had intended. "Did you see the size of that axe the general's carrying?"

"Uh-huh," Aahz replied. "Did you hear what happened to the guy who interviewed before old Red Cloak here got his turn?"

I closed my eyes and controlled my first sharp remark.

"Aahz," I said carefully. "Remember me? I'm Skeeve. I'm the one who can't hear whispers a mile away."

As usual Aahz ignored my sarcasm.

"The last guy didn't even get a chance to show his stuff," he informed me. "The chancellor took one look at the crowd he brought with him and asked how many were in his retinue. 'Eight,' the man said. 'Too many!' says the chancellor and the poor fool was dismissed immediately."

"So?" I asked bluntly.

"So, the chancellor is the one watching the purse strings," concluded Aahz. "What's more, he has more influence than the general. Look at these silly walls. Do you think a military man would leave walls half-finished if he had the final say? Somebody decided too much money was being spent constructing them, and the project was cancelled or delayed. I'm betting that somebody was the chancellor."

"Maybe they ran out of stones," I suggested.

"C'mon, kid. From what we've seen since we crossed the border this kingdom's principal crop is stones."

"But the general…"

As I spoke, I glanced in the general's direction again. To my surprise and discomfort, he was staring directly at me. It wasn't a friendly stare.

I hesitated for a moment, hoping I was wrong. I wasn't. The general's gaze didn't waver, nor did his expression soften. If anything, it got uglier.

"Aahz…" I hissed desperately, unable to tear my eyes from the general.

Now the king and the chancellor were staring in my direction too, their attention drawn by the general's gaze.

"Kid!" Aahz moaned beside me. "I thought I told you to do something about that pike!"

The pike! I had forgotten about it completely!

I pulled my eyes from the general's glare and glanced behind me as casually as I could.

Buttercup and Gleep were still standing patiently to our rear, and floating serenely above them was the guard's pike. I guess it was kind of noticeable.

"You!"

I turned toward the pavilion and the sound of the bellow. The general had stepped forward and was pointing a massive finger at me.

"Yes, you!" he roared as our eyes met once more. "Where did you get that pike? It belongs to the palace guards."

"I think you're about to have your interview, kid," Aahz murmured. "Give it your best and knock 'em stiff."

"But…" I protested.

"It beats standing in line!"

With that, Aahz took a long, leisurely step backward. The effect was the same as if I had stepped forward, which I definitely hadn't. With the attention of the entire courtyard now centered on me, however, I had no choice but to make the plunge.

VI.

"That's entertainment!"
VLAD THE IMPALER

CROSSING MY ARMS, I moved toward the pavilion, keeping my pace slow and measured.

Aahz had insisted that I practice this walk. He said it would make me look confident and self-possessed. Now that I was actually appearing before a king, I found I was using the walk, not as a show of arrogance, but to hide the weakness in my legs.

"Well?" the general rumbled, looming before me. "I asked you a question! Where did you get that pike? You'd best answer before I grow angry!"

Something in me snapped. Any fear I felt of the general and his axe evaporated, replaced by a heady glow of strength.

I had discovered on my first visit to the Bazaar at Deva that I didn't like to be pushed around by big, loud Deveels. I discovered now that I didn't like it any better when the arrogance came from a big, loud fellow Klahd.

So, the big man wants to throw his weight around, does he?

With a twitch of my mind, I summoned the pike. Without turning to look, I brought it arrowing over my shoulder in a course destined to embed it in the general's chest.

The general saw it coming and paled. He took an awkward step backward, realized it was too late for flight, and groped madly for his axe.

I stopped the pike three feet from his chest, floating it in front of him with its point leveled at his heart.

"This pike?" I asked casually.

"Ahh…" the general responded, his eyes never leaving the weapon.

"I took this pike from an overly rude soldier. He said he was following orders. Would those orders have come from you, by any chance?"

"I…um…" the general licked his lips. "I issued orders that my men deal with strangers in an expedient fashion. I said nothing about their being less than polite."

"In that case…"

I rotated the pike ninety degrees so that it now no longer threatened the general.

"…I return the pike to you so that you might give it back to the guard along with a clarification of your orders."

The general hesitated, scowling, then extended his hand to grasp the floating pike. Just before he reached it, I let it fall to the ground where it clattered noisily.

"…And, hopefully, additional instructions as to how to handle their weapons," I concluded.

The general flushed and started to pick up the pike. Then the chancellor snickered, and the general spun around to glare at him. The chancellor smirked openly and whispered something to the king, who tried to suppress a smile at his words.

The general turned to me again, ignoring the pike, and glared down from his full height.

"Who are you?" he asked in a tone which implied my name would be immediately moved to the head of the list for public execution.

"Who's asking?" I glared back, still not completely over my mad.

"The man you are addressing," the king interceded, "is Hugh Badaxe, Commander of the Royal Armies of Possiltum."

"And I am J. R. Grimble," the chancellor added hastily, afraid of being left out. "First advisor to His Majesty."

The general shot another black look at Grimble. I decided it was time to get down to business.

"I am the magician known as Skeeve," I began grandly. "I have come in response to a gracious invitation from His most Noble Majesty, Rodrick the Fifth."

I paused and inclined my head slightly to the king, who smiled and nodded in return.

"I have come to determine for myself whether I should consider accepting a position at the court of Possiltum."

The phrasing of that last part had been chosen very carefully by Aahz. It was designed to display my confidence by implying that the choice was mine rather than theirs.

The subtlety was not lost on the chancellor, who raised a critical eyebrow at my choice of words.

"Now, such a position requires confidence on both sides," I continued. "I must feel that I will be amply rewarded for my services, and His Majesty must be satisfied that my skills are worthy of his sponsorship."

I turned slightly and raised my voice to address the entire court.

"The generosity of the crown of Possiltum is known to all," I declared. "And I have every confidence that His Majesty rewards his retainers in proportion to their service to him."

There was a strangled sound behind me, from the general, I think. I ignored it.

"Therefore, all that is required is that I satisfy His Majesty...and his advisors...that my humble skills will indeed suffice his needs."

I turned to the throne once more, letting the king see my secret smile which belied the humility of my words.

"Your Majesty, my powers are many and varied. However the essence of power is control. Therefore, realizing that you are a busy man, rather than waste time with mere commercial trickeries and minor demonstrations such as we have already seen, I shall weave but three spells and trust in your wisdom to perceive the depths behind them."

I turned and stretched forth a finger to point at Buttercup and Gleep.

"Yonder are my prize pair of matched unicorns," I said dramatically. "Would your majesty be so kind as to choose one of them?"

The king blinked in surprise at being invited to participate in my demonstration. For a moment he hesitated.

"Umm...I choose the one on the left," he said finally indicating Buttercup.

I bowed slightly.

"Very well, Your Majesty. By your ward shall that creature be spared. Observe the other closely."

Actually, that was another little stunt Aahz had taught me. It's called a "magician's force," and allows a performer to offer his audience a choice without really giving them a choice. Had the king chosen Gleep, I would have simply proceeded to work on "the creature he had doomed with a word."

Slowly, I pointed a finger at Gleep and lowered my head slightly.

"Walla Walla Washington!" I said somberly.

I don't know what the words meant, but Aahz assured me they had historic precedent and would convince people I was actually doing something complex.

"Alla kazam shazam," I continued raising my other arm. "Bibbity bobbity…"

I mentally removed Gleep's disguise.

The crowd reacted with a gasp, drowning out my final "googleep."

My dragon heard his name, though, and reacted immediately. His head came up and he lumbered forward to stand docilely at my side. As planned, Aahz immediately shambled forward to a position near Gleep's head and stood watchful and ready.

This was meant to imply that we were prepared to handle any difficulty which might arise with the dragon. The crowd's reaction to him, however, overshadowed their horror at seeing a unicorn transformed to a dragon. I had forgotten how effective the "disreputable character" disguise was. Afraid of losing the momentum of my performance, I hurried on.

"This misshapen wretch is my apprentice Aahz," I announced. "You may wonder if it is within his power to stop the dragon should the beast grow angry. I tell you now…it is not!"

The crowd edged back nervously. From the corner of my eye, I saw the general's hand slide to the handle of his axe.

"…But it *is* within *my* power! Now you know that the forces of darkness are no strangers to Skeeve!"

I spun and stabbed a finger at Aahz.

"Bobbelty gook, crumbs and martyrs!"

I removed Aahz's disguise.

There was a moment of stunned silence, then Aahz smiled. Aahz's smile has been known to make strong men weak, and there were not many strong men in the crowd.

The audience half-trampled each other in their haste to backpedal from the demon, and the sound of screeches was intermixed with hastily chanted protection spells.

I turned to the throne once more. The king and the chancellor seemed to be taking it well. They were composed, though a bit pale. The general was scowling thoughtfully at Aahz.

"As a demon, my apprentice can suppress the dragon if need be…nay, ten dragons. Such is my power. Yet, power must be tempered with gentleness…gentility if you will."

I allowed my expression to grow thoughtful.

"To confuse one's enemies and receive one's allies, one needs no open show of power or menace. For occasions such as those, one's powers can be masked until one is no more conspicuous than…than a stripling."

As I spoke the final words, I stripped away my own disguise and stood in my youthful unsplendor. I probably should have used some fake magik words, but I had already used up all the ones Aahz had taught me and was afraid of experimenting with new ones.

The king and the chancellor were staring at me intently as if trying to penetrate my magical disguise with will-power alone. The general was performing a similar exercise staring at Aahz, who folded his arms and bared his teeth in a confident smile.

For a change, I shared his confidence. Let them stare. It was too late to penetrate my magik because I wasn't working any more. Though the royal troupe and the entire audience was convinced they were witnessing a powerful spell, in actually all I had done was remove the spells which had been distorting their vision. At the moment, all of us, Aahz, Buttercup, Gleep, and myself, were our normal selves, however abnormal we appeared. Even the most adept magical vision could not penetrate a nonexistent spell.

"As you see, Your Majesty," I concluded. "My powers are far from ordinary. They can make the gentle fearsome, or the mighty harmless. They can destroy your enemies or amuse your court, depending upon your whim. Say the word, speak your approval, and the powers of Skeeve are yours to command."

I drew myself up and bowed my head respectfully, and remained in that position awaiting judgement from the throne.

Several moments passed without a word. Finally, I risked a peek at the pavilion.

The chancellor and the general were exchanging heated whispers over the head of the king, who inclined his head this way and that as he listened. Realizing this could take a while, I quietly eased my head to an upright position as I waited.

"Skeeve!" the king called suddenly, interrupting his advisor's arguments. "That thing you did with the pike. Can you always control weapons so easily?"

"Child's play, Your Majesty," I said modestly. "I hesitate evern to acknowledge it as a power."

The king nodded and spoke briefly to his advisors in undertones. When he had finished, the general flushed and, turning on his heel, strode off into the palace. The chancellor looked smug.

I risked a glance at Aahz, who winked at me. Even though he was farther away, apparently his acute hearing had given him advance notice of the king's decision.

"Let all here assembled bear witness!" the chancellor's ringing voice announced. "Rodrick the Fifth, King of Possiltum, does hereby commend the magical skill and knowledge of one Skeeve and does formally name him Magician to the court of Possiltum. Let all applaud the appointment of this master magician...and then disperse!"

There was a smattering of half-hearted applause from my vanquished rivals, and more than a few glares. I acknowledged neither as I tried to comprehend the chancellor's words.

I did it! Court Magician! Of the entire selection of magicians from five kingdoms, I had been chosen! Me! Skeeve!

I was suddenly aware the chancellor was beckoning me forward. Trying to be nonchalant, I approached the throne.

"Lord Magician," the chancellor smiled. "If you will, might we discuss the matter of your wages?"

"My apprentice handles such matters," I informed him loftily. "I prefer not to distract myself with such mundane matters."

Again, we had agreed that Aahz would handle the wage negotiations, his knowledge of magik being surpassed only by his skill at haggling. I turned and beckoned to him. He responded by hurrying forward, his eavesdropping having forewarned him of the situation.

"That can wait, Grimble," the king interrupted. "There are more pressing matters which command our magician's attention."

"You need only command, Your Majesty," I said bowing grandly.

"Fine," the king beamed. "Then report to General Badaxe immediately for your briefing."

"Briefing about what?" I asked, genuinely puzzled.

"Why, your briefing about the invading army, of course," the king replied.

An alarm gong went off in the back of my mind.

"Invading army?" I asked carefully. "What invading army?"

"The one which even now approaches our borders," the chancellor supplied. "Why else would we suddenly need a magician?"

Robert Asprin

VII.

*"Numerical superiority is of no consequence.
In battle, victory will go to the best tactician."*
                              G. A. CUSTER

"CUSHY JOB, HE said! Chance to practice, he said! Piece of cake, he said!"

"Simmer down, kid!" Aahz growled.

"Simmer down? Aahz, weren't you listening? I'm supposed to stop an army! Me!"

"It could be worse," Aahz insisted.

"How?" I asked bluntly.

"You could be doing it without me," he replied. "Think about it."

I did, and cooled down immediately. Even though my association with Aahz seemed to land me in an inordinate amount of trouble, he had also been unfailing in his ability to get me out...so far. The last thing I wanted to do was drive him away just when I needed him the most.

"What am I going to do, Aahz?" I moaned.

"Since you ask," Aahz smiled. "My advice would be to not panic until we get the whole story. Remember, there are armies and there are armies. For all we know, this one might be weak enough for us to beat fair and square."

"And if it isn't?" I asked skeptically.

"We'll burn that bridge when we come to it," Aahz sighed. "First, let's hear what old Badaxe has to say."

Not being able to think of anything to say in reply to that, I didn't. Instead, I kept pace with my mentor in gloomy silence as we followed the chancellor's directions through the corridors of the palace.

It would have been easier to accept the offered guide to lead us to our destination, but I had been more than a little anxious to speak with Aahz privately. Consequently, we had left Buttercup and Gleep in the courtyard with our equipment and were seeking out the general's chambers on our own.

The palace was honeycombed with corridors to the point where I wondered if there weren't more corridors than rooms. Our trek was made even more difficult by the light, or lack thereof. Though there were numerous mountings for torches set in the walls, it seemed only about one out of every four was being used, and the light shed by those torches was less than adequate for accurate navigation of the labyrinth.

I commented on this to Aahz as further proof of the tightfisted nature of the kingdom. His curt response was that the more money they saved on overhead and maintenance, the more they would have to splurge on luxuries...like us.

He was doggedly trying to explain the concept of an "energy crisis" to me when we rounded a corner and sighted the general's quarters.

They were fairly easy to distinguish, since this was the only door we had encountered which was bracketed by a pair of matching honor guards. Their polished armor gleamed from broad shoulders as they observed our approach through narrowed eyes.

"Are these the quarters of General Badaxe?" I inquired politely.

"Are you the magician called Skeeve?" the guard challenged back.

"The kid asked you a question, soldier!" Aahz interceded. "Now are you going to answer or are you so dumb you don't know what's on the other side of the door you're guarding?"

The guard flushed bright red, and I noticed his partner's knuckles whitening on the pike he was gripping. It occurred to me that, now that I had landed the magician's job, it might not be the wisest course to continue antagonizing the military.

"Um, Aahz..." I murmured.

"Yes! These are the quarters of General Badaxe...sir!" the guard barked suddenly.

Apparently the mention of my colleague's name had confirmed my identity, though I wondered how many strangers could be wandering the halls accompanied by large scaly demons.

The final, painful "sir" was a tribute to my performance in the courtyard. Apparently the guards had been instructed to be polite, at least to me, no matter how much it hurt. Which it obviously did.

"Thank you, guard," I said loftily, and hammered on the door with my fist.

"Further," the guard observed. "The general left word that you were to go right in."

The fact that he had withheld that bit of information until after I had knocked indicated that the guards hadn't completely abandoned their low regard for magicians, but rather were finding more subtle ways of being annoying.

I realized Aahz was getting ready to start a new round with the guard and hastily opened the door and entered, forcing him to follow.

The general was standing at the window, silhouetted by the light streaming in from outside. As we entered, he turned to face us.

"Ah! Come in, gentlemen," he boomed in a mellow tone. "I've been expecting you. Do make yourselves comfortable. Help yourselves to the wine if you wish."

I found his sudden display of friendliness even more disquieting than his earlier show of hostility. Aahz, however, took it all in stride, immediately taking up the indicated jug of wine. For a moment I thought he was going to pour a bit of it into one of the goblets which shared the tray with the jug and pass it to me. Instead, he took a deep drink directly from the jug and kept it, licking his lips in appreciation. In the midst of the chaos my life had suddenly become, it was nice to know some things remained constant.

The general frowned at the display for a moment, then forced his features back into the jovial expression he had first greeted us with.

"Before we begin the briefing," he smiled, "I must apologize for my rude behavior during the interview. Grimble and I have...differed in our opinions on the existing situation, and I'm afraid I took it out on you. For that I extend my regrets. Ordinarily, I have nothing against magicians as a group, or you specifically."

"Whoa! Back up a minute, General," Aahz interrupted. "How does your feud with the chancellor involve us?"

The general's eyes glittered with a fierceness which belied the gentility of his oration.

"It's an extension of an old argument concerning allocation of funds," he said. "When news reached us of the approaching force, my advice to the king was to immediately strengthen our own army that we might adequately perform our sworn duty of defending the realm."

"Sounds like good advice to me," I interjected, hoping to improve my status with the general by agreeing with him.

Badaxe responded by fixing me with a hard glare.

"Strange that you should say that, magician," he observed stonily. "Grimble's advice was to invest the money elsewhere than in the army, specifically in a magician."

It suddenly became clear why we had been received by the guards and the general with something less than open-armed camaraderie. Not only were they getting us instead of reinforcements, our presence was a slap at their abilities.

"Okay, General," Aahz acknowledged. "All that's water under the drawbridge. What are we up against?"

The general glanced back and forth between me and Aahz, apparently surprised that I was allowing my apprentice to take the lead in the briefing. When I failed to rebuke Aahz for his forwardness, the general shrugged and moved to a piece of parchment hanging on the wall.

"I believe the situation is shown clearly by this," he said.

"What's that?" Aahz interrupted.

The general started to respond sharply, then caught himself.

"This," he said evenly, "is a map of the kingdom you are supposed to defend. It's called Possiltum."

"Yes, of course," I nodded. "Continue."

"This line here to the north of our border represents the advancing army you are to deal with."

"Too bad you couldn't get it to scale," Aahz commented. "The way you have it there, the enemy's front is longer than your border."

The general bared his teeth.

"The drawing *is* to scale," he said pointedly. "Perhaps now you will realize the magnitude of the task before you."

My mind balked at accepting his statement.

"Really, general," I chided. "Surely you're overstating the case. There aren't enough fighting men in any kingdom to form a front that long."

"Magician," the general's voice was menacing. "I did not reach my current rank by overstating military situations. The army you are facing is one of the mightiest forces the world has ever seen. It is the striking arm of a rapidly growing empire situated far to the north. They have been advancing for three years now, absorbing smaller kingdoms and crushing any resistance offered. All able-bodied men of conquered lands are conscripted for military service, swelling their ranks to the size you see indicated on the map. The only reason they are not advancing faster is that, in addition to limitless numbers of men, they possess massive war machines which, though effective, are slow to transport."

"Now tell us the bad news," Aahz commented drily.

Though I'm sure he meant to be sarcastic, the general took him seriously.

"The bad news," he growled, "is that their leader is a strategist without peer. He rose to power trouncing forces triple the size of his own numbers, and now that he has a massive army at his command, he is virtually unbeatable."

"I'm beginning to see why the king put his money into a magician," my mentor observed. "It doesn't look like you could have assembled a force large enough to stop them."

"That wasn't my plan!" the general bristled. "While we may not have been able to crush the enemy, we could have made them pay dearly enough for crossing our border that they might have turned aside for weaker lands easier to conquer."

"You know, Badaxe," Aahz said thoughtfully, "that's not a bad plan. Working together we might still pull it off. How many men can you give us for support?"

"None," the general said firmly.

I blinked.

"Excuse me, general," I pressed. "For a moment there, I thought you said…"

"None," he repeated. "I will not assign a single soldier of mine to support your campaign."

"That's insane!" Aahz exploded. "How do you expect us to stop an army like that with just magik?"

"I don't," the general smiled.

"But if we fail," I pointed out, "Possiltum falls."

"That is correct," Badaxe replied calmly.

"But…"

"Allow me to clarify my position," he interrupted. "In my estimation, there is more at stake here than one kingdom. If you succeed in your mission, it will establish that magik is more effective than military forces in defending a kingdom. Eventually, that could lead to all armies being disbanded in preference to hiring magicians. I will have no part in establishing a precedent such as that. If you want to show that magicians are superior to armies, you will have to do it with magik alone. The military will not lift a finger to assist you."

As he spoke, he took the jug of wine from Aahz's unresisting fingers, a sign in itself that Aahz was as stunned by the general's words as I was.

"My feelings on this subject are very strong, gentlemen," Badaxe continued, pouring himself some wine. "So strong, in fact, I am willing to sacrifice myself and my kingdom to prove the point. What is more, I would strongly suggest that you do the same."

He paused, regarding us with those glittering eyes.

"...Because I tell you here and now, should you emerge victorious from the impending battle, you will not live to collect your reward. The king may rule the court, but word of what happens in the kingdom comes to him through my soldiers, and those soldiers will be posted along your return path to the palace, with orders to bring back word of your accidental demise, even if they have to arrange it. Do I make myself clear?"

VIII.

"Anything worth doing, is worth doing for a profit!"
TERICIUS

WITH A MASSIVE EFFORT of self-control, I contained myself not only after we had left the general's quarters, but until we were out of earshot of the honor guard. Even when I finally spoke, I managed to keep the tell-tale note of hysteria out of my voice which would have betrayed my true feelings.

"Like you said, Aahz," I commented casually, "there are armies and there are armies. Right?"

Aahz wasn't fooled for a minute.

"Hysterics won't get us anywhere, kid," he observed. "What we need is sound thinking."

"Excuse me," I said pointedly, "but isn't 'sound thinking' what got us into the mess in the first place?"

"Okay, okay!" Aahz grimaced. "I'll admit I made a few over-sights when I originally appraised the situation."

"A few oversights?" I echoed incredulously. "Aahz, this 'cushy job' you set me up for doesn't bear even the vaguest resemblance to what you described when you sold me on the idea."

"I know, kid," Aahz sighed. "I definitely owe you an apology. This sounds like it's actually going to be work."

"Work!" I shrieked, losing control slightly. "It's going to be suicide."

Aahz shook his head sadly.

"There you go overreacting again. It doesn't have to be suicide. We've got a choice, you know."

"Sure," I retorted sarcastically. "We can get killed by the invaders or we can get killed by Badaxe's boys. How silly of me not to have realized it. For a moment there I was getting worried."

"Our choice," Aahz corrected sternly, "is to go through with this lame-brained mission, or to take the money and run."

A ray of hope broke through the dismal gloom which had burdened my mind.

"Aahz," I said in genuine awe, "you're a genius. C'mon, let's get going."

"Get going where?" Aahz asked.

"Back to the inn of course," I replied. "The sooner the better."

"That wasn't one of our options," my mentor sneered.

"But you said…"

"I said 'take the money and run' not just 'run'," he corrected. "We aren't going anywhere until we've seen Grimble."

"But Aahz…"

"'But Aahz' nothing," he interrupted fiercely. "This little jaunt has cost us a bundle. We're going to at least make it break even, if not show a small profit."

"It hasn't cost us anything," I said bluntly.

"It cost us travel time and time away from your studies," Aahz countered. "That's worth something."

"But…"

"Besides," he continued loftily, "there are more important issues at stake here."

"Like what?" I pressed.

"Well…like, um…"

"There you are, gentlemen!"

We turned to find Grimble approaching us rapidly from behind.

"I was hoping to catch you after the briefing," the chancellor continued joining us. "Do you mind if I watch with you? I know you'll be eager to start off on your campaign, but there are certain matters we must discuss before you leave."

"Like our wages," Aahz supplied firmly. Grimble's smile froze.

"Oh! Yes, of course. First, however, there are other things to deal with. I trust the general supplied you with the necessary information for your mission."

"Down to the last gruesome detail," I confirmed.

"Good, good," the chancellor chortled, his enthusiasm undimmed by my sarcasm. "I have every confidence you'll be able to deal with the riff-raff from the North. I'll have you know you were my personal choice even before the interviews. In fact, I was the one responsible for sending you the invitation in the first place."

"We'll remember that," Aahz smiled, his eyes narrowing dangerously.

A thought occurred to me.

"Say…um, Lord Chancellor," I said casually, "how did you happen to hear of us in the first place?"

"Why do you ask?" Grimble countered.

"No special reason," I assured him. "But as the interview proved so fruitful, I would like to send a token of my gratitude to that person who spoke so highly of me to you."

It was a pretty flimsy story, but the chancellor seemed to accept it.

"Well...um, actually, it was a wench," he admitted. "Rather comely, but I don't recall her name just off hand. She may have dyed her hair since you met her. It was green at the time we...er...met. Do you know her?"

Indeed I did. There was only one woman who knew of Aahz and me, much less our whereabouts. Then again, there was only one woman I knew who fit the description of being voluptuous with green hair. Tanda!

I opened my mouth to acknowledge my recognition, when Aahz dug a warning elbow into my rib.

"Glah!" I said intelligently.

"How's that again?" Grimble inquired.

"I...um, I can't place the person, just off hand," I lied. "But you know how absent-minded we magicians are."

"Of course," the chancellor smiled, for some reason relieved.

"Now that that's settled," Aahz interrupted. "I believe you mentioned something about our wages."

Grimble scowled for a moment, then broke into a good-natured grin.

"I can see why Master Skeeve leaves his business dealings to you, Aahz," he conceded.

"Flattery's nice," Aahz observed, "but you can't spend it. The subject was our wages."

"You must realize we are a humble kingdom," Grimble sighed. "Though we try to reward our retainers as best we can. There have been quarters set aside for the court magician which should be spacious enough to accommodate both of you. Your meals will be provided...that is, of course, assuming you are on time when they are served. Also, there is a possibility...no, I'd go so far as to say a certainty that His Majesty's generosity will be extended to include free stable space and food for your unicorns. How does that sound?"

"So far, pretty cheap," Aahz observed bluntly.

"What do you mean, 'cheap'?" the chancellor snarled, losing his composure for a moment.

"What you've offered so far," Aahz sneered, "is a room we won't be sleeping in, meals we won't be eating, and stable space we won't be using because we'll be in the field fighting your war for you. In exchange, you want Skeeve here to use his skills to save your kingdom. By my calculations, that's cheap!"

"Yes, I see your point," Grimble conceded. "Well, there will, of course, be a small wage paid."

"How small?" Aahz pressed.

"Sufficient to cover your expenses," the chancellor smiled. "Shall we say fifty gold pieces a month?"

"Let's say two hundred," Aahz smiled back.

"Perhaps we could go as high as seventy-five," Grimble countered.

"And we'll come down to two-twenty-five," Aahz offered.

"Considering his skills, we could pay…excuse me," the chancellor clinked. "Did you say two-twenty-five?"

"Actually," Aahz conceded, "I misspoke."

"I thought so," Grimble smiled.

"I meant two-fifty."

"Now see here…" the chancellor began.

"Look, Grimble," Aahz met him halfway. "You had three choices. You could double the size of your army, hire a magician, or lose the kingdom. Even at three hundred a month, Skeeve here is your best deal. Don't look at what you're spending, look at what you're saving."

Grimble thought about it for a few moments.

"Very well," he said grimacing, "two-fifty it is."

"I believe the figure under discussion was three hundred," I observed pointedly.

That earned me a black look, but I stood my ground and returned his stare levelly.

"Three hundred," he said, forcing the words out through gritted teeth.

"Payable in advance," Aahz added.

"Payable at the end of the pay-period," Grimble corrected.

"C'mon, Grimble," Aahz began, but the chancellor inter-rupted him holding up his hand.

"No! On that point I must remain inflexible," he insisted. "Everyone in the Royal Retinue is paid at the same time, when the vaults are opened at the end of the pay period. If we break that rule and start allowing exceptions, there will be no end to it."

"Can you at least give us a partial advance?" Aahz pressed. "Something to cover expenses on the upcoming campaign?"

"Definitely not!" Grimble retorted. "If I paid out monies for services not yet rendered, certain people, specifically Hugh Badaxe, would suspect you intended to take the money and flee without entering battle at all!"

That hit uncomfortably close to home, and I found myself averting my eyes for fear of betraying my guilt. Aahz, however, never even blinked.

"What about bribes?" he asked.

Grimble scowled.

"It is unthinkable that one of the King's retainers would accept a bribe, much less count on it as part of his income. Any attempt to bribe you should be reported immediately to His Majesty!"

"Not taking bribes, Grimble," Aahz snarled. "Giving them. When we give money out to the enemy, does that come out of our wages, or does the kingdom pay for it?"

"I seriously doubt you could buy off the army facing you," the chancellor observed skeptically. "Besides, you're supposed to carry the day with magik. That's what we're paying you for."

"Even magik is aided by accurate information," Aahz replied pointedly. "C'mon Grimble, you know court intrigue. A little advance warning can go a long way in any battle."

"True enough," the chancellor admitted. "Very well, I guess we can give you an allowance for bribes, assuming it will be kept within reason."

"How much in reason?" Aahz inquired.

"Say…five gold pieces."

"Twenty-five would…"

"Five!" Grimble said firmly.

Aahz studied his adversary for a moment, then sighed.

"Five," he said, extending his palm.

The chancellor grudgingly dug into his purse and counted out five gold pieces. In fact, he counted them twice before passing them to Aahz.

"You realize of course," he warned, "I will require an accounting of those funds after your victory."

"Of course," Aahz smiled, fondling the coins.

"You seem very confident of our victory, Lord Chancellor," I observed.

Grimble regarded me with cocked eyebrow for a moment.

"Of course I am confident, Lord Magician," he said at last. "So confident, I have staked my kingdom, and, more importantly, my reputation on your success. You will note I rate my reputation above the kingdom. That is no accident. Kingdoms rise and fall, but a chancellor can always find employment. That is, of course, providing it was not his advice which brought the kingdom to ruin. Should you fail in your campaign to save Possiltum, my career is finished. If that should happen, gentlemen, your career falls with mine."

"That has the sound of a threat to it, Grimble," Aahz observed dryly.

"Does it?" the chancellor responded with mock innocence. "That was not my intent. I am not threatening; I am stating a fact. I maintain very close contact with the chancellors of all of the surrounding kingdoms; in fact, I am related to several. They are all aware of my position in this magik-vs.-the-military issue. Should I prove wrong in my judgement, should you fail in your defense of Possiltum, they will note it. Thereafter, any magician—and you specifically, Skeeve—will be denounced as a fraud and a charlatan should you seek further employment. In fact, as the chancellors frequently control the courts, I would not be surprised if they found an excuse or a trumped-up charge which would allow them to have you put to death as a favor to me. The method of death varies from kingdom to kingdom, but the end result is the same. I trust you will keep that in mind as you plan your campaign."

With that, he turned on his heel and strode away, leaving us standing in silence.

"Well, Aahz," I said finally. "Do you have any sound advice on our situation now?"

"Of course," he retorted.

"What?" I asked.

"Now that we've got the whole story," he said solemnly, "*now* you can panic."

IX.

"There is more at stake here than our lives."
COL. TRAVIS
Alamo Pep Talk

ON THE THIRD night after leaving Possiltum's capital, we camped on a small knoll overlooking the kingdom's main north-south trail.

Actually, I use the phase "north-south" rather loosely in this instance. In three days travel, our progress was the only northward movement we had observed on this particular strip of beaten dirt. The dearth of northbound traffic was emphasized by the high volume of people bound in the opposite direction.

As we traveled, we were constantly encountering small groups and families picking their way steadily toward the capital in that unhurried yet ground-eating pace which typifies people accustomed to traveling without means of transport other than their feet. They did not seem particularly frightened or panicky, but two common characteristics marked them all as being more than casual travelers.

First, the great number of personal effects they carried was far in excess of that required for a simple pilgrimage. Whether bound in cumbersome backpacks or heaped in small, hand-pushed carts, it was obvious the southbound travelers were bringing with them as many of their worldly possessions as they could carry or drag.

Second, no one paid us any heed other than a passing glance. This was even more noteworthy than the prior observation.

Currently, our party consisted of three: myself, Aahz, and Gleep. We had left Buttercup at the palace, much to Aahz's disgust. He would have preferred to leave Gleep and bring Buttercup, but the royal orders had been firm on this point. The dragon was not to remain at the palace unless one or both of us also stayed behind to handle him. As a result, we traveled as a trio: a youth, a dragon, and a grumbling demon, not exactly a common sight in these or any other parts. The peasants flowing south, however, barely noticed us other than to give us clear road space when we passed.

Aahz maintained that this was because whatever they were running from inspired such fear that they barely noted anything or anybody in their path. He further surmised that the motivating force for this exodus could only be the very army we were on our way to oppose.

To prove his point, we attempted to question several of the groups when we encountered them. We stopped doing this after the first day due to the redundant similarities of the replies we received.

Sample:

Aahz: Hold, stranger! Where are you going?

Answer: To the capital!

Aahz: Why?

Answer: To be as near as possible to the king when he makes his defense against the invaders from the North. He'll have to try to save himself even if he won't defend the outlands.

Aahz: Citizen, you need flee no more. You have underestimated you king's concern for your safety. You see before you the new court magician, retained by His Majesty specially for the purpose of defending Possiltum from the invading army. What say you to that?

Answer: One magician?

Aahz: With my own able assistance, of course.

Answer: I say you are crazy.

Aahz: Now look…

Answer: No, *you* look, whoever or whatever you are. Meaning no disrespect to this or any other magician, you're fools to oppose that army. Magik may be well and good against an ordinary force, but you aren't going to stop that army with one magician…or twenty magicians for that matter.

Aahz: We have every confidence…

Answer: Fine, then you go north. Me, I'm heading for the capital!

Though this exchange had eventually quelled our efforts to reassure the populace, it had given rise to an argument which was still unresolved as we prepared to sleep on the third night.

"What happened to your plan to take the money and run?" I grumbled.

"Big deal," Aahz shot back. "Five whole gold pieces."

"You said you wanted a profit," I pressed. "Okay! We've got one. So it's small…but so was the effort we put into it. Considering we didn't spend anything…"

"What about the unicorn?" Aahz countered. "While they're still holding the unicorn, we've lost money on the deal."

"Aahz," I reminded him. "Buttercup didn't cost us anything, remember? He was a gift from Quigley."

"It would cost money to replace him," Aahz insisted. "That means that we lost money on the deal unless we get him back. I've told you, I want a profit…and definitely refuse to accept a loss."

"Gleep?"

Aahz's heated words had awakened my dragon, who raised his head in sleepy inquiry.

"Go back to sleep, Gleep," I said soothingly. "Everything's all right."

Reassured, he rolled onto his back and laid his head back.

Ridiculous as he looked, lying there with his four legs sticking up in the air, he had reminded me of something.

I pondered the memory for a moment, then decided to change my tactics.

"Aahz," I said thoughtfully, "what's the real reason for your wanting to go through with this?"

"Weren't you listening, kid? I said—"

"I know, I know," I interrupted. "You said it was for the profit. The only thing wrong with that is you tried to leave Gleep behind, who cost us money, instead of Buttercup, who didn't cost us anything! That doesn't ring true if you're trying to show a profit with the least possible effort."

"…Um, you know how I feel about that stupid dragon…" Aahz began.

"…And you know how I feel about him," I interrupted, "As such, you also know I'd never abandon him to save my own skin, much less for money. For some reason, you wanted to be sure I'd see this thing through…and that reason has nothing at all to do with money. Now, what is it?"

It was Aahz's turn to lapse into thoughtful silence.

"You're getting better at figuring things out, kid," he said finally.

Normally, I would have been happy to accept the compliment. This time, however, I saw it as what it was, an attempt to distract me.

"The reason, Aahz," I said firmly.

"There are several reasons, kid," he said with uncharacter-istic solemnness. "The main one is that you're not a master magician yet."

"If you don't mind my saying so," I commented drily, "that

doesn't make a whole lot of sense. If I'm short on ability, why are you so eager to shove me into this mission?"

"Hear me out, kid," Aahz said, raising a restraining hand. "I made a mistake, and that mistake has dumped us into a situation that needs a master magician. More than a master magician's abilities, we need a master magician's conscience. Do you follow me?"

"No," I admitted.

"Not surprising," Aahz sighed. "That's why I tried to trick you into completing this mission instead of explaining it. So far, all your training has been on physical abilities without developing your professional conscience."

"You've taught me to keep one eye on the profits," I pointed out defensively.

"That's not what I mean, kid. Look, forget about profitsfor a minute."

"Are you feeling okay, Aahz?" I asked with genuine concern. "You don't sound like yourself at all."

"Will you get off my back, kid?" he snarled. "I'm trying to explain something important!"

I sank into a cowed silence. Still, I was reassured. Aahz was definitely Aahz.

"When you were apprenticed to Garkin," Aahz began, "and even when you first met me, you didn't want to be a magician. You wanted to be a thief. To focus your energies behind your lessons, I had to stress how much benefit you could reap from learning magik."

He paused. I didn't say anything. There was nothing to say. He was right, both in his recollections and his interpretation of them.

"Well," he sighed. "There's another side to magik. There's a responsibility...a responsibility to your fellow practitioners, and, more importantly, to magik itself. Even though we have rivals and will probably acquire more if we live that long, and even though we may fight with them or beat them out for a job, we are all bound by a common cause. Every magician has a duty to promote magik, to see that its use is respected and reputable. The greater the magician, the greater his sense of duty."

"What's that got to do with our current situation?" I prompted.

"There's an issue at stake here, kid," he answered carefully. "You heard it from Badaxe and Grimble both. More importantly, you heard it from the populace when we talked to the peasants. Rodrick is gambling his entire kingdom on the ability of magik to do a job. Now, no one but a magician can tell how reasonable or unreasonable a task that might be. If we fail, all the laymen will see is that magik failed, and they'll never trust it again. That's why we can't walk away from this mission. We're here representing magik…and we've got to give it our best shot."

I thought about that for a few moments.

"But what can we do against a whole army?" I asked finally.

"To be honest with you," Aahz sighed. "I really don't know. I'm hoping we can come up with an idea after we've seen exactly what it is we're up against."

We sat silently together for a long time after that, each lost in our own thoughts of the mission and what was at stake.

X.

"One need not fear superior numbers if the opposing force has been properly scouted and appraised."
S. BULL

MY LAST VESTIGE of hope was squashed when we finally sighted the army. Reports of its massive size had not been overstated; if anything, they had failed to express the full impact of the force's might.

Our scouting mission had taken us across Possiltum's northern border and several days' journey into its neighbor's interior. The name of this kingdom was inconsequential. If it was not already considered part of the new Empire, it would be as soon as the news spread.

We weren't sure if we had just missed the last battle, or if the kingdom had simply surrendered. Whichever the case, there were no defending troops in evidence, just large encampments of the Empire's forces spread out in a rough line which disappeared over the horizon in either direction.

Fortunately, the army was not currently on the move, which made our scouting considerably easier. There were sentries posted at regular intervals all along the front line, but as they were not more than a given distance from the encampments, we simply traversed the line without approaching them too closely, and thus escaped detection.

Periodically, we would creep closer to an encampment or climb a tree to improve our view. Aahz seemed very absorbed in his own thoughts, both when we were actually viewing the troops and as we were traveling to new locations. Since I couldn't get more than an occasional grunt or monosyllable out of him, I occupied myself making my own observations.

The soldiers were clothed roughly the same. Standard equipment seemed to include a leather helmet and breastplate, a rough knee-length cloth tunic, sandals, sword, two javelins, and a large rectangular shield. Apparently they were not planning to move immediately, for they had pitched their tents and spent most of their time sharpening weapons, repairing armor, eating, or simply lolling about. Occasionally, a metal-encrusted soldier, presumably an officer, would appear and shout at the others, whereupon they would listlessly form ranks and drill. Their practice would usually grind to a halt as soon as the officer passed from view.

There were occasional pieces of siege equipment designed to throw large rocks or spears long distances, though we never saw them in operation. The only pieces of equipment which seemed to be used with any regularity were the signal towers. Each encampment had one of these, a rickety affair of lashed-together poles stretching roughly twenty feet in the air and surmounted by a small, square platform. Several times a day, one soldier in each encampment would mount one of these structures, and they would signal to each other with pendants or standards, The towers also did duty as clotheslines, and were periodically draped with drying tunics.

All in all, it looked like an incredibly boring existence. In fact, from my appraisal, the only thing duller than being a soldier of the Empire was spending days on end watching soldiers of the Empire!

I commented on this to Aahz as we lay belly-down on a grassy knoll, surveying yet another encampment.

"You're right, kid," he admitted absently. "Being a soldier is pretty dull work."

"How about us?" I probed, eager to keep him talking. "What we're doing isn't exactly exciting, you know!"

"You want excitement?" he asked, focusing on me for the first time in days. "Tell you what. Why don't you just stroll down there and ask the Officer of the Day for a quick run down on how their army operates? I bet that'll liven things up for you."

"I'm not that bored!" I amended hastily.

"Then what say you just keep quiet and let me do this my way," Aahz smiled and resumed his studies.

"Do what your way?" I persisted. "Exactly what is it we're trying to accomplish, anyway?"

Aahz sighed.

"We're scouting the enemy," he explained patiently. "We've got enough going against us on this campaign without rushing in uninformed."

"How much information do we need?" I grumbled. "This encampment doesn't look any different than the last five we looked at."

"That's because you don't know what you're looking for," Aahz scoffed. "What have you learned so far about the opposition?"

I wasn't ready for the question but I rose gamely to the challenge.

"Um...there are a lot of them...they're well armed...um...and they have catapults..."

"That's all?" Aahz sneered. "Brilliant! You and Badaxe make a great team of tacticians."

"Okay, so teach me!" I shot back. "What have you learned?"

"You can spend years trying to learn military theory without scratching the surface," my mentor replied sternly. "But I'll try to give you the important parts in a nutshell. To appraise a force, such as we're doing now, remember two words: 'Sam' and 'Doc'."

"'Sam' and 'Doc'," I repeated dutifully.

"Some folks prefer to remember 'Salute' but I like 'Sam' and 'Doc'," Aahz added as an aside.

"Terrific," I grimaced. "Now tell me what it means."

"They're initials to remember an information checklist," Aahz confided. "'Salute' stands for Size, Activity, Location, Unit, Time, and Equipment. That's fine as far as it goes, but it assumes no judgmental ability on the part of the scout. I prefer 'Sam' and 'Doc'. That stands for Strength, Armament, Movement, and Deployment, Organization, and Communications."

"Oh," I said, hoping he wasn't expecting me to remember all this.

"Now, using that framework," Aahz continued, "let's summarize what we've seen so far. Size: there are lots of them, enough so it's kind of pointless to try for an exact count. Movement: currently, they're just sitting there."

"I got that far all by myself," I pointed out sarcastically.

"The big key, however," Aahz continued ignoring me, "is in their Armament and Equipment. When you look at this, consider both what is there and what isn't."

"How's that again?" I asked.

"What's there is a lot of foot-schloggers, infantry, a little artillery in the form of catapults and archers, but nothing even vaguely resembling cavalry. That means they're going to be slow when they move, particularly in battle. We don't have to worry about any fast flanking moves, it'll be a toe-to-toe slugfest."

"But, Aahz..." I began.

"As to the Deployment and Organization," he pushed on undaunted, "they're strung out all over the place, probably because it's easier to forage for food that way. Then again, it displays a certain confidence on their part that they don't feel it's necessary to mass their forces. I think we're looking at their Organization, a collection of companies or battalions, each under the leadership of two or three officers, all under the guidance of a super-leader or general."

"Aahz..." I tried again.

"Communications seems to be their most vulnerable point," Aahz pushed on doggedly. "If an army this size doesn't coordinate its movements, it's in big trouble. If they're really using signal towers and runners to pass messages, we might be able to jinx the works for them."

"All of which means what?" I interrupted finally.

"Hmm? Oh, that's a capsule summary of what we're up against," Aahz replied innocently.

"I know. I know," I sighed. "But for days you've been saying you'll formulate a plan after you've seen what we're up against. Well, you've seen it. What's the plan? How can we beat 'em?"

"There's no way, kid," Aahz admitted heavily. "If I had seen one, I would have told you, but I haven't, and that's why I keep looking."

"Maybe there isn't one," I suggested cautiously.

Aahz sighed.

"I'm starting to think you're right. If so, that means we'll have to do something I really don't want to do."

"You mean give up?" I said genuinely startled, "After that big speech you gave me about responsibility and..."

"Whoa," Aahz interrupted. "I didn't say anything about giving up. What we're going to do is..."

"Gleep!"

The unmistakable sound came to us from behind, rolling up the hill from the brush filled gully where we'd left my pet.

"Kid," Aahz moaned, "will you keep that stupid dragon quiet? All we need now is to have him pull the army down our necks."

"Right, Aahz!" I agreed, worming away backwards as fast as I could.

As soon as I was clear of the crest of the hill, I rose to a low crouch and scuttled down the slope in that position. Crawling is neither a fast nor a comfortable means of travel.

As per our now-normal procedure, we had tethered Gleep to a tree...a large tree, after he had successfully uprooted several small ones. Needless to say, he wasn't wild about the idea, but it was necessary considering the delicate nature of our current work.

"Gleep!"

I could see him now, eagerly straining at the end of his rope. Surprisingly, however, for a change he wasn't trying to get to me. In fact, he was trying his best to get at a large bush which stood some distance from his tree...or at something hidden in the bush!

Cold sweat suddenly popped out on my brow. It occurred to me that Gleep might have been discovered by one of the enemy army scouts. That would be bad enough, but even worse was the possibility said scout might still be around.

I hurriedly stepped sideways into the shadow of a tree and reviewed the situation. I hadn't actually seen a scout. In fact, there was no movement at all in the indicated bush. I could sneak back and get Aahz, but if I were wrong he wouldn't be very happy over being called to handle a false alarm. I could set Gleep loose and let him find the intruder, but that would mean exposing myself.

As I stood debating my next course of action, someone slipped up behind me and put their hands over my eyes.

"Surprise!" came a soft voice in my ear.

XI.

"Should old acquaintance be forgot…"
COUNT OF MONTE CRISTO

I JUMPED!

Perhaps I should clarify. When I say, "I jumped," I mean I really jumped. Over a year ago, Aahz had taught me to fly, which is actually controlled hovering caused by reverse levitation.

Whatever it was, I did it. I went straight up in the air about ten feet and stayed there. I didn't know what had snuck up behind me, and didn't want to know. I wanted help! I wanted Aahz!

I drew a mighty breath to express this desire.

"Kinda jumpy, aren't you, handsome?"

That penetrated my panic.

Stifling my shout before it truly began, I looked down on my attacker. From my vantage point, I was treated to a view of a gorgeous golden-olive-complected face, accented by almond-cat eyes, framed by a magnificent tumble of light green hair. I could also see a generous expanse of cleavage.

"Tanda!" I crowed with delight, forcing my eyes back to her face.

"Do you mind coming down?" she called. "I can't come up."

I considered swooping down on her dramatically, but decided against it. I'm still not all that good at flying, and the effect would be lost completely if I crashed into her.

Instead, I settled for lowering myself gently to the ground a few paces from her.

"Gee, Tanda, I…glack!"

The last was squeezed forcefully from me as she swept me into a bone-crushing embrace.

"Gee, it's good to see you, handsome," she murmured happily. "How have you been?"

"I *was* fine," I noted, untangling myself briefly. "What are you doing here?"

The last time I had seen her, Tanda was part of the ill-fated group Aahz and I had seen off to dimensions unknown. Of the whole crowd, she had been the only one I was sorry to see go.

"I'm waiting for you, silly," she teased, slipping an affectionate arm around my waist. "Where's Aahz?"

"He's…" I started to point up the hill when a thought occurred to me. "Say…how did you know I had Aahz with me?"

"Oh! Don't get mad," she scolded, giving me a playful shake. "It stands to reason. Even Aahz wouldn't let you face that army alone."

"But how did you…"

"Gleep!"

My dragon had discovered his quarry was no longer hiding behind the bush. As a result, he was now straining at the end of his rope trying to reach us. The tree he was tethered to was swaying dangerously.

"Gleep!" Tanda called in a delighted voice. "How are ya, fella?"

The tree dipped to a new low as my dragon quivered with glee at having been recognized. I was quivering a little myself. Tanda has that affect on males.

Heedless of her own safety, Tanda bounded forward to kneel before the dragon, pulling his whiskers and scratching his nose affectionately.

Gleep loved it. I loved it, too. In addition to her usual soft, calf-high boots, Tanda was wearing a short green tunic which hugged her generous curves and showed off her legs just swell. What's more, when she knelt down like that, the hem rode up until…

"What's wrong with that dragon?!" Aahz boomed, bursting out of the brush behind me.

This time I didn't jump…much.

"Gee, Aahz," I began. "It's…"

I needn't have bothered trying to explain.

Tanda uncoiled and came past me in a bound.

"Aahz!" she exclaimed, flinging herself into his arms.

For a change, my mentor was caught as flat-footed as I had been. For a moment, the tangle of arms teetered on the brink of collapse, then down it went.

They landed with a resounding thump, Aahz on the bottom and therefore soaking up most of the impact.

"Still impulsive, aren't you?" Tanda leered.

"Whoosh…hah…ah…" Aahz responded urbanely.

Tanda rolled to her feet and began rearranging her tunic.

"At least I don't have to ask if you're glad to see me," she observed.

"Tanda!" Aahz gasped at last.

"You remembered?" Tanda beamed.

"She's been waiting for us, Aahz," I supplied brightly.

"That's right!" Aahz scowled. "Grimble said you set us up for this job."

Tanda winced.

"I can explain that," she said apologetically.

"I can hardly wait," Aahz intoned.

"I'm kind of curious about that myself," I added.

"Um…this could take a while, guys," she said thoughtfully. "Got anything around to drink?"

That was easily the most reasonable question asked so far today. We broke out the wine, and in no time were sitting around in a small circle quenching our thirst. Much to Aahz's disgust, I insisted we sit close enough to Gleep that he not be left out. This meant, of course, his rather aromatic breath flavored our discussion, but, as I pointed out, it was the only way to keep him quiet while we talked.

"What happened after you left?" I prodded. "Where are Isstvan and Brockhurst and Higgins? What happened to Quigley? Did they ever bring Frumple back to life, or is he still a statue?"

"Later, kid," Aahz interrupted. "First things first. You were about to explain about Grimble."

"Grimble," Tanda responded wrinkling her nose. "Did you ever notice the 'crookeder' a person is, the more possessive he is? He's the main reason I didn't wait for you at Possiltum."

"From the beginning," Aahz instructed.

"From the beginning," Tanda pursed her lips thoughtfully. "Well, I picked him up in a singles bar…he's married, but I didn't know that till later."

"What's a singles bar?" I interrupted.

"Shut up, kid," Aahz snarled.

"Well, it wasn't actually a singles bar," Tanda corrected. "It was more of a tavern. I should have known he was married. I mean, nobody that young is that bald unless he's got a wife at home."

"Skip the philosophy," Aahz moaned. "Just tell us the story, huh?"

Tanda cocked an eyebrow at him.

"You know, Aahz," she accused, "for someone as long- winded as you are when it comes to telling stories, you're awfully impatient when it comes to listening to someone else."

"And when he mentioned idiots," I supplied, "naturally you thought of us."

"Now, don't be that way," Tanda scolded. "I thought it was a good way to help out a couple friends. I knew you two were hanging out in this neck of the woods...and everybody knows what a cushy job being a court magician is."

"What did I tell you, kid?" Aahz commented.

"We must be talking about different jobs," I retorted.

"Hey," Tanda interrupted, laying a soft hand on my arm. "When I gave him your names, I didn't know about the invading army. Honest!"

My anger melted away at her touch. Right then, she could have told me she had sold my head as a centerpiece and I would have forgiven her.

"Well..." I began, but she persisted, which was fine by me.

"As soon as I found out what the real story was, I knew I had gotten you into a tight spot," she said with soft sincerity. "Like I said, I would have waited at Possiltum, but I was afraid, what with your disguises and all, that you'd recognize me before I spotted you. If you gave me the kind of greeting I've grown to expect, it could have really queered the deal. Grimble's a jealous twit, and if he thought we were more than nodding acquain-tances, he would of held back whatever support he might normally give."

"Big deal," Aahz grumbled. "Five whole gold pieces."

"That much?" Tanda sounded honestly surprised. "Which arm did you break?"

"Aahz always gets us the best possible deal," I said proudly. "At least, monetarily."

"Well," Tanda concluded, "at least I won't dig into your war funds. When I found out the mess I had gotten you into, I decided I'd work this one for free. Since I got you into it, the least I can do is help get you out."

"That's terrific," I exclaimed.

"It sure is!" Aahz agreed.

Something in his voice annoyed me.

"I meant that she was helping us," I snarled. "Not that she was doing it for free."

"That's what I meant, too, apprentice," Aahz glowered back. "But unlike some, I know what I'm talking about!"

"Boys, boys," Tanda said, separating us with her hands. "We're on the same side. Remember?"

"Gleep!" said the dragon, siding with Tanda.

As I have said, Gleep's breath is powerful enough to stop any conversation, and it was several minutes before the air cleared enough for us to continue.

"Before we were so rudely interrupted," Tanda gasped at last. "You were starting to say something, Aahz. Have you got a plan?"

"Now I do," Aahz smiled, chucking her under the chin. "And believe me, it would have been rough to do it without you."

That had an anxious sound to it. Tanda's main calling, at least the only one mentionable in polite company, was as an Assassin.

"C'mon, Aahz," I chided. "Tanda's good, but she's not good enough to take on a whole army."

"Don't bet on it, handsome," she corrected, winking at me.

I blushed, but continued with my argument.

"I still say the job's too big for one person, or three people for that matter," I insisted.

"You're right, kid," Aahz said solemnly.

"We just can't...what did you say, Aahz?"

"I said you were right," Aahz repeated.

"I thought so," I marveled. "I just wanted to hear it again."

"You'd hear it more often if you were right more often," Aahz pointed out.

"C'mon, Aahz," Tanda interrupted. "What's the plan?"

"Like the kid says," Aahz said loftily, "we need more help. We need an army of our own."

"But Aahz," I reminded him, "Badaxe said..."

"Who said anything about Badaxe?" Aahz replied innocently. "We're supposed to win this war with magik, aren't we? Well fine. With Tanda on our team, we've got a couple extra skills to draw on. Remember?"

I remembered. I remembered Aahz saying he wasn't worried about Tanda leaving with Isstvan because she could travel the dimensions by herself if things got rough. The light began to dawn.

"You mean…"

"That's right, kid," Aahz smiled. "We're going back to Deva. We're going to recruit a little invasionary force of our own!"

XII.

"This is no game for old men! Send in the boys!"
W. HAYES

I DON'T KNOW how Tanda transported us from my home dimension of Klah to Deva. If I did, we wouldn't have needed her. All I know is that at the appropriate time she commenced to chant and shift her shoulders (a fascinating process in itself), and we were there.

"There," in this case, was at the Bazaar at Deva. That phrase alone, however, does not begin to describe our new surroundings as they came into focus.

A long time ago, the dimension of Deva had undergone an economic collapse. To survive, the Deveels (whom I once knew as devils) used their ability to travel the dimensions and became merchants. Through the process of natural selection, the most successful Deveels were not the best fighters, but the best traders. Now, after countless generations of this process, the Deveels were acknowledged as the best merchants in all the dimensions. They were also acknowledged as being the shrewdest, coldest, most profit-hungry cheats ever to come down the pipe.

The Bazaar at Deva was their showcase. It was an all-day, all-night, year-round fair where the Deveels met to haggle with each other over the wares fetched back from the various dimensions. Though it was originally established and maintained by Deveels, it was not unusual to find travelers from many dimensions shopping the endless rows of displays and booths. The rule of thumb was "If it's to be found anywhere, you'll find it at the Bazaar at Deva."

I had been here once before with Aahz. At the time, we were searching for a surprise weapon to use against Isstvan. What we ended up with was Gleep and Tanda! Distractions abound at the Bazaar.

I mention this, in part, to explain why, as unusual as our foursome must have appeared, no one paid us the slightest attention as we stood watching the kaleidoscope of activity whirling about us.

Gleep pressed against me for reassurance, momentarily taken aback at the sudden change of surroundings. I ignored him. My first visit to this place had been far too brief for my satisfaction. As such,

I was rubber-necking madly trying to see as much as possible as fast as possible.

Tanda was more businesslike.

"Now that we're here, Aahz," she drawled, "do you know where we're going?"

"No," Aahz admitted. "But I'll find out right now."

Without further warning, he casually reached out and grabbed the arm of the nearest passerby, a short ugly fellow with tusks. Spinning his chosen victim around, Aahz bent to scowl in his face.

"You!" he snarled. "Do you like to fight?"

For a moment my heart stopped. All we needed now was to get into a brawl.

Fortunately, instead of producing a weapon, the tusker gave ground a step and eyed our party suspiciously.

"Not with a Pervert backed by a dragon, I don't," he retorted cautiously.

"Good!" Aahz smiled. "Then if you wanted to hire someone to do your fighting for you, where would you go?"

"To the Bazaar at Deva," the tusker shrugged.

"I know that!" Aahz snarled, "but where at the Bazaar?"

"Oh," the tusker exclaimed with sudden understanding. "About twenty rows in that direction, then turn right for another thirty or so. That's where the mercenaries hang out."

"Twenty, then up thirty," Aahz repeated carefully. "Thanks."

"A finder's fee would be appreciated more than any thanks," the tusker smiled, extending a palm.

"You're right!" Aahz agreed, and turned his back on our benefactor.

The tusker hesitated for a moment, then shrugged and continued on his way. I could have told him that Pervects in general and Aahz specifically are not noted for their generosity. "We go twenty rows that way, then up thirty," Aahz informed us.

"Yea, we heard," Tanda grimaced. "Why didn't you just ask him flat out?"

"My way is quicker," Aahz replied smugly.

"It is?" I asked skeptically.

"Look, kid," Aahz scowled. "Do you want to lead us through this zoo?"

"Well…" I retreated.

"Then shut up and let me do it, okay?"

Actually, I was more than willing to let Aahz lead the way to wherever it was we were going. For one thing, it kept him busy navigating a path through the crowd. For another, it left me with next to nothing to do except marvel at the sights of the Bazaar as I followed along in his wake.

Try as I might, though, there was just too much for one set of eyes to see.

In one booth, two Deveels argued with an elephant-headed being over a skull. At least, I think it was a skull. In another, a Deveel was putting on a demonstration for a mixed group of shoppers, summoning clouds of floating green bubbles from a tiny wooden box.

At one point, our path was all but blocked by a booth selling rings which shot bolts of lightning. Between the salesman's demonstrations and the customers trying out their purchases, the way was virtually impassible.

Aahz and Tanda never broke stride, however, confidently maintaining their pace as they walked through the thick of the bolts. Miraculously, they passed through unscathed.

Gritting my teeth, I seized one of Gleep's ears and followed in their footsteps. Again, the bolts of energy failed to find us. Apparently no Deveel would bring injury or allow anyone in his shop to bring injury to a potential customer. It was a handy fact to know.

The lightning rings brought something else to mind, however. The last time we parted company with Tanda, Aahz had given her a ring that shot a heat ray capable of frying a man-sized target on the spot. That's right...I said he *gave* it to her. You might think this was proof of the depth of his feelings for her. It's my theory he was sick. Anyway, I was reminded of the ring and curious as to what had become of it.

Increasing my pace slightly, I closed the distance between myself and the pair in the lead, only to find they were already engrossed in a heavy conversation. The din which prevails at the Bazaar stymies any attempt at serious eavesdropping, but I managed to catch occasional bits and pieces of the conversation as we walked.

"...heard...awfully expensive, aren't they?" Tanda was saying.

"...lick their weight in..." Aahz replied smugly. I moved in a little closer, trying to hear better.

"…makes you think they've got anyone here?" Tanda asked.

"With the number of bars here?" Aahz retorted, "The way I hear it, this is one of their main…"

I lost the rest of that argument. A knee-high, tentacled mess suddenly scuttled across my boots and ducked through a tent flap, closely pursued by two very frustrated-looking Deveels.

I ignored the chase and the following screams, hurrying to catch up with Aahz and Tanda again. Apparently they were discussing mercenaries, and I wanted to hear as much as possible, both to further my education, and because I might have to lead them into battle eventually.

"…find them?" Tanda was asking. "All we have is a general area."

"…easy," Aahz replied confidently. "Just listen for the singing."

"Singing?" Tanda was skeptical.

"It's their trademark." Aahz pronounced. "It also lands them in most of their…"

A Deveel stepped in front of me, proudly displaying a handful of seeds. He threw them on the ground with a flourish, and a dense black thornbush sprang up to block my path. Terrific. Normally, I would have been fascinated, but at the moment I was in a hurry.

Without even pausing to upbraid the Deveel, I took to the air, desperation giving wings to my feet…desperation assisted by a little levitation. I cleared the thornbush easily, and touched down lightly on the far side, only to be nearly trampled by Gleep as he burst through the barrier.

"Gleep?" he said, cocking his head at me curiously.

I picked myself up from the dust where I had been knocked by his enthusiasm and cuffed him.

"Watch where you're going next time," I ordered angrily.

He responded by snaking out his long tongue and licking my face. His breath was devastating and his tongue left a trail of slime. Obviously my admonishment had terrified him.

Heaving a deep sigh, I sprinted off after Aahz with Gleep lumbering along in hot pursuit.

I was just overtaking them, when Aahz stopped suddenly in his tracks and started to turn. Unable to halt my headlong sprint, I plowed into him, knocking him sprawling.

"In a hurry, handsome?" Tanda asked, eyeing me slyly.

"Gee, Aahz," I stammered bending over him, "I didn't mean to…"

From a half sitting position, his hand lashed out in a cuff that spun me half way around.

"Watch where you're going next time," he growled.

"Gleep!" said the dragon and licked my face.

Either my head was spinning more than I thought, or I had been through this scene before.

"Now quit clowning around and listen, kid."

Aahz was on his feet again, and all business.

"Here's where we part company for a while. You wait here while I go haggle with the mercenaries."

"Gee, Aahz," I whined. "Can't I…"

"No you can't!" he said firmly. "The crew I'm going after is sharp. All we need is one of your dumb questions in the middle of negotiations and they'll triple their prices."

"But…" I began.

"You will wait here," Aahz ordered. "I repeat, wait. No fights, no window shopping for dragons, just wait!"

"I'll stay here with him, Aahz," Tanda volunteered.

"Good," Aahz nodded. "And try to keep him out of trouble, okay?"

With that, he turned and disappeared into the crowd. Actually, I wasn't too disappointed. I mean, I would have liked to have gone with him, but I liked having some time alone with Tanda even more…that is, if you can consider standing in the middle of the Bazaar at Deva being alone with someone.

"Well, Tanda," I said, flashing my brightest smile.

"Later, handsome," she replied briskly. "Right now I've got some errands to run."

"Errands?" I blinked.

"Yea. Aahz is big on manpower, but I'd just as soon have a few extra tricks up my sleeve in case the going gets rough," she explained. "I'm going to duck over to the Special Effects section and see what they have in stock."

"Okay," I agreed. "Let's go."

"No you don't," she said shaking her head. "I think I'd better go this one alone. The kind of places I have in mind aren't fit for civilized customers. You and the dragon wait here."

"But you're supposed to be keeping me out of trouble!" I argued.

"And that's why I'm not taking you along," she smiled, "Now, what do you have along, in the way of weaponry?"

"Well…" I said hesitantly, "there's a sort of a sword in one of Gleep's packs."

"Fine!" she said. "Get it out and wear it. It'll keep the riff-raff at a distance. Then…um…wait for me in there!"

She pointed at a dubious-looking stone structure with a peeling sign on its front.

"What is it?" I asked, peering at it suspiciously.

"It's a 'Yellow Crescent Inn,'" she explained. "It's sort of a restaurant. Get yourself something to eat. The food's unappe-tizing, but vaguely digestible."

I studied the place for a moment.

"Actually," I decided finally, "I think I'd rather…"

Right about there I discovered I was talking to myself. Tanda had disappeared without a trace.

For the second time in my life I was alone in the Bazaar at Deva.

XIII.

"Hold the pickles, hold the lettuce."
HENRY VIII

FASCINATING AS THE Bazaar is, facing it alone can be rather frightening.

As such, I decided to follow Tanda's advice and entered the inn.

First, however, I took the precaution of tethering Gleep to the inn's hitching post and unpacking the sword. We had one decent sword. Unfortunately, Aahz was currently wearing it. That left me with Garkin's old sword, a weapon which has been sneered at by demon and demon hunter alike. Still, its weight was reassuring on my hip, though it might have been more reassuring if I had known anything about how to handle it. Unfortunately, my lessons with Aahz to date had not included swordsmanship. I could only hope it would not be apparent to the casual observer that this was my first time wearing a sword.

Pausing in the door, I surveyed the inn's interior. Unaccustomed as I was to gracious dining, I realized in a flash that this wasn't it.

One of the few pieces of advice my farmer-father had given me before I ran away from home was not to trust any inn or restaurant that appeared overly clean. He maintained that the cleaner a place was, the more dubious the quality and origin of their food would be. If he were even vaguely right, this inn must be the bottom of the barrel. It was not only clean, it gleamed.

I do not mean that figuratively. Harsh overhead lights glinted off a haphazard arrangement of tiny tables and uncomfortable looking chairs constructed of shiny metal and a hard white substance I didn't recognize. At the far end of the inn was a counter behind which stood a large stone gargoyle, the only decorative feature in the place. Behind the gargoyle was a door, presumably leading into the kitchen. There was a small window in the door through which I caught glimpses of the food being prepared. Preparation consisted of passing patties of meat over a stove, cramming them into a split roll, slopping a variety of colored pastes on top of the meat, and wrapping the whole mess in a piece of paper.

Watching this process confirmed my earlier fears. I do all the cooking for Aahz and myself, before that for Garkin and myself, and before that just for myself. While I have no delusions as to the high quality of my cooking, I do know that what they were doing to that meat could only yield a meal with the consistency and flavor of charred glove leather.

Despite the obviously low quality of the food, the inn seemed nearly full of customers. I noticed this out of the corner of my eye. I also noticed that a high percentage of them were staring at me. It occurred to me that this was probably because I had been standing in the door for some time without entering while working up my courage to go in.

Feeling slightly embarrassed, I stepped inside and let the door swing shut behind me. With fiendish accuracy, the door closed on my sword, pinning it momentarily and forcing me to break stride clumsily as I started forward. So much for my image as a swordsman.

Humiliated, I avoided looking at the other customers and made my way hurriedly to the inn's counter. I wasn't sure what I was going to do once I got there, since I didn't trust the food, but hopefully people would stop staring at me if I went through the motions of ordering.

Still trying to avoid eye contact with anyone, I made a big show of studying the gargoyle. There was a grinding noise, and the statue turned its head to return my stare. It wasn't a statue! They really had a gargoyle tending the counter!

The gargoyle seemed to be made of coarse, grey stone, and when he flexed his wings, small pieces of crushed rock and dust showered silently to the floor. His hands were taloned, and there were curved spikes growing out of his elbows. The only redeeming feature I could see was his smile, which in itself was a bit unnerving. Dominating his wrinkled face, the smile seemed permanently etched in place, stretching well past his ears and displaying a set of pointed teeth even longer than Aahz's.

"Take your order?" the gargoyle asked politely, the smile never twitching.

"Um…" I said taking a step back. "I'll have to think about it. There's so much to choose from."

In actuality I couldn't read the menu…if that's what it was. There was something etched in the wall behind the gargoyle in a language I couldn't decipher. I assume it was a menu because the prices weren't etched in the wall, but written in chalk over many erasures.

The gargoyle shrugged.

"Suit yourself," he said indifferently. "When you make up your mind, just holler. The name's Gus."

"I'll do that...Gus," I smiled, backing slowly toward the door.

Though it was my intent to exit quietly and wait outside with Gleep, things didn't work out that way. Before I had taken four steps, a hand fell on my shoulder.

"Skeeve, isn't it?" a voice proclaimed.

I spun around, or started to. I was brought up short when my sword banged into a table leg. My head kept moving, however, and I found myself face to face with an Imp.

"Brockhurst!" I exclaimed, recognizing him immediately.

"I thought I recognized you when you...hey!" the Imp took a step backward and raised his hands defensively. "Take it easy! I'm not looking for any trouble."

My hand had gone to my sword hilt in an involuntary effort to free it from the table leg. Apparently Brockhurst had interpreted the gesture as an effort to draw my weapon.

That was fine by me. Brockhurst had been one of Isstvan's lieutenants, and we hadn't parted on the best of terms. Having him a little afraid of my "ready sword" was probably a good thing.

"I don't hold any grudges," Brockhurst continued insistently. "That was just a job! Right now I'm between jobs...permanently!"

That last was added with a note of bitterness which piqued my curiosity.

"Things haven't been going well?" I asked cautiously.

The Imp grimaced.

"That's an understatement. Come on, sit down. I'll buy you a milkshake and tell you all about it."

I wasn't certain what a milkshake was, but I was sure I didn't want one if they were sold here.

"Um...thanks anyway, Brockhurst," I said forcing a smile, "But I think I'll pass."

The Imp arched an eyebrow at me.

"Still a little suspicious, eh?" he murmured. "Well, can't say as I blame you. Tell you what we'll do."

Before I could stop him, he strolled to the counter.

"Hey, Gus!" he called. "Mind if I take an extra cup?"

"Actually..." the gargoyle began.

"Thanks!"

Brockhurst was already on his way back, bearing his prize with him, some kind of a thin-sided, flimsy canister. Plopping down at a nearby table, he beckoned me over, indicating the seat opposite him with a wave of his hand.

There was no gracious course for me to follow other than to join him, though it would later occur to me I had no real obligation to be gracious. Moving carefully to avoid knocking anything over with my sword, I maneuvered my way to the indicated seat.

Apparently, Brockhurst had been sitting here before, as there was already a canister on the table identical to the one he had fetched from the counter. The only difference was that the one on the table was three quarters full of a curious pink liquid.

With great ceremony, the Imp picked up the canister from the table and poured half its contents into the new vessel. The liquid poured with the consistency of swamp muck.

"Here!" he said, pushing one of the canisters across the table to me. "Now you don't have to worry about any funny business with the drinks. We're both drinking the same thing."

With that, he raised his vessel in a mock toast and took a healthy swallow from it. Apparently he expected me to do the same. I would have rather sucked blood.

"Um…it's hard to believe things aren't going well for you," I stalled. "You look well enough."

For a change, I was actually sincere. Brockhurst looked good… even for an Imp. As Aahz had said, Imps are snappy dressers, and Brockhurst was no exception. He was outfitted in a rust-colored velvet jerkin trimmed in gold which set off his pink complexion and sleek black hair superbly. If he was starving, you couldn't tell it from looking at him. Though still fairly slender, he was as well-muscled and adroit as when I had first met him.

"Don't let appearances fool you," Brockhurst insisted, shaking his head. "You see before you an Imp pushed to the wall. I've had to sell everything: my crossbow, my pouch of magic tricks. I couldn't even raise enough money to pay my dues to the Assassins Guild."

"It's that hard to find work?" I sympathized.

"I'll tell you, Skeeve," he whispered confidentially, "I haven't worked since that fiasco with Isstvan."

The sound of that name still sent chills down my back.

"Where is Isstvan, anyway?" I asked casually.

"Don't worry about him," Brockhurst said grimly. "We left him working concession stands on the Isle of Coney, a couple dimensions from here."

"What happened to the others?"

I was genuinely curious. I hadn't had much of a chance to talk with Tanda since our reunion.

"We left Frumple under a cloud of birds in some park or other…figured he looked better as a statue than he did alive. The demon hunter and the girl took off for parts unknown one night while we were asleep. My partner, Higgens, headed back to Imper. He figured his career was over and that he might as well settle down. Me, I've been looking for work ever since, and I'm starting to think Higgens was right."

"Come on. Brockhurst," I chided. "There must be *something* you can do. I mean, this is the Bazaar."

The Imp heaved a sigh and took another sip of his drink.

"It's nice of you to say that, Skeeve," he smiled. "But I've got to face the facts. There's not a big demand for Imps anyway, and none at all for an Imp with no powers."

I knew what he meant. All the dimension travelers I had met so far—Aahz, Isstvan, Tanda, and even the Deveel Frumple—seemed to regard Imps as inferior beings. The nicest thing I had heard said about them was that they were styleless imitators of the Deveels.

I felt sorry for him. Despite the fact we had first met as enemies, it wasn't that long ago I had been a klutz nobody wanted.

"You've got to keep trying," I encouraged. "Somewhere, there's someone who wants to hire you."

"Not very likely," the Imp grimaced. "The way I am now, *I* wouldn't hire me. Would you?"

"Sure I would," I insisted. "In a minute."

"Oh, well," he sighed. "I shouldn't dwell on myself. How have things been with you? What brings you to the Bazaar?"

Now it was my turn to grimace.

"Aahz and I are in a bad spot," I explained. "We're here trying to recruit a force to help us out."

"You're hiring people?" Brockhurst was suddenly intense.

"Yeah. Why?" I replied.

Too late, I realized what I was saying.

"Then you weren't kidding about hiring me!" Brockhurst was beside himself with glee.

"Um…" I said.

"This is great," the Imp chortled, rubbing his hands together. "Believe me, Skeeve, you won't regret this."

I was regretting it already.

"Wait a minute, Brockhurst," I interrupted desperately. "There are a few things you should know about the job."

"Like what?"

"Well…for one thing, the odds are bad," I said judiciously. "We're up against an army. That's pretty rough fare considering how low the pay is."

I thought I would touch a nerve with that remark about the pay. I was right.

"How low is the pay?" the Imp asked bluntly.

Now I was stuck. I didn't have the vaguest idea how much mercenaries were normally paid.

"We…um…we couldn't offer you more than one gold piece for the whole job," I shrugged.

"Done!" Brockhurst proclaimed. "With the current state of my finances, I can't turn down an offer like that no matter how dangerous it is."

It occurred to me that sometime I should have Aahz give me a quick course in rates of exchange.

"Um…there's one other problem," I murmured thoughtfully.

"What's that?"

"Well, my partner, you remember Aahz?"

The Imp nodded.

"Well, he's out right now trying to hire a force, and he's got the money," I continued. "There's a good chance that, if he's successful, and he usually is, there won't be enough money left to hire you."

Brockhurst pursed his lips for a moment, then shrugged.

"Well," he said. "I'll take the chance. I wasn't going anywhere anyway. As I said, they haven't exactly been beating my door down with job offers."

I had run out of excuses.

"Well…" I smiled lamely. "As long as you're aware…"

"Heads up, boss," the Imp's murmur interrupted me. "We've got company."

I'm not sure which worried me more, Brockhurst calling me "boss" or the spectre-like character who had just stepped up to our table.

XIV.

"We're looking for a few good men."
B. CASSIDY

FOR A MOMENT, I thought we were being confronted by skeleton. Then I looked closer and realized there really was skin stretched over the bones, though its dusty-white color made it seem very dead indeed.

The figure's paleness was made even more corpse-like by the blue-black hooded robe that enshrouded it. It wasn't until I noted the wrinkled face with a short, bristly white beard that I realized our visitor was actually a very old man...very old.

He looked weak to the point of near-collapse, desperately clutching a twisted black walking staff which seemed to be the only thing keeping him erect. Still, his eyes were bright and his smile confident as he stood regarding us.

"Did I hear you boys right?" he asked in a crackling voice.

"I beg your pardon?" Brockhurst scowled at him.

The ancient figure sneered and raised his voice.

"I said, 'Did I hear you boys right?!'" he barked. "What's the matter? Are you deaf?"

"Um...excuse me," I interrupted hastily. "Before we can answer you, we have to know what you thought we said."

The old man thought for a minute, then bobbed his head in a sudden nod.

"You know, yer right!" he cackled. "Pretty smart, young fella."

He began to list, but caught himself before he fell.

"Thought I heard you tell Pinko here you were looking for a force to take on an army," he pronounced, jerking a thumb at Brockhurst.

"The name's Brockhurst, not Pinko!" the Imp snarled.

"Alright, Bratwurst," the old man nodded. "No need to get your dander up."

"That's Brockhurst!"

"You heard right," I interrupted again, hoping the old man would go away as soon as his curiosity was satisfied.

"Good!" the man declared. "Count me in! Me and Blackie haven't been in a good fight for a long time."

"How long is that in centuries?" Brockhurst sneered.

"Watch your mouth, Bratwurst!" the old man warned. "We may be old, but we can still teach you a thing or two about winnin' wars."

"Who's Blackie?" I asked, cutting off Brockhurst's reply.

In reply, the old man drew himself erect...well, nearly erect, and patted his walking staff.

"This is Blackie!" he announced proudly. "The finest bow ever to come from Archiah, and that takes in a lot of fine bows!"

I realized with a start that the walking staff was a bow, unstrung, with its bowstring wrapped around it. It was unlike any bow I had ever seen, lumpy and uneven, but polished to a sheen that seemed to glimmer with a life all its own.

"Wait a minute!" Brockhurst was suddenly attentive. "Did you say you come from Archiah?"

"That I did," the old man grinned. "Ajax's the name, fighting's my game. Ain't seen a war yet that could lay old Ajax low, and I've seen a lot of 'em."

"Um...could you excuse us for just a minute, sir?" Brockhurst smiled apologetically.

"Sure, son," Ajax nodded. "Take your time."

I couldn't understand the Imp's sudden change in attitude, but he seemed quite intense as he jerked his head at me, so I leaned close to hear what he had to say.

"Hire him, boss!" he hissed in my ear.

"What?" I gasped, not believing I had heard him right.

"I said hire him!" the Imp repeated. "I may not have much to offer you, but I can give you advice. Right now, my advice is to hire him."

"But he's..."

"He's from Archiah!" Brockhurst interrupted. "Boss, that dimension invented archery. You don't find many genuine Archers of any age for hire. If you've really got a war on your hands, hire him. He could tip the balance for us."

"If he's that good," I whispered back, "can we afford him?"

"One gold piece will be adequate," Ajax smiled toothily, adding his head to our conference. "I accept your offer."

"Excellent!" Brockhurst beamed.

"Wait a minute," I shrieked desperately, "I have a partner that…"

"I know, I know," Ajax sighed, holding up a restraining hand. "I heard when you told Bratwurst here."

"That's Brockhurst," the Imp growled, but he did it smiling.

"If your partner can't find help, then we're hired!" the old man laughed, shaking his head. "It's a mite strange, but these are strange times."

"You can say that again," I muttered.

I was beginning to think I had spoken too loud in my conversation with Brockhurst.

"One thing you should know though, youngster," Ajax murmured confidentially. "I'm bein' followed."

"By whom?" I asked.

"Don't rightly know," he admitted. "Haven't figured it out yet. It's the little blue fella in the corner behind me."

I craned my neck to look at the indicated corner. It was empty.

"What fella? I mean, fellow," I corrected myself.

Ajax whipped his head around with a speed that belied his frail appearance.

"Dang it!" he cursed. "He did it again! I'm telling you, youngster, that's why I can't figure what he's after!"

"Ah…sure, Ajax," I said soothingly. "You'll catch him next time."

Terrific. An Imp with no powers, and now an old archer who sees things.

My thoughts were interrupted by a gentle tap on my shoulder. I turned to find the gargoyle looming over me.

"Your order's ready, sir," he said through his perma-smile.

"My order?"

"Yes, if you'll step this way."

"There must be some mistake," I began, "I didn't…"

The gargoyle was already gone, lumbering back to his counter. I considered ignoring him. Then I considered his size and countenance, and decided I should straighten out this misunderstanding out in a polite fashion.

"Excuse me," I told my charges. "I'll be right back."

"Don't worry about us, boss," Brockhurst waved.

I wasn't reassured.

I managed to make my way to the counter without banging my sword against anything or anyone, a feat which raised my spirits for the first time this afternoon. Thus bolstered, I approached the gargoyle.

"I...um...I don't recall ordering anything," I stated politely.

"Don't blame you, either," the gargoyle growled through his smile. "Beats me how anyone or anything can eat the slop they serve here."

"But..."

"That was just to get you away from those two," the gargoyle shrugged. "You see, I'm shy. About asking you for a job, of course!"

I decided I would definitely have to keep my voice down in the future. My quiet conversation with Brockhurst seemed to have attracted the attention of half the Bazaar.

"Look...um..."

"Gus!" the gargoyle supplied.

"Yes, well, ah, Gus, I'm really not hiring..."

"I know. Your partner is," Gus interrupted. "But you're here and he isn't, so I figured I'd make our pitch to you before the second team roster is completely filled."

"Oh!" I said, not knowing what else to say.

"The way I see it," the gargoyle continued, "we could do you a lot of good. You're a Klahd, aren't you?"

"I'm from Klah," I acknowledged stiffly.

"Well, if my memory serves me correct, warfare in that dimension isn't too far advanced, technologically."

"We have crossbows and catapults," I informed him. "At least, the other side does."

"That's what I said," Gus agreed. "Practically primitive. To stop that force, all you need is air support and a little firepower. We can supply both, and we'll work cheap, both of us for one gold piece."

Now I was sure I had underestimated the market value of gold pieces. Still, the price was tempting.

"I dunno, Gus," I said cagily. "Ajax there is supposed to be a pretty good archer."

"Archers," the gargoyle snorted. "I'm talking about real firepower. The kind my partner can give you."

"Who is your partner?" I asked. "He isn't short and blue by any chance, is he?"

"Naw," Gus replied pointing to the far corner. "That's the Gremlin. He came in with the archer."

"A Gremlin?" I said, following his finger.

Sure enough, perched on a chair in the corner was a small, elfish character. Mischievous eyes danced in his soft blue face as he nodded to me in silent recognition. Reflexively, I smiled and nodded back. Apparently I owed Ajax an apology.

"I thought Gremlins didn't exist," I commented casually to Gus.

"A lot of folks think that," the gargoyle agreed. "But you can see for yourself, they're real."

I wasn't sure. In the split second I had taken my eyes off the Gremlin to speak with Gus, he had vanished without a trace. I was tempted to go looking for him, but Gus was talking again.

"Just a second and I'll introduce you to my partner," he was saying. "He's here somewhere."

As he spoke, the gargoyle began rummaging about his own body, feeling his armpits and peering into the wrinkles on his skin.

I watched curiously, until my attention was arrested by a small lizard which had crawled out of one of the gargoyle's wing folds and was now regarding me fixedly from Gus's right shoulder. It was only about three inches long, but glowed with a brilliant orange hue. There were blotchy red patterns which seemed to crawl about the lizard's skin with a life of their own. The overall effect was startlingly beautiful.

"Is that your lizard?" I asked.

"There he is!" Gus crowed triumphantly snatching the reptile from his shoulder and cupping it in his hands. "Meet Berfert. He's the partner I was telling you about."

"Hello, Berfert," I smiled, extending a finger to stroke him.

The gargoyle reacted violently, jerking the lizard back out of my reach.

"Careful, there," he warned. "That's a good way to lose a finger."

"I wasn't going to hurt him," I explained.

"No, he was about to hurt you!" Gus countered. "Berfert's a salamander, a walking firebomb. We get along because I'm one of the few beings around that won't burn to a crisp when I touch him."

"Oh," I said with sudden understanding. "So when you said 'firepower'…"

"I meant firepower," Gus finished. "Berfert cleans 'em out on the ground, and I work 'em over from the air. Well, what do you say? Have we got a deal?"

"I'll…um…have to talk it over with my partner," I countered.

"Fine," Gus beamed. "I'll start packing."

He was gone before I could stop him.

I sagged against the counter, wishing fervently for Aahz's return. As if in answer to my thoughts, my mentor burst through the door, following closely by Tanda.

My greeting died in my throat when I saw his scowl. Aahz was not in a good mood.

"I thought I told you to wait outside," he bellowed at me.

"Calm down, Aahz," Tanda soothed. "I thought he'd be more comfortable waiting in here. Besides, there's no reason to get upset. We're here and he's here. Nothing has gone wrong."

"You haven't been dealing with any Deveels?" Aahz asked suspiciously.

"I haven't even talked with any," I insisted.

"Good!" he retorted, slightly mollified. "There's hope for you yet, kid."

"I told you he could stay out of trouble," Tanda smiled triumphantly. "Isn't that right, handsome?"

Try as I might, I couldn't bring myself to answer her.

XV.

"I'll worry about it tomorrow."
S. O'HARA

"UM...ARE THE mercenaries waiting outside?" I asked finally.

"You didn't answer her question, kid," Aahz observed, peering at me with renewed suspicion."

"Don't strain your neck looking for your troops, handsome," Tanda advised me. "There aren't any. It seems our mighty negotiator has met his match."

"Those bandits!" Aahz exploded. "Do you have any idea what it would cost us if I had agreed to pay their bar bill as part of the contract? If that's a non-profit group, I want to audit their books."

My hopes for salvation sank like a rock.

"You didn't hire them?" I asked.

"No, I didn't," Aahz scowled. "And that moves us back to square one. Now we've got to recruit a force one at a time."

"Did you try..." I began.

"Look, kid," Aahz interrupted with a snarl. "I did the best I could, and I got nowhere. I'd like to see you do better."

"He already has!" Brockhurst announced, rising from his seat. "While you were wasting time, Skeeve here has hired himself a fighting team."

"He what?" Aahz bellowed turning on his critic. "Brockhurst! What are you doing here?"

"Waiting for orders in our upcoming campaign," the Imp replied innocently.

"What campaign?" Aahz glowered.

"The one on Klah, of course," Brockhurst blinked. "Haven't you told him yet, boss?"

"Boss?" Aahz roared. *"Boss?"*

"No need ta shout," Ajax grumbled, turning to face the assemblage. "We hear ya plain enough."

"Ajax!" Tanda exclaimed gleefully.

"Tanda!" the old man yelped back.

She was at him in a bound, but he smoothly interposed his bow between them.

"Easy, girl," he laughed. "None of yer athletic greetings. I'm not as young as I used to be, ya know."

"You old fraud!" Tanda teased. "You'll outlive us all." Ajax shrugged dramatically.

"That kinda depends on how good a general the youngster there is," he commented.

"Kid," Aahz growled through gritted teeth. "I want to talk to you! *Now!*"

"I know that temper!" Gus announced, emerging from the back room.

"Gus!" Aahz exclaimed.

"In the stone!" the gargoyle confirmed. "Are you in on this expedition? The boss didn't say anything about working with Perverts."

Instead of replying, Aahz sank heavily into a chair and hid his face in his hands.

"Tanda!" he moaned. "Tell me again about how this kid can stay out of trouble."

"Um...Aahz," I said cautiously. "Could I talk to you for a minute ...privately?"

"Why, I think that's an excellent idea...*boss,*" he said. The smile he turned to me wasn't pleasant.

"Kid!" Aahz moaned after I had finished my tale. "How many times do I have to tell you? This is the Bazaar at Deva! You've got to be careful what you say and to who, especially when there's money involved."

"But I told them nothing was definite until we found out if you had hired someone else," I protested.

"...But I *didn't* hire anyone else, so now the deal is final," Aahz sighed.

"Can't we get out of it?" I asked hopefully.

"Back out of a deal on Deva?" Aahz shook his head. "That would get us barred from the Bazaar so fast it would make your head spin. Remember, the Merchants Association runs this dimension."

"Well, you said you wanted outside help," I pointed out.

"I didn't expect to go that far outside," he grimaced. "An Imp, a senile Archer, and a gargoyle."

"...And a salamander," I added.

"Gus is still bumming around with Berfert?" Aahz asked, brightening slightly. "That's a plus."

"The only really uncertain factor," I said thoughtfully, "is the Gremlin."

"How do you figure that?" Aahz yawned.

"Well, he's been following Ajax. The question is, why? And will he follow us to Klah?"

"Kid," Aahz said solemnly, "I've told you before. There are no such things as Gremlins."

"But Aahz, I saw him."

"Don't let it bother you, kid," Aahz sympathized. "After a day like you've been through, I wouldn't be surprised if you saw a Jabberwocky."

"What's a..."

"Is everything set?" Tanda asked, joining our conversation.

"About as set as we'll ever be," Aahz sighed. "Though, if you want my honest opinion, with a crew like this, we're set more for a zoo than a war."

"Aahz is a bit critical of my choice in recruits," I confided.

"What's your gripe, Aahz?" she asked cocking her head. "I thought you and Gus were old foxhole buddies."

"I'm not worried about Gus," Aahz put in hastily. "Or Berfert either. That little lizard's terrific under fire."

"Well I can vouch for Ajax," Tanda informed him. "Don't let his age fool you. I'd rather have him backing my move than a whole company of counterfeit archers."

"Is he really from Archiah?" Aahz asked skeptically.

"That's what he's said as long as I've known him," Tanda shrugged. "And, after seeing him shoot, I've got no reason to doubt it. Why?"

"I've never met a genuine Archer before," Aahz explained. "For a while I was willing to believe the whole dimension was a legend. Well, if he can shoot half as well as Archers are supposed to, I've got no gripes having him on the team."

I started to feel a little better. Unfortunately, Aahz noticed my smile.

"The Imp is another story," he said grimly. "I'm not wild about working with *any* Imp, but to hire one without powers is a waste of good money."

"Don't forget he's an Assassin," Tanda pointed out. "Powers or no powers, I'll bet we find a use for him. When we were talking with the Gremlin just now..."

"Now, don't *you* start on that!" Aahz snarled.

"Start on what?" Tanda blinked.

"The Gremlin bit," Aahz scowled. "Any half-wit knows there are no such things as Gremlins."

"Do you want to tell him that?" Tanda smiled. "I'll call him over here and...oh, rats! He's gone again."

"If you're quite through," Aahz grumbled, rising from his chair, "we'd best get going. There's a war waiting for us, you know."

"Oops! That reminds me!" Tanda exclaimed, fishing inside her tunic.

"I know I shouldn't ask," Aahz signed. "But what..."

"Here!" Tanda announced, flipping him a familiar object.

It was a metal rod about eight inches long and two inches in diameter with a button on one end of it.

"A D-Hopper!" I cried, recognizing the device instantly.

"It's the same one you gave Isstvan," Tanda smiled proudly. "I lifted it from him when we parted company. You'll probably want to undo whatever you did to the controls before you use it, though."

"If I can remember for sure," Aahz scowled, staring at the device.

"I thought it might come in handy in case we get separated on this job and you need a fast exit," Tanda shrugged.

"The thought's appreciated," Aahz smiled, putting an arm around her.

"Does this mean you'll be able to teach me how to travel the dimensions?" I asked hopefully.

"Not now I won't," Aahz grimaced. "We've got a war to fight, remember?"

"Oh! Yes, of course."

"Well, get your troops together and let's go," Aahz ordered.

"Okay," I agreed, rising from my chair. "I'll get Gleep and...wait a minute! Did you say my troops?"

"You hired 'em, you lead 'em," my mentor smiled.

"But you're..."

"I'll be your military advisor, of course," Aahz continued casually. "But the job of Fearless Leader is all yours. You're the court magician, remember?"

I swallowed hard. Somehow, this had never entered into my plans.

"But what do I do?" I asked desperately.

"Well," Aahz drawled, "first, I'd advise you to move 'em outside so we can all head for Klah together...that is, unless you're willing to leave your dragon behind."

That didn't even deserve an answer. I turned to face the troops, sweeping them with what I hoped was a masterful gaze which would immediately command their attention.

No one noticed. They were all involved in a jovial conversation.

I cleared my throat noisily.

Nothing.

I considered going over to their table.

"Listen up!" Aahz barked suddenly, scaring me half to death.

The conversation stopped abruptly and all heads swiveled my way.

"Aah..." I began confidently. "We're ready to go now. Everybody outside. Wait for me by the dragon."

"Right, boss!" Brockhurst called, starting for the door.

"I'll be a minute, youngster," Ajax wheezed, struggling to rise.

"Here, Gramps," Gus said. "Let me give you a hand."

"Name's not Gramps, it's Ajax!" the Archer scowled.

"Just trying to be helpful," the gargoyle apologized.

"I kin stand up by myself," Ajax insisted. "Just 'cause I'm old don't mean I'm helpless."

I glanced to Aahz for help, but he and Tanda were already headed out.

As I turned back to Ajax, I thought I caught a glimpse of a small, blue figure slipping out through the door ahead of us. If it was the Gremlin, he was nowhere in sight when I finally reached the street.

XVI.

"Myth-conceptions are the major cause of wars!"
A. HITLER

FORTUNATELY, THE ARMY had not moved from the position it held when we left for Deva. I say fortunately because Aahz pointed out that they might well have renewed their advance in our absence. If that had happened, we would have returned to find ourselves behind the enemy lines, if not actually in the middle of one of their encampments.

Of course, he pointed this out to me after we had arrived back on Klah. Aahz is full of helpful little tidbits of information, but his timing leaves a lot to be desired.

Ajax lost no time upon our arrival. Moving with a briskness which denied his years, he strung his bow and stood squinting at the distant encampments.

"Well, youngster," he asked, never taking his eyes from the enemy's formations, "what's my first batch of targets?"

His eagerness took me a bit aback, but Aahz covered for me neatly.

"First," he said loftily, "we'll have to hold a final planning session."

"We didn't expect to have you along, Ajax," Tanda added. "Having a genuine Archer on our side naturally calls for some drastic revisions of our battle plans."

"Don't bother me none," Ajax shrugged. "Just wanted ta let you know I was ready to earn my keep. Take yer time. Seen too many wars mess up 'cause nobody bothered to do any plannin'! If ya don't mind, though, think I'll take me a little nap. Jes' holler when ya want some shootin' done."

"Ah...go ahead, Ajax," I agreed.

Without further conversation, Ajax plopped down and pulled his cloak a bit closer about him. Within a few minutes, he was snoring lightly, but I noticed his bow was still in his grip.

"Now there's a seasoned soldier," Aahz observed. "Gets his sleep when and where he can."

"You want me to do a little scouting, boss?" Gus asked.

"Um…" I hesitated, glancing quickly at Aahz. Aahz caught my look and gave a small nod.

"Sure, Gus," I finished. "We'll wait for you here."

"I'll scout in the other direction," Brockhurst volunteered.

"Okay," I nodded. "Aahz, can you give 'em a quick briefing?"

I was trying to drop the load in Aahz's lap, but he joined the conversation as smoothly as if we had rehearsed it this way.

"There are a couple things we need specific information on," he said solemnly. "First, we need a battlefield, small, with scattered cover. Gus, you check that out. You know what we're going to need. Brockhurst, see what specific information you can bring back on the three nearest encampments."

Both scouts nodded briskly.

"And both of you, stay out of sight," Aahz warned. "The information's no good to us if you don't come back."

"C'mon, Aahz," Gus admonished. "What have they got that can put a dent in the old rock?"

He demonstrated by smashing his forearm into a sapling. The tree went down, apparently without affecting the gargoyle's arm in the slightest.

"I don't know," Aahz admitted. "And I don't want to know, yet. You're one of our surprise weapons. No point in giving the enemy an advance warning. Get my meaning?"

"Got it, Aahz," Gus nodded, and lumbered off.

"Be back in a bit," Brockhurst waved, heading off in the opposite direction.

"Now that we've got a minute," I murmured to Aahz as I returned Brockhurst's wave, "would you mind telling me what our final plan is? I don't even know what the preliminary plans were."

"That's easy," Aahz replied. "We don't have one…yet."

"Well, when are we going to form one?" I asked with forced patience.

"Probably on the battlefield," Aahz yawned. "Until then it's pointless. There're too many variables."

"Wouldn't it be a good idea to have at least a general idea as to what we're going to do before we wander out on the battlefield?" I insisted. "It would do a lot for my peace of mind."

"Oh, I've already got a general idea as to what we'll be doing," Aahz admitted.

"Isn't he sweet?" Tanda grimaced. "Would you mind sharing it with us, Aahz? We've got a stake in this, too."

"Well," he began lazily, "the name of the game is delay and demoralize. The way I figure it, we aren't going to overpower them. We haven't got enough going for us to even try that."

I bit back a sarcastic observation and let him continue.

"Delay and demoralize we should be able to do, though," Aahz smiled. "Right off the bat, we've got two big weapons going for us in that kind of a fight."

"Ajax and Gus," I supplied helpfully.

"Fear and bureaucracy," Aahz corrected.

"How's that again?" Tanda frowned.

"Tanda, my girl," Aahz smiled, "you've been spoiled by your skylarking through the dimensions. You've forgotten how the man on the street thinks. The average person in any dimension doesn't know the first thing about magik, particularly about its limitations. If the kid here tells 'em he can make the sun stop or trees grow upside down, they'll believe him. Particularly if he's got a few strange characters parading around as proof of his power, and I think you'll have to admit, the crew he's got backing him this time around is pretty strange."

"What's bureaucracy?" I asked, finally getting a word in edgewise.

"Red tape...the system," Aahz informed me. "The organization to get things done that keeps things from getting done. In this case, it's called the chain-of-command. An army the size of the one we're facing has to function like a well-oiled machine or it starts tripping over its own feet. I'm betting if we toss a couple handfuls of sand into its gears, they'll spend more time fighting each other than chasing us."

This was one of the first times Aahz had actually clarified something he said. I wish he hadn't. I was more confused than I had been before.

"Um...how are we going to do all this?" I asked.

"We'll be able to tell better after you've had your first war council," Aahz shrugged.

"Aren't we having it now?"

"I meant with the enemy," Aahz scowled. "Sometime in the near future, you're going to have to sit down with one of their officers and decide how this war's going to be fought."

"Me?" I blinked.

"You are the leader of the defenses, remember?" Aahz grinned at me.

"It's part of the job, handsome," Tanda confirmed.

"Wait a minute," I interrupted. "It just came to me. I think I have a better idea."

"This I've got to hear," Aahz grinned.

"Shut up, Aahz," Tanda ordered, poking him in the ribs. "What 'cha got, handsome?"

"We've got a couple of trained assassins on our side, don't we?" I observed. "Why don't we just put 'em to work? If enough officers suddenly turn up dead, odds are the army will fall apart. Right?"

"It won't work, kid," Aahz announced bluntly.

"Why not?"

"We can bend the rules, but we can't break 'em," Aahz explained. "Wars are fought between the troops. Killing off the officers without engaging their troops goes against tradition. I doubt if your own force would stand still for it. Old troopers like Ajax would have no part of a scheme like that."

"He's right," Tanda confirmed. "Assassins take contracts on individuals in personal feuds, not against the general staff of an army."

"But it would be so easy," I insisted.

"Look at it this way, kid," Aahz put in. "If you could do it, they could do it. The way things are now, you're exempt from assassins. Would you really want to change that?"

"What do I say in a war council?" I asked.

"I'll brief you on that when the time comes," Aahz reassured me. "Right now we have other things to plan."

"Such as what?" Tanda asked.

"Such as what to do about those signal towers," Aahz retorted, jerking his head at one of the distant structures. "We probably won't have time to break their code, so the next best thing is to disrupt their signals somehow. Now, you said you picked up some special effects items back at the Bazaar. Have you got anything we could use on the signal towers?"

"I'm not sure," Tanda frowned thoughtfully. "I wish you had said something about that before I went shopping."

"What about Ajax?" I suggested.

"What about him?" Aahz countered.

"How close would he have to be to the towers to disrupt things with his archery?"

"I don't know," Aahz shrugged. "Why don't you ask him?"

Eager to follow up on my own suggestion, I squatted down next to the dozing bowman.

"Um…Ajax," I called softly.

"What 'cha need, youngster?" the old man asked, coming instantly awake.

"Do you see those signal towers?" I asked, pointing at the distant structures.

Ajax rose to his feet and squinted in the indicated direction.

"Sure can," he nodded.

"We…um…I was wondering," I explained. "Can you use your bow to disrupt their signals?"

In response, Ajax drew an arrow from beneath his cloak, cocked it, and let fly before I could stop him.

The shaft disappeared in the direction of the nearest tower. With sinking heart, I strained my eyes trying to track its flight.

There was a man standing on the tower's platform, his standard leaning against the railing beside him. Suddenly, his standard toppled over, apparently breaking off a handspan from its crosspiece. The man bent and retrieved the bottom portion of the pole, staring with apparent confusion at the broken end.

"Any other targets?" Ajax asked.

He was leaning casually on his bow, his back to the tower. He hadn't even bothered watching to see if his missile struck its mark.

"Um…not just now, Ajax," I assured him. "Go back to sleep."

"Fine by me, sonny," Ajax smiled, resettling himself. "They'll be plenty of targets tomorrow."

"How do you figure that?" I asked.

"According to that signal I just cut down," he grinned, "the army's fixin' to move out tomorrow."

"You can read the signals?" I blinked.

"Sure," Ajax nodded. "There're only about eight different codes armies use, and I know 'em all. It's part of my trade."

"And they're moving out tomorrow?" I pressed.

"That's what I said," the bowman scowled. "What's the matter, are you deaf?"

"No," I assured him hastily. "It just changes our plans is all. Go back to sleep."

Returning to our little conference, I found Aahz and Tanda engrossed in a conversation with Brockhurst.

"Bad news, kid," Aahz informed me. "Brockhurst here says the army's going to move out tomorrow."

"I know," I said. "I just found out from Ajax. Can you read the signal flags too, Brockhurst?"

"Naw," the Imp admitted. "But the Gremlin can."

"What Gremlin?" Aahz bared his teeth.

"He was here a minute ago," Brockhurst scowled, looking around.

"Well, handsome," Tanda sighed, eyeing me. "I think we just ran out of planning time. Better call your dragon. I think we're going to need all the help we can get tomorrow."

Gleep had wandered off shortly after our arrival, though we could still hear him occasionally as he poked about in the underbrush.

"You go get the dragon, Tanda," Aahz ordered. "Though it escapes me how he's supposed to be any help. The 'boss' here and I have to discuss his war council tomorrow."

Any confidence I might have built up listening to Aahz's grand plan earlier fled me. Tanda was right. We had run out of time.

XVII.

"Diplomacy is the delicate weapon of the civilized warrior."
                                                    HUN, A. T.

WE WAITED PATIENTLY for our war council. Two of us. Aahz and me. Against an army.

This was, of course, Aahz's idea. Left to my own devices, I wouldn't be caught dead in this position.

Trying to ignore that unfortunate choice of words, I cleared my throat and spoke to Aahz out of the corner of my mouth.

"Aahz?"

"Yeah, kid?"

"How long are we going to stand here?"

"Until they notice us and do something about it."

Terrific. Either we'd rot where we stood, or someone would shoot us full of arrows.

We were standing about twenty yards from one of the encampments, with nothing between us and them but meadow. We could see clearly the bustle of activity within the encampment and, in theory, there was nothing keeping them from seeing us. This is why we were standing where we were, to draw attention to ourselves. Unfortunately so far no one had noticed.

It had been decided that Aahz and I would work alone on this first sortie to hide the true strength of our force. It occurred to me that it also hid the true weakness of our force, but I felt it would be tactless to point this out.

At first, Brockhurst had argued in favor of his coming along with me instead of Aahz, claiming that as an Imp he had much more experience at bargaining than a prevect. It was pointed out to him rather forcefully by Aahz that, in this instance, we weren't bargaining for glass beads or whoopie cushions, but for a war...and if the Imp wanted to prove to Aahz that he knew more about fighting...

Needless to say, Brockhurst backed down at this point. This was good, as it saved me from having to openly reject his offer. I mean, I may not be the fastest learner around, but I could still distinctly remember Aahz getting the best of Brockhurst the last time the two of them had squared off for a bargaining session.

Besides, if this meeting went awry, I wanted my mentor close at hand to share the consequences with me.

So here we stood, blatantly exposed to the enemy, without even a sword for our defense. That was another of Aahz's brainstorms. He argued that our being unarmed accomplished three things. First, it showed that we were here to talk, not to fight. Second, it demonstrated our faith in my magical abilities to defend us. Third, it encouraged our enemy to meet us similarly unarmed.

He also pointed out that Ajax would be hiding in the tree line behind us with strung bow and cocked arrow, and would probably be better at defending us if anything went wrong than a couple of swords would.

He was right, of course, but it did nothing to settle my nerves as we waited.

"Heads up, kid," Aahz murmured. "We've got company."

Sure enough, a rather stocky individual was striding briskly across the meadow in our direction.

"Kid!" Aahz hissed suddenly. "Your disguise!"

"What about it?" I whispered back.

"It isn't!" came the reply.

He was right! I had carefully restored his "dubious character" appearance, but had forgotten completely about changing my own. Having our motley crew accept my leadership in my normal form had caused me to overlook the fact that Klahds are harder to impress than demons.

"Should I…" I began.

"Too late!" Aahz growled. "Fake it."

The soldier was almost upon us now, close enough for me to notice when he abandoned his bored expression and forced a smile.

"I'm sorry, folks," he called with practiced authority. "You'll have to clear the area. We'll be moving soon and you're blocking the path."

"Call your duty officer!" Aahz boomed back at him.

"My who?" the soldier scowled.

"Duty officer, officer of the day, commander, whatever you call whoever's currently in charge of your formation," Aahz clarified. "Somebody's got to be running things, and if you're officer material, I'm the Queen of May."

Whether or not the soldier understood Aahz's allusion (I didn't), he caught the general implication.

"Yea, there's someone in charge," he snarled, his complexion darkening slightly. "He's a very busy man right now, too busy to stand around talking to civilians. We're getting ready to move our troops, mister, so take your son and get out of the way. If you want to watch the soldiers, you'll have to follow along and watch us when we camp tonight."

"Do you have any idea who you're talking to?" I said in a surprisingly soft voice.

"I don't care who your father is, sonny," the soldier retorted. "We're trying to…"

"The name's not 'sonny,' it's Skeeve!" I hissed, drawing myself up. "Court Magician to the kingdom of Possiltum, pledged to that kingdom's defense. Now I advise you to call your officer…or do you want to wake up tomorrow morning on a lily pad?"

The soldier recoiled a step and stood regarding me suspiciously.

"Is he for real?" he asked Aahz skeptically.

"How's your taste for flies?" Aahz smiled.

"You mean he can really…"

"Look," interrupted Aahz, "I'm not playing servant to the kid because of his terrible personality, if you know what I mean."

"I see…um…" The soldier was cautiously backing toward the encampment. "I'll…um…I'll bring my officer."

"We'll be here," Aahz assured him.

The soldier nodded and retreated with noticeably greater speed than he had displayed approaching us.

"So far, so good," my mentor grinned.

"What's wrong with my personality?" I asked bluntly.

Aahz sighed.

"Later, kid. For the time being, concentrate on looking aloof and dignified, okay?"

Okay or not, there wasn't much else to do while we waited for the officer to put in his appearance.

Apparently news of our presence spread through the encampment in record time, for a crowd of soldiers gathered at the edge of the camp long before we saw any sign of the officer. It seemed all preparations to move were suspended, at least temporarily, while the soldiers lined up and craned their necks to gawk at us.

It was kind of a nice feeling to have caused such a sensation, until I noticed several soldiers were taking time to strap on weapons and armor before joining the crowd.

"Aahz!" I whispered.

"Yeah, kid?"

"I thought this was supposed to be a peaceful meeting."

"It is," he assured me.

"But they're arming!" I pointed out.

"Relax, kid," he whispered back. "Remember, Ajax is covering us."

I tried to focus on that thought. Then I saw what was apparently the officer approaching us flanked by two soldiers, and I focused on the swords they were all wearing.

"Aahz!" I hissed.

"Relax, kid," Aahz advised me. "Remember Ajax."

I remembered. I also remembered we were vastly outnumbered.

"I understand you gentlemen are emissaries of Possiltum?" the officer asked, coming to a halt in front of us.

I nodded stiffly, hoping the abruptness of my motion would be interpreted as annoyance rather than fear.

"Fine," the officer smirked. "Then, as the first representative of the Empire to contact a representative of Possiltum, I have the pleasure of formally declaring war on your kingdom."

"What is your name?" Aahz asked casually.

"Claude," the officer responded. "Why do you ask?"

"The historians like details," Aahz shrugged. "Well, Claude, as the first representative of Possiltum to meet with a representative of your Empire in times of war, it is our pleasure to demand your unconditional surrender."

That got a smile out of the officer.

"Surrender?" he chortled. "To a cripple and a child? You must be mad. Even if I had the authority to do such a thing, I wouldn't."

"That's right," Aahz shook his head in mock self-admonishment. "We should have realized. Someone in charge of a supply company wouldn't swing much weight in an army like this, would he?"

We had chosen this particular group of soldiers to approach specifically because they were a supply unit. That meant they were lightly armed and hopefully not an elite fighting group.

Aahz's barb struck home, however. The officer stopped smiling
and dropped his hand to his sword hilt. I found myself thinking
again of Ajax's protection.

"I have more than enough authority to deal with you two," he hissed.

"Authority, maybe," I yawned. "But I frankly doubt you have
the power to stand against us."

As I mentioned, I did not feel as confident as I sounded. The
officer's honor guard had mimicked his action, so that now all three
of our adversaries were standing ready to draw their swords.

"Very well," Claude snarled. "You've been warned. Now, we're
going to bring our wagons across this spot, and if you're on it when
we get here you've no one to blame but yourselves."

"Accepted!" Aahz leered. "Shall we say noon tomorrow?"

"Tomorrow?" the officer scowled. "What's wrong with right now?"

"Come, come, Claude," Aahz admonished. "We're talking about
the first engagement of a new campaign. Surely you want some
time to plan your tactics."

"Tactics?" Claude echoed thoughtfully.

"...and to pass the word to your superiors that you're leading
the opening gambit," Aahz continued casually.

"Hmm," the officer murmured.

"...and to summon reinforcements," I supplied. "Unless, of
course, you want to keep all the glory for yourself."

"Glory!"

That did it. Claude pounced on the word like a Deveel on a
gold piece. Aahz had been right in assuming supply officers don't
see combat often.

"I...uh...I don't believe we'll require reinforcements," he murmured cagily.

"Are you sure?" Aahz sneered. "The odds are only about a hundred to one in your favor."

"But he is a magician," Claude smiled. "A good officer can't be
too careful. Still, it would be pointless to involve too many
officers...er...I mean, soldiers in a minor skirmish."

"Claude," Aahz said with grudging admiration. "I can see yours
is a military mind without equal. Win or lose, I look forward to
having you as an opponent."

"And I you, sir," the officer returned with equal formality. "Shall
we say noon then?"

"We'll be here," Aahz nodded.

With that, the officer turned and strode briskly back to his encampment, his bodyguard trudging dutifully beside him.

Our comrades were bristling with questions when we reentered the tree line.

"Is it set, boss?" Brockhurst asked.

"Any trouble?" Tanda pressed.

"Piece of cake," Aahz bragged. "Right, kid?"

"Well," I began modestly. "I was a little worried when they started to reach for their swords. I would have been terrified if I didn't know Ajax was...say, where is Ajax?"

"He's up in that clump of bushes," Gus informed me, jerking a massive thumb at a thicket of greenery on the edge of the tree line. "He should be back by now."

When we found Ajax, he was fast asleep curled around his bow. We had to shake him several times to wake him.

XVIII.

"Just before the battle, Mother, I was thinking most of you…"
SONNY BARKER

A LONG, SLIMY tongue assaulted me from the darkness, accompanied by a blast of bad breath which could have only one source.

"Gleep!"

I started to automatically cuff the dragon away, then had a sudden change of heart.

"Hi, fella," I smiled, scratching his ear. "Lonely?"

In response, my pet flopped on his side with a thud that shook the ground. His serpentine neck was long enough that he managed to perform this maneuver without moving his head from my grasp.

His loyal affection brought a smile to my face for the first time since taking up my lonely vigil. It was a welcome antidote to my nervous insomnia.

I was leaning against a tree watching the pinpoints of light which marked the enemy's encampment. Even though the day's events had left me exhausted, I found myself unable to sleep, my mind awash with fear and anticipation of tomorrow's clash. Not wishing to draw attention to my discomfort, I had crept to this place to be alone.

As stealthy as I had attempted to be, however, apparently Gleep had noted my movement and come to keep me company.

"Oh, Gleep," I whispered. "What are we going to do?"

For his answer, he snuggled closer against me and laid his head in my lap for additional patting. He seemed to have unshakable faith in my ability to handle any crisis as it arose. I wished with all my heart that I shared his confidence.

"Skeeve?" came a soft voice from my right.

I turned my head and found Tanda standing close beside me. The disquieting thing about having an Assassin for a friend is that they move so silently.

"Can I talk to you for a moment?"

"Sure, Tanda," I said, patting the ground next to me. "Have a seat."

Instead of sitting at the indicated spot, she sank to the ground where she stood and curled her legs up under her.

"It's about Ajax," she began hesitantly. "I hate to bother you, but I'm worried about him."

"What's wrong?" I asked.

"Well, the team's been riding him about falling asleep today when he was supposed to be covering you," she explained. "He's taking it pretty hard."

"I wasn't too wild about it myself," I commented bitterly. "It's a bad feeling to realize that we really were alone out there. If anything had gone wrong, we would have been cut to shreds while placidly waiting for our expert bowman to intercede!"

"I know," Tanda's voice was almost too soft to be heard. "And I don't blame you for feeling like that. In a way, I blame myself."

"Yourself?" I blinked. "Why?"

"I vouched for him, Skeeve," she whispered. "Don't you remember?"

"Well, sure," I admitted. "But you couldn't have known..."

"But I should have," she interrupted bitterly. "I should have realized how old he is now. He shouldn't be here, Skeeve. That's why I wanted to talk to you about doing something."

"Me?" I asked, genuinely startled. "What do you want me to do?"

"Send him back," Tanda urged. "It isn't fair to you to endanger your mission because of him, and it isn't fair to Ajax to put him in a spot like this."

"That isn't what I meant," I murmured, shaking my head. "I meant, why are you talking to me? Aahz is the one you have to convince."

"That's where you're wrong, Skeeve," she corrected. "Aahz isn't leading this group; you are."

"Because of what he said back on Deva?" I smiled. "C'mon, Tanda. You know Aahz. He was just a little miffed. You notice he's called all the shots so far."

The moonlight glistened in Tanda's hair as she shook her head.

"I *do* know Aahz, Skeeve. Better than you do," she said. "He's a stickler for that chain-of-command. If he says you're the leader, you're the leader."

"But..."

"...besides," she continued over my protest. "Aahz is only one member of the team. What's important is that all the others are counting on you, too. On you, not on Aahz. You hired 'em, and as far as they're concerned, you're the boss."

The frightening thing was, she was right. I hadn't really stopped to think about it, but everything she had said was true. I had just been too busy with my own worries to reflect on it. Now that I realized the full extent of my responsibilities, a new wave of doubts assaulted me. I wasn't even that sure of myself as a magician, as a leader of men…let alone…

"I'll have to think about it," I stalled.

"You don't have much time," she pointed out. "You've got a war scheduled to start tomorrow."

There was a crackling in the brush to our left, interrupting our conversation.

"Boss?" came Brockhurst's soft hail. "Are you busy?"

"Sort of," I called back.

"Well, this will only take a minute."

Before I could reply, two shadows detached themselves from the brush and drew closer. One was Brockhurst, the other was Gus. I should have known from the noise the gargoyle was accompanying Brockhurst. Like Tanda, the Imp could move like a ghost.

"We were just talking about Ajax," Brockhurst informed me, squatting down to join our conference.

The gargoyle followed suit.

"Yeah," Gus confirmed. "The three of us wanted to make a suggestion to you."

"Right," Brockhurst nodded. "Gus and me and the Gremlin."

"The Gremlin?" I asked.

The Imp craned his neck to peer around him.

"He must have stayed back at camp," he shrugged.

"About Ajax," Tanda prompted.

"We think you should pull him from the team," Gus announced. "Send him back to Deva and out of the line of fire."

"It's not for us," Brockhurst hastened to clarify. "It's for him. He's a nice old guy, and we'd hate to see anything happen to him."

"He *is* pretty old," I murmured.

"Old!" Gus exclaimed. "Boss, the Gremlin says he's tailed him for over two hundred years…two hundred! According to him, Ajax was old when their paths first crossed. It won't kill him to miss this one war, but it might kill him to fight in it."

"Why is the Gremlin tailing him, anyway?" I asked.

"I've told you before, kid," a voice boomed in my ear. "Gremlins don't exist."

With that pronouncement, Aahz sank down at my side, between me and Tanda. As I attempted to restore my heart rate to normal, it occurred to me I knew an awful lot of light-footed people.

"Hi, Aahz," I said, forcing a smile. "We were just talking about…"

"I know, I heard," Aahz interrupted. "And for a change I agree."

"You do?" I blinked.

"Sure," he yawned. "It's a clear-cut breach of contract. He hired out his services as a bowman, and the first assignment you give him, he literally lays down on the job."

Actually, it had been the second assignment. I had a sudden flash recollection of Ajax drawing and firing in a smooth, fluid motion, cutting down a signal standard so distant it was barely visible.

"My advice would be to send him back," Aahz was saying. "If you want to soothe your conscience, give him partial payment and a good recommendation, but the way he is, he's no good to anybody."

Perhaps it was because of Tanda's lecture, but I was suddenly aware that Aahz had specifically stated his suggestion as 'advice,' not an order.

"Heads up, brood," Brockhurst murmured. "We've got company."

Following his gaze, I saw Ajax stumbling toward us, his ghost-like paleness flickering in the darkness like…well, like a ghost. It occurred to me that what had started out as a moment of solitude was becoming awfully crowded.

"Evenin', youngster," he saluted. "Didn't mean to interrupt nothin'! Didn't know you folks was havin' a meetin'."

"We…ah…we were just talking," I explained, suddenly embarrassed.

"I kin guess about what, too," Ajax sighed. "Wal, I was goin' to do this private-like, but I suppose the rest a' you might as well hear it, too."

"Do what, Ajax?" I asked.

"Resign," he said. "Seems to me to be the only decent thing to do after what happened today."

"It could have happened to anyone," I shrugged.

"Nice of you to say so, youngster," Ajax smiled, "but I kin see the handwriting on the wall. I'm just too old to be any good to anybody anymore. 'Bout time I admitted it to myself."

I found myself noticing the droop in his shoulders and a listless-ness that hadn't been there when we first met on Deva.

"Don't fret about payin' me," Ajax continued, "I didn't do nothin', so I figger you don't owe me nothin'. If somebody'll just blip me back to Deva, I'll get outta yer way and let you fight your war the way it should be fought."

"Well, Ajax," Aahz sighed, rising to his feet and extending his hand. "We're going to miss you."

"Just a minute!" I found myself saying in a cold voice. "Are you trying to tell me you're breaking our contract?"

Ajax's head came up with a snap.

"I expected better from a genuine Archer," I concluded.

"I wouldn't call it a breach of contract, youngster," the old bowman corrected me carefully. "More like a termination by mutual consent. I'm jes' too old…"

"Old?" I interrupted. "I knew you were old when I hired you. I knew you were old when I planned my strategy for tomorrow's fight around that bow of yours. I knew you were old, Ajax, but I didn't know you were a coward!"

There was a sharp intake of breath somewhere nearby, but I didn't see who it was. My attention was focused on Ajax. It was no longer a defeated, drooping old man, but a proud, angry warrior who loomed suddenly over me.

"Sonny," he growled. "I know I'm old, 'cause in my younger days I would have killed you for sayin' that. I never run from a fight in my life, and I never broke a contract. If you got some shootin' fer me to do tomorrow, I'll do it. Then maybe you'll see what havin' a genuine Archer on your side is all about!"

With that, he spun on his heel and stalked off into the darkness.

It had been a calculated risk, but I still found I was covered with cold sweat from facing the old man's anger. I also realized the rest of the group was staring at me in silent expectation.

"I suppose you're all wondering why I did that," I smiled.

I had hoped for a response, but the silence continued.

"I appreciate all your advice, and hope you continue to give it in the future. But I'm leading this force, and the final decisions have to be mine."

Out of the corner of my eye, I saw Aahz cock his eyebrow, but I ignored him.

"Everyone, including Ajax, said if I let him go, if I sent him back to Deva, there would be no harm done. I disagree. It would have taken away the one thing the years have left untouched…his pride. It would have confirmed to him his worst fears, that he's become a useless old man."

I scanned my audience. Not one of them could meet my eye.

"So he might get killed. So what? He's accepted that risk in every war he's fought in. I'd rather order him into a fight knowing for certain he'd be killed than condemn him to a living death as a washed-up barfly. This way, he has a chance, and as his employer, I feel I owe him that chance."

I paused for breath. They were looking at me again, hanging on my next words.

"One more thing," I snarled. "I don't want to hear any more talk about him being useless. That old man still handles a bow better than anyone I've ever seen. If I can't find a way to use him effectively, then it's my fault as a tactician, not his! I've got my shortcomings, but I'm not going to blame them on Ajax any more than I'd blame them on any of you."

Silence reigned again, but I didn't care. I had spoken my piece, and felt no compulsion to blather on aimlessly just to fill the void.

"Well, boss," Brockhurst cleared his throat getting to his feet. "I think I'll turn in now."

"Me, too," echoed Gus, also rising.

"Just one thing," the Imp paused and met my gaze squarely. "For the record, it's a real pleasure working for you."

The gargoyle nodded his agreement, and the two of them faded into the brush.

There was a soft kiss on my cheek, but by the time I turned my head, Tanda had disappeared.

"You know, kid," Aahz said, "you're going to make a pretty good leader some day."

"Thanks, Aahz," I blinked.

"...if you live that long," my mentor concluded.

We sat side by side in silence for a while longer. Gleep had apparently dozed off, for he was snoring softly as I continued petting him.

"If it isn't prying," Aahz asked finally, "what is this master plan you have for tomorrow that's built around Ajax?"

I sighed and closed my eyes.

"I haven't got one," I admitted. "I was kind of hoping you'd have a few ideas."

"I was afraid you were going to say that," Aahz grumbled.

XIX.

"What if they gave a war, and only one side came?"
LUCIFER

"WAKE UP, KID!"

I returned to consciousness as I was being forcefully propelled sideways along the forest floor, presumably assisted by the ready toe of my mentor.

After I had slid to a stop, I exerted most of my energy and raised my head.

"Aahz," I announced solemnly, "as leader of this team, I have reached another decision. In the future, I want Tanda to wake me up."

"Not a chance," Aahz leered. "She's off scouting our right flank. It's me or the dragon."

Great choice. I suddenly realized how bright it was.

"Hey!" I blinked. "How late is it?"

"Figure we've got about a minute before things start popping," Aahz said casually.

"How long?" I gasped.

Aahz's brow furrowed for a moment as he reflected on his words. Klahdish units of time still gave him a bit of trouble.

"An hour!" he smiled triumphantly. "That's it. An hour."

"That's better," I sighed, sinking back to a horizontal position.

"On your feet, kid!" Aahz ordered. "We let you sleep as late as we could, but now you're needed to review the troops."

"Have you briefed everybody?" I yawned, sitting up. "Is the plan clear?"

"As clear as it's going to be, all things considered," Aahz shrugged.

"Okay," I responded, rolling to my feet. "Let's go. You can fill me in on our new developments along the way."

Aahz and I had been up most of the night formulating today's plan, and I found I was actually eager to see it implemented.

"You should be thankful you aren't on the other side," Aahz chortled as we moved to join the others. "Old Claude's been making the most of the time we gave him."

"Keeping them busy, is he?" I smiled.

"Since sun-up," Aahz confirmed smugly. "Drilling, sharpening swords—never a dull moment in the Empire's army, that's for sure."

I wasn't sure I shared Aahz's enthusiasm for the enemy's spending lots of time sharpening their swords. Fortunately, I was spared the discomfort of replying as Gus lumbered up to us.

"You just missed Brockhurst's report," he informed us. "Still nothing on the left flank."

"Wouldn't we be able to tell from their signals if they were moving up additional support?" I asked.

"If you believe their signals," Aahz countered. "It wouldn't be the first time an army figured out the enemy had broken their code and started sending misleading messages."

"Oh," I said wisely.

"Speaking of signals," Aahz grinned. "You know the messages they were sending yesterday? The ones that went 'encountered minor resistance'?"

"I remember," I nodded.

"Well, it seems Claude has decided he needs to up the ante if he's going to get a promotion out of this. Overnight we've become 'armed opposition...must be subdued forcefully!' Neat, huh?"

I swallowed hard.

"Does that mean they'll be moving reinforcements?" I asked, trying to sound casual.

"Not a chance, kid" Aahz winked. "Claude there has turned down every offer of assistance that came down the line. He keeps insisting he can handle it with the company he's commanding.

"I'd say he's got his neck way, way out," Gus commented.

"...and we're just the ones to chop it off for him, Aahz nodded.

"Where's Ajax?" I asked, changing the subject.

"Down at the forest line picking out his firing point, Gus replied. "Don't worry, boss. He's awake."

Actually, that wasn't my worry concerning Ajax at all. In my mind's eye, I could still see his angry stance when I called him a coward the night before.

"Mornin', youngster," the bowman hailed, emerging from the bush. "Think I got us a place all picked out."

"Hi, Ajax," I replied. "Say...um...when you get a minute, I'd like to talk to you about last night."

"Think nothin' of it," Ajax assured me with a grin. "I plum fergot about it already."

There was a glint in his eye that contradicted his words, but if he was willing to pretend nothing had happened, I'd go along with it for now.

"I hate to interrupt," Aahz interrupted. "But I think friend Claude's just about ready to make his move."

Sure enough, the distant encampment was lining up in a marching formation. The hand-drawn wagons were packed and aligned, with the escort troops arrayed to the front and sides. The signal tower, despite its appearance, was apparently also portable and was being pushed along at the rear of the formation by several sweating soldiers.

"Late!" Ajax sneered. "I tell ya, youngster, armies are the same in any dimension."

"Okay, kid," Aahz said briskly. "Do your stuff. It's about time we got into position."

I nodded and closed my eyes for concentration. With a few strokes of my mental paintbrush, I altered Gus's features until the gargoyle was the mirror image of myself.

"Pretty good," Ajax commented critically, looking from Gus to me and back again.

I repeated the process, returning Aahz to his "dubious character" disguise.

"Well, we're off," Aahz waved. "Confusion to the enemy!"

Today's plan called for Gus substituting for me. The logic was that should anything to wrong, his stone flesh would not only keep him from harm, but also serve as a shield to defend Aahz.

Somehow it didn't seem right to me, to remain behind in relative safety while sending someone else to take my risks for me. It occurred to me that perhaps I had called the wrong person "coward" last night when speaking with Ajax.

The bowman seemed to accept the arrangement without question, however.

"Follow me, youngster," he cackled. "I don't want to miss any of this!"

With that, he turned and plunged into the brush, leaving me little choice but to trail along behind.

Fortunately, Ajax's chosen vantage point wasn't far. Old or not, I found he set a wicked pace.

Stringing his bow, he crouched and waited, chuckling softly in anticipation.

Settling in beside him, I took a moment to check the energy lines, the invisible streams of energy magicians draw their power from. There were two strong lines nearby, one air, one ground, which was good. While Aahz had taught me how to store the energies internally, with the amount of action scheduled for the day, I wanted all the power I could get.

We could see Aahz and Gus, striding with great dignity toward the selected combat point. The opposing force watched them in frozen silence, as they took their places.

For a moment, everyone stood in tableau.

Then Claude turned to his force and barked out an order. Immediately a half-dozen archers broke from the formation and fanned out on either side of the wagons. Moving with slow deliberation, they each drew and cocked an arrow, then leveled the bows at the two figures blocking the company's progress.

I concentrated my energies.

Claude shouted something at our comrades. They remained motionless.

I concentrated.

The bowmen loosened their missiles. Gus threw up one hand dramatically.

The arrows stopped in mid-air and fell to the ground.

The bowmen looked at each other in amazement. Claude barked another order at them. They shakily drew and fired another barrage.

This one was more ragged than the first, but I managed to stop it as well.

"Nice work, youngster," Ajax exclaimed gleefully. "That's got 'em going."

Sure enough, the neat ranks of soldiers were rippling as the men muttered back and forth among themselves. Claude noted it, too, and ordered his bowmen back into the ranks.

Round one to us!

My elation was short-lived, though. The soldiers were drawing their swords now. The two groups assigned to guarding the sides of the wagon pivoted forward, forming two wings ready to engulf our teammates. As further evidence of Claude's nervousness, he even had the troops assigned to pulling the wagons leave their posts and move up to reinforce the center of his line.

That's what we were waiting for.

"Now, Ajax!" I hissed. "Arch 'em high."

"I remember, youngster," the archer grinned. "I'm ready when you are."

I waited until he raised his bow, then concentrated an intense beam of energy at a point a few inches in front of his bow.

It was like the candle-lighting exercise, and it worked as well now as it had when we had tried it last night.

As each shaft sped from Ajax's bow, it burst into flames and continued on its flight.

Again and again, with incredible speed, the bowman sent his missiles hissing through my ignition point. It required all my concentration to maintain the necessary stream of energy, moving it occasionally as his point of aim changed.

Finally, he dropped his bow back to his side.

"That oughta do it, youngster," he grinned. "Take a look."

I did. There in the distance, behind the soldiers' lines, thin plumes of smoke were rising from the wagons. In a few moments, Claude's supply company would be without supplies.

If we had a few moments! As we watched, the men began to advance on Aahz and Gus, their swords gleaming in the sun.

"Think we'd better do something about that!" Ajax muttered, raising his bow again.

"Wait a second, Ajax!" I ordered, squinting at the distant figures.

There had been a brief consultation between Aahz and Gus, then the gargoyle stepped back and began gesturing wildly at his companion.

It took me a moment, but I finally got the message. With a smile, I closed my eyes and removed Aahz's disguise.

Pandemonium reigned. The soldiers in the front ranks took one look at the demon opposing them and stampeded for the rear, half trampling the men behind them. As word spread through the formation, it became a rout, though I seriously doubt those in the rear knew what they were running from.

If anyone noticed the burning wagons, they didn't slow once.

"Whooee!" Ajax exclaimed thumping me on the back. "That did it. Look at 'em run. You'd think those fellers never seed a Pervert before."

"They probably haven't," I commented, trying to massage some feeling back into my shoulder.

"You know," the bowman drawled, squinting at the scene below. "I got me an idea. Them fellers ran off so fast they fergot to signal to anybody. Think we should do it for 'em?"

"How?" I asked.

"Well," he grinned. "I know the signals, and you're a magician. If I told you what signal to run up, could you do it? Without anybody holdin' it?"

"Sure could," I agreed. "What'll we need for the signal?"

"Le'me think," he frowned. "We'll have to get a skull, and a couple of pieces of red cloth, and a black ball, an—"

"Wait a minute, Ajax," I said, holding up a hand. "I think there's an easier signal they'll understand. Watch this."

I sent one more blast of energy out, and the tower platform burst into flames.

"Think they'll get the message?" I smiled.

Ajax stared at the burning tower for a moment.

"Yer pretty good at that, youngster," he murmured finally. "Throwin' fire that far."

"Well," I began modestly. "We magicians can..."

"'Course," he continued. "If you can do that, then you didn't really need me and Blackie to handle those wagons, did you?"

Too late, I realized my mistake.

"Ajax, I..."

"Kinda strange, you goin' to all that trouble jes' to convince me I'm not useless."

"You're not useless." I barked. "Just because sometimes you're not necessary doesn't mean you're useless. I may be young, but I'm old enough to know that."

Ajax regarded me for a moment, then he suddenly smiled.

"Danged if you aren't right, youngst...Skeeve," he laughed. "Guess I knew it, but plum fergot it there fer a while. Let's go get some wine from that cask strapped to yer dragon. I'd like to thank you proper fer remindin' me."

We headed back to camp together.

XX.

"Chain of command is the backbone of military structure and must be strictly obeyed."
F. CHRISTIAN

THE MOOD BACK at the camp was understandably celebrative. If I had had any hopes for joining in the festivities, however, they were dashed when Aahz hailed me.

"Over here, kid!" he waved. "We've got some planning to do!"

"That's the other side o' bein' a general, youngster," Ajax murmured sympathetically. "'Tain't all speeches and glory. You go on ahead. I'll do my drinkin' with the boys."

With a jerk of his head, he indicated Gus and Brockhurst, who were already at the wine. Tanda was waiting for me with Aahz. That made my choice a little easier.

"Okay, Ajax," I smiled. "I'll catch up with you in a little bit."

"Congratulations, handsome!" Tanda winked as I joined them. "That was as neat a bit of work as I've seen in a long time."

"Thanks, Tanda," I blushed.

"I see you and Ajax are on speaking terms again," Aahz said, regarding me with cocked eyebrows. "That's not a bad trick in itself. How did you do it?"

"We...um...we had a long talk," I replied vaguely. "You said we had some planning to do?"

"More like a briefing," Aahz admitted. "Tanda here brought along a few special-effects items I think you should know about."

I had completely forgotten about Tanda's errand which had left me alone at the Bazaar. Now that I had been reminded, my curiosity soared.

"What 'cha got, Tanda?" I asked eagerly.

"Nothing spectacular," she shrugged. "Knowing Aahz was involved, I figured we'd be on a tight budget so I stuck to the basics."

"Just show him, huh?" Aahz growled. "Spare us the editorial comments."

She stuck her tongue out at him, but produced a small cloth sack from her belt.

"First off," she began. "I thought we could use a little flash powder. It never fails to impress the yokels."

"Flash powder," I said carefully.

"You set fire to it," Aahz supplied. "It burns fast and gives you a cloud of smoke."

"I've got about a dozen small bags of it here," Tanda continued, showing me the contents of her sack. "Various colors and sizes."

"Can I try one?" I asked. "I've never worked with this stuff before."

"Sure," Tanda grinned, extending the sack. "They're yours to use as you see fit. You might as well know what you've got."

I took the sack, and carefully selected one of the small bags from its interior.

"Better toss it to the ground, kid," Aahz cautioned. "Some folks can set it off in their hand, but that takes practice. If you tried it that way now, you'd probably lose a hand."

I obediently tossed the bag on the ground a few feet away. Watching it curiously, I focused a quick burst of energy on it.

There was a bright flash of light accompanied by a soft pop. Blinking my eyes, I looked at where the bag had been. A small cloud of green smoke hung in the air, slowly dissipating in the breeze.

"That's neat!" I exclaimed, reaching into the sack again.

"Take it easy," Aahz warned. "We don't have that much of the stuff."

"Oh! Right, Aahz," I replied, a little sheepish. "What else do you have, Tanda?"

"Well," she smiled. "I guess this would be the pièce-de-résistance."

As she spoke, she seemed to draw something from behind her back. I say "seemed" because I couldn't see anything. From her movements, she was holding a rod about three feet long, but there was nothing in her grasp.

"What is it?" I asked politely.

For a response, she grinned and held whatever it was in front of her. Then she opened her grip and disappeared into thin air.

"Invisibility," Aahz exclaimed. "A cloak of invisibility!"

"Couldn't afford one," came Tanda's voice from somewhere in front of us. "I had to settle for one of these."

What "one of these" was, it turned out, was a sheet of invisibility. It was a sheet of stiff material about three feet by seven feet.

Tanda had been carrying it rolled up in a tube, and her disappearance had been caused by the sheet unrolling into its normal form.

As she and Aahz chatted excitedly about her purchse, I had an opportunity to further my knowledge in the field of invisibility.

Invisible sheets, it seems were made of roughly the same material as invisible cloaks. Since the sheets were carried, not worn, they did not require the flexibility and softness necessary for a cloak. Consequently, they were considerably cheaper than the cloaks.

The effect was sort of like one-way glass. When you were on the right side of an invisible sheet, you could see through it perfectly well to observe whatever or whoever was on the other side. They, however, could not see you.

We were still discussing the potential uses of the new tool when Brockhurst hastened up to our group.

"Hey, boss!" he called. "We've got company!"

"Who? Where?" I asked calmly.

"Down on the meadow," the Imp responded, pointing. "The Gremlin says there's some kind of group forming out there."

"What Gremlin?" Aahz snarled.

"C'mon, Aahz," Tanda called, starting off. "Let's check this out."

There was indeed a group on the meadow, Empire soldiers all. The puzzling thing was their activity, or specifically their lack of it. They seemed to be simply standing and waiting for something.

"What are they doing, Aahz?" I whispered, as we studied the group from the concealment of the tree line.

"They're standing and waiting," Aahz supplied.

"I can see that," I grimaced. "But what are they waiting for?"

"Probably for us," my mentor replied.

"For us?" I blinked. "Why?"

"For a war council," Aahz grinned. "Look at it, kid. Aren't they doing the same thing we did when we wanted to talk? They're even standing in the same spot."

I restudied the group in this light. Aahz was right! The enemy was calling for a war council!

"Do you think we should go out there?" I asked nervously.

"Sure," Aahz replied. "But not right away. Let 'em sweat a little. They kept us waiting the first time, remember?"

It was nearly half an hour before we stepped from the tree line and advanced across the meadow to where the soldiers stood

waiting. I had taken the precaution of outfitting Aahz in his "dubious character" disguise for the conference. As for myself, I was bearing the invisibility sheet before me, so that though I was walking along beside Aahz, to the soldiers it appeared he was alone.

There were more soldiers at the meeting point than there had been at our first meeting with Claude. Even to my untrained eye, it was apparent that there were more than half a dozen officers present among the honor guard.

"You wish a meeting?" Aahz asked haughtily drawing to a halt before the group.

There was a ripple of quick consultation among the soldiers. Finally one of them, apparently the leader, stepped forward.

"We wish to speak with your master!" he announced formally.

"He's kinda busy right now," Aahz yawned. "Anything I can help you with?"

The leader reddened slightly.

"I am the commander of this sector!" he barked. "I demand to see Skeeve, commander of the defense, not his lackey!"

I dropped one of the bags of flash powder on the ground at my feet.

"If you insist," Aahz growled. "I'll get him. But he won't be happy."

"I'm not here to make him happy," the leader shouted. "Now be off with you."

"That won't be necessary," Aahz leered. "He's a magician. He hears and sees what his servants hear and see. He'll be along."

That was my cue. I let drop the sheet of invisibility and simultaneously ignited the bag of flash powder.

The results were spectacular.

The soldiers, with the exception of the leader, fell back several steps. To them, it looked like I had suddenly appeared from thin air, materializing in a cloud of red smoke.

For me, the effect was less impressive. As the bag of flash powder went off, it was made apparent to me that watching a cloud of smoke from a distance was markedly different from standing at ground zero.

As I was enveloped in the scarlet billows, my feeling was not of elated triumph, but rather a nearly overwhelming desire to cough and sneeze.

My efforts to suppress my reactions caused me to contort my features to the point where I must have borne more than a faint resemblance to Gus.

"Steady, Master!" Aahz cautioned.

"Aahz. Ah!" I gasped.

"Do not let your anger overcome your reason," my mentor continued hastily. "They don't know the powers they trifle with."

"I...I did not wish to be disturbed," I managed at last, regaining my breath as the smoke dissipated.

The leader of the group had held his ground through the entire proceedings, though he looked a bit paler and less sure of himself than when he had been dealing with just Aahz.

"We...um...apologize for bothering you," he began uncertainly. "But there are certain matters requiring your immediate attention...specifically the war we are currently engaged in."

I eyed him carefully. He seemed to be of a different cut than Claude had been.

"I'm afraid you have me at a disadvantage, sir," I said cagily. "You seem to know me, but I don't recall having met you before."

"We have not met before," the officer replied grimly. "If we had, be assured one of us would not be here currently. I know you by reputation, specifically your recent efforts to resist the advance of our army. For myself, I am Antonio, commander of the right wing of the left flank of the Empire's army. These are my officers."

He indicated the soldiers behind him with a vague wave of his hand. The men responded by drawing themselves more erect and thrusting their chins out arrogantly.

I acknowledged them with a slight nod.

"Where is Claude?" I asked casually. "I was under the impression he was an officer of this sector."

"You are correct," Antonio smirked. "He was. He is currently being detained until he can be properly court-martialed...for incompetence!"

"Incompetence?" I echoed. "Come now, sir. Aren't you being a little harsh? While Claude may have overstepped his abilities a bit, I wouldn't say he's incompetent. I mean, after all, he was dealing with supernatural powers, if you know what I mean."

As I spoke, I wiggled my fingers dramatically at Aahz and removed his disguise.

The jaws of the attending officers dropped, ruining their arrogant jut. Then Aahz grinned at them, and their mouths clicked shut in
unison as they swallowed hard.

Antonio was unimpressed.

"Yes, yes," he said briskly, waving a hand as if at an annoying fly.
"We have had reports—many reports—as to your rapport with demons. Claude's incompetence is in his disastrous underestimation of the
forces opposing him. Be assured, I will not be guilty of the same error."

"Don't count on it, Tony," Aahz leered. "We demons can be a
pretty tricky lot."

The officer ignored him.

"However, we are not here for idle pleasantries," he said, fixing
me with a stern gaze. "I believe we have a dispute to settle concerning right of passage over this particular piece of terrain."

"We have a dispute concerning your right of passage over the
kingdom of Possiltum," I corrected.

"Yes, yes," Antonio yawned. "Of course, if you want to stop us
from gaining Possiltum, you had best stop us here."

"That's about how we had it figured," Aahz agreed.

"Not to belabor the point, Antonio," I smiled. "But I believe
we *do* have you stopped."

"Temporarily," the officer smiled. "I expect that situation to
change shortly…shall we say, a few hours after dawn? Tomorrow?"

"We'll be here," Aahz nodded.

"Just a moment," I interrupted. "Antonio, you strike me as being a sporting man. Would you like to make our encounter tomorrow a bit more interesting? Say, with a little side wager?"

"Such as what?" the officer scowled.

"If you lose tomorrow," I said carefully. "Will you admit Claude's
defeat had nothing to do with incompetence and drop the charges
against him?"

Antonio thought for a moment, then nodded.

"Done," he said, "Normally I would fear what the reaction of
my superiors would be, but I am confident of my victory. There are
things even a demon cannot stand against."

"Such as…?" Aahz drawled.

"You will see," the officer smiled. "Tomorrow."

With that, he spun on his heel and marched off, his officers
trailing behind him.

"What do you think, Aahz?" I murmured.

"Think?" my mentor scowled. "I think you're going soft, kid. First Brockhurst, now Claude. What is this 'be kind to enemies' kick you're on?"

"I meant about tomorrow," I clarified quickly.

"I dunno, kid," Aahz admitted. "He sounded too confident for comfort. I wish I knew what he's got up his sleeve that's supposed to stop demons."

"Well," I sighed. "I guess we'll see tomorrow."

XXI.

"It takes a giant to fight a giant!"
H. PRYM

OUR PENSIVENESS WAS still with us the next day.

Our rivals were definitely up to something, but we couldn't tell exactly what it was. Tanda and Brockhurst had headed out on a scouting trip during the night and had brought back puzzling news. The Empire's soldiers had brought up some kind of heavy equipment, but it was hidden from sight by a huge box. All our scouts could say for sure was that whatever the secret weapon was, it was big and it was heavy.

Gus offered to fly over the box to take a quick peek inside, but we vetoed the idea. With the box constantly in the center of a mass of soldiers, there was no way the gargoyle could carry out his mission unobserved. So far we had kept the gargoyle's presence on our team a secret, and we preferred to keep it that way. Even if we disguised him as Aahz or myself, it would betray the fact that someone in our party was able to fly. As Aahz pointed out, it looked like this campaign would be rough enough without giving the opposition advance warning of the extent of our abilities.

This was all tactically sound and irrefutably logical. It also did nothing to reassure me as Aahz and I stood waiting for Antonio to make his opening gambit.

"Relax, kid," Aahz murmured. "You look nervous."

"I *am* nervous," I snapped back. "We're standing out here waiting to fight, and we don't know who or what we're supposed to be fighting. You'll forgive me if that makes me a trifle edgy."

I was aware I was being unnecessarily harsh on my mentor. Ajax and Gus were standing by, and Brockhurst and Tanda were watching for any new developments. The only team member unaccounted for this morning was the Gremlin, but I thought it wisest not to bring this to Aahz's attention. I assumed our elusive blue friend was off somewhere with Gleep, as my pet was also missing.

Everything which could have been done in preparation had been done. However, I still felt uneasy.

"Look at it this way, kid," Aahz tried again. "At least we know what we *aren't* up against."

What we weren't dealing with was soldiers. Though a large number of them were gathered in the near vicinity, there seemed to be no effort being made to organize or arm them for battle. As the appointed time drew near, it became more and more apparent that they were to be spectators only in the upcoming fray.

"I think I'd rather deal with soldiers," I said glumly.

"Heads up, kid," Aahz retorted nudging me with his elbow. "Whatever's going to happen is about to."

I knew what he meant, which bothered me. There was no time to ponder it, however. Antonio had just put in his appearance.

He strolled around one corner of the mammoth box deep in conversation with a suspicious-looking character in a hooded cloak. He shot a glance in our direction, smiled and waved merrily.

We didn't wave back.

"I don't like the look of this, kid," Aahz growled.

I didn't either, but there wasn't much we could do except wait. Antonio finished his conversation with the stranger and stepped back, folding his arms across his chest. The stranger waved some of the onlooking soldiers aside, then stepped back himself. Drawing himself up, he began weaving his hands back and forth in a puzzling manner. Then the wind carried the sound to me and I realized he was chanting.

"Aahz!" I gasped. "They've got their own magician."

"I know," Aahz grinned back. "But from what I can hear he's bluffing them the same way you bluffed the court back at Possiltum. He probably doesn't have any more powers than I do."

No sooner had my mentor made his observation than the side of the huge box which was facing us slowly lowered itself to the ground. Revealed inside the massive container was a dragon.

The box had been big, better than thirty feet long and twenty feet high, but from the look of the dragon he must have been cramped for space inside.

He was big! I mean, really big!

Now I've never kidded myself about Gleep's size. Though his ten-foot length might look big here on Klah, I had seen dragons on Deva that made him look small. The dragon currently facing us, however, dwarfed everything I had seen before.

He was an iridescent bluish-green his entire length, which was far more serpentine than I was accustomed to seeing in a dragon. He had massive bat wings which he stretched and flexed as he clawed his way out of the confining box. There was a silver glint from his eye sockets which would have made him look machine-like, were it not for the fluid grace of his powerful limbs.

For a moment, I was almost overcome by the beautiful spectacle he presented, emerging onto the battlefield. Then he threw his head back and roared and my admiration turned icy cold within me.

The great head turned until its eyes were focused directly on us. Then he began to stalk forward.

"Time for the better part of valor, kid," Aahz whispered tugging at my sleeve. "Let's get out of here."

"Wait a minute, Aahz!" I shot back. "Do you see that? What the keeper's holding?"

A glint of gold in the sunlight had caught my eye. The dragon's keeper had a gold pendant clasped in his fist as he urged his beast forward.

"Yea!" Aahz answered. "So?"

"I've seen a pendant like that before!" I explained excitedly. "That's how he's controlling the dragon!"

The Deveel who had been running the Dragon stall where I acquired Gleep had worn a pendant like that. The pendant was used to control dragons…unattached dragons, that is. Attached dragons can be controlled by their owner without other assistance. A dragon becomes attached to you when you feed it. That's how I got Gleep. I fed him, sort of. Actually, he helped himself to a hefty bit of my sleeve.

"Well don't just stand there, kid," Aahz barked, interrupting my reverie. "Get it!"

I reached out with my mind and took a grab at the pendant. The keeper felt it start to go and tightened his grip on it, fighting me for its possession.

"I…I can't get it Aahz," I cried. "He won't let go."

"Then hightail it outta here, kid," my mentor ordered. "Tell Ajax to bag us that keeper. Better tell Gus to stand by with Berfert just in case. I'll try to keep the dragon busy."

An image flashed in my mind. It was a view of me, Skeeve, court magician, bolting for safety while Aahz faced the dragon alone. Something snapped in my mind.

"You go!" I snapped.

"Kid, are you..."

"It's my war and my job," I shouted. "Now get going."

With that I turned to face the oncoming dragon not knowing or caring if Aahz followed my orders. I was Skeeve!

...But it was an awfully big dragon!

I tried again for the pendant, nearly lifting the keeper from his feet with my effort, but the man clung firmly to his possession, screaming orders at the dragon as he did.

I shot a nervous glance at the grim behemoth bearing down on me. If I tried to levitate out of the way, he could just...

"Look out, kid!" came Aahz's voice from behind me.

I half turned, then something barreled past me, interceding itself between me and the oncoming menace.

It was Gleep!

"Gleep!" I shouted. "Get back here!"

My pet paid me no mind. His master was being threatened, and he meant to have a hand in this no matter what I said.

No longer a docile, playful companion, he planted himself between me and the monster, lowered his head to the ground and hissed savagely, a six-foot tongue of flame leaping from his mouth as he did.

The effect on the big dragon was astonishing. He lurched to a stop and sat back on his haunches, cocking his head curiously at the mini-dragon blocking his path.

Gleep was not content with stopping his opponent, however. Heedless of the fact that the other dragon was over four times his size he began to advance stiffly, challenging his rival's right to the field.

The large dragon blinked, then shot a look behind him. Then he looked down on Gleep again, drawing his head back until his long neck formed a huge question mark.

Gleep continued to advance.

I couldn't understand it. Even if the monster couldn't flame, which was doubtful, it was obvious he had the sheer physical power to crush my pet with minimal effort. Still he did nothing, looking desperately about him almost as if he were embarrassed.

I watched in spell bound horror. It couldn't last. If nothing else, Gleep was getting too close to the giant to be ignored. Any minute now, the monster would have to react.

Finally, after a final glance at his frantic keeper, the big dragon did react. With a sigh, one of his taloned front paws lashed out horizontally in a cuff that would have caved in a building. It struck Gleep on the side of his head and sent him sprawling.

My pet was game, though, and struggled painfully to his feet, shaking his head as if to clear it.

Before he could assume his aggressive stance, however, the big dragon stretched his neck down until their heads were side by side and began to mutter and grumble in Gleep's ear. My dragon cocked his head as if listening, then "whuffed" in response.

As the stunned humans and non-humans watched, the two dragons conversed in the center of the battlefield punctuating their mutterings with occasional puffs of smoke.

I tried to edge forward to get a better idea of exactly what was going on, but the big dragon turned a baleful eye on me and let loose a blast of flame which kept me at a respectful distance. Not that I was afraid, mind you; Gleep seemed to have the situation well in hand...or talon as the case might be. Well, I had always told Aahz that Gleep was a very talon-ted dragon.

Finally, the big dragon drew himself up, turned, and majestically left the field without a backward glance, his head impressively high. Ignoring the angry shouts of the soldiers, he returned to his box and dropped his haunches to a sit with his back to the entire proceedings.

His keeper's rage was surpassed only by Antonio's. He screamed at the keeper with purpled face and frantic gestures until the keeper angrily pulled the control pendant from around his neck, handed it to the officer, and stalked off. Antonio blinked at the pendant, then flung it to the ground and started off after the keeper.

That was all the opening I needed. Reaching out with my mind, I brought the pendant winging to my hand.

"Aahz!" I began.

"I don't believe it," my mentor mumbled to himself. "I saw it, but I still don't believe it."

"Gleep!"

My pet came racing up to my side, understandably pleased with himself.

"Hi, fella!" I cried, ignoring his breath and throwing my arms around his neck in a hug. "What happened out there, anyway?"

"Gleep!" my pet said evasively, carefully studying a cloud.

If I had expected an answer, it was clear I wasn't going to get one.

"I still don't believe it," Aahz repeated.

"Look, Aahz," I remembered, holding the pendant aloft. "Now we don't have to worry about that or any other dragon. We've shown a profit!"

"So we did," Aahz scowled. "But do me a favor, huh kid?"

"What's that Aahz?" I asked.

"If that dragon, or any dragon, wanders into our camp, don't feed it! We already have one, and that's about all my nerves can stand. Okay?"

"Sure, Aahz," I smiled.

"Gleep!" said my pet, rubbing against me for more petting, which he got.

XXII.

"Hell hath no fury like a demon scorched!"
C. MATHER

OUR NEXT WAR council made the previous ones look small. This was only to be expected, as we were dealing with the commander of the entire left flank of the Empire's army.

Our meeting was taking place in a pavilion constructed specifically for that purpose, and the structure was packed with officers, including Claude. It seemed Antonio was true to his word, even though he himself was not currently present.

In the face of such a gathering, we had decided to show a bit more force ourselves. To that end, Tanda and Brockhurst were accompanying us, while Gleep snuffled around outside. Gus and Ajax we were still held in reserve, while the Gremlin had not reappeared since the confrontation of dragons.

I didn't like the officer we were currently dealing with. There was something about his easy, oily manner that set me on edge. I strongly suspected he had ascended to his current position by poisoning his rivals.

"...so, you'd like us to surrender," he was saying thoughtfully, drumming his fingers on the table before him.

"...or withdraw, or turn aside," I corrected. "Frankly, we don't care *what* you do, as long as you leave Possiltum alone."

"We've actually been considering doing just that," the commander said, leaning back in his chair to study the pavilion's canopy.

"Is that why you've been moving up additional troops all day long?" Brockhurst asked sarcastically.

"Merely an internal matter, I assure you," the commander purred. "All my officers are assembled here, and they're afraid their troops will fall to mischief if left to their own devices."

"What my colleague means," Aahz interjected, "is we find it hard to believe you're actually planning to accede to our demands."

"Why not?" the commander shrugged. "That is what you've been fighting for, isn't it? There comes a point when a commander must ask himself if it won't cost him more dearly to fight a battle

than to pass it by. So far, your resistance utilizing demons and dragons has shown us this battle could be difficult indeed."

"There are more where they come from," I interjected. "Should
the need arise."

"So you've demonstrated," the commander smiled waving a
casual hand at Tanda and Brockhurst. "Witches and devils make an
impressive addition to your force."

I deemed it unwise to point out to him that Brockhurst was an
Imp, not a Deveel.

"Then you agree to bypass Possiltum?" Aahz asked bluntly.

"I agree to discuss it with my officers," the commander
clarified. "All I ask is that you leave one of your...ah...assistants
behind."

"What for?" I asked.

I didn't like the way he was eyeing Tanda.

"To bring you word of our decision, of course," the commander shrugged. "None of my men would dare enter your camp,
even granted a messenger's immunity."

There was a mocking tone to his voice I didn't like.

"I'll stay, Skeeve," Aahz volunteered.

I considered it. Aahz had demonstrated his ability to take care
of himself time and time again. Still I didn't trust the commander.

"Only if you are willing to give us one of your officers in return
as a hostage," I replied.

"I've already said none of..." the commander began.

"He need not enter our camp," I explained. "He can remain
well outside our force, on the edge of the tree line in full view of
your force. I will personally guarantee his safety."

The commander chewed his lip thoughtfully.

"Very well," he said. "Since you have shown an interest in his
career, I will give you Claude to hold as a hostage."

The young officer paled, but remained silent.

"Agreed," I said. "We will await your decision."

I nodded to my comrades, and they obediently began filing out
of the pavilion. Claude hesitated, then joined the procession.

I wanted to tell Aahz to be careful, but decided against it. It
wouldn't do to admit my partner's vulnerability in front of the
commander. Instead, I nodded curtly to the officers and followed
my comrades.

Tanda and Brockhurst were well on their way back to the treeline. Claude, on the other hand, was waiting for me as I emerged and fell in step beside me.

"While we have a moment," he said stiffly. "I would like to thank you for interceding in my behalf with my superiors."

"Don't mention it," I mumbled absently.

"No, really," he persisted. "Chivalry to an opponent is rarely seen these days. I think…"

"Look, Claude," I growled. "Credit it to my warped sense of justice. I don't like you, and didn't when we first met, but that doesn't make you incompetent. Unpleasant, perhaps, but not incompetent."

I was harsher with him than I had intended, but I was worried about Aahz.

Finding himself thus rebuked, he sank into an uncomfortable silence which lasted almost until we reached the trees. Then he cleared his throat and tried again.

"Um…Skeeve?"

"Yeah?" I retorted curtly.

"I…um…what I was trying to say was that I am grateful and would repay your favor by any reasonable means at my disposal."

Despite my concern, his offer penetrated my mind as a potential opportunity.

"Would answering a few questions fall under the heading of 'reasonable'?" I asked casually.

"Depending upon the questions," he replied carefully. "I *am* still a soldier, and my code of conduct clearly states…"

"Tell you what," I interrupted. "I'll ask the questions, and you decide which ones are okay to answer. Fair enough?"

"So it would seem," he admitted.

"Okay," I began. "First question. Do you think the commander will actually bypass Possiltum?"

The officer avoided my eyes for a moment, then shook his head briskly.

"I should not answer that," he grimaced. "But I will. I do not feel the commander is even considering it as a serious possibility, nor does any officer in that tent. He is known as 'The Brute," even among his most loyal and seasoned troops. May I assure you he did not acquire that nickname by surrendering or capitulating while his force was still intact."

"Then why did he go through the motions of the meeting just now?" I queried.

"To gain time," Claude shrugged. "As your assistants noted he is using the delay to mass his troops. The only code he adheres to is 'Victory at all costs.' In this case, it seems it is costing him his honor."

I thought on this for a moment before asking my next question.

"Claude," I said carefully. "You've faced us in battle, and you know your own army. If your prediction is correct and the Brute attacks in force, in your opinion, what are our chances of victory?"

"Nil," the officer replied quietly. "I know it may sound like enemy propaganda, but I ask you to believe my sincerity. Even with the additional forces you displayed this evening, if the Brute sets the legions in motion they'll roll right over you. Were I in your position, I would take advantage of the cover of night to slip away, and not fear the stigma of cowardice. You're facing the mightiest army ever assembled. Against such a force there is no cowardice, only self-preservation."

I believed him. The only question was what should I do with the advice.

"I thank you for your counsel," I said formally. "And will consider your words carefully. For now, if you will please remain here in the open as promised, I must consult with my troops."

"One more thing," Claude said, laying a restraining hand on my arm. "If any harm befalls your assistant, the one you left at the meeting, I would ask that you remember I was here with you and had no part in it."

"I will remember," I nodded withdrawing my arm. "But if the Brute tries to lay a hand on Aahz, I'll wager he'll wish he hadn't."

As I turned to seek out my team, I wished I felt as confident as I sounded.

Tanda came to me readily when I caught her eye and beckoned her away from the others.

"What is it, Skeeve?" she asked as we moved away into the shadows. "Are you worried about Aahz?"

I was, though I didn't want to admit it just yet. The night was almost gone, with no signs of movement or activity from the pavilion. Still, I clung to my faith in Aahz. When that failed, I turned my mind to other exercises to distract it from fruitless worry.

"Aahz can take care of himself," I said gruffly. "There's something else I wanted your opinion on."

"What's that?" she asked cocking her head.

"As you know," I began pompously. "I am unable to see the disguise spells I cast. Though everyone else is fooled, as the originator of the spell, I still continue to see things in their true form."

"I didn't know that," she commented. "But continue."

"Well," I explained. "I was thinking that if we actually have to fight the army, we could use additional troops. I've got an idea, but I need you to tell me if it actually works."

"Okay," she nodded. "What is it?"

I started to resume my oration, then realized I was merely stalling. Instead, I closed my eyes and focused my mind on the small grove of trees ahead.

"Hey!" cried Tanda. "That's terrific."

I opened my eyes, being careful to maintain the spell.

"What do you see?" I asked nervously.

"A whole pack of demons...oops...I mean Perverts," she reported gaily. "Bristling with swords and spears. That's wild!"

It worked. I was correct when I guessed that my disguise spell could work on any living thing, not just men and beasts.

"I've never seen anything like it," Tanda marveled, "Can you make them move?"

"I don't know," I admitted. "I just..."

"Boss! Hey Boss!" Brockhurst shouted sprinting up to us. "Come quick! You'd better see this!"

"What is it?" I called, but the Imp had reversed his course and was headed for the tree line.

A sudden fear clutched at my heart.

"C'mon, Tanda," I growled and started off.

By the time we reached the tree line the whole team was assembled there, talking excitedly among themselves.

"What is it?" I barked joining them.

The group fell silent, avoiding my eyes. Brockhurst lifted a hand and pointed across the meadow.

There, silhouetted against a huge bonfire was Aahz, hanging by his neck from a crude gallows. His body was limp and lifeless as he rotated slowly at the end of the rope. At his feet, a group of soldiers were gathered to witness the spectacle.

Relief flooded over me, and I began to giggle hysterically. Hanging! If only they knew!

Alarm showed in the faces of my team as they studied my reaction in shocked silence.

"Don't worry!" I gasped. "He's okay!"

Early in my career with Aahz, I had learned that one doesn't kill pervects by hanging them. Their neck muscles are too strong! They can hang all day without being any the worse for wear. I had, of course, learned this the hard way one day when we…

"At least they have the decency to burn the body," Claude murmured from close beside me.

My laughter died in my throat.

"What?" I cried, spinning around.

Sure enough, the soldiers had cut down Aahz's 'body' and were carrying it toward the bonfire with the obvious intention of throwing it in.

Fire! That was a different story. Fire was one of the things that could kill Aahz deader than…

"Ajax!" I cried. "Quick! Stop them from…"

It was too late.

With a heave from the soldiers, Aahz arced into the roaring flames. There was a quick burst of light, then nothing.

Gone! Aahz!

I stood staring at the bonfire in disbelief. Shock numbed me to everything else as my mind reeled at the impact of my loss.

"Skeeve!" Tanda said in my ear, laying a hand on my shoulder.

"Leave me alone!" I croaked.

"But the army…"

She let the word trail off, but it made its impact. Slowly I became conscious of the world around me.

The legions, having given us our answer, were massing for battle. Drums boomed, heralding the rising sun as it reflected off the polished weapons arrayed to face us.

The Army. They had done this!

With deliberate slowness I turned to face Claude. He recoiled in fear from my gaze.

"Remember!" he cried desperately. "I had nothing to…"

"I remember," I replied coldly. "And for that reason alone I am letting you go. I would advise, however, that you choose a path to follow other than rejoining the army. I have tried to be gentle with them, but if they insist on having war, as I am Skeeve, we shall give it to them!"

XXIII.

"What is this, a Chinese fire drill?"
SUN TZU

I DIDN'T SEE where Claude went after I finished speaking with him, nor did I care. I was studying the opposing army with a new eye. Up to now I had been thinking defensively, planning for survival. Now I was thinking as the aggressor.

The legions were in tight block formations, arrayed some three or four blocks deep and perhaps fifteen blocks wide. Together they presented an awesome impression of power, an irresistible force which would never retreat.

That suited me fine. In fact, I wanted a little insurance that they would not retreat.

"Ajax!" I called without turning my head.

"Here, youngster!" the bowman replied from close beside me.

"Can Blackie send your arrows out beyond those formations?"

"I reckon so," he drawled.

"Very well," I said grimly. "The same drill as the first battle, only this time don't go for the wagons. I want a half circle of fire around their rear."

As before, the bowstring set up a rhythmic "thung" as the bowman began to loose shaft after shaft. This time, however, it seemed the arrows burst into flame more readily.

"Ease off, youngster," Ajax called. "Yer burnin 'em up before they reach the ground."

He was right. Either I was standing directly on a force line, or my anger had intensified my energies. Whatever the reason, I found myself with an incredible amount of power at my disposal.

"Sorry, Ajax," I shouted, and diverted a portion of my mind away from the ignition point.

"Tanda!" I called "Run back and get Gleep!"

"Right, Skeeve," came the reply.

I had a hunch my pet might come in handy before this brawl was done.

The front row of the army's formation was beginning to advance to the rhythmic pounding of drums. I ignored them.

"Brockhurst!"

"Here, boss!" the Imp responded stepping to my side.

"Have you spotted the commander yet?"

"Not yet," came the reply. "He's probably buried back in the middle of the formation somewhere."

"Well climb a tree or something and see if you can pinpoint him," I ordered.

"Right, boss! When I see him, do you want me to go after him?"

"No," I replied grimly. "Report back to me. I want to handle him myself."

The front line was still advancing. I decided I'd better do something about it. With a sweep of my mind, I set fire to the meadow in front of the line's center. The blocks confronted by this barrier ground to a halt while the right and left wings continued their forward movement.

"Gleep!" came a familiar voice accompanied by an even more familiar blast of bad breath.

"We're back!" Tanda announced unnecessarily.

I ignored them and studied the situation. Plumes of white smoke rising from behind the Empire's formation indicated that Ajax was almost finished with his task. Soon, the army would find itself cut off from any retreat. It was time to start thinking about our attack. The first thing I needed was more information.

"Gus!" I said thoughtfully. "I want you to take a quick flight over their formations. See if you can find a spot to drop Berfert where he can do some proper damage."

"Right, boss," the gargoyle grunted lumbering forward.

"Wait a minute," I said, a thought occurring to me. "Tanda, have you still got the invisibility sheet with you?"

"Right here!" she grinned.

"Good," I nodded. "Gus, take the sheet with you. Keep it in front of you as long as you can while you're checking them out. There's no sense drawing fire until you have to."

The gargoyle accepted the sheet with a shrug.

"If you say so, boss," he muttered. "But they can't do much to me."

"Use it anyway," I ordered. "Now get moving."

The gargoyle sprang heavily into the air and started across the meadow with slow sweeps of his massive wings. I found it hard to believe anything that big and made of stone could fly, but I was seeing it. Maybe he used levitation.

"All set, youngster," Ajax chortled, interrupting my thoughts. "Anything else I can do for ya?"

"Not just now, Ajax," I replied. "But stand by."

I was glad that portion of my concentration was free now. This next stunt was going to take all the energy I could muster.

I focused my mind on the grass in front of the advancing left wing. As testimony to the effectiveness of my efforts, that portion of the line ground to an immediate halt.

"Say!" Tanda breathed in genuine admiration. "That's neat."

The effect I was striving for was to have the grass form itself into an army of Imps, rising from the ground to confront the Empire's troops. I chose Imps this time instead of demons because Imps are shorter, and therefore require less energy to maintain the illusion.

Whatever my efforts actually achieved, it was enough to have the soldiers react. After several shouted orders from their officers, the troops let fly a ragged barrage of javelins at the grass in front of them. The weapons, of course, had no effect on their phantom foe.

"Say, youngster," Ajax said nudging me lightly. "You want me to do something about those jokers shootin' at our gargoyle?"

I turned slightly to check Gus's progress. The flying figure had passed over the center line troops, the ones my fire was holding in check. The soldiers could now see the figure behind the invisible sheet, and were reacting with enviable competence.

The archers in their formation were busy loosing their shafts at this strange figure which had suddenly appeared overhead, while their comrades did their best to reach the gargoyle with hurled javelins.

I saw all this at a glance. I also saw something else.

"Wait a minute, Ajax," I ordered. "Look at that!"

The various missiles loosed by the center line were falling to earth in the massed formations of the troops still awaiting commands. Needless to say, this was not well received, particularly as they were still unable to see the actual target of their advance force. To them, it must have appeared that by some magik or demonic possession, their allies had suddenly turned and fired on them.

8

04 | Robert Asprin

Now a few blocks began to return the fire, ordering their own archers into action. Others responded by raising their shields and starting forward with drawn swords.

The result was utter chaos, as the center-line troops tried to defend themselves from the attacks of their own reinforcements.

Mind you, I hadn't planned it this way, but I was quick to capitalize on the situation. If the presence of a gargoyle could cause this kind of turmoil, I thought it would be a good idea to up the ante a little.

With a quick brush of my mind, I altered Gus's appearance. Now they had a full-grown dragon hovering over their midst. The effect was spectacular.

I, however, did not allow myself the luxury of watching. I had learned something in this brief exchange, and I wanted to try it out.

I dissolved my Imp army, then reformed them, not in front of the troops, but in their midst!

This threw the formation into total disorder. As the soldiers struck or threw at the phantomed figures, more often than not they struck their comrades instead.

If this kept up, they would be too busy fighting each other to bother with us.

"Boss!" Brockhurst called, darting up to my side. "I've got the commander spotted!"

"Where?" I asked grimly, trying not to take my concentration from the battle raging in the meadow.

The Imp pointed.

Sure enough! There was the Brute, striding angrily from formation to formation, trying to restore order to his force.

I heard the tell-tale whisper of an arrow being drawn.

"Ajax!" I barked. "Hold your fire. He's mine...all mine!"

As I said this, I dissolved all the Imps in the Brute's vicinity, and instead changed the commander's features until he took on the appearance of Aahz.

The dazed soldiers saw a demon appear in their midst brandishing a sword, a demon of a type they knew could be killed. They needed no further prompting.

I had one brief glimpse of the Brute's startled face before his troops closed on him, then a forest of uniforms blotted him from my view.

"Mission accomplished, boss!" Gus announced, appearing beside me. "What next?"

"What...did you..." I stammered.

I had forgotten that on his return trip, the invisibility sheet would shield the gargoyle from our view. His sudden appearance had startled me.

"Berfert'll be along when he gets done with their siege equipment," Gus continued waving toward the enemy.

I looked across the meadow. He was right! The heavy equipment which had been lined up behind the army was now in flames.

Then I noticed something else.

The army wasn't fighting each other any more. I realized with a start that, between settling accounts with the Brute and Gus's reappearance, I had forgotten to maintain the Imp army.

In the absence of any visible foe, the Empire troops had apparently come to their senses and were now milling about trying to reestablish their formations.

Soon, now, they would be ready to attack again.

"What do we do next, boss?" Brockhurst asked eagerly.

That was a good question. I decided to stall while I tried to work out an answer.

"I'll draw you a diagram" I said confidently. "Somebody give me a sword."

"Here, kid. Use mine," Aahz replied passing me the weapon.

"Thanks," I said absently. "Now, this line is their main formation. If we...Aahz!?"

"Ready and able," my mentor grinned. "Sorry I'm late."

It was Aahz! He was standing there calmly with his arms folded as if he had been part of our group all along. The reactions of the others, however, showed that they were as surprised as I was at his appearance.

"But you..." I stammered. "The fire..."

"Oh, that," Aahz shrugged. "About the time I figured what they were doing, I used the D-Hopper to blink out to another dimension. The only trouble was I hadn't gotten around to re-labeling the controls yet, and I had a heck of a time finding my way back to Klah."

Relief flooded over me like a cool wave. Aahz was alive! More important, he was here! The prospects for the battle suddenly looked much better.

"What should we do next, Aahz?" I asked eagerly.

"I don't know why you're asking me," my mentor blinked innocently. "It looks like you've been doing a fine job so far all by yourself."

Terrific! Now that I needed advice, I got compliments.

"Look, Aahz," I began sternly. "We've got a battle coming up that..."

"Boss!" Brockhurst interrupted. "Something's going on out there!"

With a sinking heart, I turned and surveyed the situation again.

A new figure had appeared on the scene, an officer, from the look of him. He was striding briskly along the front of the formation, alternately shouting and waving his hands. Trailing along in his wake was a cluster of officers, mumbling together and shaking their hands.

"What in the world is that all about?" I murmured half to myself.

"Brace yourself, kid," Aahz advised. "If I'm hearing correctly, it's bad news."

"C'mon, Aahz," I sighed. "How could things get worse than they already are?"

"Easy," Aahz retorted. "That is the supreme commander of the Empire's army. He's here to find out what's holding up his left flank's advance."

XXIV.

"...and then I said to myself, 'Why should I split it two ways?'"
G. MOUSER

THE SUPREME COMMANDER'S name was Big Julie, and he was completely different than what I had expected.

For one thing, when he called for a war council, he came to us. Flanked by his entire entourage of officers, he came all the way across the meadow to stand just short of the tree line, and he came unarmed. What was more, all of his officers were unarmed, presumably at his insistence.

He seemed utterly lacking in the arrogance so prevalent in the other officers we had dealt with. Introducing him to the members of my force, I noticed he treated them with great respect and seemed genuinely pleased to meet each of them, even Gleep.

Our whole team was present for the meeting. We figured that if there was ever a time to display our power, this was it.

In a surprising show of hospitality, Aahz broke out the wine and served drinks to the assemblage. I was a little suspicious of this. Aahz isn't above doctoring drinks to win a fight, but when I caught his eye and raised an eyebrow, he responded with a small shake of his head. Apparently he was playing this round straight.

Then we got down to business.

Big Julie heard us out, listening with rapt attention. When we finished, he sighed and shook his head.

"Ah'm sorry," he announced. "But I can't do it. We've got to keep advancing, you know? That's what armies do!"

"Couldn't you advance in another direction for a while?" I suggested hopefully.

"Aie!" he exclaimed spreading his hands defensively. "What do you think I got here, geniuses? These are soldiers. They move in straight lines, know what I mean?"

"Do they have to move so vigorously?" Aahz muttered. "They don't leave much behind."

"What can I say?" Big Julie shrugged. "They're good boys. They do their job. Sometimes they get a little carried away...like the Brute."

I had hoped to avoid the subject of the Brute, but since it had come up, I decided to face it head-on.

"Say...um...Julie," I began.

"Big Julie!" one of the officers growled out of the corner of his mouth.

"Big Julie!" I amended hastily. "About the Brute. Um...he was...well...I wanted..."

"Don't mention it," Julie waved. "You want to know the truth? You did me a favor."

"I did?" I blinked.

"I was getting a little worried about the Brute, you know what I mean?" the commander raised his eyebrows. "He was getting a little too ambitious."

"In that case..." I smiled.

"Still..." Julie continued, "that's a bad way to go. Hacked apart by your own men. I wouldn't want that to happen to me."

"You should have fed him to the dragons," Aahz said bluntly.

"The Brute?" Julie frowned. "Fed to the dragons? Why?"

"Because then he could have been 'et, too'!"

Apparently this was supposed to be funny, as Aahz erupted into sudden laughter as he frequently does at his own jokes. Tanda rolled her eyes in exasperation.

Big Julie looked vaguely puzzled. He glanced at me, and I shrugged to show I didn't know what was going on either.

"He's strange," Julie announced, stabbing an accusing finger at Aahz. "What's a nice boy like you doing hanging around with strange people? Hey?"

"It's the war," I said apologetically. "You know what they say about strange bedfellows."

"You seem to be doin' all right for yourself!" Julie winked and leered at Tanda.

"You want I should clean up his act, Boss?" Brockhurst asked grimly, stepping forward.

"See!" Julie exploded. "That's what I mean. This is no way to learn warfare. Tell you what. Why don't you let me fix you up with a job, hey? What do you say to that?"

"What pay scale?" Aahz asked.

"Aahz!" I scowled, then turned back to Julie. "Sorry, but we've already got a job...defending Possiltum. I appreciate your offer, but I don't want to leave a job unfinished."

"What have I been telling you?" Julie appealed to his officers. "All the good material has been taken already. Why can't you bring me recruits like this, eh?"

This was all very flattering, but I clung tenaciously to the purpose of our meeting.

"Um...Jul...I mean, Big Julie," I interrupted. "About defending Possiltum. Couldn't you find another kingdom somewhere to attack? We really don't want to have to fight you."

"You don't want to fight?" Julie erupted sarcastically. "You think I want to fight? You think I *like* doing this for a living? You think my boys like killing and conquering all the time?"

"Well..." I began tactfully.

Big Julie wasn't listening. He was out of his seat and pacing up and down, gesturing violently to emphasize his words.

"What kind of dingbat wants to fight?" he asked rhetorically. "Do I look crazy? Do my *boys* look crazy? Everybody thinks we got some kind of weird drive that keeps us going. They think that all we want to do in the whole world is march around in sweaty armor and sharpen swords on other people's helmets. That's what you think too, isn't it? Eh? Isn't it?"

This last was shouted directly at me. By now I was pretty fed up with being shouted at.

"Yes!" I roared angrily. "That's what I think!"

"Well," Julie scowled. "You're wrong because—"

"That's what I think because if you didn't like doing it, you wouldn't do it!" I continued rising to my own feet.

"Just like that!" Julie grimaced sarcastically. "Just stop and walk away."

He turned and addressed his officers.

"He thinks it's easy! Do you hear that? Any of you who don't like to fight, just stop. Eh? Just like that."

A low chorus of chuckles rose from his assembled men. Despite my earlier burst of anger, I found myself starting to believe him. Incredible as it seemed, Julie and his men didn't like being soldiers!

"You think we wouldn't quit if we could?" Julie was saying to me again. "I bet there isn't a man in my whole army who wouldn't take a walk if he thought he could get away with it."

Again, there was a murmur of assent from his officers.

"I don't understand," I said shaking my head. "If *you* don't want to fight, and *we* don't want to fight, what are we doing here?"

"You ever hear of loan sharks?" Julie asked. "You know about organized crime?"

"Organized crime?" I blinked.

"It's like government, kid," Aahz supplied. "Only more effective."

"You'd better believe 'more effective,'" Julie nodded. "That's what we're doing here! Me and the boys, we got a list of gambling debts like you wouldn't believe. We're kinda working it off, paying 'em back in land, you know what I mean?"

"You haven't answered my question," I pointed out. "Why don't you just quit?"

"Quit?" Julie seemed genuinely astonished. "You gotta be kidding. If I quit before I'm paid up, they break my leg. You know?" His wolfish grin left no doubt that the thugs in question would do something a great deal more fatal and painful than just breaking a leg.

"It's the same with the boys here. Right boys?" He indicated his officers with a wave of his hand.

Vigorous nods answered his wave.

"And you ought to see the collection agent they use. Kid, you might be a fair magician where you come from. But," he shuddered, "this, believe me, you don't want to see."

Knowing how tough Big Julie was, I believed him.

Giving me a warm smile, he draped his arm across my shoulders.

"That's why it's really gonna break my heart to kill you. Ya know?"

"Well," I began, "you don't have to...KILL ME!"

"That's right," he nodded vigorously. "I knew you'd understand. A job's a job, even when you hate it."

"Whoa!" Aahz interrupted, holding one flattened hand across the top of the other to form a crude T. "Hold it! Aren't you over-looking something, Jules?"

"That's 'Big Julie'." one of the guards admonished.

"I don't care if he calls himself the Easter Bunny!" my mentor snarled. "He's still overlooking something."

"What's that?" Julie asked.

"Us." Aahz smiled, gesturing to the team. "Aside from the mi-nor detail that Skeeve here's a magician and not that easy to kill, he's got friends. What do you think we'll be doing while you make a try for our leader?"

The whole team edged forward a little. None of them were smiling, not even Gus. Even though they were my friends who I knew and loved, I had to admit they looked mean. I was suddenly very glad they were on my side.

Big Julie, on the other hand, seemed unimpressed.

"As a matter of fact," he smiled, "I expect you to be dying right along with your leader. That is, unless you're really good at running."

"Running from what?" Gus growled. "I still think you're over-looking something. By my count, we've got you outnumbered. Even if you were armed..."

The Supreme Commander cut him short with a laugh. It was a relaxed, confident laugh which no one else joined in on. Then the laugh disappeared and he leaned forward with a fierce scowl.

"Now, I only gonna say this once, so alla you listen close. Big Julie didn't get where he is today by overlooking nothin'. You think I'm outnumbered? Well, maybe you just better count again."

Without taking his eyes from us, he waved his hand in an abrupt motion. At the signal, one of his guards pulled a cord and the sides of the tent fell away.

There were soldiers outside. They hadn't been there when we entered the tent, but they were there now. Hoo boy were they. Ranks and ranks of them, completely surrounding the tent, the nearest barely an arm's length away. The front three rows were archers, with ar-rows nocked and drawn, leveled at our team.

I realized with a sudden calm clarity that I was about to die. The whole meeting had been a trap, and it was a good one. Good enough that we would all be dead if we so much as twitched. I couldn't even kid myself that I could stop that many arrows if they were all loosed at once. Gus might survive the barrage, and maybe the oth-ers could blip away to another dimension in time to save themselves, but I was too far away from Aahz and the D-Hopper to escape.

"I...um...thought war councils were supposed to be off- lim-its for combat." I said carefully.

"I also didn't get where I am today by playing fair." Big Julie shrugged.

"You know," Aahz drawled, "for a guy who doesn't want to fight, you run a pretty nasty war."

"What can I say?" the Supreme Commander asked, spreading
his hands in helpless appeal. "It's a job. Believe me, if there was any
other way, I'd take it. But as it is…"

His voice trailed off, and he began to raise his arm. I realized
with horror that when his hand came down, so would the curtain.

"How much time do we have to find another way?" I asked
desperately.

"You don't," Big Julie sighed.

"AND WE DON'T NEED ANY!" Aahz roared with sudden
glee.

All eyes turned toward him, including my own. He was grinning
broadly while listening to something the Gremlin was whispering in
his ear.

"What's that supposed to mean?" the Supreme Commander
demanded. "And where did this little blue fella come from? Eh?"

He glared at the encircling troops, who looked at each other in
embarrassed confusion.

"This is a Gremlin." Aahz informed him, slipping a comradely
arm around the shoulders of his confidante, "And I think he's got
the answer to our problems. All our problems. You know what I
mean?"

"What does he mean?" Julie scowled at me. "Do you unnerstand
what he's sayin'?"

"Tell him, Aahz." I ordered confidently, wondering all the while
what possible solution my mentor could have found to this mess.

"Big Julie," Aahz smiled, "what could those loan sharks of yours
do if you and your army simply disappeared?"

And so incredibly, it was ended.

Not with fireworks or an explosion or a battle. But, like a lot of
things in my life, in as crazy and off-hand a way as it had started.

And when it had ended, I almost wished it hadn't.

Because then I had to say good-bye to the team.

Saying good-bye to the team was harder than I would have
imagined. Somehow, in all my planning, I had never stopped to
consider the possibility of emerging victorious from the war.

Despite my original worries about the team, I found I had grown
quite close to each of them. I would have liked to keep them around
a little longer, but that would have been impossible. Our next stop
was the capital, and they would be a little too much to explain away.

Besides, as Aahz pointed out, it was bad for morale to let the troops find out how much their commander was being paid, particularly when it was extremely disproportionate to their own wages.

Following his advice, I paid each of them personally. When I was done, however, I found myself strangely at a loss for words. Once again, the team came to my aid.

"Well, boss," Brockhurst sighed. "I guess this is it. Thanks for everything."

"It's been a real pleasure working for you," Gus echoed. "The money's nice, but the way I figure it, Berfert and I owe you a little extra for getting us out of that slop chute. Anytime you need a favor, look us up."

"Youngster," Ajax said, clearing his throat. "I move around a lot, so I'm not that easy to track. If you ever find yourself in a spot where you think I can lend a hand, jes' send a message to the Bazaar and I'll be along shortly."

"I didn't think you visited the Bazaar that often," I asked, surprised.

"Normally I don't," the bowman admitted. "But I will now...jest in case."

Tanda was tossing her coin in the air and catching it with practiced ease.

"I shouldn't take this," she sighed. "But a girl's gotta eat."

"You earned it," I insisted.

"Yea, well, I guess we'll be going," she said, beckoning to the others. "Take care of yourself, handsome."

"Will you be coming back?" I asked hurriedly.

She made a face.

"I don't think so," she grimaced. "If Grimble saw us together..."

"I meant, ever," I clarified.

She brightened immediately.

"Sure," she winked. "You won't get rid of me that easily. Say good-bye to Aahz for me."

"Say good-bye to him yourself," Aahz growled, stepping out of the shadows.

"*There* you are!" Tanda grinned. "Where's the Gremlin? I thought you two were talking."

"We were," Aahz confirmed looking around him. "I don't understand. He was here a minute ago."

"It's as if he didn't exist, isn't it, Aahz?" I suggested innocently.

"Now look, kid!" my mentor began angrily.

A chorus of laughter erupted from the team. He spun in their direction to deliver a scathing reply, but there was a blip of light and they were gone.

We stood silently together for several moments staring at the vacant space. Then Aahz slipped an arm around my shoulder.

"They were a good team, kid," he sighed. "Now pull yourself together. Triumphant generals don't have slow leaks in the vicinity of their eyes. It's bad for the image."

XXX.

"Is everybody happy?"
MACHIAVELLI

AAHZ AND I entered the capital at the head of a jubilant mob of Possiltum citizens.

We were practically herded to the front of the palace by the crowd pressing us forward. The cheering was incredible. Flowers and other, less identifiable, objects were thrown at us or strewn in our path, making the footing uncertain enough that more than once I was afraid of falling and being trampled. The people, at least, seemed thoroughly delighted to see us. All in all, though, our triumphal procession was almost as potentially injurious to our life and limb as the war had been.

I was loving it.

I had never had a large crowd make fuss over me before. It was nice.

"Heads up, kid," Aahz murmured, nudging me in the ribs. "Here comes the reception committee."

Sure enough, there was another procession emerging from the main gates of the palace. It was smaller than ours, but made up for what it lacked in numbers with the prestige of its members.

The king was front and center, flanked closely by Grimble and Badaxe. The chancellor was beaming with undisguised delight. The general, on the other hand, looked positively grim.

Sweeping the crowd with his eyes, Badaxe spotted several of his soldiers in our entourage. His dark expression grew even darker, boding ill for those men. I guessed he was curious as to why they had failed to carry out his orders to stop our return.

Whatever he had in mind, it would have to wait. The king was raising his arms, and the assemblage obediently fell silent to hear what he had to say.

"Lord Magician," he began. "Know that the cheers of the grateful citizens of Possiltum only echo my feelings for this service you have done us."

A fresh wave of applause answered him.

"News of your victory has spread before you," he continued. "And already our historians are recording the details of your triumph...as much as is known, that is."

An appreciative ripple of laughter surged through the crowd.

"While we do not pretend to comprehend the workings of your powers," the king announced, "the results speak for themselves. A mighty army of invincible warriors, vanished into thin air, weapons and all. Only their armor and siege machines littering the empty battlefield mark their passing. The war is won! The threat to Possiltum is ended forever!"

At this, the crowd exploded. The air filled with flowers again and shouting shook the very walls of the palace.

The king tried to shout something more, but it was lost in the jubilant noise. Finally he shrugged and reentered the palace, pausing only for a final wave at the crowd.

I thought it was a rather cheap ploy, allowing him to cash in on our applause as if it were intended for him, but I let it go. Right now we had bigger fish to fry.

Catching the eyes of Grimble and Badaxe, I beckoned them forward.

"I've got to talk to you two," I shouted over the din.

"Shouldn't we go inside where it's quieter?" Grimble shouted back.

"We'll talk here!" I insisted.

"But the crowd..." the chancellor gestured.

I turned and nodded to a figure in the front row of the mob. He responded by raising his right arm in a signal. In response, the men in the forefront of the crowd locked arms and formed a circle around us, moving with near-military precision. In a twinkling, there was a space cleared in the teeming populace, with the advisors, Aahz, Gleep, myself, and the man who had given the signal standing alone at its center.

"Just a moment," Badaxe rumbled, peering suspiciously at the circle. "What's going on..."

"General!" I beamed flashing my biggest smile. "I'd like you to meet the newest citizen of Possiltum."

Holding my smile, I beckoned the mob leader forward.

"General Badaxe," I announced formally. "Meet Big Julie. Big Julie, Hugh Badaxe!"

"Nice to meet you!" Julie smiled. "The boy here, he's been tellin' me all about you!"

The General blanched as he recognized the Empire's top commander.

"You!" he stammered. "But you...you're..."

"I hope you don't mind, General," I said smoothly. "But I've taken the liberty of offering Big Julie a job...as your military consultant."

"Military consultant?" Badaxe echoed suspiciously.

"What's-a-matter," Julie scowled. "Don't you think I can do it?"

"It's not that," the general clarified hastily. "It's just that...well..."

"One thing we neglected to mention, General," Aahz interrupted. "Big Julie here is retiring from active duty. He's more than willing to leave the running of Possiltum's army to you, and agrees to give advice only when asked."

"That's right!" Julie beamed. "I just wanna sit in the sun, drink a little wine, maybe pat a few bottoms, you know what I mean?"

"But the king..." Badaxe stammered.

"...doesn't have to be bothered with it at all," Aahz purred. "Unless, of course, you deem it necessary to tell him where your new battle plans are coming from."

"Hmm," the general said thoughtfully. "You sure you'd be happy with things that way, Julie?"

"Positive!" Julie nodded firmly. "I don't want any glory, no responsibility, and no credit. I had too much of that when I was workin' for the Empire, you know what I mean? Me and the boys talked it over, and we decided..."

"The boys?" Badaxe interrupted, frowning.

"Um...that's another thing we forgot to mention, General," I smiled. "Big Julie isn't the only new addition to Possiltum's citizenry."

I jerked my head at the circle of men holding back the crowd.

The general blinked at the men, then swiveled his head around noting how many more like them were scattered through the crowd. He blanched as it became clear to him both where the Empire's army had disappeared to, and why his men had been unsuccessful in stopping our return to the capital.

"You mean to tell me you..." Badaxe began.

"Happy Possiltum citizens all, General!" Aahz proclaimed, then dropped his voice to a more confidential level. "I think you'll find that if you should ever have to draft an army, these new citizens will train a lot faster than your average plow pusher. You know what I mean?"

Apparently the general did. His eyes glittered at the thought of the new force we had placed at his command. I could see him mentally licking his chops in anticipation of the next war.

"Big Julie!" he declared with a broad smile. "You and your...er...boys are more than welcome to settle here in Possiltum. Let me be one of the first to congratulate you on your new citizenship."

He extended his hand, but there was an obstruction in his way. The obstruction's name was J. R. Grimble.

"Just a moment!" the chancellor snarled. "There's one minor flaw in your plans. It is my intention to advise the king to disband Possiltum's army."

"What?" roared Badaxe.

"Let me handle this, General," Aahz soothed. "Grimble, what would you want to do a fool thing like that for?"

"Why, because of the magician, of course," the chancellor blinked. "You've demonstrated he is quite capable of defending the kingdom without the aid of an army, so I see no reason why we should continue to bear the cost of maintaining one."

"Nonsense!" Aahz scolded. "Do you think the great Skeeve has nothing to do with his time but guard your borders? Do you want to tie up your high-cost magician doing the job a low-cost soldier could do?"

"Well..." Grimble scowled.

"Besides," Aahz continued. "Skeeve will be spending considerable time on the road furthering his studies...which will, of course, increase his value to Possiltum. Who will guard your kingdom while he's away, if not the army?"

"But the cost is..." Grimble whined.

"If anything," Aahz continued ignoring the chancellor's protests. "I should think you'd want to expand your army now that your borders have increased in size."

"What's that? Grimble blinked. "What about our borders?"

"I thought it was obvious," Aahz said innocently. "All these new citizens have to settle somewhere...and there is a lot of land up for grabs just north of here. As I understand it, it's completely unguarded at the moment. Possiltum wouldn't even have to fight for it, just move in and settle. That is, of course, provided you have a strong army to hold it once you've got it."

"Hmm," the chancellor said thoughtfully, stroking his chin with his hand.

"Then again," Aahz murmured quietly. "There's all the extra tax money the new citizens and land will contribute to the exchanger."

"Big Julie!" Grimble beamed. "I'd like to welcome you and your men to Possiltum."

"I'm welcoming him first!" Badaxe growled. "He's *my* advisor."

As he spoke, the general dropped his hand to the hilt of his axe, a move which was not lost on the chancellor.

"Of course, General," Grimble acknowledged, forcing a grin. "I'll just wait here until you're through. There are a few things I want to discuss with our new citizens."

"While you're waiting, Grimble," Aahz smiled. "There are a few things we have to discuss with you."

"Such as what?" the chancellor scowled.

"Such as the Court Magician's pay!" my mentor retorted.

"Of course," Grimble laughed. "As soon as we're done here we'll go inside and I'll pay him his first month's wages."

"Actually," Aahz drawled. "What we wanted to discuss was an increase."

The chancellor stopped laughing.

"You mean a bonus, don't you?" he asked hopefully. "I'm sure we can work something out, considering…"

"I mean an increase!" Aahz corrected firmly. "C'mon, Grimble. The kingdom's bigger now. That means the magician's job is bigger and deserves more pay."

"I'm not sure I can approve that," the chancellor responded cagily.

"With the increase of your tax base," Aahz pressed, "I figure you can afford…"

"Now let's be careful," Grimble countered. "Our overhead has gone up right along with that increase. In fact, I wouldn't be surprised if…"

"C'mon, Gleep," I murmured to my pet. "Let's go see Buttercup."

I had a feeling the wage debate was going to last for a while.

XXVI.

"All's well that ends well."
E. A. POE

I WAS SPENDING a leisurely afternoon killing time in my immense room within the palace.

The bargaining session between Aahz and Grimble had gone
well for us. Not only had I gotten a substantial wage increase, I was
also now housed in a room which was only a little smaller than
Grimble's, which, in turn, was second only to the king's in size. What
was more, the room had a large window, which was nice even if it
did look out over the stables. Aahz had insisted on this, hinting darkly
that I might be receiving winged visitors in the night. I think this
scared me more than it did Grimble, but I got my window.

When I chose, I could look down from my perch and keep an
eye on Gleep and Buttercup in the stables. I could also watch the
hapless stable boy who had been assigned to catering to their every
need. That had been part of the deal, too, though I had pushed for
it a lot harder than Aahz.

Aahz was housed in the adjoining room, which was nice though
smaller than mine. The royal architects were scheduled to open a
door in our shared wall, and I had a hunch that when they did, the
room arrangement would change drastically. For the moment, at
least, I had a bit of unaccustomed privacy.

The room itself, however, was not what was currently commanding my attention. My mind was focused on Garkin's old brazier. I had been trying all afternoon to unlock its secrets, thus far
without success. It stood firmly in the center of the floor where I
had first placed it, stubbornly resisting my efforts.

I perched on my windowsill and studied the object glumly. I could
levitate it easily enough, but that wasn't what I wanted. I wanted it to
come alive and follow me around the way it used to follow Garkin.

That triggered an idea in my mind. It seemed silly, but nothing
else had worked.

Drawing my eyebrows together, I addressed the brazier without focusing my energies on it.

"Come here!" I thought.

The brazier seemed to waiver for a moment, then it trotted to my side, clacking across the floor on its spindly legs.

It worked! Even though it was a silly little detail, the brazier's obedience somehow made me feel more like a magician.

"Hey, kid!" Aahz called barging through my door without knocking. "Have you got a corkscrew?"

"What's a corkscrew?" I asked reflexively.

"Never mind," My mentor sighed. "I'll do it myself." With that, he shifted the bottle of wine he was holding to his left hand, and inserted the claw on his right forefinger into the cork. The cork made a soft pop as he gently eased it from the neck of the bottle, whereupon the cork was casually tossed into a corner as Aahz drank deeply of the wine.

"Ahh!" he gasped emerging for breath. "Terrific bouquet!"

"Um...Aahz?" I said shyly, leaving my window perch and moving to the table. "I have something to show you."

"First, could you answer a question?" Aahz asked.

"What?" I frowned.

"Why is that brazier following you around the room?"

I looked, and was startled to find he was right! The brazier had scuttled from the window to the table to remain by my side. The strange part was that I hadn't summoned it.

"Um...that's what I was going to show you," I admitted. "I've figured out how to get the brazier to come to me all by itself...no levitation or anything."

"Swell," Aahz grimaced. "Now, can you make it stop?"

"Um...I don't know," I said, sitting down quickly in one of the chairs.

I didn't want to admit it, but while we were talking I had tried several mental commands to get the brazier to go away, all without noticeable effect. I'd have to work this out on my own once Aahz had left.

"Say, Aahz," I said casually, propping my feet on the table. "Could you pour me some of that wine?"

Aahz cocked my eyebrow at me, then crossed the room slowly to stand by my side.

"Kid," he said gently. "I want you to look around real carefully. Do you see anybody here except you and me?"

"No," I admitted.

"Then we're in private, not in public...right?" he smiled.

"That's right," I agreed.

"Then get your own wine, apprentice!" he roared, kicking my chair out from under me.

Actually, it wasn't as bad as it sounds. I exerted my mind before I hit the floor and hovered safely on thin air. From that position, I reached out with my mind and lifted the bottle from Aahz's hand, transferring it to my own.

"If you insist," I said casually taking a long pull on the bottle.

"Think you're pretty smart, don't you!" Aahz snarled, then he grinned. "Well, I guess you are, at that. You've done pretty well...for an amateur."

"A professional," I corrected. "A *salaried* professional."

"I know," Aahz grinned back. "For an amateur, you're pretty smart. For a professional you've got a lot to learn."

"C'mon, Aahz!" I protested.

"...But that can wait for another day," Aahz conceded. "You might as well relax for a while and enjoy yourself...while you can."

"What's that supposed to mean?" I frowned.

"Nothing!" Aahz shrugged innocently. "Nothing at all."

"Wait a minute, Aahz," I said sharply, regaining my feet. "I'm a court magician now, right?"

"That's right, Skeeve," my mentor nodded.

"Court magician is the job you pushed me into because it's so easy, right?" I pressed.

"Right again, kid," He smiled, his nodding becoming even more vigorous.

"Then nothing can go wrong? Nothing serious?" I asked anxiously.

Aahz retrieved his wine bottle and took a long swallow before answering.

"Just keep thinking that, kid," he grinned. "It'll help you sleep nights."

"C'mon, Aahz!" I whined. "You're supposed to be my teacher. If there's something I'm missing, you've got to tell me. Otherwise I won't learn."

"Very well, apprentice," Aahz smiled, evilly emphasizing the word. "There are a few things you've overlooked."

"Such as?" I asked, writhing under his smile.

"Such as Gus, Ajax, and Brockhurst, who you just sent back to Deva without instructions."

"Instructions?" I blinked.

"Tanda we don't have to worry about, but the other three…"

"Wait a minute, Aahz." I interrupted before he got too far from the subject. "What instructions?"

"Instructions not to talk about our little skirmish here." Aahz clarified absently. "Tanda will know enough to keep her mouth shut, but the others won't."

"You think they'll talk?"

"Is a frog's behind watertight?" Aahz retorted.

"What's a frog?" I countered.

"Money in their pockets, fresh from a successful campaign against overwhelming odds…of course they'll talk!" Aahz thundered. "They'll talk their fool heads off to anyone who'll listen. What's more, they'll embellish it a little more with each telling until it sounds like they're the greatest fighters ever to spit teeth and you're the greatest tactician since Gronk!"

"What's wrong with that?" I inquired, secretly pleased. I didn't know who Gronk was, but what Aahz was saying had a nice ring to it.

"Nothing at all." Aahz responded innocently. "Except now the word will be out as to who you are, where you are, and what you are…also that you're for hire and that you subcontract. If there's anyplace in all the dimensions that folks will take note of information like that, it's the Bazaar."

Regardless of what my mentor may think, I'm not slow. I realized in a flash the implications of what he was saying…realized them and formulated an answer.

"So we suddenly get a lot of strange people dropping in on us to offer jobs, or looking for work." I acknowledged. "So what? All that means is I get a lot of practice saying 'No.' Who knows, it might improve my status around here a little if it's known that I regularly consult with strange beings from other worlds."

"Of course," Aahz commented darkly, "there's always the chance that someone at the Bazaar will hear that the other side is thinking of hiring you and decide to forcibly remove you from the roster. Either that or some young hotshot will want to make a name for himself by taking on this unbeatable magician everyone's talking about."

I tried not to show how much his grim prophecy had unnerved me. Then I realized he would probably keep heaping it on until he saw me sweat. Consequently, I sweated…visibly.

"I hadn't thought of that, Aahz." I admitted. "I guess I did overlook something there."

"Then again, there's Grimble and Badaxe." Aahz continued as if he hadn't heard me.

"What about Grimble and Badaxe?" I asked nervously.

"In my estimation," Aahz yawned, "The only way those two would ever work together would be against a common foe. In my further estimation, the best candidate for that 'common foe' position is you!"

"Me?" I asked in a very small voice.

"You work it out, kid." my mentor shrugged. "Until you hit the scene there was a two-way power struggle going as to who had the king's ear. Then you came along, and not only saved the kingdom, you increased the population, expanded the borders, and added to the tax base. That makes you the most popular and therefore the most influential person in the king's court. Maybe I'm wrong, but I don't think Grimble and Badaxe are going to just sigh and accept that. It's my guess they'll double-team you and attack anything you say or do militarily and monetarily, and that's a tough one-two punch to counter."

"Okay. Okay. So there were two things I overlooked." I interrupted. "Except for that…"

"And of course there's the people Big Julie and his men owe money to." Aahz commented thoughtfully. "I wonder how long it will be before they start nosing around looking for an explanation as to what happened to an entire army? More important, I wonder who they'll be looking for by name to provide them with that explanation?"

"Aahz?"

"Yea, kid?"

"Do you mind if I have a little more of that wine?"

"Help yourself, kid. There's lots."

I had a hunch that was going to be the best news I would hear for a long time.

Myth

Directions

I.

"Dragons and Demons and Kings, Oh my!"
THE COWARDLY KLAHD

"THIS PLACE STINKS!" my scaley mentor snarled, glaring out the window at the rain.

"Yes, Aahz," I agreed meekly.

"What's that supposed to mean?" he snapped, turning his demon's speckled gold eyes on me.

"It means," I gulped, "that I agree with you. The Kingdom of Possletum, and the palace specifically, stink to high heaven—both figuratively and literally."

"Ingratitude!" Aahz made his appeal to the ceiling. "I lose my powers to a stupid practical joker, and instead of concentrating on getting them back, I take on some twit of an apprentice who doesn't have any aspirations higher than being a thief, train him, groom him, and get him a job paying more than he could spend in two lifetimes, and what happens? He complains! I suppose you think you could have done better on your own?"

It occurred to me that Aahz's guidance had also gotten me hung, embroiled in a Magik duel with a Master magician, and recently in the unenviable position of trying to stop the world's largest army with a handful of down-at-the-heels demons. It also occurred to me that this was not the most tactful time to point out these minor nerve-jangling incidents.

"I'm sorry, Aahz," I grovelled. "Possletum is a pretty nice kingdom to work for."

It stinks!" he declared, turning to the window again.

I stifled a sigh. A magician's lot is not a happy one. I stole that saying from a tune Aahz sings off and on...key. More and more, I was realizing the truth of the jingle. As the court magician to my king I had already endured a great deal more than I had ever bargained for.

Actually the King of Posseltum isn't my king. I'm his Royal Magician, an employee at best.

Aahz isn't my demon, either. I'm his apprentice, trying desperately to learn enough Magik to warrant my aforementioned lofty title.

Gleep is definitely my dragon, though. Just ask Aahz. Better still, ask anyone in the Court of Possletum. Anytime my pet wrecks havoc with his playful romping, I get the blame and J.R. Grimble, the King's chancellor, deducts the damages from my wages.

Naturally, this gets Aahz upset. In addition to managing my Magik career, Aahz also oversees our finances. Well, that's something of an understatement. He shamelessly bleeds the kingdom for every monetary consideration he can get for us (which is considerable) and watches over our expenses. When it comes to spending our ill-gotten wealth, Aahz would rather part with my blood. As you might guess, we argue a lot over this.

Gleep is understanding though; which is part of the reason I keep him around. He's quite intelligent and understanding for a baby dragon with a one word vocabulary. I spend a considerable amount of time telling him my troubles, and he always listens attentively without interrupting or arguing or shouting about how stupid I am. This makes him better company than Aahz.

It says something about one's lifestyle when the only cane you can get sympathy from is a dragon.

Unfortunately, on this particular day I was cut off from my pet's company. It was raining, and when it rains in Possletum, it doesn't kid around. Gleep is too big to live indoors with us, and the rain made the courtyard impassable, so I couldn't reach the stables where he was quartered. What was more, I couldn't risk roaming the halls of the castle for fear of running into the king. If that happened, he would doubtless ask when I was going to do something about the miserable weather. Weather control was not one of my current skills, and I was under strict orders from Aahz to avoid the subject at all costs. As such, I was stuck waiting out the rain in my own quarters. That in itself wouldn't be so bad, if it wasn't for the fact that I shared those quarters with Aahz.

Rain made Aahz grouchy, or I should say grouchier than usual. I'd rather be locked in a small cage with an angry spider-bear than be alone in a room with Aahz when he's in a bad mood.

"There must be something to do," Aahz grumbled, begging to pace the floor. "I haven't been this bored since the Two Hundred 1 Year Siege."

"You could teach me about dimension travel," I suggested hopefully.

This was one area of Magik Aahz had steadfastly refused to teach me. As I mentioned earlier, Aahz is a demon, short for "dimension traveler." Most of my close friends these days were demons, and I was eager to add dimension traveling to my meager list of skills.

"Don't make me laugh, kid." Aahz laughed harshly. "At the rate you're learning, it would take more than two hundred years to teach it to you."

"Oh," I said, crestfallen. "well—you could tell me about the Two Hundred Year Siege."

"The Two Hundred Year Siege," Aahz murmured dreamily, smiling slightly to himself. Large groups of armed men have been known to turn pale and tremble visibly before Aahz's smile.

"There isn't much to tell," he began, leaning against a table and hefting a large pitcher of wine. "It was me and another magician, Diz-Ne. He was a snotty little upstart…you remind me a bit of him."

"What happened?" I urged, anxious to get the conversation away from me.

"Well, once he figured out he couldn't beat me flat out, he went defensive," Aahz reminisced. "He was a real nothing Magikally, but he knew his defense spells. Kept me off his back for a full two hundred years, even though we drained most of the Magik energies of that dimension in the process."

"Who won?" I pressed eagerly.

Aahz cocked an eyebrow at me over the lip of the wine pitcher.

"I'm telling the story, kid," he pointed out. "You figure it out." I did, and swallowed hard.

"Did you kill him?"

"Nothing that pleasant," Aahz smiled. "What I did to him once I got through his defenses will last a lot longer than two hundred years—but I guarantee you, he won't get bored."

"Why were you fighting?" I asked in a desperate effort to forestall the images my mind was manufacturing.

"He welched on a bet," my mentor shrugged, hefting the wine again.

"That's all?"

"That's enough," Aahz insisted grimly. "Setting's a serious matter —in any dimension."

"Um—Aahz?" I frowned. "Weren't Big Julie and his men running from gambling debts when we met them?"

That's the army I mentioned earlier. Big Julie and his men were currently disguised as happy citizens of Possletum. "That's right, kid," Aahz nodded.

"Then that's why you said the loansharks would probably come looking for them," I declared triumphantly.

"Wrong," Aahz said firmly.

"Wrong?" I blinked.

"I didn't say they'd `probably' come looking," he corrected. "I said they would come looking. Bank on it. There are only two questions involved here: When are they coming, and what are you going to do about it?"

"I don't know about the 'when,' " I commented with careful deliberation, "but I've given some thought to what I'm going to do."

"And you've decided—" Aahz prompted.

"To grab our money and run!" I declared. "That's why I want to learn dimension travel. I figure there won't be anywhere in this dimension we could hide, and that means leaving Klah for greener, safer pastures."

Aahz was unmoved.

"If push comes to shove," he yawned, "we can use the D-Hopper. As long as we've got a mechanical means of traveling to other dimensions, there's no need for you to learn how to do it magically."

"Com'on, Aahz!" I exploded. "Why won't you teach me? What makes dimension traveling so hard to learn?"

Aahz studied me for a long moment, then heaved a big sigh. "All right, Skeeve," he said. "If you listen up, I'll try to sketch it out for you."

I listened. With every pore, I listened. Aahz didn't call me by my given name often, and when he did, it was serious.

"The problem is that to travel the dimensions, even using pentacles for beacons—gateways, requires knowing your desti-nation dimension…knowing it almost as well as your home dimension. If you don't, then you can get routed into a dimension you aren't even aware of, and be trapped there with no way out."

He paused to take another drink from the wine pitcher.

"Now, you've only been in one dimension besides Klah," he continued. "That was Deva, and you only saw the Bazaar. You know the Bazaar well enough to know it's constantly changing and rearranging. You don't know it well enough to have zeroed in on the few permanent fixtures you could use to home in on for a return trip, so effectively, you don't know any other dimensions well enough to be sure of your destination if you tried to jump magikally. That's why you can't travel the dimensions without using the D-Hopper! End of lecture."

'I blinked.

"You mean the only reason I can't do it magikally is because I don't know the other dimensions?" I asked.

"That's the main reason," Aahz corrected.

"Then let's go!" I cried, leaping to my feet. "I'll get the D-Hopper and you can show me a couple new dimensions while we're waiting for the rain to stop."

"Not so fast, kid!" Aahz interrupted, holding up a restraining hand. "Sit down."

"What's wrong? I challenged.

"Do you really think that possibility hadn't occurred to me?" he asked, an edge of irritation creeping into his voice.

I thought about it, and sat down again.

"Why don't you think it's a good idea?" I querried in a more humble tone.

"There are a few things you've overlooked in your en-thusiasm," he intoned dryly. "First of all, remember that in another dimension, you'll be a demon. Now, except for Deva, which makes its money on cross-dimension trade, most dimen-sions don't greet demons with flowers and red carpets. The fact is, a demon is likely to be attacked on sight by whoever's around with whatever's handy."

He leaned forward to emphasize his words. "What I'm trying to say is, it's dangerous! Now, if we went touring and ran into trouble, what do we have to defend ourselves? I've lost my powers and yours are still so undeveloped as to be practically non-existant. Who's going to handle the natives?"

"How dangerous is it?" I asked hesitantly.

"Let me put it to you this way, kid," Aahz sighed. "You spend a lot of time griping about how I keep putting your life in jeopardy with my blatant disregard for danger. Right?"

"Right." I nodded vigorously.

"Well, now I'm saying the trip you're proposing is dangerous. Does that give you a clue as to what you'll be up against?"

I leaned back in my chair and stretched, trying to make it look nonchalant..

"How about sharing some of that wine?" I suggested casually. For a change, Aahz didn't ignore the request. He tossed the pitcher into the air as he rose and strode to the window again.

Reaching out with my mind, I gently grabbed the pitcher and brought it floating to my outstretched hand without spilling a drop.

As I said, I am the Court Magician for Possletum. I'm not without powers.

"Don't let it get you down, kid," Aahz called from the window. "If you keep practicing, someday we can take that tour under your protection. But until you reach that level, or until we find you a magikal bodyguard, it'll just have to wait."

"I suppose you're right, Aahz," I conceded. "It's just that sometimes…"

There was a soft "BAMF!" as the ether was rent asunder and a demon appeared in the room. Right there! In my private quarters in the Possletum Royal Palace!

Before I could recover from my surprise or Aahz could move to intervene, the demon plopped itself onto my lap and planted a big, warm kiss full on my mouth.

"Hi, Handsome!" it purred. "How's tricks?"

II.

"When old friends get together, everything else fades to insignificance."
WAR, FAMINE, PESTILENCE, AND DEATH

TANANDA!" I EXCLAIMED, recovering from shock sufficiently
to fasten my arms around her waist in an energetic hug.

"In the flesh!" she winked, pressing hard against me.

My temperature went up several degrees, or maybe it was the
room. Tananda has that effect on me—and rooms. Lusciously
curvacious, with a mane of light green hair accenting her lovely olive
complexion and features, she could stop a twenty-man brawl with a
smile and a deep sigh.

"He isn't the only one in the room, you know," Aahz commented dryly.

"Hi, Aahz!" my adorable companion cried, untangling herself
from my lap and throwing herself into Aahz's arms.

The volume of Tananda's affections is exceeded only by her
willingness to share them. I had a secret belief, though, that Tananda
liked me better than she liked Aahz. This belief was tested for strength
as their greeting grew longer and longer.

"Um…what brings you to these parts?" I interrupted at last.

That earned me a dark look from Aahz, but Tananda didn't bat
an eye.

"Well," she dimpled. "I could say I was just in the neighborhood
and felt like dropping by, but that wouldn't be true. The fact is, I need
a little favor."

"Name it," Aahz and I declared simultaneously.

Aahz is tight-fisted and I'm chicken, but all bets are off when it
comes to Tananda. She had helped us out of a couple tight spots in
the past, and we both figured we owed her. The fact she had helped
us *into* as many tight spots as she had helped us out of never entered
our minds. Besides—she was awfully nice to have around.

"It's nothing really," she sighed. "I have a little shopping to
do and was hoping I could borrow one of you two to help me
carry things."

"You mean today?" Aahz frowned.

"Actually, for the next couple days," Tananda informed him, "Maybe as long as a week."

"Can't do it," Aahz sighed. "I have to referee a meeting between Big Julie and General Badaxe tomorrow. Any chance you could postpone it until next week?"

"Ummm...you weren't the one I was thinking of, Aahz," Tananda said, giving the ceiling a casual survey. "I was thinking Skeeve and I could handle it."

"Me?" I blinked.

Aahz scowled.

"Not a chance," he declared. "The kid can't play step-and-fetch-it for you. It's beneath his dignity."

"No it isn't!" I cried. "I mean, if it wouldn't be beneath you, Aahz, how could it be beneath me?"

"I'm not the Court Magician of Possletum!" he argued.

"I can disguise myself!" I countered. "That's one of my best spells. You've said so yourself."

"I think your scaley green mentor is just a lee-tle bit jealous," Tananda observed, winking at me covertly.

"Jealous?" Aahz exploded. "Me? Jealous of a little..." He broke off and looked back and forth between Tananda and myself as he realized he was being baited.

"Oh—I suppose it would be okay," he grumbled at last. "Go ahead and take him—even though it's beyond me what you expect to find in this backwater dimension worth shopping for."

"Oh, Aahz!" Tananda laughed. "You're a card. Shopping in Klah? I may be a little flighty from time to time, but I'm not crazy."

"You mean we're headed for other dimensions?" I asked eagerly.

"Of course," she nodded. "We have quite an itincrary ahead of us. First, we'll hop over to..."

"What's an itinerary?" I asked.

"Stop!" Aahz shouted, holding up a hand for silence. "But I was just..."

"Stop!"

"We were..."

"Stop!"

Our conversation effectively halted, we turned our attention to Aahz. With melodramatic slowness, he folded his arms across his chest.

"No," he said.

"No?" I shrieked. "But Aahz…"

"But Aahz nothing," he barked back. "I said 'No' and I meant it."

"Wait a minute," Tananda interceded, stepping between us. "What's the problem, Aahz?"

"If you think I'm going to let my apprentice go traipsing around the dimensions alone and unprotected…"

"I won't be alone," I protested. "Tananda will be there."

"…a prime target for any idiot who wants to bag a demon," Aahz continued, ignoring my outburst, "just so you can have a beast of burden for your shopping jaunt, well you'd better think again."

"Are you through?" Tananda asked testily.

"For the moment," Aahz nodded, matching her glare for glare.

"First of all," she began, "as Skeeve pointed out, if you'd bothered to listen, he won't be alone. I'll be with him. That means, second of all, he won't be unprotected. Just because I let my membership with the Assassins Guild expire doesn't mean I've forgotten everything."

"Yea, Aahz," I interjected.

"Shut up, kid," he snapped.

"Third of all," Tananda continued, "you've got to stop thinking of Skeeve here as a kid. He stopped Big Julie's army, didn't he? And besides, he is your apprentice. I assume you've taught him something over the last couple of years."

That hit Aahz in his second most sensitive spot. His vanity. His most sensitive spot is his money pouch.

"Well…" he waivered.

"Com'on, Aahz," I pleaded. "What could go wrong?" "The mind boggles," he retorted grimly.

"Don't exaggerate, Aahz," Tananda reprimanded. "Exaggerate!" my mentor exploded anew. "The first time I took Mr. Wonderful here off-dimension, he bought a dragon we neither need nor want and nearly got killed in a brawl with a pack of cutthroats."

"A fight which he won, as I recall," Tananda observed.

"The second time we went out," Aahz continued undaunted, "I left him at a fast-food joint where he promptly recruits half the deadbeats at the Bazaar fora fighting force."

"They won the war!" I argued.

"That's not the point," Aahz growled. "The point is, every time the kid here hits another dimension, he ends up in trouble. He draws it like a magnet."

"This time I'll be there to keep an eye on him," Tananda soothed.

"You were there the first two times," Aahz pointed out grimly.

"So were you!" she countered.

"That's right!" Aahz agreed. "And both of us together couldn't keep him out of trouble. Now do you see why I want to keep him right here in Klah?"

"Hmm," Tananda said thoughtfully. "I see your point, Aahz."

My heart sank.

"I just don't agree with it," she concluded.

"Damn it, Tananda…" Aahz began, but she waved him to silence.

"Let me tell you a story," she smiled. "There was this couple see, who had a kid they thought the world of. They thought so much of him, in fact, that when he was born they sealed him in a special room. Just to be sure nothing would happen to him, they screened everything that went into the room; furniture, books, food, toys, everything. They even filtered the air to be sure he didn't get any diseases."

"So?" Aahz asked suspiciously.

"So—on his eighteenth birthday, they opened the room and let him out," Tananda explained. "The kid took two steps and died of excitement."

"Really?" I asked, horrified.

"It's exaggerated a bit," she admitted, "but I think Aahz gets the point."

"I haven't been keeping him sealed in," Aahz mumbled. "There've been some real touch-and-go moments, you know. You've been there for some of them."

"But you have been a little overprotective, haven't you, Aahz?" Tananda urged gently.

Aahz was silent for several moments, avoiding our eyes. "All right," he sighed at last. "Go ahead, kid. Just don't come crying to me if you get yourself killed."

"How could I do that?" I frowned.

Tananda nudged me in the ribs and I took the hint.

"There are a few things I want settled before you go," Aahz declared brusquely, a bit of his normal spirit returning.

He began moving back and forth through the room, gathering items from our possessions.

"First," he announced, "here's some money of your own for the trip. You probably won't need it, but you always walk a little taller with money in your pouch."

So saying, he counted out twenty gold pieces into my hands. Realizing I had hired a team of demons to fight a war for five gold pieces, he was giving me a veritable fortune!

"Gee, Aahz…" I began, but he hurried on.

"Second, here's the D-Hopper." He tucked the small metal cylinder into my belt. "I've set it to bring you back here. If you get into trouble, if you think you're getting into trouble, hit the button and come home right then. No heroics, no jazzy speeches. Just hit and get. You understand me?"

"Yes, Aahz," I promised dutifully.

"And finally," he announced, drawing himself up to his full height, "the dragon stays here. You aren't going to drag your stupid pet along with you and that's final. I know you'd like to have him with you, but he'd only cause problems."

"Okay, Aahz," I shrugged.

Actually, I had figured on leaving Gleep behind, but it didn't seem tactful to point that out.

"Well," my mentor sighed, sweeping us both with a hard gaze, "I guess that's that. Sorry I can't hang around to see you off, but I've got more pressing things to do."

With that he turned on his heels and left, shutting the door behind him more forceably than was necessary.

"That's funny," I said, staring after him. "I didn't think he had anything important to do. In fact, just before you showed up, he was complaining about being bored."

"You know, Skeeve," Tananda said softly, giving me a strange look, "Aahz is really quite attached to you."

"Really?" I frowned. "What makes you say that?"

"Nothing," she smiled. "It was just a thought. Well, are you ready to go?"

"As ready as I'll ever be," I declared confidently. "What's our first stop? The Bazaar at Deva?"

"Goodness no!" she retorted, wrinkling her nose. "We're after something really unique, not the common stuff they have at the Bazaar. I figure we're going to have to hit some out-of-the-way dimensions, the more-out-of-the-way the better."

Despite my confidence, an alarm gong went off in the back of my mind at this declaration.

"What were we looking for, anyway?" I asked casually.

Tananda shot a quick glance at the door, then leaned forward to whisper in my ear.

"I couldn't tell you before," she murmured conspiratorally, "but we're after a birthday present. A birthday present for Aahz!"

III.

"That's funny, I never have any trouble with service when I'm shopping."
K. KONG

EVER SINCE HE took me on as an apprentice, Aahz has complained that I don't practice enough. He should have seen me on the shopping trip! In the first three days after our departure from Klah I spent more time practicing magik than I had in the previous year.

Tananda had the foresight to bring along a couple of translator pendants which enabled us to understand and be understood by the natives in the dimensions we visited. That was fine for communications, but there remained the minor detail of our physical appearance. Disguises were my job.

Besides flying Aahz had taught me one other spell which had greatly enhanced my ability to survive dubious situations; that was the ability to change the outward appearance of my own, or anyone else's, physical features. Tagging along with Tananda, this skill got a real workout.

The procedure was simple enough. We would arrive at some secluded point, then creep to a spot where I would observe a few members of the local population. Once I had laid eyes on them I could duplicate their physical form for our disguises and we could blend with the crowd. Of course, my nerves had to be calmed so I wouldn't jump out of my skin when catching a passing glance of the being standing next to me.

If from this you conclude that the dimensions we visited were inhabited by people who looked a little strange...you're wrong. The dimensions we visited were peopled by beings who looked *very* strange.

When Tananda decides to tour out-of-the-way dimensions, she doesn't kid around. None of the places we visited looked normal to my untraveled eyes but a few in particular stand out in my memory as being exceptionally weird.

Despite Tananda's jokes about rental agencies, Avis turned out to be populated with bird-like creatures with wings and feathers. In that dimension I not only had to maintain our disguises, I had to fly us from perch to perch as per the local method of transportation.

Instead of traversing their market center as I had expected, we spent considerable time viewing their national treasures. These treasures turned out to be a collection of broken pieces of colored glass and bits of shiny metal which to my eye were worthless—but Tananda studied them with quiet intensity.

To maintain our disguises, we had to eat and drink without hands—which proved to be harder than it sounded. Since the food consisted of live grubs and worms, I passed on any opportunity to sample the local cuisine. Tananda, however, literally dove into (remember—no hands!) a bowlful. Whether she licked her lips because she found the fare exceptionally tasty or if she was attempting to catch a few of the wriggly morsels that were trying to escape their fate was not important; I found the sight utterly revolting. To avoid having to watch her, I tried the local wine.

The unusual drinking style meant that I ended up taking larger swallows than I normally would, but that was okay as the wine was light and flavorful. Unfortunately, it also proved to be much stronger than anything I had previously sampled. After I had nearly flown us into a rather large tree Tananda decided it was time for us to move to another dimension.

As a footnote to that particular adventure, the wine had two side effects: first I developed a colossal headache and second I became violently nauseous. The latter was because Tananda gleefully told me how they make wine on Avis. To this day I can't hear the name Avis without having visions of flying through the air and a vague tinge of air-sickness. As far as I'm concerned, when rating dimensions on a scale of ten, Avis will always be a number two.

Another rather dubious dimension we spent considerable time in was Gastropo. The length of our stay there had nothing to do with our quest. Tananda decided, after relatively few stops, that the dimension had nothing to offer of a quality suitable for Aahz's present. What delayed us was our disguises.

Let me clarify that before aspersions are cast on my admittedly limited abilities, the physical appearance part was easy. As I've said, I'm getting quite good at disguise spells. What hung us up was the manner of locomotion. After flying from tree to tree in Avis, I would have thought I was ready to get from point A to point B in any conceivable way. Well, as Aahz has warned me, the dimensions are an endless source of surprises.

The Gastropods were snails—large snails, but snails none-the-less. Spiral shells, eyes on stalks—the whole bit. I could handle that. What I couldn't get used to was inching my way along with the rest of the local pedestrians—excuse me, pod-estrians.

"Tananda," I growled under my breath. "How long are we going to stay in this god-awful dimension?"

"Relax, Handsome," she chided, easing forward another inch. "Enjoy the scenery."

"I've been enjoying this particular hunk of scenery for half a day," I complained. "I'm enjoying it so much I've memorized it."

"Don't exaggerate," my guide scolded. "This morning we were on the other side of that tree."

I closed my eyes and bit back my first five or six responses to her correction. "How long?" I repeated.

"I figure we can split after we turn that corner."

"But that corner's a good twenty-five feet away!" I protested. "That's right," she confirmed. "I figure we'll be there by sundown."

"Can't we just walk over there at normal speed?"

"Not a chance; we'd be noticed."

"By who?"

"Whom. Well, by your admirer, for one."

"My what?" I blinked.

Sure enough, there was a Gastropod chugging heroically along behind us. When it realized I was looking at it, it began to wave its eye-stalks in slow, but enthusiastic, motions.

"It's been after you for about an hour," Tananda confided. "That's why I've been hurrying."

"That does it!" I declared, starting off at a normal pace. "C'mon, Tananda, we're getting out of here."

Shrill cries of alarm were being sounded by the Gastropods as I rounded the corner, followed, shortly, by my guide.

"What's the matter with you?" she demanded. "We could—"

"Get us out—now!" I ordered.

"But—"

"Remember how I got my dragon?" I barked. "If I let an amorous snail follow me home, Aahz will disown me as his apprentice. Now, are you going to get us out of here, or do I use the D-Hopper and head for home?"

"Don't get your back up," she soothed, beginning her ritual to change dimensions. "You shouldn't have worried though, we're looking for cargo—not S-cargo."

We were in another dimension before I could ask her to explain why she was giggling. So it went, dimension after dimension until I gave up trying to predict the unpredictable and settled for coping with the constants. Even this turned out to be a chore. For one thing, I had some unexpected problems with Tananda. I had never noticed it before, but she's really quite vain. She didn't just want to look like a native—she wanted to look like an attractive native.

Anyone who thinks beauty is a universal concept should visit some of the places we did. Whatever grotesque form I was asked to duplicate Tananda always had a few polite requests for improving her appearance. After a few days of "the hair should be more matted," or "shouldn't my eye be a bit more bloodshot?" or "a little more slime under the armpits," I was ready to scream. It probably wouldn't have been so annoying if her attention to detail had extended just a little bit to my appearance. All I'd get was—"You? You look fine." That how I know she's vain; she was more interested in her own appearance than mine.

That wasn't the only thing puzzling about Tananda's behavior. Despite her claim that we were on a shopping trip, she steadfastly avoided the retail sections of the dimensions we visited. Bazaars, farmers' market, flea markets and all the rest were met with the same wrinkled nose (when there was a nose) and "we don't want to go there." Instead she seemed to be content as a tourist. Her inquiries would invariably lead us to national shrines or the public displays of royal treasures. After viewing several of these we would retire to a secluded spot and head off for the next dimension.

In a way this suited me fine. Not only was I getting a running, flying and crawling tour of the dimensions, I was doing it with Tananda. Tananda is familiar with the social customs of over a hundred dimensions and in every dimension she was just that—familiar. I rapidly learned that in addition to beauty, morality varied from dimension to dimension. The methods of expressing affection in some of the dimensions we visited defy description but invariably make me blush at the memory. Needless to say, after three days of this I was seriously trying to progress beyond the casual friendship level with my shapely guide. I mean, Tananda's interpretation of casual friendship was already seriously threatening the continued smooth operation of my heart—not to mention other organs.

There was a more pressing problem on my mind, however. After three days of visiting strange worlds, I was hungry enough to bite my own arm for the blood. They say if you're hungry enough you'll eat anything. Don't you believe it. The things placed before me and called food were unstomachable despite starvation. I know; I tried occassionally, out of desperation, only to lose everything else in my stomach along with the latest offering. Having Tananda sitting across from me, joyfully chewing tentacled things that oozed out of her mouth and wriggled didn't help.

Finally I expressed my distress and needs to Tananda.

"I wondered why you hadn't been eating much," she frowned. "But I thought maybe you were on a diet, or something. I wish you'd spoken up sooner."

"I didn't want to be a bother," I explained lamely.

"It isn't that," she waved. "It's just that if I had known two dimensions ago there were half a dozen humanoid dimension nearby that we could have hopped over to. Right now, there's only one that would fit the bill without us having to go through a couple of extra dimensions along the way."

"Then let's head for that one," I urged. "The sooner I eat the better off we'll be." I wasn't exaggerating. My stomach was beginning to growl so loudly it was a serious threat to our disguises.

"Suit yourself," she shrugged, pulling me behind a row of hedges that tinkled musically in the breeze. "Personally, though, it's not a dimension I normally stop in."

Again the alarm sounded in the back of my head, despite my hunger. "Why not?" I asked suspiciously.

"Because they're weird there—I mean, really weird," she confided.

Images flashed across my mind of the beings we'd already encountered. "Weirder than the native we've been imitating?" I gulped. "I thought you said they'd be humanoid?"

"Not weird physically," Tananda chided, taking my hand. "Weird mentally. You'll see."

"What's the name of the dimension? I called desperately as she closed her eyes to begin our travels. The scenery around us faded, there was a rush of darkness, then a new scene burst brightly and noisily into view.

"Jahk," she answered, opening her eyes since we were there.

IV.

" 'Weird' is a relative, not an absolute term."
BARON FRANK N. FURTER

YOU RECALL MY account of our usual modus operandi on hitting a new dimension? How we would arrive inconspicuously and disguise ourselves before mingling with the native? Well, however secluded Tananda's landing point in Jahk might be normally—it wasn't when we arrived.

As the dimension came into focus it was apparent that we were in a small park, heavily overgrown with trees and shrubs. It was not the flora of the place which caught and held my attention, however, it was the crowd. What crowd? you might ask. Why, the one carrying blazing torches and surrounding us, of course. Oh—that crowd!

Well, to be completely honest, they weren't actually sur-rounding us. They were surrounding the contraption we were standing on. I had never really known what a contraption was when Aahz had used the word in conversation, and being Aahz he wouldn't define the word when I asked him to. Now that I was here, however, I recognized one on sight. The thing we were standing on had to be a contraption.

It was some sort of wagon—in that it was large and had four wheels. Beyond that I couldn't tell much about it, because it was completely covered by tufts of colored paper. That's right, I said paper—light fluffy stuff that would be nice if you had a cold, runny nose. But this paper was mostly yellow and blue. Looming over us was some kind of monstrous, dummy warrior complete with helmet—also covered with tufts of blue and yellow paper.

Of all the things that had flashed across my mind when Tananda warned me that the Jahk's were weird, the one thing that had not occurred to me was that they were blue-and-yellow-paper freaks.

"Get off the float!"

This last was shouted at us from someone in the crowd. "I beg your pardon," I shouted back.

"The float! Get off of it!"

"C'mon Handsome," Tananda hissed, hooking my elbow in hers.

Together we leaped to the ground. As it turned out we were barely in time. With a bloodthirsty howl, the crowd surged forward and tossed their torches onto the contraption we had so recently abandoned. In moments it was a mass of flames the heat of which warmed the already overheated crowd. They danced and sang, joyfully oblivious to the destruction of the contraption.

Edging away from the scene, I realized with horror that it was being duplicated throughout the park. Wherever I looked there were bonfires set on contraptions and jubilant crowds.

"I think we arrived at a bad time," I observed.

"What makes you say that?" Tananda asked.

"Little things," I explained, "like the fact they're in the middle of torching the town."

"I don't think so," my companion shrugged. "when you torch a town you don't usually start with the parks."

"Okay, then you tell me just what they're doing."

"As far as I can tell, they're celebrating."

"Celebrating what?"

"Some kind of victory. As near as I can tell, everyone's shouting—we won! we won!"

I surveyed the blazes again. "I wonder what they'd do if they lost?"

Just then a harried looking individual strode up to us. His no-nonsense business-like manner was an island of sanity in a sea of madness. I didn't like it. Not that I have anything against sanity, mind you. It's just that up 'til now we have been pretty much ignored. I feared that was about to change.

"Here's your pay," he said brusquely, handing us each a pouch. "Turn in your costume at the Trophy Building." With that he was gone, leaving us open mouthed and holding the bags.

"What was that all about?" I managed to say.

"Beats me," Tananda admitted. "They lost me when they called that contraption a float."

"Then I'm right! It is a contraption," I exclaimed with delight. "I knew they had to be wrong; a float is airtight and won't sink in water."

"I thought it was made with ice cream and ginger-ale?" Tananda frowned.

"With what and what?" I blinked.

"Great costumes—really great!" someone shouted to us as they staggered by.

"Time to do something about our disguises," Tananda murmured as she waved to the drunk.

"Right," I nodded, glad we could agree on something.

The disguises should have been easy after my recent experience in other dimensions. I mean the Jahks were humanoid and I had lots of ready models to work from. Unfortunately I encountered problems.

The first was pride. Despite the teeming masses around us, I couldn't settle on two individuals whose appearance I wanted to duplicate. I never considered myself particularly vain; I've never considered myself as being in top physical condition—of course, that was before I arrived in Jahk.

Every being I could see was extremely off-weight—either over or under. If a specific individual wasn't ribs-protruding thin to the point of looking brittle, he was laboring along under vast folds of fat which bunched and bulged at waist, chin and all four cheeks. Try as I might, I couldn't bring myself to alter Tananda or myself to look like these wretched specimens.

My second problem was that I couldn't concentrate, anyway. Disguise spells, like any other magik, require a certain amount of concentration. In the past I've been able to cast spells in the heat of battle or embarrassment. In our current situation I couldn't seem to get my mind focused.

You see there was this song—well, I think it was a song. Anyway the crowd acted like it was singing a rhythmic chant; the chant was incredibly catchy. Even in the short time we'd been there I'd almost mastered the lyrics—which is a tribute to the infectious nature of the song rather than any indication of my ability to learn lyrics. The point is that every time I tried concentrating on our disguises, I found myself singing along with the chant instead. Terrific!

"Any time you're ready, Handsome."

"What's that, Tananda?"

"The disguises," she prompted glancing about nervously.

spell will work better when you aren't humming."

"I—er, um—I can't seem to find two good models," I alibied lamely.

"Are you having trouble counting up to two all of a sudden?" she scowled. "By my count you've got a whole parkful of models."

"But none I want to look like—want us to look like," I amended quickly.

"Check me on this," Tananda said, pursing her lips. "Two days ago you disguised us as a pair of slimy slugs, right?"

"Yes, but—"

"And before that as eight-legged dogs?"

"Well, yes, but—"

"And you never complained about how you looked in your disguise then, right?"

"That was different," I protested.

"How?" she challenged.

"Those were—well, things! These are humanoids and I know what humanoids should look like."

"What they *should* look like isn't important," my guide argued. "What matters is what they *do* look like. We've got to blend with the crowd—and the sooner the better."

"But—" I began.

"—Because if we don't," she continued sternly, "we're going to run into someone who's both sober and unpreoccupied—which will give us the choice between being guest-of-honor at the next bonfire they light or skipping this dimension before you've had anything to eat."

"I'll try again," I sighed, scanning the crowd once more.

In a desperate effort to comply with Tananda's order, I studied the first two individuals my eyes fell on, then concentrated on duplicating their appearance without really considering how they looked.

"Not bad," Tananda commented dryly, surveying her new body. "Of course, I always thought I looked better as a woman."

"You want a disguise, you get a disguise," I grumbled.

"Hey, Handsome," my once-curvaceous comrade breathed, laying a soft, but hairy, hand on my arm. "Relax, we're on the same side. Remember?"

My anger melted away at her touch—as always. Maybe someday I'll develop an immunity to Tananda's charms. Until then I'll just enjoy them. "Sorry, Tananda," I apologized. "Didn't mean to snap at you—log it off to hunger."

"That's right," she exclaimed, clicking her fingers, "we're supposed to be finding you some food. It completely slipped my mind again what with this racket going on. C'mon, let's see what the blue-plate special is today."

Finding a place to eat turned out to be more of a task than either of us anticipated. Most of the restaurants we came across were either closed or only serving drinks. I half-expected Tananda to suggest that we drink our meal, but mercifully that possibility wasn't mentioned.

We finally located a little sidewalk cafe down a narrow street and elbowed our way to a small table, ignoring the glares of our fellow diners. Service was slow, but my companion sped things up a bit by emptying the contents of one of our pouches onto the table-top thus attracting the waiter's attention. In short order we were presented with two bowls of steaming whatever. I didn't even try to identify the various lumps and crunchies. It smelled good and tasted better and after several days of enforced fasting, that was all that mattered to me. I glutted myself and was well into my second bowl by the time Tananda finished her first. Pushing the empty dish away she begain to study the crowd on the street with growing interest.

"Have you figured out yet what's going on?" she asked. "MMurppg!?" I replied through a mouthful of food. "Hmmm?" she frowned.

"I can't tell for sure," I said, swallowing hard. "Everybody's happy because they won something, but darned if I can hear what they won."

"Well," Tananda shrugged. "I warned you they were weird."

Just then the clamor in the streets soared to new heights, drowning out any efforts at individual conversation. Craning our necks in an effort to locate the source of the disturbance, we beheld a strange phenomenon. A wall-to-wall mob of people was marching down the street, chanting in unison and sweeping along, or trampling, any smaller groups it encountered. Rather than expressing anger or resentment at this intrusion, the people around us were jumping up and down and cheering, hugging each other with tears of pure joy in their eyes. The focus of everyone's attention seemed to be sitting on a liter borne aloft by the stalwarts at the head of the crowds. I was fortunate enough to get a look at it as it passed by—Fortunate in that I could see it without having to move. The crowds were such that I couldn't move if I'd wanted to, so it was just as well that it passed close by.

To say they carried a statue would be insufficient. It was the ugliest thing I had ever seen in my life and that included everything I'd just seen on this trip with Tananda. It was small, roughly twice the size of my head and depicted a large, four-legged toad holding a huge eyeball in its mouth. Along its back, instead of warts,were the torsos, heads and arms of tiny Jahks intertwined in truly grotesque eroticism. These figures were covered with the warty protrusions one would expect to have found on the toad itself. As a crowning touch, the entire thing had a mottled gold finish which gave the illusion of splotches crawling back and forth on the surface.

I was totally repulsed by the statue, but it was obvious the crowd around me did not share these feelings. They swept forward in a single wave, joining the mob and adding their voices to the chant which could still be heard long after the procession had vanished from sight. Finally we were left in relative quiet on a street deserted save for a few random bodies of those not swift enough to either join or evade the mob.

"Well," I said casually, clearing my throat. "I guess we know what they won, now. Right?"

There was no immediate response. I shot a sharp glance at my companion and found her staring down the street after the procession.

"Tananda," I repeated, slightly concerned.

"That's it," she said with sudden, impish glee.

"That's what?" I blinked.

"Aahz's birthday present," she proclaimed.

I peered down the street, wondering what she was looking at. "What is?" I asked.

"That statue," she said firmly.

"That statue?" I cried, unable to hide my horror.

"Of course," she nodded, "it's perfect. Aahz will have never seen one, much less owned one."

"How do you figure that?" I pressed.

"It's obviously one-of-a-kind," she explained. "I mean, who could make something like that twice?"

She had me there, but I wasn't about to give up the fight. "There's just one little problem. I'm no expert on psychology, but if that pack we just saw is any decent sample, I don't think the folks around here are going to be willing to sell us their pretty statue."

"Of course not, silly," she laughed, turning to her food again. "That's what makes it priceless. I never planned to buy Aahz's present."

"But if it isn't for sale, how do we get it?" I frowned, fearing the answer.

Tananda choked suddenly on her food. It took me a moment to realize she was laughing. "Oh, Skeeve," she gasped at last, "you're such a kidder."

"I am?" I blinked.

"Sure," she insisted looking deep into my eyes. "Why do you think it was so important for you to come along on this trip. I mean, you've always said you wanted to be a thief."

V.

"Nothing is impossible. Anything can be accomplished
with proper preparation and planning."
PONCE DE LEON

IT WAS ROUGHLY twelve hours later, the start of a new day. We were still in Jahk. I was still protesting. At the very least, I was sure this latest madcap project was not in line with Aahz's instructions to stay out of trouble.

Tananda, on the other hand, insisted that it would not be any trouble—or it might not be any trouble. We wouldn't know for sure until we saw what kind of security the locals had on the statue. In the meantime, why assume the worst?

I took her advice. I assumed the best. I assumed the security would be impenetrable and that we'd give the whole idea up as a lost cause.

So it was, with different but equally high hopes, we set out in search of the statue.

The town was deathly still in the early morning light. Apparently everyone was sleeping off the prior night's festi-vities—which seemed a reasonable pastime all things considered.

We did manage to find one open restaurant, however. The owner was wearily shoveling out the rubble left by the celebrating crowds, and grudgingly agreed to serve us breakfast.

I had insisted on this before setting out. I mean, worried or not, it takes more than one solid meal to counterbalance the effects of a three-day stretch without food.

"So," I declared once we were settled at the table. "How do we go about locating the statue?"

"Easy," Tananda winked. "I'll ask our host a few subtle questions when he serves our food."

As if summoned by her words, the owner appeared with two steaming plates of food, which he plopped on the table in front of us with an unceremonious 'klunk."

"Thanks," I nodded, and was answered with an unenthusiastic grunt.

"Say, could we ask you a couple questions?" Tananda purred.

"Such as?" the man responded listlessly.

"Such as where do they keep the statue?" she asked bluntly.

I choked on my food. Tananda's idea of interrogation is about as subtle as a flogging, I keep forgetting she's a long standing drinking partner of Aahz's.

"The statue?" our host frowned.

"The one that was being carried up and down the streets yesterday," Tananda clarified easily.

"Oh! You mean the Trophy," the man laughed. "Statue. Hey that's a good one. You two must be new in town."

"You might say that," I confirmed dryly. I had never been that fond of being laughed at—particularly early in the morning.

"Statue, Trophy, what's the difference," Tananda shrugged. "Where is it kept?"

"It's on public display in the Trophy Building, of course," the owner informed us. "If you want to see it, you'd best get started early. After five years, everyone in the city's going to be showing up for a look-see."

"How far is it to..." Tananda began, but I interrupted her.

"You have a whole building for trophies?" I asked with forced casualness. "How many trophies are there?"

"Just the one," our host announced. "We put up a building especially for it. You two must really be new not to know that."

"Just got in yesterday," I confirmed. "Just to show you how new we are, we don't even know what the trophy's for."

"For?" the man gaped. "Why, its for winning the Big Game, of course."

"What Big Game?"

The question slipped out before I thought. It burst upon the conversation like a bombshell, and our host actually gave ground a step in astonishment. Tananda nudged my foot warningly under the table, but I had already realized I had made a major blunder.

"I can see we have a lot to learn about your city, friend," I acknowledged smoothly. "If you have the time, we'd appreciate your joining us in a glass of wine. I'd like to hear more about this 'Big Game.' "

"Say, that's nice of you," our host declared, brightening noticeably. "Wait right here. I'll fetch the wine."

"What was that all about?" Tananda hissed as soon as he had moved out of earshot.

"I'm after some information," I retorted. "Specifically, about the Trophy."

"I know that," she snapped. "The question is `why?'"

"As a thief," I explained loftily, "I feel I should know as much as possible about what I'm trying to steal."

"Who ever told you that?" Tananda frowned. "All you want to know about a target item is how big it is, how heavy it is, and what it will sell for. Then you study the security protecting it. Learning a lot about the item itself is a handicap, not an advantage."

"How do you figure that?" I asked, my curiosity aroused in spite of myself.

My companion rolled her eyes in exasperation.

"Because it'll make you feel guilty," she explained. "When you find out how emotionally attached the current owner is to the item, or that he'll be bankrupt without it, or that he'll be killed if it's stolen, then you'll be reluctant to take it. When you actually make your move, guilt can make you hesitate, and hesitant thieves either end up in jail or dead."

I was going to pursue the subject further, but our host chose that moment to rejoin us. Balancing a bottle and three glasses in his hands, he hooked an extra chair over to our table with his foot.

"Here we go," he announced, depositing his load in front of us. "The best in the house—or the best that's left after the celebrations. You know how that is. No matter how much you stock in advance, it's never enough."

"No we don't know," I corrected. "I was hoping you could tell us."

"That's right," he nodded, filling the glasses. "You know I still can't believe how little you know about politics."

"Politics?" I blinked. "What does the Big Game have to do with politics?"

"It has everything to do with politics," our host proclaimed mightily. "That's the point. Don't you see?"

"No," I admitted bluntly.

The man sighed.

"Look," he said, "this land has two potential capitols. One is Veygus, and this one, as you know, is Ta-hoe."

I hadn't known it, but it seemed unwise to admit my ignorance. I'm slow, but not dumb.

"Since there can only he one capitol at any given time," our host continued, "the two cities compete for the privilege each year. The winner is the capitol and gets to be the center of government for the next year. The Trophy is the symbol of that power, and Veygus has had it for the last five years. Yesterday we finally won it back."

"You mean the Big Game decides who's going to run the land?" I exclaimed, realization dawning at last. "Excuse my asking, but isn't that a bit silly?"

"No sillier than any other means of selecting governmental leadership," the man countered, shrugging his boney shoulders. "It sure beats going to war. Do you think it's a coincidence that we've been playing the game for five hundred years and there hasn't been a civil war in that entire time?"

"But if the Big Game has replaced civil war, than what..."I began, but Tananda interrupted.

"I hate to interrupt," she interrupted, "but if we're going to beat the crowds, we'd better get going. Where did you say the Trophy Building was, again?"

"One block up and six blocks to the left," our host supplied. "You'll know it by the crowds. I'll set the rest of the bottle aside and we can finish it after you've seen the Trophy."

"We'd appreciate that," Tananda smiled, paying him for our meal.

Apparently she had succeeded in using the right currency, for the owner accepted it without batting an eye and waved a fond farewell as we started off.

"I was hoping to find out more about this 'Big Game,'" I grumbled as we passed out of earshot.

"No you weren't," my guide corrected. "I wasn't?" I frowned. "No. You were getting involved," she pointed out. "We're here to get a birthday present, not to get embroiled in local politics." "I wasn't getting involved," I protested. "I was just trying to get a little information."

Tananda sighed heavily.

"Look, Skeeve," she said, "Take some advice from an old dimension traveler. Too much information is poison. Every dimension has its problems, and if you start learning the gruesome details, it occurs to you how simple it would be to help out. Once you see a problem and a solution, you feel almost obligated to meddle. That always leads to trouble, and we're supposed to be avoiding trouble this trip, remember?"

I almost pointed out the irony of her advising me to avoid trouble while enroute to engineer a theft. Then it occurred to me that if the theft didn't bother her, but local politics did, I might be wise to heed her advice. As I've said, I'm slow, but not dumb.

As predicted, the Trophy Building was crowded despite the early hour. As we approached, I marveled anew at the physique of the natives—or specifically, the lack thereof.

Tananda did not seem to share my fascination with the natives, and threaded her way nimbly through the throng, leaving me to follow behind. There was no organized line, and by the time we got through one of the numerous doors, the throng was thick enough to impede our progress. Tananda continued making her way closer to the Trophy, but I stopped just inside the door. My advantage of height gave me a clear view of the Trophy from where I was.

If anything, it was uglier seen plainly than it had been viewed from a distance.

"Isn't it magnificent?" the woman standing next to me sighed.

"It took me a moment to realize she was speaking to me. My disguise made me look shorter, and she was talking to my chest.

"I've never seen anything like it," I agreed lamely.

"Of course not," she frowned. "It's the last work done by the great sculptor Watgit before he went mad."

It occurred to me that the statue might have been done after he went mad. Then it occurred to me that it might have driven him mad—especially if he had been working from a live model. I became so lost in the horrible thought that I started nervously when Tananda reappeared at my side and touched my arm.

"Let's go, handsome," she murmured. "I've seen enough."

The brevity of her inspection gave me hope.

"There's no hope, eh?" I sighed dramatically. "Gee, that's tough. I had really been looking forward to testing my skills."

"That's good," she purred, taking my arm. "Because I think I see a way we can pull this caper off."

I wasn't sure what a caper was, but I was certain that once I found out I wouldn't like it. I was right.

VI.

"Now you see it, now you don't."
H. SHADOWSPAWN

"ARE YOU POSITIVE there was no lock on the door?" I asked for the twenty-third time.

"Keep it down," Tananda hissed, laying a soft hand on my lips, though none too gently. "Do you want to wake everybody?"

She had a point. We were crouched in an alley across from the Trophy Building, and as the whole idea of our waiting was to be sure everyone was asleep, it was counterproductive to make so much noise we kept them awake. Still, I had questions I wanted answered.

"You're sure?" I asked again in a whisper.

"Yes, I'm sure," Tananda sighed. "You could have seen for yourself if you had looked."

"I was busy looking at the statue," I admitted.

"Uh-huh," my partner snorted. "Remember what I said about getting over-involved with the target? You were supposed to be checking security, not playing art connoisseur."

"Well, I don't like it," I declared suspiciously, eager to get the conversation off my shortcomings. "It's too easy. I can't believe they'd leave something they prize as highly as that Trophy in an unlocked, unguarded building."

"There are a couple things you've overlooked," Tananda chided. "First of all, that statue's one of a kind. That means any thief who stole it would have some real problems trying to sell it again. If he even showed it to anyone here in Ta-hoe, they'd probably rip his arms off."

"He could hold it for ransom," I pointed out.

"Hey, that's pretty good," my guide explained softly, nudging me in the ribs. "We'll make a thief of you yet! However, that brings us to the second thing you overlooked."

"Which is?"

"It's not unguarded," she smiled.

"But you said…" I began.

"Sshh!" she cautioned. "I said there would be no guards in the building with the Trophy."

I closed my eyes and regained control of my nerves, particularly those influenced by blind panic.

"Tananda," I said gently. "Don't you think it's about time you shared some of the details of your master plan with me?"

"Sure, handsome," she responded, slipping an arm around my waist. "I didn't think you were interested."

I resisted an impulse to throttle her.

"Just tell me," I urged. "First off, what is the security on the Trophy."

"Well," she said, tapping her chin with one finger, "As I said, there are no guards in the building. There is, however, a silent alarm that will summon guards. It's triggered by the nightingale floor."

"The what?" I interrupted.

"The nightingale floor," she repeated. "It's a fairly common trick throughout the dimensions. The wooden floor around the Trophy is riddled with deliberately loosened boards that creak when you step on them. In this case, they not only creak, they trip an alarm."

"Wonderful!" I grimaced. "So we can't set foot in the room we're supposed to steal something out of. Anything else?"

I was speaking sarcastically, but Tananda took me seriously.

"Just the magikal wards around the statue itself," she shrugged.

"Magikal wards?" I gulped. "You mean there's magik in this dimension?"

"Of course there is," Tananda smiled. "You're here." "I didn't set any wards," I exclaimed.

"That isn't what I meant," Tanda chided. "Look, you tapped into the magikal force lines to disguise us. That means there's magik here for anyone trained to use it—not just us, anyone. Even if none of the locals are adept, there's nothing stopping someone from another dimension from dropping in and using what's here."

"Okay, okay," I sighed. "I guess I wasn't thinking. I guess the next question is, "How are we supposed to beat the funny floor and the wards."

"Easy," she grinned. "The wards are sloppy. Someone set up a 'fence' instead of a 'dome' when they cast the wards. All you have to do is levitate the Trophy over the wards and float it across the floor into our waiting arms. We never even have to set foot in the room."

"Whoa!" I cautioned, holding up a hand. "There's one problem with that. I can't do it."

"You can't? she blinked. "I thought levitation was one of your strongest spells."

"It is," I admitted. "But that statue's heavy. I couldn't levitate it from a distance. It has something to do with what Aahz calls leverage. I'd have to be close, practically standing on top of it."

"Okay," she said at last. "We'll just have to switch to Plan B."

"You have a Plan B?" I asked, genuinely impressed.

"Sure," she grinned. "I just made it up. You can fly us both across the floor and over the wards. Then we latch onto the Trophy and fly back to Klah from inside the wards."

"I don't know," I frowned.

"Now what's wrong?" my guide scowled.

"Well, flying's a form of levitation," I explained. I've never tried flying myself and someone else, and even if I can do it, we'll be pushing down on the floor as hard as if we were walking on it. It might set the alarm off."

"If I understand flying," Tananda pondered, "our weight would be more dispersed than if we were walking, but you're right. There's no point in taking the extra risk of flying us both across the floor."

She snapped her fingers suddenly.

"Okay. Here's what we'll do," she exclaimed, leaning forward. "You fly across to the Trophy alone while I wait by the door. Then, when you're in place, you can use the D-Hopper to bring yourself and the Trophy back to Klah, while I blip back magikally."

For some reason, the thought of dividing our forces in the middle of a theft bothered me.

"Say...um, Tananda," I said, "it occurs to me that even if we set off the alarm, we would be long gone by the time the guards arrived. I mean, if they haven't had war for over five hundred years, they're bound to be a little sloppy turning out."

"No," Tananda countered firmly. "If we've got a way to completely avoid alerting the guards, we'll take it. I promised Aahz to keep you out of trouble, and that means..."

She broke off suddenly, staring across the street.

"What is it?" I hissed, craning my neck for a better look.

In response, she pointed silently at the darkened Trophy Building.

A group of a dozen cloaked figures had appeared from the shadows beside the building. They looked briefly up and down the street, then turned and disappeared into the building.

"I thought you said there wouldn't be any guards in the building!" I whispered frantically.

"I don't understand it," Tananda murmured, more to herself than to me. "It's not laid out for a guard force."

"But if there are guards, we can't..." I began, but Tananda silenced me with a hand on my arm.

The group had reemerged from the building. Moving more slowly than when we had first seen them, they edged their way back into the shadows and vanished from sight.

"That's a relief," Tananda declared letting out a pent-up breath. "It's just a pack of drunks sneaking an after hours at the Trophy."

"They didn't act like drunks," I commented doubtfully.

"Com'on, handsome," my guide declared, clapping a hand on my shoulder. "It's time we got this show on the road. Follow me."

Needless to say, I didn't want to go, but I was even more reluctant to be left behind. This left me no choice but to follow as she headed across the street. As I went, though, I took the precaution of fumbling out my D-Hopper. I didn't like the feel of this, and wanted to be sure my exit route was at hand in case of trouble.

"In you go!" Tananda ordered, holding the door open. "Be sure to sing out when you're in position. I want to be there to see Aahz's face when you give him the trophy."

"I can't see anything," I protested, peering into the dark building.

"Of course not!" Tananda snapped. "It's dark. You know where the Trophy is, though, so get going."

At her insistence, I reached out with my mind and pushed gently against the floor. As had happened a hundred times in practice, I lifted free and began to float toward the estimated position of the statue.

As I went, it occurred to me I had neglected to ask Tananda how high the wards extended. I considered going back or calling to her, but decided against it. Noise would be dangerous, and time was precious. I wanted to get this over with as soon as possible. Instead, I freed part of my mind from the task of flying and cast about in front of me, seeking the tell-tale aura of the magikal wards. There were none.

"Tananda!" I hissed, speaking before I thought. "The wards are down!"

"Impossible," came her response from the door. "You must be in the wrong spot. Check again."

I tried again, casting about the full extent of the room. Nothing. As I peered about, I realized my eyes were acclimating to the darkness.

"There are no wards," I called softly. "I'm right over the pedestal and there are no wards."

Something was tugging at my consciousness. Something I had seen was terribly wrong, but my attention was occupied scanning for the wards.

"If you're over the pedestal," Tananda called, "then drop down and get the Trophy. And hurry! I think I hear someone coming."

I lowered myself to the floor, gently as I remembered the creaky boards, and turned to the pedestal. Then it burst upon me what was wrong.

"It's gone!" I cried.

"What?" Tananda gasped, her silhouette appearing in the doorway.

"The Trophy! It's gone!" I exclaimed, running my hands over the vacant pedestal.

"Get out, Skeeve," Tananda called, suddenly full volume. I started for the door, but her voice stopped me.

"No! Use the D-Hopper. Now!"

My thumb went to the activator button on the device I had been clutching, but I hesitated.

"What about you?" I called. "Aren't you coming?"

"After you're gone," she insisted. "Now get go…"

Something came flying out of the dark and struck her silhouette. She went down in a boneless heap.

"Tananda!" I shouted, starting forward.

Suddenly the doorway was filled with short silhouettes swarming all over Tananda's prone form.

I waivered for a moment in indecision.

"There's another one inside!" someone called.

So much for indecision. I hit the button.

There was the now familiar rush of darkness…and I was back in my quarters on Klah.

Aahz was seated at a table with his back to me, hut he must have heard the BAMF of my arrival.

"It's about time!" he growled. "Did you enjoy your little..."

He broke off as he turned and his eyes took in the expression on my face.

"Aahz," I cried, stumbling forward. "We're in trouble."

His fist came down in a crash which splintered the table. "I knew it!" he snarled.

VII.

"NOW LET'S SEE if I've got this straight," Aahz grumbled, pacing the length of the room. "You got away without a scratch, but Tananda got caught. Right?"

"I couldn't help it!" I moaned, shaking my head. "They were all over her and you said..."

"I know, I know," my mentor waved. "You did the right thing. I'm just trying to get a clear picture of the situation. You're sure this was in Jahk? The weird dimension with the short, pale guys? Skinny or overweight?"

"That's right," I confirmed. "Do you know it?"

"I've heard of it," Aahz shrugged, "but I've never gotten around to visiting. It's talked around a bit on the gambling circuit."

"Must be because of the Big Game," I suggested brightly.

"What I can't figure," Aahz mused, ignoring my comments, "is what you two were doing there."

"Um...it was sort of because of me," I admitted in a small voice.

"You?" Aahz blinked, halting his pacing to stare at me. "Who told you about Jahk?"

"No one," I clarified hastily. "It wasn't that I asked to go to Jahk specifically. I was hungry, and Tananda said Jahk was the closest dimension where I could find something to eat."

"I know how that is," my mentor grimaced. "Eating is always a problem when you're traveling the dimensions—even the humanoid ones."

"It's even rougher when you aren't even visiting humanoid dimensions," I agreed.

"Is that a fact?" Aahz murmured, eyeing me suspiciously. "Which dimensions did you visit, anyway?"

"Um...I can't remember all the names," I evaded. "Tananda—um—felt there would be less chance of trouble in some of the out of the way dimensions."

"What did the natives look like?" Aahz pressed.

"Aren't we getting off the subject?" I asked desperately. "The real issue is Tananda."

Surprisingly, the ploy worked.

"You're right, kid," Aahz sighed. "Okay. I want you to think hard. You're sure you don't know who jumped her or why?"

My conversational gambit had backfired. The question placed me in a real dilemma. On the one hand, I couldn't expect Aahz to come up with a rescue plan unless he knew the full situation. On the other, I wasn't particularly eager to admit what we were doing when Tananda was captured.

"Um…" I said, avoiding his eyes. "I think I can remember a few things about those other dimensions after all. There was one where…"

"Wait a minute," Aahz interrupted. "You were the one who said we should focus on Tananda's problem. Now don't go straying off…"

He stopped in mid sentence to examine me closely. "You're holding out on me, kid," he announced in a cold voice that allowed no room for argument. "Now give! What haven't you told me about this disaster?"

His words hung expectantly in the air, and it occurred to me I couldn't stall any longer.

"Well…" I began, clearing my throat. "I'm not *sure,* but I think the ones who grabbed Tananda were the city guardsmen."

"Guardsmen?" Aahz frowned. "Why would they want to put the grab on Tananda? All you were doing was getting a bite to eat and maybe a little shopping."

I didn't answer, taking a sudden interest in studying my feet in close detail.

"That is all you were doing, wasn't it?"

I tried to speak, but the words wouldn't come.

"What were you doing?" Aahz growled. "Come on. Out with it. I should have known it wasn't just…Hey! You didn't kill anyone, did you?"

Strong hands closed on my shoulders and my head was tossed about by a none too gentle shaking.

"We didn't kill anyone!" I shouted, the process difficult because my jaw was moving in a different direction than my tongue. "We were just stealing…"

"Stealing!?!"

The hands on my shoulders released their grip so fast I fell to the floor. Fortunately, I had the presence of mind to break my fall with my rump.

"I don't believe it! Stealing!" Aahz made his appeal to the ceiling. "All this because you tried to steal something."

My rump hurt, but I had other more pressing matters to deal with. I was desperately trying to phrase my explanation when I realized with some astonishment that Aahz was laughing.

"Stealing!" he repeated. "You know, you really had me going for a minute there, kid. Stealing! And I thought it was something important."

"You mean, you aren't mad?" I asked incredulously.

"Mad? Now!" he proclaimed. "Like the old saying goes, 'you can take the boy out of thieving…Heck! Most demons are thieves. It's the only way to get something if you don't have any native coinage."

"I thought you'd really be upset," I stammered, still unwilling to believe my good fortune.

"Now, don't get me wrong, kid," my mentor amended sternly, "I'm not overjoyed with your venture into thievery. You're supposed to be studying magik…the kind that will get you a raise as a court magician, not the kind that ends up with you running down a dark alley. Still, all things considered, you could have done a lot worse on your first solo trip through the dimension."

"Gee, thanks, Aahz," I beamed.

"So, let's see it," he smiled, extending a palm. "See what?" I blinked.

"What you stole," he insisted. "If you came here direct from the scene of the crime, I assume you still have it with you."

"Umm…actually," I gulped, avoiding his eyes again. "I—that is, *we* didn't get it. It's still back on Jahk somewhere."

"You mean to say you went through all this hassle, got Tananda captured, and came running back here with your tail between your legs, and you didn't even bother to pick up what you were trying to steal?"

The storm clouds were back in Aahz's face. I realized I was on the brink of being in trouble again.

"But you said…" I protested.

"I know you aren't supposed to be a thief!" my mentor roared. "But once you set your hand to it, I expect you to at least be a successful thief! To think an apprentice of mine can't even put together a workable plan..."

"It was Tananda's plan," I offered weakly.

"It was?" Aahz seemed slightly mollified. "Well, you should have checked it over yourself before you joined in."

"I did," I protested. "As far as I can tell it should have worked."

"Oh really?" came the sarcastic reply. "All right. Why don't you tell me all about this plan that didn't work after you okayed it."

He dragged up a chair and sat in front of me, leaving me little option but to narrate the whole story. I went over the whole thing for him; the plan, the nightingale floor, the magik wards, every-thing—except what we were trying to steal, and why. By the time I had finished, his jeering smile had faded to a thoughtful frown.

"You're right, kid," he admitted at last. "It should have worked. The only thing I can figure is that they moved your target some-where else for safekeeping—but that doesn't make sense. I mean, why would they set up all the security arrangements if the target was going to be kept somewhere else? And that group hanging around the building before you went in sounds a bit suspicious."

He thought for a few more minutes, then sighed and shrugged his shoulders. "Oh well," he proclaimed. "Nobody wins all the time. It didn't work and that's that. Com'on kid. Let's get some sleep."

"Sleep?" I gasped. "What about Tananda?"

"What about her?" Aahz frowned.

"They're holding her prisoner in Jahk!" I exclaimed. "Aren't we going to try to rescue here?"

"Oh that!" my mentor laughed. "Don't worry about her. She'll be along on her own in a little while."

"But they're holding her prisoner!" I insisted.

"You think so?" Aahz grinned. "Stop and think a minute, kid. How are they going to hold her? Remember, she can hop dimen-sions any time she wants. The only reason she didn't come back at the same time you did is that she got knocked cold. As soon as she wakes up, she'll be back. Mark my words."

Something about his logic didn't ring true, but I couldn't put my finger on it.

"What if they execute her before she wakes up?" I asked.

"Execute her?" Aahz frowned. "For what? The heist didn't work, so they've still got their whatever. I can't see anyone getting upset enough to have her executed.

"I dunno, Aahz," I said. "The whole city seemed pretty worked up over the Trophy, and…"

"Trophy?" Aahz interrupted. "You mean the Trophy from the Big Game? What does that have to do with anything?"

"That's…um, that's what we were trying to steal," I explained.

"The Trophy?" Aahz exclaimed. "You two didn't aim small, did you? What did you want with—no, on second thought don't tell me. That woman's logic always makes my head hurt."

"But now you see why I'm afraid they might execute her," I pressed, secretly relieved at not having to disclose the motive for our theft.

"It's a possibility," Aahz admitted, "but I still think they'd let her wake up first. Public trials are dramatic, especially for something as big as trying to steal the Big Game Trophy. Heck, Tananda's enough of a sport that she might even stick around for the trial before popping back here."

"You really think so?" I pressed.

"I'm sure of it," Aahz declared confidently. "Now let's get some sleep. It sounds like it's been a long day for you."

I grudgingly retired to my bed, but I didn't go to sleep immediately. There was still something eluding my mental grasp—something important. As I lay there, my mind began wandering back over my trip—the sights, the smells, the strange beings…

"Aahz!" I shouted, bolting upright. "Aahz! Wake up!"

"What is it?" my mentor growled sleepily, struggling to rise. "I just remembered! I was handling our disguises for the whole trip."

"So what?" Aahz growled. "It's good practice for you, but…"

"Don't you see?" I insisted. "If I'm here and Tananda's unconscious in Jahk, then she hasn't got a disguise! They'll be able to see she isn't one of them—that she's a demon!"

There was a frozen moment of silence, then Aahz was on his feet, looming over me.

"Don't just sit there, kid," he growled. "Get the D-Hopper. We're going to Jahk!"

VIII.

"Once more into the breach…"
ZARNA, THE HUMAN CANNONBALL

FORTUNATELY, THERE WAS a setting for Jahk on our D-Hopper though Aahz had to search a bit to find it.

I wanted to go armed to the teeth, but my mentor vetoed the plan. Under cross-examination I had had to admit that I hadn't seen anyone in that dimension wearing arms openly except the city guards, and that was that. My ability to disguise things was weak when it came to metal objects, and swords and knives would have made us awfully conspicuous walking down the street. As Aahz pointed out, the one time you don't want to wear weapons is when they're more likely to get you into trouble than out of it.

I hate it when Aahz makes sense.

Anyway, aside from a few such minor squabbles and disputes, our departure from Klah and our subsequent arrival at Jahk was smooth and uneventful. In hindsight, I realize that was the last thing to go right for some time.

"Well, kid," Aahz exclaimed, looking about him eagerly, "Where do we go?"

"I don't know," I admitted, scanning the horizon.

Aahz frowned. "Let me run this by you slowly," he sighed. "You've been here before, and I haven't. Now, even your limited brain should realize that that makes you the logical guide. Got it?"

"But I haven't been here before," I protested. "Not here! When Tananda and I arrived, we were in a park in Ta-hoe!"

At the moment, Aahz and I were standing beside a dirt road, surrounded by gently rolling meadows and a scattering of very strange trees. There wasn't even an outhouse in sight, much less the booming metropolis I had visited.

"Don't tell me, let me guess," Aahz whispered, shutting his eyes as if in pain. "Tananda handled your transport on the way in the first time. Right?"

"That's right," I nodded. "You made me promise to keep the D-Hopper set for Klah, and…"

"I know, I know," my mentor waved impatiently. "I must say, though, you pick the damndest times to be obedient. Okay! So the D-Hopper's set for a different Drop Zone than the one Tananda uses. We'll just have to dig up a native guide to get us oriented."

"Terrific!" I grimaced. "And where are we supposed to find a native guide?"

"How about right over there?" Aahz smirked, pointing.

I followed the line of his extended talon. Sure enough, not a stone's throw away was a small pond huddled in the shade of a medium sized tree. Seated, leaning against the tree, was a young native. The only thing that puzzled me was that he was holding one end of a short stick, and there was a string which ran from the stick's other end to the pond.

"What's he doing?" I asked suspiciously.

"From here, I'd say he's fishing," Aahz proclaimed.

"Fishing? Like that?" I frowned. "Why doesn't he just..."

"I'll explain later," my mentor interrupted. "Right now we're trying to get directions to Ta-hoe. Remember?"

"That's right!" I nodded. "Let's go."

I started forward, only to be stopped short by Aahz's heavyhand on my shoulder.

"Kid," he sighed, "aren't you forgetting something?"

"What?" I blinked.

"Our disguises, dummy," he snarled. "Your lazy old teacher would like to be able to ask our questions without chasing him all around the landscape for the answers."

"Oh! Right, Aahz."

Embarrassed by the oversight, I hastily did my disguise bit, and together we approached the dozing native.

"Excuse me, sir," I began, clearing my throat. "can you tell us the way to Ta-hoe?"

"What are you doing out here?" the youth demanded, without opening his eyes. "don't you know the land between Veygus and Ta-hoe is a no-man's land until the war's over?"

"What did he say?" Aahz scowled.

"What was that?" the youth asked, his eyes snapping open.

For a change, my mind grasped the situation instantly. I was still wearing my translator pendant from my travels with Tananda, but Aahz didn't have one. That meant that I could understand and be understood by both Aahz and the native, neither of them could decipher what the other was saying. Our disguise was in danger of being discovered by the first native we'd met on our rescue mission. Terrific.

"Umm. Excuse me a moment, sir," I stammered at the youth.

Thinking fast, I removed the pendant from around my neck and looped it over my arm. Aahz understood at once, and thrust his hand through the pendant, grasping my forearm with an iron grip. Thus, we were both able to utilize the power of the pendant.

Unfortunately, the native noticed this by-play. His eyes, which had opened at the sound of Aahz's voice, now widened to the point of popping out as he looked from one of us to the other.

"Fraternity initiation," Aahz explained conspiratorially, winking at him.

"A what?" I blinked.

"Later, kid." my mentor mumbled tensely. "Get the conversation going again."

"Right. Ummm…what was that you were saying about a war?"

"I was saying you shouldn't be here," the youth replied, regaining some of his bluster, but still eyeing the pendant suspiciously. "Both sides have declared this area off-limits to civilians until after the war's over."

"When did this war start?" I asked.

"Oh, it won't actually start for a week or so," the native shrugged "We haven't had a war for over five hundred years and everyone's out of practice. It'll take them a while to get ready—but you still shouldn't be here."

"Well, what are you doing here?" Aahz challenged. "You don't look like a soldier to me."

"My dad's an officer," the youth yawned. If a Ta-hoer patrol finds me out here, I'll just tell 'em who my father is and they'll keep their mouths shut."

"What if a patrol from Vey-gus finds you?" I asked curiously.

"The Veygans?" he laughed incredulously. "They're even more unprepared than Ta-hoe is. They haven't even got their uniforms designed yet, much less organized enough to send out patrols."

"Well, we appreciate the information," Aahz announced. "Now if you'll just point out the way to Ta-hoe, we'll get ourselves off your battlefield."

"The way to Ta-hoe?" the youth frowned. "You don't know the way to Ta-hoe? That's strange."

"What's strange?" my mentor challenged. "So we're new around here. So what?"

The youth eyed him passively.

"It's strange," he observed calmly, "because that road only runs between Veygus and Ta-hoe. Perhaps you can explain how it is that you're traveling a road without knowing either where you're going or where you're coming from?"

There was a moment of awkward silence, then I withdrew my arm from the translator pendant.

"Well, Aahz," I sighed, "How do we talk our way out of this one?"

"Put your arm back in the pendant," Aahz hissed. "He's getting suspicious."

"He's already suspicious," I pointed out. "The question is what do we do now?"

"Nothing to it," my mentor winked. "Just watch how I handle this."

In spite of my worries, I found myself smiling in eager anticipation. Nobody can spin a lie like Aahz once he gets rolling. "The explanation is really quite simple," Aahz smiled, turning to the youth. "You see, we're magicians who just dropped in from another world. Having just arrived here, we are naturally disoriented."

"My, what a clever alibi," I commented dryly.

Aahz favored me with a dirty look.

"As I was saying," he continued, "we have come to offer our services to the glorious city of Ta-hoe for the upcoming war."

It occurred to me that that last statement was a little suspicious. I mean, we had clearly not known about the war at the beginning of this conversation. Fortunately, the youth overlooked this minor detail.

"Magicians?" he smiled skeptically. "You don't look like magicians to me."

"Show him, kid," Aahz instructed.

"Show him?" I blinked.

"That's right," my mentor nodded. "Drop the disguises, one at a time."

With a shrug, I slipped my arm back into the translator pendant and let my disguise fall away.

"I am Skeeve," I announced, "and this…" I dropped Aahz's disguise, "…is my friend and fellow magician, Aahz."

The effect on the youth couldn't have been greater if we had lit a fire under him. Dropping his pole, he sprang to his feet and began backing away until I was afraid he'd topple into the pond. His eyes were wide with fright, and his mouth kept opening and shutting, though no sounds came forth.

"That's enough, kid," Aahz winked. "He's convinced."

I hastily reassembled the disguises, but it did little to calm the youth.

"Not a bad illusion, eh sport?" my mentor leered at him.

"I...I..." the youth stammered. Then he paused and set his lips. "Ta-hoe's that way."

"Thanks," I smiled. "We'll be on our way now."

"Not so fast, kid," Aahz waved. "What's your name, son?"

"Griffin...sir," the youth replied uneasily.

"Well, Griffin," Aahz smiled, "How would you like to show us the way."

"Why?" I asked bluntly.

"Wake up kid," my mentor scowled. "We can't just leave him here. He knows who and what we are."

"I know," I commented archly. "You told him."

"...and besides," he continued as if I hadn't spoken, "he's our passport if we meet any Army patrols."

"I'd rather not..." Griffin began.

"Of course," Aahz interrupted. "There is another possibility. We could kill him here and now."

"I insist you let me escort you!" the youth proclaimed. "Welcome, comrade!" I beamed.

"See, kid?" my mentor smiled, clapping me on the shoulder. "I told you you could settle things without my help."

"Ummm...there is one thing, though," Griffin commented hesitantly.

"And that is..." Aahz prompted.

"I hope you won't hold it against me if your services aren't accepted," the youth frowned.

"You doubt our powers?" my mentor scowled in his most menacing manner.

"Oh, it's not that," Griffin explained quickly. "It's just that...you see...well, we already have a magician."

"Is that all," Aahz laughed. "Just leave him to us."

When Aahz says "us" in regard to magik, he means me.

However bad things had gone so far, I had an uncomfortable foreboding they were going to get worse.

IX.

"War may be Hell...but it's good for business!"
THE ASSOCIATION FOR MERCHANTS,
MANUFACTURERS, AND MORTICIANS

TA-HOE WAS A beehive of activity when we arrived. Prepara-tions
for the upcoming war were in full swing, and everybody was doing
something. Surprisingly enough, most of the prepara-tions were of
a non-military nature.

"What is all this?" I asked our native guide.

"I told you," he explained. "We're getting ready for a war with
Veygus."

"This is getting ready for a war?" I said, gazing incredulously
about.

"Sure," Griffin nodded. "Souvenirs don't make themselves,
you know."

There wasn't a spear or uniform in sight. Instead, the citizens
were busily producing pennants, posters, and lightweight shirts with
"Win the War" emblazoned across them.

"It's the biggest thing to hit Ta-hoe in my lifetime," our guide
confided. "I mean, Big Game souvenirs are a stock item. If you
design it right, you can even hang on to any overstock and sell it the
following year. This war thing caught everybody flatfooted. A lot of
people are complaining that they weren't given sufficient warning to
cash in on it. There's a resolution before the council right now to
postpone hostilities for another month. The folks who deal in knit-
ted hats and stadium blankets are behind it. They claim that declaring
war on such short notice will hurt their businesses by giving unfair
advantage to the merchants who handle stuff like bumper stickers
and posters, that can be cranked out in a hurry."

I couldn't understand most of what he was talking about, but
Aahz was enthralled.

"These folks really know how to run a war!" he declared with
undisguised enthusiasm. "Most dimensions make their war profits
off munitions and weapons contracts. I'll tell you, kid, if we weren't
in such a hurry, I'd take notes."

It's a rare thing for Aahz to show admiration for anyone, much less a whole dimension, and I'd never before heard him admit there was anything he could learn about making money. I found the phenomena unnerving.

"Speaking of being in a hurry," I interjected, "would you mind telling me *why* we're on our way to talk to Ta-hoe's magician?"

"That's easy," my mentor smiled. "For the most part, magi-cians stick together. There's a loyalty to others in the same line of work that transcends any national or dimensional ties. With any luck, we can enlist his aid in springing Tananda loose."

"That's funny," I observed dryly. "The magicians I've seen so far were usually at each other's throats. I got the definite impression they'd like nothing better than to see competing magicians, and us specifically, expire on the spot."

"There is that possibility," Aahz admitted, "but look at it this way. If he won't help us, then he'll probably be our major opponent and we'll want to get a fix on what he can and can't do before we make our plans. Either way, we want to see him as soon as possible."

You may have noticed. Aahz's appraisals of a situation are usually far from reassuring. Some day I might get used to that, but in the meantime I'm learning to operate in a constant state of blind panic.

For a moment, our path was blocked by a crowd listening to a young rabble-rouser who spoke to them from atop a jury-rigged platform. As near as I could make out, they were protesting the war.

"I tell you, the council is withholding information from us!" A growl arose from the assemblage.

"As citizens of Ta-hoe, we have the right to know the facts about this war!"

The response was louder and more fevered.

"How are we supposed to set the odds for this war, much less bet intelligently, if we don't know the facts?"

The crowd was nearing frenzied hysterics as we finally edged past.

"Who are these people?" I asked.

"Bookies," Griffin shrugged. "The council'd better watch its step. They're one of the strongest lobbies in Ta-hoe."

"I tell you, it's awe-inspiring," Aahz murmured dreamily. "We've got to stand up for our rights! Demand the facts!" the rabble-rouser was screaming. "We've got to know the lineups, the battle plans, the…"

"They're barking up the wrong tree," Griffin commented. "They haven't gotten the information because the military hasn't devised a plan yet."

"Why don't you tell them?" I suggested.

Our guide cocked an eyebrow at me. "I thought you were in a hurry to see the magician," he countered.

"Oh, that's right," I returned, a little embarrassed by the oversight.

"Say, Griffin," Aahz called. "I've been meaning to ask. What started the war, anyway?"

For the first time since we'd met him, our youthful guide showed an emotion other than boredom or fear.

"Those bastards from Veygus stole our Trophy," he snarled angrily. "Now we're going to get it back or know the reason why."

For a change, I didn't need an elbow in the ribs from Aahz to remember to keep quiet. I got one anyway.

"Stole your Trophy, eh?" my mentor commented innocently. "Know how they did it?"

"A pack of 'em pulled a hit-and-run raid the day after the Big Game," Griffin proclaimed bitterly. "They struck just after sundown and got away before the guardsmen could respond to the alarm."

The memory of the group entering and leaving the Trophy Building while Tananda and I waited flashed across my mind. That explained a couple questions that had been bothering me, like 'where did the statue go?' and 'how did the guards arrive so fast?' We hadn't triggered any alarms! The group from Veygus had…inadvertently setting us up for the guards!

"I'd think you'd take better care of the Trophy, if it means so much to you," Aahz suggested.

Griffin spun on him, and I thought for a minute he was actually going to throw a punch. Then, at the last moment, he remembered that Aahz was a magician and dropped his arms to his side. I heaved a quiet sigh of relief. I mean, Aahz is strong! I was impressed with his strength in my own dimension of Klah, and here on Jahk, I looked strong compared to the natives. If Griffin had thrown a punch, Aahz would have ripped him apart…literally!

"Our security precautions on the Trophy were more than adequate," our guide announced levelly, "under normal circumstances. The thieves had magical assistance."

"Magical assistance?" I said, finally drawn from my silence. "That's right." Griffin nodded vigorously. "How else could they have moved such a heavy statue before the guards arrived?" "They could have done it without magic," Aahz offered. "Say if they had a lot of strong men on the job."

"Normally, I'd agree with you," our guide admitted, "but in this case, we actually captured the demon that helped them."

For a long moment there was silence. Neither Aahz nor I wanting to ask the next question...afraid of what the answer might be. Finally, Aahz spoke. "A demon, you say?" he asked, smiling his broadest. "What happened to it?"

His tone was light and casual, but there was a glint in his eye I didn't like. I found myself in the unique position of worrying about the fate of an entire dimension.

"The demon?" Griffin frowned. "Oh, the magician's holding it captive. Maybe he'll let you see it when you meet him."

"The magician? The one we're going to see?" Aahz pressed.

"He's got the demon?"

"That's right," our guide answered. "Why do you ask?"

"Is she still unconscious?" I blurted.

The elbow from Aahz almost doubled me over this time, but it was too late. Griffin had stopped in his tracks and was studying me with a new intensity.

"How did you know it was unconscious?" he asked suspiciously. "And why do you refer to it as 'she?'"

"I don't know," I covered smoothly. "Must have been something you said."

"I said we'd captured a demon," he argued, "not how, and as far as its sex goes..."

"Look," Aahz interrupted harshly. "Are we going to stand around arguing all day, or are you going to take us to the magician?"

Griffin stared at us hard for a moment, then shrugged his shoulders.

"We're here," he announced, pointing at a door in the wall.

The magician lives there."

"Well, don't just stand there, son," Aahz barked. "Knock on the door and announce us."

Our guide heaved a sigh of disgust, but obediently walked over and hammered on the indicated door.

"Aahz!" I hissed. "What are we going to say?"

"Leave it to me, kid," he murmured back. "I'll try to feel him out a little, then we'll play it by ear from there."

"What are we supposed to do with our ears?" I frowned. Aahz rolled his eyes. "Kid…" he began.

Just then, the door opened, exposing a wizen old man who blinked at the sunlight.

"Griffin!" he exclaimed. "What brings you here?"

"Well, sir," our guide stammered, "I—that is, there are two gentleman who want to speak with you. They say…Well, they're magicians."

The old man started at this and shot a sharp glance in our direction before he covered his reaction with a friendly smile.

"Magicians, you say! Well, come right in, gentlemen. Lad, I think you'd better wait outside here. Professional secrets and all that, you know."

"Um…actually, I thought I'd be on my way now," Griffin murmured uneasily.

"Wait here." There was steel in the old man's voice now. "Yes, sir," our guide gulped, licking his lips.

I tried to hide my nervousness as we followed the magician into his abode. I mean, aside from the fact that we didn't have the vaguest idea of this man's power, and that we had no guarantee we'd ever get out of this place alive, I had nothing to worry about. Right?

"Aahz," I whispered. "Have you got a fix on this guy yet?"

"It's a little early to say," my mentor replied sarcastically. "In the meantime, I've got a little assignment for you."

"Like what?" I asked.

"Like, check his aura. Now."

One of the first things I had learned from Aahz was how to check auras, the field of magik around people or things. It seemed a strange thing to do just now, but I complied, viewing our host with unfocused eyes.

"Aahz," I gasped. "He's got an aura! The man's actually radiating magik. I can't do anything against someone that powerful."

"It's possible there is another explanation, kid," Aahz murmured. "He could be wearing a disguise spell like we are."

"Do you think so?" I asked hopefully.

"Well," my mentor drawled, "he's wearing a translator pendant, the same as we are. That makes it a good bet that he's about from this dimension. Besides, there's something familiar about his voice."

Our conversation ground to a halt as we reached our destination, a small room sparsely furnished with a large table surrounded by several chairs.

"If you'll be seated, gentlemen," our host said, gesturing to the chairs, "perhaps you'll be good enough to tell me what it is you wish to speak to me about."

"Not so fast," Aahz challenged, holding up a hand. "We're used to knowing who we're dealing with. Could you do us the courtesy of removing your disguise before we start?"

The magician averted his eyes and began to fidget nervously. "You spotted it, eh?" he grumbled. "It figures. As you've probably guessed already, I'm relatively new to this profession. Not in your class at all, if you know what I mean."

An immense wave of relief washed over me, but Aahz remained undaunted.

"Just take off the disguise, huh?" he insisted.

"Oh, very well," our host sighed and began fumbling in his pocket.

We waited patiently until we found what he was looking for.

Then the lines of his features began to waver…his body grew taller and fuller…until at last we saw.

"I thought so!" Aahz crowed triumphantly.

"Quigley!" I gasped.

"This is embarrassing," the demon hunter grumbled, slouching down into his chair.

X.

"Old heroes never die; they reappear in sequels"
M. MORECOCK

PHYSICALLY, QUIGLEY WAS unchanged from when we first met him. Tall, long-boned and muscular, he still looked as if he'd be more at home in armor swinging a sword than sitting around in magician robes sipping wine with us. However, here we were, gathered in a conference which bore little resemblance to the formal interview I had originally anticipated.

"I was afraid you two would be along when I realized it was Tananda the guards captured," the ex-demon hunter grumbled.

"Afraid?" I frowned, genuinely puzzled. "Why should you be afraid of us?"

"Oh come now, lad," Quigley smiled bitterly, "I appreciate your efforts to spare my feelings, but the truth of the matter is plain. My magikal powers don't hold a candle next to yours. I know full well that now that you're here you'll be able to take my job away from me without much difficulty. Either that, or make me look silly in front of my employers so that they'll fire me outright."

"That's ridiculous," I cried, more than slightly offended. "Look Quigley, I promise you we'll neither steal your job nor make you look silly while we're here."

"Really?" Quigley asked, brightening noticeably.

"You're being a little hasty with your promises, aren't you, kid?" Aahz interrupted in a warning tone.

"Com'on, Aahz," I grimaced. "You know that isn't why we're here."

"But kid…"

I ignored him, turning back to Quigley.

"I promise you, Quigley. No job stealing, and nothing that will endanger your position. The truth is, I've already got a magician's job of my own. I'm surprised Tananda hasn't told you."

Strangely enough, instead of relaxing, Quigley seemed even more ill at ease and avoided my gaze.

"Well, actually, lad," he murmured uncomfortably, "Tananda hasn't said anything since she was turned over to my custody."

"She hasn't?" I asked, surprised. "That's funny. Usually the trouble is getting her to stop talking."

"Quite right," Quigley laughed uneasily. "Except this time-well—she hasn't regained consciousness yet."

"You mean she's still out cold?" Aahz exclaimed, surging to his feet. "Why didn't you say so? Come on, Quigley, wheel her out here. This might be serious."

"No, no. You misunderstand," Quigley waved. "She hasn't regained consciousness because I've kept a sleep spell on her."

"A sleep spell?" I frowned.

"That's right," Quigley nodded. "Tananda taught it to me herself. It's the first spell I learned, actually. Really very simple. As I understand it, all members of the Assassin's Guild are required to learn it."

"Why?" Aahz interrupted.

"I never really gave it much thought," Quigley blinked. "I suppose it would help them in their work. You know, if you came on a sleeping victim, the spell would keep him from waking up until after you'd finished the job. Something like that."

"Not that!" Aahz moaned. "I know how assassins operate better than you do. I meant, why are you using a sleep spell on Tananda?"

"Why, to keep her from waking up, of course," Quigley shrugged.

"Brilliant," I muttered. "Why didn't we think of that?"

"Shut up, kid," my mentor snarled. "Okay, Quigley, let's try this one more time. Why don't you want to wake her up? I thought you two got along pretty well last time I saw you."

"We did," Quigley admitted, blushing. "But I'm a working magician now. If I let her wake up…well, I don't flatter myself about my powers. There would be nothing I could do to keep her from escaping."

"You don't want her to escape?" I blinked.

"Of course not. It would mean my job," Quigley smiled. "That's why I'm so glad you promised not to do anything that would jeopardize my position."

My stomach sank.

"Smooth move, kid," Aahz commented dryly. "Maybe next time you'll listen when I try to advise you."

I tried to say something in my own defense, but nothing came to mind, so I shut my mouth and used the time to feel miserable.

"Well, gentlemen," Quigley beamed, rubbing his hands together. "Now that that's settled, I suppose you'll be wanting to get on your way to wherever you're going."

"Not so fast, Quigley," Aahz declared, sinking back into his chair and propping his feet up on the table. "If nothing else, I think you owe us an explanation. The last time we saw you, you were a demon-hunter, heading off through the dimension with Tananda to learn more about magik. Now, I was under the distinct impression you intended to use that knowledge to further your old career. What brought you over to our side of the fence?"

Quigley thought for a moment, then shrugged and settled back in his own chair.

"Very well," he said. "I suppose I can do that, seeing as how we were comrades-in-arms at one point."

He paused to take a sip of wine before continuing.

"Tananda and I parted company with the others shortly after we discovered your little joke. We thought it was quite amusing, particularly Tananda, but the others seemed quite upset, especially Isstvan, so we left them and headed off on our own."

The demon-hunter's eyes went slightly out of focus as he sank back into his memories, "We traveled the dimensions for some time. Quite a pleasant time, I might add. I learned a lot about demons and a little about magik, and it set me to thinking about my chosen line of work as a demon-hunter. I mean, demons aren't such a bad lot once you get to know them, and magik pays considerably better than swinging a sword."

"I hope you're paying attention, kid," Aahz grinned, prodding my shoulder.

I nodded, but kept my attention on Quigley.

"Then," the demon-hunter continued, "circumstances arose that prompted Tananda to abandon me without money or a way back to my own dimension."

"Wait a minute," Aahz interrupted. "That doesn't sound like Tananda. What were these 'circumstances' you're referring to?"

"It was a misunderstanding, really," Quigley explained, flushing slightly. "Without going into lurid details, the end result involved my spending a night with a female other than Tananda."

"I can see why she'd move on without you," Aahz frowned, "But not why she'd take your money."

"Well actually, it was the young lady I was with at the time who relieved me of my coinage," the demon-hunter admitted, blushing a deeper shade of red.

"Got it," Aahz nodded. "Sounds like along with magik and demons, there are a few things you have to learn about women."

I wouldn't have minded a few lessons in the department myself, but I didn't think this was the time to bring it up.

"Anyway," Quigley continued hastily, "there I was, stranded and penniless. It seemed the only thing for me to do was to go to a Placement Service."

"A Placement Service?" Aahz blinked. "Just where was this that you were stranded?"

"Why, the Bazaar at Deva, of course," the demon-hunter replied. "Didn't I mention that?"

"The Bazaar at Deva," my mentor sighed. "I should have known. Oh well, keep going."

"There's really not that much more to tell." Quigley shrugged. "There were no openings for a demon-hunter, but they managed to find me this position here in Jahk by lying about how much magik I knew. Since then, things have been pretty quiet—or they were before the guards appeared at my door carrying Tananda."

I was starting to wonder if any court magician was really qualified for his position.

"And you aren't about to let Tananda go. Right?" Aahz finished.

"Don't misunderstand," Quigley insisted, gnawing his lip. "I'd like to let her go. If nothing else it would do a lot for patching up the misunderstanding between Tananda and myself. Unfortu-nately, I just don't see any way I could let her escape without losing my job on grounds of incompetence."

"Say, maybe we could get you a job in Possletum!" I suggested brightly.

"Kid," Aahz smiled, "are you going to stop that tongue of yours all by yourself, or do I have to tear it out by the roots?" I took the hint and shut up.

"Thank you, lad," Quigley said, "but I couldn't do that. Unlike yourself, I'm still trying to build a reputation as a magician. How would it look if I left my first job in defeat with my tail between my legs?"

"You haven't got a tail," Aahz pointed out.

"Figure of speech," Quigley shrugged.

"Oh," my mentor nodded. "Well, if you think a hasty retreat from one's first job is unusual, my friend, you still have a lot to learn about the magik profession."

"Haven't I been saying that?" Quigley frowned.

I listened to their banter with only half an ear. The rest of me was floating on Quigley's implied compliment. I'm getting quite good at hearing indirect compliments. The direct ones are few and far between.

Come to think of it, I was getting a reputation as a magician. No one could deny we beat Isstvan at his own game—and I had actually recruited and commanded the team that stopped Big Julie's army. Why, in certain circles, my name must be...

"Bullshit! " Aahz roared, slapping his hand down on the table hard enough to make the chairs jump. "I tell you she didn't steal the damn Trophy! "

I collected my shattered nerves and turned my attention to the conversation once more.

"Oh come now, Aahz, " Quigley grimaced. "I traveled with Tananda long enough to know she's not above stealing something that caught her eye—nor are you two, I'd imagine. "

"True enough, " Aahz admitted easily, "but you can bet your last baseball card that if any of us went after your Trophy, we wouldn't be caught afterward. "

"My last what? " Quigley frowned. "Oh, no matter. Look, even if I believed you I couldn't do anything. What's important is the Council believes Tananda was involved, and they wouldn't even consider releasing her unless they got the Trophy back first. "

"Oh yea? " Aahz smiled, showing all his teeth. "How many Council members are there and how are they guarded? "

"Aahz!" Quigley said sternly. "If anything happened to the Council, I'm afraid I'd see it as a threat to my job and therefore a direction violation of Master Skeeve's promise."

My mentor leaned back in his chair and stared at the ceiling. The heavy metal wine goblet in his hand crumpled suddenly, but aside from that there was no outward display of his feelings.

"Urn...Quigley?" I ventured cautiously. I still had a vivid image in my mind of my tongue in Aahz's grasp instead of the wine goblet.

"Yes, lad?" Quigley asked, cocking an eyebrow at me.

"What did you say would happen if the Trophy were returned?"

Aahz's head swiveled around slowly until our gazes met, but his gold speckled eyes were thoughtful now.

"Well, I didn't say, actually," Quigley grumphed, "but that would change everything. With the Trophy back, the council would be ecstatic and definitely better disposed toward Tananda...Yes, if the Trophy were returned, I think I could find an excuse to release her."

"Is that a promise?"

I may be ignorant, but I'm a fast learner.

Quigley studied me for a moment before answering. "Very well," he said at last. "Why do you ask?"

I shot a glance at Aahz. One eyelid slowly closed in a wink, then he went back to studying the ceiling.

"Because," I announced, relief flooding over me, "I think I've come up with a way we can free Tananda, protect your job, and stop the War in one fell swoop."

XI.

"What do you mean 'You've got a little job for me'?"
HERCULES

STEAL THE TROPHY back from Vey-gus. Just like that," Aahz grumbled for the hundredth time.

"We're doomed," Griffin prophesied grimly.

"Shut up, Griffin," I snarled.

It occured to me I was picking up a lot of Aahz's bad habits lately.

"But I keep telling you, I don't know Veygus," the youth protested. "I won't be any help at all. Please, can't I go back to Ta-hoe?"

"Just keep walking," I sighed.

"Face it son," Aahz smiled, draping a casual arm over our guide's shoulder. "We aren't going to let you out of our sight until this job's over. The sooner we get to Vey-gus, the sooner you'll be rid of us."

"But why?" Griffin whined.

"We've gone over this before," my mentor sighed. "This heist is going to be rough enough without Veg-gus hearing about it in advance. Now the only way we can be sure you don't tell anyone is to keep you with us. Besides, you're our passport through the Ta-hoe patrols if we meet any."

"The patrols are easy to avoid," the youth insisted. "And I won't tell anyone about your mission, honest. Isn't there any way I can get you to trust me?"

"Well," Aahz *drawled judiciously,* "I guess there is one thing that might do the trick."

"Really?" our guide asked hopefully.

"What da ya think, Skeeve?" my mentor called. "Do you feel up to turning our friend here into a rock or a tree or something until the job's over?"

"A rock or a tree?" the youth gulped, wide-eyed.

"Sure," Aahz shrugged. "I wouldn't have suggested it myself. There's always a problem finding the *right* rock or tree to change back. Sometimes it takes years of searching. Sometimes the magician just gives up."

"Can't you guys walk any faster?" Griffin challenged, quickening his pace. "We'll never get to Vey-gus at this rate."

"I guess that settles that," I smiled, winking at Aahz to show I appreciated his bluff.

"Steal the Trophy from Vey-gus," my mentor replied, picking up his witty repartee where he had left it. "Just like that." So much for changing the subject.

"Com'on Aahz, give me a break," I defended glibly. "You agreed to this before I proposed it."

"I didn't say anything," he argued.

"You winked," I insisted.

"How do you know I didn't just get something in my eye?" he countered.

"I don't," I admitted. "Did you?"

"No." he sighed. "I winked. But only because it looked like the only way out of the situation you got us into."

He had me there.

"How we got into this spot is beside the point," I decided. "The real question is how are we going to steal the Trophy."

"I see," Aahz grunted. "When you get us into trouble, it's beside the point."

"The Trophy," I prompted.

"Well..." my mentor began slowly, rising to the bait. "We won't be able to make any firm plans until we see the layout and size up the guards. How 'bout it, Griffin? What are we liable to be up against? How good are these Veygans?"

"The Veygans?" our guide grimaced. "I wouldn't worry about them if I were you. They couldn't guard a pea if they swallowed it."

"Really inept, uh?" Aahz murmured cocking an eyebrow. 'Inept? They're a joke," Griffin laughed. "There isn't a Veygan alive who knows how to spell strategy, much less use it."

"I thought you said you didn't know anything about Veygus," I commented suspiciously.

"Well...I don't actually," the youth admitted, "but I've seen their team play in the Big Game, and if that's the best they can muster..."

"You mean everything you've been saying was speculation based on the way their team plays?" Aahz interrupted. "That's right," Griffin nodded.

"The same team that's been beating the pants off Ta-hoe for the last five years?"

Our guide's head came up as if he had just been slapped. "We won this year!" he declared fiercely.

"Whereupon they turned around and stole the Trophy right out from under your noses," my mentor pointed out. "It sounds to me like they may not be as inept as you'd like to think they are."

"They get lucky once in a while," Griffin muttered darkly.

"You might want to think it through a bit," I advised. "I mean, do you really want to go around claiming your team was beaten by a weak opponent? If Ta-hoe is so good and Veygus is so feeble, how do you explain five losses in a row? Luck isn't enough to swing the game *that* much."

"We got overconfident," our guide confided. "It's a constant danger you have to guard against when you're as good as we are."

"I know what you mean," Aahz nodded. "My partner and I have the same problem."

Well, modesty has never been Aahz's strong suit. Still it was nice to hear him include me in his brash statements. It made me feel like my studies were finally bearing fruit, like I was making progress.

"Aside from the military, what are we up against?" my mentor asked. "How about the magik you keep mentioning? Do they have a magician?"

"They sure do," Griffin nodded vigorously. "Her name's Massha. If you have any troubles at all, it will be with her. She's mean."

"Is that 'mean' in abilities, or in temperament?" Aahz cross-examined.

"Both," our guide asserted firmly. "You know, I've never been totally convinced our magician is as good as he claims to be, but Massha's a real whiz. I couldn't even start to count the fantastic things I've seen her do."

"Um…what makes you think her temperament is mean?" I asked casually, trying to hide my sagging confidence.

"Well, let me put it this way," Griffin explained. "If there was a messy job to be done, and you could think of three ways to do it, she'd find a fourth way that was nastier than the other three ways combined. She has a real genius for unpleasantness."

"Terrific," I grimaced.

"How's that again?" our guide frowned.

"Skeeve here always likes a challenge," Aahz explained hastily, draping a friendly arm around my shoulders.

I caught the warning, even without him digging his talons in until they nearly drew blood. He did it anyway, making it a real effort to smile.

"That's right," I laughed to hide my gasp. "We've handled heavy-weights before."

Which was true. What I neglected to mention and tried hard not to think about was that we survived the encounters by a blend of blind luck and bald-faced deceit.

"Good," Griffin beamed. "Even if you don't manage to steal the Trophy, if you can take Massha out of action, Ta-hoe can win the war easily."

"You know, Griffin," Aahz commented, cocking an eyebrow, "for someone who doesn't know Veygus, you seem to know an awful lot about their magician."

"I sure do," our guide laughed bitterly. "She used to be Ta-hoe's magician until Veygus hired her away. I used to run errands for her and…" He suddenly stopped in mid-stride and mid-sen-tence simultaneously. "Hey! That's right." he exclaimed. "I can't go along with you if you're going to see Massha. She knows me! If the Veygans find out I'm from Ta-hoe, they'll think I'm a scout. I'd get torn apart."

"Don't worry," I soothed, "we aren't going anywhere near Massha."

"Yes, we are," Aahz corrected. "We are?" I blinked.

"Kid, do I have to explain it to you all over again? We've got to check out the local magikal talent, the same as we did when we hit Ta-hoe."

"And look where that got us," I muttered darkly.

"Look where who got us?" Aahz asked innocently. "I didn't quite hear that."

"All right! All right!" I surrendered. "We'll go see Massha. I guess I'll just have to whip up a disguise for Griffin so he won't be spotted."

"She'll recognize my voice," our guide protested.

"Don't talk!" I ordered, without clarifying if it was an immedi-ate or future instruction.

"This time, I think he's right," Aahz interrupted thoughtfully. "It would probably be wisest to leave Griffin behind for this venture."

"It would?" I blinked.

"Hey! Wait a minute," Griffin interjected nervously. "I don't want to be a rock or a stone."

"Oh, I'm sure we can work out something a bit less drastic," my mentor smiled reassuringly. "Excuse us for a moment while we confer."

I thought Aahz was going to pull me aside for a private conversation, but instead he simply slipped off his translator pendant. After a bit of browbeating, Quigley had supplied us with an extra, so now we each had one. Removing them allowed us to converse without fear of being overheard, while at the same time keeping Griffin within an arm's length. I followed suit and removed mine.

"What gives, Aahz?" I asked as soon as I was free of the pendant. "Why the change in plans?"

"The job's getting a little too complex," he explained. "It's time we started reducing our variables."

"Our what?" I puzzled.

"Look!" Aahz gritted. "We're going to have our hands full trying to elude the military and this Massha gal without trying to keep an eye on Griffin, too. He can't be any great help to us, and if he isn't a help, he's a hindrance."

"He shouldn't be too much trouble," I protested.

"Any trouble will be too much trouble," my mentor corrected firmly. "So far, he's an innocent bystander we've dragged into this. That means if we take him into Veygus, we should be confident we can bring him out again. Now, are you that confident? Or don't you mind the thought of leaving him stranded in a hostile town."

Aahz doesn't give humanitarian arguments often, but when he does, they always make sense.

"Okay," I sighed. "But what do we do with him? You know I can't turn him into a rock or a tree. Not that I would if I could."

"That's easy," Aahz shrugged. "You put a sleep spell on him. That should keep him out of mischief until we get back here."

"Aahz," I said gently, closing my eyes. "I don't know how to cast a sleep spell. Remember?"

"That's no problem," my mentor winked. "I'll teach you."

"Right now?" I questioned incredulously.

"Sure. Didn't you hear Quigley? It's easy," Aahz declared confidently. "Of course, you realize it isn't really a 'sleep' spell. It's more like suspended animation."

"Like what?" I blinked.

"It's a magikal slowing of the body's metabolism," he clarified helpfully. "If it were sleep as you perceive it, then you'd run into problems of dehydration and…"

"Aahz!" I interrupted, holding up a hand. "Is the spell easier than the explanation?"

"Well, yes," he admitted. "But I thought you'd like to know."

"Then just teach me the spell. Okay?"

XII.

"Out of the frying pan, into der fire.*"*
THE SWEDISH CHEF

FORTUNATELY, THE SLEEP spell was as easy to learn as Aahz
had promised, and we left Griffin snoozing peacefully in a patch of
weeds along the road.

We took the precaution of circling Veygus to enter the city from
a direction other than Ta-hoe. As it turned out it was a pointless
exercise. Everyone in Veygus was too busy with their own business
to even notice us, much less which direction we were coming from.

"This is really great!" Aahz chortled, looking about the streets as
we walked. "I could develop a real fondness for this dimension."

The war activities in Veygus were the same as we had witnessed
in Ta-hoe, except the souvenirs were being made in red and white
instead of blue and gold. I was starting to wonder if anyone was
ever going to get around to actually fighting the war, or if they were
all too busy making money.

"Look at that, Aahz!" I exclaimed, pointing.

There was a small crowd gathered, listening to a noisy orator.
From what I could hear, their complaint was the same one we heard
back in Ta-hoe: that the government's withholding information about
the war was hampering the odds-makers.

"Yea. So?" my mentor shrugged.

"I wonder if they're bookies, too," I speculated.

"There's one way to find out," Aahz offered.

Before I could reply, he had sauntered over to someone at the
back of the crowd and engaged them in an animated conversation.
There was nothing for me to do but wait…and worry.

"Good news, kid," he beamed, rejoining me at last.

"Tell me," I pressed. "I could use some good news right about now."

"They're giving three-to-one odds against Ta-hoe in the upcoming war."

It took me a moment to realize that was the extent of his information. "That's it?" I frowned. "That's your good news? It sounds
to me like we've badly underestimated Veygus's military strength."

"Relax, kid," Aahz soothed. "Those are the same odds they're offering in Ta-hoe against Veygus. Local bookies always have to weight the odds in favor of the home team. Otherwise no one will bet against them."

Puzzled, I shook my head. "Okay, so they're actually evenly matched," I shrugged. "I still don't see how that's good news for us."

"Don't you see?" my mentor urged. "That means the bookies are operating independently instead of as a combine. If we play our cards right, we could show a hefty profit from this mess."

Even though annoyed that Aahz could be thinking of money at a time like this, I was nonetheless intrigued with his logic. I mean, after all, he *did* train me.

"By betting?" I asked. "How would we know which side to bet for?"

"Not 'bet for,' bet against," Aahz explained..."And we'd bet equal amounts against both sides."

I thought about this a few moments, nodding knowingly all the while, then gave up. "I don't get it," I admitted. "Betting the same amount for...excuse me, against...both sides, all we do is break even."

Aahz rolled his eyes in exasperation. "Think it through kid," he insisted. "At three to one odds we can't do anything but win. Say we bet a thousand against each team. If Ta-hoe wins, then we pay a thousand in Ta-hoe and collect three thousand in Veygus, for a net profit of two thousand. If Veygus wins, we reverse the process and still come out two thousand ahead."

"That's not a bad plan," I said judiciously, "but I can see three things wrong with it. First, we don't have a thousand with us to bet..."

"We could hop back to Klah and get it," Aahz countered.

"...second, we don't have the time..."

"It wouldn't take that long," my mentor protested.

"third, if our mission's successful, there won't be a war."

Aahz's mouth was open for a response, and that's where it stayed-open, and blissfully noiseless as he thought about my argument.

"Got you there, didn't I, Aahz?" I grinned.

"I wonder what the odds are that there won't be a war," he mused, casting a wistful eye at the crowd of bookies.

"Com'on, Aahz," I sighed, tugging bravely at his arm, "we've got a heist to scout."

"First," he corrected firmly, "we have to check out this Massha character."

I had hoped he had forgotten, but then, this adventure was not being typified by its phenomenally good luck.

We picked our way across Veygus, occasionally stopping people to ask directions, and arrived at last outside the dwelling of the town magician. It was an unimposing structure, barely inside the eastern limits of the city, and exuded an intriguing array of aromas.

"Not much of a hangout for a powerful magician, eh, Aahz?" I commented, trying to bolster my sagging courage.

"Remember where you were living when we first met?" my mentor retorted, never taking his eyes from the building.

I did. The one-room clapboard shack where I had first studied magik with Garkin made this place look like a veritable palace.

"What I can't figure out is why Massha settled for this place," Aahz continued, talking as much to himself as to me. "If what Griffin said is true, she could have had any place in town to work from. Tell you what, kid. Check for force lines, will you?"

I obediently closed my eyes and stretched out my mind, searching for those invisible currents of magikal power which those in the profession tap for their own use. I didn't have to look hard.

"Aahz!" I gasped. "There are four...no five...force lines intersecting here. Three in the air and two in the ground."

"I thought so," my mentor nodded grimly. "This location wasn't chosen by accident. She's got power to spare, if she knows how to use it."

"But what can we do if she's that powerful?" I moaned.

"Relax, kid," Aahz smiled. "Remember, the power's there for anyone to use. You can tap into it as easily as she can."

"That's right," I said, relaxing slightly, but not much. "Okay, what's our plan."

"I don't really know," he admitted, heading for the door. "We'll just have to play this by ear."

Somehow that phrase rang a bell in my memory. "Say—um—Aahz," I stammered. "Remembering how things went back in Tahoe, this time let's play it by your ear. Okay?"

"You took the words right out of my mouth," Aahz grinned. "Just remember to check her aura as soon as we get inside. It'll help to know if she's local or if we're dealing with imported help."

So saying, he raised his hand and began rapping on the door. I say 'began' because between the second and third rap, the door flew open with alarming speed.

"What do you...well, hel-lo there, boys."

"Are...um...are you Massha, the magician?" Aahz stammered, both taken aback and stepping back.

"Can you imagine anyone else fitting the description?" came the throaty chuckle in response.

She was right. I had not seen anyone on Jahk—heck, in several dimensions, who looked anything like the figure framed in the open door. Massha was immense, in girth if not in height. She filled the doorway to overflowing—and it wasn't that narrow a door. Still, size alone doth not a pageant make. Massha might have been overlooked as just another large woman were it not for her garments.

Purple and green warred with each other across her tent-like dress, and her bright orange hair draped across one shoulder in dirty strings did nothing toward encouraging an early settlement. And jewelry! Massha was wearing enough in the way of earrings, rings and necklaces to open her own store. She wasn't a sample case, she was the entire inventory!

Her face was nothing to write home about—unless you're really into depressing letters. Bad teeth were framed by fleshy chapped lips, and her pig-like eyes peering from the depths of her numerous smile wrinkles were difficult to distinguish from her other skin blemishes.

I've seen some distinctive looking women in my travels, but Massha took the cake, platter, and tablecloth.

"Did you boys just come to stare?" the apparition asked, "or can I do something for you?"

"We...um...we need help," Aahz managed.

I wasn't sure if he was talking about our mission or our immediate situation, but either way I agreed with him whole-heartedly.

"Well, you came to the right place," Massha leered. "Step into my parlor and we'll discuss what I've got that you want—and vice-versa."

Aahz followed her into the building, leaving me no choice but to trail along. He surprised me, though, by dropping back slightly to seek my advice.

"What's the word, kid?" he hissed.

ᘯASSHA

©PᴿFOGLIO·82

"How about 'repulsive?'" I suggested.

That earned me another dig in the ribs.

"I meant about her aura. What's the matter, did you forget?"

As a matter of fact, I had. Now that I had been so forcefully reminded, though, I hurriedly checked for magikal emanations.

"She's got—no, wait a minute," I corrected. "It isn't her, it's her jewelry. It's magikal, but she isn't."

"I thought so," Aahz nodded. "Okay. Now we know what we're dealing with."

"We do?" I asked.

"She's a mechanic," my mentor explained hurriedly. "Gimmick magik with her jewelry. Totally different than the stuff I've been teaching you."

"You mean you think I could beat her in a fair fight?"

"I didn't say that," he corrected. "It all depends on what kind of jewelry she's got—and from what we've seen so far, she's got a lot."

"Oh," I sagged. "What are we going to do?"

"Don't worry, kid," Aahz winked. "Fair fights have never been my specialty. As long as she doesn't know you're a magician, we've got a big advantage."

Any further questions I might have had were forgotten as we arrived at our destination. Having just left Quigley's dwelling, I was unprepared for what Massha used for an office.

To say it was a bedroom would be an understatement. It was the gaudiest collection of tassles, pillows, and erotic statues I had seen this side of the Bazaar at Deva. Colors screamed and clawed at each other, making me wonder if Massha were actually colorblind. As fast as the thought occurred to me, I discarded it. No one could select so many clashing colors by sheer chance.

"Sit down, boys," Massha smiled, sinking onto the parade-ground-sized bed. "Take off your things and we'll get started."

My life flashed before my eyes. While I had secretly dreamed of a career as a ladies' man, I had never envisioned it starting like this! If I had, I might have become a monk.

Even, Aahz, with his vast experience, seemed at a loss. "Well, actually," he protested. "We don't have much time…"

"You misunderstand me," Massha waved, fanning the air with a massive hand. "What I meant was, take off your disguises."

"Our disguises?" I blurted, swallowing hard.

In reply, she held aloft her left hand, the index finger extended for us to see. The third—no—it was the fourth—ring was blinking a brilliant purple.

"This little toy says you're not only magicians, you're disguised," she grinned. "Now, I'm as sociable as the next person but I like to see who I'm doing business with. In fact, I insist!"

As she spoke, the door behind us slammed shut and locked with an audible click.

So much for our big advantage.

XIII.

"If you can't dazzle them with dexterity, baffle *them with bullshit!"*
Prof. H. Hill

THERE WAS A long silent moment of frozen immobility. Then Aahz turned to me with an exaggerated shrug.

"Well," he sighed, "I guess she's got us dead to rights. There's no arguing with technology, you know. It never makes mistakes."

I almost missed his wink, and even then I was slow to realize what he was up to.

"With your permission, dear lady..." Making a half bow at Massha, he began making a series of graceful passes with his hand in the air in front of him.

It was all very puzzling. Aahz had lost all his magikal powers back when...Then it hit me. Massha thought we were both magicians! Aahz was trying to maintain the illusion and could very well pull it off—if I got busy and backed his move.

As inconspicuously as possible, I closed my eyes and got to work stripping away his disguise.

"A Pervert!" Massha crowed in tribute to my efforts. "Well whadaya know. Thought you walked funny for a Jahk."

"Actually," Aahz corrected smoothly, "as a native of Perve I prefer to be called a 'pervect.'"

"I don't care what ya call yerself," she winked lewdly, "I'm more interested in how ya act."

I was just beginning to enjoy my mentor's discomfort when Massha turned her attentions on me.

"How 'bout you, sport?" she pressed. "You don't say much, let's see what yer hiding."

I resisted an impulse to clutch wildly at my clothes, and instead set about restoring my normal appearance.

"A Kland—and a young one at that," Massha proclaimed, cocking her head as she examined me. "Well, no matter, by the time old Massha's through with you...say!"

Her eyes suddenly opened wide and her gaze darted to Aahz, then back to me.

"A Klahd traveling with a Pervert...your name wouldn't be Skeeve, would it?"

"You've heard of me?" I blinked, both startled and flattered.

"Heard of you?" she laughed, "The last time I dropped into the Bazaar, that's all anyone was talking about."

"Really? What were they saying?" I urged.

"Well, the word is that you put together a team of six and used 'em to stop a whole army. It's the most effective use of manpower anyone's pulled off in centuries."

"It was actually eight, if you include Gleep and Berfert," I admitted modestly.

"Who?" she frowned.

"A dragon and a salamander," I explained. "It was such a successful venture I'd like to be sure everyone involved gets some credit."

"That's decent of you," Massha nodded approvingly. "Most folks I know in the trade try to hog all the glory when their plans work and only mention the help if they need someone to blame for failure."

"If you know Skeeve, here," Aahz smiled, elbowing his way into the conversation, "then surely you know who I am."

"As a matter of fact, I don't," Massha shrugged. "I heard there was a loudmouthed Pervert along, but no one mentioned his name."

"Oh really?" Aahz asked, showing a suspicious number of teeth. "A loudmouthed Pervert, eh? And just who did you hear that from?"

"Um...in that case," I interrupted hastily, "allow me to introduce my friend and colleague, Aahz."

"Aahz?" Massha repeated, raising an eyebrow. "As in..."

"No relation," Aahz assured her.

"Oh," she nodded.

"Mind if I have some wine?" my mentor asked, gesturing grandly at the wine pitcher on a nearby table. "It's been a long dry trip."

This time I was ready, and covertly levitated the pitcher into his waiting hand. The thought of embarrassing him by leaving the wine where it was never entered my mind. We were still in a tight spot, and anything we could do to keep Massha off balance was a good gambet.

"So, what are a pair of big leaguers like you doing in Jahk?" Massha asked, leaning back into her silken pillows. "You boys wouldn't be after my job, would you?"

It occurred to me that all the employed magicians I was meeting shared a common paranoia about losing their jobs.

'I assure you," Aahz interjected quickly, "taking your job away from you is the furthest thing from our minds. If nothing else, we couldn't pass the physical."

I almost asked 'the physical what?'" but restrained myself. Verbal banter was Aahz's forte, and for the time being my job was to give him room to operate.

"Flattery will get you everywhere," Massha chuckled appreciatively, "except around a direct question—and you haven't answered mine. If you aren't looking for work, what are you doing here?"

That was a good question, and thankfully Aahz had an answer ready.

"We're just on a little vacation," he lied, "and dropped by Jahk to try to make some of our money back in the gambling set."

"Gambling?" Massha frowned. "But the Big Game is over."

"The Big Game," Aahz snorted. "I'll level with you. We don't know enough about spectator sports to bet on 'em, but we do know wars—and we hear there's one brewing. I figure if we can't bet more intelligently than a bunch of yokels who haven't seen a war in five hundred years, we deserve to lose our money."

"That explains what you're doing in Jahk," Massha nodded thoughtfully, "but it doesn't say what you're doing here—'in my office' here. What can I do for you you can't do for yourselves?"

"I could give you a really suggestive answer," Aahz smirked, "but the truth is, we're looking for information. From where we sit, magik could swing the balance one way or the other in this war. What we'd like is a little inside information as to how much of a hand you expect to have in the proceedings, and if you expect any trouble with the opposition."

"The opposition? You mean Ta-hoe's magician?"

She threw back her head and laughed, "I guarantee you, boys, I can handle...what's his name...Quigley...with one hand. That is, of course, providing that one hand is armed with a few of my toys."

She wiggled her fingers to illustrate her point and the ring colors glittered and danced like a malevolent rainbow.

"That's fine for the war," Aahz nodded. "but how about here in town? What's to keep Ta-hoe from stealing the Trophy back before the war?"

"Oh, I've got a few gizmos over at the Trophy Building that'll fry anyone who tries to heist it—especially if they try to use magaik. Any one of 'em alone is fallible, but the way I've got 'em set, disarming one means setting off another. Nobody's taking that Trophy any where without my clearing it."

"Sounds good," my mentor smiled, though I noticed it was a little forced. "As long as you have total control on the Trophy's security, it isn't likely anything will go wrong."

"Not total control," Massha corrected. "The army's respon-sible for it when it's on parade."

"Parade?" I blurted. "What parade?"

"I know it's dumb," she grimaced. "That's why I refuse any responsibility for it. In fact, I had it written into my contract. I don't give demonstrations and I don't do parades."

"What parade?" Aahz repeated.

"Oh, once a day they carry the Trophy through the streets to keep the citizens fired up. You'd think they'd get tired of it, but so far everyone goes screaming bonkers every time it comes in view."

"I assume it has a military escort," Aahz commented.

"Are you kidding? Half the army tags along when it does the rounds. They spend more time escorting that Trophy around than they do drilling for the war."

"I see," my mentor murmured. "Well, I guess that tells us what we need to know. We should be on our way."

Before he could move, Massha was at the end of the bed, clasping his leg. "What's the hurry?" she purred. "Doesn't Massha get a little something in return for her information?"

"As a matter of fact," Aahz said, struggling to extract his leg, "there is something that might be valuable to you."

"I know there is," Massha smiled, pulling herself closer to him.

"Did you know that Quigley has summoned up a demon to help him?"

"He what?"

Massha released her hold on Aahz's leg to sit bolt upright. "That's right," Aahz nodded, moving smoothly out of reach.

"From what we hear, he's holding it captive in his workshop. I can't imagine any reason for his doing that unless he plans to use it in the war."

"A demon, eh?" Massha muttered softly, staring absently at the far wall. "Well, well, whatdaya know. I didn't think Quigley had it in him. I don't suppose you've heard anything about its powers?"

"Nothing specific," Aahz admitted, "but I don't think he'd summon anything weaker than he is."

"That's true," Massha nodded. "Well, I should be able to handle them both."

I recognized her tone of voice. It was the way I sounded when I'm trying to convince myself I'm up to handling one of Aahz's plans.

"Say, Massha," my mentor explained, as if a thought had just struck him. "I know we're supposed to be on vacation, but maybe we can give you a hand here."

"Would you?" she asked eagerly.

"Well, it's really in our own best interest if we're betting money on the war," he smiled. "Otherwise we wouldn't get involved. As it is, though, I think we can get the demon away from Quigley, or at least neutralize is so it won't help him at all."

"You'd do that for me? As a favor?" Massha blinked.

"Sure," Aahz waved. "Just don't be surprised at anything we do and whatever you do, don't try to counter any of our moves. I won't make any guarantees, but I think we can pull it off. If we do, just remember you owe us a favor someday."

Anyone who knew Aahz would have been immediately suspicious if he offered to do anything as a favor. Fortunately, Massha didn't know Aahz, and she seemed both solicitous and grateful as she waved goodbye to us at the door.

"Well, kid," Aahz grinned, slapping me on the back. "Not bad for an afternoon's work, if I do say so myself. Not only did we scout the opposition, we neutralized it. Big bad Massha won't move against us no matter what we do, for fear of disrupting our plans against Quigley."

As I had restored our disguises before we emerged onto the street, Aahz's back slap didn't arrive on my back—and it hit me with more force than I'm sure he intended. All in all, it did nothing to improve my already black mood.

"Sure, Aahz," I growled. "Except for one little detail."

"What's that?"

"We can't steal Tananda away from Quigley because he'd lose his job and we promised we wouldn't do anything to jeopardize his position. Remember?"

"Skeeve, Skeeve," my mentor chuckled, shaking his head. "I haven't overlooked anything. You're the one who hasn't thought things through."

"Okay," I snapped. "So I'm slow! Explain it to me."

"Well, first of all, as I just mentioned, we don't have to worry about Massha for a while."

"But…" I began, but he cut me off.

"Second of all," he continued, "I said 'free or neutralize.' Now, we already know Quigley isn't about to use Tananda in the war, so Massha's going to owe us a favor whether we do anything or not."

"But we're supposed to be rescuing Tananda," I protested, "and that means stealing the Trophy."

"Right!" Aahz beamed. "I'm glad you finally caught on."

"Huh?" I said intelligently.

"You haven't caught on," my mentor sighed. "Look, kid. The mission's still on. We're going to steal the Trophy."

"But I can't bypass Massha's traps at the Trophy Building."

"Of course not," Aahz agreed. "That's why we're going to steal it from the parade."

"The parade?" I blinked. "In broad daylight with half the army and the whole town watching?"

"Of course," Aahz shrugged. "It's the perfect situation."

It occurred to me that either my concept of a perfect situation was way out of line, or my mentor had finally lost his mind!

XIV.

"As any magician will tell you Myth Direction
is the secret of a successful steal."
D. HENNING

"DON'T YOU SEE kid? The reason it's a perfect situation is that everyone's sure it can't be stolen!"

It was the same answer Aahz had given the last ten times I asked, so I gave him my usual rebuttal.

"The reason they're sure is because it can't be stolen. At least half the population of Veygus will be looking. Aahz, and they'll be looking right at the Trophy we're trying to steal! Someone's bound to notice."

"Not if you follow your instructions, they won't," my mentor winked. "Trust me."

I wasn't reassured. Not that I didn't trust Aahz, mind you. His ability to get me into trouble is surpassed only by his ability to bail me out again. I just had a hunch his bailing abilities were going to be tested to their limits this time.

I was about to express this to Aahz when a roar went up from the crowd around us, ending any hope for conversation. The Trophy was just coming into view.

We had chosen our post carefully. This point was the closest the procession came to the North wall of Veygus...and hence it was the closest the Trophy came to the gate opening onto the road to Ta-hoe.

In line with Aahz's plan, we waved our fists in the air and jumped up and down as the Trophy passed by with its military escort. It was pointless to shout, however. The crowd was making so much noise that two voices more or less went unnoticed, and we needed to save our lung power for the heist itself. Working our way to the back of the mob also proved to be no problem. By simply not fighting back when everyone else elbowed in front of us soon moved us to our desired position.

"So far, so good," Aahz murmured, scanning the backs in front of us to be sure we were unobserved.

"Maybe we should quit while we're ahead," I suggested hopefully.

"Shut up and start working," he snapped back in a tone that left no room for argument.

With an inward sigh, I closed my eyes and began making subtle changes in our disguises.

When I first learned the disguise spell, it was specifically to alter the facial features and body configurations of a being to resemble another. Later, after considerable practice, I learned to change the outward appearance of inanimate objects, providing they had once been alive. Aahz had seized this modification for a new application...specifically to change the configuration of our clothes. By the time I was done, we not only looked like Jahks, we were dressed in the uniforms of Veygan soldiers.

"Good enough, kid," Aahz growled, clapping me on the shoulder. "Let's go!"

With that, he plunged headlong into the crowd, clearing a path for me to emerge on the street behind the Trophy procession. Clearing paths through moveable objects, like people, is one of the things Aahz does best.

"Make way!" he bawled. "One side! Make way!"

Close behind him, I added my bellow to the din.

"Ta-hoers!" I called. "At the South wall! Ta-hoers!"

That's one of the things I do best—scream in panic.

For a moment, no one seemed to hear us. Then a few heads turned. A couple voices took up my call.

"Ta-hoers!" they cried. "We're being attacked."

The word spread through the crowd ahead of us like wildfire, such that when we reached the rear-guard of the procession, it had ground to a halt. The soldiers milled about, tangling weapons with bodies around them as they tried simultaneously to scan the crowd, rooftops, and sky.

"Ta-hoers!" I shouted, pushing in among them.

"Where?"

"The South wall."

"Where?"

"The South wall."

"Who?"

"Ta-hoers!"

"Where?"

This nonsense might have continued endlessly, except for the appearance of an officer on the scene. He was noticeably more intelligent than the soldiers around him...which was to say he might have won a debate with a turnip.

"What's going on here?" he demanded, his authoritative voice silencing the clamor in the ranks.

"Ta-hoers, sir!" I gasped, still a bit out of breath from my performance. "They're attacking in force at the South wall!"

"The South wall?" the officer frowned. "But Ta-hoe is north of here."

"They must have circled around the city," I suggested hastily. "They're attacking the South wall."

"But Ta-hoe is north of here," the man insisted. "Why would they attack the South wall?"

His slow-wittedness was exasperating. It was also threatening to totally disrupt our plan, which hinged on momentum.

"Are you going to stand here arguing while those yellow and blue idiots take the city?" Aahz demanded, shouldering his way past me. "If everybody gets killed because of your indecision, the Council will bust you back to the ranks."

That possibility wasn't very logical, so, of course, the fool took it to heart. Drawing his sword, he turned to the men around him.

"To the South wall," he ordered. "Follow me!"

"To the South wall!"

The cry went up as the soldiers wheeled and dashed back down the street.

"To the South wall!" I echoed, moving with them.

Suddenly, a powerful hand seized my shoulder and slammed me against a wall hard enough to knock the air out of my lungs. "To the South wall!"

It was Aahz, leaning back to keep me pinned between him and the wall as he waved the soldiers past.

At last, he turned his head slightly to address me directly. "Where ya' going?" he asked curiously.

"To the South wall?" I suggested in a small voice.

"Why?"

"Because the Ta-hoers...oh!"

I felt exceptionally stupid. I also felt more than slightly squashed. Aahz is no featherweight.

"I think better when I can breathe," I pointed out meekly. The ground slipped up and crashed into me as Aahz shifted his weight forward.

"Quit clowning around, kid," he snarled, hauling me to my feet. "We've still got work to do."

As I've said before, Aahz has an enviable grasp of the obvious. A dozen soldiers were still clustered around the Trophy, its litter now resting on the ground. There was also the minor detail of the crowd of onlookers still milling about arguing over this latest change in events.

"What are we going to do, Aahz?" I hissed.

"Just leave everything to me," he retorted confidently. "Okay," I nodded.

"Now here's what I want you to do..."

"What happened to 'leave everything to you?" ' I grumbled. "Shut up and listen," he ordered. "I want you to change my face and uniform to match that officer we talked to."

"But..."

"Just do it!"

In a moment the necessary adjustments were made and my mentor was on his way, striding angrily toward the remaining soldiers.

"What are you doing there?" he bawled. "Get to the South wall with the others!"

"But...we were...our orders are to guard the Trophy," the nearest soldier stammered in confusion.

"Defend it by keeping the Ta-hoers out of the city," Aahz roared. "Now get to the South wall! Anyone who tries to stay behind I'll personally charge with cowardice in the face of the enemy. Do you know what the punishment for that is?"

Apparently they did, even if I didn't. Aahz's question went unanswered as the soldiers sprinted off down the street toward the South wall.

So much for the Trophy's military escort. I did wonder, though, what my mentor planned to do about the milling crowd   "Citizens of Veygus," Aahz boomed, as if in answer to my silent question. "Our fair city is under attack. Now, I know all of you will want to volunteer to help the Army in this battle, but to e effective you must be disciplined and orderly. To that end, I want all volunteers to line up here in front of me for instructions. Any who are unable to

serve should return to their homes at this time, so the militia will
have room to maneuver. All right, volunteers assemble!"

Within seconds, Aahz and I were left alone in the street. The
crowd of potential volunteers had evaporated like water spilled on
a hot griddle.

"So much for the witnesses," my mentor grinned, winking at me.

"Where'd they all go?" I asked, craning my neck to look around.

"Home, of course," Aahz smirked. "No one likes the draft—
particularly when it effects them personally."

I wet my finger and tested the breeze. "There's not that much
wind today," I announced suspiciously.

For some reason, this statement seemed to annoy my mentor.
He rolled his eyes and started to say something, then changed his
mind.

"Look, let's just grab the Trophy, okay?" he snarled. "That 'South
wall' bit won't fool the Army forever, and I for one don't want to
be here when they get back."

For once, we were in total agreement.

"Okay, Aahz," I nodded. "How do we get it out of the city?"

"That's easy," he waved. "Remember, I'm not exactly a
weakling."

With that, he strode over to the Trophy and simply picked it up
and tucked it under his arm, balancing it casually on his hip. "But
Aahz…" I began.

"I know what you're going to say," he admonished, holding up
a hand, "and you're right. It would be easier to steal a cart. What
you're overlooking is that a cart is personal property, while the Trophy belongs to the whole city."

"But Aahz…"

"That means," he continued hastily, "that everyone assumes someone else is watching the Trophy, so we can walk away with it. If we
stole a cart, the owner would spot it in a minute and raise the alarm.
Now, having successfully liberated the Trophy, it would be really
dumb to get arrested for stealing a cart, wouldn't it?"

"I didn't mean 'how are we going to move it!'" I blurted. "I
meant 'how are we going to get it past the guards at the North gate?'"

"What's that?" Aahz frowned.

"They aren't going to let us just walk past them carrying that
Trophy, and I can't disguise it. It's a metal!"

"Hmmm...you're right, kid," my mentor nodded thoughtfully. "Well, maybe we can...oh swell!"

"What is it?" I asked fearfully.

"The soldiers are coming back," he announced, cocking his head to listen. Aahz has exceptionally sharp hearing. "Oh well, we're just going to have to do this the fast way. Break out the D-Hopper."

"The what?" I blinked.

"The D-Hopper!" he insisted. "We'll just take this back to Klah with us."

I hurriedly fumbled the D-Hopper out of my pouch and passed it to Aahz for setting.

"What about Tananda?"

"We'll use this gizmo to bring the Trophy back later and spring her," Aahz mumbled. "I hadn't figured on using this just now. There's always a possibility that...oh well. Hang on, kid.

Here we go."

I crowded close to him and waited as he hit the button to activate the Hopper. Nothing happened.

XV.

"—Or was it unlock the safe then swim to the surface?"
H. HOUDINI

"NOTHING HAPPENED."

"I know it," Aahz groaned, glaring at the D-Hopper. "That's the trouble with relying on mechanical gadgets. The minute you rely on them, they let you down."

"What's wrong?" I pressed.

"The damn thing needs recharging," Aahz spat. "And there's no way we can do it before the Army gets here."

"Then let's hide until…"

"Hide where?" my mentor snapped. "Do you want to ask one of the citizens to hide us? They might have a few questions about the Trophy we're lugging along."

"Okay, you suggest something!" I snarled.

"I'm working on it," Aahz growled, looking around. "What we need is…there!"

Before I could ask what he was doing, he strode into a nearby shop, tugged an animal skin off the wall, and began wrapping it around the Trophy.

"Terrific," I observed dryly. "Now we have a furry Trophy. I don't think it will fool the guards."

"It will, once you disguise it," Aahz grinned.

"I told you, I can't," I insisted. "It's a metal!"

"Not the Trophy, dummy!" he snapped. "The skin. Get to work! Change it to anything. No…make it a wounded soldier!" I wasn't sure it would work, but I closed my eyes and gave it a try. One wounded soldier—complete with a torn, bloodstained uniform and trailing feet.

"Not bad, kid," Aahz nodded, sticking the bundle under his arm.

As usual, I couldn't see the effects of my work. When I looked, I didn't see an officer of the guard with a wounded comrade under his arm. I saw Aahz holding a suspiciously lumpy package.

"Are you sure it's okay?" I asked doubtfully.

"Sure," Aahz nodded. "Just...oops! Here they come. Leave everything to me."

That had a suspiciously familiar ring to it, but I didn't have many other options at the moment. The soldiers were in sight now, thundering down on us with grim scowls set fiercely on their faces.

"That way! Quick! They're getting away."

Aahz's bellow nearly startled me out of my skin, but I held my ground. I'm almost used to his unexpected gambits—almost. "After them!" Aahz repeated. "Charlie's hit!"

"Who's Charlie?" I frowned.

"Shut-up, kid," my mentor hissed, favoring me with a glare before returning his attention to the soldiers.

They had slowed their headlong dash and were looking down the sidestreets as they came, but they hadn't changed course. The only fortunate thing was that the officer Aahz was impersonating was nowhere in sight.

"Don't you understand?" Aahz shouted. "They've got the Trophy! That way!"

That did it. With a roar of animal rage, the soldiers wheeled and started off in the direction Aahz had indicated.

"Boy," I murmured in genuine admiration. "I wouldn't want to be holding that Trophy when they caught up with me."

"It could be decidedly unpleasant," Aahz agreed. "So if you don't mind, could we be on our way? Hmmm?"

"Oh! Right, Aahz."

He was already on his way, eating up great hunks of distance with his strong, hurried stride. As I hastened to keep up with him, I resolved not to ask about his plans for getting past the guards at the North gate. I was only annoying him with my constant questions, and besides, the answers only unsettled me.

As we drew nearer to the gate, however, my nervousness grew stronger and my resolve weaker.

"Ummm...do you want me to change the disguise on the Trophy?" I asked tentatively.

"No," came the brusk reply. "But you could mess us up a little."

"Mess us up?" I blinked.

"A little dirt and blood on the uniforms," Aahz clarified. "Enough to make it look like we've been in a fight."

I wasn't sure what he had up his sleeve, but I hastened to adjust our disguises. That isn't as easy as it sounds, incidentally. Try closing your eyes and imagining dirty uniforms in detail while walking down a strange street at a near-trot. Fortunately, my life with Aahz had trained me to work under desperate conditions, so I completed my task just as we were coming up on the gate.

As a tribute to my handiwork, the guard didn't even bother to address us directly. He simply gaped at us for a moment, then started hollering for the Officer of the Guard. By the time that member appeared, we were close enough to count his teeth as his jaw dropped.

"What's going on here?" he demanded finally, recovering his composure.

"Fighting in the streets," Aahz gasped in a realistic imitation of a weary warrior. "They need your help. We're your relief."

"Our relief?" the officer frowned. "But that man's unconscious and you look like…fighting, did you say?"

"We're fit enough for gate duty," Aahz insisted, weakly pulling himself erect. "Anything to free a few more able-bodied men for the fighting."

"What fighting?" the officer screamed, barely suppressing an impulse to shake Aahz back to his senses.

"Riots," my mentor. blinked. "The bookies have changed the odds on the War and won't honor earlier bets. It's awful."

The officer blanched and recoiled as if he had been struck. "But that means…my life savings are bet on the war. They can't do that."

"You'd better hurry," Aahz insisted. "If the mobs tear the bookies apart, no one will get their money back."

"Follow me! All of you!" the officer bellowed, though it wasn't necessary. The guards were already on their way. Apparently the officer wasn't the only one with money in the bookies' care.

The officer started after them, then paused to sweep us with an approving stare.

"I don't know if you'll get a medal for this," he announced grimly, "but I won't forget it. You have my personal thanks."

"Don't mention it turkey," Aahz murmured as the man sprinted off.

"You know, I bet he won't forget this…ever," I smiled. "Feeling pretty smug, aren't you, kid," Aahz commented, cocking a critical eyebrow at me.

"Yes," I confirmed modestly.

"Well, you should," he laughed, clapping me on the back. "I think, however, we'd best celebrate at a distance."

"Quite right," I agreed, gesturing grandly to the open gate. "After you."

"No, after you!" he countered, imitating my gesture.

Not wanting to waste additional time arguing, we walked side by side through the now unguarded North gate of Veygus, bearing our prize triumphantly with us.

That should have been it. Having successfully recaptured the Trophy, it should have been an easy matter to return to Ta-hoe, exchange the Trophy for Tananda, and relax in a celebration party back at Klah. I should have known better.

Any time things seem calm and tranquil, something happens to disrupt matters. If unforeseen outside complications don't arise, then either Aahz's temper flares or I open my big mouth. In this case, there were no outside complications, but there our luck ran out. Neither one of us was to blame—we both were. Aahz for his temper, me for my big mouth.

We were nearly back to the place where he had hidden Griffin, when Aahz made an unexpected request.

"Say, kid," he said. "How about dropping the disguises for a while."

"Why?" I asked, logically.

"No special reason," he shrugged. "I just want to look at this Trophy that's caused everyone so much trouble."

"Didn't you see it back at Veygus?" I frowned.

"Not really," my mentor admitted. "At first I was busy chasing away the soldiers and the civilians, and after that it was something big and heavy to carry. I never really stopped to study it.

It took mere seconds to remove the disguises. They're easier to break down than to build, since I can see what the end result is supposed to look like.

"Help yourself," I announced.

"Thanks, kid," Aahz grinned, setting the Trophy down and hastily unwrapping it.

The Trophy was as ugly as ever; not that I had expected it to change. If anything, it looked worse up close, as Aahz was doing.

Then he backed up and looked again. Finally he walked around it, studying the monstrosity from all angles.

For some reason, his silent scrutiny was making me uneasy. "Well, what do you think?" I asked, in an effort to get the conversation going again.

He turned slowly to face me, and I noticed his scales were noticeably darker than normal.

"That's it?" he demanded, jerking a thumb over his shoulder at the statue. "That's the Trophy? You got Tananda captured and put us through all this for a dismal hunk of sculpture like that?"

Something clicked softly in my mind, igniting a small ember of anger. I mean, I've never pretended to admire the Trophy, but it *had* been Tananda's choice.

"Yes, Aahz," I said carefully. "That's it."

"Of all the dumb stunts you've pulled, this takes the cake!" my mentor raged. "You neglect your studies, cost us a fortune, not to mention putting everybody's neck on the chopping block, and for what?"

"Yes, Aahz," I managed.

"And Tananda! I knew she was a bit dippy, but this! I've got a good mind to leave her right where she is."

I tried to say something, but nothing came out.

"All I want to hear from you, apprentice, is why!"

He was looming over me now.

"Even feeble minds need a motive. What did you two figure to do with this pile of junk once you stole it? Tell me that!"

"It was going to be your birthday present!" I shouted, the dam bursting at last.

Aahz froze stock-still, an expression of astonishment spreading slowly over his face.

"My...my birthday present?" he asked in a small voice.

"That's right, Aahz," I growled. "Surprise. We wanted to get you something special. Something no one else had, no matter how much trouble it was. Sure was stupid of us, wasn't it?"

"My birthday present," Aahz murmured, turning to stare at the Trophy again.

"Well, it's all over now," I snarled savagely. "Us feeble-minded dolts bit off more than we could chew and you had to bail us out. Let's spring Tananda and go home. Maybe then we can forget the whole thing—if you'll let us."

Aahz was standing motionless with his back to me. Now that I had vented my anger, I found myself suddenly regretful for having ground it in so mercilessly.

"Aahz?" I asked, stepping in behind him. "Hey! Com'on, we've got to give it back and get Tananda."

Slowly he turned his head until our gazes met. There was a far-away light in his eyes I had never seen before.

"Give it back?" he said softly. "What daya mean 'Give it back'? That's my birthday present!"

XVI.

"...and then the fun began."
N. BONAPARTE

I HAD ATTENDED war councils before. I hadn't been wild about
it as a pastime even then, but I had done it. On those occasions,
however, our side was the only one with the vaguest skills in magik.
This time, all three sides would have magicians in attendance. My joy
knew definite bounds; in fact, I didn't want to be there at all.

"Maybe they won't come," I suggested hopefully.

"With their precious Trophy on the line?" Aahz grinned. "Not a
chance. They'll be here."

"If they got the messages," I corrected. "Griffin may have just
headed for the horizon."

My mentor cocked an eyebrow at me. "Think back to the days
before you were an apprentice, kid," he suggested. "If a magician
gave you a message to deliver, would you try to get away?"

"Well..." I conceded.

"They'll be here," he concluded firmly. "I just hope Quigley gets
here first."

My last hope gone, I resigned myself to the meeting and turned
my attention to our immediate surroundings.

"Can you at least tell me why we're meeting here?" I asked.
"Why not in the forest where we'd have some trees to duck behind
if things get ugly? What's so special about this statatorium?"

"That's stadium, kid," my mentor corrected, rolling his eyes.
"And there're three good reasons to set up the meeting here.
First of all, both the Veygans and the Ta-hoers know where it is.
Second, they both acknowledge it as neutral ground."

"And third?" I prompted.

"You said it yourself," Aahz shrugged. "There's no cover. Nothing
at all to hide behind."

"That's good?"

"Think it through, kid," my mentor sighed. "If we can hide
behind a tree, so could someone else. The difference is, they have
more people to hide."

"You mean they might try to ambush us?" I blinked.

"It's a possibility. I only hope that having the meeting in the open like this will lower the probability."

One thing I have to admit about Aahz. Any time I'm nervous, I can count on him to say just the right thing to convert my nervousness to near-hysteric panic.

"Um...Aahz," I began carefully. "Isn't it about time you let me in on this master plan of yours?"

"Sure," my mentor grinned. "We're going to have a meeting with representatives from both Veygus and Ta-hoe."

"But what are you going to say to them?" I pressed.

"You're missing the point, kid. The reason I'm meeting with both of them at once is because I don't want to have to repeat myself. Now, if I explain everything to you now, I'll only have to repeat myself at the meeting. Understand?"

"No," I announced, bluntly. "I don't. I'm supposed to be your apprentice, aren't I? Well, how am I going to help out if I don't know what's going on?"

"That's a good point," Aahz conceded. "I wish you had raised it earlier."

"Because now it's too late. Our guests are arriving."

I turned to look in the direction he was pointing and discovered he was right. A small group had emerged from one of the entrances halfway up the side of the stadium and was filing down the stairs toward the field where we were waiting. Watching them descend, I was struck again by the enormity of the stadium. I had realized it was large when we first arrived and I saw the rows and rows of seats circling the field. Now, however, seeing how tiny the group looked in this setting made me all the more aware of exactly how large the stadium really was. As we waited, I tried to imagine the seats filled with thousands upon thousands of people all staring down at the field and the very thought of it made me uneasy. Fortunately, the odds of my ever actually seeing it were very very low.

The group was close enough now for us to distinguish between individuals. This didn't do us much good, though, as we didn't know any of the individuals involved. I finally recognized Griffin in their ranks, and from that figured out it was the Ta-hoe delegation approaching. Once I realized that, I managed to spot Quigley bringing up the rear. I would have recognized him sooner, but he was disguised as a Jahk, which threw me for a moment. Actually, it made sense. I mean, Aahz and I were currently disguised as Jahks, so it was only logical that Quigley would also be hiding his extra-dimensional origins as well. Sometimes it bothers me that I seem to habitually overlook the obvious.

"That's far enough!" Aahz boomed.

The group halted obediently a stone's throw away. it occurred to me it might be better if they were a little more than a stone's throw away, but I kept quiet.

"We're ready to discuss the return of the Trophy," one of the delegates called, stepping forward.

"We're not," my mentor retorted.

This caused a minor stir in the group and they began to mumble darkly among themselves.

"Aahz!" I urged.

"What I mean to say," Aahz added hastily, "is that what we have to say will wait until the other delegation arrives. In the meantime, I wish a word with your Master Magician."

There was a brief huddle, then Quigley came forward to join us. Even at a distance I could see he was upset.

"Hi, Quigley," Aahz grinned."How's tricks?"

"I certainly hope you have an explanation for this," the exdemon hunter snapped, ignoring the cordial greeting. "Explanation for what?" my mentor countered innocently. "You promised...or rather, Master Skeeve did...that you two wouldn't do anything to endanger my job."

"And we haven't," Aahz finished.

"Yes, you have!" Quigley insisted. "The Council expects me to use my magik to get the Trophy away from you at this meeting. If I don't, I can kiss my job goodbye."

"Don't worry," my mentor soothed. "We've taken that into account."

"We have?" I murmured in wonder.

Aahz shot me a black look and continued.

"I guarantee that by the end of the meeting the Council won't expect you to perform any magik against us."

"You mean you'll give the Trophy back voluntarily?" Quigley asked, brightening noticeably. "I must say that's decent of you."

"No, it isn't," Aahz corrected, "and we're not going to give it back. All I said was they wouldn't expect you to get it for them with magik."

"But..."

"The reason I wanted to talk with you," Aahz interrupted, "was to clarify a little something from our previous conversation."

"What's that?" Quigley frowned.

"Well, you promised to release Tananda if the Trophy was returned. Now, if Ta-hoe has a change to take the Trophy back...and then doesn't do it, is the deal still on? Will you let her go?"

"I...I suppose so," the ex-demon hunter acquiesced, gnawing his lip. "But I can't imagine them not wanting it."

"Wanting something and being able to take it are two different things," Aahz grinned.

"But I'm supposed to be helping them with my magik!"

"Not this time, you aren't," my mentor corrected. "I've already told you that..."

"Is this a private chat, boys? Or can anybody join in?"

We all turned to find Massha lumbering towards us. The rest of the Veygus delegation waited behind her, having apparently arrived while we were talking to Quigley.

"Good God! What's that?" Quigley gasped, gaping at Massha's approaching bulk.

"That's Massha," I volunteered casually. "You know, the Veygan's magician?"

"That's Massha?" he echoed, swallowing hard.

"If you'll excuse us for a moment," Aahz suggested, "there are a few things we have to discuss with her before the meeting."

"Of course, certainly."

The ex-demon hunter beat a hasty retreat, apparently relieved at being able to avoid a face to face meeting with his rival.

"The Council there tells me that was Quigley you were just talking to," Massha announced, tracking his flight with her eyes.

"Is that true?"

"Umm...yes," I admitted.

"You boys wouldn't be trying to double-cross old Massha, would you?" her tone was jovial, but her eyes narrowed suspiciously.

"My dear lady!" Aahz gasped. "You wound me! Didn't we promise to neutralize Quigley's demon for you?"

"You sure did."

"And it would be extremely difficult to engineer that without at least being on speaking terms with Quigley. Wouldn't it?"

"Well...yes."

"So no sooner do we start working on the project than you accuse us of double-crossing you! We should leave right now and let you solve your own problems."

I had to suppress a smile. Aahz looking indignant is a comical sight at best. Massha, however, swallowed it hook, line and sinker.

"Now, don't be that way," she pleaded. "I didn't mean to get ya all out of joint. Besides, do you blame me for being a little suspicious after you up and made off with the Trophy?"

Aahz sighed dramatically. "Didn't we say not to be surprised at anything we did? Geez! I guess it's what we should expect, trying to deal with someone who can't comprehend the subtlety of our plans."

"You mean stealing the Trophy is part of your plan to neutralize the demon?" Massha asked, wide-eyed with awe.

"Of course!" Aahz waved. "Or it was. You see, Quigley got the demon to help get the Trophy away from Veygus. Now, if Veygus doesn't have the Trophy, he doesn't need the demon, right?"

"Sounds a little shakey to me," the sorceress frowned.

"You're right," Aahz acknowledged. "That's why I was so glad when the k...I mean, when Master Skeeve here came up with this new plan."

"I did?"

Aahz's arm closed around my shoulders in an iron grip which eliminated any thoughts of protest from my mind.

"He's so modest," my mentor explained. "You've heard what a genius tactician he is? Well, he's come up with a way to neutralize the demon...*and* give Veygus a good chance at retrieving the Trophy."

"I'm dying to hear it," Massha proclaimed eagerly.

"Me, too," I mumbled. Aahz's grip tightened threateningly.

"Then I guess we're ready to get started," he declared. "You'd better rejoin your delegation. Wouldn't want it to look like we're playing favorites. And remember...agree with us no matter what we say. We're on your side."

"Right!" she winked, and headed off.

"Say, um, Aahz," I managed at last.

"Yea, kid?"

"If you're on Quigley's side *and* on Massha's side, who's on my side?"

"I am, of course."

I had been afraid he was going to say something like that. It was becoming increasingly clear that Aahz was going to come out of this in pretty good shape no matter how it ran. I didn't have much time to ponder the point, though.

Aahz was beckoning the groups forward to start the meeting.

XVII.

"I'm sure we can talk things out like civilized people."
J. WAYNE

"I SUPPOSE YOU'RE all wondering why I called you here," my mentor began with a grin.

I think he intended it as a joke. I've gotten so I recognize his "waiting for a laugh" grin. Unfortunately, he was trying it on the wrong crowd. Jahks aren't generally noted for their sense of humor."

"I assume it's to talk about the Trophy," a distinguished individual from the Ta-hoe group observed dryly. "Otherwise we're wasting our time."

"Oh, it's about the Trophy," Aahz assured him hastily. "Which you stole from us!" a Veygan contributed venomously. "…after you stole it from us!" the Ta-hoer speaker shot back. "Only after you cheated us out of it at the Big Game." "That call was totally legal! The rules clearly state…" "That rule hasn't been enforced for three hundred years.

There are four rulings on record which have since contradicted…"

"Gentlemen, please!" Aahz called, holding up his hands for order. "All that is water under the drawbridge, as well as being totally beside the point. Remember, neither of you currently have the Trophy. *We* do."

There was a moment of tense silence as both sides absorbed this observation. Finally, the Ta-hoer speaker stepped forward. "Very well," he said firmly. "Name your price for its return.

The Ta-hoe Council is prepared to offer…"

"Veygus will top any offer Ta-hoe makes."

"And Ta-hoe will double any offer that Veygus makes," the speaker shot back.

This was starting to sound pretty good to me. Maybe I've been hanging around with Aahz too long, but the potential financial benefits of our situation impressed me as being ex-ceptionally good. The only foreseeable difficulty was Aahz's insistence that he was going to keep his birthday present.

"...if you try anything, our magician will..."

"Your magician! We fired her. If she tries anything, our magician will..."

The raging debate forced its way into my consciousness again. That last bit sounded like it could get very ugly very quickly. I snuck a nervous glance at Aahz, but as usual he was way ahead of me.

"Gentlemen, gentlemen!" he admonished, raising his hands once more.

"Who are you calling a gentleman?"

"And ladies," my mentor amended, squinting at the source of the voice. "What-da-ya know. ERA strikes again."

"What's an eerah?" the Ta-hoe spokesman frowned, echoing my thoughts exactly.

"It seems," Aahz continued, ignoring the question entirely, "that our motives have been misconstrued. We didn't appropriate the Trophy to ransom it. Quite the contrary. It has been our intention all along to see that it goes to its rightful owners."

An ugly growl arose from the Veygans.

"Excellent!" beamed the Ta-hoe spokesman. "If you won't accept a reward, will you at least accompany us back to town as our guests. There's sure to be celebrating and..."

"I said 'the rightful owner.'" Aahz smiled, cutting him off.

The spokesman paused, his smile melting to a dangerous scowl. "Are you saying we aren't the rightful owners?" he snarled. "If you thought Veygus had a better claim, why did you steal it in the first place?"

"Let me run it past you one more time," my mentor sighed. "The Trophy's going to its rightful owner. That lets Veygus out, too."

That took the spokesman aback. I didn't blame him. Aahz's logic had me a bit confused, too. ..and I was on his side!

"If I understand it correctly," Aahz continued grandly, "the Trophy's goes to the winning team—that wins the Big Game—as their award for being the year's best team. Is that right? "Of course," the spokesman nodded.

"Why do you assume the team that wins the Big Game is the best team?" Aahz asked innocently.

"Because there are only two teams. So it follows logically that..."

"That's where you're wrong," my mentor interrupted. "There is another team."

"Another team?" the spokesman blinked.

"That's right. A team that neither of your teams has faced, much less beaten. Now, we maintain that until that team is defeated, neither Ta-hoe nor Veygus has the right to declare their team the year's best!"

My stomach did a flip-flop. I was getting a bad feeling about this.

"That's ridiculous!" called the Veygus spokesman. "We've never heard of another team. Whose team is this, anyway?"

"Ours," Aahz smiled. "And we're challenging both your teams to a game, a three-way match, right here in thirty days...Winner takes all."

Bad feeling confirmed. For a moment, I considered altering my disguise and sneaking out with one of the delegations. Then I realized that option was closed. Both groups had stepped back well out of ear-shot to discuss Aahz's proposal. That put them far away, so that I couldn't join them without being noticed. With nothing else to do, I turned on Aahz.

"This is your plan?" I demanded. "Setting us up to play a game we know absolutely nothing about against not one but two teams, who've been playing it for five hundred years? That's not a plan, that's a disaster!"

"I figure it's our best chance to spring Tananda and keep the Trophy," my mentor shrugged.

"It's a chance to get our heads beaten in," I corrected. "There's got to be an easier way."

"There was," Aahz agreed. "Unfortunately, you eliminated it when you promised we wouldn't do anything to endanger Quigley's job."

I hate it when Aahz is right. I hate it almost as much as getting caught in my own stupid blunders. More often than not, those two phenomena occur simultaneously in my life.

"Why didn't you tell me about this plan before?" I asked to hide my discomfort.

"Would you have gone along with it if I had?"

"No."

"That's why."

"What happens if we refuse your challenge?" the Ta-hoe spokesman called.

"Then we consider ourselves the winners by default," Aahz replied.

"Well, Veygus will be there," came the decision from the other group.

"And so will Ta-hoe," was the spontaneous response.

"If I might ask," the Ta-hoe spokesman queried, "Why did you pick a date thirty days from now?"

"It'll take time for you to lay out a triangular field," my mentor shrugged. "And besides, I thought your merchants would require more than a week to prepare their souvenirs. There were nods in both groups for that reasoning.

"Then it's agreed?" Aahz prompted.

"Agreed!" roared Veygus. "Agreed!" echoed Ta-hoe.

"Speaking of merchandizing," the Ta-hoe spokesman commented, "what is the name of your team? We'll need it before we can go into production of the souvenirs.

"We're called The Demons," Aahz said winking at me. In flash I saw what his plan really was. "Would you like to know why?"

"Well...I would assume it's because you play like demons," the Ta-hoe spokesman stammered.

"Not 'like' demons!" my mentor grinned. "Shall we show them, partner?"

"Why not," I smiled, closing my eyes.

In a moment, our disguises were gone, and for the first time the delegates had a look at what was opposing them.

"As I was saying," Aahz announced, showing all his teeth, "not 'like' demons."

It was a good gambit, and it should have worked. Any sane person would quake at the thought of taking on a team of demons. No sacrifice would be too great to avoid the confrontation. We had overlooked one minor detail, however. Jahks are not sane people.

"Excellent," the Ta-hoe spokesman exclaimed.

"What?" Aahz blinked, his smile fading.

"This should keep the odds even," the spokesman continued.

"That's what we were discussing...whether you could field a good enough team to make a fight of it. But now...well, everyone will want to see this matchup."

"You...aren't afraid of playing against demons?" my mentor asked slowly.

Now it was the spokesman's turn to smile.

"My dear fellow," he chortled, "if you had ever seen our teams play, you wouldn't have to ask that question."

With that, he turned and rejoined his delegation as the two groups prepared to withdraw from the meeting.

"Didn't you listen in on their conversations?" I hissed.

"If you'll recall," Aahz growled back, "I was busy talking with you at the time."

"Then we're stuck," I moaned.

"Maybe not," he corrected. "Quigley! Could we have a word with you?"

The ex-demon hunter lost no time in joining us.

"I must say," he chortled. "You boys *did* an excellent job of getting me out of a tight spot there. Now it's a matter of pride for them to win the Trophy back on the playing field."

"Swell," Aahz growled. "Now how about your part of the deal? Ta-hoe has its chance, so there's no reason for you to keep Tananda."

"Mmm...yes and no," Quigley corrected. "It occurs to me that if I release her now, then you'll have the Trophy *and* Tananda, and would therefore have no motive to return for the game. To fulfill your promise, to give Ta-hoe a chance for the Trophy, the game will have to take place. Then I'll release Tananda."

"Thanks a lot," my mentor spat.

"Don't mention it," the ex-demon hunter waved as he went to rejoin his group.

"Now what do we do?" I asked.

"We form a team," Aahz shrugged. "Hey, Griffin!"

"What is it now?" the youth growled.

"We have one more job for you," my mentor smiled. "All you have to do is help us train our team. There are...a few points of the game that aren't very clear to us."

"No," said Griffin firmly.

"Now look, short stuff..."

"Wait a minute, Aahz," I interrupted. "Griffin, this time we aren't threatening you. I'm offering you a job at good wages to help us."

"What!?" Aahz shrieked.

"Shut up, Aahz."

"You don't understand," Griffin interrupted in turn. "Neither threats nor money will change my mind. I helped you steal the Trophy from Veygus, but I won't help you against my own team. I'd die before I'd do that."

"There are worse things than dying," Aahz suggested ominously.

"Let it drop, Aahz," I said firmly. "Thanks anyway Griffin. You've been a big help when we needed you, so I won't fault you for holding back now. Hurry up. The others are waiting." We watched as he trotted off to join his delegation.

"You know, kid," Aahz sighed at last, "sometime we're going to have to have a long talk about these lofty ideals of yours."

"Sure, Aahz," I nodded. "In the meantime, what are we going to do about this game?"

"What else can we do?" my mentor shrugged. "We put together a team."

"Just like that," I winced. "And where are we going to find the players, much less someone who can tell us how the game is played?"

"Where else," Aahz grinned, setting the D-Hopper. "The Bazaar at Deva!"

XVIII.

"What's the point-spread on World War III?"
R. REAGAN

AT SEVERAL OTHER points in this tale, I've referred to the Bazaar at Deva. You may be wondering about it. So do I...and I've been there!

Deva is the home dimension of the Deveels, acknowledged to be the best traders anywhere. You may find references to them in your folklore. Deals with Deveels are usually incredible and frequently disastrous. I've dealt with only two Deveels personally. One got me hung (not hung-over from drink—but hung up by the neck!) and the other sold me my dragon, Gleep. I like to think that makes me even, but Aahz insists I'm batting zero—whatever that means.

Anyway, there is a year-round, rock the clock Bazaar in that dimension where the Deveels meet to trade with each other. Everything imaginable and most things that aren't are available there. All you have to do is bargain with the Deveels. Fortunately, the Bazaar is large enough that there is much duplication, and sometimes you can play the dealers off against each other.

I had been here twice before, both times with Aahz. This was however, the first time I had been here when it was raining.

"It's raining," I pointed out, scowling at the overhanging clouds. They were a dark orange, which was quite picturesque, but did nothing toward making getting wet more pleasant.

"I know it's raining," Aahz retorted tersely. "Com'on. Let's step in here while I get my bearings."

'Here," in this case, was some sort of invisible bubble enveloping one stall which seemed to be doing an admirable job of keeping the rain out. I've used magik wards before to keep out unwelcome intruders, but it had never occurred to me to use it against the elements.

"Buying or looking, gentlemen?" the proprietor asked, sidling up to us.

I glanced at Aahz, but he was up on his tiptoes surveying the surroundings.

"Um...looking, I guess."

"Then stand in the rain!" came the snarling reply. "Force fields cost money, you know. This is a display, not a public service."

"What's a force field?" I stalled.

"Out!"

"Com'on kid," Aahz said. "I know where we are now."

"Where?" I asked suspiciously.

"In the stall of the Bazaar's rudest dealer," my mentor explained, raising his voice. "I wouldn't have believed it if I hadn't heard him with my own ears."

"What's that?" the proprietor scowled.

"Are you Garbelton?" Aahz asked, turning his attention on the proprietor. "Well...yes."

"Your reputation precedes you, sir," my mentor intoned loftily, "and is devastatingly accurate. Come, Master Skeeve, we'll take our business elsewhere."

"But, gentlemen!" Garbelton called desperately, "if you'll only reconsider..."

The rest was lost as Aahz gathered me up and strode off into the rain.

"What was that all about?" I demanded, breaking stride to jump a puddle. Aahz stepped squarely in it, splashing maroon mud all over my legs. Terrific.

"That? Oh, just a little smokescreen to save face. It isn't good for your reputation to get thrown out of places...particularly for not buying."

"You mean you hadn't heard of him before? Then how did you know his name?"

"It was right there on the stall's placard," Aahz grinned. "Sure gave him a turn, though, didn't I? There's nothing a Deveel hates as much as losing a potential customer...except for giving a refund."

As much as I care for Aahz and appreciate the guidance he's given me, he can be a bit stomach-turning when he starts gloating. "We're still out in the rain," I pointed out.

"Ah, But now we know where we're going."

"We do?"

Aahz groaned, swerving to avoid a little old lady who was squatting in the middle of the thoroughfare chortling over a cauldron. As we passed, a large hairy paw emerged from the cauldron's depth, but the lady whacked it with her wooden spoon and it retreated out of sight. Aahz ignored the entire proceedings.

"Look, kid," he explained, "we're looking for two things here. First, we need to recruit some players for our team."

"How can we recruit for the team when we don't know the first thing about the game?" I interrupted.

"Second," my mentor continued tersely, "we have to find someone who can fill us in on the details of the game."

"Oh."

Properly mollified, I plodded along beside him in silence for several moments, sneaking covert glances at the displays we were passing. Then something occurred to me.

"Say…ummmm, Aahz?"

"Yea, kid?"

"You never answered my question. Where are we going?"

"To the Yellow Crescent Inn."

"The Yellow Crescent Inn?" I echoed, brightening slightly. "Are we going to see Gus?"

"That's right," Aahz grinned. "Gus is a heavy better. He should be able to put us in touch with a reliable bookie. Besides he owes us a favor. Maybe we can get him for the team."

"Good," I said, and meant it.

Gus is a gargoyle. He was part of the crew we used to stop Big Julie's army and I trust him as much as I do Aahz…maybe a little more. Anyone who's used the expression "heart of stone" to mean insensitive has never met Gus. I assume his heart is stone, the rest of him is, but he's one of the warmest, most sympathetic beings I've ever met. He's also without a doubt the stablest being that I've met through Aahz. If Gus joined our team, I'd worry a lot less…well, a little less. Then again, he might be too sensible to get involved in this madcap scheme. And as for the bookies…

"Hey, Aahz," I blinked. "What do we need a bookie for?"

"To brief us on the game, of course."

"A bookie from Deva is going to tell us how to play the game on Jahk?"

"It's the best we can do," Aahz shrugged. "You heard Griffin. Nobody on Jahk will give us the time of day, much less help us put a team together. Cheer up, though. Bookies are very knowledgeable in spectator sports, and the ones here on Deva are the best."

I pondered this for several moments, then decided to ask the question that had been bothering me since the meeting.

"Aahz? When you issued the challenge, did you really expect to play the game?"

My mentor stopped dead in his tracks and whirled to face me.

"Do you think I'd issue a challenge without intending to fight?" he demanded. "Do you think I'm a big-mouthed bluffer who'd rather talk his way out of trouble than fight?"

"It had crossed my mind," I admitted.

"Well, you're right," he grinned, resuming his stride. "You're learning pretty fast—for a Klahd. No, I really thought they'd back down when we dropped our disguises. That and I didn't think Quigley would see through the ploy and call our hand."

"He's learning fast, too," I commented. "I'm afraid he could become a real problem."

"Not a chance," my mentor snorted. "You've got him beat cold in the magik department."

"Except I've promised not to move against him," I observed glumly.

"Don't let it get you down," Aahz insisted, draping an arm around my shoulders. "We've both made some stupid calls on this one. All we can do is play the cards we're dealt."

"Bite the bullet, eh?" I grimaced.

"That's right. Say, you really are learning quick."

I still didn't know what a bullet was, but I was picking up some of Aahz's pet phrases. At least now I could give the illusion of intelligence.

The Yellow Crescent Inn was in sight now. I expected Aahz to quicken his pace...I mean, it was raining. Instead, however, my mentor slowed slightly, peering at a mixed group of beings huddled under a tent-flap.

"Hel-lo!" he exclaimed. "What have we here?"

"It looks like a mixed group of beings huddled under a tentflap," I observed dryly, or as dryly as I could manage while dripping wet.

"It's a crap game," Aahz declared. "I can hear the dice."

Trust a Pervert to hear the sound of dice on mud at a hundred paces.

"So?" I urged.

"So I think we've found our bookie. The tall fellow, thereat the back of the crowd. I've dealt with him before."

"Are we going to talk to him now?" I asked eagerly.

"Not 'we,'" Aahz corrected. "Me. You get in enough trouble in clean-cut crowds without my taking you into a crap game. You're going to wait for me in the Inn. Gus should be able to keep an eye on you."

"Oh, all right."

I was disappointed, but willing to get out of the rain.

"And don't stop to talk to anyone between here and there. Do you hear me?"

"Yes, Aahz," I nodded, starting off at a trot.

"And whatever you do, don't eat the food!"

"Are you kidding?" I laughed. "I've been here before."

The food at the Yellow Crescent Inn is dubious at best. Even after dimension hopping with Tananda and seeing what was accepted as food elsewhere, I wouldn't put anything from that place in my mouth voluntarily.

As I approached, I could see through the door that the place was empty. This usually surprised me. I mean, from my prior experience, there was actually a good-sized crowd in there, and I would have expected the rain to increase the number of loiterers.

Gus wasn't in sight, either; but the door was open, so I pushed my way in, relieved to be somewhere dry again. I shouldn't have been.

No sooner had I gained entry when something like a large hand closed over the top of my head and I was hoisted bodily from my feet.

"Little person!" a booming voice declared. "Crunch likes little persons. Crunch likes little persons better than Big Macs. How do you taste, little person?"

With this last, I was rotated until I was hanging face to face with my assailant. In this case, I use the term 'back' loosely. It had felt like I was being picked up by a big hand because I was being picked up by a big hand. At the other end of the big hand was the first and only Troll it had been my misfortune to meet...and he looked hungry.

XIX.

"Why should I have to pay a troll just to cross a bridge?"
B. G. GRUFF

WHILE I HAD never seen a troll before, I knew that this was one. I mean, he fit the description: tall, scraggly hair in patches, long rubbery limbs, misshapen face with runny eyes of unequal size. If it wasn't a troll, it would do until something better worse—came along.

I should have been scared, but strangely I wasn't. For some time now I had been ducking and weaving through some tight situations trying to avoid trouble. Now, Big Ugly here wanted to hassle me. This time, I wasn't buying.

"Why little person not answer Crunch?" the troll demanded, shaking me slightly.

"You want an answer?" I snarled. "Try this!"

Levitation is one of my oldest spells, and I used it now. Reaching out with my mind, I picked up a chair and slammed it into his face.

He didn't even blink.

Then I got scared.

"What's going on out here!" Gus bellowed, charging out of the kitchen. "Any fights, and I'll…Skeeve!!"

"Tell your customer here to put me down before I tear off his arm and feed it to him!" I called, my confidence returning with the arrival of reinforcements.

I needn't have said anything. The effect of Gus's words on the troll was nothing short of miraculous.

"Skeeve?" my assailant gaped, setting me gently on my feet. "I say. Bloody good to make your acquaintance. I've heard so much about you, you know. Chumly here."

The hand which had so recently fastened on my head now seized my hand and began pumping it gently with each adjective.

"Ummm…a pleasure, I'm sure," I stammered, trying vainly to retrieve my hand. "Say, weren't you talking differently before?"

"Oh, you mean Crunch?" Chumly laughed. "Beastly fellow. Still, he serves his purpose. Keeps the rif-raff at a distance, you know."

"What he's trying to say," Gus supplied, "is that it's an act he puts on to scare people. It's lousy for business when he drops in for a visit, but it does mean we can talk uninterrupted. That's about the only way you can talk to Chumly. He's terribly shy."

"Oh, tosh," the troll proclaimed, digging at the floor with his toe. "I'm only giving the public what it wants. Not much work for a vegetarian troll, you know."

"A vegetarian troll?" I asked incredulously. "Weren't you about to eat me a minute ago?"

"Perish the thought," Chumly shuddered. "Presently I would have allowed you to squirm free and run...except, of course, you wouldn't. Quite a spirited lad, isn't he?"

"You don't know the half of it," the gargoyle answered through his perma-grin. "Why, when we took on Big Julie's army..."

"Chumly!" Aahz exclaimed, bursting through the door. "Aahz," the troll answered. "I say, this is a spot of all right. What brings you..."

He broke off suddenly, eycing the Deveel who had followed Aahz into the inn.

"Oh, don't mind the Geek here," my mentor waved. "He's helping us with some trouble we're having."

"The Geek?" I frowned.

"It's a nickname," the Deveel shrugged.

"I knew it," Gus proclaimed, sinking into a chair. "Or I should have known it when I saw Skeeve. The only time you come to visit is when there's trouble."

"If you blokes are going to have a war council, perhaps I'd better amble along," Chumly suggested.

"Stick around," Aahz instructed. "It involves Tananda."

"Tananda?" the troll frowned. "What has that bit of fluff gone and gotten herself into now?"

"You know Tananda?" I asked.

"Oh quite," Chumly smiled. "She's my little sister."

"Your sister?" I gaped.

"Rather. Didn't you notice the family resemblance?"

"Well...I, ah..." I fumbled.

"Don't let him kid you," my mentor grinned. "Tananda and Chumly are from Trollia, where the men are Trolls and the women are Trollops. With men like this back home, you can understand why Tananda spends as much time as she does dimension hopping."

"That's quite enough of that," Chumly instructed firmly. "I want to hear what's happened to little sister."

"In a bit," Aahz waved. "First let's see what information the Geek here has for us."

"I can't believe I let you pull me out of a hot crap game to meet with this zoo," the Deveel grumbled.

"Zoo?" echoed Gus. He was still smiling, but then, he always smiled. Personally, I didn't like the tone of his voice.

Apparently Aahz didn't either, as he hastened to move the conversation along.

"You should thank me for getting you out," he observed, "before the rest of them figured out that you'd switched the dice."

"You spotted that?" the Geek asked, visibly impressed. "Then maybe it's just as well I bailed out. When a Pervert can spot me..."

"That's Pervect!" Aahz corrected, showing all his teeth.

"Oh! Yes...of course," the Deveel amended, pinking visibly.

For his sake, I hoped he had some good information for us. In an amazingly short time he had managed to rub everyone wrong. Then again, Deveels have never been noted for their personable ways.

"So what can you tell us about the game on Jahk," I prompted.

"How much are you paying me?" the Geek yawned.

"As much as the information's worth," Aahz supplied grimly.

"Probably more."

The Deveel studied him for a moment, then shrugged.

"Fair enough," he declared. "You've always made good on your debts, Aahz. I suppose I can trust you on this one."

"So what can you tell us?" I insisted.

Now it was my turn to undergo close scrutiny, but the gaze turned on me was noticeably colder than the one Aahz had suffered. With a lazy motion, the Geek reached down and pulled a dagger from his boot and tossed it aloft with a twirl. Catching it with his other hand, he sent it up again, forming a glittering arch from hand to hand, never taking his eyes from mine.

"You're pretty mouthy for a punk Klahd," he observed. "Are you this mouthy when you don't have a pack of goons around to back your move?"

"Usually," I admitted. "And they aren't goons, they're my friends."

As I spoke, I reached out once more with my mind, caught the knife, gave it an extra twirl, then stopped it dead in the air, its point hovering bare inches from the Deveel's throat. Like I said, I was getting a little tired of people throwing their weight around.

The Geek didn't move a muscle, but now he was watching the knife instead of me.

"In case you missed it the first time around," Gus supplied, still smiling, "this 'punk Klahd's' name is Skeeve. The Skeeve." The Deveel pinked again. I was starting to enjoy having a reputation.

"Why don't you sit down, Geek," Aahz suggested, "and tell the k...Skeeve...what he wants to know?"

The Deveel obeyed, apparently eager to move away from the knife. That being the case, I naturally let it follow him.

Once he was seated, I gave it one last twirl and set it lightly on the table in front of him. That reassured him somewhat, but he still kept glancing at it nervously as he spoke.

"I...um...I really don't have that much information," he began uncomfortably. "They only play one game a year, and the odds are usually even."

"How is the game played?" Aahz urged.

"Never seen it, myself," the Geek shrugged. "It's one of those get-the-ball-in-the-net games. I'm more familiar with the posi-tions than the actual play."

"Then what are the positions?" I asked.

"It's a five-man team," the Deveel explained. "Two forwards, or Fangs, chosen for their speed and agility; one guard or Intercep-tor, for power; a goal-tender or Castle, who is usually the strongest man on the team; and a Rider, a mounted player who is used both for attack and defense."

"Sounds straightforward enough," my mentor commented.

"Can't you tell us anything at all about the play?" I pressed.

"Well, I'm not up on the Strategies," the Geek frowned. "But I have a general idea of the action. The team in possession of the ball has four tries to score a goal. They can move the ball by running, kicking, or throwing. Once the ball is immobilized, the try is over and they line up for their next try. Of course, the defense tries to stop them."

"Run, kick, or throw," Aahz murmured. "Hmmm...Sounds like defense could be a problem. What are the rules regarding conduct on the field?"

"Players can't use edged weapons on each other," the Deveel recited. "Any offenders will be shot down on the spot."

"Sensible rule," I said, swallowing hard. "What else?"

"That's it," the Geek shrugged.

"That's it?" Aahz exclaimed. "No edged weapons? That's it?"

"Both for the rules and my knowledge of the game," the Deveel confirmed. "Now, if we can settle accounts, I'll be on my way."

I wanted to cross-examine him, but Aahz caught my eye and shook his head.

"Would you settle for a good tip?" he asked.

"Only if it was a really good tip," the Geek responded dourly. "Have you heard about the new game on Jahk? The three-way brawl that's coming up?"

"Of course," the Deveel shrugged.

"You have?" I blinked. I mean we had only just set it up!

"I have a professional stake in keeping up on these things."

"Uh-huh!" my mentor commented judiciously. "How are the odds running?"

"Even up for Ta-hoe and Veygus. This new team is throwing everyone for a loop, though. Since no one can get a line on them, they're heavy underdogs."

"If we could give you an inside track on this dark-horse team," Aahz said, looking at the ceiling, "would that square our account?"

"You know about the Demons?" the Geek asked eagerly. "If you do, it's a deal. With inside info, I could be the only one at the Bazaar with the data to fix the real odds."

"Done!" my mentor declared. "We're the Demons."

That got him. The Geek sagged back in his chair for a moment, open mouthed. Then he cocked his head at us. "You mean, you're financing the team?"

"We are the team…or part of it. We're still putting it together."

The Deveel started to say something, then changed his mind. Rising silently, he headed for the door, hesitated with one hand on the knob, then left without saying a word.

Somehow, I found his reaction ominous.

"How 'bout that, kid," Aahz chortled. "I got the information without paying a cent!"

"I don't like the way he looked," I announced, still staring at the door.

"Com'on. Admit it! I just got us a pretty good deal."

"Aahz?" I said slowly. "What is it you always told me about dealing with Deveels?"

"Hmmm? Oh, you mean, 'If you think you've made a good deal with a Deveel…!'"

He broke off, his jubilance fading.

"'first count your fingers, then your limbs, then your relatives!'"

I finished for him. "Are you sure you got a good deal?" Our eyes met, and neither of us were smiling.

XX.

"What are friends *for?"*
R. M. NIXON

WE WERE STILL pondering our predicament, when Chumly interrupted our thoughts.

"You blokes do seem to be having a bit of difficulty," he said draping an arm around both of our shoulders. "but if it wouldn't be too much trouble, could you enlighten me as to what all this has to do with Tananda?"

Normally, this would sound like a casual request. When one pauses to consider, however, that the casual request was coming from a troll half again as tall as we were, and capable of mashing our heads like normal folks squash grapes, the request takes on a high priority no matter how politely it's phrased.

"Well, you know this game we're talking about?" Aahz began uneasily.

"Tananda's the prize," I finished lamely.

Chumly was silent. Then his grip on my shoulder tightened slightly.

"Forgive me," he smiled. "For a moment there I thought you said my little sister is the prize in some primitive, spectator brawl."

"Actually," Aahz explained hastily, trying to edge away, "The kid, here, was there when she was captured."

"…But it was Aahz that got her involved in the game," I countered, edging in the other direction.

"You chaps got her into this?" the troll asked softly, his grip holding us firmly in place. "I thought you were trying to rescue her."

"Whoa! Everybody calm down!" Gus ordered, stepping into the impending brawl. "Nobody wrecks this place but me. Chumly, let's all sit down and hear this from the top."

I was pretty calm myself…at least, I wasn't about to start a fight. Still, Gus's suggestion was a welcome change in direction from the one the conversation was headed in.

This time, I needed no prompting to let Aahz do the talking, While he gets trapped in oversights from time to time, if given free rein, he can and has talked us out of some seemingly impossible situations. This was no exception. Though he surprised me by sticking to the truth, by the time he was done, Chumly's frozen features had softened to a thoughtful stare.

"I must say," the troll commented finally, "it seems little sister has done it to herself this time. You seem to have tried everything you could to affect her release."

"We could give the Trophy back," I suggested.

Aahz kicked me under the table.

"Out of the question," Chumly snorted. "It's Aahz's gift fair and square. If Tananda got herself in trouble acquiring it, that's bloody well her problem. You can't expect Aahz to feel responsible."

"Yes, I can," I corrected.

"No," the troll declared. "The only acceptable solution is to trounce these blighters soundly at their own game. I trust you'll allow me to fill a position on your team?"

"I'd had my hopes," my mentor grinned.

"Count me in, too," Gus announced, flexing his stone wings. "Can't let you all go into a brawl like this without my steadying influence."

"See, kid?" Aahz grinned. "Things are looking up already."

"Say, Aahz," I said carefully. "It occurs to me...you know that Rider position? Well, it seems to me we'd have a big psychological advantage if our Rider was sitting on top of a dragon."

"You're right."

"Aw, com'on, Aahz! Just because Gleep's a bit...Did you say 'you're right?'"

"Right. Affirmative. Correct," my mentor nodded. "Some-times you come up with some pretty good ideas."

"Gee, Aahz..."

"...But not that stupid little dragon of yours," he insisted. "We're going to use that monster we got with Big Julie's army."

"But Aahz..."

"But Aahz nothing! Com'on, Gus! Close up shop here. We're heading for Klah to pick up a dragon!"

Now, Klah is my home dimension, and no matter what my fellow dimension travelers say, I think it's a pretty nice one to live in. Still, after spending extensive time in some other dimensions, however pleasantly familiar the sights of Klah seem, they do look a little drab.

Aahz had surprised me by bringing us well North of Possletum, instead of at our own quarters in the Royal Palace. I inquired about this, and for a change my mentor gave me a straight answer.

"It's all in how you set the D-Hopper," he explained. "You've got eight dials to play with, and they let you control both which dimension you're going to as well as where you are when you arrive."

"Does that mean we could use it to go from one place to another in the same dimension?" I asked.

"Hmmm," Aahz frowned. "I really don't know. It never occurred to me to try. We'll have to check into it sometime."

"Well then, why did you pick this arrival point?"

"That's easy," my mentor grinned, gesturing at our colleagues. "I wasn't sure what our reception at the palace would be like if we arrived with a troll and a gargoyle."

He had me there. At the Bazaar disguises had been unnecessary, and I had gotten so used to seeing strange beings around me it had completely slipped my mind that our group would be a strange sight to the average Klahd.

"Sorry, Aahz," I flushed. "I forgot."

"Don't worry about it," my mentor waved. "If it had been important I would have said something to you before we left the Bazaar. I just wanted to shake you up a little to remind you to pay attention to details. The real reason we're here instead of at the palace is, we want to see Big Julie, and I'm too lazy to walk the distance if we could cover it with the D-Hopper."

Despite his reassurances, I got to work correcting my oversight. To redeem myself, I decided to show Aahz I had been practicing during my tour with Tananda. Closing my eyes, I concentrated on disguising Gus and Chumly at the same time.

"Not bad, kid," Aahz commented. "They're a little villanous looking, but acceptable."

"I thought it would help us avoid trouble if they looked a little mean," I explained modestly.

"Not bad?" Chumly snarled. "I look like a Klahd!"

"I think you look cute as a Klahd," Gus quipped.

"Cute? CUTE?" Chumly bristled. "Who ever heard of a cute troll? I say, Aahz, is this really necessary?"

"Unfortunately, yes," my mentor replied, his grin belying his expression of sympathy. "Remember, you aren't supposed to be a troll just now. Just a humble citizen of this lower than humble dimension."

"Why aren't you disguised?" the troll asked suspiciously, obviously unconvinced.

"I'm already known around here as the apprentice of the Court Magician," Aahz countered innocently. "Folks are used to seeing me like this."

"Well," Chumly grumbled, "there'll be bloody Hell to pay if anyone I know sees me looking like this."

"If anyone you know sees you like this, they won't recognize you," I pointed out cautiously.

The troll thought about that for a moment, then slowly nodded his head.

"I suppose you're right," he conceded at last. "Let's off to find this Big Julie, hmmm? The less time I spend looking like this, the better."

"Don't get your hopes too high," Aahz cautioned. "We're going to do our training in this dimension, so you might as well get used to being a Klahd for a while."

"Bloody Hell," was the only reply.

TRUE TO HIS plans for retirement, Big Julie was relaxing on the lawn of his cottage, drinking wine when we arrived. To the casual observer, he might seem nothing more than a spindley old man basking in the sun. Then again, the casual observer wouldn't have known him when he was commanding the mightiest army ever to grace our dimension. This was probably just as well. Julie was still hiding from a particularly nasty batch of loan sharks who were very curious as to why he and his men gave up soldiering…and hence their ability to pay back certain old gambling debts.

"Aye! Hello boys!" he boomed, waving enthusiastically. "Long time no see, ya know? Pull up a chair and have some wine. What brings you out this way, eh?"

"A little bit of pleasure and a lot of business," Aahz explained, casually gathering to his bosom the only pitcher of wine in sight. We've got a little favor to ask."

"If it's mine, it's yours," Julie announced. "What da ya need?"
"Is there any more wine?" I asked hastily.

Long years of experience had taught me not to expect Aahz to share a pitcher of wine. One Was barely enough for him. "Sure. I got lots. Badaxe is inside now getting some."

"Badaxe?" Aahz frowned. "What's he doing here?"

"At the moment, wondering what you're doing here," came a booming voice.

We all turned to find the shaggy-mountain form of Possle-tum's General framed in the doorway of the cottage, a pitcher of wine balanced in each hand. Hugh Badaxe always seemed to me to be more beast than man, though I'll admit his curly dark hair and beard when viewed in conjunction with his favorite animal skin cloak contributed greatly to the image. Of course, beasts didn't use tools, while Badaxe definitely did. A massive double-edged axe dangled constantly from his belt, at once his namesake and his favorite tool of diplomacy.

"We just dropped in to have a few words with Big Julie here," my mentor replied innocently.

"What about?" the general demanded. "I thought we agreed that all military matters would be brought to me before seeking Big Julie's advice. I am the Commander of Possletum's army, you know."

"Now Hugh," Julie soothed, "the boys just wanted to ask me for a little favor, that's all. If it involved the army, they would've come to you. Right, boys?"

Aahz and I nodded vigorously. Gus and Chumly looked blank. We had overlooked briefing them on General Badaxe and his jealousies regarding power.

"You see?" Julie continued. "Now sit down and have some wine while I talk to the boys. Now, then, Aahz, what sort of favor can I do for you?"

"Nothing much," my mentor shrugged. "We were wondering if we could borrow your dragon for a little while."

"My dragon? What do you need my dragon for? You've already got a dragon."

"We need a big dragon," Aahz evaded.

"A big dragon?" Julie echoed, frowning. "It sounds like you boys are into something dangerous."

"Don't worry," I interjected confidently, "I'll be riding the dragon in the game, so nothing…"

"Game?" Badaxe roared. "I knew it. You're going into a war game without even consulting me."

"It's not a war game," I insisted.

"Yes, it is," Aahz corrected.

"It is?" I blinked.

"Think about it, kid," my mentor urged. "Any spectator sport with teams is a form of wargaming."

"Then why wasn't I informed?" Badaxe blustered. "As Commander of Possletum's armed forces, any war games to be held fall under my jurisdiction.

"General," Aahz sighed, "the game isn't going to be played in this kingdom."

"Any military...oh!" Badaxe paused, confused by this turn of events. "Well, if it involves any members of my army..."

"It doesn't," my mentor interrupted. "This exercise only involves a five-man team, and we've filled it without drawing on the army's resources."

A bell went off in my mind. I ran a quick check, which only confirmed my fears.

"Um...Aahz..." I began.

"Not now, kid," he growled, "You see, general, all your paranoid fears were..."

"Aahz!" I insisted.

"What is it?" my mentor snarled, turning on me.

"We haven't got five players, only four."

XXI.

"We've got an unbeatable team."
SAURON

"FOUR?" AAHZ ECHOED blankly.

"I count real good up to five," I informed him loftily. "and you, me, Gus and Chumly only make four. See? One, two , three…"

"All right! I get the message," my mentor interrupted, scowling at our two comrades. "Say Gus! I don't suppose Berfert's along, is he?"

"Com'on, Aahz," I chided, "we can't claim a salamander as a team member.

"Shut up, kid. How 'bout it, Gus?"

"Not this time," the gargoyle shrugged. "he ran into a ladyfriend of his, and they decided to take a vacation together."

"A lady friend?" Aahz asked, arching an eyebrow.

"That's right," Gus nodded. "You might say she's an old flame."

"An old flame," the troll grinned. "I say, that's rather good." For a change, I got the joke, and joined Gus and Chumly in a hearty round of laughter, while Badaxe and Julie looked puzzled. Aahz rolled his eyes in exasperation.

"That's all I need," he groaned. "One member short, and the ones I've got are half-wits. When you're all quite through, I'm open to suggestions as to where we're going to find a fifth team member."

"I'll fill the position," Badaxe said calmly.

"You?" I gulped, my laughter forgotten.

"Of course," the general nodded. "It's my duty."

"Maybe I didn't make myself clear," Aahz interjected. "Possle-tum isn't involved in this at all."

"But its magician and his apprentice are," Badaxe added pointedly. "You're both citizens of Possletum, and rather promi-nent citizens at that. Like it or not, my duty is to protect you with any means at my disposal—and in this case, that means me."

I hadn't thought of that. In a way, it was kind of nice. Still, I wasn't wild about the general putting himself in danger on our account.

"Ummm...I appreciate your offer, general," I began carefully, "but the game's going to be played a long way from here."

"If you can survive the journey, so can I," Badaxe countered firmly.

"But you don't understand!"

"Kid," Aahz interrupted in a thoughtful tone, "why don't you introduce him to his potential teammates?"

"What? Oh, I'm sorry. General Badaxe, this is Gus, and that's Chumly."

"No," my mentor smiled. "I mean introduce him."

"Oh!" I said. "General, meet the rest of our team."

As I spoke, I dropped the disguise spell, revealing both gargoyle and troll in their true forms.

"Gus!" Big Julie roared. "I thought I recognized your voice."

"Hi, Julie!" the gargoyle waved. "How's retirement?"

"Pretty dull. Hey, help yourself to some wine!"

"Thanks."

Gus stepped forward and took the two pitchers of wine from the general's nerveless grip, passing one to Chumly. It occurred to me that I was the only one of the crew who wasn't getting a drink out of this.

The general was transfixed, his eyes darting from gargoyle to troll and back again. He had paled slightly, but to his credit he hadn't given ground an inch.

"Well, Badaxe," Aahz grinned, "still want to join the team?" The general licked his lips nervously, then tore his eyes away from Gus and Chumly.

"Certainly," he announced. "I'd be proud to fight alongside such...worthy allies. That is, if they'll have me."

That dropped it in our laps.

"What do you think, Skeeve?" Aahz asked. "You're the boss."

Correction. That dropped it in my lap. Aahz had an annoying habit of yielding leadership just when things got sticky. I was beginning to suspect it wasn't always coincidence.

"Well, Lord Magician?" Badaxe rumbled. "Will you accept my services for this expedition?"

I was stuck. No one could deny Badaxe's value in a fight, but I had never warmed to him as a person. As a teammate..."

"Gleep!"

The warning wasn't soon enough! Before I could brace myself, I was hit from behind by a massive force and sent sprawling
on my face. The slimy tongue worrying the back of my head and
the accompanying blast of incredibly bad breath could only have
one source.

"Gleep!" my pet announced proudly, pausing briefly in his efforts to reach my face.

"What's that stupid dragon doing here?" Aahz bellowed, unmoved by our emotional reunion.

"Ask Badaxe," Julie grinned. "He brought him."

"He did?" my mentor blinked, momentarily stunned out of
his anger.

I was a bit surprised myself. Pushing Gleep away momen-tarily
I scrambled to my feet and shot a questioning glance at the general.

For the first time since and including our original confron-tation,
Hugh Badaxe looked uncomfortable. The fierce warrior who wouldn't
flinch before army, magician, or demon couldn't meet our eyes.

"He was…well, with you two gone he was just moping around,"
the general mumbled. "No one else would go near him and I
thought…well, that is…it seemed logical that…"

"He brought him out to play with my dragon," Julie explained
gleefully. "It seems the fierce general here has a weak spot for
animals."

Badaxe's head came up with a snap. "The dragon served the
Kingdom well in the last campaign," he announced hotly. "It's only
fair that someone sees to his needs—as a veteran."

His bluster didn't fool anyone. There was no reason why he
should feel responsible for my dragon. Even if he did, it would
have been easy for him to order some of his soldiers to see to my
pet rather than attending to it personally as he had done. The truth
of the matter was that he liked Gleep.

As if to confirm our suspicions, my pet began to frolic around
him, waggling head and tail in movements I knew were reserved
for playmates. The general stoically ignored him…which is not that
easy to do.

"Um…General?" I said carefully.

"Yes?"

I was fixed by a frosty gaze, daring me to comment on the
dragon's behavior.

"About our earlier conversation," I clarified hastily. "I'm sure I speak for the rest of the team when I say we're both pleased and honored to have you on our side for the upcoming war game."

"Thank you, Lord Magician," he bowed stiffly. "I trust you will find your confidence in me is not misplaced."

"Now that that's settled," Aahz chortled, rubbing his hands together. "Where's the big dragon? We've got some practicing to do."

"He's asleep," Julie shrugged.

"Asleep?" Aahz echoed.

"That's right. He got into the barn, ate up over half the livestock in the place. Now he's sleepin' like a rock, you know? Probably won't wake up for a couple of months at best."

"A couple of months!" my mentor groaned. "Now what are we going to do? The kid's got to have something to ride in the game!" "Gleep!" my pet said, rolling on the ground at my feet. Aahz glared at me.

"He said it, I didn't," I declared innocently.

"Don't think we've got much choice, Aahz," Gus pointed out. "If you aren't used to them, any dragon would seem rather frightening," Chumly supplied.

"All right! All right!" Aahz grimaced, throwing up his hands in surrender. "If you're all willing to risk it, I'll go along. As long as he doesn't drive me nuts by always saying…"

"Gleep?" my pet asked, swiveling his head around to see what Aahz was shouting about.

"Then we're ready to start practicing?" I asked hastily.

"As ready as we'll ever be, I guess," Aahz grumbled, glaring at the dragon.

"I know this isn't my fight," Big Julie put in, "but what kinda strategies have you boys worked up."

"Haven't yet," my mentor admitted. "But we'll think of something."

"Maybe I can give you a hand. I used to be pretty good with small unit tactics. You know what I mean?"

THE NEXT FEW weeks were interesting. You notice I didn't say 'instructive,' just interesting. Aside from learning to work together as a team, there was little development among the individuals of our crew.

You could argue that with the beings we had on the team there was little development to be done. That was their opinion. Nor was it easy to argue with them. With the exception of myself, their physical condition ranged from excellent to unbelievable. What was more, they were all seasoned veterans of countless battles and campaigns. From what we had seen of the Jahks, any one of our team was more than a match for five of our opponents—and together...

Maybe that's what bothered me: the easy assurance on everyone's part that we could win in a walk. I know it bothered Big Julie.

"You boys are over-confident," he'd scold, shaking his head in exasperation. "There's more to fighting than strength. Know what I mean?"

"We've got more than strength," Aahz yawned. "There's speed, agility, stamina, and with Gus along, we've got air cover. Then again, Skeeve there has a few tricks up his sleeve as a magician."

"You forgot 'experience,'" Julie countered. "These other guys, they've been playing this game for what? Five hundred years now? They might have a trick or two of their own."

With that stubborn argument, Julie would threaten, wheedle, and cajole us into practicing. Unfortunately, most of the practice centered around me.

Staying on Gleep's back was rough enough. Trying to keep my seat while throwing or catching a ball proved to be nearly impossible. Gleep was no help. He preferred chasing the ball himself or standing stock still while scratching himself with a hind leg to following orders from me. I finally had to cheat a little, resorting to magik to keep me upright on my mount's back. A little levitation, a little flying, and suddenly my riding skills improved a hundred fold. If Aahz suspected I was using something other than my sense of balance, he didn't say anything.

The problem of catching and throwing the ball was solved by the addition of a staff to my argument. Chumly uprooted a hefty sized sapling, and the general used his ever-present belt axe to trim away branches and roots. The result was an eleven foot club with which I could either knock the ball along the ground or swat it out of the air if someone had thrown or kicked it aloft. The staff was a bit heavier than I would have liked, but the extra weight moved the ball farther each time I hit it. Of course, I used a little magik to steer the ball, too, so I didn't miss often and it usually went where I wanted it to go.

Gleep, on the other hand, went where he wanted to go. While my club occasionally helped both to set him in motion and to institute minor changes in his direction once he was moving, total control had still eluded me when the day finally arrived for our departure.

The five of us (six including Gleep) gathered in the center of our practice meadow and said our goodbyes to Julie.

"I'm sorry I can't come with you, boys," he declared mournfully, "but I'm not as young as I used to be, you know?"

"Don't worry," Aahz waved, "we'll be back soon. You can come to our victory celebration."

"There you go again," Julie scowled, "I'm warning you, don't celebrate until after the battle. After five hundred years..."

"Right, Julie," Aahz interrupted hastily. "You've told us before. We'd better get going now or we'll miss the game. Wouldn't want to lose by default."

With that, he checked to see we were all in position and triggered the D-Hopper.

A moment later, we were back on Jahk.

XXII.

"No matter what the game, no matter what the rules,
the same rules apply to both sides!"
HOYLE'S LAW

THE STADIUM HAD undergone two major changes since the last time Aahz and I were here.

First, the configuration of the field had been changed. Instead of a rectangle, the chalk lines now outlined a triangle with netted goals at each corner. I assumed that was to accommodate a three-way instead of a two-way match.

The second change was people. Remember how I said I didn't even want to imagine what the stadium would be like full of people? Well, the reality dwarfed anything my imagination could have conjured up. Where I had envisioned neat rows of people to match the military precision of the seats, the stands were currently a chaotic mass of color and motion. I don't know why they bothered providing seats. As far as I could tell, nobody was sitting down.

A stunned hush had fallen over the crowd when we appeared. This was understandable. Beings don't appear out of thin air very often, as we had assembled.

At Aahz's instruction, I had withheld any disguises from our team in order to get maximum psychological impact from our normal appearance. We got it.

The crowd gaped at us, while we gaped at the crowd. Then they recovered their composure and a roar trumpeted forth from a thousand throats simultaneously. The bedlam was deafening.

"They don't seem very intimidated," I observed dryly.

I didn't expect to be heard over the din, but I had forgotten Aahz's sharp ears.

"Ave Caesar. Salutes e moratorium. Eh, kid?" he grinned.

I didn't have the foggiest what he was talking about, but I grinned back at him. I was tired of staring blankly every time he made a joke.

"Hey, boss. We've got company," Gus called, jerking his head toward one side of the stadium.

"Two companies, actually," Chumly supplied, staring in the opposite direction.

Swivelling my head around, I discovered they were both right. Massha was bearing down on us from one side, while old Greybeard was waddling forward from the other. It seemed both Veygus and Ta-hoe wanted words with us.

"Hell-o boys," Massha drawled, arriving first. "Just wanted to wish you luck with your...venture."

This might have sounded strange coming from a supporter of the opposition. It did to me. Then I remembered that Massha thought we were out to neutralize Quigley's "demon." Well, in a way we were.

Aahz, as usual, was way ahead of me.

"Don't worry, Massha," he grinned. "We've got everything well in hand."

It never ceases to amaze me the ease with which my mentor can lie.

"Just be sure you stay out of it," he continued smoothly. "It's a rather delicate plan, and any miscellaneous moving parts could foul things up."

"Don't worry your green little head about that," she winked, "I know when I'm outclassed. I was just kinda hoping you'd introduce me to the rest of your team."

I suddenly realized that throughout our conversation, she hadn't taken her eyes off our teammates. Specifically, she was staring sideways at Hugh Badaxe. This didn't change as Aahz made the proper introductions.

"Massha, this is Gus."

"Charmed, madam," the gargoyle responded.

"...and Chum...er. . Crunch."

"When fight? Crunch likes fighting," Chumly declared, dropping into his troll act.

Massha didn't bat an eye. She was busy running both of them up and down the General's frame.

"And this is Hugh Badaxe."

With a serpentine glide, Massha was standing close to the General.

"So pleased to meet 'cha, Hugh...you don't mind if I call you Hugh, do you?" she purred.

"Harmmph...I...that is," Badaxe stammered, visibly uncomfortable.

I could sympathize with him. Having Massha focus her attention on one was disquieting to say the least. Fortunately, help arrived
just then in the form of the Ta-hoe delegate.

"Good afternoon, gentlemen," he chortled, rubbing his hands
together gleefully. "Hello, Massha."

"Actually," she returned icily, "I was just leaving."

She leaned forward and murmured something in the General's
ear before departing for her seat in the stands. Whatever it was,
Badaxe flushed bright red and avoided our eyes.

"We were afraid you wouldn't arrive in time," Greybeard continued, ignoring Massha's exist. "Wouldn't want to disappoint the
fans with a default, would we? When are you expecting the rest of
your team?"

"The rest of our team?" I frowned. "I thought the rules only
called for five players plus a riding mount."

"That's right," Greybeard replied, "but...oh well, I admire your
confidence. So there're only the five of you, eh? Well, well. That will
change the odds a bit."

"Why?" I demanded suspiciously.

"Are the edges on that thing sharp?" the spokesman asked, spy-
ing the General's axe.

"Razor," Badaxe replied haughtily.

"But he won't use it on anyone," I added hastily suddenly remembering the 'no edged weapons' rule. I wasn't sure what the
General's reaction would be if anyone tried to take his beloved axe
away from him.

"Oh, I have no worries on that score," Greybeard responded
easily. "As with all games, the crossbowmen will be quick to eliminate any player who chooses to ignore the rules."

He waved absently at the sidelines. We looked in the indicated
direction, and saw for the first time that the field was surrounded by
crossbowmen, alternately dressed in the blue and yellow of Ta-hoe
and the red and white of Veygus. This was a little wrinkle the Geek
had neglected to mention. He had told us about the rules, but not
how they were enforced.

At the same time, I noticed two things which I had previously
missed while scanning the stands.

The first was Quigley, sitting front and center on the Ta-hoe
side. What was more important was that he had Tananda with him.

She was still asleep, floating horizontally in the air in front of him. Apparently he didn't want to miss the game, and didn't trust us enough to leave her unguarded back at his workshop. He saw me staring and waved. I didn't wave back. Instead, I was about to call Aahz's attention to my find when I noticed the second thing.

Griffin was at the edge of the field, jumping up and down and frantically waving his arms to get my attention. As soon as he saw I was watching him, he began vigorously beckoning to me. Aahz was engrossed in conversation with the Ta-hoe spokesman, so I ambled off to see what Griffin wanted. "Hello, Griffin," I smiled. "How've you been?"

"I just wanted to tell you," he gasped, breathless from his exertions, "I've changed sides. If there's anything I can do to help you, just sing out."

"Really?" I drawled, raising an eyebrow. "And why the sudden change of heart, not to mention allegiances?"

"Call it my innate sense of fair play," he grimaced. "I don't like what they're planning to do to you. Even if my old team is involved, I don't like it."

"What are they planning to do to us?" I demanded, suddenly attentive.

"That's what I wanted to warn you about," he explained.

"The two teams had a meeting about this game. They decided that however much they hated each other, neither side wanted to see the Trophy go to a bunch of outsiders."

"That's only natural," I nodded, "but what..."

"You don't understand!" the youth interrupted hastily.

"They're going to double-team you! They've declared a truce with each other until they've knocked you off the field. When the game starts you'll be up against two teams working together against your one!"

"Kid! Get back here!"

Aahz's bellow reminded me there was another conference going on. "I've got to go, Griffin," I declared. "Thanks for the warning."

"Good luck!" he called. "You're going to need it."

I trotted back onto the field, to find the assemblage waiting for me with expectant expressions.

"They want to see the Trophy," Aahz informed me with a wink.

"As per our original agreement," the Ta-hoe spokesman added stiffly. "It should be here to be awarded to the victorious team."

"It is here." I announced firmly.

"I beg your pardon?" Greybeard blinked, looking around. "Show him, kid," my mentor grinned.

"All right," I nodded, "everybody stand back."

In many ways it was harder to produce the statue using magik than it would have been to do it with physical labor. I had to agree with Aahz, though, that this way was far more dramatic.

Stretching my levitation capacities to their utmost, I went to work. A large hunk of turf was lifted from the center of the field and set aside. Then the exposed dirt was shoved aside, and finally the Trophy rose into view. I let it hover in midair while I rearranged the dirt and replaced the turf, then let it settle majestically to rest in all its magnificent, ugly splendor.

The crowd roared its approval, though whether for my magik or the Trophy itself I wasn't sure.

"Pretty good," Aahz exclaimed, slapping me gently on the back.

"Gleep," my pet exclaimed, adding his slimy tongue to the offered congratulations.

"Very clever," Greybeard admitted. "We never thought to look there. A little rough on the field, though, isn't it?"

"It'll get torn up this afternoon anyway," my mentor shrugged. "Incidentally, when's game time?"

As if in answer to his question, the stands exploded in bedlam. I hadn't thought the stadium could get any noisier, but this was like a solid wall of sound pressing in on us from all sides.

The reason for the jubilation was immediately obvious. Two columns of figures had emerged from a tunnel at the far end of the stadium and were jogging onto the field.

The blue and yellow tunics of one column contrasted with the scarlet and white tunics of the other, but served nicely to identify them as our opponents. This, however, was not their most noteworthy feature.

The Ta-hoe team was wearing helmets with long, sharp spikes on the top, while their counterparts from Veygus had long, curved horns emerging from either side of their helmets giving them an animalistic appearance. Even more noticeable, all the players were big. Bigger than any Jahk I had encountered to date. Easily as big as Chumly, but brawnier with necks so short their heads seemed to emerge directly from their shoulders.

As I said earlier, I count real good up to five, and there were considerably more than five players on each team.

XXIII.

"Life is full of little surprises."
PANDORA

AS I WAS prone to do in times of crises, I turned to my mentor for guidance. Aahz, in turn, reacted with the calm levelheadedness I've grown to expect.

Seizing the Ta-hoe spokesman by the front of his tunic, Aahz hoisted him up until his feet were dangling free from the ground. "What is this!!" he demanded.

"glaah...Sakle..." the fellow responded.

"Um...Aahz?" I intervened. "He might be a little more coherent if he could breathe."

"Oh! Right," my mentor acknowledged, lowering the spokesman until he was standing once more. "All right. Explain!"

"Ex...explain what?" Greybeard stammered, genuinely puzzled. "Those are the teams from our respective cities. You can tell them apart by their helmets and..."

"Don't give me that!" Aahz thundered. "Those aren't Jahks. Jahks are skinny or overweight!"

"Oh! I see," the spokesman said with dawning realization. "I'm afraid you've been mislead. Not all Jahks are alike. Some are fans, and some are players—athletes. The fans are...a little out of shape, but that's to be expected. They're the workers who keep the cities and farms running. The players are a different story. All they do is train and so on. Over the generations, they've gotten noticeably larger than the general population of fans."

"Generally larger?" Aahz scowled, glaring down the field.

"It's like they're another species!"

"I've seen it happen in other dimension," Gus observed, "but never to this extent."

"Well, Big Julie warned us about over-confidence," Chumly sighed.

"What was that?" Greybeard blinked.

"Want fight," Chumly declared, dropping back into character. "Crunch likes fight."

"Oh," the spokesman frowned. "Very well. If there's nothing else, I'll just…"

"Not so fast," I interrupted. "I want to know why there are so many players. The game is played by five-man teams, isn't it?"

"That's right," Greybeard nodded. "The extra players are replacements…you know, for the ones who are injured or killed during the game."

"Killed?" I swallowed.

"As I said," the spokesman called, starting off, "I admire your confidence in only bringing five players."

"Killed?" I repeated, turning desperately to Aahz.

"Don't panic, kid," my mentor growled, scanning the opposition. "It's a minor setback, but we can adapt our strategies."

"How about the old 'divide and conquer' gambit," Badaxe suggested, joining Aahz.

"That's right," Gus nodded. "They're not used to playing a three-way game. Maybe we can play them off against each other."

"It won't work," I declared flatly.

"Don't be so negative, kid," Aahz snapped. "Sometimes old tricks are the best."

"It won't work because they won't be playing against each other…just us."

I quickly filled them in on what Griffin had told me earlier. When I finished , the team was uncomfortably silent.

"Well," Aahz said at last, "things could be worse."

"How?" I asked bluntly.

"Gleep?"

My dragon had just spotted something the rest of us had missed. The other teams were bringing their riding beasts onto the field. Unlike the players, the beasts weren't marked with the team colors …but then, it wasn't necessary. There was no way they could be confused with each other.

The Veygus beast was a cat-like creature with an evilly flattened head—nearly as long as Gleep, it slank along the ground with a fluid grace which was ruined only by the uneven gait of its oversized hindlegs. Though its movements were currently slow and lazy, it had the look of something that could move with blinding speed when it wanted to. It also looked very, very agile, I was sure the thing could corner like…well, like a cat.

The Ta-hoe mount was equally distinctive, but much more difficult to describe. It looked like a small, armored mound with its crest about eight feet off the ground. I would have thought it was an over-sized insect, but it had more than six legs. As a matter of fact, it had hundreds of legs which we could see when it moved, which it seemed to do with equal ease in any direction. When it stopped, its armor settled to the ground, both hiding and guarding its tiny legs. I couldn't figure out where its eyes were, but I noticed it never ran into anything…at least accidentally.

"Gleep?"

My pet had pivoted his head around to peer at me. If he was hoping for an explanation or instructions, he was out of luck. I didn't have the vaguest idea of how to deal with the weird creatures. Instead, I stroked his mustache in what I hoped was a reassuring fashion. Though I didn't want to admit it to my teammates, I was becoming less and less confident about this game…and I hadn't been all that confident to begin with.

"Don't look now," Gus murmured, "but I've spotted Tananda."

"Where?" Chumly demanded, craning his neck to see where the gargoyle was pointing.

Of course, I had seen Tananda earlier and had forgotten to point her out to the others. I felt a little foolish, but then, that was nothing new. To cover my embarrassment, I joined the others in staring towards Tananda's floating form.

Quigley noticed us looking his way and began to fidget nervously. Apparently he was not confident enough in his newfound powers to feel truly comfortable under our mass scrutiny. His discomfort affected his magik…at least his levi-tation. Tananda's body dipped and swayed until I was afraid he was going to drop her on her head.

"If that magician's all that's in our way," Gus observed, "it occurs to me we would just sashay over there and take her back."

"Can't," Aahz snapped, shaking his head. "The kid here promised we wouldn't do anything to make that magician look bad."

"That's fine for you two," the gargoyle countered, "but Chumly and I didn't promise a thing."

"I say, Gus," Chumly interrupted, "we can't go against Skeeve's promise. It wouldn't be cricket."

"I suppose you're right," Gus grumbled. "I just thought it would be easier than getting our brains beaten out playing this silly game."

I agreed with him there. In fact, I was glad to find something I could agree with. Chumly's argument about crickets didn't make any sense at all.

"It occurs to me, Lord Magician," Badaxe rumbled, "that the promise you made wasn't the wisest of pledges."

"Izzat so?" Aahz snarled, turning on him. "Of course, General, you speak from long experience in dealing with demons."

"Well…actually…"

"Then I'd suggest you keep your lip buttoned about Lord Skeeve's wisdom and abilities. Remember, he's your ticket back out of here. Without him, it's a long walk home." Chastised, the General retreated, physically and verbally.

"Gee, thanks Aahz."

"Shut up, kid," my mentor snarled. "He's right. It was a dumb move."

"But you said…"

"Call it reflex," Aahz waved. "A body's got to earn the right to criticize my apprentice…and that speciman of Kladish military expertise doesn't qualify."

"Well…Thanks anyway," I finished lamely.

"Don't mention it."

"Hey, Aahz," Chumly called. "Let's get this…Trophy out of the center of the field and put it somewhere safe."

"Like where?" my mentor retorted, "we're the only ones in the stadium I trust."

"How about in our goal?" Gus suggested, pointing to the wide net at our corner of the triangle.

"Sounds good," Aahz agreed. "I'll be back in a second, kid."

I had gotten so used to the bedlam in the stadium that I barely noticed it. As my teammates started to move the Trophy, however, the chorus of boos and catcalls that erupted threatened to deafen me. My colleagues responded with proper aplomb, shaking fists and making faces at their decriers. The crowd loved it. If they loved it anymore, they'd charge down onto the field and lynch the lot of us.

I was about to suggest to my comrades that they quit baiting the crowd, when General Badaxe beckoned me over for a conference.

"Lord Magician," he began carefully, "I hope you realize I meant no offense with my earlier comments. I find that I'm a trifle on edge. I've never fought a war in front of an audience before."

"Forget it, Hugh," I waved. "You were right. In hindsight it was a bad promise. Incidentally…it's Skeeve. If we're in this mess together, it's a little silly to stand on formality."

"Thank you…Skeeve," the General nodded. "Actually I was hoping I could speak with you privately on a personal matter."

"Sure," I shrugged. "What is it?"

"Could you tell me a little more about that marvelous creature I was just introduced to earlier?"

"Marvelous creature?" I blinked. "What marvelous creature?"

"You know…Massha."

"Massha?" I laughed. Then I noticed the General's features were hardening. "I mean, oh that marvelous creature. What do you want to know?"

"Is she married?"

"Massha? I mean…no, I don't think so."

The General heaved a sigh of relief. "Is there a chance she'll ever visit us in Possletum?"

"I doubt it," I replied. "But if you'd like I could ask her."

"Fine," the General beamed, bringing a hand down on my shoulder in a bone-jarring display of friendship. "I'll consider that a promise."

"A what?" I blinked. Somehow the words had a familiar ring to it.

"I know how you honor your promises," Badaxe continued. "Fulfill this pledge, and you'll find I can be a friend to prize…just as I can be an enemy to be feared if crossed. Do we understand each other?"

"But I…

"Hey, kid," Aahz shouted. "Hurry up and get on that stupid dragon! The game's about to start!"

I had been so engrossed in my conversation with Badaxe I had completely lost track of the other activities on the field.

The team from Ta-hoe and Veygus had retired to the sidelines, leaving five players apiece on the field. The Cat and The Bug each had riders now, and were pacing and scuttling back and forth in nervous anticipation.

At midfield, where the Trophy had been, a Jahk stood wearing a black and white striped tunic and holding a ball. I use the phrase 'ball' rather loosely here. The object he was holding was a cube of what appeared to be black, spongy substance. A square ball! One more little detail the Geek had neglected to mention.

Without bothering to take my leave from the General, I turned and sprinted for Gleep. Whatever was about to happen, I sure didn't want to face it afoot.

XXIV.

"This contest has to be the dumbest thing I've ever seen."
H. COSSELL

I WAS BARELY astride Gleep when the Jahk at midfield set the 'ball' down and started backing toward the sidelines. "Hey Aahz!" I called. "What's with the guy in the striped tunic?"

"Leave him alone," my mentor shouted back. "He's a neutral." Actually, I hadn't planned on attacking him, but it was nice to know he wasn't part of the opposition.

I was the last of the team to get into place. Aahz and Chumly were bracketting me as the Fangs, Gus was behind me, waiting to take advantage of his extra mobility as Guard; and Badaxe was braced in the mouth of the goal as Castle. We seemed about as ready as we would ever be.

"Hey, kid!" Aahz called. "Where's your club?"

I was so engrossed in my own thoughts it took a minute for his words to sink in. Then I panicked. For a flash moment I thought I had left my staff back in Klah. Then I spotted it lying in the grass at our entry point. A flick of my mind brought it winging to hand.

"Got it, Aahz!" I waved.

"Well, hang onto it, and remember…"

A shrill whistle blast interrupted our not-so-private confer-ence and pulled our attention down-field. The Cat and the Bug were heading for the ball at their respective top speeds, with the rest of their teammates charging alone in their wakes.

The game was on, and all we were doing was standing around with our mouths open.

As usual, Aahz was the first to recover.

"Don't just stand there with your mouth open!" he shouted. "Go get the ball."

"But I…"

"GLEEP!"

What I had intended to point out to Aahz was that the Cat was almost at the ball already. Realizing there was no way I could get there first, I felt we should drop back and tighten our defense. My pet, however, had other ideas.

Whether he was responding to Aahz's command to "get the ball" (which was unlikely), or simply eager to meet some new play-mates (which was highly probable), the result was the same. He bounded forward, cutting me off in mid-sentence and setting us on a collision course with the Cat.

The crowd loved it.

Me, I was far less enthusiastic. The Cat's rider had the ball now, but he and his mount were holding position at midfield instead of immediately advancing on our goal. Presumably this was to allow his teammates to catch up, so he could have some cover. This meant he wouldn't have to venture among us alone.

That struck me as being a very intelligent strategy. I only wished I could follow it myself. Gleep's enthusiasm was placing me in the position I had hoped to avoid at all costs—facing the united strength of both of the opposing teams without a single teammate to sup-port me. For the first time since our opponents had taken the field, I stopped worrying about surviving until the end of the game. Now I was worried about surviving until the end of the first play!

My hopes improved for a moment when I realized we would reach the Cat and its rider well ahead of their teammates. The feeling of hope faded rapidly, however, as my rival uncoiled his weapon.

Where I was carrying a staff, he had a whip...a long whip. The thing was twenty feet long if it was an inch. No, I'm not exaggerat-ing. I could see its length quite clearly as the rider let it snake out toward my head.

The lash fell short by a good foot, though it seemed much closer at the time. Its sharp crack did produce one result, however. Gleep stopped in his tracks, throwing me forward on his neck as I fought to keep my balance. An instant behind the whip attack, the Cat bounded forward, its teeth bared and ears flat against its skull, and one of its forepaws darted out to swat my dragon on the nose.

Though never noted for his agility, Gleep responded by trying to jump backwards and swap ends at the same time. I'm not sure how successful he was, because somewhere in the middle of the maneuver, he and I parted company.

Normally such a move would not have unsettled me. When Gleep had thrown me in practice, I had simply flown clear, delicately settled to the ground at a distance. This time, however, I was already off balance and the throw disoriented me completely. Realizing I was airborne, I attempted to fly...and succeeded in slamming into the turf with the grace of a bag of garbage. This did nothing toward improving my disorientation.

Lying there, I wondered calmly which parts of me would fall off if I moved. There was a distant roaring in my ears, and the ground seemed to be trembling beneath me. From far away, I could hear Aahz shouting something. Yes, just lying here seemed like an excellent idea.

"...up, kid!" came my mentor's voice. "Run!"

Run? He had to be kidding. My head was clearing slowly, but the ground was still shaking. Rolling over, I propped one eye open to get my bearings, and immediately wished I hadn't.

It wasn't in my head! The ground really was shaking! The Bug was bearing down on me full tilt, displaying every intention of trampling me beneath its multiple tiny feet. It didn't even occur to me that this would be a ridiculous way to go. All that registered was that it was a way to go, and somehow that thought didn't appeal to me.

I sprang to my feet and promptly fell down again. Apparently I hadn't recovered from my fall as much as I thought I had. I tried again and got as far as my hands and knees. From there I had a terrific view of my doom thundering down on me, and there was nothing I could do about it!

Then Aahz was there. He must have jumped over me in midstride to get into position, but he was there, half-way between the charging Bug and me. Feet spread and braced, knees bent to a crouch, he faced the charge unflinching. Unflinching? He threw his arms wide and bared his teeth in challenge.

You want to fight?" he roared. "Try me."

The Bug may not have understood his words, but it knew enough about body language to realize it was in trouble. Few beasts or beings in any dimension have the courage or stupidity to try to face down a Pervect when it has a full mad on, and Aahz was mad. His scales were puffed out until he appeared twice his normal breadth, and they rippled dangerously from the tensed muscles underneath. Even his color was a darker shade of green than normal, pulsing angrily as my mentor vented his emotions.

Whatever intelligence level the Bug might possess, it was no fool. It somehow managed to slow from a full charge to a dead stop before coming within Aahz's reach. Even the frantic goadings from its rider's hooked prod couldn't get it to resume its charge. Instead, it began to cautiously edge sideways, trying to bypass Aahz completely.

"You want to fight?" my mentor bellowed, advancing toward the beast. "Com'on! I'm ready."

That did it! The Bug put it into reverse, skuttling desperately backward despite the frantic urgings of its rider and the hoots from the crowd.

"I say, you lads seem to have things in hand here."

A powerful hand fastened on my shoulder and lifted. In fact, it lifted me until my feet were dangling free from the ground. "Um...I can walk now, Chumly," I suggested.

"Oh, terribly sorry," the troll apologized, setting me gently on the ground. "Just a wee bit distracted is all."

"Gleep!"

A familiar head snaked into view from around Chumly's hip to peer at me quizzically.

"You were a big help!" I snarled, glad for the chance to vent my pent-up nervous energy.

"Gleep," my pet responded, hanging his head.

"Here, now," the troll chided. "Don't take it out on your mate, here. He got surprised, that's all. Can't blame him for getting a little spooked under fire. What?"

"But if he hadn't..." I began.

"Now are you ready to get rid of that stupid dragon?" Aahz demanded, joining our group.

"Don't take it out on Gleep," I flared back. "He just got a little fired is all."

"How's that again?" my mentor blinked.

"Gleep!" proclaimed my pet, unleashing his tongue on one of his aromatic, slimy licks. This time, to my relief Aahz was the recipient.

"Glaah!" my mentor exclaimed, scrubbing at his face with the back of his hand. "I may be violently sick!"

"The Beast's just showing his appreciation for your saving his master," Chumly laughed.

"That's right," I agreed. "If you hadn't…"

"Forget it," Aahz waved. "No refugee from a wine-making festival's going to do his dance on my apprentice while I'm around."

For once, I knew what he was talking about. "'Refugee from a wine-making festival' that's pretty good, Aahz," I grinned.

"No it wasn't," my mentor snarled. "In fact, so far this afternoon, nothing's been good. Why are we standing around talking?"

"Because the first play's over," Chumly supplied. "Also, I might add, the first score."

We all looked down field toward our goal. The field was littered with bodies, fortunately theirs, not ours. Whatever had happened, we had given a good accounting of ourselves. Stretcher bearers and trainers were tending to the fallen and wounded with well practiced efficiency. The players still on their feet, both on the field and on the sidelines, were dancing around hugging each other and holding their index fingers aloft in what I supposed was some sort of religious gesture to the gods. Badaxe was sagging weakly against one of our four goalposts while Gus fanned him with his wings.

"The score," the troll continued casually, "is nothing to nothing to one…against us. Not the best of starts, what?"

For one instant I thought we had scored. Then I remembered that in this game, points are scored against a team. Therefore "nothing to nothing to one" meant we were behind by a point.

"Don't worry," Aahz snarled. "We'll get the point back, with interest! If they want to play rough, so can we. Right?"

"Quite right," Chumly grinned.

"Ummm…" I supplied hesitantly.

"So let's fire up!" my mentor continued. "Chumly, get Gus and Badaxe up her for a strategy session. Kid, get back on that dragon—and this time try to stay up there, huh?"

I started to obey, then turned back to him. "Ummm…Aahz?"

"Yea, kid?"

"I didn't say it too well a minute ago, but thanks for saving me."

"I said forget it."

"No, I won't," I insisted defiantly. "You could have been killed bailing me out, and I just wanted you to know that I'll pay you back someday. I may not be very brave where I'm concerned, but I owe you my life on top of everything else and it's yours anytime you need it."

"Wait a minute, kid," my mentor corrected. "Any risks I take are mine, understand? That includes the ones I take pulling your tail out of the fire once in a while. Don't mess up my style by making me responsible for two lives."

"But Aahz..."

"If I'm in trouble and you're clear, you skedadle. Got it? Especially in this game. In fact, here..."

He fumbled in his belt pouch and produced a familiar object.

"Here's the D-Hopeer. It's set to get you home. You keep it and use it if you have to. If you see a chance to grab Tananda and get out of here, take it! Don't worry about me."

"But..."

"That's an order, apprentice. If you want to argue it, wait until we're back to Klah. In the meantime, just do it! Either you agree or I'll send you home right now."

Our eyes locked for long moments, but I gave ground first. "All right, Aahz," I sighed. "But we're going to have this out once we get home."

"Fine," he grinned, clapping me on the shoulder. "For now though, get on that stupid dragon of yours and try to keep him pointed in the right direction. We've got some points to score!"

XXV.

"If you can't win fair: just win!"
U. S. Grant

WE NEEDED TO score some points, and to do that, we needed the ball.

That thought was foremost in my mind as we lined up again. One way or another, we were going to get that ball.

When the whistle sounded, I was ready for it. Reaching out with my mind, I brought the ball winging to my grasp. Before our team could form up around me, however, the whistle sounded again and the Jahk in the striped tunic came trotting toward us waving his arms.

"Now what?" Aahz growled. Then aloud, he called, "What's wrong, Ref?"

"There's been a protest," the referee informed him. "Your opponents say you're using magik."

"So what?" my mentor countered. "There's no rule against it."

"Well, not officially," the ref admitted, "but it's been a gentleman's agreement for some time."

"We're not gentlemen," Aahz grinned. "So get out of our way and let us play."

"But if you can use magik, so can your opponents," the striped tunic insisted.

"Let 'em," Aahz snarled. "Start the game."

A flash of inspiration came to me. "Wait a minute, Aahz," I called. "Sir, we're willing to allow the use of magik against us *if,* and only if, the magicians do it from the field."

"What?" the ref blinked.

"You heard him," Aahz crowed. "If your magicians join the team and take their lumps like our magician does, then they're free to use whatever skills and abilities they bring onto the field with them. Otherwise they can sit in the bleachers with the spectators and keep their magik out of it."

"That seems fair," the Jahk nodded thoughtfully. "I'll so inform the other teams."

"I say," Chumly commented as the referee trotted off. "That was a spot of clear thinking."

"Tactically superb," Badaxe nodded.

"That's the kind of generalmanship that beat Big Julie's army," Gus supplied proudly.

I waved modestly, but inside I was heady from the praise. "Let's save the congratulations until after the game, shall we?" Aahz suggested icily.

It was an annoyingly accurate observation. There was still a long battle between us and the end of the game, and the other teams were already lining up to pit their best against our clumsy efforts. In grim silence, we settled down to go to work.

I won't attempt to chronicle the afternoon play by play. Much of it I'm trying to forget, though sometimes I still bolt upright out of a sound sleep sweating at the memory. The Jahks were tough and they knew their business. The only thing holding them at bay was the sheer strength and ferocity of my teammates and some inspired magik by yours truly.

However, a few incidents occurred prior to the game's climax which would be criminal neglect to omit from my account.

Gleep came of age that afternoon. I don't know what normally matures dragons, but for my pet adulthood arrived with the first play of the afternoon. Gone was the playfulness which lead to my early unseating. Somewhere in that puzzling brain of his, Gleep thought things over and arrived at the conclusion that we had some serious business on our hands.

I, of course, didn't know this. When the ball ended up in my hands, I was counting on my other teammates for protection. Unfortunately, our opponents had anticipated this and planned accordingly. Three players each swarmed over Aahz and Chumly, soaking up incredible punishment to keep them from coming to my support. The two Riders converged on me.

I saw them coming and panicked. I mean, the Cat was faster than us and the Bug seemed invulnerable. Frantically, I looked around for some avenue of escape. I needn't have worried.

Instead of bolting, Gleep stood his ground, his head lowered menacingly. As the Cat readied itself for a pounce, my pet loosed a jet of fire full in its face, singeing its whiskers and setting it back on its haunches.

I was so astonished I forgot to watch the Bug moving up on our flank. Gleep didn't. His tail lashed out to intercept the armored menace. There was a sound like a great church bell gonging, and the Bug halted its forward progress and began wandering aimlessly in circles.

"Atta boy, Gleep!" I cheered, balancing the ball on his back for a moment so I could thump his side.

That was a mistake. No sooner had I released the hold on the ball when one of the Jahks leaped high to pluck it from its resting spot. I took a wipe at him with my staff but he dodged to one side and I missed. Unfortunately for him, the dodge brought him within Chumly's reach.

The Troll snaked out one of his long arms over the shoulder of a blocker, picked up the ball carrier by his head, and slammed him violently to the ground.

"Big Crunch catch," he called, winking at me.

The ball carrier lay still, and the stretcher team trotted onto the field again. The lineup of players on the sideline had decreased noticeably since the game started. In case you haven't noticed, things were pretty rough on the field.

"Tell me I didn't see that," Aahz demanded, staggering to my side.

"Um..: Chumly's tackle or Gleep stopping the two Riders?" I asked innocently.

"I'm talking about your giving the ball away," my mentor corrected harshly. "Now that the dragon's coming through for us, you start..."

"Do you really think he's doing a good job?" I interrupted eagerly. "I always said Gleep had a lot of potential."

"Don't change the subject," Aahz growled. "You..."

"Com'on, you two," Gus called. "There's a game on."

"Got to go," I waved, guiding my pet away from my sputtering mentor. "We'll talk after the game."

Our defense finally solidified, and we meted out terrible punishment to any Jahk foolish enough to head for our goal with the ball in his arms. We even managed to score some points, though it took a little help from my magik to do it.

The first point we scored was against the Veygans. It was a variation of Aahz's original "divide and conquer" plan. The Veygans had the ball and were bringing it down-field when we plowed into them at midfield. As per my instructions, I waited until the brawl was getting heated, then used a disguise spell on Gus, altering his appearance so he looked like one of the Ta-hoe players, complete with a spiked helmet. Having been forewarned, the change didn't startle him at all. Instead, he started dancing around, waving his arms wildly.

"Here!" he shouted. "I'm open! Over here!"

The ball carrier was zig-zagging desperately with Aahz in hot pursuit. He saw an ally in a position to score and lobbed the ball to him without breaking stride. Gus gathered the ball in and started for the Veygus goal.

"Double-cross!"

The first shout was from Chumly, but the Veygus players quickly picked it up. Spurred by indignation, they turned on the Ta-hoe players who a moment ago had been their allies. The Ta-hoers were understandably surprised, but reacted quickly, defending themselves while at the same time laying down a blocking pattern for Gus.

The Veygan Castle had been up-field when the play broke, but the goal-tender braced himself as Gus swept down on him. The only pursuit close enough to count was Chumly, who appeared intent on hauling down the ball carrier from behind. At the crucial moment, however, he charged past the gargoyle and piled into the goal tender. Gus scored untouched.

"That's zero to one to one now!" I crowed.

"Before you get too caught up in celebrating," Aahz advised, "you'd better do something about that!"

I followed his finger and realized that fights were breaking out throughout the stands. It seemed the fans didn't like the double-cross any more than the players had.

To avert major bloodshed, I removed Gus's disguise as he came back up the field. Within seconds, the fans and the opposing teams realized they had been had. Hostilities between the rival factions ceased immediately. Instead, they focused their emotions on us. Terrific.

The uniform change bit had been effective, but with the new attentiveness in the opposition, I was pretty sure it wouldn't work twice.

I'm particularly proud of our second goal, in that it was my idea from start to finish. I thought it up and executed it without the help or consultation of my teammates. Of course, that in itself caused some problems...but I'm getting ahead of myself.

The idea occurred to me shortly after my staff broke. I was swinging at the ball when one of the Ta-hoe players somehow got his head in the way. He was sidelined, but I was left with two pieces of what used to be a pretty good club. As we waited for play to resume, I found myself marveling anew at the sheer size of our opponents and wishing we had bigger players on our side. It occurred to me, too late of course, that I could have used disguise spells to make our team seem bigger when we first appeared. Now our rivals already knew how big, or to be specific, how small we were, so that trick wouldn't work.

I was starting to berate myself for this oversight,when the idea struck. If a disguise spell could make us look bigger, it could also make us look smaller. It was almost a good idea, but not quite. If one or all of us "disappeared" our opponents would notice immediately. What we needed was a decoy.

I found myself considering the two pieces of broken staff I was holding. There was a stunt I pulled once when we were fighting Big Julie. Then it had been a desperation gambit. Of course, we weren't exactly cruising along now.

"Get the ball to me!" I called to my teammates. "I've got an idea."

"What kind of an idea?" Aahz asked.

"Just get me the ball." I snapped back.

I didn't mean to be short with him, but if this plan was going to work, I needed all my concentration, and Aahz's banter wasn't helping.

Closing my eyes, I began to draw and focus power. At the same time, I began forming the required images in my mind.

"Head's up, kid!" Aahz shouted with sudden urgency.

My eyes popped open...and the ball was there. I wasn't quite as ready as I would have liked to have been but the time was now and I had to go for it.

I'll detail what happened next so you can appreciate the enormity of my accomplishment. In live time, it took no longer than an eyeblink to perform.

Dropping the two halves of the staff, I caught the ball with my hands. Then, I cast two spells simultaneously. (Four, actually but I don't like to brag.)

For the first, I shrank the images of Gleep and myself until we were scant inches high. Second, I changed the appearance of the two staff halves until what was seen was full sized reproductions of me astride my pet.

Once that was accomplished, I used my remaining energy to fly us toward the Ta-hoe goal. That's right, I said 'fly.'" Even in our diminutive form, I wanted us well above the eye-level of our opponents.

Flying both Gleep and myself took a lot of effort. So much, in fact, that I was unable to animate the images we left behind. I had realized this before I started, but figured that suddenly stationary targets would only serve as a diversion for our real attack.

It seemed to work. We were unopposed until we reached the Ta-hoe goal. Then my mischievous sense of humor got the better of me. Landing a scant arm's length from the goalie, I let our disguises drop.

"Boo!" I shouted.

To the startled player, it appeared that we suddenly popped out of thin air. A life time of training fell away from him in a second, and he fainted dead away.

With a properly dramatic flourish, I tossed the ball into the goal.

One to one to one! A tie game!

The team was strangely quiet when Gleep and I triumphant-ly returned to our end of the field.

"Why the long faces?" I laughed. "We've got 'em on the run now!"

"You should have told us you had a gambit going," Gus said carefully.

"There wasn't time," I explained. "Besides, there's no harm done."

"That's not entirely accurate," Chumly corrected, pointing up field.

There was a pile of Jahks where I had left the staff pieces. The stretcher teams were busy untangling the bodies and carting them away.

"He was trying to protect you…or what he thought was you," Badaxe observed acidly.

"What." Then I saw what they were talking about. At the bottom of the pile was Aahz. He wasn't moving.

XXVI.

"Winning isn't the most important thing; it's the only thing."
                                        J. CAESAR

"HE'LL BE ALL right," Gus declared, looking up from examining our fallen teammate. "He's just out cold."

We were gathered around Aahz's still form, anxiously awaiting the gargoyle's diagnosis. Needless to say, I was relieved my mentor was not seriously injured. General Badaxe, however, was not so easily satisfied.

"Well, wake him up!" he demanded. "And be quick about it."

"Back off, General," I snarled, irritated by his insensitivity.

"Can't you see he's hurt?"

"You don't understand," Badaxe countered, shaking his head. "We need five players to continue the game. If Aahz doesn't snap out of it..."

"Wake up, Aahz!" I shouted, reaching out a hand to shake his arm.

It was bad enough that my independent scoring drive had resulted in Aahz getting roughed up. If it cost us the game..."Save it, Skeeve," Gus sighed. "Even if he woke up, he wouldn't be able to play. That was a pretty nasty pounding he took. I mean, I don't think there's anything seriously wrong with him, but if he tried to mix it up with anyone in his current condition..."

"I get the picture," I interrupted. "And if we wake him up, Aahz is just stubborn enough to want to play."

"Right," the gargoyle nodded. "You'll just have to think of something else."

I tried, I really did. The team kept fussing over Aahz to stall for time, but nothing came to me in the way of a plan. Finally the referee trotted over to our huddle.

"How's your player?" he asked.

"Ah...just catching his breath," Badaxe smiled, trying to keep his body between the official and Aahz.

"Don't give me that," the stripe-tuniced Jahk scowled. "I can see. He's out cold, isn't he?"

"Well, sort of," Gus admitted.

"'Sort of nothing," the ref scowled. "If he can't play and you don't have a replacement, you'll have to forfeit the game."

"We're willing to play with a partial team," the gargoyle suggested hastily.

"The rules state you must have five players on the field. No more, no less," the official declared, shaking his head.

"All right," Badaxe nodded. "Then we'll keep him on the field with us. We'll put him off to one side where he won't get hurt and then we'll play with a four-man team."

"Sorry," the ref apologized, "but I can't let him stay on the field in that condition. It's a rough game, but we do have some ethics when it comes to the safety of the players."

"Especially when you can use the rules to force us out of the game," Gus spat.

I thought the slur would draw an angry response from the official, but instead the ref only shook his head sadly.

"You don't understand," he insisted. "I don't want to dis-qualify your team. You've been playing a hard game and you deserve a chance to finish it. I hate to see the game stopped with a forfeit... especially when the score's tied. Still, the rules are the rules, and if you can't field a full team, that's that. I only wished you had brought some replacements."

"We've got a replacement!" I exploded suddenly.

"We do?" Gus blinked.

"Where?" frowned the ref.

"Right there!" I announced, pointing to the stands.

Tananda was still floating in plain sight in front of Quigley. "The captive demon?" the official gasped.

"What do you think we are? Muppets?" Gus snarled, recovering smoothly.

"Muppets? What...I don't think..." the ref stammered. "You don't have to," I smiled. "Just summon the Ta-hoe magician and I'm sure we can work something out."

"But...Oh, very well."

The official trotted off toward the stands while the rest of the team crowded around me.

"You're going to have a woman on the team?" Badaxe demanded.

"Let me explain," I waved. "First of all, Tananda isn't..."

"She's not actually a woman," Chumly supplied. "She's my sister. And when it comes to the old rough and tumble, she can beat me four out of five times."

"She isn't? I mean, she is?" Badaxe struggled. "I mean, she can?"

"You bet your sweet axe she can," Gus grinned.

"Gleep," said the dragon, determined to get his two cents worth in.

"If you're all quite through," I said testily. "I'd like to finish. What I was about to say was that Tananda isn't going to play." There was a moment of stunned silence as the team absorbed this.

"I don't get it," Gus said at last. "If she isn't going to play, then what…"

"Once she's here and revived, we're going to grab her and the Trophy and head back for Klah," I announced. "The ref's about to hand us the grand prize on a silver platter."

"But what about the game?" Badaxe scowled.

I closed my eyes, realizing for a moment how Aahz must feel when he has to deal with me.

"Let me explain this slowly," I said carefully. "The reason we're in this game is to rescue Tananda and grab the Trophy. In a few minutes we're going to have them both, so there'll be no reason for us to keep getting our heads beaten in. Understand?"

"I still don't like quitting the field before the end of a battle," the General grumbled.

"For crying out loud!" I exploded, "This is a game, not a war!"

"Are we talking about the same field?" Chumly asked innocently.

Fortunately, I was spared having to formulate an answer to that one as Quigley chose that moment to arrive, Tananda floating in his wake.

"What's this the ref says about using Tananda in the game?" he demanded.

"That's right," I lied. "We need her to finish the game. Now if you'll be so good as to wake her up, we'll just…"

"But she's my hostage," the magician protested.

"Com'on, Quigley," I argued. "We aren't taking her anyplace. She'll be right here on the field in full sight of you and everybody else."

"And you can all skip off to another dimension any time you want," Quigley pointed out. "No deal."

That was uncomfortably close to the truth, but if there's one thing I've learned from Aahz, it's how to bluff with a straight face.

"Now look Quigley," I snarled. "I'm trying to be fair about this, but it occurs to me you're taking advantage of my promise."

"Of course," the magician nodded. "But tell you what. Just to show you I'm a sport, I'll let you have Tananda."

"Swell," I grinned.

"If…and I repeat, if you let me keep Aahz in exchange."

"What?" I exclaimed. "I mean, sure. Go ahead. He's already out cold."

"Very well," he nodded. "This will just take a few seconds."

"What does this do to our plans?" Gus asked, drawing me aside.

"Nothing," I informed him through gritted teeth. "We go as soon as it's clear."

"What?" the gargoyle gaped. "What about Aahz?"

"It's his orders," I snarled. "Before the game started he made me promise that if he got in trouble I wouldn't endanger myself or the team trying to save him."

"And you're going to skip out on him?" Gus sneered. "After all he's done for you?"

"Now don't you start on me, Gus!" I grimaced. "I don't want to…"

"Hi, handsome," Tananda chirped, joining our discussion. "If it isn't too much trouble, could someone fill me in as to why this august assemblage has assembled, why we're standing in the middle of a pasture, and what all these people are doing staring at us? And where's Quigley going with Aahz?"

"There's no time," I declared. "We've got to get going."

"Get going where?" she frowned.

"Back to Klah," Gus grumbled. "Skeeve here is in the middle of abandoning Aahz."

"He's what?" Tananda gasped.

"Gus…" I warned.

"Save it, handsome. I'm not budging until someone tells me what's going on, so you might as well start now."

It took surprisingly little time to bring her up to date once I got started. I deliberately omitted as many details as possible to keep from getting Tananda riled. I had enough problems on my hands without fighting her, too! It seemed to work, as she listened patiently without comment or frown.

"and so that's why we've got to get out of here before play resumes," I finished.

"Bull feathers," she said firmly.

"I'm glad you...how's that again?" I sputtered.

"I said 'Bull feathers,'" she repeated. "You guys have been knocked around, trampled, and otherwise beaten on for my sake and now we're going to run? Not me! I say we stay right here and teach these Bozos a lesson."

"But..."

"I don't know if your D-Hopper can move the whole team," she continued, "but I'll bet it can't do the job if we aren't cooperating."

"That's telling him," Gus chortled.

"...so retreat is out. Now, if you're afraid of getting hurt, just stay out of our way. We aren't leaving until we finish what you and Aahz started."

"Well, said," Badaxe nodded.

"Count me in," the gargoyle supplied.

"You'll be the death of me yet, little sister," Chumly sighed.

I managed to get a grip on Gleep's nose before he could add his vote to the proceedings.

"Actually," I said slowly, "Aahz had always warned me about how dangerous it is to travel dimensions alone. And if I'm going to stay here, it occurs to me the safest place would be surrounded by my teammates."

"All right, Skeeve!" Gus grinned, clapping me on the back. "Then it's decided," Tananda nodded. "Now then, handsome, what's the plan."

Somehow, I had known she was going to say that.

"Give me a minute," I pleaded. "A second ago the plan was to just split, remember? These plans don't just grow on trees, you know."

I plunged into thought, considering and discarding ideas as they came to me. That didn't take long. Not that many ideas were occurring to me. I found myself staring at Chumly. He was craning his neck to look at the stands.

"What are you doing?" I asked, irritated by his apparent lack of concern with our situation.

"Hmmm? Oh. Sorry, old boy," the troll apologized. "I was just curious as to how many Deveels were in the crowd. There's a lot of them."

"There are?" I blinked, scanning the crowd. "I don't see any."

"Oh, they're disguised, of course," Chumly shrugged. "But you can see their auras if you check. With the odds that were being given on this bloody game, it was a sure thing they'd be here."

He was right. I'd been so preoccupied with the game I had never bothered to check the stands. Now that I looked, I could see the auras of other demons scattered throughout the crowd.

"It's too bad we can't cancel their disguises," I muttered to myself.

"Oh, we could do that easy enough," the troll answered.

"We could?"

"Certainly. Deveels always use the cheapest, easiest disguises available. I know a spell that would restore their normal appearance quick enough."

"You do?" I pressed. "Could it cover the whole stadium?"

"Well, not for a terribly long time," Chumly said, "but it would hold for a minute or two. Why do you ask?"

"I think I've got an idea," I explained. "Be back in a minute."

"Where are you going?" the troll called after me as I started for the sidelines.

"To talk to Griffin," I retorted, not caring that the explanation didn't really explain anything.

XXVII.

"Ask not for whom the bell tolls—"
M. ALI

THE BALL CARRIER was somewhere under Gleep when the whistle blew. That wouldn't have been too bad, if it weren't for the fact that Chumly had already thrown the ball carrier to the ground and jumped on him prior to my pet joining in the fracas. *As* I said before, Gleep had really gotten into the spirit of things.

"I say," came an agonized call from the troll, "do you mind?"

"Sorry!" I apologized, backing the dragon onto more solid footing.

"Say, Skeeve," Gus murmured, sliding up beside me, "How much longer until we're set for the 'big play?'"

"Should be any minute now," I confided. "Why do you ask?"

"He's afraid of additional casualties you and that dragon will inflict on the team while we're stalling for time," Badaxe chimed in sarcastically.

"Gleep," my pet commented, licking the General's face.

"You might as well forget the 'hard guy' act, Hugh," the gargoyle observed. "The dragon's got you pegged as a softie."

"Is that so?" Badaxe argued, gasping a bit on Gleep's breath. "Well, allow me to point out that with the master plan about to go into effect, we don't have the ball!"

"Skeeve'll get it for us when we need it," Tananda protested, rising to my defense. "He always comes through when we need him. You've just never followed him into battle before."

"I believe I can testify," Chumly growled, limping back to join us, "that it's safer to be following him than in front of him."

"Sorry about that, Chumly," I winced. "It's just that Gleep…"

"I know, I know," the troll interrupted. " 'Spooked under fire'…remember, I gave you that excuse originally. He seems to have recovered admirably."

"I hate to interrupt," Gus interrupted. "But isn't that our signal?"

I followed his gaze to the sidelines. Griffin was there waving his arms wildly. When he saw he had my attention, he crossed the fingers on both hands, then crossed his forearms over his head. Thai was the signal.

"All right," I announced. "Fun time is over. The messages have been delivered. Does everyone remember what they're supposed to do?"

As one, the team nodded, eager grins plastered on their faces. I don't know what they were so cheerful about. If any phase of this plan didn't work, some or all of us would be goners.

"Tananda and Chumly make one team. Badaxe, you stick with Gus. He's your ticket home," I repeated needlessly.

"We know what to do," the General nodded.

"Then let's do it!" I shouted, and wheeled Gleep into position.

This time, as the ball came into play, we did not swarm toward the ball carrier. Instead, our entire team back-pedaled to cluster in the mouth of our goal.

Our opponents hesitated, looking at each other. We had emptied over three quarters of their reserve teaching them to respect our strength, and now that lesson was bearing fruit. No one seemed to want to be the one to carry the ball into our formation. They weren't sure what we were up to but they didn't want any part of it.

Finally, the ball carrier, a Ta-hoe player, turned and threw the ball to his Rider, apparently figuring the Bug had the best chance of breaking through to the goal. That's what I had been waiting for.

Reaching out with my mind, I brought the ball winging, not to me, but to Hugh Badaxe. In a smooth, fluid motion, the axe came off the General's belt and struck at the missile. I had never seen Hugh use his axe before, and I'll admit I was impressed. Weapon and ball met, and the weapon won. The ball fell to the ground in two halves as the axe returned to its resting place on the General's belt.

The crowd was on its feet, screaming incoherently. If they didn't like that, they didn't really get upset over our next move.

"Everybody, mount up!" I shouted.

On cue, Tananda jumped on Chumly's back and Badaxe did the same with Gus. I levitated half the ball to each twosome, then did a fast disguise spell.

What our opponents saw now was three images of me astride three images of Gleep. Each image of me had half a ball proudly in its possession.

The more mathematically oriented of you might realize that that adds up to three halves. Very good. Fortunately for us, Jahks aren't big on math. The question remains, however, of where did the third half come from?

You don't think I was standing by idly while all this was going on, do you? While my teammates were mounting up, I took advantage of the confusion to do one more levitation/disguise job. As a result, the Trophy was now resting in front of me on Gleep's back disguised as half a ball. It was the same stunt I had pulled in Veygus, but this time I draped my shirt over it.

"Chumly!" I called. "Start your spell!"

"Done!" he waved back.

"We meet back at Klah!" I shouted.

"Now go for it!"

My teammates started up opposite sidelines, heading for both our opponents' goals simultaneously. I waited a few beats for them to draw off the tacklers, then started for my objective. Gleep and I were going for Aahz.

With all due modesty, my plan worked brilliantly. The appearance of Deveels throughout the crowd sent the Jahks into a state of panic. The crossbowmen were too busy tryin' to get a shot of these new invaders to pay any attention to me. Well...most of them were. One or two bolts whisked past me, but they were poorly aimed. For some reason the beings shooting at me seemed a bit rattled.

I caught sight of Quigley, standing on his seat and waving his arms. Catchy phrases like "Begone foul spirits!" and "I vanquish thee!" were issuing from his lips as he did his routine.

This didn't surprise me. Not that I felt Quigley was particularly quick thinking in a crises. It had to do with the messages I had sent to both him and Massha before the play started.

The messages were simple:

STAND BY TO REPEL AN INVASION OF DEMONS! P.S. GO THROUGH THE MOTIONS. I'LL TAKE CARE OF THE DEMONS.

SKEEVE

I caught his eye and winked at him. In return, one of his "demon dispelling" waves got a little limp-wristed as he nodded slightly, bidding me adeiu. In the middle of saving his employers from an invasion of demons, who could blame him if a few departed who were supposed to stay put.

Aahz's unconscious body came wafting toward us in response to my mental summons. Gleep stretched out his long neck and caught my mentor's tunic in his mouth as he floated by.

It wasn't quite the way I planned it but I was in no position to be choosy. Tightening my legs around Gleep's middle, I hit the button on the D-Hopper, and...

The walls of my room were a welcome change from the hostile stadium.

"We did it!" I exclaimed, then was startled by the volume of my voice. After the din of the stadium, my room seemed incredibly quiet.

"Kid," came a familiar voice, "would you tell your stupid dragon to put me down before I die from his breath?"

"Gleep?" my pet asked, dropping my mentor in an undignified heap.

"Aahz?" I blinked. "I thought you were..."

"Out cold? Not hardly. Can you think of a better way to get Tananda out on the field? For a while there I was afraid you wouldn't figure it out and call for a replacement."

"You mean you were faking all along?" I demanded. "I was scared to death! You could have warned me, you know."

"Like you warned me about your vanishing act?" he shot back. "And what happened to my orders to head for home once Tananda was in the clear?"

"Your orders?" I stammered. "Well..."

There was a soft "BAMF" and Gus and Badaxe were in the room. Gus was holding the General cradled in his arms like a babe, but they both seemed in good spirits.

"Beautiful!" Hugh chortled, hugging the gargoyle around the neck. "If you ever need a back-up man..."

"If you ever need a partner." Gus corrected, hugging him back. "You and I could..."

"BAMF!"

Chumly and Tananda appeared sprawling on the bed. Both her nostrils were bleeding, but she was laughing uproariously. Chumly was panting for breath and wiping tears of hilarity from his big moon eyes.

"I say," he gasped. "That was a spot of fun. We haven't double-teamed anyone like that since the last family reunion, when Auntie Tizzie got Tiddley and…"

"What happened?" I bellowed.

"We won!" Gus cheered. "One and a half to one and a half to one! They never knew what hit 'em."

"It's one for the record book," Tananda agreed, dabbing at her nose.

"For the record book?" Gus challenged, "this game'll fill a book by itself."

"Aahz, old bean," Chumly called. "Do you have any wine about? The assemblage seems up for a celebration."

"I know where it is," Badaxe waved, starting for the barrels we had secreted under the work table.

"Hold it!!" Aahz roared. "Halt, stop, desist, and TIME OUT!!"

"I think he wants our attention," Tananda told the group.

"If you're all quite through," my mentor continued, shooting her a black look. "I have one question."

"What's that?" Tananda asked in her little girl voice.

"Quit bleeding on the bed," Aahz scowled. "It lacks class. What I want to know is, did any of you superstars think to pickup the Trophy? That was the objective of this whole fiasco, you know."

The team gestured grandly at me. With a grin, I let the disguise drop away from the Trophy.

"Ta-da!" I warbled. "Happy Birthday, Aahz."

"Happy Birthday!!" the team echoed.

Aahz looked at their grins, then at the Trophy, then at their grins again.

"All right," he sighed. "Break out the wine."

The roar of approval for this speech rivaled anything that had come from the stands that afternoon as the team descended on the wine barrels like a swarm of hungry humming mice.

"Well, Aahz," I grinned, levitating the Trophy to the floor and sliding from Gleep's back. "I guess that just about winds it up."

I was starting for the wine barrels when a heavy hand fell on my shoulder.

"There are *a few* loose ends to be tied up," my mentor drawled.

"Like what?" I asked fearfully.

"Like the invitation you gave Massha to drop by for a visit."

"Invitation?" I echoed in a small voice.

"Badaxe told me about it," Aahz grimaced. "Then there's a little matter of a quick trip to Deva."

"To Deva?" I blinked. "What for? I mean, swell, but…"

"I've got to pick up our winnings," my mentor informed me. "I took the time to place a few small bets on the game while we were there. Profits don't just happen, you know."

"When do we start," I asked eagerly.

"We don't," Aahz said firmly. "This time I'm going alone. There's something about you and the Bazaar that just don't mix well."

"But Aahz…"

"…And besides," he continued, grinning broadly, "there's one more loose end from this venture that will be occupying your time. One which only you can handle."

"Really?" I said proudly. "What's that?"

"Well," my mentor said, heading for the wine, "you can start thinking about how we're going to get that stupid dragon out of our room. He's too big to fit through the door or window."

"Gleep!" said my pet, licking my face.

Hit
or Myth

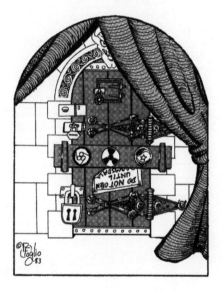

I.

"There's something to be said for relatives...it has to be said because it's
unprintable!"
A. EINSTEIN

PERHAPS IF I hadn't been so preoccupied with my own thoughts
when I walked into my quarters that day, I wouldn't have been caught
unawares. Still, who expects to get caught in a magical attack just
walking into their own room?

Okay, okay! So I am the Court Magician of Possiltum, and maybe
I have been getting a bit of a reputation lately. I still should be able to
walk into my own room without getting jumped! I mean, if a magician isn't safe in his own quarters, can he be safe anywhere?

Scratch that question!

It's the kind of thing my teacher says to convince me that choosing magic for a career path is not the best way to insure living out
one's normal life span. Of course, it doesn't take much convincing.
Actions speak louder than words, and the action since I signed on as
his apprentice has been loud enough to convince me that a magician's
life is not particularly quiet. I mean, when you realize that within days
of meeting him, we both got lynched by an angry mob...as in hung
by the neck...

But I digress.

We started out with me simply walking into my room. Yea,
simple! There was a demon waiting for me, a Pervect to be exact.
This in itself wasn't unusual. Aahz, the teacher I mentioned earlier, is
a Pervect. In fact, he shares my quarters with me. What was unusual
was that the demon waiting for me wasn't Aahz!

Now I haven't met many Pervects...heck, the only one I know
is Aahz...but I know Aahz very well, and this Pervect wasn't him!

This demon was shorter than my mentor, his scales were a lighter
shade of green, and his gold eyes were set closer together. What's
more, he wasn't smiling...and Aahz always smiles, even when he's
mad...especially when he's mad. To the average eye Aahz and this
stranger might look alike, but to me they were as different as a
Deveel and an Imp. Of course, there was a time when I couldn't tell

the difference between a Deveel and an Imp. It says something about the company I've been keeping lately.

"Who are you?" I demanded.

"You Skeeve?"

"Yea. Me Skeeve. Who you?"

For an answer, I suddenly felt myself snatched into the air by an invisible hand and spun end over end until I finally stopped dangling head down four feet off the floor.

"Don't get smart with me, punk. I understand you're holding a relative of mine in some kind of bondage. I want him back. Understand?"

He emphasized his point by lowering me to within a few inches of the floor, then using that surface to rap my head sharply.

I may not be the greatest magician ever, but I knew what he was doing. He was using his mind to levitate me about the room. I've done it myself to small objects from time to time. Of course, it occurred to me that I wasn't a small object and that I was dealing with someone a bit better versed in the magical arts than myself. As such, I deemed it wiser to keep my temper and my manners.

"You know Aahz?"

"Sure do. And I want him back."

The latter was accompanied by another head rap. So much for holding my temper.

"Then you should know him well enough to know that nobody holds him against his will!"My head started for the floor again, but stopped short of its target. From my inverted position I could get a partial view of the demon tapping himself thoughtfully on the chin.

"That's true," he murmured. "All right…"

I was turned into an upright position once more.

"Let's take it from the top. Where's Aahz, and what's keeping him in this backwater dimension?"

"I think and talk better with my feet on the ground."

"Hmm? Oh! Sorry."

I was lowered into a normal standing position. Now that I was self-supporting again, I realized the interrogation had left me with a splitting headache.

"He's back in General Badaxe's quarters arguing military tactics," I managed. "It was so boring I came back here. He should be along soon. They were almost out of wine when I left."

"Tactics and wine, eh?" my visitor grimaced. "That sounds like Aahz. What's the rest of it? Why is he staying around a no-where dimension like Klah and how did he get mixed up with the Great Skeeve?"

"You've heard of me?"

"Here and there around the dimensions," the demon ack-nowledged. "In some circles they think you're pretty hot stuff. That's why I started wondering if you'd managed to cage Aahz somehow. I was braced for a real battle royale when you walked in.

"Well, actually I'm not all that good," I admitted. "I've only really started making headway in the last couple years since I started studying under Aahz. I'd still be a total nothing if he hadn't lost his powers and taken me on as an apprentice."

"Bingo!" my visitor declared, holding up his hand. "I think you just explained everything. Aahz lost his powers and took on a new apprentice! No wonder he hasn't been home in a while. And all this talk about the Great Skeeve is just a standard Aahz-managed hype job for a new talent. Right?"

"We have taken on a few rough assignments," I said defensively.

"In which Aahz choreographed, then set you up to take the credit. Right?"

"What's 'choreographed'?" I asked. Obviously the family simi-larity was more than scale deep.

"Well, I hope you're up to operating on your own, Skeeve, 'cause I'm taking your mentor back to Perv with me."

"But you don't have to rescue him from me!" I protested. "He's free to come and go as he wants."

"I'm not saving him from you, I'm saving him from Aahz. Our colleague has an overblown sense of responsibility that isn't always in his own best interest. Do you know how lucrative a practice he's letting fall apart on Perv while he clowns around with you?"

"No," I admitted.

"Well, he's losing money every day he's gone...and that means the family is losing money."

Right there I gave up the argument. Early on in my association with Aahz I learned the futility of trying to talk a Pervect out of money. The fact that Aahz was willing to sacrifice a steady income to work with me was an incredible tribute to our friendship...or his sense of duty. Of course, there's more than one way to win an argument.

"Well, as I said before, I can't keep him here," I said innocently. "If you can convince him he's not needed any more…"

"No way, punk," the demon sneered. "We both know that won't get him to desert an apprentice. I'm going to lure him back to Perv with a blatant lie. And you're going to keep your mouth shut."

"But…"

"…Because if you don't, I'll make sure there's nothing left to keep him in Klah…meaning you! Now before you even think about trying to match magic with me, remember something. You've been studying under Aahz for a couple years now. I graduated after over three hundred years of apprenticeship. So far, I'm willing to live and let live. You should be able to earn a living on what you've learned so far, maybe even pick up a few new tricks as you go along. *However,* if you cross me now, there won't be enough of you to pick up with a sponge. Do we understand each other?"

I was suddenly aware why nobody we met in our dimension-crawling ever wanted to tangle with a Pervect. I was also aware that someone had just walked into the room behind me.

"Rupert!"

"Uncle Aahz!"

The two pounded each other on the back. I gave them lots of room.

"Hey kid, this is my nephew Rupert…but I see you've already met."

"Unfortunately," I grumbled.

That earned me a black look from Rupert, but Aahz missed it completely.

"So what brings you to Klah, nephew? A bit off your normal prowl pattern, isn't it?"

"It's Dad. He wants you."

"Sorry," Aahz was suddenly his normal self again. "I've got too many irons in the fire here to get drawn into some family squabble."

"But he's dying."

That stopped Aahz for a moment.

"My brother? Nonsense. He's too tough to kill. He could even beat me in an unfair fight."

"He got into a fight with Mom."

A look of concern crossed Aahz's face. I could see he was wavering.

"That serious, huh? I don't know, though. If he's really dying, I don't see what I can do to help."

"It shouldn't take long," Rupert urged. "He said something about his will."

I groaned inwardly. Trust a Pervect to know a Pervect's weaknesses.

"Well, I guess my business here can keep for a few days," Aahz declared with false reluctance. "Stay out of trouble, kid. I'll be back as soon as I can."

"Let's get going," Rupert suggested, hiding his triumphant grin. "The sooner we get to Perv, the sooner you can be back."

"But Aahz…"

"Yea, kid?"

I saw Rupert's brow darken.

"I…I just wanted to say 'goodbye.'"

"Hey, don't make a big thing of this, kid. It's not like I was going forever."

Before I could respond, Rupert clapped an arm around Aahz's shoulder and they both faded from view. Gone.

Somehow I couldn't make myself believe it had happened. My mentor had been spirited away…permanently. Whatever I had learned from Aahz would have to do, because now I was totally on my own.

Then I heard a knock at my door.

II.

"When things are blackest, I just tell myself 'cheer up, things could be worse!'
And sure enough, they get worse!"
SKEEVE

I DECIDED THAT as Court Magician of Possiltum, my response should be gracious.

"Go away!"

That was gracious. If you knew what my actual thoughts were, you'd realize that. Very few people ever visited me in my chambers, and I didn't want to see any of them just then.

"Do you know who you're talking to?" came a muffled voice from the other side of the door.

"No! And I don't care! Go away!"

"This is Rodrick the Fifth. Your King!"

That stopped me. Upset or not, that title belonged to the man who set and paid my wages. As I said earlier, I have learned a few things from Aahz.

"Do you know who you're talking to?" I called back, and hoped.

There was a moment's pause.

"I assume I'm talking to Skeeve the Magnificent, Court Magician of Possiltum. At best, he'll be the one to bear the brunt of my wrath if I'm kept waiting outside his chambers much longer."

So much for hoping. These things never work in real life the way they do in jokes.

Moving with undignified haste, I pounced on the door handle and wrenched it open.

"Good afternoon, Lord Magician. May I come in?"

"Certainly, Your Majesty," I said, standing aside. "I never refuse a fifth."

The King frowned.

"Is that a joke? If so, I don't get the point."

"Neither do I," I admitted calmly. "It's something Aahz my apprentice says."

"Ah, yes. Your apprentice. Is he about?"

Rodrick swept majestically into the room, peering curiously into the corners as if he expected Aahz to spring forth from the walls.

"No. He's...out."

"Good. I had hoped to speak with you alone. Hmmm...these are really quite spacious quarters. I don't recall having been here before."

That was an understatement. Not only had the King never visited my room in his palace, I couldn't recall having seen him when he wasn't either on the throne or in its near vicinity.

"Your Majesty has never graced me with his presence since I accepted position in his court," I said.

"Oh. Than, that's probably why I don't recall being here," Roderick responded lamely.

That in itself was strange. Usually the King was quite glib and never at a loss for words. In fact, the more I thought about it, the stranger this royal visit to my private chambers became. Despite my distress at Aahz's unplanned and apparently permanent departure, I felt my curiosity beginning to grow.

"May I ask the reason for this pleasant, though unexpected audience?"

"Well..." the King began, then shot one more look about the room. "Are you sure your apprentice isn't about?"

"Positive. He's...I sent him on a vacation."

"A vacation?"

"Yes. He's been studying awfully hard lately."

The King frowned slightly.

"I don't remember approving a vacation."

For a moment, I thought I was going to get caught in my own deception. Then I remembered that in addition to the various interdimensional languages, Aahz had also been teaching me to speak "bureaucrat."

"I didn't really feel your authorization was necessary," I said loftily. "Technically, my apprentice is not on your Majesty's payroll. I am paying him out of my wages, which makes him my employee, subject to my rules including vacations...or dismissal. While he is subject to your laws, as is any subject of Possiltum, I don't feel he actually is governed by Subparagraph G concerning palace staff!"

My brief oration had the desired effect: it both confused and bored my audience. Aahz would have been proud of me. I was particularly pleased that I had managed to sneak in that part about dismissals. It meant that when Aahz didn't return, I could claim that I had dismissed him without changing the wage paid me by the crown.

Of course, this got me brooding again about Aahz not coming back.

"Well, whatever. I'm glad to see your philosophy regarding vacations mirrors my own, Lord Magician. Everyone should have a vacation. In fact, that's why I came to see you this afternoon."

That threw me.

"A vacation? But your Majesty, I don't need a vacation." That threw the King.

"You? Of course not. You and that apprentice of yours spend most of your time gallivanting around other worlds. You've got a lot of nerve asking for a vacation."

That did it. All the anger I had been storing up since Rupert's arrival exploded.

"I didn't ask for a vacation!"

"Oh! Yes. Of course."

"And furthermore, that 'gallivanting around other worlds' you mentioned is stock and trade for magicians, court or otherwise. It enables us to work our wonders…like saving your kingdom from Big Julie's army. Remember?"

"How could I forget. I…"

"If, however, your Majesty feels I have been lax in fulfilling my duties as his court Magician, he need only ask for my resignation and it's his. If he recalls, he approached me for this position. I didn't ask for that either!"

"Please, Lord Magician," Rodrick interrupted desperately, "I meant no offense. Your services have been more than satisfactory. In fact, any reluctance I expressed regarding your vacation was based on a fear of having to run the kingdom for a period without your powers available. If you really feel you want a vacation, I'm sure we could work out something to…"

"I don't want a vacation. All right? Let's drop the subject."

"Certainly. I just thought…very well." Shaking his head slightly, he headed for the door.

Winning the argument put me in a much better mood. After the beating my ego had taken from Rupert, it was nice to hear someone say they thought my powers were worth something.

It occurred to me, however, that winning the argument with the man who paid my wages might not have been the wisest way to bounce back.

"Your Majesty?"

The King stopped.

"Aren't you forgetting something?"

He frowned.

"Like the original reason for your visit? Since I wasn't asking for a vacation, and you weren't offering one, I assume you had something else on your mind?"

"Oh, yes. Quite right. But all things considered, this might not be the time to discuss it."

"What? Because of our misunderstanding? Think nothing of it, your Majesty. These things happen. Rest assured I am still your loyal retainer, ready to do anything in my power to assist you in the management of your kingdom."

As I said before, I was getting pretty good at shoveling when the situation called for it.

Rodrick beamed.

"I'm glad to hear that, Master Skeeve. That is precisely why I came to you today."

"And how may I be of service?"

"It's about a vacation."

I closed my eyes.

For a brief moment, I knew...knew, mind you...how Aahz felt. I knew what it felt to be sincerely trying to help someone, only to find that that someone seems bound and determined to drive you out of your mind.

The King saw my expression and continued hastily, "Not a vacation for you. A vacation for me!"

That opened my eyes. Figuratively and literally.

"You, your Majesty? But Kings don't take vacations." "That's the whole point."

Rodrick began pacing the floor nervously as he spoke.

"The pressures of being a King mount up like they do on any other job. The difference is that as a King you never get a break. No time to rest and collect your thoughts, or even just sleep late. From the coronation when the crown hits your head until it's removed by voluntary or forcible retirement, you are the King."

"Gee, that's tough, your Majesty. I wish there was something I could do to help."

The King stopped pacing and beamed at me again.

"But you can! That's why I'm here!"

"Me? I can't approve a vacation for you! Even if it were in my power, and it isn't, the kingdom needs a king on the throne all the time. It can't spare you, even for one day!"

"Exactly! That's why I can't leave the throne unattended. If I wanted a vacation, I'd need a stand-in."

An alarm bell went off in my mind.

Now, however much Aahz may have nagged me about being a slow student, I'm not stupid. Even before I met Aahz. —heck, before I learned my letters...I knew how to add two and two to get four. In this case, one two was the King's need for a stand-in; the second two was his presence in my quarters, and the four was...

"Surely your Majesty can't mean me!"

"Of course I mean you," Rodrick confirmed. "The fact is, Lord Magician, I had this in mind when I hired you to your current position."

"You did?"

I could feel the jaws of the trap closing. If this was indeed why the King had hired me, I would be ill-advised to refuse the assignment. Rodrick might decide my services were no longer needed, and the last thing I needed with Aahz gone was to get cut off from my source of income. I wasn't sure what the job market was like for ex-court magicians, but I was sure I didn't want to find out first hand.

"As you said earlier, the powers of the Court Magician are at my disposal, and one of the powers you demonstrated when we first met was the ability to change your own shape, or the shape of others, at will."

The disguise spell! It was one of the first spells Aahz had taught me and one of the ones most frequently used over our last several adventures. After all the times it's bailed me out of tight spots, who would have guessed it would be the spell to get me into trouble? Well, there was the time it had gotten me hung..."

"But, your Majesty, I couldn't possibly substitute for you. I don't know how to be a King!"

"Nothing to it," Rodrick smiled. "The nice thing about being a King is that even when you're wrong, no one dares to point it out."

"But..."

"And besides, it will only be for one day. What could possibly go wrong in one day?"

III.

"Once a knight, always a knight, But once a King is once too often!"
SIR BELLA OF EASTMARCH

NOW, I DON'T want you to think I'm a pushover. I drove a hard bargain with the King before giving in. I not only managed to get him to agree to a bonus, but to cough up a hefty percentage in advance before accepting the assignment. Not bad for a fledgling magician who was over a barrel.

Of course, once I accepted, I was no longer over a barrel, I was in over my head!

The more I thought about it, the worse the idea of standing in for the King seemed. The trouble was, I didn't have a choice...or did I? I thought about it some more and a glimmer of hope appeared.

There was a way out! The only question was, how far could I run in a day? While not particularly worldly (or off-worldly for that matter) I was pretty sure that double-crossing kings wasn't the healthiest of pastimes.

It was going to be a big decision, definitely the biggest I ever had to make on my own. The King (or to be exact, his stand-in) wasn't due to make an appearance until noon tomorrow, so I had a little time to mull things over. With that in mind, I decided to talk it out with my last friend left in the palace.

"What do you think, Gleep? Should I take it on the lam, or stick around and try to bluff it out for one day as king?" The response was brief and to the point.

"Gleep!"

For those of you who've tuned in to this series late, Gleep is my pet. He lives in the Royal Stables. He's also a twenty-foot long blue dragon...half grown. (I shudder to think what he'll be like when he's fully grown! Groan!) As to his witty conversation, you'll have to forgive him. He only has a one-word vocabulary, but he makes up for it by using that word a lot. Wordy or not, I turned to him in this moment of crisis because with Aahz gone, he was the only one in this dimension who would be even vaguely sympathetic to my problem. That in itself says a lot about the social life of a magician.

"Come on, Gleep, get serious. I'm in real trouble. If I try to stand in for the King, I might make a terrible mistake...like starting a war or hanging an innocent man. On the other hand, if I double-cross the King and disappear, you and I would spend the rest of our lives as hunted fugitives."

The unicorn in the next stall snorted and stamped a foot angrily.

"Sorry, Buttercup. The three of us would be hunted fugitives."

War unicorns aren't all that common, even in Royal Stables. That particular war unicorn was mine. I acquired him as a gift shortly after I acquired Gleep. As I said before, this life-style is more than a little zooish.

"In a kingdom with a bad king, a lot of people would get hurt," I reasoned, "and I'd be a terrible king. Heck, I'm not all that good a magician."

"Gleep," my pet argued sternly.

"Thanks for the vote of confidence, but it's true. I don't want to hurt anybody, but I'm not wild about being a hunted fugitive, either."

Tired of verbalizing his affection, Gleep decided to demonstrate his feelings by licking my face. Now, aside from leaving a slimy residue, my dragon's kisses have one other side effect. His breath is a blast of stench exceeded only by the smell of Pervish cooking.

"G...Gleep, old boy," I managed at last, "I love you dearly, but if you do that twice a week, we may part company...permanently!"

"Gleep?"

That earned me a hurt expression, which I erased simply enough by scratching his head. It occurred to me that dragons had survived because each of them only became emotionally attached to one being in its lifetime. If their breath reached the entire population instead of a single individual, they would have been hunted into extinction long ago. No, it was better that only one person should suffer than..."

Another part of my mind grabbed that thought and started turning it over.

"If I run, then I'll be the only one in trouble, but if I try to be king, the whole kingdom suffers! That's it! I have to leave. It's the only decent thing to do. Thanks, Gleep!"

"Gleep?"

My pet cocked his head in puzzlement.

"I'll explain later. All right. It's decided. You two stock up on food while I duck back to my room to get a few things. Then it's 'Goodbye Possiltum!'"

I've had pause to wonder what would have happened if I'd followed my original plan: just headed for my room, gathered up my belongings, and left. The timing for the rest of the evening would have changed, and the rest of this story would have been totally different. As it was, I made a slight detour. Halfway to my room, Aahz's training cut in. That is, I started thinking about money.

Even as a hunted fugitive, money would come in handy...and the King's advance would only last so long. With a little extra cash, I could run a lot farther, hide a lot longer...or at the very least live a lot better..."

Buoyed by these thoughts, I went looking for J. P. Grimble.

The Chancellor of the Exchequer and I had never been what you would call close friends. Blood enemies would be a better description. Aahz always maintained that this was because of my growing influence in court. Not so. The truth was that my mentor's greed for additional funding was surpassed only by Grimble's reluctance to part with the same. Literally the same, since my wages came out of those coffers so closely guarded by the Chancellor.

I found him, as expected, in the tiny cubicle he used for an office. Scuttlebutt has it he repeatedly refused larger rooms, trying desperately to impress the rest of the staff by setting an example of frugality. It didn't work, but he kept trying and hoping.

His desk was elbow deep in paper covered by tiny little numbers which he alternately peered at and changed while moving various sheets from stack to stack. There were similar stacks on the floor and on the only other available chair, leading me to believe he had been at his current task for some time. Seeing no available space for sitting or standing, I elected to lean against the door frame.

"Working late, lord Chancellor?"

That earned me a brief, dark glare before he returned to his work.

"If I were a magician, I'd be working late. As Chancellor of the Exchequer, these are my normal hours. For your information, things are going rather smoothly. So smoothly, in fact, I may be able to wrap up early tonight, say in another three or four hours."

"What are you working on?"

"Next year's Budget and Operating Plan, and it's almost done. That is, providing someone doesn't want to risk incurring my permanent disfavor by trying to change a number on me at the last minute."

The last was accompanied by what can only be described as a meaningful stare.

I ignored it.

I mean, what the heck! l was already on his bad side, so his threats didn't scare me at all.

"Then it's a good thing I caught you before you finished your task," I sand nonchalantly. "I want to discuss something with you that will undoubtedly have an impact on your figures. Specifically, a change in my pay scale."

"Out of the question!" Grimble exploded. "You're already the highest paid employee on the staff, including myself. It's outrageous that you would even think of asking for a pay increase."

"Not a pay increase, Lord Chancellor, a pay cut."

That stopped him.

"A pay cut?"

"Say, down to nothing."

He leaned back in his chair and regarded me suspiciously.

"I find it hard to believe that you and your apprentice are willing to work for nothing. Forgive me, but I always distrust noble sacrifice as a motive. Though I dislike greed, at least it's a drive I can understand."

"Perhaps that's why we've always gotten along so well," I purred. "However, you're quite right. I have no intention of working for free. I was thinking of leaving the court of Possiltum to seek employment elsewhere."

The chancellor's eyebrows shot up.

"While I won't argue your plan, I must admit it surprises me. I was under the impression you were quite enamored of your position here in 'a soft job,' I believe is how your scaly apprentice describes it. What could possibly entice your to trade the comforts of court life for an uncertain future on the open road?"

"Why, a bribe, of course," I smiled. "A lump sum of a thousand gold pieces."

"I see," Grimble murmured softly. "And who's offering this bribe, if I might ask?"

I stared at the ceiling.

"Actually, I was rather hoping that *you* would."

THERE WAS A bit of haggling after that, but mostly on the terms of our agreement. Grimble really wanted Aahz and me out of his accounts, though I suspect he would have been less malleable if he had realized he was only dealing with me. There was a bit of name calling and breast beating, but the end result is what counts, and that end result was my heading for my quarters, a thousand gold pieces richer in exchange for a promise that it was the last money I would ever receive from Grimble. It was one more reason for my being on my way as soon as possible.

With light heart and heavy purse, I entered my quarters.

Remember the last time I entered my quarters? How there was a demon waiting for me? Well, it happened again.

Now don't get me wrong. This isn't a regular occurrence in my day-to-day existence. One demon showing up unannounced is a rarity. Two demons...well, no matter how you looked at it, this was going to be a red-letter day in my diary.

Does it seem to you I'm stalling? I am. You see, this demon I knew, and her name was Massha!

"Well hel-lo, high roller! I was just in the neighborhood and thought I'd stop by and say 'Hi!'"

She started forward to give me a hug, and I hastily moved to put something immobile between us. A 'hi!' and a hug might not sound like a threat to you. If not, you don't know Massha!

I have nothing against hello hugs. I have another demon friend named Tananda (yes, I have a lot of demon friends these days) whose hello hugs are high points in my existence. Tananda is cute, curvaceous, and cuddly. Okay, so she's also an assassin, but her hello hugs can get a rise out of a statue.

Massha, on the other hand, is not cute and cuddly. Massha is immense...and then some. I didn't doubt the sincere goodwill behind her greeting. I was just afraid that if she hugged me, it would take days to find my way out again...and I had a getaway to plan.

"Um...Hi, Massha. Good to see you...all of you."

The last time I had seen Massha, she was disguised as a gaudy circus tent, except it wasn't a disguise. It was actually the way she dressed. This time, though, she had apparently kicked out the jams…along with her entire wardrobe and any modicum of good taste. Okay, she wasn't completely naked. She was wearing a leopard-skin bikini, but she was showing enough flesh for four normal naked people. A bikini, her usual wheelbarrow full of jewelry, light green lipstick that clashed with her orange hair, and a tattoo on her bicep. That was Massha. Class all the way.

"What brings you to Klah? Aren't you still working Jahk?" I asked, mentioning the dimension where we met.

"The boys will just have to work things out without me for a while. I'm on a little…vacation."

There was a lot of that going around.

"But what are you doing here?"

"Not much for small talk, are you? I like that in a man."

My skin started to crawl a little on that last bit, but she continued.

"Well…while I'm here, I thought I'd take another little peek at your General Badaxe, but that's not the real reason for my visit. I was hoping you and me could talk a little…business."

My life flashed before my eyes. For a moment, neither Aahz's departure nor the King's assignment was my biggest problem… pun intended.

"Me?" I managed at last.

"That's right, hot stuff. I've been giving it a lot of thought since you and your scaly green sidekick rolled through my territory, and yesterday I made up my mind. I've decided to sign on as your apprentice."

IV.

"Duty: A fee paid for transacting in good(s)."
U.S. DEPT. OF COMMERCE

"BUT YOUR MAJESTY, he promised me he'd pay the other half before spring, and…"

"I did not."

"Did too."

"Liar!"

"Thief!"

"Citizens," I said, "I can only listen to one side at a time. Now then, you! Tell me what you remember being said."

That's right. I said. There I was, sitting on the very throne I had decided to avoid at all cost.

Actually, this king business wasn't all that rough. Rodrick had briefed me on basic procedure and provided me with a wardrobe, and from there it was fairly simple. The problems paraded before me weren't all that hard to solve, but there were lots of them.

At first I was scared, then for a while it was fun. Now it was just boring. I had lost count of how many cases I had listened to, but I had developed a new sympathy for Rodrick's desire to get away for a while. I was ready for a vacation before lunch rolled around. It was beyond my comprehension how he had lasted for years of this nonsense.

You may wonder how I went from talking with Massha to sitting on the throne. Well, I wonder myself from time to time, but here's what happened as near as I can reconstruct it.

Needless to say, her request to work as my apprentice caught me unprepared.

"M…my…but Massha. You already have a job as a court magician. Why would you want to apprentice yourself to me?"

In response, Massha heaved a great sigh. It was a startling phenomenon to watch. Not just because there was so much of Massha moving in so many different directions, but because when she was done, she seemed to have deflated to nearly half her original size. She was no longer an imposing figure, just a rather tired looking fat woman.

"Look, Skeeve," she said in a low voice that bore no resemblance to her normal vampish tones. "If we're going to work together, we've got to be honest with each other. Court magician or not, we both know that I don't know any magic. I'm a mechanic…a gimmick freak. I've got enough magic baubles to hold down a job, but any bozo with a big enough bankroll could buy the same stuff at the Bazaar at Deva.

"Now, mind you, I'm not complaining. Old Massha's been kicked around by some of the best and nobody's ever heard her complain. I've been happy with what I have up to now. It's just when I saw you and your rat pack put one over on both city-states at the Big Game with some real magic, I knew there was something to learn besides how to operate gimmicks. So whattaya say? Will you help me learn a little of the stuff I really got into the magic biz for?"

Her honesty was making me more than a little uncomfortable. I wanted to help her, but I sure didn't want an apprentice right now. I decided to stall.

"Why did you choose magic for a profession, anyway?" That got me a sad smile.

"You're sweet, Skeeve, but we were going to be honest with each other, remember? I mean, look at me. What am I supposed to do for a living? Get married and be a housewife? Who would have me? Even a blind man could figure out in no time flat that I was more than he had bargained for…a lot more. I resigned myself to the way I look a long time ago. I accepted it and covered up any embarrassment I felt with loud talk and flamboyant airs. It was only natural that a profession like magic that thrives on loud talk and flamboyant airs would attract me."

"We aren't all loud talk," I said cautiously.

"I know," she smiled. "You don't have to act big because you've got the clout to deliver what you promise. It impressed me on Jahk, and everyone I talked to at the Bazaar on Deva said the same thing. 'Skeeve doesn't strut much, but don't start a fight with him.' That's why I want you for my teacher. I already know how to talk loud."

Honesty and flattery are a devastating one-two punch. Whatever I thought about her before, right now Massha had me eating out of the palm of her hand. Before I committed myself to anything I might regret later, I decided to try fighting her with her own weapons.

"Massha…we're going to be honest with each other, right? Well, I can't accept you as an apprentice right now for two reasons. The first is simple. I don't know that much magic myself. No matter what kind of scam we pull on the paying customers, including the ones on Deva, the truth is that I'm just a student. I'm still learning the business myself."

"That's no problem, big bwana," Massha laughed, regaining some of her customary composure. "Magic is like that: the more you learn, the more you find there is to know. That's why the really big guns in our business spend all their time closeted away studying and practicing. You know some magic, and that's some more than I know. I'll be grateful for anything you're willing to teach me."

"Oh." I said, a bit surprised that my big confession hadn't fazed her at all. "Well, there's still the second reason."

"And that is?"

"That I'm in a bit of trouble myself. In fact, I was just getting ready to sneak out of the kingdom when you showed up." A small frown wrinkled Massha's forehead.

"Hmm…" she said, thoughtfully. "Maybe you'd better give me some of the details of this trouble you're in. Sometimes talking it out helps, and that's what apprentices are for."

"They are?" I countered skeptically. "I've been apprenticed twice, and I don't remember either of the magicians I studied under confiding in me with their problems."

"Well, that's what Massha's for. Listening happens to be one of the few things I'm really good at. Now give. What's happened to put a high-stepper like you on the run?"

Seeing no easy alternative, I told her about the King's assignment and my subsequent deal with Grimble. She was right. She was an excellent listener, making just enough sympathetic noise to keep me talking without actually interrupting my train of thought.

When I finally wound down, she sighed and shook her head. "You're right. You've got a real problem there. But I think there are a few things you've overlooked in reaching your final decision."

"Such as…?"

"Well, first you're right. A bad king is worse than a good king. The problem is that a bad king is better than no king at all. Roddie Five is counting on you to fill his chair tomorrow, and if you don't show up, the whole kingdom goes into a panic because the king has disappeared."

"I hadn't thought about it that way," I admitted.

"Then there's the thing with Grimble. We all pick up a little extra 'cash when we can, but in this case if it comes out that Grimble paid you to skip out when the King was counting on you, his head goes on the chopping block for treason."

I closed my eyes.

That did it. It was bad enough to hurt the faceless masses, but when the mass had a face, even if it was Grimble's, I couldn't let him face a treason charge because of my cowardice.

"You're right," I sighed. "I'm going to have to sit in for the King tomorrow."

"With me as your apprentice?"

"Ask me after tomorrow...if I'm still alive. In the meantime, scurry off and say 'Hello' to Badaxe. I know he'll be glad to see you."

"Your majesty?"

I snapped back to the present, and realized the two arguers were now looking at me, presumably to render a decision.

"If I understand this case correctly," I stalled, "both of you are claiming ownership of the same cat. Correct?"

Two heads bobbed in quick agreement.

"Well, if the two of you can't decide the problem between you, it seems to me there's only one solution. Cut the cat in two and each of you keep half."

This was supposed to inspire them to settle their difference with a quick compromise. Instead they thanked me for my wisdom, shook hands, and left smiling, presumably to carve up their cat.

It occurred to me, not for the first time today, that many of the citizens of Possiltum don't have both oars in the water. What anyone could do with half a dead cat, or a whole dead cat for that matter, was beyond me.

Suddenly I was very tired. With an offhanded wave I beckoned the herald forward.

"How many more are waiting out there?" I asked.

"That was the last. We deliberately kept the case load light today so your Majesty could prepare for tomorrow." "Tomorrow?"

The question slipped out reflexively. Actually, I didn't really care what happened tomorrow. My assignment was done. I had survived the day, and tomorrow was Rodrick's problem.

"Yes, tomorrow...when your bride arrives."

Suddenly I was no longer tired. Not a bit. I was wide awake and listening with every pore.

"My bride?" I asked cautiously.

"Surely your Majesty hasn't forgotten. She specifically scheduled her arrival so that she would have a week to prepare for your wedding."

Case load be hanged. Now I knew why dear Rodrick wanted a vacation. I also knew, with cold certainty, that he wouldn't be back tonight to relieve me of my duties. Not tonight, and maybe not ever.

V.

"The only thing worse than a sorcerer is a sorcerer's apprentice."
M. MOUSE

FOR ONCE, I successfully surpressed the urge to panic. I had to!

Without Aahz around to hold things together until I calmed down, I couldn't afford hysterics.

Instead, I thought...and thought.

I was in a jam, and no matter how I turned it over in my mind, it was going to take more than just me to get out of it.

I thought of Massha.

Then I thought about suicide.

Then I thought about Massha again.

With firm resolve and weak knees, I made my decision. The question was, how to locate Massha? The answer came on the heels of the question. Standing in for the king had been nothing but a pain so far. It was about time I started making it work for me for a change.

"Guard!"

A uniformed soldier materialized by the throne with impressive speed.

"Yes, your Majesty?"

"Pass the word for General Badaxe. I'd like to see him."

"Umm...begging your Majesty's pardon. He's with a lady just now."

"Good. I mean, bring them both."

"But..."

"Now."

"Yes, your Majesty!"

The guard was gone with the same speed with which he had appeared.

I tried not to grin. I had never gotten along particularly well with the military of Possiltum. Of course, the fact that my first exposure to them was when Aahz and I were hired to fight their war for them might have something to do with it. Anyway, the thought of some poor honor guard having to interrupt his general's tete-a-tete was enough to make me smile, the first in several days.

Still, sending a guard to fetch the person I wanted to see was certainly better than chasing them down myself. Perhaps being a king did have its advantages.

Two hours later, I was still waiting. In that time, I had more than ample opportunity to reconsider the benefit of issuing kingly summons. Having sent for Badaxe, I was obligated to wait for him in the throne room until he appeared.

At one point I considered the horrible possibility that he had taken Massha riding and that it might be days before they were located. After a little additional thought, I discarded the idea. There wasn't a steed in the Kingdom, including Gleep, who could carry Massha more than a few steps before collapsing.

I was still contemplating the image of Massha, sitting indignant on the ground with horse's legs protruding grotesquely from beneath her rump, when the herald sprang into action.

"Now comes General Badaxe...and a friend."

With that, the man stood aside. Actually, he took several sideways steps to stand aside.

I've already described Massha's bulk. Well, Hugh Badaxe wasn't far behind her. What he lacked in girth, he made up for in muscle. My initial impression of the General remained unchanged; that he had won his rank by taking on the rest of the army...and winning. Of course, he was wearing his formal bearskin, the clean one, which made him appear all the larger. While I had been there when they met, I had never actually seen Badaxe and Massha standing side by side before. The overall effect was awe-inspiring. Together, they might have been a pageant of a barbarian invasion gone decadent...if it weren't for the General's axe. His namesake, a huge, double-bitted hand axe, rode comfortably in its customary place on the General's right hip, and the glitter from it wasn't all decorative. Here, at least, was one barbarian who hadn't let decadence go to his sword arm.

"Your Majesty."

Badaxe rumbled his salutation as he dropped to one knee with an ease that denied his size. One could almost imagine the skull of a fallen enemy crackling sharply beneath that descending knee. I forced the thought from my mind.

"Greetings, General. Won't you introduce me to your... companion?"

"I...certainly, your Majesty. May I present Massha, Court Magician of Ta-hoe, and friend of both myself and Lord Skeeve, Magician to your own court here at Possiltum."

"Charmed, your Majesty."

I realized with a start that Massha was about to attempt to imitate Badaxe by dropping to one knee. Even if she were able to execute such a maneuver, it would require sufficient effort as to invite ridicule from the other court retainers present...and somehow I didn't want that.

"Ah...there is no need for that," I asserted hastily. "It was not our intention to hold formal court here, but rather an informal social occasion."

That caused a minor stir with the court, including the general who frowned in slight puzzlement. Still, I was already committed to a line of conversation, so I blundered on.

"In fact, that was the only reason for the summons. I wished to meet the lady dazzling enough to lure our general from his usual position by my side."

"Your Majesty gave his permission for my absence today," the general protested.

"Quite right. As I said, this is a social gathering only. In fact, there are too many people here for casual conversation. It is our wish that the court be adjourned for the day and the room cleared that I might speak freely with this visiting dignitary."

Again there was a general ripple of surprise, but a royal order was a royal order, and the various retainers bowed or curtsied to the throne and began making their way out.

"You too, General. I would speak with Massha alone."

Badaxe began to object, but Massha nudged him in the ribs with an elbow, a blow which would have been sufficient to flatten most men, but was barely enough to gain the general's attention. He frowned darkly, then gave a short bow and left with the others.

"So, you're a friend of our lord Magician," I asked after we were finally alone.

"I have that...honor, your Majesty," Massha replied cautiously. "I hope he's...well?"

"As a matter of fact, he's in considerable trouble right now."

Massha heaved a great sigh.

"I was afraid of that. Something to do with his last assignment?"

I ignored the question.

"General Badaxe seems quite taken with you. Are you sure you want to stay in the magic biz? Or are you going to try your hand at a new lifestyle?"

Massha scowled at me.

"Now how did you hear that? You haven't been torturing your own magician, have you?"

I caught the small motion of her adjusting her rings, and decided the time for games was over.

"Hold it, Massha! Before you do anything, there's something I have to show you."

"What's that?"

I had already closed my eyes to remove my disguise spell...faster than I ever had before.

"Me," I said, opening my eyes again.

"Well, I'll be...you really had me going there, hot stuff."

"It was just a disguise spell," I waved off-handedly.

"Nice. Of course, it almost got you fried. Why didn't you let me know it was you?"

"First of all, I wanted to see if my disguise spell was good enough to fool someone who was watching for it. This is my first time to try to disguise my voice as well as my appearance. Secondly...well, I was curious if you had changed your mind about being my apprentice."

"But why couldn't you have just asked me...I see. You're really in trouble, aren't you? Bad enough that you didn't want to drag me into an old promise. That's nice of you, Skeeve. Like I said before, you run a class act."

"Anybody would have done the same thing," I argued, trying to hide my embarrassment at her praise.

She snorted loudly.

"If you believed that, you wouldn't have survived as long as you have. Anyway, apprentice or not, a friend is a friend. Now out with it. What's happened?"

Sitting on the steps to the throne, I filled her in about the forthcoming wedding and my suspicions about the king's conveniently scheduled vacation. I tried to sound casual and matter-of-fact about it, but towards the end my tone got rather flat.

When I was done, Massha gave a low whistle of sympathy.

"When you big leaguers get in trouble, you don't kid around, do you? Now that you've filled me in, I'll admit I'm a little surprised you're still here."

I grimaced.

"I'm a little slow from time to time, but you only have to lecture me once. If one day without a king is bad for a kingdom, a permanent disappearance could be disastrous. Anyway, what I need right now is someone to track down the real king and get him back here, while I keep bluffing from the throne."

Massha scowled.

"Well, I've got a little trinket that could track him, if you've got something around that he's worn, that is…"

"Are you kidding? You think court magicians dress this way in Possiltum? Everything I'm wearing and two more closet-fulls in his quarters belong to the king."

"But what I can't figure out is why you need me? Where's your usual partner…whatsisname…Aahz? It seems to me he'd be your first choice for a job like this. Wherever he is, can't you just pop over to that dimension and pull him back for a while?"

Lacking any other option, I decided to resort to the truth, both about Aahz's permanent departure and my own lack of ability to travel the dimensions without a D-Hopper. When I was done, Massha was shaking her head.

"So you're all alone and stranded here and you were still going to give me an out instead of pressuring me into helping? Well, you got my help, Mister, and you don't have to bribe me with an apprenticeship, either. I'll get your king back for you…before that wedding. Then we'll talk about apprentices."

I shook my head.

"Right idea, but wrong order. I wasn't going to bribe you with an apprenticeship, Massha. I told you before I don't know much magic, but what I know I'll be glad to teach you…whether you find the King or not. I'm not sure that's an apprenticeship, but it's yours if you want it."

She smiled, a smile quite different from her usual vamp act.

"We'll argue about it later. Right now, I've got a king to find."

"Wait a minute! Before you go, you're pretty good with gadgets, right? Well, I've got a D-Hopper in my quarters. I want you to show me two settings: the one for Deva, and the one for Klah. You see,

I'm not all that noble. If things get too rough or it takes you longer than a week to find the king, I want a little running room. If I'm not here when you get back, you can look for your 'noble' Skeeve at the Yellow Crescent Inn at the Bazaar at Deva."

Massha snorted.

"You're putting yourself down again, Hot Stuff. You're going to try before you run, which is more than I can say for most in our profession. Besides, whatever you think your motives are, they're deeper than you think. You just asked me to show you two settings. You only need one to run."

VI.

"Good information is hard to get. Doing anything with it is even harder!"
L. SKYWALKER

I HAD LONG since decided that the main requirement for Royalty or its impersonators was an immunity to boredom. Having already chronicled the true tedious nature of performing so-called "duties of state," I can only add that waiting to perform them is even worse.

There was certainly no rush on my part to meet the king's bride-to-be, much less marry her. After word had come that her arrival would be delayed by a full day, however, and as the day waxed into late afternoon waiting for her "early morning" reception, I found myself wishing that she would get here so we could meet and get it over with already.

All other royal activity had ground to a halt in an effort to emphasize the importance of Possiltum's greeting their bride-to-be. I hardly thought it was necessary, though, as the citizens decked the street with flowers and lined up three deep in hopes of catching a glimpse of this new celebrity. The wait didn't seem to dampen their spirits, though the flowers wilted only to be periodically replaced by eager hands. If nothing else, this reception was going to put a serious dent in Possiltum's flower crop for awhile. Of course, it might also put a dent in all our crops, for the streets remained packed with festive people who showed not the slightest inclination to return to their fields or guild shops when word was passed of each new delay.

"Haven't the citizens anything better to do with their time than stand around the streets throwing flowers at each other?" I snarled, turning from the window. "Somebody should be keeping the kingdom during all this foolishness."

As usual, J. R. Grimble took it on himself to soothe me.

"Your Majesty is simply nervous about the pending reception. I trust his wisdom will not allow his edginess to spill over onto his loyal subjects?"

"I was assured when she crossed the border that she would be here this morning. Morning! Ever see the sun set in the morning before?"

"Undoubtedly she was delayed by the condition of the roads," General Badaxe offered. "I have told your Majesty before that our roads are long overdue for repair. In their current state, they hinder the passage of travelers...and troops should our fair land come under attack."

Grimble bared his teeth.

"And his Majesty has always agreed with me that repairing the roads at this time would be far too costly...unless the General would be willing to significantly reduce the size of his army that we might use the savings from wages to pay for the road work?"

The General purpled.

"Reduce the size of the army and you'll soon lose that treasury that you guard so closely, Grimble."

"Enough, gentlemen," I said, waving them both to silence. "As you've both said, we've discussed this subject many times before."

It had been decided that rather than having the King of Possiltum sit and fidget in front of the entire populace, that he should sweat it out in private with his advisors until his bride actually arrived. Royal image and all that. Unfortunately this meant that since morning I had been confined in a small room with J. R. Grimble and Hugh Badaxe for company. Their constant bickering and sniping was sufficient to turn my already dubious mood into something of record foulness.

"Well, while we're waiting, perhaps you can each brief me on your opinions of my future bride and her kingdom."

"But your Majesty, we've done that before. Many times." "Well, we'll do it again. You're supposed to be my advisors,

aren't you? So advise me. General Badaxe, why don't you start?" Badaxe shrugged.

"The situation is essentially unchanged from our last briefing. Impasse is a small kingdom; tiny really—less than a thousand citizens altogether. They claim the entire Impasse mountain range, from which the kingdom gets its name, and which is the bulk of their military defense. Their claim stands mostly because the mountains are treacherous and there is little or no reason to venture there. At least ninety-five percent of their population is concentrated along the one valley through the mountains. They have no formal military, but rather a militia, which suffices as there are no less than five passes in the main valley where a child with a pile of rocks could hold off an army... and they have plenty of rocks. Their main vulnerability is food. The terrain is such that they are unable to support even their small population, and as they are still at odds with the kingdom at the other end of the valley who originally owned it, they are forced to buy all their food from us…at prices even a generous man would call exorbitant."

"Supply and demand," Grimble said with a toothy smile.

"Wait a minute, General," I interrupted. "If I understand this right, Impasse is not a threat to us militarily because of its size. If anything, it guards our flank against attack from the pass. Right?"

"Correct."

"Which it is already doing."

"Also correct."

Seeing an opening, I hurried on.

"We can't attack them, but from what you say they don't have anything we want. So why are we bothering with this marriage/alliance?"

The General looked pointedly at Grimble.

"Because even though Impasse is people-few and crop-light, they are sitting on the largest deposit of precious metal on the continent," The Chancellor of the Exchequer supplied.

"Precious met…oh! You mean gold."

"Precisely. With the alliance, Possiltum will become the richest kingdom ever."

"That hardly seems like sufficient reason to get married," I mumbled.

"Your Majesty's opinions on the subject are well known to us," Grimble nodded. "You have expressed them often and long every time the possibility of this marriage was broached. I am only glad that you finally gave your consent when the citizens of Possiltum threatened to revolt if you didn't accept the betrothal offer."

"That was only after you spread the word that such an alliance would significantly lower taxes, Grimble, Badaxe scowled.

"I said it might lower taxes," the Chancellor corrected innocently. "Can I help it if the common folk jumped to conclusions?"

Now that I had a clearer picture of the situation, I might have mustered a bit of sympathy for the King's predicament, if he hadn't stuck me in it in his stead.

"Enough about Impasse. Now give me your opinions of my bride-to-be."

There was a brief moment of uncomfortable silence.

"Impasse doesn't have a monarchy," Grimble said carefully. "That is, until recently. It was more a tribal state, where the strongest ruled. When the last king died, however, his daughter Hemlock somehow managed to take over and maintain the throne, thereby establishing a royal line of sorts. Exactly how she did it is unclear."

"Some say that prior to the king's death she managed to gain the…loyalty of all the able-bodied fighters in the kingdom, thereby securing her claim from challenge," Badaxe supplied.

I held up a restraining hand.

"Gentlemen, what you're telling me are facts. I asked for your opinions."

This time, there was a long uncomfortable silence.

"That good, eh?" I grimaced.

"Your Majesty must remember," Grimble protested, "we are being asked to express our hidden feelings about a woman who will soon be our Queen."

"Not until the marriage," I growled. "Right now, I am your king. Get my drift?"

They got it, and swallowed hard.

"The words 'cold-blooded' and 'ruthless' come to mind," the general said, "and that's the impression of a man who's made a career of the carnage of war."

"I'm sure the rumors that she murdered her father to gain control of the kingdom are exaggerated," Grimble argued weakly.

"But your Majesty would be well advised to insist on separate sleeping quarters, and even then sleep lightly…and armed," the general concluded firmly.

"No difficulty should be encountered with separate quarters," Grimble leered. "It's said Queen Hemlock has the morals of an alley cat."

"Terrific," I sighed.

The Chancellor favored me with a paternal smile.

"Oh, there's no doubt that the entire kingdom, myself included, admires your Majesty for the sacrifices he is willing to make for his people."

The trouble was, only I knew who the King was willing to sacrifice!

I studied Grimble's smile through hooded eyes, seeking desperately through my mind for something to disrupt his smug enjoyment of the situation. Suddenly, I found it.

"I've been meaning to ask, does anyone know the current where-abouts of our Court Magician?"

Grimble's smile disappeared like water on a hot skillet. "He's…gone, your Majesty."

"What? Out on another of his miscap adventures?"

The Chancellor averted his eyes.

"No I mean he's…gone. Tendered his resignation and left."

"Tendered his resignation to whom?" I pressed. "On whose authority has he quit his post during this, my darkest hour?"

"Ahh…mine, your Majesty."

"What was that, Grimble? I couldn't quite hear you."

"Mine. I told him he could go."

Grimble was sweating visibly now, which was fine by me. In fact, an idea was beginning to form in my mind.

"Hmm…knowing you, Lord Chancellor, I would suspect money is behind the Great Skeeve's sudden departure."

"In a way," Grimble evaded, "you might say that."

"Well, it won't do," I said firmly. "I want him back…and before this accursed marriage. What's more, since you approved his departure, I'm holding you personally responsible for his return."

"B…But your Majesty! I wouldn't know where to start looking. He could be anywhere by now."

"He can't have gone far," Badaxe volunteered casually. "His dragon and unicorn are still in the Royal Stables."

"They are?" the Chancellor blinked.

"Yes," the General smiled, "as you might know if you ever set foot outside your counting house."

"See, Grimble," I said. "The task I set before you should be easy for a man of your resources. Now off with you. The longer you tarry here, the longer it will be before you find our wayward magician."

The Chancellor started to say something, then shrugged and started for the door.

"Oh, Grimble," I called. "Something you might keep in mind. I heard a rumor that the Great Skeeve has recently been disguising himself as me for an occasional prank. Like as not the scamp is parading around somewhere with the royal features on his face. That tidbit alone should help you locate him."

"Thank you, your Majesty," the Chancellor responded glumly, reminded now of the shape-changing abilities of his supposed quarry.

I wasn't sure, but I thought General Badaxe was stifling a laugh somewhere in the depths of his beard as his rival trudged out.

"How about you, General? Do you think your men could assist in passing word of my royal summons to the Great Skeeve?"

"That won't be necessary, your Majesty."

With sudden seriousness he approached me, laid a hand on my shoulder, and stared into my eyes.

"Lord Magician," he said, "the King would like to see you."

VII.

"There is no counter for a spirited woman except spirited drink."
R. BUTLER

"YOU'VE KNOWN FOR some time that I'm a fighting man. What *you don't* seem to realize is what that implies."

We were sitting over wine now, in a much more relaxed conversation than when I had been pretending to be King Rodrick.

"Fighting men recognize people as much by movement and mannerism as they do by facial feature. It's a professional habit. Now, you had the appearance and voice of the King, but your carriage and gestures were that of the Great Skeeve, not Rodrick the Fifth."

"But if you knew I was an imposter, why didn't you say something?"

The General drew himself up stiffly.

"The King had not taken me into his confidence in this matter, nor had you. I felt it would have been rude to intrude on your affairs uninvited."

"Weren't you afraid that I might be a part of some plot to murder the King and take his place?"

"Lord Magician, though we met as rivals, prolonged exposure to you has caused my respect for you to grow to no small matter. Both in your convincing Big Julie and his army to defect from the Mob and join Possiltum as honest citizens, and in fighting at your side in the Big Game when you risked life and limb to rescue a comrade in peril, you have shown ingenuity, courage, and honor.

While I may still speak of you from time to time in less than glowing terms, my lowest opinion of you does not include the possibility of your having a hand in murdering your employer."

"Thank you, General."

"..And besides, only a total idiot would want to assume Rodrick's place so soon before his marriage to Queen Hemlock." I winced.

"So much for your growing respect."

"I said 'ingenuity, courage, and honor.' I made no mention of intelligence. Very well, then, a total idiot or someone under orders from his king."

"How about a bit of both?" I sighed.

"I suspected as much." Badaxe nodded. "Now that we're speaking candidly, may I ask as to the whereabouts of the King?"

"Good question."

In a few depressing sentences, I brought him up to date on my assignment and Rodrick's disappearance.

"I was afraid something like this would happen," the General said when I concluded. "The King has been looking desperately for some way out of this marriage, and it looks like he's found it. Well, needless to say, if there's anything I can do to help, just ask."

"Thanks, General. As a matter of fact, I…"

"As long as it doesn't go against the good of the kingdom," Badaxe amended. "Like helping you to escape. Possiltum needs a king, and for the time being, you're it!"

"Oh. Well…how about using your men to help find the king?"

Badaxe shook his head.

"Can't do it. Massha has that assignment. If I sent my men to back her up, she'd think I didn't have any faith in her."

Terrific! I had an ally, if I could get around his loyalties and amorous entanglements.

The General must have noticed my expression.

"Anything else I'll be willing to do."

"Like what?"

"Well…like teaching you to defend yourself against your bride-to-be."

That actually sounded promising.

"Do you think we'll have enough time?"

With that, there was a heavy knocking at the door.

"Your Majesty! The carriage of Queen Hemlock is approaching the palace!"

"No," said the General, with disheartening honesty.

WE BARELY MADE it to our appointed places ahead of the Queen's procession. The throne of Possiltum had been tempor-arily moved to a position just inside the doors to the palace, and only by sprinting through the corridors with undignified abandon were Badaxe and I able to reach our respective positions before the portals were thrown open.

"Remind me to have a word with you about the efficiency of your army's early warning system," I said to the General as I sank into my seat.

"I believe it was the Court Magician who complained about the excessive range of the military spy system," Badaxe retorted. "Perhaps your Majesty will see fit now to convince him of the necessity of timely information."

Before I could think of a sufficiently polite response, the Queen's party drew to a halt at the foot of the stairs.

The kingdom of Impasse had apparently spared no expense on the Queen's carriage. If it was not actually fashioned of solid gold, there were sufficient quantities of the metal in the trim and decorations as to make the difference academic. I took secret pleasure that Grimble was not present to gloat at the scene. The curtains were drawn, allowing us to see the rich embroidery upon them, but not who or what was within. A team of eight matched horses completed the rig, though their shaggy coats and short stature suggested that normally the mountainfolk put them to far more practical use than dragging royalty around the countryside.

With the carriage, however, any semblance of decorum about the Queen's procession vanished.

Her escort consisted of at least twenty retainers, all mounted and leading extra horses, though whether these were relief mounts or the bride's dowry I couldn't tell. The escort was also all male, and of a uniform appearance; broad-shouldered, narrow-waisted, and musclebound. They reminded me of miniature versions of the opposing teams Aahz and I had faced during the Big Game, but unlike those players, these men were armed to the teeth. They fairly bristled with swords and knives, glittering from boot-tops, arm sheaths, and shoulder scabbards, such that I was sure the combined weight of their weapons offset that of the golden coach they were guarding. These weren't pretty court decorations, but well handled field weapons worn with the ease fighting men accord the tools of their trade.

The men themselves were dressed in drab tunics suited more for crawling through thickets with knives clenched in their teeth than serving as a royal escort. Still, they wrinkled their broad, flat features into wide smiles as they alternately gawked at the building and waved at the crowd which seemed determined to unload the earlier noted surplus of flowers by burying the coach with them. The escort may have seemed sloppy and undisciplined in the eyes of Badaxe or Big Julie, but I wouldn't want to be the one to try to take anything away from them; Queen, coach, kingdom, or even a flower they had taken a fancy to.

Two men in the procession were notable exceptions to the rule. Even on horseback they looked to be head and shoulder taller than the others and half again as broad. They had crammed their massive frames into tunics which were clean and formal, and appeared to be unarmed. I noted, however, that instead of laughing or waving, they sat ramrod stiff in their saddles and surveyed their surroundings with the bored, detached attention to detail I normally associated with predators...big predators.

I was about to call Badaxe's attention to the pair when the carriage door opened. The woman who appeared was obviously akin to most of the men in the escort. She had the same broad, solid build and facial features, only more so. My first impression was that she looked like the bottom two-thirds of an oak door, if the door were made of granite. Unsmiling, she swept the area with a withering stare, then nodded to herself and stepped down.

"Lady in waiting," Badaxe murmured.

I'm not sure if his comment was meant to reassure me, but it did. Only after did it occur to me that the General had volunteered the information to keep me from running, which I had been seriously considering.

The next figure in view was a radical departure from the other Impassers in the party. She was arrow thin and pale with black stringy black hair that hung straight past her shoulders. Instead of the now expected round, flat face, her features looked like she had been hung up by her nose to dry. She wasn't unpleasant to look at, in fact, I guessed that she was younger than I was, but the pointed nose combined with a pair of dark, shiny-alert eyes gave her a vaguely rodent appearance. Her dress was a long-sleeved white thing that would have probably looked more fetching on a clothes-hanger. Without more than a glance at the assembled citizens she gathered up what slack there was in the skirt, hopped down from the carriage, and started up the stairs toward me with the athletic, leggy grace of a confirmed tomboy.

" That is Queen Hemlock," the General supplied.

Queen Hemlock

I had somehow suspected as much, but having received confirmation, I sprang into action. This part, at least, I knew how to handle, having had it drilled into me over and over again by my advisors.

I rose to my feet and stood regally until she reached the throne, then timed my bow to coincide with her curtsey...monarch greeting monarch and all that.

Next, I was supposed to welcome her to Possiltum, but before I could get my mouth open, she came up with her own greeting.

"Sorry I didn't curtsey any lower, but I'm not wearing a thing under this dress. Rod, it's beastly hot here in the lowlands," she said, giving me a wide but thin-lipped smile.

"Aahh..." I said carefully.

Ignoring my response, or lack thereof, she smiled and waved at the throng, which responded with a roar of approval.

"What idiot invited the rabble?" she asked, the smile never leaving her face.

"Aahh..." I repeated.

General Badaxe came to my rescue.

"No formal announcement was made, your Majesty, but word of your arrival seems to have leaked out to the general populace. As might be expected, they are very eager to see their new Queen."

"Looking like this?" she said, baring her teeth and waving to those on the rooftops. "Six days on the road in this heat without a bath or a change of clothes and instead of a discreet welcome, half the kingdom gets to see me looking like I was dragged along behind the coach instead of riding in it. Well, it's done and we can't change it. But mind you, if it happens again...General Badaxe, is it? I thought so. Anyway, as I was saying, if it happens again, heads will roll...and I'm not speaking figuratively."

"Welcome to Possiltum," I managed at last.

It was a considerably abbreviated version of the speech I had planned to give, but it was as much as I could remember under the circumstances.

"Hello, Roddie," she said without looking at me, still waving at the crowd. "I'm going to scamper off for my quarters in a second. Be a love and try not to get underfoot during the next week...there's so much to do. Besides, it looks like you're going to have your hands full with other business."

"How's that?"

"You've got a wee bit of trouble coming your way, at least, according to the gentleman I met on the road. Here he comes now. Bye."

"But…"

Queen Hemlock had already disappeared, vanishing into the depths of the palace like a puff of smoke. Instead, I found myself focusing on the man who had stepped from the carriage and was currently trudging up the stairs toward my throne. I observed that he had the same weasel features and manners of J. R. Grimble. Mostly, though, I noticed that the two broadshouldered predators previously assumed to be part of the Queen's escort, had suddenly materalized at his side, towering over him like a pair of bookends… mean looking bookends.

I sat down, in part because the approaching figure did not seem to be royalty, but mostly because I had a feeling I wanted to be sitting down for this next interview.

The man reached my throne at last, drew himself up, and gave a curt nod rather than a bow. This, at least, looked polite, since his flankers didn't acknowledge my presence at all.

"Forgive me for intruding on such a festive occasion, your Majesty," the man said, "but there are certain matters we need to discuss."

"Such as…?"

"My name is Shai-ster, and I represent a…consortium of businessmen. I wish to confer with one of your retainers concerning certain employees of ours who failed to report in after pursuing our interests in this region."

As I mentioned earlier, I was getting pretty good at speaking 'bureaucrat." This man's oration, however, lost me completely. "You want to what about who?"

The man sighed and hung his head for a moment.

"Let me put it to you this way," he said at last. "I'm with the Mob, and I want to see your Magician, Skeeve. It's about our army, Big Julie's boys, that sort of disappeared after tangling with him. Now do you understand me?"

VIII.

"Choose your friends carefully. Your enemies will choose you!"
Y. ARAFAT

WITHIN A FEW days of Queen Hemlock's arrival, the palace of Possiltum had the happy, relaxed air of a battlefield the night before the battle. The Queen's party and the mob representatives were housed in the palace as "royal guests," giving me a two-front war whether I wanted it or not.

Queen Hemlock was not an immediate problem; she was more like a time bomb. With specific orders to 'stay out of her way," I didn't have to deal with her much, and even General Badaxe admitted that if she were going to try to kill me, it wouldn't be until after the wedding when she was officially Queen of Possiltum. Still, as the wedding day loomed closer, I was increasingly aware that she would have to be dealt with.

The Mob representatives, however, were an immediate problem. I had stalled them temporarily by telling them that the Court Magician was not currently in the palace, but had been sent for, and as a token of good faith had given them the hospitality of the palace. They didn't drink much, and never pestered me with questions about "Skeeve's" return. There was no doubt in my mind, however, that at some time their patience would be exhausted and they would start looking for the Court Magician themselves. I also had a feeling that 'some time' would be real soon.

Needing all the help I could get, I had Badaxe send one of his men for Big Julie. With minimal difficulty we smuggled him into the palace, and the three of us held a war council. On Badaxe's advice, I immediately dropped my disguise and brought our guest up to date on the situation.

"Ah'm sorry," Julie said to open the meeting, "but I don't see where I can help you, know what I mean?"

Terrific. So much for Big Julie's expert military advice.

"I'd like to help," he clarified. "You've done pretty good by me and the boys. But I used to work for the Mob, you know? I know what they're like. Once they get on your trail, they never quit. I tried to tell you that before."

"I don't see what the problem is," General Badaxe rumbled. "There are only three of them, and their main spokesman's a noncombatant to boot. It wouldn't take much to make sure they didn't report anything to anybody...ever again."

Big Julie shook his head.

"You're a good man, Hugh, but you don't know what you're dealing with here. If the Mob's scouting party disappears, the Big Boys will know they've hit paydirt and set things in motion. Taking out their reps won't stop the Mob...it won't even delay them. If anything, it will speed the process up!"

Before Badaxe had a chance to reply, I interrupted with a few questions of my own.

"Wait a minute, Big Julie. When we first met, you were commanding the biggest army this world had ever seen. Right?"

"That's right," he nodded. "We was rolling along pretty good until we met you."

"And we didn't stop you militarily. We just gave you a chance to disappear as soldiers and retire as citizens of Possiltum. You and your boys were never beaten in as fight."

"We were the best," Big Julie confirmed proudly. "Anybody messed with us, they pulled back a bloody stump with no body attached, know what I mean?"

"Then why are you all so afraid of the Mob? If they try anything, why don't you and your boys just hook up with General Badaxe's army and teach 'em a lesson in maneuvers?"

The ex-commander heaved a deep sigh.

"It don't work that way," he said. "If they was to march in here like an army, sure, we could send 'em packing. But they won't. They move in a few musclemen at a time, all acting just as polite as you please so there's nothing you can arrest 'em for. When enough of 'em get here, though, they start leaning on your citizens. Little stuff, but nasty. If somebody complains to you, that somebody turns up dead along with most of their family.

Pretty soon, all your citizens are more afraid of the Mob than they are of you. Nobody complains, nobody testifies in court. When that happens, you got no more kingdom. The Mob runs every-thing while you starve. You can't fight an invasion like that with an army. You can't fight it at all!"

We all sat in uncomfortable silence for a while, each avoiding the other's gaze while we racked our brains for a solution.

"What I don't understand," Badaxe said at last, "is if the system you describe is so effective and so unstoppable, why did they bother having an army at all?"

"I really hate to admit this," Big Julie grimaced, "but we was an experiment. Some of the Mob's bean-counters got it into their heads that even though an army was more expensive, the time savings of a fast takeover would offset the additional cost. To tell you the truth, I think their experiment was a washout."

That one threw me.

"You mean to say your army wasn't effective?"

"Up to a point we were. After that, we were too big. It costs a lot to keep an army in the field, and toward the end there, it was costing more to support my boys for a week than we were getting out of the kingdoms we were conquering. I think they were getting ready to phase us out...and that's why it's taken so long for them to come looking for their army."

I shook my head quickly.

"You lost me on that last loop, Big Julie. Why did they delay their search?"

"Money," he said firmly. "I'll tell you, nothing makes the Big Boys sit up and take notice like hard cash. I mean, they wrote the book when it came to money motivation."

"Sounds like Grimble," Badaxe muttered. "Doesn't anybody do anything for plain old revenge anymore?"

"Stow it, General," I ordered, leaning forward. "Keep going, Big Julie. What part does money have in this?"

"Well, the way I see it, the Mob was already losing money on my army, you know? To me, that means they weren't about to throw good gold after bad. I mean, why spend more money looking for an army that, when you find it, is only going to cost you more money?"

"But they're here now."

"Right. At the same time Possiltum's about to become suddenly rich. It looks to me like the Big Boys have found a way to settle a few old scores and turn a profit at the same time."

"The wedding!" I said. "I should have known. That means that by calling off the wedding, I can eliminate two problems at once; Queen Hemlock, *and* the Mob!"

Badaxe scowled at me.

"I thought we had already discarded that option. Remember Grimble and the citizenry of Possiltum?"

Without thinking, I slammed the flat of my hand down on the table with a loud slap.

"Will you forget about Grimble and the citizenry of Possiltum? I'm tired of being in a box, General, and one way or another I'm going to blast a way out!"

From the expressions of my advisors, I realized I might have spoken louder than I had intended. With a conscious effort, I modulated my tone and my mood.

"Look, General...Hugh," I said carefully. You may be used to the pressures of command, but this is new to me. I'm a magician, remember? Forgive me if I get a little razzled trying to find a solution to the problem that your...I mean, our King has dropped in my lap. Okay?"

He nodded curtly, but still didn't relax.

"Now, your point has merit," I continued, "but it overlooks a few things. First, Grimble isn't here. When and if he does get back, he'll have the king in tow, and friend Rodrick can solve the problem for us...at least the problem with the Queen. As for the citizenry of Possiltum...between you and me I'm almost ready to face their protests rather than have to deal with Queen Hemlock. Now if you weigh the disappointment of our people over having to continue the status quo against having both the Queen *and* the Mob move in on a permanent basis, what result do you get? Thinking of the welfare of the kingdom, of course!"

The General thought it over, then heaved a great sigh.

"I was never that much in favor of the wedding, anyway," he admitted.

"Just a minute, boys," Big Julie said, holding up a weary hand. "It's not quite that easy. The money thing may have slowed up their search a bit, but now that the Mob is here, there are a couple other matters they're gonna want to settle."

"Such as?" I asked, dreading the answer.

"Well, first off there's me and my boys. Nobody just walks away from the Mob, you know. Their pay scale is great, but their retirement plan stinks."

"I thought you said they didn't want their army anymore," Badaxe grumbled.

"Maybe not as an army, but they can always use manpower.

They'll probably break us up and absorb us into various positions in the organization."

"Would you be willing to go back to work for them?"

Big Julie rubbed his chin with one hand as he considered the General's question.

"I'd have to talk to the boys," he said. "Like I said, this kingdom's been pretty good to us. I'd hate to see anything happen to it because we were here…especially if we'd end up working for them again anyway."

"No," I said flatly.

"But…"

"I said 'No!' You've got a deal with Possiltum, Big Julie. More important, you've got a deal with me. We don't turn you over to the Mob until we've tried everything we can do to defend you."

"And how do you propose to defend them from the Mob?" Badaxe asked, sarcastically.

"I don't know. I'm working on it. Maybe we can buy them off. Offer them Queen Hemlock to hold for ransom or something."

"Lord Magician!"

"Okay, okay. I said I was still working on it, didn't I? What's next, Big Julie? You said there were a couple things they wanted besides money."

"You," he said bluntly. "The Mob isn't going to be happy until they get the Great Skeeve, Court Magician of Possiltum." "Me?" I said in a small voice.

"The Mob didn't get to the top by ignoring the competition. You've made some pretty big ripples with your work, and the biggest as far as they're concerned is making their army disappear. They know you're big. Big enough to be a threat. They're gonna want you neutralized. My guess is that they'll try to hire you, and failing that, try for some sort of non-aggression deal."

"And failing that…?" Badaxe asked, echoing my thoughts. Big Julie shrugged.

"Failing that, they're gonna do their best to kill you."

IX.

"I don't know why anyone would be nervous about going to see royalty."
P. IN BOOTS

"BUT WHY DO I have to come along?" Badaxe protested, pacing along at my side as we strode towards the Queen's chambers.

"Call it moral support," I growled. "Besides, I want a witness that I went into the Queen's chambers…and came out again, if you get my drift."

"But if this will only solve one of our problems…"

"Then it will be one less problem for us to deal with. Shh! Here we are."

I had switched back to my Rodrick disguise. That combined with the General's presence was enough to have the Honor Guards at the Queen's chambers snap to rigid attention at our approach. I ignored them and hammered on the door, though I did have a moment to reflect that not long ago, I thought the biggest problem facing a king was boredom!

"For cryin' out loud!" came a shrill voice from within. "Can't you guards get anything right? I told you I didn't want to be disturbed!"

One of the guards rolled his eyes in exasperation. I favored him with a sympathetic smile, then raised an eyebrow at Badaxe.

"King Rodrick the Fifth of Possiltum seeks an audience with Queen Hemlock!" he bellowed.

"I suppose it's all right," came the reply. "How about first thing in the morning?"

"Now," I said.

I didn't say it very loud, but it must have carried. Within a few heartbeats the door flew open, exposing Queen Hemlock… literally. I can't describe her clothing because she wasn't wearing any. Not a stitch!

"Roddie!" she chirped, oblivious to the guards and Badaxe, all of whom gaped at her nakedness. "Come on in. What in the world are you doing here?"

"Wait for me," I instructed Badaxe in my most commanding tone.

"C...certainly, your Majesty!" he responded, tearing his eyes away from the Queen long enough to snap to attention. With that, I stepped into the Queen's lair.

"So, what have you got for me?" She shut the door and leaned back against it. The action made her point at me, even though her hands were behind her back.

"I beg your pardon?"

"The audience," she clarified. "You wanted it, you got it. What's up?"

Somehow under the circumstances, I found that to be another embarrassing question.

"I...um...that is...could you please put something on? I'm finding your attire, or lack thereof, to be quite distracting."

"Oh, very well. It is beastly hot in here, though."

She flounced across the room and came up with a flimsy something which she shrugged into, but didn't close completely.

"Right after the wedding," she declared, "I want that window enlarged, or better yet, the whole wall torn out. Anything to get a little ventilation in this place."

She plopped down in a chair and curled her legs up under her. It eased my discomfort somewhat, but not much.

"Ahh...actually, that's what I'm here to talk to you about."

"The window?" she frowned.

"No. The wedding."

That made her frown even more.

"I thought it was agreed that I would handle all the wedding arrangements. Oh, well, if you've got any specific changes, it isn't too late to..."

"It isn't that," I interrupted hastily. "It's...well, it's come to my attention that the high prices Possiltum is charging your kingdom for food is forcing you into this marriage. Not wishing to have you enter into such a bond under duress, I've decided to cut our prices in half, thereby negating the need for our wedding."

"Oh, Roddie, don't be silly. That's not the reason I'm marrying you!"

Rather than being upset, the Queen seemed quite amused at my suggestion.

"It isn't?"

"Of course not. Impasse is so rich that we could buy your yearly crop at double the prices if we wanted to and still not put a dent in our treasury."

My stomach began to sink.

"Then you really want this marriage? You aren't being forced into it for political reasons?"

The Queen flashed all her teeth at me in a quick smile.

"Of course there are political reasons. I mean, we are royalty, aren't we? I'm sure you're a pleasant enough fellow, but I can get all the pleasant fellows I want without marrying them. Royalty marries power blocks, not people."

There was a glimmer of hope in what she was saying, and I pounced on it with all fours.

"Which brings us to the other reason we should call off the wedding," I said grandly.

The Queen's smile disappeared.

"What's that?" she said sharply.

For my reply, I let drop my disguise spell.

"Because I'm not Royalty. I'm people."

"Oh, that," the Queen shrugged. "No problem. I knew that all along."

"You did?" I gulped.

"Sure. You were embarrassed...twice. Once when I arrived at the palace, and again just now when I opened the door in my all-together. Royalty doesn't embarrass. It's in the blood. I knew all long you weren't Rodrick. It's my guess you're the Great Skeeve, Court Magician. Right? The one who can shape change?"

"Well, it's a disguise spell, not shape changing, but except for that, you're right."

Between Badaxe and Queen Hemlock, I was starting to wonder if anyone was really fooled by my disguise spells.

The Queen uncoiled from her seat and began pacing back and forth as she spoke, oblivious to her nakedness which peeked out of her wrap at each turn.

"The fact that you aren't the king doesn't change my situation, if anything it improves it. As long as you can keep your disguise up enough to fool the rabble, I'll be marrying two power blocks instead of one."

"Two power blocks," I echoed hollowly.

"Yes. As the 'king' of Possiltum, you control the first block I was after: land and people. Impasse by itself isn't large enough to wage an aggressive war, but uniting the respective powers of the two kingdoms, we're unstoppable. With your armies backed by my capital, I can sweep as far as I want, which is pretty far, let me tell you. There's nothing like growing up in a valley where the only view is the other side of the valley to whet one's appetite for new and unusual places."

"Most people content themselves with touring," I suggested. "You don't have to conquer a country to see it."

"Cute," Queen Hemlock sneered. "Naive, but cute. Let's just say I'm not most people and let it ride, okay? Now then, for the second power base, there's you and your magic. That's a bonus I hadn't expected, but I'm sure that, given a day or two, I can expand my plans to take advantage of it."

At one time, I thought I had been scared by Massha. In hindsight, Massha caused me only faint discomfort. Talking with Queen Hemlock, I learned what fear was all about! She wasn't just a murderess, as Badaxe suspected. She was utter mayhem waiting to be loosed on the world. The only thing between her and the resources necessary to act out her dreams was me. Me, and maybe...

"What about King Rodrick?" I blurted out. "If he shows up, the original wedding plans go into effect."

"You mean he's still alive?" she exclaimed, arching a thin eyebrow at me. "I've overestimated you, Skeeve. Alive he could be a problem. No matter. I'll alert my escort to kill him on sight if he appears before the wedding. After we're married, it would be a simple matter to declare him an imposter and have him officially executed."

Terrific. Thanks to my big mouth, Massha would be walking into a trap if she tried to return the King to the castle. If Queen Hemlock's men saw him, then...

"Wait a minute!" I exclaimed. "If I'm walking around disguised as the King, what's to keep your men from offing me by mistake?"

"Hmm. Good thing you thought about that. Okay! Here's what we'll do."

She dove into her wardrobe and emerged with a length of purple ribbon.

"Wear this in full view whenever you're outside your chambers," she instructed, thrusting it into my hands. "It'll let my men know that you're the man I want to marry instead of their target."

I stood with the ribbon in my hand.

"Aren't you making a rather large assumption, your Majesty?"

"What's that?" she frowned.

"That I may not want to marry you?"

"Of course you do," she smiled. "You've already got the throne of Possiltum. If you marry me, you not only have access to my treasury, it also rids you of your other problem."

"My other problem?"

"The Mob, silly. Remember? I rode in with their representative. With my money, you can buy them off. They'll forget anything if the price is high enough. Now, isn't being my husband better than running from their vengeance and mine for the rest of your life?"

I had my answer to that, but in a flash of wisdom kept it to myself. Instead, I said my goodbyes and left.

"From your expression, I take it that your interview with the Queen was less than a roaring success," Badaxe said dryly.

"Spare me the 'I told you so's,' General," I snarled. "We've got work to do."

Shooting a quick glance up and down the corridor, I cut my purple ribbon in half on the edge of his axe.

"Keep a lookout for Massha and the King," I instructed. "If you see them, be sure Rodrick wears this. It'll make his trip through the palace a lot easier."

"But where are you going?"

I gave him a tight smile.

"To see the Mob representatives. Queen Hemlock has graciously told me how to deal with them!"

X.

"Superior firepower is an invaluable tool when entering into negotiations."
G. PATTON

THE MOB REPRESENTATIVES had been housed in one of the less frequented corners of the palace. In theory, this kept them far from the hub of activity while Badaxe and I figured out what to do with them. In fact, it meant that now that I was ready to face them, I had an awfully long walk to reach my destination.

By the time I reached the proper door, I was so winded I wasn't sure I'd have enough breath to announce my presence. Still, on my walk I had worked up a bit of a mad against the Mob. I mean, who did they think they were, popping up and disrupting my life this way? Besides, I was too unnerved by Queen Hemlock to try anything against her, which left the Mob as the only target for my frustration.

With that in mind, I drew a deep breath and knocked on the door.

I needn't have worried about announcing myself. Between the second and third knocks, the door opened a crack. My third knock hit the door before I could stop it, but the door remained unmoved by the impact.

"Hey, Shai-ster! It's the King!"

"Well, let him in, you idiot!"

The door opened wide, revealing one of Shai-ster's massive bodyguards, then a little wider to allow me entry space past him. "Come in, come in, your Majesty," the Mob's spokesman said, hurrying forward to greet me. "Have a drink...Dummy! Get the King something to drink!"

This last was addressed to the second hulking muscleman who heaved himself off the bed he had been sprawled upon. With self—conscious dignity he picked up the end of the bed one-handed, set it down again, then picked up the mattress and extracted a small, flat bottle from under it.

I wondered briefly if this was what Big Julie meant when he referred to the Mob tradition of "going to the mattresses." Somehow the phrase had always brought another image to mind... something involving women.

Accepting the flask from his bodyguard, Shai-ster opened the top and offered it to me, smiling all the while.

"Am I correct in assuming that your Majesty's visit indicates news of the whereabouts of his court magician? Perhaps even an estimated time as to when he is expected back?"

I accepted the flask, covertly checking the locations of the bodyguards before I answered. One was leaning against the door, while the other stood by the bed.

"Actually, I can do better than that. The Great Skeeve..." I closed my eyes and dropped my disguise spell.

"Is here."

The bodyguards started visibly at my transformation, but Shai-ster remained unmoved except for a narrowing of the eyes and a tightening of his smile.

"I see. That simplifies things a bit. Boys, give the Great Skeeve here a chair. We have some business to discuss."

His tone was not pleasant, nor were the bodyguards smiling as they started for me.

Remember how Rupert jumped me so easily? Well, he took me by surprise, and had three hundred years plus of magical practice to boot. Somehow, I was not particularly surprised by the bodyguards' action...in fact, I had been expecting it and had been gathering my powers for just this moment.

With a theatric wave of my hand and a much more important focusing of my mental energies, I picked the two men up and spun them in midair. Heck, I wasn't adverse to stealing a new idea for how to use levitation...even from Rupert. I did like a little originality in my work, though, so instead of bouncing them on their heads, I slammed them against the ceiling and held them pinned there.

"No, thanks," I said as casually as I could, "I'd rather stand." Shai-ster looked at his helpless protectors, then shot a hard stare at me.

"Perhaps this won't be as simple as I thought," he admitted. "Say, you've got a unicorn, don't you?"

"That's right," I confirmed, surprised by the sudden change in topic.

"I don't suppose you'd be particularly scared if you woke up in the morning and found him in your bed...not all of him, just his head?"

"Scared? No, not particularly. In fact, I'm pretty sure I'd be mad enough to quit playing games and get down to serious revenge."

The Mob spokesman sighed heavily.

"Well, that's that. If we can't make a deal, we'll just have to do this the hard way. You can let the boys down now. We'll be heading back in the morning."

This time, it was my turn to smile.

"Not so fast. Who said I didn't want to make a deal?"

For the first time since I met him, Shai-ster's poise was shaken.

"But...I thought...if you can..."

"Don't assume, Shai-ster. It's a bad habit for businessmen to get into. I just don't like to get pushed around, that's all. Now then, as you said earlier, I believe we have some business to discuss."

The spokesman shot a nervous glance at the ceiling. "Um...could you let the boys down first? It's a bit distracting."

"Sure."

I closed my eyes and released the spell. Mind you, unlike the disguise spell, I don't have to close my eyes to remove a levitation spell. I just didn't want to see the results.

The room shook as two loud crashes echoed each other. I distinctly heard the bed assume a foolproof disguise as kindling. I carefully opened an eye.

One bodyguard was unconscious. The other rolled about, groaning weakly.

"They're down," I said, needlessly.

Shai-ster ignored me.

"Big bad bodyguards! Wait'll the Big Boys hear how good dumb muscle is against magic!"

He paused to kick the groaner in the side.

"Groan quieter! Mister Skeeve and I have some talking to do."

Having already completed one adventure after antagonizing the military arm of a large organization, I was not overly eager to add another entire group of plug-uglies to my growing list of enemies.

"Nothing personal," I called to the bodyguard who was still conscious. "Here! Have a drink."

I levitated the flask over to him, and he caught it with a weak moan I chose to interpret as 'thanks.'

"You said something about a deal?" Shai-ster said, turning to me again.

"Right. Now, if my appraisal of the situation is correct, the Mob wants three things: Big Julie's army back, me dead or working for them, and a crack at the new money coming into Possiltum after the wedding."

The Mob spokesman cocked his head to one side.

"That a bit more blunt than I would have put it, but you appear to have captured the essential spirit of my clients' wishes. My compliments on your concise summation."

"Here's another concise summation to go with it. Hands off Big Julie and his crew; he's under my protection. By the same token, Possiltum is my territory. Stay away from it or it will cost you more than you'll get. As to my services, I have no wish to become a Mob employee. I would consider an occasional assignment as an outside contractor for a specific fee, but full-time employment is out."

The Mob spokesman was back in his element, face stony and impassive.

"That doesn't sound like much of a deal."

"It doesn't?"

I reviewed the terms quickly in my mind.

"Oh! Excuse me. There is one other important part of my offer I neglected to mention. I don't expect your employers to give up their objectives without any return at all. What I have in mind is a swap: an army and maybe a kingdom for an opportunity to exploit an entire world."

Shai-ster raised his eyebrows.

"You're going to give us the world? Just like that? Lord Magician, I suspect you're not bargaining with a full deck."

"I didn't say I would give you the world, I said I would give you access to a world. Brand new territory full of businesses and people to exploit; one of the richest in the universe."

The spokesman frowned.

"Another world? And I'm supposed to take your word as to how rich it is and that you can give us access?"

"It would be nice, but even in my most naive moments I wouldn't expect you to accept a blind bid like that. No, I'm ready to give you a brief tour of the proposed world so that you can judge for yourself."

"Wait a minute," Shai-ster said, holding up his hands. "This is so far beyond my negotiating parameters that even if I liked what I saw, I couldn't approve the deal. I need to bring one of the Big Boys in on this decision."

This was better than I had hoped. By the time he could bring one of the Mob's hierarchy to Possiltum, I could deal with some of my other problems.

"Fine. Go and fetch him. I'll hold the deal until your return." The spokesman gave one of his tight-lipped smiles.

"No need to wait," he said. "My immediate superior is on call specifically for emergencies such as this."

Before I could frame a reply, he opened the front of his belt-buckle and began rubbing it, all the while mumbling under his breath.

There was a quick flash of light, and an old, hairy-jowled man appeared in the room. Looking round, he spied the two body-guards sprawled on the floor and gripped the sides of his face with his open hands in an exaggerated expression of horror.

"Mercy!" he wheezed in a voice so hoarse I could barely understand him. "Shai-ster, you bad boy. If there was trouble, you should have called me sooner. Oh, those poor, poor boys."

The Mob spokesman's face was once again blank and impassive as he addressed me.

"Skeeve, Lord Magician of Possiltum, let me introduce Don Bruce, the Mob's fairy godfather."

XI.

"Tell you what. Let me sweeten the deal a bit for you..."
BEELZEBUB

"OH! THIS IS simply mar-velous! Who would have ever thought... another dimension, you say?"

"That's right," I said off-handedly. "It's called Deva."

Of course, I was quite in agreement with Don Bruce. The Bazaar on Deva was really something, and every time I visited it, I was impressed anew. It was an incredible tangle of tents and displays stretching as far as the eye could see in every direction, crammed full of enough magical devices and beings to defy anyone's imagination and sanity. It was the main crossroads of trade for the dimensions. Anything worth trading money or credits for was here.

This time, however, I was the senior member of the expedition. As much as I wanted to rubberneck and explore, it was more important to pretend to be bored and worldly...or other-worldly as the case might be.

Don Bruce led the parade, as wide-eyed as a farm-kid in his first big city, with Shai-ster, myself, and the two bodyguards trailing along behind. The bodyguards seemed more interested in crowding close to me than in protecting their superiors, but then again, they had just had some bad experiences with magic.

"The people here all look kinda strange," one of them muttered to me. "You know, like foreigners."

"They are foreigners...or rather you are," I said. "You're on their turf, and a long way from home. These are Deveels."

"Devils?" the man responded, looking a little wild-eyed. "You're tellin' me we're surrounded by devils?"

While it was reassuring to me to see the Mob's bully-boys terrified by something I had grown used to, it also occurred to me that if they were too scared, it might ruin the deal I was trying to set up.

"Look...say, what is your name, anyway?"

"Guido," the man confided, "and this here's my cousin Nunzio."

"Well look, Guido. Don't be thrown by these jokers. Look at them. They're storekeepers like storekeepers anywhere. Just because they look funny doesn't mean they don't scare like any-body else."

"I suppose you're right. Say, I meant to thank you for the drink back there at the castle."

"Don't mention it," I waved. "It was the least I could do after bouncing you off the ceiling. Incidentally, there was nothing per-sonal in that. I wasn't trying to make you two look bad, I was trying to make myself look good...if you see the difference."

Guido's brow furrowed slightly.

"I...think so. Yeah! I get it. Well, it worked. You looked real good. I wouldn't want to cross you, and neither would Nunzio. In fact, if we can ever do you a favor...you know, bend someone a little for you...well , just let us know."

"Hey, what's that?"

I looked in the direction Don Bruce was pointing. A booth was filled with short painted sticks, all floating in midair. "I think he's selling magic wands," I guessed.

"Oh! I want one. Now, don't go anywhere without me."

The bodyguards hesitated for a moment, then followed as Don Bruce plunged into negotiations with the booth's proprietor, who gaped a bit at his new customer.

"Does he always dress like that?" I asked Shai-ster. "You know, all in light purple?"

The Mob spokesman raised an eyebrow at me.

"Do you always dress in green when you travel to other dimensions?"

Just to be on the safe side, I had donned another disguise before accompanying this crew to Deva. It occurred to me that if I were successful in my negotiations, it wouldn't be wise to be known at the Bazaar as the one who introduced organized crime to the dimension.

Unfortunately, this had dawned on me just as we were prepar-ing to make our departure, so I hadn't had much time to choose someone to disguise myself as. Any of my friends were out, as were Massha, Quigley, Garkin...in desperation I settled on Rupert...I mean, there was one being I owed a bad turn or two. Consequently, I was currently parading around the Bazaar as a scaly green Pervert...excuse me, Pervect.

"I have my reasons," I dodged loftily.

"Well, so has Don Bruce," Shai-ster scowled. "Now if you don't mind, I've got a few questions about this place. If we try to move in here, won't language be a problem? I can't understand anything these freaks are saying."

"Take a look," I instructed, pointing.

Don Bruce and the Deveel proprietor were haggling ear-nestly, obviously having no difficulty understanding each other, however much they disagreed.

"No Deveel worth his salt is going to let a little thing like language stand in the way of a sale."

"Hey, everybody! Look what I got!"

We turned to find Don Bruce bearing down on us, proudly waving a small rod the same color as his clothes.

"It's a magic wand!" he exclaimed. "I got it for a song."

"A song plus some gold, I'd wager," Shai-ster observed dryly. "What does it do?"

"What does it do?" Don Bruce grinned. "Watch this."

He swept the wand across the air with a grand gesture, and a cloud of shiny dust sparkled to the ground.

"That's it?" Shai-ster grimaced.

Don Bruce frowned at the wand.

"That's funny. When the guy back there did it, he got a rainbow."

He pointed the wand at the ground and shook it...and three blades materialized out of thin air, lancing into the dust at our feet.

"Careful!" Shai-ster warned, hopping back out of range. "You'd better read the instructions on that thing."

"I don't need instructions," Don Bruce insisted. "I'm a fairy godfather. I know what I'm doing."

As he spoke, he gestured emphatically with the wand, and a jet of flame narrowly missed one of the bodyguards.

"..But this can wait," Don Bruce concluded, tucking the wand into his waistband. "We've got business to discuss."

"Yes. We were just..." Shai-ster began.

"Shuddup! I'm talking to Skeeve here."

The force behind Don Bruce's sudden admonishment, combined with the Shai-ster's quick obedience, made me hastily revise my opinion of the Mob leader. Strange or not, he was a force to be recognized.

"Now then, Mister Skeeve, what's the police situation around here?"

"There aren't any."

Shaister's eyebrows shot up.

"Then how do they enforce the laws?" he asked, forgetting himself.

"As far as I can tell, there are no laws either."

"How 'bout that, Shai-ster?" Don Bruce laughed. "No police, no laws, no lawyers. You'd be in trouble if you were born here."

I started to ask what a lawyer was, but the godfather saved me from my own ignorance by plunging into the next question. "How about politicians?"

"None."

"Unions?"

"None."

"Bookies?"

"Lots," I admitted. "This is the gambling capital of the dimensions. As near as I can tell, though, they all operate independently. There's no central organization."

Don Bruce rubbed his hands together gleefully.

"You listening to this, Shai-ster? This is some world Mister Skeeve is givin' us here."

"He's not giving it to us," Shai-ster corrected. "He's offering access to it."

"That's right," I said quickly. "Exploiting it is up to your organization. Now, if you don't think your boys can handle it..."

"We can handle it. A layout like this? It's a piece of cake." Guido and Nunzio exchanged nervous glances, but held their silence as Don Bruce continued.

"Now if I understand this right, what you want in return for letting us into this territory is that we lay off Big Julie and Possiltum. Right?"

I count real good up to three.

"And me," I added. "No 'getting even with the guy who thrashed our army plans,' no `join the Mob or die' pressure. I'm an independent operator and happy to stay that way."

"Sure, sure," Don Bruce waved. "Now that we've seen how you operate, no reason we can't eat out the same bowl. If anything, we owe you a favor for opening up a new area to our organization."

Somehow, that worried me.

"Um...tell you what. I don't want any credit for this...inside the Mob or outside. Right now, nobody but us knows I had a hand in this. Let's keep it that way, okay?"

"If that's what you want," Don Bruce shrugged. "I'll just tell the Big Boys you're too rough for us to tangle with, and that's why we're going to leave you alone. Anytime our paths cross, we go ahead with your approval or we back off. Okay?"

"That's what I want."

"Deal?"

"Deal."

We shook hands ceremoniously.

"Very well," I said. "Here's what you need to travel between here and home."

I fished the D-Hopper out of my sleeve.

"This setting is for home. This one is for here. Push this button to travel."

"What about the other settings?" Shai-ster asked.

"Remember the magic wand?" I countered. "Without instruc-tions, you could get lost with this thing. I mean, really lost."

"Come on, boys," Don Bruce said, setting the D-Hopper. "We gotta hurry home. There's a world here to conquer, so we gotta get started before somebody else beats us to it. Mister Skeeve, a plea-sure doin' business with you."

A second later, they were gone.

I should have been elated, having finally eliminated one set of problems from my horizon. I wasn't.

Don Bruce's last comment about world conquering reminded me of Queen Hemlock's plans. Now that the Mob was neutralized, I had other problems to solve. As soon as I got back to the palace, I would have to...

Then it hit me.

The Mob representatives had taken the D-Hopper with them when they left. That thing was my only route back to Klah! I was stranded at the Bazaar with no way back to my own dimension!

XII.

"I'm making this up as I go along!"
I. JONES

BUT I DIDN'T panic. Why should I?

Sure, I was in a bit of a mess, but if there was one place in all the dimensions I could be confident of finding help, it was here at the Bazaar. Anything could be had here for a price, and thanks to Aahz's training, I had made a point of stocking my pouch with money prior to our departure from Klah.

Aahz!

It suddenly occurred to me that I hadn't thought about my old mentor for days. The crises that had erupted shortly after his departure had occupied my mind to an extent where there was no time or energy left for brooding. Except for the occasional explanation of his absence, Aahz was playing no part in my life currently. I was successfully handling things without him.

Well...

Okay. I had successfully handled some things without him...the Mob for example. Of course, the training he had gotten me into earlier in our relationship had also provided me with confidence under fire...another much-needed commodity these days.

'Face it, kid,' I said to myself in my best imitation of Aahz. `You owe a lot to your old mentor.'

Right. A lot. Like not making him ashamed of his prize pupil...say by leaving a job half done.

With new resolve, I addressed my situation. First, I had to get back to Klah...or should I look for a solution right here?

Rather than lose time to indecision, I compromised. With a few specific questions to the nearest vendor, I set a course for my eventual destination, keeping an eye out as I went for something that would help me solve the Queen Hemlock problem.

This trip through the Bazaar was different from my earlier visits. Before, my experience had been of wishing for more time to study the displays at leisure while hurrying to keep up with Aahz. This time, it was me that was pushing the pace, dismissing display after display with a casual 'interesting, but no help with today's problem.' Things seemed to have a different priority when responsibility for the crisis was riding on my shoulders.

Of course, I didn't know what I was looking for. I just knew that trick wands and instant thunderstorms weren't it. Out of desperation, I resorted to logic.

To recognize the solution, I needed to know the problem. The problem was that Queen Hemlock was about to marry me instead of Rodrick. Scratch that. Massha was bringing Rodrick back, and I couldn't help her. I just had to believe she could do it. The problem was Queen Hemlock.

Whether she married me or Rodrick, she was determined to use Possiltum's military strength to wage a war of expansion. If her husband, whoever it was, tried to oppose her, he would find himself conveniently dead.

Killing the Queen would be one solution, but somehow I shrank from cold-blooded murder...or hot-blooded murder for that matter. No. What was needed was something to throw a scare into her. A big scare.

The answer walked past me before I recognized it. Fortu-nately, it was moving slowly, so I turned and caught up with it in just a few steps.

Answers come in many shapes and sizes. This one was in the form of a Deveel with a small tray display hung by a strap around his neck.

"What you just said, was it true?"

The Deveel studied me.

"I said 'Rings. One size fits all. Once on, never off.'" "That's right. Is it true?"

"Of course. Each of my rings are pre-spelled. Once you put it on, it self-adjusts so that it won't come off, even if you want it to." "Great. I'll take two."

"...Because to lose a ring of such value would be tragedy indeed. Each one worth a king's ransom..."

I rolled my eyes.

"Look," I interrupted. "I know it's a tradition of the Bazaar to bargain, but I'm in a hurry. How much for two? Bottom price."

He thought for a moment and named a figure. My training came to the fore and I made a counteroffer one-tenth of his.

"Hey! You said 'no haggling,'" he protested. "Who do you think you are?"

Well, it was worth a try. According to Massha, I was getting a bit of a reputation at the Bazaar.

"I think I'm the Great Skeeve, since you asked."

"...And the camel you rode in on," the vendor sneered. "Everyone knows the Great Skeeve isn't a Pervert."

The disguise! I had forgotten about it completely. With a mental wave, I restored my normal appearance.

"No, I'm a Klahd," I smiled. "And for your information, that's Pervect!"

"You mean you're really...no, you must be. No one else would voluntarily look like a Klahd...or defend Perverts...excuse me, Pervects."

"Now that that's established," I yawned, "how much for two of your rings?"

"Here," he said, thrusting the tray forward. "Take your pick, with my compliments. I won a bundle betting on your team at the Great Game. All I ask is permission to say that you use my wares."

It was with a great deal of satisfaction that I made my selection and continued on my way. It was nice to have a reputation, but nicer to earn it. Those two little baubles now riding in my pouch were going to get me out of the Possiltum dilemma...if I got back in time...and if Massha had found the King.

Those sobering thoughts brought my hat size back to normal in a hurry. The time to gloat was after the battle, not before. Plans aren't victories, as I should be the first to know.

With panic once again nipping at my heels, I quickened my pace until I was nearly running by the time I reached my final destination: the Yellow Crescent Inn.

Bursting through the door of the Bazaar's leading fast food establishment, I saw that it was empty of customers except for a troll munching on a table in the corner.

Terrific.

I was expecting to deal with Gus, the gargoyle proprietor, but I'd settle for the troll.

"Skeeve!" the troll exclaimed. "I say, this is a surprise. What brings you to the Bazaar?"

"Later, Chumly. Right now I need a lift back to Klah. Are you busy with anything?"

The troll set his half-eaten table to one side and raised the eyebrow over one mismatched moon eye.

"Not to be picky about formality," he said, "but what happened to 'Hello, Chumly. How are you?'"

"I'm sorry. I'm in a bit of a hurry. Can we just..."

"Skeeve! How's it going, handsome?"

A particularly curvaceous bundle of green-haired loveliness had just emerged from the ladies' room.

"Oh. Hi, Tananda. How 'bout it, Chumly?"

Tananda's smile of welcome disappeared, to be replaced by a puzzled frown.

"'Oh. Hi, Tananda?'" she repeated, shooting a look at the troll. "Does anything strike you as strange about that rather low-key greeting, big brother?"

"No stranger than the greeting I just got," Chumly confided. "Just off-hand, I'd say that either our young friend here has forgotten his manners completely, or he's gotten himself into a spot of trouble."

Their eyes locked and they nodded.

"Trouble," they said together.

"Cute," I grimaced. "Okay, so I'm in a mess. I'm not asking you to get involved. In fact, I think I've got it worked out myself. All I want is for you to pop me back to Klah."

Brother and sister stepped to my side.

"Certainly," Chumly smiled. "You don't mind if we tag along, though, do you?"

"But I didn't ask you to..."

"When have you had to ask for our help before, handsome?" Tananda scolded, slipping an arm around my waist. "We're your friends, remember?"

"But I think I've got it handled..."

"...In which case, having us along won't hurt," the troll insisted.

"Unless, of course, something goes wrong," Tananda sup-plied. "In which case, we might be able to lend a hand."

"...And if the three of us can't handle it, we'll be there to pull you out again," Chumly finished.

I should have known better than to try to argue with the two of them when they were united.

"But...if...well, thanks," I managed. "I didn't really expect this. I mean, you don't even know what the trouble is."

"You can tell us later," Tananda said firmly, starting her conjuring to move us through the dimensions. "Incidentally, where's Aahz?"

"That's part of the problem," I sighed.

And we were back!

Not just back on Klah, back in my own quarters in the palace. As luck would have it, we weren't alone. Someday I'll have time to figure out if it was good luck or bad.

The King was trussed up hand and foot on my bed, while Massha and J. R. Grimble were each enjoying a goblet of wine, and apparently each other's company. At least, that was the scene when we arrived. Once Massha and Tananda set eyes on each other, the mood changed dramatically.

"Slut," my new apprentice hissed.

"No-talent mechanic," Tananda shot back.

"Is that freak on our payroll?" Grimble interrupted, staring at Chumly.

"Spoken like a true bean-counter," the troll sneered. I tried to break it up.

"If we can just…"

That brought Grimble's attention to me.

"You!" he gasped. "But if you're Skeeve, then who's…"

"King Rodrick of Possiltum," I supplied, nodding to the bound figure on the bed. "And now that everybody knows each other, can you all shut up while I tell you what our next move is?"

XIII.

"Marriage, being a lifelong venture, must be approached with care and caution."
BLUEBIRD

THE WEDDING WENT off without a hitch.

I don't know why I had been worried. There were no interruptions, no missed lines, nobody protested or even coughed at the wrong time. As was previously noted, Queen Hemlock had handled the planning to the last minute detail…except for a few surprises we were holding back.

That's why I was worried! My cronies and I knew that as gaudy and overdone as the Royal Wedding was, it was only the warm-up act for the main event. There was also the extra heat on me of knowing that I hadn't shared all of my plans with my co-conspirators. It seemed that was another bad habit I had picked up from Aahz.

Grimble and Badaxe were at their usual places as mismatched bookends to the throne, while Chumly, Tananda, Massha, and I, courtesy of my disguise spells and Badaxe's pull as general, were lined up along the foot of the throne as bodyguards. Everything was set to go…if we ever got the time!

As dignitary after dignitary stepped forward to offer his or her congratulations and gifts, I found little to occupy my thoughts except how many things could go wrong with my little scheme. I had stuck my neck out a long way with my plan, and if it didn't work, a lot of people would be affected, starting with the king and subjects of Possiltum.

The more I thought, the more I worried until, instead of wishing the dignitaries would hurry, I actually found myself hoping they would take forever and preserve this brief moment of peace.

Of course, no sooner did I start hoping things would last, and they were over. The last well-wisher was filing out and the Queen herself rising to leave when Grimble and Badaxe left their customary positions and stepped before the throne.

"Before you go, my dear," Rodrick said, "our retainers wish to extend their compliments."

Queen Hemlock frowned slightly, but resumed her seat.

"The Chancellor of the Exchequer stands ready to support their majesties in any way," Grimble began. "Of course, even with the new influx of wealth into the treasury, we must watch needless expenses. As always, I stand ready to set the example in cost savings, and so have decided that to purchase a present for you equal to my esteem would be a flagrant and unnecessary expense, and therefore…"

"Yes, yes, Grimble," the King interrupted. "We understand and appreciate your self-sacrifice. General Badaxe?"

Grimble hesitated, then yielded the floor to his rival.

"I am a fighting man, not a speechmaker," the General said abruptly. "The army stands ready to support the kingdom and the throne of Possiltum. As for myself…here is my present."

He removed the axe from his belt and laid it on the stairs before the throne.

Whether he was offering his pet weapon or his personal allegiance, I found the gesture eloquent beyond words. "Thank you, General Badaxe, Grimble," Queen Hemlock said loftily. "I'm sure I can…"

"My dear," the King interrupted softly. "There is another retainer."

And I was on.

Screwing up my courage, I dropped my disguise and stepped before the throne.

"Your majesties, the Great Skeeve gives you his congratulations on this happy event."

The Queen was no fool. For one beat her eyes popped open and on the next she was staring at the King. You could almost hear her thoughts: 'If the Magician is there, then the man I just married is…"

"That's right, your majesty. As you yourself said in our earlier conversations, 'Royalty has married royalty. While it might have been nice dramatically to savor that moment, I noticed the Queen's eyes were narrowing thoughtfully, so I hurried on.

"Before you decide how to express your joy," I warned, "perhaps I should explain my gift to the throne."

Now the thoughtful gaze was on me. I expressed my own joy by sweating profusely.

"My gift is the wedding rings now worn by both king and queen. I hope you like them, because they won't come off."

Queen Hemlock made one brief attempt to remove her ring, then her eyes were on me again. This time, the gaze wasn't thoughtful.

"Just as the fate of the kingdom of Possiltum is linked to the throne, as of the moment you donned those rings, your fates are linked to each other. By the power of a spell so simple it cannot be broken or countered, when one of you dies, so does the other."

The Queen didn't like that at all, and even the King showed a small frown wrinkle on his forehead, as if contemplating something he had not previously considered. That was my signal to clarify things for him…that there was an implication to the rings that I hadn't mentioned to him.

"This is not intended as a 'one-sided' gift, for just as Queen Hemlock must now protect the health and well-being of her king, so must King Rodrick defend his queen against all dangers. . all dangers."

The King was on his feet now, eyes flashing.

"What is that supposed to mean, Lord Magician?"

As adept as I was becoming at courtly speech, there were things which I felt were best said in the vernacular.

"It means if you or anybody else kills her, say, on your orders, then, you're dead. Now SIT DOWN AND LISTEN!!"

All the anger and frustration I had felt since figuring out the King was trying to double-cross me, but had been too busy to express, found its vent in that outburst. It worked. The King sank back into his chair, pale and slightly shaken.

I wasn't done, though. I had been through a lot, and a few words weren't enough to settle my mind.

"Since I accepted this assignment, I've heard nothing but how ruthless and ambitious Queen Hemlock is. Well, that maybe true, BUT SHE ISN'T GETTING ANY PRIZE EITHER! Right now, King Rodrick, I have more respect for her than I have for you. She didn't abandon her kingdom in the middle of a crisis."

I began to pace back and forth before the thrones as I warmed to my topic.

"Everybody talks about 'our duty to the throne.' It's the guiding directive in the walk-a-day life of commoners. What never gets mentioned is 'the throne's duty to the people.'"

I paused and pointed directly at the King.

"I sat in that chair for a while. It's a lot of fun, deciding people's lives for them. Power is heady, and the fringe benefits are great! All that bowing and scraping, not to mention one heck of a wardrobe. Still, it's a job like any other, and with any job you sometimes have to do things you don't like. Badaxe doesn't just parade and review his troops, he has to train them and lead them into battle…you know, as in 'I could get killed out here' battle. Grimble spends ungodly hours poring over those numbers of his for the privilege of standing at your side.

"Any job has its pluses and minuses, and if the minuses outweigh the pluses, you screw up your courage and quit…unless, of course, you're King Rodrick. Then, instead of abdicating and turning the pluses and minuses over to someone else, you stick someone else with doing the job in your name and sneak out a back door. Maybe that's how people do their jobs where you were raised, but I think it's conduct a peasant would be ashamed of.

I faced them, hands defiantly on my hips.

"Well, I've done my job. The kingdom has been protected from the immediate threat. With any luck, you two will learn to work together. I trust King Rodrick can dilute the Queen's ambition. I only hope that Queen Hemlock's fiery spirit can put a little more spine and courage into the King."

This time it was Queen Hemlock who was on her feet.

"Are you going to let him talk to you like that, Roddie? You're the king. Nobody pushes a king around."

"Guards!" Rodrick said tightly. "Seize that man."

It had worked! King and Queen were united against a common foe…me! Now all I had to do was survive it.

One more mind pass, and my comrades stood exposed as the outworlders they were.

Queen Hemlock, unaccustomed to my dealings with demons, dropped into her seat with a small gasp., The King simply scowled as he realized the real reason for the presence of my friends.

"Your Majesties," Badaxe said, stepping forward. "I am sworn to protect the throne and would willingly lay down my life in your defense. I do not see a physical threat here, however. If anything, it occurs to me both throne and kingdom would be strengthened if the Great Skeeve's words were heard and heeded."

"I am not a fighting man," Grimble said, joining Badaxe, "so my duty here is passive. I must add, though, that I also feel the Lord Magician's words have merit and should be said to every ruler."

His eyes narrowed and he turned to face me.

"I challenge, though, whether they should be said by a retainer to the court. One of our first duties is to show respect to the throne, in word and manner."

"That much we agree on, Grimble," Badaxe nodded, adding his glare to the many focused on me.

"Strange as it may sound," I said, "I agree, too. For that reason, I am hereby tendering my resignation as Court Magician of Possiltum. The kingdom is now secure militarily and financially, and in my opinion there is no point in it bearing the expense of a full-time magician. especially one who has been insolent to the throne. There is no need to discuss severance pay. The King's reward for my last assignment, coupled with the monies I have already received from the Exchequer, will serve my needs adequately. I will simply gather my things and depart."

I saw Grimble blanch slightly when he realized that I would not be returning his bribe. I had faith in his ability to hide anything in his stacks of numbered, sheets, though.

With only the slightest of nods to the throne, I gathered my entourage with my eyes and left.

Everything had gone perfectly. I couldn't have asked for the proceedings to have turned out better. As such, I was puzzled as to why I was sweat-drenched and shaking like a leaf by the time I reached my own quarters.

XIV.

"Some farewells are easier than others."
P. MARLOWE

"SO, WHERE DO you go from here?" Tananda asked.

She and Chumly were helping me pack. We had all agreed that having incurred the combined wrath of the King and Queen, it would be wisest to delay my departure as little as possible. Massha was off seeing to Gleep and Buttercup as well as saying her goodbyes to Badaxe.

"I don't really know," I admitted. "I was serious when I said I had accumulated enough wealth for a while. I'll probably hole up someplace and practice my magic for a while...maybe at that inn Aahz and I used to use as a home base."

"I say, why don't you tag along with little sister and me?" Chumly suggested. "We usually operate out of the Bazaar at Deva. It wouldn't be a bad place for you to keep your hand in, magic-wise."

It flashed through my mind that the Mob must have started its infiltration of the Bazaar by now. It also occurred to me that, in the pre-wedding rush, I hadn't told Tananda or Chumly about that particular portion of the caper. Having remembered, I found myself reluctant to admit my responsibility for what they'd find on their return.

"I dunno, Chumly," I hedged. "You two travel pretty light. I've got so much stuff, I'd probably be better off settling down somewhere permanent."

It was a pretty weak argument, but the troll seemed to accept it...maybe because he could see that mountain of gear we were accumulating, trying to clear my quarters.

"Well, think it over. We'd be glad to have you. You're not a bad sort to have around in a tight spot."

"I'll say," Tanda agreed with a laugh. "Where did you find those rings, anyway?"

"Bought them from a street vendor at the Bazaar."

"On Deva?" Chumly said with a frown. "Two spelled rings like that must have set you back a pretty penny. Are you sure you have enough money left?"

Now it was my turn to laugh.

"First of all, they aren't spelled. That was just a bluff I was running on their royal majesties. The rings are plain junk jewelry...and I got them for free."

"Free?"

Now Tananda was frowning.

"Nobody gets anything for free at the Bazaar."

"No, really. They were free...well, the vendor did get my permission to say that I use his wares, but that's the same as free, isn't it? I mean, I didn't pay him any money."

As I spoke, I found myself suddenly uncertain of my 'good deal.' One of my earliest lessons about dealing with Deveels was 'If you think you've made a good deal with a Deveel, first count your fingers, then your limbs, then your relatives...

"Permission to use your name?" Tananda echoed. "For two lousy rings? No percentage or anything? Didn't Aahz ever teach you about endorsements?"

There was a soft BAMPH in the air.

"Is someone taking my name in vain?"

And Aahz was there, every green scaly inch of him, making his entrance as casually as if he had just stepped out.

Of the three of us, I was the first to recover from my surprise. Well, at least I found my voice.

"Aahz!"

"Hi, kid. Miss me?"

"But Aahz!"

I didn't know if I should laugh or cry. What I really wanted to do was embrace him and never let go. Of course, now that he was back, I would do no such thing. I mean, our relationship had never been big in the emotional displays department.

"What's the matter with everybody?" my mentor demanded. "You all act like you never expected to see me again."

"We...Aahz! I..."

"We didn't," Tananda said flatly, saving me from making an even bigger fool of myself.

"What little sister means," Chumly put in, "is that it was our belief that your nephew, Rupert, had no intention of letting you return from Perv."

Aahz gave a derisive snort.

"Rupert? That upstart? Don't tell me anybody takes him seriously."

"Well, maybe not if your powers were in full force," Tananda said, "but as things are…"

"Rupert?" Aahz repeated. "You two have known me a long time, right? Then you should get it through your heads that nobody holds me against my will."

Somehow that quote sounded familiar. Still, I was so glad to have Aahz back, I would have agreed to anything just then.

"Yeah!" I chimed eagerly. "This is Aahz! Nobody pushes him around."

"There!" my mentor grinned. "As much as I hate to agree with a mere apprentice, the kid knows what he's talking about…this time."

Chumly and Tananda looked at each other with that special gaze that brother and sister use to communicate non-verbally.

"You know, big brother," Tananda said, "this mutual admira-tion society is getting a bit much for my stomach. How about you?"

"Ectually," the troll responded. "I wasn't hearing all that much mutual admiration. Somehow the phrase 'mere apprentice' sticks in my mind."

"Oh come on, you two," Aahz waved. "Get real, huh? I mean, we all like the kid, but we also know he's a trouble magnet. I've never met anyone who needs looking after as badly as he does. Speaking of which…"

He turned his yellow eyes on me with that speculative look of his.

"I notice you're both here…and I definitely heard my name as I phased in. What I need more than fond 'hellos' is a quick update as to exactly what kind of a mess we have to bail the Great Skeeve out of this time."

I braced myself for a quick but loud lesson about 'endorse-ments,' whatever that was, but the troll surprised me.

"No mess," he said, leaning back casually. "Little sister and I just dropped by for a visit. In fact, we were just getting ready to leave."

"Really?" my mentor sounded both surprised and suspicious. "Just a visit? No trouble?"

"Well, there was a little trouble," Tananda admitted. "Some-thing to do with the King…"

"I knew it!" Aahz chortled, rubbing his hands together.

"…But Skeeve here handled it himself," she finished pointedly. "Currently, there are no problems at all."

"Oh."

Strangely, Aahz seemed a bit disappointed.

"Well, I guess I owe you two some thanks, then. I really appreciate your watching over Skeeve here while I was gone. He can…"

"I don't think you're listening, Aahz," Chumly said, looking at the ceiling. "Skeeve handled the trouble. We just watched."

"Oh, we would have pitched in if things got tight," Tananda supplied. "You know, the way we do for you, Aahz. As it turned out, we weren't needed. Your 'mere apprentice' was more than equal to the task."

"Finished the job rather neatly, you know?" the troll added. "In fact, I'm hard pressed to recall when I've seen a nasty situation dealt with as smoothly or with as little fuss."

"All right, all right," Aahz grimaced. "I get the message. You can fill me in on the details later. Right now, the kid and I have some big things to discuss…and I mean big."

"Like what?" I frowned.

"Well, I've been giving it a lot of thought, and I figure it's about time we left Possiltum and moved on."

"Urn, Aahz?" I said.

"I know, I know," he waved. "You think you need practice. You do, but you've come a long way. This whole thing with the trouble you handled only proves my point. You're ready to…"

"Aahz?"

"All right. I know you've got friends and duties here, but eventually you have to leave the nest. You'll just have to trust my judgment and experience to know when the time is right to…"

"I've already quit!"

Aahz stopped in midsentence and stared at me.

"You have?" he blinked.

I nodded and pointed at the pile of gear we had been packing. He studied it for a moment as if he didn't believe what he was seeing.

"Oh," he said at last. "Oh well, in that case, I'll just duck over to talk to Grimble and discuss your severance pay. He's a tight fisted bird, but if I can't shake five hundred out of him, I'll know the reason why."

"I know the reason why," I said carefully.

Aahz rolled his eyes.

"Look, kid. This is my field of expertise, remember? If you go into a bargaining session aiming low, they'll walk all over you.

You've got to…"

"I've already negotiated for a thousand!"

This time, Aahz's 'freeze' was longer…and he didn't look at me.

"A thousand?" he said finally. "In gold?"

"Plus a hefty bonus from the King himself," Tananda supplied helpfully.

"We've been trying to tell you, Aahz old boy," Chumly smiled. "Skeeve here has been doing just fine without you."

"I see."

Aahz turned away and stared silently out the window.

I'll admit to being a bit disappointed. I mean, maybe I hadn't done a first-rate job, but a little bit of congratulations would have been nice. The way my mentor was acting, you'd think he…

Then it hit me. Like a runaway war-chariot it hit me. Aahz was jealous! More than that, he was hurt!

I could see it now with crystal clarity. Up until now I had been blinded by Aahz's arrogant self-confidence, but suddenly the veil was parted.

Aahz's escape from Perv wasn't nearly as easy as he was letting on. There had been a brawl—physical, verbal, or magical—some hard feelings, and some heavy promises made or broken. He had forced his way back to Klah with one thing on his mind: his apprentice…his favorite apprentice, was in trouble. Upon returning, what was his reception? Not only was I not in trouble, for all appearances, I was doing better without him!

Tananda and Chumly were still at it, merrily chattering back and forth about how great I was. While I appreciated their support, I wished desperately I could think of a way of getting it through to them that what they were really doing was twisting a knife in Aahz.

"Umm…Aahz?" I interrupted. "When you've got a minute, there are a few things I need your advice on."

"Like what?" came the muffled response. "From the sound of things, you don't need anybody, much less a teacher with no powers of his own."

Tananda caught it immediately. Her gadfly manner dropped away like a mask and she signaled desperately to Chumly. The troll was not insensitive, though. His reaction was to catch my eye with a pleading gaze.

It was up to me. Terrific.

"Well, like…um."

And Massha exploded into the room.

"Everything's ready downstairs, hot stuff, and...oh! Hi there, green and scaly. Thought you were gone for good." Aahz spun around, his eyes wide.

"Massha?" he stammered. "What are you doing here?"

"Didn't the man of the hour here tell you?" she smiled, batting her expansive eyelashes. "I'm his new apprentice."

"Apprentice?" Aahz echoed, his old fire creeping into his voice.

"Um...that's one of the things I wanted to talk to you about, Aahz," I smiled, meekly.

"Apprentice?" he repeated, as if he hadn't heard. "Kid, you and I have got to talk...NOW!"

"Okay, Aahz. As soon as I..."

"Now!"

Yep. Aahz was back.

"Um, if you'll excuse us, folks, Aahz and I have to..."

For the second time, there was a BAMPH in the room.

This one was louder, which was understandable, as there were more beings involved. Specifically, there were now four

Deveels standing in the room...and they didn't look happy. "We seek the Great Skeeve," one of them boomed.

My heart sank. Could my involvement with the Mob have been discovered so fast?

"Who's asking?"

Aahz casually placed his bulk between me and the intruders. Tananda and Chumly were also on their feet, and Massha was edging sideways to get a clear field of fire. Terrific. All I needed to complete my day was to have my friends soak up the trouble I had started.

"We are here representing the merchants of the Bazaar on Deva, seeking an audience with the Great Skeeve."

"About what?" my mentor challenged.

The Deveel fixed him with an icy glare.

"We seek the Great Skeeve, not idle chit-chat with a Pervert."

"Well, this particular Per-vect happens to be the Great Skeeve's business manager, and he doesn't waste his time with Deveels unless I clear them."

I almost said something, but changed my mind. Concerned or not, this was not the time to take a conversation away from Aahz. The Deveel hesitated, then shrugged.

"There is a new difficulty at the Bazaar," he said. "A group of organized criminals has gained access to our dimension threatening to disrupt the normal flow of business unless they are paid a percentage of our profits."

Tananda and Chumly exchanged glances, while Massha raised an eyebrow at me. I studied the ceiling with extreme care. Aahz alone was unruffled.

"Tough. So what does that have to do with the Great Skeeve?" he demanded.

Anticipating the answer, I tried to decide whether I should fight or run.

"Isn't it obvious?" the Deveel frowned. "We wish to retain his services to combat this threat. From what we can tell, he's the only magician around up to the job."

That one stopped me. Of all the strange turns events could have taken, this had to be the most unanticipated and...well, bizarre!

"I see," Aahz murmured, a nasty gleam in his eye. "You realize, of course, that the Great Skeeve's time is valuable and that such a massive undertaking would require equally massive remuneration?"

Every alarm in my system went off.

"Um...Aahz?"

"Shut up, k...I mean, be patient, Master Skeeve. This matter should be settled in a moment."

I couldn't watch.

Instead, I went to the window and stared out. Listening over my shoulder, I heard Aahz name an astronomical figure, and realized there might be a way out of this yet. If Aahz was greedy enough, and the Deveels stingy enough...

"Done!" said the spokesman.

"Of course, that's only an advance," Aahz pressed. "A full rendering will have to wait until the job is completed."

"Done," came the reply.

"And that is the fee only. Expenses will be reimbursed separately."

"Done! The advance will be awaiting your arrival. Anything else?"

In tribute to the Deveel's generosity, Aahz was unable to think of any other considerations to gouge out of them.

There was another BAMPH, and the delegation was gone. "How about that!" Aahz crowed. "I finally put one over on the Deveels!"

"What's that thing you always say about anyone who thinks they've gotten a good deal from a Deveel, Aahz?" Tananda asked sweetly.

"Later," my mentor ordered. "Right now we've got to get our things together and pop over to the Bazaar to scout the opposition."

"We already know what the opposition is."

"How's that, kid?"

I turned to face him.

"The opposition is the Mob. You remember, the organized crime group that was sponsoring Big Julie's army?"

A frown crossed Aahz's face as he regarded me closely. "And how did you come by that little tidbit of information, if I may ask?"

I regarded him right back.

"That's the other little thing I wanted your advice on."

XV.

"In a war against organized crime, survival is a hit or myth proposition."
—M. BOLAN

"NOW LET ME see if I've got this right," Aahz scowled, pacing back and forth in front of our worried gazes. "What we've got to do is keep the Mob from taking over the Bazaar, without letting them know we're opposing them or the Deveels know we were the ones who loosed the Mob on the Bazaar in the first place. Right?"

"You can do it, Aahz," I urged eagerly.

This time, it required no false enthusiasm on my part. While I had done an adequate job operating on my own, when it came to premeditated deviousness, I was quick to acknowledge my master. There might be someone out there in the multitude of dimensions better than Aahz at finding under-handed ways out of dilemmas, but I haven't met them yet.

"Of course I can do it," my mentor responded with a confident wink. "I just want everyone to admit it isn't going to be easy. All this talk about the Great Skeeve has made me a little insecure."

"A little?" Tananda smirked.

"I think it's a bit of all right," Chumly said, nudging his sister with an elbow. "I've always heard how formidable Aahz is when he swings into action. I, for one, am dying to see him handle this rather sticky situation all by himself."

Aahz's shoulders sagged slightly as he heaved a small sigh. "Whoa! Stop! Perhaps in my enthusiasm I overspoke. What I meant to say is that my slimy but agile mind can provide a plan to pull off this assignment. Of course, the execution of said plan will rely upon abilities and goodwill of my worthy colleagues. Is that better, Chumly?"

"Quite," the troll nodded.

"Now that that's settled," Gus interrupted impatiently, "can we get on with it? This is my place of business, you know, and the longer I keep the place closed, the more money I lose."

For those of you who missed the earlier references, Gus is a gargoyle. He is also the owner/proprietor of the Yellow Crescent

Inn, the Bazaar's leading fast-food establishment and our current
field headquarters. Like Chumly and Tananda, he's helped me out of
a couple scrapes in the past and, as soon as he heard about our
current crisis, volunteered again. Like anyone who earns their living
at the Bazaar, however, he habitually keeps one eye on the cash reg-
ister. Even though he had closed his doors to give us a base of
operations for the upcoming campaign, there was still a reflexive
bristling over missed profits.

An idea struck me.

"Relax, Gus," I ordered. "Come up with a daily figure for your
normal trade, bump it for a decent profit, and we'll reimburse you
when this thing's over."

"What!" my mentor screeched, losing momentary control. "Are
you out of your mind, kid? Who do you think is paying for this,
anyway?"

"The merchants of Deva," I answered calmly. "We're on an
expense account, remember? I think renting a place while we're on
assignment isn't an unreasonable expense, do you?"

"Oh. Right. Sorry, Gus. Old reflexes."

Aahz's confusion was momentary. Then his eyes narrowed
thoughtfully.

"In fact, if we put all of you on retainer, your help will fall
under the heading of 'consultant fees' and never come near our own
profits. I like it."

"Before you get too carried away," Tananda put in quickly, "I
think big brother and I would rather work for a piece of the action
than on a flat fee."

"But, honey," Massha blinked, "you haven't even heard his plan
yet. What makes you think a percentage will net you more than a
fee?...just between us girls?"

"Just between us girls," Tananda winked, "you've never worked
with Aahz before. I have, and while he may not be the pleasantest
being to team with, I have unshakeable faith in his
profit margins."

"Now that we're on the subject," Aahz said, staring hard at Massha,
"we never have worked together before, so let's get the rules straight
early on. I've got my own style, see, and it usually doesn't allow much
time for 'please' and 'thank you' and explanations. As long as you do
what you're told, when you're told, we'll get along fine. Right?"

"Wrong!"

My reply popped out before Massha could form her own response. I was vaguely aware that the room had gotten very quiet, but most of my attention was on Aahz as he slowly cranked his head around to lock gazes with me.

"Now look, kid…" he began dangerously.

"No you look, Aahz," I exploded. "I may be your apprentice, but Massha is mine. Now if she wants to dump that agreement and sign on with you, fine and dandy. But until she does, she's my student and my responsibility. If you think she can help, then you suggest it to me and I decide whether she's up to it. There's one lesson you've drummed into my head over and over, mentor mine, whether you meant to or not. Nobody leans on your apprentice but you…nobody! If you didn't want to teach that lesson, then maybe you'd better be more careful with the example you set the next time you take on an apprentice."

"I see," Aahz murmured softly. "Getting pretty big for your britches, aren't you, kid?"

"Not really. I'm very much aware of how little I know, thank you. But this is my assignment, or at least it was accepted in my name, and I mean to give it my best shot…however inadequate that might be. Now for that assignment, I need your help Aahz…heck, I'll always probably need your help. You're my teacher and I've got a lot to learn. But, I'm not going to roll over and die without it. If getting your help means turning my assignment and my apprentice over to you, then forget it. I'll just have to try to handle things without you."

"You'll get your brains beat out."

"Maybe. I didn't say I'd win, just that I'd try my best. You bring out my best, Aahz. You push me into things that scare me, but so far I've muddled through somehow. I need your help, but I don't have to have it. Even if you don't want to admit it to me, I think you should admit it to yourself."

With that, we both lapsed into silence.

Me, I couldn't think of anything else to say. Up until now, I had been carried along by my anger and Aahz's responses. All of a sudden, my mentor wasn't responding. Instead, he stared at me with expressionless yellow eyes, not saying a thing.

It was more than a little unnerving. If there is one characteristic of Aahz's I could always count on, it was that he was expressive.

Whether with facial expression, gestures, grunts, or verbal explosions, my mentor usually let everyone in the near vicinity know what he felt or thought about any event or opinion expressed. Right now, though, I didn't know if he was about to explode or just walk away.

I began having regrets over instigating this confrontation. Then I toughened up. What I had said was right and needed to be said. It flashed across my mind that I could lose Aahz over this argument. My resolve wavered. Right or not, I could have said it better…gentler. At least I could have picked a time when all our friends weren't watching and listening. Maybe…

Aahz turned away abruptly, shifting his stance to face Tananda and Chumly.

"Now I'm ready to believe you two," he announced. "The kid here really did handle that mess on Klah all by himself, didn't he?"

"That's what we've been trying to tell you, old boy," the troll winked. "Your apprentice is growing up, and seems to us more than capable of standing on his own two feet lately."

"Yeah, I noticed."

He looked at me again, and this time his eyes were expressive. I didn't recognize the expression, but at least there was one.

"Kid…Skeeve," he said. "If I've ever wondered why I bothered taking you under my wing, you just gave me the answer. Thanks."

"Um…Thanks. I mean, you're welcome. No. I mean…"

As always, I was very glib in the face of the unexpected. I had gotten used to weathering Aahz's tirades, but this I didn't know how to handle. Fortunately my pet came to my rescue.

"Gleep?" he queried, shaking his head in through the door.

"But if you take anything I've showed you, I mean spell one, and teach it to that dragon," my mentor roared, "you and I are going to go a couple rounds. Do we understand each other, apprentice?"

"Yes, Aahz."

Actually, I didn't. Still, this didn't seem like the time to call for a clarification.

"Butt out, Gleep," I ordered. "Go play with Buttercup or something."

"Gleep!" and my dragon's head was gone as fast as it had appeared.

"Say, hot stuff," Massha drawled. "As much as I appreciate your standing up for me, I'm kinda curious to hear what Big Green has for a plan."

"Right!" I nodded, glad to be off the hot seat. "Sorry, Aahz, I didn't mean to interrupt. What's the plan?"

"Well first," Aahz said, taking his accustomed place as center of attention once more, "I've got a question for Gus. What's the Mob been doing so far to move in?"

"Judging from what I heard," the gargoyle responded, "a bunch of them move in on a merchant and offer to sell him some 'insurance.' You know, 'pay us so much of your revenue and nothing happens to your business.' If anyone's slow to sign up, they arrange a small demonstration of what could go wrong: some 'accidental' breaking of stock or a couple plug-uglies standing outside hassling customers. So far it's been effective. Deveels don't like to lose business."

"Good," my mentor grinned, showing every last one of his numerous pointed teeth. "Then we can beat them."

"How?"

If nothing else, I've gotten quite good at feeding Aahz straight lines.

"Easy. Just ask yourselves this: If you were a Deveel and paid the Mob to protect your business, and things started going wrong anyway, what would you do?"

"I can answer that one," Massha said. "I'd either demand better protection, scream for my money back, or both."

"I don't get it," I frowned. "What's going to happen to a Mob-protected business?"

"We are," Aahz grinned.

"What our strategist is trying to say," Chumly supplied, "is that the best defense is a good offense. Not terribly original, but effective nonetheless."

"You're darn right it's effective," my mentor exclaimed. "Instead of us defending against the Mob, we're going to start a crime wave right here at the Bazaar. Then let's see how good the Mob is at defending against us!"

XVI.

"It's always easier to destroy than to create."
ANY GENERAL, ANY ARMY, ANY AGE.

"HEY GUIDO! HOW'S it going?"

The big bodyguard spun around, scanning the crowd to see who had hailed him by name. When he saw me, his face brightened.

"Mister Skeeve!"

"Never expected to run into you here!" I lied.

From Gus's description, I had known that both Guido and his cousin Nunzio were part of the Mob's contingent at the Bazaar. This 'chance meeting' was the result of nearly half a day's worth of searching and following rumors.

"What are you doing here?" he asked confidentially. "Shop-ping for a few little items to wow 'em with back at Possiltum?"

"Just taking a bit of a vacation. That new queen and I don't get along so well. I thought things might ease up if I disappeared for a while."

"Too bad. If you was shoppin', I could line you up with some 'special deals,' if you know what I mean."

"You guys are really moving in, then?" I marveled. "How is it going? Any problems?"

"Naw," the bodyguard bragged, puffing out his chest. "You was right. These Deveels are like shopkeepers anywhere. Lean on 'em a little and they fall in line."

"Don't tell me you're handling this all by yourself! I mean, I know you're good, but..."

"Are you kiddin'? I'm an executive now...well, at least a team leader. Both Nunzio and me have a dozen men to order around, courtesy of our 'extensive knowledge of the Bazaar.' Pretty good, huh?"

"You mean you're running the whole operation?"

"That's Shai-ster's job. Me and Nunzio report to him, but it's us gives the orders to the boys."

I looked around expectantly.

"Is your team around? I'd like to meet them."

"Naw. We worked this area a couple days ago. I'm on my way to meet 'em and give out today's assignments. We're going after the area by the livestock pens today."

"How about Nunzio's team?"

"They're about three hours west of here. You know, this is a really big place!"

I put on my most disappointed face.

"Too bad, I would have liked to have met some of the ones who do the real work."

"Tell ya' what," Guido exclaimed, "why don't you drop by Fat's Spaghetti Parlor sometimes? That's where we're all hanging out. If we're not there, they can tell you where we are."

"I'll do that. Well, don't work too hard…and be careful. These guys can be meaner than they look."

"Piece of cake," he laughed as he headed off.

I was still waving merrily at his retreating figure as the rest of my 'gang' faded out of the crowd around me.

"Did you get all that?" I asked out of the corner of my mouth.

"Two teams, neither one in this area. Shai-ster's running the show and therefore holding the bag," Tananda recited. "This area is both clear and under protection."

"Fat's Spaghetti Parlor is their headquarters, which is where we can find Shai-ster," Chumly completed. "Anything else?"

"Yeah," Aahz grinned. "Skeeve has a standing invite to drop by, and when he does, they're ready to tell him which team is working what area that day. Nice work."

"Lucky," I admitted with no embarrassment. "Well, shall we start?"

"Right," Aahz nodded. "Just like we planned, Tananda and Chumly are a team. Gus, you're with me. Skeeve and Massha, you start here. We all move out in different directions and space our hits so there's no pattern. Okay?"

"One more thing," I added. "Keep an eye on your disguises. I'm not sure of the exact range I can hold that spell at. If your disguise starts to fade, change direction to parallel mine."

"We meet back at the Yellow Crescent Inn," Gus finished. "And all of you watch your backs. I don't stock that much first aid gear."

"Good thought," I said. "Okay. Enough talk. Let's scatter and start giving the Mob a headache."

The other two teams had melted into the crowd of shoppers before I had even turned to Massha.

"Well, anything catch your eye for us to have a go at?"

"You know, you're starting to sound a bit like that troll."

That sounded a bit more abrupt than was Massha's normal style. I studied her curiously.

"Something bothering you?"

"Just a little nervous, I guess," she admitted. "Has it occurred to you that this plan has a major flaw? That to implement it potentially means getting the entire Bazaar after us, as well as the Mob?"

"Yes, it has."

"Doesn't it scare you?"

"Yes, it does."

"Well, how do you handle it?"

"By thinking about it as little as possible," I said flatly. "Look, apprentice, aside from doing shtick in court for the amusement of the masses, this profession of ours is pretty dangerous. If we start dwelling on everything that can go wrong in the future, we'll either never move or blunder headlong into the present because our minds aren't on what we're doing right now. I try to be aware of the potential danger of a situation, but I don't worry about trouble until it happens. It's a little shaky, but it's worked so far."

"If you say so," she sighed. "Oh well, gear me up and let's get started."

With a pass of my mind, I altered her features. Instead of being a massive woman, she was now a massive man...sort of. I had been experimenting with color lately, so I made her purple with reddish sideburns that ran all the way down her arms to her knuckles. Add some claw-like horns at the points of the ears and rough-textured, leathery skin on the face and hands, and you had a being I wouldn't want to mess with.

"Interesting," Massha grimaced, surveying what she could see of herself. "Did you make this up yourself, or is there a nasty dimension I haven't visited yet?"

"My own creation," I admitted. "The reputation you're going to build I wouldn't wish on any dimension I know of. Call it a

Hoozit from the dimension Hoo."

"Who?"

"You've got it."

She rolled her eyes in exasperation.

"Hot stuff, do me a favor and only teach me magic, okay? Keep your sense of humor for yourself. I've already got enough enemies."

"We still need a target," I said, slightly hurt.

"How about that one? It looks breakable."

I looked where she was pointing and nodded.

"Good enough. Give me a twenty count head start. If they're not protected, I'll be back out. If you don't see me in twenty, they're fair game. Do your worst."

"You know, she smiled, rubbing her hands together, "this could be fun."

"Just remember that I'm in there before you decide exactly what today's 'worst' is."

The display she had chosen was a small, three-sided tent with a striped top. It was lined with shelves that were crowded with an array of stoppered bottles of all sizes and colors. As I entered, I noticed was something in each of the bottles—smoky things that shifted as if they were alive.

"May I help you, sahr?" The Deveel proprietor asked, baring what he doubtless thought was a winning smile.

"Just browsing," I yawned. "Actually, I'm seeking refuge from gossip. All anyone can talk about is this pack of ruffians that's selling insurance."

The Deveel's face darkened and he spat out the door.

"Insurance! Extortion I call it. They ruined two of my treasures before I could stop them long enough to subscribe to their services. It was a dark day when they first appeared at the Bazaar."

"Yes, yes. Believe me, I've heard it before."

Having established that this shop was indeed under the protection of the Mob, I turned my attention to the displays.

With studied nonchalance, I plucked up a small bottle, no more than a hand's-width high, and peered at the contents. Murky movement and a vague sparkle met my gaze.

"Be careful," the proprietor cautioned. "Once a Djin is released, it can only be controlled if you address it by name."

"A Djin?"

The Deveel swept me with a speculative gaze. Since I wasn't doing the heavy work, I wasn't in disguise and looked like...well, me.

"I believe in Klah, they're referred to as Genies."

"Oh. You have quite a collection here."

The Deveel preened at the praise.

"Do not be fooled by the extent of my poor shop's selection, young sahr. They are extremely rare. I personally combed the far reaches of every dimension…at great personal expense, I might add…to find these few specimens worthy of…"

I had been wondering when Massha was going to make her entrance. Well, she made it. Hoo-boy, did she make it. Right through the side of the tent.

With an almost musical chorus, the stand along that wall went over, dumping the bottles onto the floor. The released Djin rose in a cloud and poured out the open tent side, shrieking with inhuman joy as they went.

The Deveel was understandably upset.

"You idiot!" he shrieked. "What are you doing?"

"Pretty weak shelves," Massha muttered in a gravelly-bass voice.

"Weak shelves?"

"Sure. I mean, all I did was this…"

She shoved one of the remaining two shelves, which toppled obligingly into the last display.

This time the Djin didn't even bother using the door. They streaked skyward, taking the top of the tent with them as they screamed their way to freedom.

"My stock! My tent! Who's going to pay for this?"

"That's Hoozit," Massha retorted, "and I'm certainly not going to pay. I don't have any money."

"No money?" the proprietor gasped.

"No. I just came in here to get out of the rain."

"Rain? Rain? But it isn't raining!"

"It isn't?" my apprentice blinked. "Then, good-bye."

With that she ambled off, making a hole in yet another tent side as she went.

The Deveel sank down in the shattered remains of his display and cradled his face in his hands.

"I'm ruined!" he moaned. "Ruined!"

"Excuse me for asking," I said. "But why didn't you call out their names and get them under control?"

"Call out their names? I can't remember the name of every Djin I collect. I have to look them up each time I sell one."

"Well, at least that problem's behind you."

That started him off again.

"Ruined!" he repeated needlessly. "What am I going to do?" "I really don't know why you're so upset," I observed. "Weren't you just saying that you were insured?"

"Insured?"

The Deveel's head came up slowly.

"Certainly. You're paying to be sure things like this don't happen, aren't you? Well, it happened. It seems to me whoever's protecting your shop owes you an explanation, not to mention quite a bit of money."

"That's right!" the proprietor was smiling now. "More the latter than the former, but you're right!"

I had him going on now. All that was left to be done was the coup de grace.

"Tell you what. Just so your day won't be a total washout, I'll take this one. Now you won't have to stay open with just one Djin in stock."

I flipped him the smallest coin in my pouch. True to his heritage, he was sneering even as he plucked it out of the air.

"You can't be serious," he said. "This? For a Djin? That doesn't even cover the cost of the bottle!"

"Oh come, come, my good man," I argued. "We're both men of the world...or dimensions. We both know that's clear profit."

"It is?" he frowned.

"Of course," I said, gesturing at the broken glass on the floor. "No one can tell how many bottles were just broken. I know you'll just include this one on the list of lost stock and collect in full from your insurance in addition to what I just gave you. In fact, you could probably add five or six to the total if you were really feeling greedy."

"That's true," the Deveel murmured thoughtfully. "Hey, thanks! This might not turn out so bad after all."

"Don't mention it," I shrugged, studying the small bottle in my hand. "Now that we're in agreement on the price, though, could you look up the name of my Djin?"

"I don't have to. That one's new enough that I can remember. It's name is Kalvin."

"Kalvin?"

"Hey, don't laugh. It's the latest thing in Djins."

XVII.

"The best laid plans often go a fowl."
WILE E. COYOTE

"WELL, EXCEPT FOR that, how are things going?"

"Except for that?" Shai-ster echoed incredulously. "Except for that? Except for that things are going rotten. This whole project is a disaster."

"Gee, that's tough," I said, with studied tones of sympathy.

I had gotten to be almost a permanent fixture here at Fat's Spaghetti Palace. Every night I dropped by to check the troops' progress...theirs and mine.

It was nice to be able to track the effectiveness of your activities by listening to the enemy gripe about them. It was even nicer to be able to plan your next move by listening to counter-attacks in the discussion stage.

"I still don't get it," Guido protested, gulping down another enormous fork-full of spaghetti. "Everything was goin' terrific at first. No trouble at all. Then BOOM, it hits the fan, know what I mean?"

"Yeah! It was like someone was deliberately workin' to put us out of business."

That last was from cousin Nunzio. For the longest time I thought he was physically unable to talk. Once he got used to having me around, though, he opened up a little. In actuality, Nunzio was shy, a fact which was magnified by his squeaky little voice which seemed out of place coming from a muscleman.

"I warned you that Deveels can be a nasty lot," I said, eager to get the subject away from the possibility of organized resistance. "And if the shopkeepers are sneaky, it only stands to reason that the local criminal element would have to have a lot on the ball. Right, Guido?"

"That's right," the goon nodded vigorously, strands of spaghetti dangling from his mouth. "We criminal types can beat any honest citizen at anything. Say, did I ever tell you about the time Nunzio and me were..."

"Shut up, dummy!" Shai-ster snapped. "In case you haven't noticed, we're footing the bill for these local amateurs. We're getting our brains beat out financially, and it's up to you boys to catch up with the opposition and return the favor…physically."

"They're scared of us," Guido insisted. "Wherever we are, they aren't. If we can't find 'em, they can't be doin' that much damage."

"You know, brains never were your long suit, Guido," Shai-ster snarled. "Let me run this past you once real slow. So far, we've paid out six times as much as we've taken in. Add all our paychecks and expenses to that, and you might have a glimmer as to why the Big Boys are unhappy."

"But we haven't been collecting very long. After we've expanded our clientele…"

"We'll be paying claims on that many more businesses," Shai-ster finished grimly. "Don't give me that 'we'll make it up on volume' guff. Either an operation is self-supporting and turning a profit from the beginning, or it's in trouble. And we're in trouble so deep, even if we could breathe through the tops of our heads we'd still be in trouble."

"Maybe if we got some more boys from back home…" Nunzio began.

Shai-ster slapped his hand down on the table, stopping his lieutenant short.

"No more overhead!" he shouted. "I'm having enough trouble explaining our profit/loss statement to the Big Boys without the bottom line getting any worse. Not only are we not going to get any more help, we're going to start trimming our expenses, and I mean right now. Tell the boys to…what are you grinning at?"

This last was directed at me.

"Oh, nothing," I said innocently. "It's just that for a minute there you sounded just like someone I know back on Klah…name of Grimble."

"J. R. Grimble?" Shai-ster blinked.

Now it was my turn to be surprised.

"Why yes. He's the Chancellor of the Exchequer back at Possiltum. Why, do you know him?"

"Sure. We went to school together. Chancellor of the Exchequer, huh? Not bad. If I had known he was working the court of Possiltum, I would have stuck around and said 'hi' when I was there."

Somehow, the thought of Shai-ster and Grimble knowing each other made me uneasy. There wasn't much chance of the two of them getting together and comparing notes, and even if they did, Grimble didn't know all that much about my modus operandi. Still, it served as a grim reminder that this was a very risky game I was playing, with some very dangerous people.

"I still think there's another gang out there somewhere," Nunzio growled. "There's too much going down for it to be independent operators."

"You're half right," Shai-ster corrected. "There's too much going down for it to be a gang. Nobody's into that many things...not even us!"

"You lost me there, Shai-ster," I said, genuinely curious. The mobster favored me with a patronizing smile.

"That's right. As a magician, you don't know that much about how organized crime works. Let me try to explain. When the Mob decides to move in, we hit one specialty field at a time. .you know, like protection or the numbers. Like that. Focusing our efforts yields a better saturation as well as market penetration."

"That makes sense," I nodded, not wanting to admit he had lost me again.

"Now you take a look at what's happening here. We're getting all sorts of claims; vandalism, shoplifting, armed robbery, even a couple cases of arson. It's too much of a mix to be the work of one group. We're dealing with a lot of small-time independents, and if we can make an example of a few of them, the others will decide there are easier pickings elsewhere."

In a way, I was glad to hear this. I owed Aahz one more back-pat. He was the one who had decided that the efforts of our team were too limited. To accelerate our "crime wave," he had introduced the dubious practice of "insurance fraud" to Deva...and the Deveels were fast learners.

Is your stock moving too slow? Break it yourself and turn in a claim for vandalism. Trying to sell your shop, but nobody wants to buy, even at a discount? Torch the place and collect in full. Better still, want to fatten up your profit margin a little? Dummy up a few invoices and file a claim for "stolen goods." All profit, no cost.

The Deveels loved it. It let them make money and harass the Mob at the same time. No wonder Shai-ster's table was fast disappearing under a mountain of claims and protests.

It was terrific...except for the part about making an example out of everyone they caught. I made a mental note to warn the team about being extra careful.

"If it's not a gang, and they aren't working against us," Nunzio scowled, "why is everything happening in our areas? My dad taught me to be suspicious of coincidences. He got killed by one."

"How do you know it's just happening in our area?" Shai-ster countered. "Maybe we picked a bad area of the Bazaar to start our operation. Maybe the whole Bazaar is a bad area. Maybe we should have been suspicious when Skeeve here told us there were no police. You get this much money floating around with no police, of course there'll be crooks around."

"So what are we supposed to do?" Guido snarled, plucking his napkin from under his chin and throwing it on the table. "My boys can't be two places at once. We can't watch over our current clients and sign on new accounts, too."

"That's right," Shai-ster agreed, "so here's what we're going to do. First, we split up the teams. Two-thirds of the boys patrol the areas we've got under protection. The others go after new clients...but we don't just take anybody. We investigate and ask questions. We find out how much trouble a new area or a new shop has had before we take them as a client. Then we know who the bad risks are, and if we protect them at all, they pay double. Capish?"

Both Guido and Nunzio were thinking, and it was obvious the process hurt.

"I dunno," Nunzio squeaked at last. "Sumpin' sounds kinda funny about that plan."

"Crime wouldn't pay if the government ran it," I murmured helpfully.

"What's that?" Shai-ster snapped.

"Oh, just something my teacher told me once." I shrugged. "Hey! Skeeve's right," Guido exclaimed.

"What you're sayin' is that we're going to be policemen and insurance investigators."

"Well, I wouldn't use those words..."

"'Well' nothin'. We ain't gonna do it!"

"Why not?"

"C'mon, Shai-ster. We're the bad guys. You know, crooks. What's it going to do to our reputation if it gets back to the Mob that we've turned into policemen?"

"They'll think we're valuable employees who are working hard to protect their investment."

"Yeah?" Guido frowned, unconvinced.

"Besides, it's only temporary," Shai-ster soothed. "Not only that, it's a smoke screen for what we'll really be doing." "What's that?" I asked blandly.

Shai-ster shot a quick look around the restaurant, then leaned forward, lowering his voice.

"Well, I wasn't going to say anything, but remember that I was telling you about how the Mob focuses on one field at a time? The way I see it, maybe we picked the wrong field here at Deva. Maybe we shouldn't have tried the protection racket."

"So you're going to change fields?" I urged.

"Right," Shai-ster smiled. "We'll put the protection racket on slow-down mode for a while, and in the meantime start leaning on the bookies."

"Now you're talking," Guido crowed. "There's always good money to be made at gambling."

"Keep your voice down, you idiot. It's supposed to be a secret."

"So who's to hear?" Guido protested.

"How about them?"

Shai-ster jerked his thumb toward a table of four enormous beings, alternately stuffing their faces and laughing uproariously.

"Them? That's the Hutt brothers. They're in here about once a week. They're too busy with their own games to bother us."

"Games? Are they gamblers?"

"Naw...well, except maybe Darwin. He's the leader of the pack. But he only gambles on businesses."

"Which one is he?"

"The thinnest one. I hear his fiancee has him on a diet. It's making him mean, but not dangerous to us."

Shai-ster turned back to our table.

"Well, keep your voice down anyway. How about it, Skeeve? The gambling, I mean. You've been here at the Bazaar before. Do you know any bookies we can get hold of?"

"Gee, the only one I know of for sure is the Geek," I said. "He's a pretty high-roller. If you boys are going to try to pull a fast one on him, though, don't tell him I was the one who singled him out."

Shai-ster gave me a broad wink.

"Gotcha. But anything we get from him, you're in for a percentage. You know, a finder's fee. We don't forget our friends."

"Gee, thanks," I managed, feeling more than a little guilty. "Well, I'd better be going. C'mon, Gleep."

"Gleep!" echoed my dragon, pulling his head up out of a tub of spaghetti at the sound of his name.

Fats had taken an instant liking to my pet, founded I suspect on Gleep's newfound capacity for the maggot-like stuff barely hidden by blood-red sauce that was the parlor's mainstay.

I had never been able to screw up my courage enough to try spaghetti, but my dragon loved it. Knowing some of the dubious things, edible and in, living and non, that also met with Gleep's culinary approval, this did little toward encouraging me to expand my dietary horizons to include this particular dish. Still, as long as I had Gleep along, we were welcome at Fats, even though my pet was starting to develop a waddle reminiscent of the parlor's proprietor.

"Say, Skeeve. Where do you keep your dragon during the day?"

I glanced over to find Shai-ster studying my pet through narrowed, thoughtful eyes.

"Usually he's with me, but sometimes I leave him with a dragon-sitter. Why?"

"I just remembered an 'interruption of business' claim we had to pay the other day...had to pay! Heck, we're still paying it. Anyway, this guy sells dragons, see, except for over a week now he hasn't sold a one. Usually sells about three a day and says since he paid us to be sure nothing happens to his business, we should make up the difference in his sales drop...and, you know, those things are expensive!"

"I know," I agreed, "but what does that have to do with Gleep?"

"Probably nothing. It's just that this guy swears that just before everything went to pot, some little dragon came by and talked to his dragons. Now they won't roar or blow fire or nothing. All they do is sleep and frolic...and who wants to buy a dragon that frolics, you know?"

"Talked to his dragons?" I asked uneasily.

For some reason, I had a sudden mental image of Gleep confronting Big Julie's dragon, a beast that dwarfed him in size, and winning.

"Well...they didn't exactly talk, but they did huddle up and put their heads together and made mumbly puffy noises at each other. Wouldn't let this guy near 'em until it was over. The only thing he's sure of is the little one, the one he says messed up his business, said something like 'Peep!' Said it a couple of times."

"Peep?" I said.

"Gleep!" answered my dragon.

Shai-ster stared at him again.

"C'mon, Shai-ster," Guido said, giving his superior a hearty shove. "Talking dragons? Somebody's pullin' your leg. Sounds to me like he got a bad shipment of dragons and is trying to get us to pay for them. Tell him to take a hike."

"It's not that easy," Shai-ster grumbled, "but I suppose you're right. I mean, all dragons look pretty much alike."

"True enough," I called, heading hastily for the nearest exit. "C'mon, Peep...I mean, Gleep!"

Maybe Shai-ster's suspicions had been lulled, but I still had a few of my own as we made our way back to the Yellow Crescent Inn.

"Level with me, Gleep. Did you do anything to louse up somebody's dragon business?"

"Gleep?" answered my pet in a tone exactly like my own when I'm trying too hard to sound innocent.

"Uh-huh. Well, stay out of this one. I think we've got it in hand without you getting in the line of fire."

"Gleep."

The answer was much more subdued this time, and I realized he was drooping noticeably.

"Now don't sulk. I just don't want anything to happen to you. That's all."

I was suddenly aware that passers-by were staring at us. As strange as the Bazaar was, I guess they weren't used to seeing someone walking down the street arguing with a dragon.

"Let's hurry," I urged, breaking into a trot. "I don't know what we can do about the Mob moving in on the bookies, but I'm sure Aahz will think of something."

XVIII.

"Life can be profitable, if you know the odds."

RIPLEY

THE SPORTS ARENA we were in was noticeably smaller than the stadium on Jahk where we had played in the Big Game, but no less noisy. Perhaps the fact that it was indoors instead of being open-air did something to the acoustics, but even at half-full the crowd in the arena made such a din I could barely hear myself think.

Then again, there was the smell. The same walls and ceiling that botched up the acoustics did nothing at all for ventilation. Even a few thousand beings from assorted dimensions in these close quarters produced a blend of body odors that had my stomach doing slow rolls...or maybe it was just my nerves.

"Could you explain to me again about odds?"

"Not now," the Geek snarled, nervously playing with his program. "I'm too busy worrying."

"I'll give it a try, hot stuff," Massha volunteered from my other side. "Maybe I can say it in less technical jargon than our friend here."

"I'd appreciate it," I admitted.

That got me a black look from the Geek, but Massha was already into it.

"First, you've got to understand that for the most part, bookies aren't betting their own money. They're acting as agents or go-betweens for people who are betting different sides of the same contest. Ideally, the money bet on each side evens out, so the bookie himself doesn't have any of his own money riding on the contest."

"Then how do they make their money?"

"Sometimes off a percentage, sometimes...but that's another story. What we're talking about is odds. Okay?"

"I guess so," I shrugged.

"Now, the situation I described is the ideal. It assumes the teams or fighters or whatever are evenly matched. That way, some people bet one side, some the other, but overall it evens out. That's even odds or 1-1."

She shifted her weight a bit, ignoring the glares from our fellow patrons when the entire row of seats wobbled in response.

"But suppose things were different. What if, instead of an even match, one side had an advantage...like say if Badaxe were going to fight King Rodrick?"

"That's easy," I smiled. "Nobody would bet on the King."

"Precisely," Massha nodded. "Then everybody would bet one side, and the bookies would have to cover all the bets with their own money...bets they stood a good chance of losing."

"So they don't take any bets."

"No. They rig things so that people will bet on the king." I cocked an eyebrow at her.

"They could try, but I sure wouldn't throw my gold away like that. I'd back Badaxe."

"Really?" Massha smiled. "What if, instead of betting one gold piece to win one gold piece, you had to bet ten gold pieces on Badaxe to win one back?"

"Well..."

"Let me make it a little harder. How about if you bet one gold piece on the King, and he won, that instead of getting one gold piece back, you got a hundred?"

"I...um...might take a long shot on the King," I said, hesitantly. "There's always a chance he could get lucky. Besides, if I lose, I'm only out one gold piece."

"And that's how bookies use odds to cover themselves. Now, how they figure out how many bets they need on the King at 'x' odds to cover the bets they have on Badaxe at 'y' odds is beyond me."

I looked at the Deveel next to me with new respect.

"Gee, Geek. I never really realized how complicated your work is."

The Deveel softened a bit. They're as susceptible to flattery as anyone else.

"Actually, it's even more complicated than that," he admitted modestly. "You've got to keep track of several contests at once, sometimes even use the long bets from one to cover the short bets on another. Then there are side bets, like who will score how often in which period in the Big Game. It isn't easy, but a sharp being can make a living at it."

"So what are the odds tonight?"

The Deveel grimaced.

"Lousy. It's one of those Badaxe and the King matchups, if I was following your example right. In this case, the team you'll see in red trunks are Badaxe. They're hotter than a ten dollar laser and have won their last fifteen bouts. The weak sisters...the King to you...will be in white trunks and haven't won a bout in two years. When the Mob put their bet down, the odds were running about two hundred to one against the whites."

I whistled softly.

"Wow. Two hundred in gold return on a one-gold-piece bet. Did you remember to act surprised when they put their money down?"

"I didn't have to act," the Geek said through tight lips. "Not with the size bet they came up with. Being forewarned, I had expected they wouldn't be going small, but still..."

He shook his head and lapsed into silence.

I hadn't really paused to consider the implication of the odds, but I did now. If betting one piece could get you two hundred back, then a bet of a thousand would have a potential payback of two hundred thousand! And a ten thousand bet...

"How big was their bet?" I asked fearfully.

"Big enough that if I lose, I'll be working for the Mob for the rest of my life to pay it off...and Deveels don't have short life-spans."

"Wait a minute. Didn't Aahz tell you that if you lost, we'd cover it out of our expense money?"

"He did," the Deveel said. "And he also pointed out that if you were covering my losses, you'd also take all winnings if things went as planned. I opted to take the risk, and the winnings, myself."

Massha leaned forward to stare.

"Are you that confident, or that greedy?"

"More the latter," the Geek admitted. "Then again, I got burnt rather badly betting against Skeeve here in the Big Game. I figure it's worth at least one pass backing the shooter who's working a streak."

I shook my head in puzzlement. "Aren't you afraid of losing?"

"Well, it did occur to me that it might be me and not the Mob who's being set up here. That's why I'm sitting next to you. If this turns out to be a double cross..."

"You're pretty small to be making threats, Geek," Massha warned.

"...And you're too big to dodge fast if I decide I'm being had," the Deveel shot back.

"Knock it off, both of you," I ordered. "It's academic anyway. There won't be any problems...or if there are, I'll be as surprised as you are, Geek."

"More surprised, I hope," the Deveel sneered. "I'm half expecting this to blow up, remember?"

"But Aahz has assured me that the fix is in."

"Obviously. Otherwise, the Mob wouldn't be betting so heavily. The question is, which fix is going to work, theirs or yours?"

Just then a flurry of activity across the arena caught my eye. The Mob had just arrived...in force. Shai-ster was there, flanked by Guido and Nunzio and backed by the remaining members of the two teams currently assigned to the Bazaar. Seen together and moving, as opposed to individually feeding their faces at Fats', they made an impressive group. Apparently others shared my opinion. Even though they were late, no one contested their right to prime seats as they filed into the front row. In fact, there was a noticeable bailing out from the desired seats as they approached.

It was still a new enough experience for me to see other beings I knew in a crowd at the Bazaar that I stood up and waved at them before I realized what I was doing. Then it dawned on me!

If they saw me sitting with the Geek and then lost a big bet, they might put two and two together and get five!

I stopped waving and tried to ease back into my seat, but it was too late. Guido had spotted my gyrations and nudged Shaister to point me out. Our eyes met and he nodded acknowledgement before returning to scanning the crowd.

Crestfallen, I turned to apologize to the Geek, only to find myself addressing a character with a pasty complexion and hairy ears who bore no resemblance at all to the Deveel who had been sitting beside me.

I almost...almost!...looked around to see where the Geek had gone. Then I did a little mental arithmetic and figured it out.

A disguise spell!

I'd gotten so used to fooling people myself with that spell that when someone did the same to me, I was completely taken in.

"Still kinda new at this intrigue stuff, aren't you?" he observed dryly from his new face.

Fortunately I was saved the problem of thinking up a suitable response by the entrance of the contestants. With the scramble of planning and launching our counter-offensive, I hadn't really been briefed on what the Mob was betting on except that it would be a tag-team wrestling match. No one said what the contestants would be like, and I had assumed it would be like the matches I had seen back on Klah. I should have known better. The two teams were made up of beings who barely stood high enough to reach my waist! I mean they were small! They looked like kids…if you're used to having kids around with four arms each.

"What are those?" I demanded.

"Those are the teams," the Geek said helpfully. "I mean, what are they? Where are they from?"

"Oh. Those are Tues."

"And you bet on them? I mean, I've heard of midget wrestling, but this is ridiculous!"

"Don't knock it," the Deveel shrugged. "They're big on the wrestling circuit. In fact, teams like this are their dimension's most popular export. Everyone knows them as the Terrible Tues. They're a lot more destructive than you'd guess from their size."

"This is a put-on, right?"

"If you really want to see something, you should catch their other export. It's a traveling dance troupe called the Tue Tours." Massha dropped a heavy hand on my shoulder. "Hot stuff, remember our deal about my lessons?"

"Later, Massha. The match is about to start."

Actually, it was about to finish. It was that short, if you'll pardon the expression.

The first member of the favored red trunk team simply strolled out and pinned his white-trunked rival. Though the pin looked a bit like someone trying to wrap a package with tangled string, the red-trunker made it seem awfully easy. All efforts of his opponent's partner to dislodge the victor were in vain, and the bout was over.

"Well, that's that," the Geek said, standing up. "A pleasure doing business with you, Skeeve. Look me up again if you tie on to a live one."

"Aren't you going to collect your bet?" The Deveel shrugged.

"No rush. Besides, I think your playmates are a little preoccupied just now."

I looked where he was pointing, and saw Shai-ster storming toward the dressing rooms with Guido and Nunzio close behind.

None of them looked particularly happy, which was understandable, given the circumstances.

"Whoops. That's my cue. See you back at the Yellow Crescent,
Massha."

And with that, I launched myself in an interceptor course with
the angry mobsters.

XIX.

"These blokes need to be taught to respect their superiors."
GEN. CORNWALLIS

I ALMOST MISSED them. Not that I was moving slow, mind you.

It's just that they had a real head of steam on.

"Hi guys!" I called, just as Shai-ster was raising a fist to hammer on the dressing room door. "Are you going to congratulate the winners, too?"

Three sets of eyes bored into me as my 'friends' spun around. "Congratulate!" Guido snarled. "I'll give 'em congratulate."

"Wait a minute," Shai-ster interrupted. "What did you mean, 'too?'"

"Well, that's why I'm here. I just won a sizable bet on the last match."

"How sizable?"

"Well, sizable for me," I qualified. "I stand to collect fifty gold pieces."

"Fifty," Guido snorted. "You know how much we lost on that fiasco?"

"Lost?" I frowned. "Didn't you know the Reds were favored?"

"Of course we knew," Shai-ster snarled. "That's why we were set to make a killing when they lost."

"But what made you think they were going to…Oh! Was that what you were talking about when you said you were going into gambling?"

"That's right. The red team was supposed to take a graceful dive in the third round. We paid them enough…more than enough, actually."

He sounded so much like Grimble I couldn't resist taking a cheap shot.

"Judging from the outcome, it sounds to me that you paid them a little less than enough."

"It's not funny. Now, instead of recouping our losses, we've got another big loss to explain to the Big Boys."

"Oh come on, Shai-ster," I smiled. "How much can it cost to fix a fight?"

"Not much," he admitted. "But when you figure in the investment money we just lost, it comes to…"

"Investment money?"

"He means the bet," Guido supplied.

"Oh. Well, I suppose that's the risk you take when you try to make a killing."

An evil smile flitted across Shai-ster's face.

"Oh, we're going to make a killing, all right," he said. "It's time the locals at this Bazaar learned what it means to cross the Mob."

With that, he nodded at Guido who opened the dressing room door.

All four wrestlers were sharing the same room, and they looked up expectantly as we filed in. That's right. I said we. I kind of tagged along at the end of the procession and no one seemed to object.

"Didn't you clowns forget something out there?" Shai-ster said for his greeting. "Like who was supposed to win?"

The various team members exchanged glances. Then the smallest of the red team shrugged.

"Big deal. So we changed our minds."

"Yeah," his teammate chimed in. "We decided it would be bad for our image to lose...especially to these stumblebums." That brought the white team to its feet.

"Stumblebums?" one of them bellowed. "You caught us by surprise, that's all. We was told to take it easy until the third round."

"If you took it any easier, you'd be asleep. We were supposed to be wrestling, not dancing."

Shai-ster stepped between them.

"So you all admit you understood your original instructions?"

"Hey, get off our backs, okay? You'll get your stinking money back, so what's your beef, anyway?"

"Even if you gave us a full refund," Shai-ster said softly, "there's still a matter of the money we lost betting on you. I don't suppose any of you are independently wealthy?"

"Oh, sure," one of the reds laughed. "We're just doin' this for kicks."

"I thought not. Guido. Nunzio. See what you can do about squaring accounts with these gentlemen. And take your time. I want them to feel it, you know?"

"I dunno, Shai-ster," Guido scowled. "They're awfully small. I don't think we can make it last too long."

"Well, do your best. Skeeve? Would you join me outside? I don't think you're going to want to see this."

He was closer to being right than he knew. Even though I had been through some rough and tumble times during recent years, that didn't mean I enjoyed it—even to watch.

The door was barely shut behind us when a series of thuds and crashes erupted inside. It was painful just to listen to, but it didn't last long.

"I told them to take their time," Shai-ster said, scowling at the silence. "Oh well, I guess…"

The door opened, revealing one of the white team.

"If you've got any more lessons out there, I suggest you send them in. These two didn't teach us much at all."

He shut the door again, but not before we caught a glimpse of the two bodyguards unconscious on the floor. Well, Guido was on the floor. Nunzio was kind of standing on his head in the corner. "Tough little guys," I remarked casually. "It must be the four arms. Think you could find work for them in the Mob?" Shai-ster was visibly shaken, but he recovered quickly.

"So they want to play rough. Well that's fine by me."

"You aren't going in there alone, are you?" I asked, genuinely concerned.

He favored me with a withering glance.

"Not a chance."

With that, he put his fingers in his mouth and blew a loud blast. At least, that's what it looked like. I didn't hear a thing. Before I could ask what he was doing, though, a thunder of footsteps announced the arrival of two dozen Mob reinforcements. Neat trick. I guess the whistle had been too high for me to hear…or too low.

"They got Guido and Nunzio," Shai-ster shouted before the heavies had come to a complete halt. "Let's show 'em who's running things around here. Follow me!"

Jerking the door open, he plunged into the dressing room with the pack at his heels.

I'm not sure if Shai-ster had ever actually been in a fight before, much less led a team into a fight. I am, however, sure he never tried it again.

The screams of pain and anguish that poured out of that room moved me to take action. I walked a little further down the hall and did my waiting there. It turned out my caution was needless. The wall didn't collapse, nor did the ceiling or the building itself. Several hunks of plaster did come loose, however, and at one point some-one poked a hole in the wall…with his head.

It occurred to me that if the fight fans in the arena really wanted to get their money's worth, they should be down here. Additional thought made me decide it was just as well they didn't. There were already more than enough beings crowded into that dressing room…which was as good a reason as any for my staying in the hall.

Eventually the sounds of battle died away, leaving only omi-nous silence. I reminded myself that I had every confidence in the outcome. As the length of silence grew, I found it necessary to re-mind myself several times.

Finally the door opened, and the four Tues filed out laughing and chatting together.

"Cute," I called. "Don't hurry or anything. I can worry out here all day."

One of the white team ran up and gave me a hug and a kiss. "Sorry, handsome. We were having so much fun we forgot about you."

"Um…could you do something about the disguises before you kiss me again?"

"Whoops. Sorry about that!"

The taller red team member closed his eyes, and the Tues were gone. In their places stood Aahz, Gus, Tananda, and Chumly. That's why I hadn't been worried…much.

"Nice work, Gus," I said, nodding my approval. "But I still think I could have handled the disguises myself."

"Have you ever seen a Tue before?" Aahz challenged.

"Well…no."

"Gus has. That's why he handled the disguises. End of discussion."

"Used to have a secretary named Etheyl," the gargoyle explained, ignoring Aahz's order. "She was a big fan of the wrestling circuit."

"A secretary?" I blinked.

"Sure, haven't you ever heard of a Tue Fingered Typist?"

"Enough!" Aahz insisted, holding up his hand. "I vote we head back to the Yellow Crescent Inn for a little celebration. I think we've thwarted the Mob enough for one night."

"Yeah," Tananda grinned. "That'll teach 'em to pick on some-one their own size."

"But you are their size," I frowned.

"I know," she winked. "That's the point."

"I say, are you sure, Aahz?" Chumly interjected. "I mean, we gave them a sound thrashing, but will it hold them until morning?"

"If they're lucky," my mentor grinned. "Remember, once they wake up, they're going to have to report in to their superiors."

"Do you think they'll try to recoup their losses with another stab at gambling?" I asked.

"I hope so," Aahz said, his grin getting broader. "The next big betting event on the docket is the unicorn races, and we've got that covered easily."

"You mean Buttercup? You can't enter him in a race. He's a war-unicorn."

"I know. Think about it."

XX.

"Figure the last thing you would expect the enemy to do,
then count on him doing precisely that!"
RICHELIEU

THE MOB DID not try another gambit right after their disastrous attempt to move in on Deva's bookies. In fact, for some time afterward, things were quiet…too quiet, as Aahz put it.

"I don't like it," he declared, staring out the front window of the Yellow Crescent Inn. "They're up to something. I can feel it."

"Fats says they haven't been around for nearly a week," I supplied. "Maybe they've given up."

"Not a chance. There's got to be at least one more try, if for nothing else than to save face. And instead of getting ready, we're sitting around on our butts."

He was right. For days now, the team's main activity had been hanging around Gus's place waiting for some bit of information to turn up. Our scouting missions had yielded nothing, so we were pretty much reduced to relying on the normal Bazaar gossip network to alert us to any new Mob activity.

"Be reasonable, Aahz," Chumly protested. "We can't plan or prepare without any data to work with. You've said yourself that action in an absence of information is wasted effort, eh what? Makes the troops edgy."

Aahz stalked over to where the troll was sprawled.

"Don't start quoting me at me! You're the one who usually argues with everything I say. If everybody starts agreeing with me, we aren't using all the mental resources we can."

"But you're the one saying that we should be planning," I pointed out.

"Right," my mentor smiled. "So we might as well get started. In absence of hard facts, we'll have to try to second-guess them. Now, where is the Bazaar most vulnerable to Mob takeover? Tananda, have you seen…Tananda?"

She abandoned her window-gazing to focus on the discussion. "What was that, Aahz? Sorry. I was watching that Klahd coming down the street dressed in bright purple."

"Purple!?"

Massha and I said it together.

I started to race her for the window, then changed my mind. What if I won? I didn't want to be between the window and her mass when she finally got there. Instead, I waited until she settled into position, then eased in beside her.

"That's him all right," I said out loud, confirming my unvoiced thoughts. "That's Don Bruce. Well, now we know what the Mob's been doing. They've been whistling up the heavy artillery. The question is, what is he doing here at the Bazaar? When we get the answer to that, we'll be able to plan our next move."

"Actually, the question should be what is he doing here at the Yellow Crescent Inn," Gus commented dryly from my elbow. "And I think we're about to get the answer."

Sure enough, Don Bruce was making a beeline for the very building we were watching him from. With his walk, it had taken me a minute to zero in on his direction.

"All right. We know who he is and that he's coming here. Now, let's quit gawking like a bunch of tourists."

Aahz was back in his familiar commander role again. Still, I noticed he was no quicker to leave the window than any of the rest of us.

"Everybody sit down and act natural. Skeeve, when he gets here, let me do the talking, okay?"

"Not a chance, Aahz," I said, sinking into a chair. "He's used to dealing with me direct. If we try to run in a middleman he'll know something's up. Sit at this table with me, though. I'm going to need your advice on this one."

By the time Don Bruce opened the door, we were all sitting; Aahz and I at one table, and two others accommodating Massha and Gus, and the Chumly Tananda team respectively. I noticed that we had left two-thirds of the place empty to sit at adjoining tables, which might have looked a little suspicious. I also noticed we had reflexively split up into two-person teams again, but it was too late to correct either situation.

"Hi there," Don Bruce called, spotting me at once. "Thank goodness I found you here. This Bazaar is great fun to wander, but simply beastly at finding what or who you're looking for."

"You were looking for me?"

This was not the best news I had heard all day. Despite his affected style of speech, I had a healthy respect for Don Bruce. From what I had scen of the Mob, it was a rough group, and I figured no one could hold down as high a position as Don Bruce did, unless there was some real hard rock under that soft exterior. Friendly greeting or not, I began to feel the fingers of cold fear gripping my stomach.

"That's right. I've got to have a meet with you, you know? I was hoping I could speak with you in private."

The last thing in the world I wanted right now was to be alone with Don Bruce.

"It's all right," I said expansively. "These are my friends. Any business I have with your...organization we're in on together...I mean, can be discussed in front of them."

"Oh, very well."

The Mob chieftain flounced onto a chair at my table.

"I didn't mean to be rude, and I do want to meet you all. It's just that first thing there are some pressing matters to deal with."

"Shoot," I said, then immediately wished I had chosen another word.

"Well, you know we're trying to move in on this place, and you know it hasn't been going well...no, don't deny it. It's true. Shai-ster has mentioned you often in his reports, so I know how well informed you are."

"I haven't seen Shai-ster lately, but I do know he's been working hard at the project."

"That's right," Aahz chimed in. "From what Skeeve's been telling us, Shai-ster is a good man. If he can't pull it off, you might as well pack up and go home."

"He's an idiot!" Don Bruce roared, and for a moment we could see the steel inside the velvet glove. "The reason you haven't seen him is that I've pulled him from the project completely. He thought we should give up, too."

"You aren't giving up?" I said, fearfully.

"I can't. Oh, if you only knew what I go through on the Council. I made such a thing out of this Deva project and how much it could do for the Mob. If we pulled out now, it would be the same as saying I don't know a good thing when I see it. No sir.

Call it family politics or stubborn pride, we're going to stay right here."

My heart sank.

"But if the operation is losing money..." I began, but he cut me off with a gesture.

"So far...but not for long. You see, I've figured out for myself what's going wrong here."

"You have? How? I mean, this is your first visit here since the project started."

I was starting to sweat a bit. Don Bruce was regarding me with an oily reptilian smile I didn't like at all.

"I saw it in the reports," he declared. "Clear as the nose on your face. That's why I know Shai-ster's an idiot. The problem was right there in front of him and he couldn't see it. That problem is you."

My sweat turned cold. At the edge of my vision I saw Tananda run her fingers through her hair, palming one of her poison darts in the process, and Massha was starting to play with her rings. Chumly and Gus exchanged glances, then shifted in their chairs slightly. Of our entire team, only Aahz seemed unconcerned.

"You'll have to be a little clearer for the benefit of us slow folks," he drawled. "Just how do you figure that Skeeve here is a problem?"

"Look at the facts," Don Bruce said, holding up his fingers to tick off the count.

"He's been here the whole time my boys were having trouble; he knows the Bazaar better than my boys; he knows magic enough to do things my boys can't handle; and now I find out he's got a bunch of friends and contacts here."

"So?" my mentor said softly.

"So? Isn't it obvious? The problem with the operation is that he should have been working for us all along."

By now I had recovered enough to have my defense ready. "But just because I...what?"

"Sure. That's why I'm here. Now I know you said before you didn't want to work for the Mob full time. That's why I'm ready to talk a new deal with you. I want you to run the Mob's operation here at the Bazaar...and I'm willing to pay top dollar."

"How much is that in gold?"

Aahz was leaning forward now.

"Wait a minute! Whoa! Stop!" I interrupted. "You can't be serious. I don't have the time or the know-how to make this a profitable project."

"It doesn't have to be profitable," Don argued. "Break even would be nice, or even just lose money slower. Anything to get the council to look elsewhere for things to gripe about at our monthly Meetings. You could do it in your extra time."

I started to say something, but Aahz put a casual hand on my shoulder. I knew that warning. If I tried to interrupt or correct him, that grip would tighten until my bones creaked.

"Now let me see if I've got this right," he said, showing all his teeth. "You want my man here to run your operation, but you don't care if it doesn't show a profit?"

"That's right."

"Of course, with things as shaky as they are now, you'd have to guarantee his salary."

Don Bruce pursed his lips and looked at me.

"How much does he cost?"

"Lots," Aahz confided. "But less than the total salary of the force you've got here now."

"Okay. He's worth it."

"Aahz..." I began, but the grip on my shoulder tightened.

..And you aren't so much concerned with the Mob's reputation here on Deva as you are with how the Council treats you, right?"

"Well...yea. I guess so."

"...So he'd have free rein to run the operation the way he saw fit. No staff forced on him or policies to follow?"

"No. I'd have to at least assign him a couple bodyguards. Anybody running a Mob operation has got to have a couple of the Family's boys to be sure nothing happens to him."

Aahz scowled.

"But he's already got..."

"How about Guido and Nunzio?" I managed, through gritted teeth. Abruptly the grip on my shoulder vanished.

"Those losers?" Don Bruce frowned. "I was going to have a severe talk with them after this disaster, but if you want 'em, they're yours."

"But since you're the one insisting on them, they don't show up on our overhead. Right?" Aahz said firmly.

I leaned back, working my shoulder covertly, and tried to ignore the horrified stares my friends were exchanging. I didn't know for sure what Aahz was up to, but knew better than to get in his way when he smelled money.

I could only cross my fingers and hope that he knew what he was doing...for a change.

XXI.

"Stayin' alive! Stayin' alive!"
V. DRACULA

THE REPRESENTATIVES OF the Bazaar Merchants didn't look happy, but then Deveels never do when they're parting with money.

"Thank you gentlemen," Aahz beamed, rubbing his hands together gleefully over the substantial pile of gold on the table.

"You're sure the Mob is gone?" the head spokesman asked, looking plaintively at the gold.

"Positive. We've broken their reign of terror and sent them packing."
The Deveel nodded.

"Good. Now that that's settled, we'll be going."

"...Of course," Aahz yawned, "there's no guarantee they won't be back tomorrow."

That stopped the delegation in their tracks.

"What? But you said..."

"Face it, gentlemen. Right now, the only thing between the Mob and the Bazaar is the Great Skeeve here, and once he leaves..."

The Deveels exchanged glances.

"I don't suppose you'd consider staying," one said hopefully. I favored him with a patronizing smile.

"I'd love to, but you know how it is. Expenses are high, and I've got to keep moving to eke out a living."

"But with your reputation, clients will be looking for you. What you really need is a permanent location so you can be found."

"True enough," Aahz smiled. "But to be blunt, why should we give you for free what other dimensions are willing to pay for? I should think that if anybody could understand that, you Deveels would."

"Now we're getting to the heart of the matter," the lead spokesman sighed, pulling up a chair. "Okay. How much?"

"How much?" Aahz echoed.

"Don't give me that," the Deveel snapped. "Innocence looks ridiculous on a Pervert. Just tell us what kind of retainer would be necessary to keep the Great Skeeve around as the Bazaar's magician in residence."

Aahz winked at me.

"I'm sure you'll find his fee reasonable," he said. "Well, reasonable when you stop to think what you're getting for your money. Of course, the figure I'm thinking of is just for making the Bazaar his base of operations. If any specific trouble arises, we'll have to negotiate that separately."

"Of course," the Deveel winced.

I settled back to wait patiently. This was going to take a while, but I was confident of the eventual outcome. I also knew that whatever fee Aahz was thinking of originally just got doubled when the Deveel made that 'Pervert' crack. As a Pervect, Aahz is very sensitive about how he's addressed...and this time I wasn't about to argue with him.

"I love it!" Aahz crowed, modestly. "Not only are we getting a steady income from both the Mob and the Deveels, we don't have to do a thing to earn it! This is even better than the setup we had at Possiltum."

"It's a sweet deal, Aahz."

"And how about this layout? It's a far cry from that shack you and Garkin were calling home when we first met."

Aahz and I were examining our new home, provided as an extra clause in our deal with the Bazaar merchants. It was huge, rivaling the size of the Royal Palace at Possiltum. The interesting thing was that from the outside it looked no bigger than an average Bazaar stall.

"Of course, holding out for a lifetime discount on anything at the Bazaar was a stroke of genius, if I do say so myself."

"Yeah, Aahz. Genius."

My mentor broke off his chortling and self-congratulations to regard me quizzically.

"Is something bothering you, Skeeve? You seem a little subdued."

"It's nothing, really."

"Come on. Out with it," he insisted. "You should be on top of the world right now, not moping around like you just heard that your dragon has a terminal illness or something."

"Well, it's a couple of things," I admitted grudgingly. "First, I've got a bad feeling about those deals you just put together."

"Now wait a minute," my mentor scowled. "We talked all this out before we went after the merchants and you said that double-dealing wouldn't bother you."

"It doesn't. If anything, I'm glad to see both the Mob and the Deveels getting a little of their own back for a change."

"Then what's wrong? I got you everything I could think of!"

"That's what's wrong."

My mentor shook his head sharply as if to clear his vision. "I've got to admit, this time you lost me. Could you run that one past again, slow?"

"Come on, Aahz. You know what I'm talking about. You've gotten me more money than I could spend in a lifetime, a beautiful house...not just anywhere, mind you, but at the Bazaar itself...steady work anytime I want it...in short, everything I need to not only survive, but prosper. Everything."

"So?"

"So are you setting me up so you can leave? Is that what this is all about?"

I had secretly hoped that Aahz would laugh in my face and tell me I was being silly. Instead, he averted his eyes and lapsed into silence.

"I've been thinking about it," he said finally. "You're doing pretty well lately and, like you say, this latest deal will insure you won't starve. The truth of the matter is that you really don't need me anymore."

"But Aahz!"

"Don't 'but Aahz' me! All I'm doing is repeating what you shoved down my throat at the beginning of this caper. You don't need me. I've been giving it a lot of thought, and you're right. I thought you always wanted to hear me say that."

"Maybe I don't like being right," I said plaintively. "Maybe I wish I did need you more and things could go on forever like they have in the past."

"That's most of growing up, kid," Aahz sighed. "Facing up to reality whether we like it or not. You've been doing it, and I figure it's about time I did the same. That's why I'm going to stick around."

"But you don't have to...what?"

My mentor's face split in one of his expansive grins.

"In this case, the reality that I'm facing is that whether you need me or not, I've had more fun since I took you on as an apprentice than I've had in centuries. I'm not sure exactly what's going to happen to you next, but I wouldn't miss it for all the gold on Deva."

"That's great!"

"Of course, there's still a lot I can teach you, just like there's a lot I have to learn from you."

"From me?" I blinked.

"Uh huh. I've been learning from you for some time now, kid. I was just never up to admitting it before. You've got a way of dealing with people that gets you respect, even from the ones who don't like you. I haven't always been able to get that. Lots of folks are afraid of me, but not that many respect me. That's why I've been studying your methods, and have every intention of continuing."

"That's...umm...interesting, Aahz. But how come you're telling me this now?"

"Because if I stay around, it'll be on one condition: that you wake up and accept the fact that you're a full partner in our relationship. No more of this 'apprentice' crud. It's getting too rough on my nerves."

"Gee, Aahz...I..."

"Deal?"

"Deal."

We shook hands solemnly, and I remembered he had refused this simple act when he first accepted me as an apprentice. A full partner. Wow!

"Now what's the other thing?"

"Hmm, excuse me?"

"If I recall correctly, you said there were a couple things bothering you. What's the other?"

"Well...it's this house."

"What about the house?" Aahz exploded, slipping easily back into his old patterns. "It's got enough room for us and our friends and your bodyguards when they show up and Buttercup and Gleep and anyone else who wanders by."

"That's true."

"What's more, we got it for free. It's a good deal."

"Say that again, Aahz."

"I said, 'it's a good...' Oh."

"From the Deveels, right?"

"Oh come on, Skeeve. It's just a house. What could be wrong?"

"To use your phrase, 'The mind boggles.' I've been trying to spot the catch, and I want you to check me to see if my facts and logic are correct."

"Okay."

"Now. Deveels are experts at dimension travel. If I under-stand it right, they manage these 'bigger inside than outside' houses by offsetting the dimensions just a bit. That is, if we numbered the dimensions, and Deva was one, then our door is in dimension one and the rest of our house is in dimension one point four or something."

"Now that's one I hadn't thought about before," Aahz admitted. "The Deveels have been pretty tight-lipped about it. Makes sense, though. It would be rough to play the poverty-stricken shopowner with a place like this just over your shoulder. If I had thought about it I would have realized a Deveel needs someplace secret to keep his wealth."

"So we've effectively been given our own dimension," I continued; "An unlisted dimension that's all ours. For free, no less."

"That's right," Aahz nodded, but there was a note of doubt in his voice now.

"What I wonder about is how many of these offset dimensions do the Deveels have access to, and why is this particular one standing vacant? What's in this dimension?"

"Our house?" my mentor suggested tentatively.

"And what else?" I urged. "I've noticed there are no windows. What's outside our back door that the Deveels were so eager to give away?"

"Back door?"

I pulled away the tapestry to reveal the door I had spotted during our first tour. It was heavy wood with strange symbols painted on it. It also had a massive beam guarding it, and several smaller but no less effective-looking locks around the edge.

"I tried to say something at the time, but you kept telling me to shut up."

"I did, didn't I."

We both stared at the door in silence for several minutes. "Tell you what," Aahz said softly. "Let's save investigating this for another day."

"Right," I agreed, without hesitation.

"And until we do, let's not mention this to the others."

"My thoughts precisely."

"And, partner?"

"Yes, Aahz?"

"If anyone knocks at this door, don't answer unless I'm with you."

Our eyes met, and I let the tapestry fall back into place.

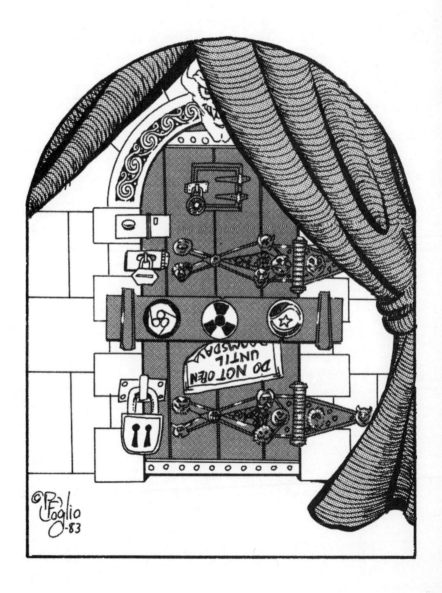

Myth-ing
Persons

I.

"Reputations are fine up to a point. After that they become a pain!"
                                                    D. JUAN

THERE IS SOMETHING sinfully satisfying about doing something you know you aren't supposed to. This was roughly my frame of mind as I approached a specific nondescript tent at the Bazaar at Deva with my breakfast under my arm...guilty, but smug.

"Excuse me, young sahr!"

I turned to find an elderly Deveel waving desperately at me as he hurried forward. Normally I would have avoided the encounter, as Deveels are always selling something and at the moment I wasn't buying, but since I wasn't in a hurry I decided to hear what he had to say.

"I'm glad I caught you in time," he said, struggling to catch his breath. "While I don't usually meddle, you really don't want to go in there!"

"Why not? I was just..."

"Do you know who lives there?"

"Well, actually I thought..."

"That is the dwelling of the Great Skeeve!"

Something about this busybody irritated me. Maybe it was the way he never let me finish a sentence. Anyway, I decided to string him along for a while."

"The Great Skeeve?"

"You never heard of him?" The Deveel seemed genuinely shocked. "He's probably the most powerful magician at the Bazaar."

My opinion of the busybody soared to new heights, but the game was too much fun to abandon.

"I've never had too much faith in magicians," I said with studied casualness. "I've found for the most part their powers are overrated."

The oldster rolled his eyes in exasperation.

"That may be true in most cases, but not when it comes to the Great Skeeve! Did you know he consorts with Demons and has a dragon for a familiar?"

I favored him with a worldly smile.

"So what? Deva is a crossroads of the dimensions. Dimension travelers, or Demons as you call them, are the norm around here. As a Deveel, your main livelihood comes from dealing with Demons. As for the dragon, there's a booth not eight rows from here that sells dragons to anyone with the price."

"No, no! You don't understand! Of course we all deal with Demons when it comes to business. The difference is that this Skeeve is actually *friends* with them...invites them into his home and lives with them. One of his permanent house guests is a Pervert, and I don't know of a single Deveel who would stoop that low. What's more, I've heard it said that he has underworld connections."

The game was growing tiresome. Any points the Deveel had made with his tribute to the Great Skeeve had been lost with interest when he started commenting on Demons.

"Well, thank you for your concern," I said, holding out my hand for a handshake. "I promise you I'll remem-ber everything you've said. What was your name again?"

The Deveel grabbed my hand and began pumping it vigorously.

"I am Aliman, and glad to be of assistance," he said with an ingratiating smile. "If you really want to show your gratitude, re-member my name. Should you ever be in need of a *reputable* magician, I have a nephew who's just getting started in the business. I'm sure we could arrange some discount prices for you. Tell me, what is *your* name so I can tell him who to watch for?"

I tightened my grip slightly and gave him my widest smile. "Well, my friends call me Skeeve."

"I'll be sure to tell...SKEEVE?"

The Deveel's eyes widened, and his complexion faded from red to a delicate pink.

"That's right," I said, retaining my grip on his hand. "Oh, and for your information Demons from Perv are called Pervects, not Perverts...and he's not my house guest, he's my partner."

The Deveel was struggling desperately now, trying to free his hand.

"Now then, how many customers have you scared away from my business with your tales about what a fearsome person I am?"

The Deveel tore loose from my grip and vanished into the crowds, sounding an incoherent scream of terror as he went. In short, Aliman left. Right?

I watched him go with a certain amount of mischievous satisfaction. I wasn't really angry, mind you. We literally had more money
than we could use right now, so I didn't begrudge him the customers. Still, I had never really paused to consider how formidable our
operation must look from the outside. Viewing it now through a
stranger's eyes, I found myself more than a little pleased. Considering the dubious nature of my beginning, we had built ourselves quite
a reputation over the last few years. I had been serious when I told
Aliman that I didn't have much faith in magicians. My own reputation was overrated to say the least, and if I was being billed as a
powerful magician, it made the others of my profession more than
a little suspect in my eyes. After several years of seeing the inside of
the magic business, I was starting to wonder if *any* magician was
really as good as people thought.

I was so wrapped up in these thoughts as I entered our humble
tent that I had completely forgotten that I was supposed to be sneaking in. I was reminded almost immediately.

The reminder came in the form of a huge man who loomed up
to block my path. "Boss," he said in a squeaky little voice that was
always surprising coming from such a huge body, "you shouldn't ought
to go out alone like that. How many times we got to tell you…"

"It's all right, Nunzio," I said, trying to edge around him. "I just
ducked out to get some breakfast. Want a bagel?"

Nunzio was both unconvinced and undaunted in his scolding.

"How are we supposed to be your bodyguards if you keep
sneaking off alone every chance you get? Do you know what Don
Bruce would do to us if anything happened to you?"

"C'mon, Nunzio. You know how things are here at the Bazaar.
If the Deveels see me with a bodyguard, the price of everything
goes through the ceiling. Besides, I like being able to wander around
on my own once in a while."

"You can afford the higher prices. What you can't afford is to
set yourself up as a target for every bozo who wants the rep of
bagging the Great Skeeve."

I started to argue, but my conversation with Aliman flashed
across my mind. Nunzio was right. There were two sides to having
a reputation. If anyone believed the rumors at the Bazaar and still
meant me harm, they would muster such firepower for the attempt
that my odds for survival would be nonexistent.

"Nunzio," I said slowly, "you may be right, but in all honesty what could you and Guido do to stop a magical attack on me?"

"Not a thing," he said calmly. "But they'd probably try to knock off your bodyguards first, and that might give you time to get away or hit them yourself before they could muster a second attack."

He said it easily, like you or I might say "The sun rises in the east," but it shook me. It had never really occurred to me how expendable bodyguards are, or how readily they accept the dangers of their profession.

"I'll try to remember that in the future," I said with a certain degree of grave humility. "What's more, I think I owe you and Guido an apology. Where is Guido, anyway?"

"Upstairs arguing with His Nibs," Nunzio grinned. "As a matter of fact, I was looking for you to break it up when I found you had snuck out again."

"Why didn't you say so in the first place?"

"What for? There's no rush. They'll be arguing until you get there. I figured it was more important to convince you to quit going out alone."

I groaned a little inside, but I had learned long ago the futility of arguing priorities with Nunzio.

"Well, thanks again for the advice, but I'd better get upstairs before those two kill each other."

With that I headed across the courtyard for the fountain stairs to our offices...

Courtyard? Fountain stairs?

What happened to the humble tent I was walking into a minute ago?

*Weelll...*I said I was a magician, didn't I? Our little stall at the Bazaar is bigger on the inside than it is on the outside. Lots bigger. I've lived in royal palaces that weren't as big as our "humble tent." I can't take any credit for this particular miracle, though, other than the fact that it was my work that helped earn us our current residence. We live here rent-free courtesy of the Devan Merchants Association as partial payment for a little job we did for them a while back. That's also how I got my bodyguards...but that's another story.

Devan Merchants Association, you ask? Okay. For the uninitiated, I'll go over this just once. The dimension I'm currently residing in is Deva, home of the shrewdest deal-drivers in all the known dimensions. You may have heard of them. In my own home dimension they were called devils, but I have since learned the proper pronun-ciation is Deveels. Anyway, my gracious living quarters are the result of my partner and I beating the Deveels at their own game...which is to say we got the better of them in a deal. Don't tell anyone, though. It would ruin their reputation and maybe even cost me a cushy spot. You see, they still don't know they've been had.

Anyway, where was I? Oh, yes. Heading for the offices. Nor-mally after sneaking out I would stop by the stables to share break-fast with Gleep, but with a crisis on my hands I decided to forgo the pleasure of my pet's company and get to work. Gleep. He's the dragon Aliman was talking about...and I'm *not* going to try to con-dense *that* story. It's just too complicated.

Long before I reached the offices I could hear their voices raised in their favorite "song." The lyrics changed from time to time, but I knew the melody by heart.

"Incompetent bungler!"

"Who are you calling an incomplete bungler?" "I stand cor-rected. You are a *complete* bungler!"

You better watch your mouth! Even if you are the boss's part-ner, one more word and I'll..."

"You'll what? If you threw a punch the safest place to be would be where you're aiming."

"Izzat so?"

It sounded like I had arrived in the nick of time. Taking a deep breath, I casually strolled into the teeth of the fracas.

"Hi, guys." I pretended to be totally unaware of what was go-ing on. "Anyone want a bagel?"

"No, I don't want a bagel!" came the sneering response from one combatant. "What I want is some decent help."

"...and while you're at it see what you can do about getting me a little respect!" the other countered.

The latter comment came from Guido, senior of my two body-guards. If anything, he's bigger and nastier than his cousin Nunzio.

The former contribution came from Aahz. Aahz is my partner. He's also a demon, a Pervect to be exact, and even though he's slightly shorter than I am, he's easily twice as nasty as my two body-guards put together.

My strategy had worked in that I now had their annoyance focused on me instead of each other. Now, realizing the potential devastation of their respective temperaments individually, much less collectively, I had cause to doubt the wisdom of my strategy.

"What seems to be the trouble?"

"The trouble," Aahz snarled, "is that your ace body-guard here just lost us a couple of clients."

My heart sank. I mentioned earlier that Aahz and I have more money than we know what to do with, but old habits die hard. Aahz is the tightest being I've ever met when it comes to money, and, living at the Bazaar at Deva, that's saying something! If Guido had really lost a potential customer, we'd be hearing about it for a long time.

"Ease up a minute, partner," I said more to stall for time than anything else. "I just got here, remember? Could you fill me in on a few of the details?"

Aahz favored Guido with one more dark stare. "There's not all that much to tell," he said. "I was in the middle of breakfast…"

"He was drinking another meal," Guido translated scornfully.

"…when mush-for-brains here bellows up that there are some customers waiting downstairs in reception. I called back that I'd be down in a few, then finished my meal."

"He kept them waiting at least half an hour. You can't expect customers to…"

"Guido, could you hold the editorial asides for one round? Please?" I interceded before Aahz could go for him. "I'm still trying to get a rough idea of what happened, remember? Okay, Aahz. You were saying?"

Aahz took a deep breath, then resumed his account.

' "Anyway, when I got downstairs, the customers were nowhere to be seen. You'd think your man here would be able to stall them or at least have the sense to call for reinforcements if they started getting twitchy."

"C'mon, Aahz. Guido is supposed to be a bodyguard, not a receptionist. If some customers got tired of waiting for you to show up and left, I don't see where you can dodge the blame by shifting it to…"

"Wait a minute, Boss. You're missing the point. They didn't leave!"

"Come again?"

"I left 'em there in the reception room, and the next thing I know Mr. Mouth here is hollerin' at me for losing customers. They never came out! Now, like you say, I'm supposed to be a body-guard. By my figuring we've got some extra people wandering the premises, and all this slob wants to do is yell about whose fault it is."

"I know whose fault it is," Aahz said with a glare. "There are only two ways out of that reception room, and they didn't come past me!"

"Well they didn't come past *me!*" Guido countered. I started to get a very cold feeling in my stomach. "Aahz," I said softly.

"If you think I don't know when…"

"AAHZ!"

That brought him up short. He turned to me with an angry retort on his lips, then he saw my expression. "What is it, Skeeve? You look as if…"

"There are more than two ways out of that room."

We stared at each other in stunned silence for a few moments, then we both sprinted for the reception room, leaving Guido to trail along behind.

The room we had selected for our reception area was one of the largest in the place, and the only large room with easy access from the front door. It was furnished in a style lavish enough to impress even those customers spoiled by the wonders of the Bazaar who were expecting to see the home office of a successful magician. There was only one problem with it, and that was the focus of our attention as we dashed in.

The only decoration that we had kept from the previous owners was an ornate tapestry hanging on the north wall. Usually I'm faster than Aahz, but this time he beat me to the hanging, sweeping it aside with his arm to reveal a heavy door behind it.

Our worst fears were realized.

The door was unlocked and standing ajar.

II.

"Success often hinges on choosing a reliable partner."
REMUS

WHAT'S THAT?" GUIDO demanded, taking advantage of our stunned silence.

"It's a door," I said.

"An open door, to be specific," Aahz supplied.

" I can see that for myself!" the bodyguard roared. "I meant what is it doing here?"

"It would look pretty silly standing alone in the middle of the street now, wouldn't it?" Aahz shot back.

Guido purpled. As I've said, these two have a positive talent for getting under each other's skins.

"Now look, all I'm askin'…"

"Guido, could you just hang on for a few minutes until we decide what to do next? Then we'll explain, I promise."

My mind was racing over the problem, and having Aahz and Guido going at each other did nothing for my concentration.

"I think the first thing we should do, partner," Aahz said thoughtfully, "is to get the door closed so that we won't be…interrupted while we work this out."

Rather than answer, I reached out a cautious toe and pushed the door shut. Aahz quickly slipped two of the bolts in place to secure it.

That done, we leaned against the door and looked at each other in silence.

"Well? What do you think?" I asked at last.

"I'm in favor of sealing it up again and forgetting the whole thing."

"Think it's safe to do that?"

"Don't know, really. Not enough information."

We both turned slowly to level thoughtful stares at Guido.

"Say, uh, Guido, could you tell us a little more about those customers who came in this morning?"

"Nothing doin'." Guido crossed his arms. "You're the guys who insist on 'information for information.' Right? Well, I'm not telling you anything more until somebody tells me about that door. I mean,

I'm supposed to be your bodyguard and nobody bothers to tell me there's another way into this place?"

Aahz bared his teeth and started forward, but I caught him by the shoulder.

"He's right, partner. If we want his help, we owe him an explanation."

We locked eyes again for a moment, then he shrugged and retreated.

"Actually, Guido, the explanation is very simple…"

"That'll be a first," the bodyguard grumbled.

In a bound, Aahz was across the room and had Guido by the shirt front.

"You wanted an explanation? Then SHUT UP AND LET HIM EXPLAIN!"

Now Guido is no lightweight, and he's never been short in the courage department. Still, there's nothing quite like Aahz when he's really mad.

"O—Okay! Sorry! Go ahead, Boss. I'm listening." Aahz released his grip and returned to his place by the door, winking at me covertly as he went.

"What happened is this," I said, hiding a smile. "Aahz and I found that door when we first moved in here. We didn't like the looks of it, so we decided to leave it alone. That's all."

"That's all!? A back door that even you admit looks dangerous and all you do is ignore it? And if that wasn't bad enough, you don't even bother to tell your bodyguards about it? Of all the lamebrained, half…"

Aahz cleared his throat noisily, and Guido regained control of himself…rapidly.

"Aahh…what I mean to say is…oh well. That's all behind us now. Could you give *me a* little more information now that the subject's out in the open? What's on the other side of that door, anyway?"

"We don't know," I admitted.

"YOU DON'T KNOW?" Guido shrieked.

"What we *do* know," Aahz interrupted hastily, "is what *isn't* on the other side. What isn't there is any dimension we know about."

Guido blinked, then shook his head. "I don't get it. Could you run that past me again…real slow?"

"Let me try," I said. "Look, Guido, you already know about dimensions, right? How we're living in the dimension Deva, which is an entirely different world than our own home dimension of Klah? Well, the people here, the Deveels, are masters of dimension travel to a point where they build their houses across the dimension barriers. That's how come this place is bigger on the inside than it is on the outside. The door is in Deva, but the rest of the house is in another dimension. That means if we go through that door, the back door that we've just shown you, we'd be in another world…one we know nothing about. That's why we were willing to leave it sealed up rather than stick our noses out into a completely unknown situation."

"I still think you should have checked it out," the bodyguard insisted stubbornly.

"Think again," Aahz supplied. "You've only seen two dimensions. Skeeve here has visited a dozen. I've been to over a hundred myself. The Deveels you see here at the Bazaar, on the other hand, know over a thousand different dimensions."

"So?"

"So we think they gave us this place because it opens into a dimension that *they* don't want…'don't want' as in 'scared to death of'. Now, you've seen what a Deveel will brave to turn a profit. Do *you* want to go exploring in a world that's too mean for *them* to face?"

"I see what you mean."

"Besides," Aahz finished triumphantly, "take an-other look at that door. It's got more locks and bolts than three ordinary bank vaults."

"*Somebody* opened it," Guido said pointedly.

That took some of the wind out of Aahz's sails. Despite himself, he shot a nervous glance at the door.

"Well…a good thief with a lockpick working from this side…"

"Some of these locks weren't picked, Aahz."

I had been taking advantage of their discussion to do a little snooping, and now held up one of my discoveries for their inspection. It was a padlock with the metal shackle snapped off. There were several of them scattered about, as if someone had gotten impatient with the lock-pick and simply torn the rest of them apart with his hands.

Guido pursed his lips in a silent whistle. "Man, that's strong. What kind of person could to that?"

"That's what we've been trying to get you to tell us," Aahz said nastily. "Now, if you don't mind, what were those customers like?"

"Three of them…two men and a woman…fairly young-looking, but nothing special. Klahds by the look of em. Come to think of it, they did seem a bit nervous, but I thought it was just because they were coming to see a magician."

"Well, now they're on the other side of the door." Aahz scooped up one of the undamaged locks and snapped it into place. "I don't think they can pick locks, or break them if they can't reach 'em. They're there, which is their problem, self-inflicted I might add, and we're here. End of puzzle. End of problem."

"Do you really think so, Aahz?"

"Trust me."

Somehow that phrase struck a familiar chord in my memory, and the echoes weren't pleasant. I was about to raise this point with Aahz when Nunzio poked his head in the door.

"Hey, Boss. You got visitors."

"See?" my partner exclaimed, beaming. "I told you things could only get better! It's not even noon and we've got more customers."

"Actually," Nunzio clarified, "it's a delegation of Deveels. I think it's the landlord."

"The landlord?" Aahz echoed hollowly.

"See how much better things have gotten?" I said with a disgusted smirk. "And it's not even noon."

"Shall I run 'em off, Boss?" Guido suggested.

"I think you'd better see 'em," Nunzio advised. "They seem kind'a upset. Something about us harboring fugitives."

Aahz and I locked gazes in silence, which was only natural as there was nothing more to be said. With a vague wave that bordered on a nervous tick, I motioned for Nunzio to show the visitors in.

As expected, it was the same delegation of four from the Devan Chamber of Commerce who had originally hired us to work for the Bazaar, headed by our old adversary, Hay-ner. Last time we dealt with him, we had him over a barrel and used the advantage mercilessly. While he had agreed to our terms, I always suspected it had hurt his Devan pride to cut such a generous deal and that he had been waiting ever since to pay us back. From the smile on his face as he entered our reception room, it appeared he felt his chance had finally come.

"Aahh, Master Skeeve," he said. "How good of you to see us so promptly without an appointment. I know how busy you are, so I'll

come right to the point. I believe there are certain individuals in residence here that our organization is *most* anxious to speak with. If you
would be so kind as to summon them, we won't trouble you further."

"Wait a minute, Hay-ner," Aahz put in before I could respond.
"What makes you think the people you're looking for are here?"

"Because they were seen entering your tent less than an hour
ago and haven't come out yet," said the largest of Hay-ner's back-
up team.

I noticed that unlike Hay-ner, he wasn't smiling. In fact, he looked
down-right angry.

"He must mean the ones who came in earlier," Nunzio suggested helpfully. "You know, Boss, the two guys with the broad."

Aahz rolled his eyes in helpless frustration, and for once I was
inclined to agree with him.

"Umm, Nunzio," I said, staring at the ceiling. "why don't you
and Guido wait outside while we take care of this?"

The two bodyguards trooped outside in silence, though I noticed
that Guido glared at his cousin with such disdain that I suspected a
stern dressing-down would take place even before I could get to him
myself. The Mob is no more tolerant than magicians of staff members who say more than they should in front of the opposition.

"Now that we've established that we all know who we're talking about and that they're here," Hay-ner said, rubbing his hands
together, "call them out and we'll finish this once and for all."

"Not so fast," I interrupted. "First of all, neither of us have laid
eyes on those folks you're looking for, because, second of all, they
aren't here. They took it on the lam out the back door before we
could meet them."

"Somehow, I don't expect you to take our word for it," Aahz
added. "So feel free to search the place."

The Deveel's smile broadened, and I was conscious of cold
sweat breaking out on my brow.

"That won't be necessary. You see, whether I believe you or not
is of little consequence. Even if we searched, I'm sure you would be
better at hiding things than we would be at finding them. All that
really matters is that we've established that they did come in here,
and that makes them *your* responsibility."

I wasn't sure exactly what was going on here, but I *was* sure that
I was liking it less and less with each passing moment.

3

"Wait a minute, Hay-ner," I began. "What do you mean 'We're responsible'? Responsible for what?"

"Why, for the fugitives, of course. Don't you remember? When we agreed to let you use this place rent-free, part of the deal was that if anyone of this household broke any of the Bazaar rules, and either disappeared off to another dimension or otherwise refused to face the charges, that you would personally take responsibility for their actions. It's a standard clause in any Bazaar lease."

"Aahz," I said testily, "you cut the deal. Was there a clause like that in it?"

"There was," he admitted. "But I was thinking of Tananda and Chumley at the time...and we'll stand behind them anytime. Massha, too. It never occurred to me that they'd try to claim that anyone who walked through our door was a member of our household. I don't see how they can hope to prove..."

"We don't have to prove that they're in your household," Hayner smiled. "You have to prove they aren't."

"That's crazy," Aahz exploded. "How can we prove..."

"Can it, Aahz. We can't prove it. That's the point. All right, Hayner. You've got us. Now what exactly have these characters done that we're responsible for and what are our options? I thought one of the big sales points of the Bazaar was that there weren't any rules here."

"There aren't many," the Deveel said, "but the few that do exist are strictly enforced. The specific rule your friends broke involves fraud."

He quickly held up a hand to suppress my retort.

"I know what you're going to say. Fraud sounds like a silly charge with all the hard bargaining that goes on here at the Bazaar, but to us it's a serious matter. While we pride ourselves in driving a hard bargain, once the deal is made you get the goods you were promised. Sometimes there are specific details omitted in describing the goods, but anything actually *said* is true. That is our reputation and the continued success of the Bazaar depends on that reputation being scrupulously maintained. If a trader or merchant sells something claiming it to be magical and it turns out to have no powers at all, that's fraud...and if the perpetrators are allowed to go unpunished, it could mean the end of the Bazaar as we know it."

"Actually," I said drily, "all I was going to do was protest you billing them as our friends, but I'll let it go. What you haven't mentioned is our options."

Hay-ner shrugged. "There are only three, really. You can pay back the money they took falsely plus a twenty-five percent fine, accept permanent banishment from the Bazaar, or you can try to convince your fr—aahh, I mean the fugitives to return to the Bazaar to settle matters themselves."

"I see…Very well. You've had your say. Now please leave so my partner and I can discuss our position on the matter."

Aahz took care of seeing them out while I plunged into thought as to what we should do. When he returned, we both sat in silence for the better part of an hour before either of us spoke.

"Well," I said at last, "what do you think?"

"Banishment from the Bazaar is out!" Aahz snarled. "Not only would it destroy our reputations, I'm not about to get run out of the Bazaar *and* our home over something as idiotic as this!"

"Agreed," I said grimly. "Even though it occurs to me that Hay-ner is bluffing on that option. He wants us to stick around the Bazaar as much as we want to stay. He was the one who hired us in the first place, remember? I think he's expecting us to ante up and pay the money. That way he gets back some of the squeeze he so grudgingly parted with. Somehow the idea of giving in to that kind of pressure really galls me."

Aahz nodded. "Me too."

There followed several more minutes of silence.

"Okay," Aahz said finally, "who's going to say it?"

"We're going to have to go after them." I sighed.

"Half right," Aahz corrected. "*I'm* going to have to go after them. Partner or not, we're talking about hitting a totally new dimension here, and it's too dangerous for someone at your level of magical skill."

"*My* level? How about you? You don't have any powers at all. If it's too dangerous for me, what's supposed to keep you safe?"

"Experience," he said loftily. "I'm used to doing this, and you aren't. End of argument."

"'End of argument' nothing! Just how to you propose to leave me behind if I don't agree?"

"That's easy," Aahz grinned. "See who's standing in the corner?"

I turned to look where he was pointing, and that's the last thing I remembered for a long time.

III.

"Reliable information is a must for successful planning."
C. COLUMBUS

HEY! HOT STUFF! Wake up!! You okay?"

If I led a different kind of life, those words would have been uttered by a voluptuous vision of female loveliness. As it was, they were exclaimed by Massha.

This was one of the first things that penetrated the fogginess of my mind as I struggled to regain consciousness. I'm never at my best first thing in the morning, even when I wake up leisurely of my own accord. Having wakefulness forced upon me by someone else only guaran-tees that my mood will be less than pleasant.

However groggy I might be feeling, though, there was no mistaking the fact that it was Massha shaking me awake. Even through unfocused eyes, her form was unmistakable. Imagine, if you will, the largest, fattest woman you've ever met. Now expand that image by fifty percent in all directions, top it off with garish orange hair, and false eyelashes and purple lipstick, and adorn it with a wheelbarrow load of gaudy jewelry. See what I mean? I could recognize Massha a mile away on a dark night...blindfolded.

"Of course I'm okay, *apprentice!*" I snarled. "Don't you have any lessons you're supposed to be practicing or something?"

"Are you *sure?*" she pressed mercilessly.

"Yes, I'm sure. Why do you ask? Can't a fellow take a little nap without being badgered about it?"

"It's just that you don't usually take naps in the middle of the reception room floor."

That got my attention, and I forced my eyes into focus. She was right! For some reason I was sprawled out on the floor. Now what could have possessed me to...

Then it all came back! Aahz! The expedition into the new dimension!

I sat bolt upright...and regretted it immediately. A blinding headache assaulted me with icepick intensity, and my stomach flipped over and landed on its back with all the grace of a lump of overcooked oatmeal.

Massha caught me by the shoulder as I started to list. "Steady there, High Roller. Looks like your idea of 'okay' and mine are a little out of synch."

Ignoring her, I felt the back of my head cautiously and discovered a large, tender lump behind my ear. If I had had any doubts as to what had happened, they were gone now.

"That bloody Pervert!" I said, flinching at the new wave of pain brought on by the sound of my own voice. "He must have knocked me out and gone in alone!"

"You mean Aahz? Dark, green, and scaly himself? I don't get it. Why would your own partner sucker-punch you?"

"So he could go through the door without me. I made it very clear that I didn't want to be left behind on this caper."

"Door? What door?" Massha said with a frown. "I know you two have your secrets, Boss, but I think you'd better fill me in on a few more details as to exactly what's going on around here."

As briefly as I could, I brought her up to date on the day 's events, including the explanation as to why Aahz and I had never said anything about the house's myster-ious back door. Being a seasoned dimension traveler her-self, she grasped the concept of an unlisted dimension and its potential dangers much more rapidly than Guido and Nunzio.

"What I don't understand is even if he didn't want you along, why didn't he take *someone* else as a back-up?"

"Like who?" I said with a wry grimace. "We've already established that you're *my* apprentice and he doesn't give you orders without clearing them through me. He's never been impressed with Guido and Nunzio. Tananda and Chumley are off on their own contracts and aren't due back for several days. Even Gus is taking a well-earned vacation with Berfert. Besides, he knows good and well that if he started building a team and excluded me, there'd be some serious problems before the dust settled. I wouldn't take something like that lying down!"

"Don't look now, but you just did," my apprentice pointed out dryly, "though I have to admit he sort of forced it on you."

With that, she slid a hand under each of my armpits and picked me up, setting me gently on my feet.

"Well, now what? I supposed you're going to go charging after him with blood in your eye. Mind if I tag along? Or are you bound and determined to be as stupid as he is?"

As a matter of fact, that was exactly what I had been planning to do. The undisguised sarcasm in her voice combined with the unsettling wobbliness of my legs, however, led me to reconsider.

"No," I said carefully. "One of us blundering around out there is enough...or one too many, depending on how You count it. While I still think I should have gone along, Aahz has dealt this hand, so it's up to him to play it out. It's up to me to mind the store until he gets back."

Massha cocked an eyebrow at me.

"That makes sense," she said, "though I'll admit I'm a little surprised to hear you say it."

"I'm a responsible businessman now." I shrugged. "I can't afford to go off half-cocked like a rash kid anymore. Besides, I have every confidence in my partner's ability to handle things."

Those were brave words, and I meant them. Two days later, however, this particular 'responsible businessman' was ready to go off *fully* cocked. Guido and Nunzio ceased to complain about my sneaking off alone...mostly because I didn't go out at all! In fact, I spent most of my waking hours and all of my sleeping hours (though I'll admit I didn't sleep much) in the reception room on the off-chance that I could greet Aahz on his triumphant return.

Unfortunately, my vigil went unrewarded.

I did my best to hide my concern, but I needn't have bothered. As the hours marched on, my staff's worries grew until most of my time was spent telling them, 'No, he isn't back yet. When he gets here, I'll let you know." Even Guido, who never really got along with Aahz, took to stopping by at least once an hour for a no-progress report.

Finally, as a salve for my own nerves, I called every-one into the reception room for a staff meeting.

"What I want to know is how long are we just going to sit around before we admit that something's gone wrong?" Guido muttered for the fifth time.

"How long do you figure it takes to find a fugitive in a strange dimension?" I shot back. "How long would it take you to find them if they were on Klah, Guido? We've got to give him some time."

"How much time?" he countered. "It's already been two days..."

"Tananda and Chumley will be back any time now," Massha interrupted. "Do you think they'll just sit around on their hands when they find out that Aahz is out there all alone?"

"I thought _you_ were the one who thought that going after him was a stupid idea?"

"I still do. Now do you want to know what I think of the idea of doing _nothing?_"

Before I could answer, a soft knock sounded at the door...the back door!

"See!" I crowed triumphantly. "I told you he would be back!"

"That doesn't sound like his knock," Guido observed suspiciously.

"And why should he knock?" Massha added. "The door hasn't been locked since he left."

In my own relief and enthusiasm, their remarks went unnoticed. In a flash I was at the door, wrenching it open while voicing the greeting I had been rehearsing for two days.

"It's about time, part...ner."

It wasn't Aahz.

In fact, the being outside the door didn't look anything at all like Aahz. What was doubly surprising, though, was that I recognized her!

We had never really met...not to exchange names, but shortly after meeting Aahz I had been strung up by an angry mob while impersonating her, and I had seen her in the crowd when I successfully "interviewed" for the job of court magician at Possletum.

What I had never had a chance to observe first-hand was her radiant complexion framed by waves of sun-gold hair, or the easy grace with which she carried herself, or the "It's the Great Skeeve, right? Behind the open mouth?"

Her voice was so musical it took me a few moments to zero in on what she had said and realize that she was expecting an answer.

"Aahh...yes. I mean, at your service."

"Glad to finally meet you face-to-face," she said briskly, glancing at Guido and Massha nervously. "I've been looking for an excuse for a while, and I guess this is it. Got some news for you...about your apprentice."

I was still having problems focusing on what she was saying. Not only was her voice mesmerizing, she was easily the loveliest woman I had ever met...well, girl actually. She couldn't have been much older than me. What's more, she seemed to like me. That is, she kept smiling hesitantly and her deep blue eyes never left mine. Now, I had gotten respect from my colleagues and from beings at the Bazaar who knew my reputation, but never from anyone who looked like...

Then her words sank in.

"My apprentice?"

I stole an involuntary glance at Massha before I realized the misunderstanding.

"Oh, you mean, Aahz. He's not my apprentice any more. He's my partner. Please come in. We were just talking about him."

I stood to one side of the door and invited her in with a grand sweeping gesture. I'd never tried it before, but I had seen it used a couple of times while I was working the court at Possletum, and it had impressed me.

"Umm—Boss? Could I talk to you for a minute?"

"Later, Guido."

I repeated the gesture, and the girl responded with a quick smile that lit up the room.

"Thanks for the invite," she said, but I'll have to take a rain check. I really can't stay. In fact, I shouldn't be here at all. I just thought that someone should let you know that your friend…Aahz is it? Anyway, your friend is in jail."

That brought me back to earth in a hurry.

"Aahz? In jail? For what?"

"Murder."

"MURDER!" I shrieked, dropping all attempts to be urbane. "But Aahz wouldn't…"

"Don't shout at me! Oh, I knew I shouldn't have come. Look, I know he didn't do it. That's why I had to let you know what was going on. If you don't do something they're going to execute him…and they know how to execute demons over here."

I spun around to face the others.

"Massha! Go get your jewelry case. Guido, Nunzio! Gear up. We're going to pay a little call on our neighbors." I tried to keep my voice calm and level, but somehow the words came out a bit more intense than I had, intended.

"Not so fast, Boss," Guido said. "There's somethin you oughta know first."

"Later. I want you to…"

"NOW, Boss. It's important!"

"WHAT IS IT!"

Needless to say, I was not eager to enter into any prolonged conversations just now.

"She's one of 'em."

"I beg your pardon?"

"The three that went out through the back door. The ones your partner is chasing. She's the broad."

Thunderstruck, I turned to the girl for confirmation, only to find the doorway was empty. My mysterious visitor had disappeared as suddenly as she had arrived.

"This could be a trap, you know," Massha said thoughtfully.

"She's right." Guido nodded. "Take it from someone who's been on the lam himself. When you're running from the law and there are only a couple of people who can find you, it gets real tempting to eliminate that link. We've only got her word that your partner's in trouble."

"It wouldn't take a mental giant to figure out that you and Aahz are the most likely hunters for the Deveels to hire. After all, they knew whose house they were cutting through for their getaway," Massha added.

Guido rose to his feet and started pacing.

"Right," he said. "Now suppose *they've* got Aahz. Can you think of a better way to bag the other half of the pair than by feeding you a line about your partner being in trouble so you'll come charging into whatever trap they've laid out? The whole set-up stinks, Boss. I don't know about strange dimensions, but I *do* know about criminals. As soon as you step through that door, you're gonna be a sitting duck."

"Are you *quite* through?"

Even to my ears my voice sounded icy, but for a change I didn't care.

Guido and Massha exchanged glances, then nodded silently.

"Very well. You may be right, and I appreciate your concern for my well-being. HOWEVER..."

My voice sank to a deadly hiss.

"...what if you're wrong? What if our fugitive is telling the truth? You've all been on my case about not doing anything to help Aahz. Do you really think I'm just going to sit here while my partner AND friend burns for a crime he didn't commit...on the off-chance that getting involved *might* be dangerous to me?"

With great effort I forced my tones back to normal.

"In ten minutes I'm going through that door after Aahz...and if I'm walking into a trap, it had better be a good one. Now do any of you want to come with me, or am I going it alone?"

IV.

"It's useless to try to plan for the unexpected...by definition!"
A. Hitchcock

ACTUALLY, IT WAS more like an hour before we were really ready to go, though for me it seemed like a lot longer. Still, even I had to admit that not taking the proper preparations for this venture would not only be foolish, it would be downright suicidal!

It was decided that Nunzio would stay behind so there would be someone at our base to let Tananda and Chumley know what was going on when they returned.

Needless to say, he was less than thrilled by the assignment.

"But I'm supposed to be your bodyguard!" he argued. "How'm I supposed to guard you if I'm sittin' back here while you're on the front lines?"

"By being sure our support troops get the information they need to follow us," I said.

As much as I disliked having to argue with Nunzio, I would rather dig in my heels against half a dozen Mobtype bodyguards than have to explain to Tananda and Chumley why they weren't included in this rescue mission.

"We could leave a note."

"No.

"We could..."

"NO! I want you *here*. Is that plain enough?"

The bodyguard heaved a heavy sigh. "Okay, Boss. I'll hang in here until they show up. Then the three of us will..."

"No!" I said again. "Then Tananda and Chumley will come in after us. You're going to stay here."

"But Boss...

"Because if Hay-ner and his crew show up again, someone has to be here to let them know we're on the job and that we haven't just taken off for the tall timber. Assuming for the moment that we're going to make it back, we need our exit route, and you're going to be here making sure it stays open. All we need is for our hosts to move in a new tenant while we're gone...say, someone who decides to brick up this door while we're on the other side."

Nunzio thought this through in silence.

"What if you don't come back?" he asked finally. "We'll burn that bridge when we come to it," I sighed.

"But remember, we aren't that easy to kill. At least one of us will probably make it back."

Fortunately, my mind was wrenched away from that unpleasant train of thought by the arrival of Guido. "Ready to go, Boss."

Despite the desperateness of the situation and the haunting time pressures, I found myself gaping at him. "What's that?" I managed at last.

Guido was decked out in a long dark coat and wearing a wide-brimmed hat and sunglasses.

"These? These are my work clothes," he said proudly. "They're functional as well as decorative."

"They're what?"

"What I mean is, not only do people find 'em intimidating, the trench coat has all these little pockets inside, see? That's where I carry my hardware."

"But..."

"Hi, Hot Stuff. Nice outfit, Guido."

"Thanks! I was just telling the Boss here about it."

Massha was dressed...or should I say undressed in *her* work clothes. A brief vest struggled to cover even part of her massive torso, while an even briefer bottom was on the verge of surrendering its battle completely.

"Ummm...Massha?" I said carefully. "I've always meant to ask. Why don't you...ummm...wear more?"

"I like to dress cool when we're going into a hot situation," she winked. "You see, when things speed up, I get a little nervous...and the only thing worse than havin' a fat broad around is havin' *a sweaty* fat broad around."

"I think it's a sexy outfit," Guido chimed in. "Re-minds me of the stuff my old man's moll used to wear."

"Well thanks, Dark and Deadly. I'd say your old man had good taste...but I never tasted him."

I studied them thoughtfully as they shared a laugh over Massha's joke. Any hope of a quiet infiltration of this unknown dimension was rapidly disintegrating. Either Guido or Massha alone was eye-catching, but together they were about as inconspicuous as a circus parade and an army maneuver sharing the same road. Then it occurred to me that, not knowing what things were like where we were heading, they might fit in and I would stand out. It was a frightening thought. If everybody there looked like this...

I forced the thought from my mind. No use scaring myself any more than I had to before there was information to back it up. What was important was that my two assistants were scared. They were trying hard not to show it, but in doing so, each was dropping into old patterns, slipping behind old character masks. Guido was playing his "tough gangster" bit to the hilt, while Massha was once more assuming her favorite "vamp" character with a vengeance. The bottom line, though, was that, scared or not, they were willing to back my move or die trying. It would have been touching, if it weren't for the fact that it meant they were counting on me for leadership. That meant I had to stay calm and confident...no matter how scared I felt myself. It only occurred to me as an afterthought that, in many ways, leadership was the mask I was learning to slip behind when things got tight. It made me wonder briefly if *anyone* ever really knew that they were doing or felt truly confident, or if life was simply a mass game of role-playing.

"Okay. Are we ready?" I asked, shrugging off my wandering thoughts. "Massha? Got your jewelry?"

"Wearing most of it, and the rest is right here," she said, patting the pouch on her belt.

While I will occasionally make snide mental comments about my apprentice's jewelry, it serves a dual purpose. Massha's baubles are in reality a rather extensive collection of magical gimmicks she has accumulated over the years. How extensive? Well, before she signed on as my apprentice to learn real magic, she was holding down a steady job as the magician for the city-state of Ta-hoe on the dimension of Jahk solely on the strength of her collected mechanical "powers." While I agreed with Aahz that real magic was preferable to mechanical in that it was less likely to malfunction (a lesson learned from first-hand experience) I sure didn't mind having her arsenal along for back-up.

"You know that tracking ring? The one you used to find the king? Any chance there's an extra tucked away in your pouch?"

"Only have the one," she said, waggling the appropriate finger.

I cursed mentally, then made the first of what I feared would be many unpleasant decisions on this venture.

"Give it to Nunzio. Tananda and Chumley will need it to find us."

"But if we leave it behind, how are we going to find your partner?"

"We'll have to figure out something, but we can't afford to divide our forces. Otherwise, even if we get Aahz, we could still end up wandering around out there trying to find the other half of the rescue team."

"If you say so, Hot Stuff," she grimaced, handing over the ring, "but I hope you know what you're doing."

"So do I, Massha, so do I. Okay, gang, let's see what our back-yard is *really* like!"

FROM the outside, our place looked a lot more impressive than the side that showed in the Bazaar. It really did look like a castle...a rather ominous one at that, squatting alone on a hilltop. I really didn't study it too close, though, beyond being able to recognize it again for our trip out. As might be expected, my main attention was focused on the new dimension itself.

"Kinda dark, ain't it."

Guido's comment was more statement than question, and he was right.

Wherever we were, the lighting left a lot to be desired. At first I thought it was night, which puzzled me, as so far in my travels all dimensions seemed to be on the same sun-up and sun-down schedule. Then my eyes adjusted to the gloom and I realized the sky was simply heavily overcast...to a point where next to no light at all penetrated, giving a night-like illusion to the day.

Aside from that, from what I could see, this new land seemed pretty much like any of the others I had visited: Trees, underbrush, and a road leading to or from the castle, depending on which way you were facing. I think it was Tananda who was fond of saying "If you've seen one dimension, you've seen them all." Chumley, her brother, argued that the reason for the geologic similarities was that all the dimensions we traveled were different realities off the same base. This always struck me as being a bit redundant..."They're all alike because they're the same? c'mon Chumley!", but his rebuttals always left me feeling like I'd been listening to someone doing readings in another language, so of late I've been tending to avoid the discussions.

"Well, Hot Stuff, what do we do now?"

For a change, I had an answer for this infuriating question.

"This road has to go somewhere. Just the fact that it exists indicates we aren't alone in this dimension."

"I thought we already knew that," Guido said under his breath. "That's why we're here."

I gave him my best dark glare.

"I believe there was *some* debate as to whether or not we were being lied to about Aahz being held prisoner. If there's a road here, it's a cinch that neither my partner nor the ones he was chasing built it. That means we have native types to deal with...possibly hostile."

"Right," Massha put in quickly. "Put a sock in it, Guido. I want to hear our plan of action, and I don't like being kept waiting by hecklers."

The bodyguard frowned, but kept his silence.

"Okay. Now, what we've got to do is follow this road and find out where it goes. Hug the side of the road and be ready to disappear if you hear anybody coming. We don't know what the locals look like, and until I have a model to work from, it's pointless for me to try to disguise us."

With those general marching orders, we made our way through the dark along the road, moving quietly to avoid tipping our hand to anyone ahead of us. In a short time we came up to our first decision point. The road we were on ended abruptly when it met another, much larger thoroughfare. My assistants looked at me expectantly. With a shrug I made the arbitrary decision and led them off to the right down this new course. As we went, I reflected with some annoyance that even though both Massha and Guido knew that I was as new to this terrain as they were, it somehow fell to me to choose the path.

My thoughts were interrupted by the sound of voices ahead, coming our way. The others heard it too, and without word or signal we melted into the underbrush. Squatting down, I peered through the gloom toward the road, anxious to catch my first glimpse of the native life I forms.

I didn't have long to wait. Two figures appeared, a young couple by the look of them, talking and laughing merrily as they went. They looked pretty normal to me, which was a distinct relief, considering the forms I had had to imitate in some of the other dimensions.

They were humanoid enough to pass for Klands...or Jahks, actually, as they were a bit pale. Their dress was not dissimilar from my own, though a bit more colorful. Absorbing all this in a glance, I decided to make my first try for information. I mean, after all my fears, they were so familiar it was almost a letdown, so why not bull ahead? Compared with some of the beings I've had to deal with in the past, this looked like a piece of cake.

Signaling the others to stay put, I stepped out onto the road behind my target couple.

"Excuse me!" I called "I'm new to this area and in need of a little assistance. Could you direct me to the nearest town?"

Translation pendants were standard equipment for dimension travel, and as I was wearing one now, I had no fear of not being understood.

The couple turned to face me, and I was immediately struck by their eyes. The "whites" of their eyes glowed a dark red, sending chills down my spine. It occurred to me that I might have studied the locals a bit longer before I tried to pass myself off as a native. It also occurred to me that I had already committed myself to this course of action and would have to bluff my way through it regardless. Finally, it occurred to me that I was a suicidal idiot and that I hoped Massha and Guido were readying their back-up weapons to save me from my own impatience.

Strangely enough, the couple didn't seem to notice anything unusual about my appearance.

"The nearest town? That would be Blut. It's not far, we just came from there. It's got a pretty wild night life, if you're into that kind of thing."

There was something about his mouth that nagged at the edges of my mind. Unfortunately, I couldn't look at it directly without breaking eye contact, so, buoyed by my apparent acceptance, I pushed ahead with the conversation.

"Actually, I'm not too big on night life. I'm trying to run down an old friend of mine I've lost touch with. Is there a post office or a police station in Blut I could ask at?"

"Better than that," the man laughed. "The one you want to talk to is the Dispatcher. He keeps tabs on every-body. The third warehouse on your left as you enter town. He's converted the whole second floor into an office. If he can't help you, nobody can."

As vital as the information was, I only paid it partial attention. When the man laughed, I had gotten a better look at his mouth. His teeth were…

"Look at his teeth!" the girl gasped, speaking for the first time.

"My teeth?" I blinked, realizing with a start that she was staring at me with undisguised astonishment.

Her companion, in the meantime, had paled noticeably and was backing away on unsteady legs.

"You…you're…Where did you come from?"

Trying my best to maintain a normal manner until I had figured out what was going on, I moved forward to keep our earlier conversational distance.

"The castle on the hill back there. I was just…"

"THE CASTLE!?!"

In a flash the couple turned and sprinted away from me down the road.

"Monster!! Help!! MONSTER!!!"

I actually spun and looked down the road behind me, trying to spot the object of their terror. Looking at the empty road, however, it slowly began to sink in. They were afraid of *me!* Monster?

Of all the reactions I had tried to anticipate for our reception in this new land, I had never in my wildest imaginings expected this.

Me? A monster?

"I think we've got problems, High Roller," Massha said as she and Guido emerged from the brush at my side.

"I'll say. Unless I'm reading the signs all wrong, they're afraid of me."

She heaved a great sigh and shook her head.

"That's not what I'm talking about. Did you see their teeth?"

"I saw his," I said. "The canines were long and pointed. Pretty weird, huh?"

"Not all that weird, Hot Stuff. Think about it. My bet is that you were just talking to a couple of vampires!"

V.

"To survive, one must be able to adapt to changing situations."
TYRANNOSAURUS REX

VAMPIRES," I SAID carefully.

"Sure. It all fits." Massha nodded. "The pale skin, the sharp fangs, the red eyeliner, the way they turned into bats..."

"Turned into bats?"

"You missed it, Boss," Guido supplied. "You were lookin' behind you when they did it. Wildest thing I ever saw. One second they was runnin' for their lives, and the next they're flutterin' up into the dark. Are all the other dimensions like this?"

"Vampires..."

Actually, my shock wasn't all that great. Realizing the things Aahz and I had run into cruising the so-called "known and safe" dimensions, I had expected something a bit out of the ordinary in this one. If anything, I was a bit relieved. The second shoe had been dropped... and it really wasn't all that bad! That is, it could have been worse. (If hanging around with Aahz had taught me any-thing, it was that things could always be worse!) The repetitive nature of my conversational brilliance was merely a clever ploy to cover my mental efforts to both digest this new bit of information and decide what to do with it.

"Vampires are rare in any dimension," my apprentice replied, stepping into the void to answer Guido's question

"What's more, they're pretty much feared universally What I can't figure out is why those two were so scared of Skeeve here."

"Then again," I said thoughtfully, "there's the question of whether or not we can safely assume the whole dimension is popu-lated with beings like the two we just met. I know it's a long shot, but we might have run into the only two vampires in the place."

"I dunno, High Roller. They acted pretty much at home here, and they sure didn't think you'd find anything unusual about *their* appearance. My guess is that they're the norm and we're the exceptions around here."

"Whatever," I said, reaching a decision at last, "they're the only two examples we have to work with so far, so that's what we'll base our actions on until proven different."

"So what do we do against a bunch of vampires?"

As a bodyguard, Guido seemed a bit uneasy about our assessment of the situation.

"Relax," I smiled. "The first order of business is to turn on the old reliable disguise spell. Just a few quick touch-ups and they won't be able to tell us apart from the natives. We could walk through a town of vampires and they'd never spot us."

With that, I closed my eyes and went to work. Like I told the staff, this was going to be easy. Maintain everyone's normal appearance except for paler skin, longer canines, and a little artful reddening of the eyes, and the job was done.

"Okay," I said, opening my eyes again. "What's next?"

"I don't like to quote you back at yourself, Hot Stuff," you trying to say we still have the same appearance as before I cast the spell?"

One of the problems with casting a disguise spell is that as the caster, I can never see the effects. That is, I see people as they really are whether the spell is on or not. I had gotten so used to relying on the effects of this particular spell that it had never occurred to me that it might not work.

Massha and Guido were looking at each other with no small degree of concern.

"Ummm...maybe you forgot."

"Try again."

"That's right! This time remember to..."

"Hold it, you two," I ordered in my most commanding tone. "From your reactions, I perceive that the answer to my questions is 'yes.' That is, that the spell didn't work. Now just ease up a second and let me think. Okay?"

For a change they listened to me and lapsed into a respectful silence. I might have taken a moment to savor the triumph if I wasn't so worried about the problem.

The disguise spell was one of the first spells I had learned, and until now was one of my best and most reliable tools. If it wasn't working, something was seriously wrong. Now I knew that stepping through the door hadn't lessened my knowledge of that particular spell, so that meant that if something was hay-wire, it would have to be in the...

"Hey, Hot Stuff! Check the force lines!"

Apparently my apprentice and I had reached the conclusion si-multaneously. A quick magical scan of the sky overhead and the surrounding terrain confirmed my worst fears. At first I thought there were no force lines at all. Then I realized that they were there, but so faint thatit took nearly all of my reserve power just to detect them "What's all this about force lines?" Guido demanded. Massha heaved an impatient sigh.

"If you're going to run with this crowd, Dark and Deadly, you'd best start learning a little about the magic biz...or at least the vo-cabulary. Force lines are invisible streams of energy that flow through the ground and the air. They're the source of power we tap into when we do our bibbity-bobbity-boo schtick. That means that in a land like this one, where the force lines are either non-existent or very weak..."

"...you can't do squat," the bodyguard finished for her. "Hey, Boss! If what she says is true, how come those two you just met could still do that bat-trick?"

"By being very, *very* good in the magic department. To do so much with so little means they don't miss a trick...pardon the pun...in tapping and using force lines. In short, they're a lot better than either Massha or me at the magic game."

"That makes sense." Massha nodded. "In any dimension I've been in that had vampires, they were some of the strongest magic-slingers around. If this is what they have to train on, I can see why they run hog-wild when they hit a dimension where the force lines are both plentiful and powerful."

I rubbed my forehead, trying desperately to think and to fore-stall the headache I felt coming on. Right on schedule, things were getting worse!

"I don't suppose you have anything in your jewelry collection that can handle disguises, do you?"

Despite our predicament, Massha gave a low laugh.

"Think about it, High Roller. If I had anything that could do disguises, would I walk around looking like this?"

"So we get to take on a world of hot-shot magic types with our own cover fire on low ammo," Guido summarized.

"Okay. So it'll be a little tougher than I thought at first. Just remember my partner has been getting along pretty well these last few years without any powers at all."

"Your partner is currently sitting in the hoosegow for murder," Guido said pointedly. "That's why we're here in the first place. Remember?"

"Besides," I continued, ignoring his comment (that's another skill I've learned from Aahz), "it's never been our intention `to take on the whole world." All we want to do is perform a quick hit and run. Grab Aahz and get back out with as little contact with the natives as possible. All this means is that we've got to be a little more careful. That's all."

"What about running down the trio we started out to retrieve?"

I thought briefly about the blonde who had warned us of Aahz's predicament.

"That's part of being more careful," I announced solemnly. "If...I mean, *when* we get Aahz out of jail, we'll head for home and count ourselves as lucky. So we...pay off the Deveels. It's a...cheap price to...pay for..."

I realized the staff was looking at me a little askance. I also realized that my words had been gradually slowing to a painful broken delivery as I reached the part about paying off the Deveels.

I cleared my throat and tried again.

"Ummm, let's just say we'll reappraise the situation once we've reached Aahz. Okay?"

The troops still looked a little dubious, so I thought it would be best if I pushed on to the next subject.

"As to the opposition, let's pool our knowledge of vampires so we have an idea of what we're up against. Now, we know they can shapechange into bats or dogs"

"...or just into a cloud of mist," Massha supplied.

"They drink blood," Guido said grimly.

"They don't like bright light, or crosses..."

"...and they can be killed by a stake through their heart or..."

"They drink blood."

"Enough with the drinking blood! Okay, Guido?"

I was starting to get more than a little annoyed with my bodyguard's endless pessimism. I mean, none of us was particularly pleased by the way things were going, but there was nothing to be gained by dwelling on the negatives.

"Sorry, Boss. I guess looking on the dark side of things gets to be a habit in my business."

"Garlic!" Massha exclaimed suddenly.

"What's that?"

"I said `garlic'," she repeated. "Vampires don't like garlic!"

"That's right! How about it, Guido? Do you have any garlic along?"

The bodyguard actually looked embarrassed.

"Can't stand the stuff," he admitted "The other boys in the Mob used to razz me about it, but it makes me break out in a rash."

Terrific. We probably had the only Mob member in existence who was allergic to garlic. Another brilliant idea shot to hell.

"Well," I said, heaving a sigh, "now we know what we're up against."

"Ummm...say, Hot Stuff?" Massha said softly. "All kidding aside. Aren't we a little overmatched on this one? I mean, Dark and Deadly here can hold up his end on the physical protection side, but I'm not sure my jewelry collection is going to be enough to cover us magically."

"I appreciate the vote of confidence," Guido smiled sadly, "but I'm not sure my hardware is going to do us a lick of good against vampires. With the Boss out of action on the magic side..."

"Don't count me out so fast. My magic may not be at full power, but I can still pull off a trick or two if things
really get rough."

Massha frowned. "But the force lines..."

"There's one little item I've omitted from your lessons so far, apprentice," I said with a smug little grin. "It hasn't really been necessary what with the energy so plentiful on Deva...as a matter of fact, I've kind of gotten out of the habit myself. Anyway, what it boils down to is that you don't always tap into a force line to work magic. You can store the energy internally like a battery so that it's there when you need it. While we've been talking, I've been charging up, so I can provide a bit of magical cover as needed. Now, I won't be able to do anything prolonged like a constant disguise spell, and what I've got I'll want to use carefully because it'll take a while to recharge after each use, but we won't be relying on your jewelry completely."

I had expected a certain amount of excitement from the staff when they found out I wasn't totally helpless. Instead, they looked uncomfortable. They exchanged glances, then looked at the sky, then at the ground.

"Ummm...does this mean we're going on?" Guido said at last.

"That's right," I said, lips tight. "In fact, I probably would have gone on even if my powers were completely gone. Somewhere out there my partner's in trouble, and I'm not going to back away from at least *trying* to help him. I'd do the same if it was one of you, but we're talking about Aahz here. He's saved my skin more times than I care to remember. I can't just..."

I caught myself and brought my voice back under control.

"Look," I said, starting again. "I'll admit we never expected this vampire thing when we started out, and the limited magic handicap is enough to give anyone pause. If either or both of you want to head back, you can do it without hard feelings or guilt trips. Really. The only reason I'm pushing on is that I know me. Whatever is up ahead, it can't be any worse than what I would put myself through if I left Aahz alone to die without trying my best to bail him out. But that's me. If you want out, go ahead."

"Don't get your back up, Hot Stuff," Massha chided gently. "I'm still not sure how much help I'm going to be, but I'll tag along. I'd probably have the same problem if anything happened to you and I wasn't there, that you'd have if anything happened to Aahz. I *am* your apprentice, you know."

"Bodyguarding ain't much, but it's all I know," Guido said glumly. "I'm supposed to be guardin' that body of yours, so where it goes, I go. I'm just not wild about the odds, know what I mean?"

"Then it's settled," I said firmly. "All right. As I see it, our next stop is Blut."

"Blut," Massha echoed carefully.

"That's right. I want to look up this Dispatcher character and see what he has to say. I mean, a town is a town, and we've all visited strange towns before. What we really need now is information, and the nearest source seems to be Blut."

"The Dispatcher," Massha said without enthusiasm."

"Blut," Guido repeated with even less joyful antici-pation.

It occurred to me that while my assistants were bound and determined to stay with me on this caper, if I wanted wholehearted support, I'd better look for it from the natives...a prospect I didn't put much hope in at all.

VI.

"An agent is a vampire with a telephone!"
ANY EDITOR

REMEMBER HOW I said that if you've seen one town, you've seen 'em all? Well, forget it. Even though I've visited a lot of dimensions and seen a lot of towns, I had to admit that Blut looked a little strange.

Everything seemed to be done to death in basic black. (Perhaps "done to death" is an unfortunate turn of a phrase. Whatever.) Mind you, when I say everything, I mean *everything* Cobblestones, walls, roof tiles, every-thing had the same uninspired color scheme. Maybe by itself the black overtones wouldn't have seemed too ominous, if it weren't for the architectural decorations that seemed to abound everywhere you looked. Stone dragons and snakes adorned every roof peak and ledge, along with the inescapable gargoyles and, of course, bats. I don't mean "bats" here, I mean "BATS"!!! Big bats, little bats, bats with their wings half open and others with their wings spread wide…BATS!!! The only thing they all seemed to have in common (besides being black) was mouths full of needle-sharp teeth…an image which did nothing to further the confidence of my already nervous party. I myself felt the tension increasing as we strode down the street under the noses of those fierce adornments. One almost expected the stone figures to come to life and swoop down on us for a pint or two of dinner.

"Cheerful sort of place, isn't it?" Massha asked, eyeing the rooftops.

"I don't like to complain, Boss," Guido put in, lying blatantly, "but I've been in friendlier-looking graveyards."

"Will you both keep your mouths shut!" I snarled, speaking as best I could through tightly pressed lips. "Remember our disguises."

I had indeed turned on my disguise spell as we entered town, but in an effort to conserve magical energy, I had only turned our eyes red. If any of the others on the street, and there were lots of them, happened to spot our non-vampirish teeth, the balloon would go up once and for all. Then again, maybe not. We still hadn't figured out why the couple we met on the road had been so afraid of

me, but I wasn't about to bank the success of our mission on anything as flimsy as a hope that the whole town would run at the sight
of our undisguised features.

Fortunately, I didn't have to do any magical tinkering with our
wardrobe. If anything, we were a little drab compared to most of
the vampires on the street. Though most of them appeared rather
young, barely older than me, they came in all shapes and sizes, and
were decked out in some of the most colorful and outrageous garb
it has ever been my misfortune to encounter as they shouted to each
other or wove their way in and out of taverns along the street.

It was night now, the clouds having cleared enough to show a
star-studded night sky, and true to their billing, vampires seemed to
love the night life.

"If everybody here is vampires," Guido said, ignoring my
warning, "how do they find anybody to bite for blood?"

"As far as I can tell," Massha answered, also choosing to overlook the gag order, "they buy it by the bottle."

She pointed to a small group of vampires sitting on a low wall
merrily passing a bottle of red liquid back and forth among themselves. Despite our knowledge of the area, I had subconsciously
assumed they were drinking wine. Confronted by the inescapable
logic that the stuff they were drinking was typed, not aged, my
stomach did a fast roll and dip to the right.

"If you two are through sightseeing," I hissed, "let's try to find
this Dispatcher character before someone invites us to join them for
a drink."

With that, I led off my slightly subdued assistants, nodding and
waving at the merrymaking vampires as we went. Actually, the go-
ings on looked like a lot of fun, and I might have been tempted to
join in, if it weren't for the urgency of our quest...and, of course,
the fact that they *were* vampires.

Following the instructions I had gleaned from the couple on the
road before their panicky flight, we found the Dispatcher's place
with no problem. Leaving Guido outside as a lookout, Massha and
I braved the stairs and entered the Dispatcher's office.

As strange as Blut had appeared, it hadn't prepared me for the
room we stepped into.

There were hundreds of glass pictures lining the walls, pictures
which depicted moving, living things much like looking into a rack

of fishbowls. What was more, the images being displayed were of incredible violence and unspeakable acts being performed in seemingly helpless victims. The overall effect was neither relaxing nor pleasant...definitely not something I'd want on the wall at home.

I was so entranced by the pictures, I almost missed the Dispatcher himself until he rose from his desk.

Perhaps "rose" is the wrong description. What he actually did was hop down to the floor from his chair which was high to begin with, but made higher by the addition of a pillow to the seat.

He strode forward, beaming widely, with his hand extended for a handshake.

"Hi there Vilhelm's the name Your problem is my problem Don't sit down Standing problems I solve for free Sitting problems I charge for Reasonable rates Just a minor percentage off the top What can I do for you?"

That was sort of all one sentence in that he didn't pause for breath. He did, however, seize my hand, pump it twice, then repeated the same procedure with Massha, then grabbed my hand again...all before he stopped talking.

All in all, it was a little overpowering. I had a flash impression of a short, stocky character with plump rosy cheeks and a bad case of the fidgets. I had deliberately tried not to speculate on what the Dispatcher would look like, but a cherub vampire still caught me a little off-guard.

"I...ummm...how did you know I have a problem?"

That earned me an extra squeeze of the hand and a wink.

"Nobody comes in here unless they've got a problem," he said, finally slowing down his speech a bit. "I mean, I could always use a bit of help, but does anyone leap forward to lend a hand? Fat chance. Seems like the only time I see another face in the flesh is when it means more work for me. Prove me wrong...please! Tell me you came in here to take over for an hour or so to let me duck out for a bite to drink."

"Well, actually, we've got a problem and we were told..."

"See! What did I tell you? All right. What have you got? A standing or a sitting problem? Standing problems I handle for..."

He was off again. In a desperate effort to keep our visit short, I interrupted his pitch.

"We're looking for a friend who..."

"Say no more! A friend! Just a second!"

With that he vaulted back into his chair, grabbed the top off a strange-looking appliance on his desk, diddled with it briefly, then started talking into it.

"Yea Darwin? Vilhelm. I need...sure..."

Leaning back in his chair, he tucked the gadget under one side of his head and grabbed another.

"This is Vilhelm. Is Kay around?...Well, put her on when she's done..."

The second gadget slid in under the same ear as the first and he reached for yet another.

"I know I shouldn't ask this," I murmured to Massha, "but what's he doing?"

"Those are telephones," she whispered back as a fourth instrument came into play. "You talk into one end of it and whoever's at the other end can hear you and talk back. It beats running all over town to find an answer."

By this time, the little vampire had so many instruments hung from his shoulders and arms he looked like he was being attacked by a nest of snakes. He seemed to be handling it well, though, talking first into one, then another, apparently keeping multiple conversations going at once like a juggler handles a basket full of balls.

"Gee, that's kind of neat!" I exclaimed. "Do you think we could get some of these for our place at the Bazaar?"

"Believe me, they're more trouble than they're worth," Massha said. "In nothing flat you find you're spending all your time on the phone talking to people and not accomplishing anything. Besides, ever since they broke up the corporation..."

"I think I've got it!" Vilhelm announced, jumping down to floor-level again. "I've got one friend for you definite, but to be honest with you he's only so-so. I've got call-backs coming on two others, so let's see what they're like before you commit on the definite. Okay?"

"Ummm...I think there's some kind of mistake here," I said desperately, trying to stop the madness before it progressed any further. "I'm not trying to find a *new* friend. I'm trying to locate a friend I already have who may be here in town."

He blinked several times as this news sank in. He started to turn back to his phones in an involuntary motion, then waved a hand at them in disgusted dismissal.

"Heck with it," he said with a sigh. "If they can come up with anything, I can always fob 'em off on someone else for a profit. Now then, let's try this again. You're looking for someone specific. Are they are a townie or a transient? It *would* help if you gave me a little something to go on, you know."

He seemed a little annoyed, and I would have liked to do or say something to cheer him up. Before I could think of anything, however, my apprentice decided to join the conversation.

"This is quite a layout you've got, Fast Worker. Mind if I ask exactly what it is you do?"

As always, Massha's "people sense" proved to be better than mine. The little vampire brightened noticeably at the compliment, and his chest puffed out as he launched into his narration.

"Well, the job was originally billed as Dispatcher...you know, as in Dispatcher of Nightmares. But anyway, like any job, it turned out to involve a lot of things that aren't on the job description. Now it's sort of a combination of dispatcher, travel agent, lost and found, and missing persons bureau."

"Nightmares?" I questioned, unable to contain myself.

"Sure. Anything that comes out of Limbo, be it dreams or the real thing, comes through here. Where're you from that you didn't know that?"

Obviously, I wasn't wild about continuing on the subject of our place of origin.

"Ahhh, can you really help us find our friend? He's new in town, like us."

"That's right. You're looking for someone. Sorry. I get a little carried away sometimes when I talk about my work. New in town, hmmm? Shouldn't be that hard to locate. We don't get that many visitors."

"He might be in jail," Massha blurted out before I realized what she was going to say.

"In jail?" The vampire frowned. "The only outsider in jail right now is...Say! Now I recognize you! The eyes threw me for a minute. You're Skeeve, aren't you?"

"Screen 97B!" he declared proudly, gesturing vaguely over his shoulder. "There's someone a dozen dimensions over from here, runs a hot dog stand, who features you in his most frequent nightmares. You, a dragon, and a Pervert. Am I correct in assuming that the current resident in our fair jail is none other than your sidekick Aahz?"

"To be correct, that's Pervect, not Pervert...but except for that you're right. That's my partner you've got locked up there, and we aim to get him out."

I was probably talking too much, but being recognized in a dimension I'd never heard of had thrown me off balance. Then again, the Dispatcher didn't seem all that hostile at the discovery. More curious than anything else.

"Well, well. Skeeve himself. I never expected to meet you in person. Sometime you must tell me what you did to that poor fellow to rate the number-one slot on his hit parade of nightmares."

"What about Aahz?" I said impatiently.,

"You know he's up for murder, don't you?"

"Heard it. Don't believe it. He's a lot of things, but a murderer isn't one of them."

"There's a fair amount of evidence." Vilhelm shrugged. "But tell me. What's with the vampire get-up. You're no more a vampire than I'm a Klahd."

"It's a long story. Let's just say it seemed to be the local uniform."

"Let's not," the dispatcher grinned. "Pull up a chair...free of charge, of course. I've got time and lots of questions about the other dimensions. Maybe we can trade a little information while you're here."

VII.

"I don't see anything thrilling about it!"
M. JACKSON

I REALLY DON'T see how you can drink that stuff," I declared, eyeing Vilhelm's goblet of blood.

"Funny," he smiled in return, "I was about to say the same thing. I mean, you know what W. C. Fields said about water!"

"No, What?"

"Now let me get this straight," Guido interrupted before I could get any answer. "You're sayin' you vampire guys don't really drink blood from people?"

"Oh, a few do," the Dispatcher said with a shrug. "But it's an acquired taste, like steak tartare. Some say it's a gourmet dish, but I could never stand the stuff myself. I'll stick with the inexpensive domestic varieties any night."

We were all sprawled around the Dispatcher's office at this point, sipping our respective drinks and getting into a pretty good rap session. We had pulled Guido in off door watch and I had dropped our disguises so my energy reserve wasn't being drained."

The Dispatcher had played with his phones, calling from one to the other. Then he put them all down and announced that he had them on "hold," a curious expression since it was the first time in half an hour he hadn't been holding one.

Vilhelm himself was turning out to be a priceless source of information, and, as promised, had a seemingly insatiable curiosity about otherworldly things.

"Then how do you account for all the vampire legends around the other dimensions," Massha said skeptically.

The Dispatcher made a face.

"First of all, you've got to realize who you're dealing with. Most of the ones who do extensive touring outside of Limbo are 'old money' types. We're talking about the idle rich…and that usually equates to bored thrillseekers. Working stiffs like me can't afford to take that kind of time away from our jobs. Heck, I can hardly manage to get my two weeks each year. Anyway, there are a lot more of us around the dimensions than you might realize. It's just that the level-headed ones are content to maintain a low profile and blend with the natives. They content them-selves with the blood of domestic livestock, much the way we do here at home. It's the others that cause the problems. Like any group of tourists, there's always a few who feel that just because they're in another world or city, the rules don't apply...and that includes common manners and good taste. They're the ones who stir up trouble by getting the locals up in arms about 'bloodsucking monsters.' If it makes you feel any better, you human types have a pretty bad rep yourselves here in Limbo."

That caught my attention.

"Could you elaborate on that last point, Vilhelm? What problem could the locals have with us?"

The Dispatcher laughed.

"The same one you humans have with us vampires. While humans aren't the leading cause of death in vampires any more than vampires are a leading cause of death in humans, it's certainly one of the more publicized and sensational ways to go."

"Is that why the first locals we met took off like bats out of hell...if you'll pardon the expression?" Massha asked.

"You've got it. I think you'll find that the citizens of Blut will react the same way to you that you would if you ran into a vampire in your home dimension."

"I don't notice you bein' particularly scared of us," Guido said suspiciously.

"One of the few advantages of this job. After a few years of monitoring the other dimensions, you get pretty blase about demons. As far as I can tell, most of 'em are no worse than some of the folks we've got around here."

This was all very interesting, but I was getting a little fidgety about our mission.

"Since you know we aren't all evil or on a permanent vampire hunt, what can you tell us about the mess Aahz is in? Can you give us any help there?"

"I dunno," the Dispatcher said, rubbing his jaw thoughtfully. "Until I found out who he was, I was ready to believe he was guilty as sin. There's an awful lot of evidence against him."

"Such as?" I pressed.

"Well, he was caught with a stake and mallet in his hand, and there are two eyewitnesses who say they saw him kill one of our citizens and scatter his dust to the winds."

"Wait a minute. You mean you ain't got no *corpus delecti?*" Guido said, straightening in his chair. "Sorry to interrupt, Boss, but you're playin' in my alley now. This is somethin' I know a little about. You can't go on trial for murder without a corpse, know what I mean?"

"Maybe where you come from," Vilhelm corrected, "but things get a little different when you're dealing with vampires. If we *had a* body, or even just the pile of dust, we could revive him in no time flat. As it is, the problem is when there's *no* body…when a vampire's been reduced to dust and the dust scattered. That's when it's impossible to pull 'em back into a functional mode."

"But if there isn't a body, how do you know the victim is dead at all?" I asked.

"There's the rub," Vilhelm agreed. "But in this case, there's a matter of two eyewitnesses."

"Two of 'em, eh?" Massha murmured thoughtfully. "Would you happen to have descriptions of these two peepers?"

"Saw 'em myself. They were both off-worlders like yourselves. One was a young girl, the blonde and innocent type. The other was a pretty sleazy-looking guy. It was her who sold us on the story, really. I don't think anyone would have believed him if he said that werewolves were furry."

My heart sank. I had wanted very badly to believe the girl who had warned us of Aahz's danger was somehow an innocent by-stander in the proceedings. Now it looked as if

"Do the descriptions sound familiar, Hot Stuff? Still think Guido and I were being paranoid when we said this might be a set-up? Sounds like they framed your partner, then came back after you to complete the set."

I avoided her eyes, staring hard at the wall monitors. "There might be another explanation, you know." My apprentice gave out a bark of laughter.

"If there is, I'm dying to hear it. Face it, High Roller, any way you look at it the situation stinks. If they cooked up a frame that tight on Green and Scaly on such short notice, I'm dying to see what kind of a trap they've got waiting for you now that they've had time to get ready *before* inviting you to step in."

It occurred to me that I had never been that mouthy when I was an apprentice. It also occurred to me that now I understood why Aahz had gotten so angry on the rare occasions when I had voiced an opinion...and the rarer times when I was right.

"I think I missed a lap in this conversation somewhere." Vilhelm frowned. "I take it you know the witnesses?"

Massha proceeded to bring the Dispatcher up to date, with Guido growling counterpoint to the theme. For once I was glad to let them do the talking. It gave me a chance to collect my scattered thoughts and try to formulate a plan. When they finished, I still had a long way to go on both counts.

"I must admit, viewed from the light of this new information, the whole thing does sound a little suspicious," the vampire said thoughtfully.

"*A little* suspicious!" Massha snorted. "It's phonier than a smiling Deveel!"

"Tell ya what," Guido began, "just give us a few minutes alone with these witnesses of yours and we'll shake the truth out of 'em."

"I'm afraid that will be a little difficult," the Dispatcher said, eyeing the ceiling. "You see, they haven't been around for a while. Disappeared right after the trial."

"The trial!?" I snapped, abandoning my efforts to collect my wits. "You mean the trial's already been held?" The vampire nodded.

"That's right. Needless to say, your friend was found guilty."

"Why do I get the feeling he didn't get a suspended sentence for a first offense?" Guido growled under his breath.

"As a matter of fact, he's been slated for execution at the end of the week," Vilhelm admitted.

That got me out of my seat and pacing.

"We've got to do something," I said needlessly. "How about it, Vilhelm? Can you help us out at all? Any chance of getting the verdict reversed or at least a stay of execution?"

"I'm afraid not. Character witnesses alone wouldn't change anything, and as for new evidence, it would only be your word against the existing witnesses...and you've already admitted the defendant is a friend of yours. Mind you, I believe you, but there are those who would suspect you'd say anything or fabricate any kind of tale to save your partner."

"But can you *personally* give us a hand?"

"No, I can't," the vampire said, turning away. "You all seem like real nice folks, and your friend is probably the salt of the earth, but I have to live here and deal with these people for a long time. If I sided with outsiders against the town legal system, my whole career would go down the drain whether I was right or not. It's not pretty and I don't like it, but that's the way things are."

"We could fix it so you like it a lot less!" Guido said darkly, reaching into his coat.

"Stop it, Guido," I ordered. "Let's not forget the help Vilhelm's *already* given us. It's a lot more than we expected to get when we first came into this dimension, so don't go making enemies out of the only friend we've got locally. Okay?"

The bodyguard sank back into his chair, muttering something I was just as glad I didn't hear, but his hand came out of his coat empty and stayed in sight.

"So what do we do now, Hot Stuff?" Massha sighed.

"The only thing I can think of is to try to locate those witnesses before the execution date," I said. "What I can't figure is how to go about looking without getting half the town down on our necks."

"What we really need is a bloodhound," Guido grumbled.

"Say, that's not a bad idea!" Vilhelm exclaimed, coming to life. "Maybe I can help you after all!"

"You got a bloodhound?" the bodyguard said, raising his eyebrows.

"Even better," the vampire declared. "I don't know why I didn't think of it before. The ones you need to get in touch with are the Woof Writers."

I studied him carefully to see if this were some kind of joke.

"The Woof Writers?" I repeated at last.

"Well, that's what we in Blut call them behind their backs. Actually, they're a husband-wife team of were-wolves who are on a big crusade to raise sympathy for humans."

"Werewolves," I said carefully.

"Sure. We got all kinds here in Limbo. Anyway, if anyone in this dimension will be willing to stick their necks out for you, they're the ones. They do their own thing and don't really give a hang what any of the other locals think about it. Besides, werewolves are second to none when it comes to sniffing out a trail."

"Werewolves."

Vilhelm cocked his head at me curiously.

"Am I imagining things, Skeeve, or didn't you just say that?"

"What's more," Massha smiled sweetly, "he'll probably say it again. It bears repeating."

"Werewolves," I said again, just to support my apprentice.

"Boss," Guido began, "I don't want to say this, but nobody said anything about werewolves when we..."

"Good," I interrupted brusquely. "You don't want to say it, and I don't want to hear it. Now that we're in agreement, let's just pass on it and..."

"But Boss! We can't team up with werewolves."

"Guido, we just went over this. We're in a tight spot *and* in a strange dimension. We can't afford to be choosy about our allies."

"You don't understand, Boss. I'm allergic to 'em!"

I sank down into a chair and hid my face in my hands.

"I thought you were allergic to garlic," I said through my fingers.

"That, too," the bodyguard said. "But mostly I'm allergic to furry things like kitties or fur coats or..."

"...or werewolves," Massha finished for him. "Frankly, Dark and Deadly, one starts to wonder how you've been able to function effectively all these years."

"Hey, it doesn't come up all that often, know what I mean?" Guido argued defensively. "How many times have *you* been attacked by somethin' furry?"

"Not as often as I'd like!" Massha leered.

"Enough, you two," I ordered, raising my head. "Guido, have you ever actually been near a werewolf?"

"Well, no. But..."

"Then until we know for sure, we'll assume you're *not* allergic to them. Okay? Vilhelm, exactly where do we find these Woof Writers of yours?"

VIII.

"First, let's decide who's leading and who's following."
F. ASTAIRE

BOSS, JUST WHERE the hell is Pahkipsee?"

I found myself wondering if all bodyguards spent most of their time complaining, or if I had just gotten lucky.

"Look, Guido. You were there and heard the same instructions I did. If Vilhelm was right, it should be just up the road here a couple more miles."

"...a rather dead bedroom community, fit only for those not up to the fast-lane life-style of the big city," Massha quoted in a close imitation of the vampire's voice.

Guido snickered rudely.

"Why do I get the feeling you didn't particularly warm to Vilhelm, Massha?" I suppressed a grin of my own.

"Maybe it's because he's the only guy we've met she hasn't made a pass at?" Guido suggested.

Massha favored him with an extended tongue and crossed eyes before answering.

"Oh, Vilhelm's okay," she said. "Kinda cute, too...at least the top of his head was. And he did admit that in general vampires were more partial to cities and parties while werewolves preferred the back-to-nature atmos-phere of rural living. I just didn't like the crack, that's all. I grew up on a farm, you know. Country breakfasts have a lot to do with my current panoramic physique. Besides, something inside says you shouldn't trust a smiling vampire...or at least you shouldn't trust him too far."

I had been about to mention the fact that I had grown up on a farm, too, but withheld the information. Obviously, farm food hadn't particularly affected my physique, and I didn't want to rob my apprentice of her excuse.

"If he had wanted to do us harm, all he would have had to do was blow the whistle on us while we were still in town," I pointed out. "Let's just take things at face value and assume he was really being as nice as he seemed...for all our peace of minds."

I wished I was as confident as I sounded. We were a long way out in the boondocks, and if Vilhelm had wanted to send us off on a wild goose chase, he couldn't have picked a better direction to start us off in.

"Yeah, well I'd feel a lot better if we weren't being followed," Guido grumbled.

I stopped in my tracks. So did Massha…in her tracks, that is. The bodyguard managed to stumble into us before bringing his own forward progress to a halt.

"What is it, Boss? Something wrong?"

"For a minute there, I thought I heard you say that we were being followed."

"Yeah. Since we left the Dispatcher's. Why does…you mean you didn't know?"

I resisted an impulse to throttle him.

"No, Guido. I didn't know. You see, my bodyguard didn't tell me. He was too busy complaining about the road conditions to have time to mention anything as trivial as someone following us."

Guido took a few shaky steps backward.

"Hey! C'mon, Boss. Don't be like that. I thought you knew! Honest. Whoever's back there isn't doin' such a hot job of hiding the fact that they're dogging our trail. Any idiot could've spotted…I mean…"

"Keep going, Dark and Deadly," Massha urged. "You're digging yourself in further with every word, in case you hadn't noticed."

With great effort I brought myself back under control. "Whatever," I said. "I don't suppose you have any idea who it is?"

"Naw. There's only one of 'em. Unless…"

His voice trailed off into silence and he looked suddenly worried.

"Out with it, Guido. Unless what?"

"Well, sometimes when you're getting *really* tricky about tailing someone, you put one real clumsy punk out front so's they can be spotted while you keep your real ace-hitter hidden. I hadn't stopped to think of that before. This turkey behind us could be a decoy, know what I mean?"

"I thought you used decoys for ducks, not turkeys," Massha scowled.

"Well, if that's what's happening, then *we're* sitting ducks, if it makes you feel any better."

"Could both of you just be quiet for a few minutes and let me think?" I said, suddenly impatient with their banter.

"Well, maybe it isn't so bad," Guido said in a doubtful voice. "I'm pretty sure I would have spotted the back-up team if there was one."

"Oh sure," Massha sneered. "Coming out of a town full of vampires that can change themselves into mist whenever they want. Of course you'd spot them."

"Hey. The Boss here can chew on me if he wants, but I don't have to take that from you. You didn't even spot the turkey, remember?"

"The only turkey I can see is..."

"Enough!" I ordered, having arrived at a decision despite their lack of cooperation. "We have to find out for sure who's behind us and what they want. This is as good a place as any, so I suggest we all retire into the bushes and wait for our shadow to catch up with us...No, Massha. I'll be over here with Guido. You take the other side of the road."

That portion of my plan had less to do with military strategy than with an effort on my part to preserve what little was left of my nerves. I figured the only way to shut the two of them up was to separate them.

"I'm sorry, Boss," Guido whispered as we crouched side by side in the brush. "I keep forgettin' that you aren't as into crime as the boys I usually run with."

Well, I had been half right. Massha on the other side of the road was being quiet, but as long as he had someone to talk to, Guido was going to keep on expressing his thoughts and opinions. I was starting to understand why Don Bruce insisted on doing all the talking when the bodyguards were around. Encouraging employees to speak up as equals definitely had its drawbacks.

"Will you keep your voice down?" I tried once more. "This is supposed to be an ambush."

"Don't worry about that, Boss. It'll be a while before they catch up, and when they do, I'll hear 'em before..."

"Is that you, Skeeve?"

The voice came from the darkness just up the road.

I gave Guido my darkest glare, and he rewarded it with an apologetic shrug that didn't look particularly sincere to me.

Then it dawned on me where I had heard that voice before.

"Right here," I said, rising from my crouch and stepping onto the road. "We've been waiting for you. I think it's about time we had a little chat."

Aside from covering my embarrassment over having been discovered, that had to be my best understatement in quite a while. The last time I had seen this particular person, she was warning me about Aahz's imprisonment "Good." She stepped forward to meet me. "That's why I've been following you. I was hoping we could..."

Her words stopped abruptly as Guido and Massha rose from the bushes and moved to join us.

"Well, look who's here," Massha said, flashing one of her less pleasant smiles.

"If it isn't the little bird who sang to the vampires," Guido leered, matching my apprentice's threatening tone.

The girl favored them with a withering glance, then faced me again.

"I was hoping we could talk alone. I've got a lot to say and not much time to say it. It would go faster if we weren't interrupted."

"Not a chance, Sweetheart," Guido snarled. "I'm not goin' to let the Boss out of my sight with you around."

"...besides which, I've got a few things to tell you myself," Massha added, "like what I think of folks who think frames look better on people than on paintings."

The girl's eyes never left mine. For all her bravado, I thought I could detect in their depths an appeal for help.

"Please," she said softly.

I fought a brief skirmish in my mind, and, as usual, common sense lost.

"All right."

"WHAT! C'mon, Boss. You can't let her get you alone! If her pals are around..."

"Hot Stuff, if I have to sit on you, you aren't going to..."

"Look!" I said, wrenching my eyes away from the girl to confront my mutinous staff. "We'll only go a few steps down the road there, in plain sight. If anything happens you'll be able to pitch in before it gets serious."

"But..."

"...and you certainly can't think *she's* going to jump me. I mean, it's a cinch she isn't carrying any concealed weapons."

That was a fact. She had changed outfits since the last time I saw her, probably to fit in more with the exotic garb favored by the party-loving vampires. She was wear-ing what I've heard referred to as a "tank top" which left her midsection and navel delightfully exposed, and the open-sided skirt (if you can call two flaps of cloth that) showed her legs up past her hips. If she had a weapon with her, she had swallowed it. Either that, or...I dragged my thoughts back to the argument.

"The fact of the matter is that she isn't going to talk in front of a crowd. Now, am I going to get a chance to hear another view-point about what's going on, or are we going to keep groping around for information with Aahz's life hanging in the balance?"

My staff fell silent and exchanged glances, each waiting for the other to risk the next blast.

"Well, okay," Massha agreed at last. "But watch yourself, Hot Stuff. Remember, poison can come in pretty bottles."

So, under the ever-watchful glares of my assistants, I retired a few steps down the road for my first words alone with...

"Say, what is your name, anyway?"

"Hmmm? Oh. I'm Luanna. Say, thanks for backing me up. That's a pretty mean-looking crew you hang around with. I had heard you had a following, but I hadn't realized how nasty they were."

"Oh, they're okay once you get to know them. If you worked with them on a day-to-day basis, you'd find out that they...heck, none of us are really as dangerous or effective as the publicity hype cuts us out to be."

I was suddenly aware of her eyes on me. Her expression was strange...sort of a bitter half-smile.

"I've always heard that *really* powerful people tended to under-state what they can do, that they don't have to brag. I never really believed it until now."

I really didn't know what to say to that. I mean, my reputation had gotten big enough that I was starting to get used to being recognized and talked about at the Bazaar, but what she was displaying was neither fear nor envy. Among my own set of friends, admiration or praise was always carefully hidden within our own brand of rough humor or teasing. Faced with the undiluted form of the same thing, I was at a loss as to how to respond.

"Ummm, what was it you wanted to talk to me about?"

Her expression fell and she dropped her eyes.

"This is so embarrassing. Please be patient with me, Skeeve...is it all right if I call you Skeeve? I haven't had much experience with saying 'I'm sorry'...heck, I haven't had much experience with people at all. Just partners and pigeons. Now that I'm here, I really don't know what to say.

"Why don't we start at the beginning?" I wanted to ease her discomfort. "Did you really swindle the Deveels back at the Bazaar?"

Luanna nodded slowly without raising her eyes.

"That's what we do. Matt and me. That and running, even though I think sometimes we're better at running than working scams. Maybe if we were better at conning people, we wouldn't get so much practice at running."

Her words thudded at me like a padded hammer. I had wanted very badly to hear that she was innocent and that it had all been a mistake. I mean, she was so pretty, so sweet, I would have bet my life that she was innocent, yet here she was openly admitting her guilt to me.

"But why?" I managed at last. "I mean, how did you get involved in swindling people to begin with?"

Her soft shoulders rose and fell in a helpless shrug.

"I don't know. It seemed like a good idea when Matt first explained it to me. I was dying to get away from the farm, but I didn't know how to do anything but farmwork for a living...until Matt explained to me how easy it was to get money away from people by playing on their greed.

"Promise them something for nothing," he said, "or for so little that they think *they're* swindling *you.*" When he put it that way, it didn't seem so bad. It was more a matter of being smart enough to trick people who thought they were taking advantage of you."

"...by selling them magical items that weren't." I finished for her. "Tell me, why didn't you just go into the magic trade for real?"

Her head came up, and I caught a quick flash of fire in her sad blue eyes.

"We didn't know any magic, so we had to fake it. You probably can't understand that, since you're the real McCoy. I knew that the first time I saw you at Possletum. We were going to try to fake our way into the Court Magician spot until you showed up and flashed a bit of real magic at the crown. Even Matt had to admit that we were outclassed, and we kind of faded back before anyone asked us to show what we could do. I think it was then that I..."

She broke off, giving me a startled, guilty look as if she had been about to say something she shouldn't. "Go on," I urged, my curiosity piqued.

"It's nothing, really," she said hastily. "Now it's your turn. Since I've told you my story, maybe you won't mind me asking how you got started as a magician."

That set me back a bit. Like her, I had been raised on a farm. I had run away, though, planning to seek my fortune as a master thief, and it was only my chance meeting with my old teacher Garkin and eventually Aahz that had diverted my career goals toward magic. In hind-sight, my motives were not discernibly better than hers, but I didn't want to admit it just now. I kind of liked the way she looked at me while laboring under the illusion that I was someone noble and special.

"That's too long a tale to go into just now," I said brusquely. "There are still a few more answers I'd like from you. How come you used our place as a getaway route from Deva?"

"Oh, that was Vic's idea. We teamed up with him just before we started working our con at the Bazaar. When it looked like the scam was starting to turn sour, he said he knew a way-off dimension that no one would be watching. Matt and I didn't even know it was your place until your doorman asked if we were there to see you. Matt was so scared about having to tangle with you that he wanted to forget the whole thing and find another way out, but Vic °showed us the door and it looked so easy we just went along with him."

"Of course, it never occurred to you that we'd get stuck with the job of trying to bring you back."

"You better believe it occurred to us. I mean, we didn't think you'd *have* to do it. We expected you'd be mad at us for getting you involved and come after us yourself. Vic kept saying that we shouldn't worry, that if you found us here in Limbo that he could fix it so you wouldn't be able to take us back. I didn't know he was thinking about setting up a frame until he sprang it on your partner."

I tried to let this console me, but it didn't work.

"I notice that once you found out that Aahz was being framed, you still went along with it."

"Well...I didn't want to, but Vic kept saying that if you two were as good as everyone said, that your partner could get out of jail by himself. We figured that he'd escape before the execution, but with the whole dimension hunting him as a fugitive that he'd be too busy running for home to bother about catching us."

I was starting to get *real* anxious to meet this guy Vic. It also occurred to me that of all the potential problems our growing reputation could bring down on us, this was one we had never expected.

"And you believed him?"

Luanna made a face, then shrugged.

"Well...you're supposed to be able to do some pretty incredible things, and I don't want you to think I don't

believe in your abilities, but I was worried enough that I sneaked back to let you know what was going on...just in case."

It was almost funny that she was apologizing for giving us the warning. Almost, but not quite. My mind kept running over what might have happened if she *had* believed in me completely.

"I guess my only other question is who is this citizen that Aahz is supposed to have killed?"

"Didn't anybody tell you?" she blinked. "It's Vic. He's from this dimension...you know, a vampire. Anyway, he's hiding out until the whole thing's resolved one way or another. I don't think even Matt knows where he is. Vampires are normally suspicious, and after I sneaked out the first time, he's even gotten cagey around us. He just drops in from time to time to see how we're doing."

Now I *knew* I wanted to meet friend Vic. If I was lucky, I'd meet him before Aahz did.

"Well, I do appreciate you filling me in on the problem. Now, if you'll just come back to Blut with us and explain things to the authorities, my gratitude will be complete."

Luanna started as if I had stuck her with a pin.

"Hold on a minute! Who said anything about going to the authorities? I can't do that! That would be double-crossing *my* partners. I don't want to see you or your friends get hurt, but I can't sacrifice my own to save them."

An honest crook is both incongruous and infuriating. Aahz had often pointed this out to me when some point in my ethic kept me from going along with one of his schemes, and now I was starting to understand what he was talking about.

"But then why are you here?"

"I wanted to warn you. Vic has been thinking that you might come into Limbo after your partner, and he's setting up some kind of trap if you did. If he was right, I thought you should know that you're walking into trouble. I figured that if you came, you'd look up the Dispatcher, so I waited there and followed you when you showed up. I just wanted to warn you is all. That and..."

She dropped her eyes again and lowered her voice until I could hardly hear her.

"...I wanted to see you again. I know it's silly, but..."

As flattering as it was, this time I was unimpressed.

"Yeah, sure." I interrupted. "You're so interested in me you're willing to let my partner sit on a murder rap just so you can watch me go through my paces."

"I already explained about that," she said fiercely, stepping forward to lay a hand on my arm.

I stared at it pointedly until she removed it.

"Well," she said in a small voice. "I can see that there's nothing more I can say. But, Skeeve? Promise me that you won't follow me when I leave? You or your friends? I took a big risk finding you. Please don't make me regret it."

I stared at her for a long moment, then looked away and nodded.

"I know you're disappointed in me, Skeeve," came her voice, "but I can't go against my partners. Haven't you ever had to do something you didn't want to do to support your partner?"

That hit home...painfully.

"Yes, I have," I said, drawing a ragged breath. "I'm sorry, Luanna. I'm just worried about Aahz, that's all. Tell you what. Just to show there're no hard feelings, can I have a token or something? Something to remember you by until I see you again?"

She hesitated, then pulled a gossamer-thin scarf from somewhere inside her outfit. Stepping close, she tucked it into my tunic, then rose on her tiptoes and kissed me softly.

"It's nice of you to ask," she said. "Even if I don't mean anything to you at all, it's nice of you to ask."

With that, she turned and sprinted off down the road into the darkness.

I stared after her.

"You're letting her go!?"

Suddenly Massha was at my side, flanked by Guido. "C'mon, Boss. We gotta catch her. She's your partner's ticket off death row. Where's she goin'?"

"To meet up with her partners in crime," I said. "Including a surprisingly lively guy named Vic...surprising since he's the one that Aahz is supposed to have killed."

"So we can catch 'em all together. Nice work, Hot Stuff. Okay, let's follow her and..."

"No!"

"Why not?"

"Because I promised her."

There was a deathly silence as my assistants digested this information.

"So she walks and Green and Scaly dies, is that it?"

"You're sellin' out your partner for a skirt? That musta been some kiss."

I slowly turned to face them, and, mad as they were, they fell silent.

"Now listen close," I said quietly, "because I'm not going to go over it again. If we tried to follow her back to their hideout, and she spotted us, she'd lead us on a wild goose chase and we'd never catch up with them...and we need that so-called corpse. I don't think her testimony alone will swing the verdict."

"But Boss, if we let her get away..."

"We'll find them," I said. "Without us dogging her footsteps, she'll head right back to her partners."

"But how will we..."

In answer, I pulled Luanna's scarf from my tunic. "Fortunately, she was kind enough to provide us with a means to track her, once we recruit the necessary werewolf."

Guido gave my back a slap that almost staggered me.

"Way to go, Boss," he crowed. "You really had me goin' for a minute. I thought that chickie had really snowed you."

I looked up to find Massha eyeing me suspiciously.

"That *was* quite a kiss, Hot Stuff," she said. "If I didn't know better, I'd think that young lady is more than a little stuck on you...and you just took advantage of it."

I averted my eyes, and found myself staring down the road again.

"As a wise woman once told me," I said, "sometimes you have to do things you don't like to support your partner...Now, let's go find these Woof Writers."

IX.

*"My colleagues and I feel that independents like Elf Quest
are nothing but sheep in wolves clothing!"*
                                        S. LEE

THE WOOF WRITERS turned out to be much more pleasant than
I had dared hope, which was fortunate as my werewolf disguises
were some of the shakiest I'd ever done. Guido was indeed allergic
to werewolves as feared (he started sneezing a hundred yards from
their house) and was waiting outside, but even trying to maintain
two disguises was proving to be a strain on my powers in this magic-
poor dimension. I attempted to lessen the drain by keeping the
changes minimal, but only succeeded in making them incredibly un-
convincing even though my assistants assured me they were fine. No
matter what anyone tells you, believe, me, pointy ears alone do not a
wolf make.

You might wonder why I bothered with disguises at all? Well,
frankly, we were getting a little nervous. Everyone we had talked to
or been referred to in this dimension was so *nice!* We kept waiting
for the other shoe to drop. All of our talks and discussions of possible traps had made us so skittish that we were now convinced that
there was going to be a double-cross somewhere along the way.
The only question in our minds was when and by whom.

With that in mind, we decided it would be best to try to pass
ourselves off as werewolves until we knew for sure , the Woof
Writers were as well-disposed toward humans as Vilhelm said they
were. The theory was that if they weren't, the disguises might give us
a chance to get out again before our true nature was exposed. The
only difficulty with that plan was that I had never seen a werewolf in
my life, so not only was I working with a shortage of energy, I was
unsure as to what the final result should look like. As it turned out,
despite their knowledgeable advice, my staff didn't know either.

While we're answering questions from the audience, you might
ask, if neither I nor my assistants knew what a werewolf looked
like, how I knew the disguises were inadequate? Simple. I deduced
the fact after one look at real werewolves. That and the Woof

Writers told me so. Didn't I tell you they were great folks? Of course, they let us sweat for a while before admitting that they knew we were poorly disguised humans all along, but I myself tend to credit that to their dubious sense of humor. It's Massha who insists it was blatant sadism. Of course, she was the one who had to eat a bone before they acknowledged the joke.

Anyway, I was talking about the Woof Writers. It was interesting in that I had never had much opportunity to watch a husband-wife team in action before (my parents don't count). The closest thing to the phenomenon I had witnessed was the brother-sister team of Tananda and Chumley, but they spent most of their conversational time trying to "one-down" each other. The Woof Writers, in contrast, seemed to take turns playing "crazy partner-sane partner." They never asked my opinion, but I felt that she was much better at playing the crazy than he. He was so good at playing the straight that when he did slip into crazy mode, it always came as a surprise.

"Really, dear," Idnew was saying to Massha "wouldn't you like to slip out of that ridiculous disguise into something more comfortable? A werewolf with only two breasts looks so silly."

"Idnew," her husband said sternly, "you're making our guests uncomfortable. Not everyone feels as easy about discussing their bodies as you do."

"It's the artist in me," she returned. "And besides, Drahcir, who was it that set her up to eat a bone?—and an old one at that. If you were a little more conscientious when you did the shopping instead of stocking up on junk food…"

"Oh, don't worry about me, Hairy and Handsome," Massha interceded smoothly, dropping into her vamp role. "I've got no problems discussing my body, as long as we get equal time to talk about yours. I've always liked my men with a lot of facial hair, if you get my drift."

I noticed Idnew's ears flatten for a moment before returning to their normal upright position. While it may have been nothing more than a nervous twitch, it occurred to me that if we were going to solicit help from these two, it might not be wise to fan any embers of jealousy that might be lying about.

"Tell me," I said hastily, eager to get the subject away from Massha's obvious admiration of Drahcir, "What got you started campaigning for better relationships between humans and werewolves?"

"Well, there were many factors involved," Drahcir explained, dropping into the lecturer mode I had grown to know so well in such a short time. "I think the most important thing to keep in mind is that the bad reputation humans have is vastly overrated. There is actually very little documented evidence to support the legends of human misconduct. For the most part, werewolves tend to forget that, under the proper conditions, we turn into humans. Most of them are afraid or embarrassed and hide themselves away until it passes, but Idnew and I don't. If anything we generally seize the opportunity to go out and about and get the public used to seeing harmless humans in their midst. Just between us, though, I think Idnew here likes to do it because it scares the hell out of folks to be suddenly confronted by a human when they aren't expecting it. In case you haven't noticed, there's a strong exhibitionist streak in my wife. For myself, it's simply a worthy cause that's been neglected for far too long."

"The other factor, which my husband has neglected to mention," Idnew put in impishly, "is that there's a lot of money in it."

"There is?" I asked.

My work with Aahz had trained me to spot profit opportunities where others saw none, but this time the specific angle had eluded me.

"There…umm…are certain revenues to be gleaned from our campaign," Drahcir said uneasily, shooting a dark glance at his wife. "T-shirts, bumper stickers, lead miniatures, fan club dues, greeting cards, and calendars, just to name a few. It's a dirty job, but somebody's got to do it. Lest my wife leave you with the wrong impression of me, however, let me point out that I'm supporting this particular cause because I *really* believe in it. There are lots of ways to make money."

"…and he knows them all, don't you dear?" Idnew said with a smile.

"Really?" I interrupted eagerly. "Would you mind running over a few? Could I take notes?"

"Before you get carried away, High Roller," Massha warned, "remember why we came here originally."

"Oh! Right! Thanks, Massha. For a minute there I…Right!"

It took me a few seconds to rechannel my thoughts. While Aahz's training has gotten me out of a lot of tight spots and generally improved my standard of living, there are some unfortunate side effects.

Once I got my mind back on the right track, I quickly filled the werewolves in on our current problem. I kept the details sketchy, both because I was getting tired of going back and forth over the same beginning, and to keep from having to elaborate on Luanna's part in causing our dilemma. Still, the Woof Writers seemed quite enthralled by the tale, and listened attentively until I was done.

"Gee, you're really in a spot," Idnew said when I finally ground to a halt. "If there's anything we can do to help..."

"We can't," Drahcir told us firmly. "You're behind on your deadlines, Idnew, and I've got three more appearances this month...not to mention answering the mail that's piled up the last two weekends I've been gone."

"Drahcir..." Idnew said, drawing out his name.

"Don't look at me like that, dear," her husband argued before she had even started her case, "and don't cock your head, either. Someone's liable to shove a gramo-phone under it. Remember, *you're* the one who keeps pointing out that we have to put more time into our work."

"I was talking about cutting back on your personal appearances," Idnew argued. "Besides, this is important."

"So's meeting our deadlines. I'm as sympathetic to their problem as you are, but we can't let the plight of one small group of humans interfere with our work on the big picture."

"But *you're* the one who insists that deadlines aren't as important as..."

She broke off suddenly and semaphored her ears toward her husband.

"Wait a minute. Any time you start talking about 'big pictures' and 'grand crusades'...is our bank account low again?"

Drachir averted his eyes and shifted his feet uncomfortably.

"Well, I was going to tell you, but I was afraid it might distract you while you were trying to work..."

"All right. Let's have it," his wife growled, her hackles rising slightly. "What is it you've invested our money in this time?"

I was suddenly very uncomfortable. Our little discussion seemed to be dissolving into a family fight I felt I had no business being present for. Apparently Massha felt the same thing.

"Well, if you can't help us, that's that," she said, getting to her feet. "No problem. A favor's not a favor if you have to be argued into it. C'mon, Hot Stuff. We're wasting our time *and* theirs."

Though in part I agreed with her, desperation prompted me to make one last try.

"Not so fast, Massha. Drachir is right. Time's money. Maybe we could work out some kind of a fee to compensate them for their time in helping us. Then it's not a favor, it's a business deal. Face it, we *really* need their help in this. The odds of us finding this Vic character on our own are pretty slim."

Aahz would have fainted dead away if he had heard me admitting how much we needed help *before* the fee was set, but that reaction was nothing compared to how the Woof Writers took my offer.

"What did you say?" Drahcir demanded, rising to all fours with his ears back.

"I said that maybe you'd help us if we offered to pay you," I repeated, backing away slightly. "I didn't mean to insult you…"

"You can't insult Drahcir with money," his wife snapped. "He meant what did you say about Vic?"

"Didn't I mention him before?" I frowned. "He's the vampire that Aahz is supposed to have…"

There was a sudden loud flapping sound in the rafters above our heads, like someone noisily shaking a newspaper to scare a cat off a table. It worked…not on the cat (I don't think the werewolves owned one) but on Massha and me. My apprentice hit the floor, covering her head with her hands, while I, more used to sudden danger and being more svelte and agile, dove beneath the coffee table.

By the time we recovered from our panicky…excuse me, our shrewd defensive maneuvers, there was nothing to see except the vague shape of someone with huge wings disappearing out the front door.

"This one's all yours, dear," Drahcir said firmly, his posture erect and unmoved despite the sudden activity. "Come on, honey," his wife pleaded. "You're so much better at explaining things. You're supposed to help me out when it comes to talking to people."

"It's a skill I polished at those personal appearances you're so critical of," he retorted stiffly.

"Would *somebody* tell me what's going on?" I said in tones much louder than I usually use when I'm a guest in someone's home.

Before I could get an answer, the door burst open again utterly destroying what little was left of my nervous system.

"Hey, Boss! Did you s—se—Wha—wa…"

"Outside, Guido!" I ordered, glad to have someone I could shout at without feeling guilty. "Blow your nose…and I'm *fine,* thanks! Nice of you to ask!"

By the time my bodyguard had staggered back out-side, his face half buried in a handkerchief, I had managed to regain most of my composure.

"Sorry for the interruption," I said as nonchalantly as I could, "but my colleague *does* raise an interesting question. What *was* that?"

"Scary?" Massha suggested.

Apparently she had recovered her composure a little better than I had. I closed my eyes and reflected again on the relative value of cheeky apprentices.

"That," Drahcir said loftily, barely in time to keep me from my assistant's throat, "was Vic…one of my wife's weird artist friends who dropped in unannounced for a prolonged stay *and,* unless I miss my guess, the criminal you're looking for who framed your partner."

"He wasn't really a friend of mine," Idnew put in in a small voice. "Just a friend of a friend, really. Weird artist types tend to stick together and pass around the locations of crash spaces. He was just another charity case down on his luck who…"

"…who is currently winging his way back to his accomplice with the news that we're on their trail," I finished with a grimace.

"Isn't that 'accomplices' as in plural?" Massha asked softly.

I ignored her.

"Oh, Drahcir," Idnew said, "now we have to help them. It's the only way we can make up for having provided a hideout for the very person they were trying to find."

"If I might point out," her husband replied, "we've barely met these people. We don't really owe them an explanation, much less any help. Besides, you still have a deadline to meet and…"

"Drahcir!" Idnew interrupted. "It could get real lonely sleeping in the old kennel while I work day and night on a deadline, if you catch my meaning."

"Now, dear," Drahcir said, sidling up to his wife, "before you go getting into a snit, hear me out. I've been thinking it over and I think there's a way we can provide assistance without biting into our own schedules. I mean, we *do* have a friend…one who lives a little north of here…who's temporarily between assignments and could use the work. I'm sure he'd be willing to do a little tracking for them at a fraction of the fee that we'd charge for the same service."

He was obviously talking in the veiled references partners use to communicate or check ideas in front of strangers, as his words went completely over my head, but drew an immediate reaction from Idnew.

"Oh, Drahcir!" she exclaimed excitedly, all trace of her earlier anger gone. "That's perfect! And he'll just *love* Massha."

"There's still the question of whether or not we can get him here in time," her husband cautioned. "And of course I'll want a percentage off the top as a finder's fee…"

"WHAT!" I exclaimed.

"I agree," Idnew said firmly. "A finder's fee is totally…"

"No! Before that," I urged. "What did you say about there not being enough time? I thought the execution wasn't scheduled until the end of the week!"

"That's right," Drahcir said. "But the end of the week is tomorrow. Your friend is slated to be executed at high midnight."

"C'mon, Massha," I ordered, heading for the door. "We're heading back to Blut."

"What for?" she demanded. "What can we do without a tracker?"

"We've tried being nice about this, and it isn't working," I responded grimly. "Now we do it the other way. You wanted action, apprentice? How do you feel about giving me a hand with a little jailbreak?"

X.

"What's wrong with a little harmless crime once in a while?"
M. Blaise

BUT I'M TELLING you, Boss, jailbreak is a bad rap. With you
operating at only half power in the magic department, there's no
tellin' what can go wrong, and then…"

"Before we get all worked up about what can go wrong, Guido,"
I said, trying to salvage something constructive out of the conversation, "could you give me a little information on exactly how hard it
is to break someone out of jail? Or haven't you been involved in any
jail-breaks, either?"

"Of course I've been along on some jailbreaks," the bodyguard declared, drawing himself up proudly. "I've been an accomplice on *three*
jailbreaks. What kind of Mob member do you take me for, anyway?"

With a heroic effort I resisted the temptation to answer that
particular rhetorical question.

"Okay. So how about a few pointers? This is my first jailbreak,
and I want it to go right."

I was all set to settle in for a fairly lengthy lecture, but instead of
launching into the subject, Guido looked a bit uncomfortable.

"Umm…actually, Boss, I don't think you'd want to use any of
the plans I followed. You see, all three of 'em were busts. None of
'em worked, and in two of the capers the guy we were tryin' to save
got killed. That's how I know about what a bad rap a jailbreak is,
know what I mean?"

"Oh, swell! Just swell! Tell me, *Mister* bodyguard with your allergies and zero-for-three record at jailbreak, did you ever do *anything* for the Mob that worked?"

A gentle hand fell on my shoulder from behind.

"Hey! Ease up a little, High Roller," Massha said softly. "I know
you're worried about your partner, but don't take it out on Guido…or
me, either, for that matter. We may not be much, but we're here and
trying to help as best we can when we'd both just as soon be back at
the Bazaar. You're in a bad enough spot without starting a two-front
war by turning on your allies."

I started to snap at her, but caught myself in time. Instead, I drew a long ragged breath and blew it out slowly. She was right. My nerves were stretched to the breaking point...which served me right for not following my own advice.

We were currently holed up at the Dispatcher's, the only place I could think of for an in-town base of operations, and as soon as we had arrived, I had insisted that both Massha and Guido grab a bit of sleep. We had been going nonstop ever since stepping through the door into Limbo, and I figured that the troops would need all the rest they could get before we tried to spring Aahz. Of course, once I had convinced them of the necessity of racking out, I promptly ignored my own wisdom and stayed up thinking for the duration.

The rationalization I used for this insane action was that I wanted some extra time uninterrupted to recharge my internal batteries, so whatever minimal magic I had at my disposal would be ready for our efforts. In actuality, what I did was worry. While I had indeed taken part in several criminal activities since teaming up with Aahz, they had all been planned by either Aahz or Tananda. This was my first time to get involved in masterminding a caper, and the stakes were high. Not only Aahz's but "Sorry, Guido," I said, trying to restructure my thinking. "I guess I'm more tired than I realized. Didn't mean to snap at you."

"Don't worry, Boss," the bodyguard grinned. "I've been expectin' it. All the big operators I've worked with get a little crabby when the heat's on. If anything, your temper gettin' short is the best thing I've seen since we started this caper.

That's why I've been so jumpy myself. I wasn't sure if you weren't taking the job seriously, or if you were just too dumb to know the kind of odds we were up against. Now that you're acting normal for the situation, I feel a lot better about how it's goin' to come out in the end."

Terrific! Now that I was at the end of my rope, our eternal pessimist thought things were going great.

"Okay," I said, rubbing my forehead with one finger, "we haven't got much information to go on, and what we do know is bad. According to Vilhelm, Aahz is being held in the most escape-proof cell they have, which is the top floor of the highest tower in town. If we try to take him from the inside, we're going to have to fool or fight every guard on the way up *and* down. To me, that means our best bet is to spring him from the outside."

My assistants nodded vigorously, their faces as enthusiastic as if I had just said something startlingly original and clever.

"Now, with my powers at low ebb, I don't think I can levitate that far *and* spring the cell. Massha, do you have anything in your jewelry collection that would work for rope and climbing hooks?"

"N—no," she said hesitantly, which surprised me. She usually had a complete inventory of her nasty pretties on the tip of her tongue.

"I saw a coil of rope hangin' just inside the door," Guido supplied.

"I noticed it, too," I acknowledged, "but it isn't nearly long enough. We'll just have to use up my power getting up to the cell and figure some other way of opening the window."

"Ummm...you don't have to do that, High Roller," Massha said with a sigh. "I've got something we can use."

"What's that?"

"The belt I'm wearing with all my gear hung on it. It's a levitation belt. The controls aren't horribly reliable, but it should do to get us to the top of the tower."

I cocked an eyebrow at my apprentice.

"Wait a minute, Massha. Why didn't you mention this when I asked?"

She looked away quickly."You didn't ask about a belt. Only about rope and climbing hooks."

"Since when do I have to ask you specific questions...or any questions, for that matter, to get your input?"

"All right," she sighed. "If you really want to know, I was hoping we could find a way to do this without using the belt."

"Why?"

"It embarrasses me."

"It what?"

"It embarrasses me. I look silly floating around in the air. It's okay for skinny guys like you and Guido, but when I try it, I look like a blimp. All I'd need is Goodyear tattooed on my side to make the picture complete."

I closed by eyes and tried to remember that I was tired and that I shouldn't take it out on my friends. The fact that Massha was worried about appearances while I was trying to figure out a way to get us all out of this alive wasn't really infuriating. It was...flattering! That was it! She was so confident of my abilities to get us through this crisis that she had time to think about appearances! Of course, the possibility of betraying that confidence set me off in another round of worrying. Wonderful. "You okay, Boss?"

"Hmmm? Yeah. Sure, Guido. Okay. Now Massha floats up to the window, which leaves you and me free to..."

"Hold it, Hot Stuff," Massha said, holding up a hand. "I think I'd better explain a little more about this belt. I bought it in an `as-is' rummage sale, and the controls are not all they should be."

"How so?"

"Well, the 'up' control works okay, but the `altitude' is shaky so you're never sure how much you can lift or how high it will go. The real problem, though, is the `down' control. There's no tapering-off effect, so it's either on or off."

I was never particularly good at technical jargon, but flying was something I knew so I could almost follow her.

"Let me see if I've got this right," I said. "When you go up, you aren't sure how much power you'll have, and when you land..."

"...it ain't gentle," she finished for me. "Basically, you fall from whatever height you're at to the ground."

"I don't know much about this magic stuff," Guido commented dryly, "but that doesn't sound so good. Why would you use a rig like that, anyway?"

"I don't...at least not for flying," Massha said. "Remember, I told you I think it makes me look silly? All I use it for is a utility belt...you know, like Batman? I mean, it's kind of pretty, and it isn't easy to find belts in my size."

"Whatever," I said, breaking into their fashion discussion. "We're going to use it tonight to get up to the cell even if it means rigging some kind of ballast system. Now all we need to figure out is how to open the cell window and a getaway plan. Guido, it occurs to me that we might pick up a few lessons on jailbreaks from your experiences even if they *were* unsuccessful. I mean, negative examples can be as instructive as positive examples. So tell me, in your opinion what went wrong in the plans you followed in the past?"

The bodyguard's brow furrowed as it took on the unaccustomed exercise of thought.

"I dunno, Boss. It seems that however much planning was done, something always came up that we hadn't figured on. If I had to hang our failures on any one thing, I'd say it was just that... overplanning. I mean, after weeks of lectures and practice sessions, you get a little overconfident, so when something goes wrong you're caught flatfooted, know what I mean?"

Nervous as we were, that got a laugh from both Massha and me.

"Well, that's one problem we won't have to worry about," I said. "Our planning time is *always* minimal, and for this caper we're going to have to put it together in a matter of hours."

"If you take hours, you'll never pull it off," Vilhelm said, entering our planning room just in time to hear my last comment.

"What's that supposed to mean?" Massha growled.

"Say, are you *sure* you guys are on the level?" the vampire said, ignoring my apprentice. "It occurs to me that I've only got your word on all this...that Vic is still alive and all. If you're taking advantage of my good nature to get me involved in something crooked..."

"He's alive," I assured him. "I've seen him myself since we were here last...but you didn't answer the question. What was that you were saying about what would happen if we took hours to plan the jailbreak?" The Dispatcher shrugged.

"I suppose you guys know what you're doing and I should keep my mouth shut, but I was getting a little worried. I mean, it's sundown already, and if you're going to make your move before the execution, it had better be soon."

"How do you figure that?" I frowned. "The action isn't slated until high midnight. I had figured on waiting a while until it was dark and things quieted down around town a little."

"Are you kidding?" the vampire said with a start, his eyebrows going up to his hairline. "That's when...oh, I get it. You're still thinking in terms of your off-dimension timetables. You've got to...umm, you might want to be sitting down for this, Skeeve."

"Lay it on me," I said, rubbing my forehead again. "What have I overlooked now? Even without the blindfold and the cigarette I'd just as soon take the bad news standing up."

"Well, you've got to remember that you're dealing with a city of vampires here. Sundown is the equivalent of dawn to us. That's when things *start* happening, not when they start winding down! That means..."

"...that high midnight is a major traffic time and the longer we wait, the more people there will be on the street," I said, trying to suppress a groan.

Once the basic oversight had been pointed out, I could do my own extrapolations...with all their horrible con-sequences. Trying to fight back my own panic, I turned to my assistants.

"Okay, troops. We're on. Guido, grab that rope you saw. We may need it before this is over."

The bodyguard's eyes widened with astonishment. "You mean we're going to start the caper right now? But Boss! We haven't planned..."

"Hey, Guido," I said, flashing a grin that was almost sane. "you were the one who said that overplanning was a problem. Well, if you're right, this should be the most successful jailbreak ever!"

XI.

"Nice jail. Looks strong."
H. HOUDINI

VILHELM WAS RIGHT about one thing. The streets were nowhere nearly as crowded as they had been the times we navigated their length well after sundown. Only a few stray beings wandered here and there, mostly making deliveries or sweeping down the sidewalks in front of their shops prior to opening. Except for the lack of light, the streets looked just like any town preparing for a day's business...that and the red eyes of the citizens.

We hugged the light as we picked our way across town...

That's right. I said "hugged the light." I try to only make the same mistake a dozen times. In other dimensions, we would have "hugged the dark" to avoid being noticed or recognized. Here, we "hugged the light." Don't laugh. It worked.

Anyway, as we picked our way through the streets of Blut, most of my attention was taken up with the task of trying to map a good getaway route. Getting Aahz out of jail I would deal with once we got there. Right now I was worried about what we would do once we had him out...a major assumption, I know, but I had so little optimism that I clung to what there was with all fours.

The three of us looked enough like vampires in appearance to pass casual inspection. There was no way however, that we could pass off my scaly green partner as a native without a disguise spell, and I wasn't about to bet on having any magical energy left after springing Aahz. As such, I was constantly craning my neck to peer down side-streets and alleys, hoping to find a little-traveled route by which we could spirit our fugitive colleague out of town without bringing the entire populace down on our necks. By the time we reached our destination, I was pretty sure I could get us back to the Dispatcher's by the route we were following, and *positively* sure that if I tried to take us there by the back routes, I would get us totally and helplessly lost.

"Well, Boss. This is it. Think we can crack it?"

I don't think Guido really expected an answer. He was just talking to break the silence that had fallen over us as we stood looking at our target.

The Municipal Building was an imposing structure, with thick stone walls and a corner tower that stretched up almost out of sight into the darkness. It didn't look like we could put a dent in it with a cannon...if we had a cannon, which we didn't. I was used to the tents of the Bazaar or the rather ramshackle building style of Klah. While I had been gradually getting over being overawed by the construction prevalent here in Blut, this place intimidated me. I'd seen shakier looking mountains!

"Well, one thing's for certain," I began, almost under my breath.

"What's that?"

"Staring at it isn't going to make it any weaker." Neither of my assistants laughed at my joke, but then again, neither did I.

Shaking off a feeling of foreboding, I turned to my staff.

"All right, Guido. You stay down here and keep watch. Massha? Do you think that belt of yours can lift two? It's time I went topside and took a good look at this impregnable cell."

My apprentice licked her lips nervously and shrugged.

"I don't know, Hot Stuff. I warned you that the controls on this thing don't work right. It could lift us right into orbit for all I know."

I patted her shoulder in what I hoped was a reassuring way. "Well, give it a try and we'll find out."

She nodded, wrapped one arm around my chest, and used her other hand to play with the jewels on her belt buckle.

There was a sparkle of light, but beyond that nothing.

"Not enough juice," she mumbled to herself.

"So turn it up already," I urged.

Even if the vampires tended to avoid light, we were lit up like a Christmas tree and bound to attract attention if we stayed at ground level much longer.

"Cross your fingers," she said grimly and touched the jewels again.

The light intensified and we started up fast...too fast.

"Careful, Boss!" Guido shouted and grabbed my legs as they went past him.

That brought our progress to a halt...well, almost.

Instead of rocketing up into the night, we were rising slowly, almost imperceptibly.

"That's got it, High Roller!" Massha exclaimed, shifting her grip to hang onto me with both arms. "A little more ballast than I had planned on, though."

I considered briefly telling Guido to let go, but rejected the thought. If the bodyguard released his grip, we'd doubtless resume our previous speed...and while a lot of folks at the Bazaar talked about my meteoric rise, I'd just as soon keep the phrase figurative. There was also the minor detail that we were already at a height where it would be dangerous for Guido to try dropping back to the street. There was that, and his death-grip on my legs.

"Don't tell me, let me guess," I called down to him "You're acrophobic, too?"

The view of Blut that was unfolding beneath us was truly breathtaking. Truly! My life these days was so cluttered with crisis and dangers that a little thing like looking down on buildings didn't bother me much, but even I was finding it hard to breathe when confronted up close with sheer walls adorned with stone creatures. Still, until I felt his fingernails biting into my calves, it had never occurred to me that such things might upset a rough-and-tumble guy like Guido.

"Naw. I got nothin' against spiders," he replied nervously. "It's heights that scare me."

I let that one go. I was busy studying the tower which could be viewed much more clearly from this altitude. If anything, it looked stronger than the portion of the building that was below us. One feature captured my attention, though. The top portion of the tower, the part I assumed was Aahz's cell, was shaped like a large dragon's head. The window I had been expecting was actually the creature's mouth, with its teeth serving as bars.

I should have anticipated something like that, realizing the abundance of stone animals on every other building in town. Still, it came as a bit of a surprise...but a pleasant surprise. I had been trying to figure a way to get through iron bars, but stone teeth might be a bit easier. Maybe with Aahz working from the inside and us working from the outside, we could loosen the mortar and...

I suddenly realized that in a few moments we would be level with the cell...and that a few moments after that we'd be past it!

Unless something was done, and done fast, to halt our upward progress, we'd only have time for a few quick words with Aahz before parting company permanently. With time running out fast, I cast about for a solution.

The wall was too far away to grab onto, and there was no way to increase our weight, unless...

When Aahz first taught me to fly, he explained the process as "levitation in reverse." That is, instead of using the mind to lift objects, you push against the ground and lift yourself. Focusing my reservoir of magical energy, I used a small portion to try *flying* in reverse. Instead of pushing up, I pushed down!

Okay. So I was desperate. In a crisis, I'll try anything, however stupid. Fortunately, this stupid idea worked!

Our upward progress slowed to a halt with me hanging at eye-level with the cell's dragon mouth.

Trying not to show my relief, I raised my voice.

"Hey, Aahz! When are visiting hours?"

For a moment there was no response, and I had a sudden fear that we were hanging a hundred feet in the air outside an empty cell. Then my partner's unmistakable countenance appeared in the window.

"Skeeve?" he said in a skeptical voice. "Skeeve! What are you doing out there?"

"Oh, we were just in the neighborhood and thought we'd drop in," I replied in my best nonchalant voice. "Heard you were in a bit of trouble and thought we'd better get you out before it got serious."

"Who's we?" my partner demanded, then he focused on my assistants. "Oh no! Those two? Where are Tananda and Chumley? C'mon, Skeeve. I need a rescue team and you bring me a circus act!"

"It's the best I could do on short notice," I shot back, slightly annoyed. "Tananda and Chumley aren't back from their own work yet, but I left a message for them to catch up with us if they could. Of course, I'm not sure how much help they'll be. In case you're wondering why I'm being carried by my apprentice instead of flying free, this particular dimension is exceptionally low on force lines to tap in to. If anything, I think I'm pretty lucky that I brought `these two' along instead of ending up with a whole team of for-real magicians who are too proud to use gimmicks. It's thanks to `these

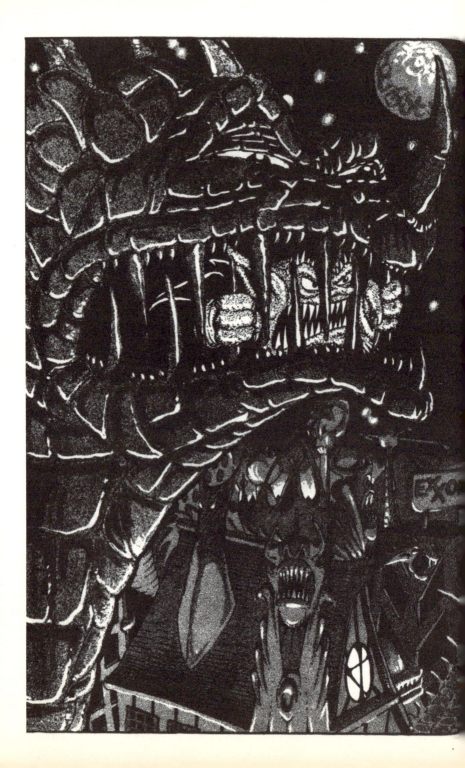

two' that I made it this far at all. Now, do you want our help, or do you want to wait for the next team to float past? I mean, you're in no rush, are you?"

"Now don't get your back up, partner," Aahz said soothingly. "You caught me a little off-guard is all. So tell me, just how do you figure to get me out of here?"

That brought me back to earth…or as close to it as I could get while suspended in mid-air.

"Umm…actually, Aahz, I was kinda hoping *you* might have a few ideas on the subject. You're usually pretty good at coming up with plans to get us out of tight spots."

"What I want to know," Guido snarled, turning slightly in the wind, "is how come your partner hasn't figured a way out of there all by himself, if he's so all-fired smart?"

I started to rebuke my bodyguard, but slowly his words sank in. That was a good question! Aahz was strong…I mean STRONG! By rights he should have been able to rip the stone teeth out of the window all by himself. What *was* keeping him here?

"Oh, I'm having so much fun in here I just couldn't bear to leave," Aahz barked back. "I'm in here because I can't get out, that's why. What's more, if any of you have any ideas about how to get me out, I think now's a real good time to share them with the rest of us."

"Wait a minute, Aahz," I said. *"Why* can't you get out…and how did they catch you in the first place?"

"I was framed," my partner retorted, but I noticed his voice was a bit more subdued.

"We already know that," I pressed. "What I want to know is why you didn't just bust a few heads and sprint for home? You've never been particularly respectful of local authority before."

To my surprise, Aahz actually looked embarrassed.

"I was drugged," he said in a disgusted tone. "They put something in my drink, and the next thing I knew I had a stake and mallet in my hands and a room full of officials. Whatever it was they used, it kept me groggy all the way through the trial…I mean I couldn't walk straight, much less defend myself coherently, and after that I was in *here!"*

"The old Mickey Finn trick!" Massha snorted, rocking our entire formation. "I'm surprised someone as off-worldly as you could get caught by such a corny stunt."

"Yeah. It surprised me, too!" Aahz admitted. "I mean, that gag is so old, who would really expect anyone to try it at all?"

"Only if you figured the mark was louder than he was smart," Guido sneered.

"Is that so!" my partner snapped, ready to renew their old rivalry. "Well, when I get out of here, you and me can…"

"Stop it, you two," I ordered. "Right now the problem is to get us *all* out of here before the balloon goes up…no offense, Massha. Now spill, Aahz. What's so special about this cell that's keeping you bottled up?"

My partner heaved a great sigh.

"Take another look at it, Skeeve. *A close* look."

I did. It still looked the same to me: a tower room on the shape of a dragon's head.

"Yeah. Okay. So?"

"So remember where we are. This thing was built to hold *vampire* criminals. You know, beings with super-human strength that can change into mist?"

My gaze flew back to the dragon's head.

"I don't get it," I admitted. "How can any stone cell hold beings like that?"

"That's the point." Aahz winced. "A stone cell *can't!* This thing is made of *living stone*. If whoever's inside tries to bust out, it swallows them. If they try to turn into mist, it inhales them."

"You mean…"

"Now you're getting the picture."

He flashed his toothy grin at me despite his obvious depression.

"The cell is alive!"

Startled by this revelation, I looked at the tower top cell again. As if it had been waiting for the right cue, the dragon's head opened its eyes and looked at me.

XII.

"For the right person, the impossible is easy!"
DUMBO

TO EVERYONE'S SURPRISE, particularly my own, I didn't find the revelation about the true nature of Aahz's confinement at all discouraging. If anything, I was doubly pleased. Not only did I have an immediate idea for how to beat the problem, I had arrived at it before my knowledge-able partner...well before, as a matter of fact, as he had been pondering his dilemma for days whereas I had only just received the information. Of course, he was probably not in a position to see the easy solution that I could.

"What are you grinning at?" he demanded. "If there's anything funny about this, it eludes me completely."

Unlike my own amiable self, Aahz tends to show his worry by getting mad. Come to think of it, he tends to express almost any emotion by *getting* mad. Well, at least he's consistent.

"Tell me," I said, eyeing the dragon's head, "you say this thing's alive. How alive is it?"

"What do you mean, `how alive is it'?" Aahz scowled. "It's alive enough to swallow me if it gets it into it's head. That's alive enough for me.

"I mean, can it hear and see?"

"Who cares?" my partner said, in a dazzling display of charm and curiosity that makes him so lovable. "I hadn't planned on asking it out for a date."

I stared thoughtfully at the beast.

"I was just wondering if it could hear me...say, if I said that I thought it was the ugliest building decoration I've seen here in town?"

The dragon's head rewarded me by narrowing its eyes into an evil glare.

"I think it can hear you, Boss," Guido said, shifting his grip nervously. "It doesn't look like it liked that last comment."

"Oh, swell!" Aahz grumbled. "Tell you what, partner. Why don't *you* come in here and sit on this thing's tongue instead of me before you start getting it all riled up?"

"I was just checking." I smiled. "To tell the truth, I think it's the most incredible thing I've seen since I started traveling the dimensions. I just said that other to test its reactions."

The dragon stopped glaring, but it still looked a little bit suspicous and wary.

"Well, find some other reaction to test, okay?" my partner snapped. "For some obscure reason, I'm a little nervous these days, and every time this thing moves its tongue I age a few centuries."

I ignored his grumbling and shook one of my legs. "Hey, Guido! Are you still paying attention down there?"

His grip tightened fiercely.

"Of course I'm paying attention, you little...I mean, yeah, Boss. There's not much else to do while we're hangin' here, know what I mean? And quit jerking your leg around...please?"

I found his verbal slip rather interesting, but now wasn't the time to investigate further.

"Well, listen up," I said. "Here's what I want you to do. I want you to let go with one hand and pass the rope up tome..."

"No way, Boss! Have you seen how far down it is? I'm not lettin' go no matter what you..."

"...because if you don't," I continued as if he hadn't interrupted, "I'm going to start squirming around until either you lose your grip with both hands or Massha loses her grip on me. Whichever way it goes, you'll fall. Get my drift? Now for once could you just follow orders without a lot of back-talk? We don't have much time to pull this off."

There was a stricken silence below as Guido absorbed my ultimatum and weighed the possibilities.

"Pull what off?" Aahz demanded. "Why doesn't anybody tell me anything? If this master plan of yours is riding on that sorry excuse for a bodyguard, you might as well give up right now. I've told you all along that he was too lily-livered to be any good at..."

"Who's lily-livered?!" Guido shouted. "Look, Big Mouth, as soon as we get you out of there, you and me are going to settle this once and..."

"First, we've got to get him out, Guido," I interrupted. "The rope."

"Right, Boss. One rope coming up. We'll see who's lily-livered. The last person who called me that was my mom, and by the time I got done with her..."

Our whole formation began to rock dangerously as he fumbled through his coat one-handed in search of the rope. For a minute, I was afraid he was mad enough to let go with both hands to speed his search.

"Easy there, Guido," I cautioned. "We can…"

"Here it is, Boss!" he said, flipping the rope up so violently that it almost whacked me in the face. "I hope you can use it to hang the son of a…"

"Hanging isn't enough!" Aahz taunted. "It takes more than a piece of rope to do me in."

"Yeah. It takes a little girl with blue eyes and a spiked drink," my bodyguard sneered back. "If you think I'm going to let you live *that* one down…"

I forced myself to ignore them. While it was tempting to rally to Luanna's defense, there were other more pressing matters to attend to.

Moving as carefully as I could, I looped one end of the rope up and around Massha's waist. It took a couple of tries and a lot more rope than I would have liked, but finally I managed to catch the dangling end and tie it off securely.

"What's with the rope, Hot Stuff?" Massha said calmly, the only one of our group who had managed to keep her cool through the entire proceedings.

"Well, with any luck, in a little while we're going to be heading down…with Aahz," I explained. "Even though I know you're strong, I don't think your hands are strong enough to keep a grip on all three of us while we make the trip. This is to be sure we don't lose anyone *after* we spring the cell."

"Speaking of that," Aahz called, "I'm still waiting to hear how you're going to get me out of this thing. You might even say I'm *dying* to find out."

He wasn't the only one. The dragon's head was watching my every movement through slitted eyes. I'm not sure how much pride it took in its job, but it was obvious the beast wasn't getting ready to overwhelm us with its cooperation.

Everything was as ready as I could make it, so I decided it was time to play my trump card.

"There's nothing to it, really," I told my partner with a smile. "Talk to me."

It isn't often I catch my old mentor totally by surprise...I get him upset on a fairly regular basis, but total surprise was a real rarity. This was one of those golden times.

"Say WHAT?" Aahz exclaimed loudly.

"Trust me, Aahz," I insisted. "I know what I'm doing. Just talk to me. Tell me a story. How did you first meet Garkin?"

"Oh, that," he said, rolling his eyes expressively.

"Well, we were at the same boring cocktail party, see...you know, one of those dreary affairs where the crowd has you pinned against the wall and you get stuck talking to whatever the tide washes up against you? Anyway, he was trying to impress some little bit of fluff with his magic, which really wasn't all that hot in those days...let me tell you, partner, anytime you start getting depressed with your lack of progress in the magic business, remind me to tell you what your old teacher Garkin was like when we first met. But, as I was saying, out of respect for the craft, I just had to wander over and show them what the *real* stuff looked like...not that I had any interest in her myself, mind you..."

I felt Guido tugging on my pantleg.

"Say, Boss," he complained. "What is this? I thought we were in a hurry."

"This is what we needed the time for," I whispered back.

"For *this?*" he grumbled. "But Boss, if we don't get started..."

"We're started," I answered. "Now pay attention to what he's saying."

I was afraid our side comments might have distracted Aahz, but I needn't have worried. As per normal, once my partner got on a verbal roll, he wasn't that easy to stop.

"...so there we were, just the three of us, mind you, and remember, our clothes were five floors away at this point..."

"What's going on, Hot Stuff?" Massha hissed from her position above me. "I *know you*'ve heard this story before. Heck, *I've* heard it four times myself."

"Keep your eye on the dragon," I advised her. "And be ready to act fast."

I was going through the motions of reacting to Aahz's story and fielding the impatient questions of my assistants as best I could, but my real attention was focused on the dragon's head. My strategy was already working Aahz's droning account of past glories were starting to take effect.

The dragon's eyes were definitely starting to glaze.

"...of course, after all that, I just *had* to take her home with me. It was the least I could do for the poor thing under the circumstances."

Aahz was winding up his story already! I had to keep him going just a little bit longer.

"Was that the party where you met Tananda?" I said, deliberately feeding him another cue.

"Tananda? No. That's another story completely. I met her when I was sitting in on a cut-throat game of dragon poker over at the Geek's. We had a real pigeon on the line, the kind of idiot who would bet a busted Corp's a' Corp's into a Unicorn Flush showing, you know? Well, I was a little low on funds just then, so..."

Guido was getting restless again.

"Boss, how much longer are we gonna..."

"Not much longer," I interrupted. "Get hold of the rope. We're about to move."

"...now I was holding Ogres back-to-back...or was it Elves? No, it was Ogres. I remember because Tananda had Elves wrapped up. Of course, we didn't know that until the end of the hand. Anyway, as soon as the Geek opened, I bumped him back limit, and Tananda..."

That did it. I should have known a hand-by-hand, bet-by-bet description of dragon poker would do the trick.

Without any warning at all, the dragon yawned...long and wide.

Aahz broke off his narration, a momentous event in itself, and blinked his surprise.

"Quick, Aahz! Jump for it!"

Bewildered as he was, there was nothing wrong with my partner's reflexes. He was out of the dragon's mouth in a flash, diving through the air to catch the rope below Guido.

As soon as his hands closed on our lifeline, several things happened at the same time.

With the extra weight on Massha's levitation belt, our whole formation started to sink at an alarming rate...my apprentice lost her grip on me, giving me minor rope burns as I clutched madly for the rope, almost too late to follow the advice I had been so freely giving to everyone else...and the dragon closed his mouth.

I caught one last glimpse of the beast before we sank from sight, and I honestly don't think he even knew we were gone. His eyelids were at half-mast, and the eyes themselves were out of focus from boredom. Aahz's stories tended to have that effect on even vaguely-intelligent beings. I had simply found a practical application for the phenomenon.

"I've gotta change the controls, Hot Stuff!" Massha called, alerting me once more to our current situation. The ground was rushing up to meet us with frightening speed.

I remembered the faulty controls that held all of us at their mercy.

"No! Wait, Massha! Let me try..."

Exerting my last ounce of reserve power, I worked at levitating our whole crew. Under normal circumstances, I could lift three people easily and four or five in a pinch. Here in Limbo, using everything I had with Massha's belt assisting me, I barely managed to slow our descent to a moderate crawl.

"What happened there, partner?" Aahz called. "How did you know that thing was going to yawn?"

"Call it a lucky guess," I grunted, still concentrating on keeping us from crashing. "I'll explain later."

"Check the landing zone," Guido warned.

I sneaked a peak.

We had been at our task longer than I thought. The sidewalk below was crowded with vampires strolling here and there as Blut's legendary nightlife fired up.

"I don't think we can bluff our way through this one," Aahz said calmly. "Any chance you can steer us around the corner into the alley? There doesn't seem to be as much of a crowd there."

Before I could answer, something flashed past us from above with a flutter of leather wings.

"JAILBREAK!" it screamed, banking around the corner. "Murderer on the loose! JAILBREAK!"

XIII.

"I've never seen so damn many Indians."
G. A. CUSTER

THE WORDS OF alarm had an interesting effect on the crowd below. After a brief glance to see us descending into their midst, to a man they turned and ran. In a twinkling, the street was empty.

"What's going on?" I called to Aahz, unable to believe our good fortune.

"Beats me!" my partner shouted back. "I guess none of the normal citizenry want to tangle with an escaped murderer. Better get us down fast before they figure out how badly outnumbered we are."

I didn't have to be told twice. Our escape had just gotten an unexpected blessing, but I wasn't about to make book on how long it would last. I cut my magical support, and we dropped swiftly toward the pavement.

"What was that that blew the whistle on us?" Massha said, peering up into the darkness where our mysterious saboteur had disappeared.

"I think it was that Vic character," Guido answered from below me. "I got a pretty good look at him when he bolted past me back at the Woof Writers."

"Really?" I asked, half to myself, twisting around to look after the departed villain. "That's one more we owe him."

"Later," Aahz commanded, touching down at last. "Right now we've got to get out of here."

Guido was beside him in a second. I had to drop a ways, as with the extra weight removed from the rope, we had ceased to sink.

"C'mon, Massha!" I called. "Cut the power in that thing. It's not that far to fall."

"I'm trying!" she snapped back, fiddling with the belt buckle once more. "The flaming thing's malfunctioning again!"

The belt setting had changed. Holding the rope, I could feel that there was no longer an upward pull. Unfortunately, Massha wasn't sinking, either. Instead, she hovered in mid-air about fifteen feet up.

"Hey, Boss! We got company!"

I followed by bodyguard's gaze. There was a mob forming down the street to our left, and it didn't look happy. Of course, it was hard to tell for sure, but I had the definite impression that their eyes were glowing redder than normal, which I was unable to convince myself was a good sign.

"Maasshhha!" I nagged, my voice rising uncontrollably as I tugged on the rope.

"It's jammed!" she whimpered. "Go on, take off, Hot Stuff. No sense in all of us getting caught."

"We can't just leave you here," I argued.

"We don't have time for a debate," Aahz snarled. "Guido! Get up there ahead of us and keep the street open. We can't afford to get cut off. Okay, let's go!"

With that, he snatched the rope out of my hand and took off running down the street away from the crowd with Guido out front in point position and Massha floating over his head like a gaudy balloon. For once, I didn't object to him giving orders to my bodyguard.I was too busy sprinting to keep up with the rest of my group.

If the watching mob was having any trouble deciding what to do, the sight of us fleeing settled it. With a howl, they swarmed down the street in pursuit.

When I say "with a howl," I'm not speaking figuratively. As they ran, some of the vampires transformed into large, fierce-looking dogs, others into bats, presumably to gain more speed in the chase. While Aahz and I had been chased by mobs before, this was the first pack of pursuers who literally bayed at our heels. I must say I didn't care much for the experience.

"Where are we going, Aahz?" I panted.

"Away from them!" he called back.

"I mean, eventually," I pressed. "We're heading the wrong way to get back to our hideout."

"We can't hole up until we've shaken our fan club," my partner insisted. "Now shut up and run."

I had certain doubts about our ability to elude our pursuers while towing Massha overhead to mark our position, but I followed Aahz's instructions and pumped the pavement for all I was worth. For one thing, if I pointed out this obvious fact to my partner, he might simply let go of the rope and leave my apprentice to fend for herself. Then again, the option to running was to stand firm and face the mob. All in all, running seemed like a *real* good idea.

Guido was surprisingly good at clearing a path for us. I had never really seen my bodyguard in action, but with his constant carping and allergy problems throughout this venture, I was tending to discount his usefulness. Not so. The vampires we encountered in our flight had not heard the alarm and were unprepared for the whirlwind that burst into their midst. Guido never seemed to break stride as he barreled into victim after victim, but whatever he did to them was effective. None of the fallen bodies which marked his progress attempted to interfere with Aahz or I...heck, they didn't even move.

"River ahead, Boss!" he called over his shoulder.

"What's that?" I puffed, realizing for the first time how out of shape I had grown during my prosperous stay at the Bazaar.

"A river!" he repeated. "The street we're on is going to dead-end into a river in a few blocks. I can see it from here. We're going to have to change direction or we'll get pinned against the water."

I wondered whether it wouldn't be a good idea for us to just plunge into the river and put some moving water between us and the vampires, as I seemed to recall a legend that that was one of the things that could stop them. Then it occurred to me that my bodyguard probably couldn't swim.

"Head right!" Aahz shouted. "There! Up that alley."

Guido darted off on the indicated course with my partner and I pounding along about fifteen paces behind him. We had built up a bit of a lead on our pursuers, though we could still hear their cries and yelps a block or so back, and for the first time I started to have the hope that we might actually elude them. Now that we were out of their line of sight...

"Look out..."

There was a sudden cry from above, and Massha came crashing to the ground, gaining the dubious distinction of being the first person I've ever witnessed doing a belly-flop on dry land. I'm sure the ground didn't actually shake, but the impact was enough to leave that impression. I experienced a quick flash of guilt, realizing that my first thought was not for the well-being of my apprentice, but rather unbridled relief that she hadn't landed on one of us.

"I think the controls just came unstuck," Aahz said, rather unnecessarily to my thinking.

"Are you all right, Massha?" I said, crouching over her.

"Wha—ha..." came the forced reply.

"Of course, she's not all right," Aahz snapped, assuming translator duties. "At the very least she's got the wind knocked out of her."

Whatever the exact extent of the damages were suffered from her fall, my apprentice wasn't even trying to rise. I would have liked to give her a few minutes recovery time, but already the sounds of our pursuers were drawing closer.

"Can you carry her, Aahz?"

"Not on my best day," my partner admitted, eyeing Massha's sizable bulk. "How about you? Have you got enough juice left to levitate her?"

I shook my head violently.

"Used it all supervising our aerial maneuvers back at the jail."

"Hey, Boss!" Guido hissed, emerging from the shadows behind us. "The alley's blocked. This is the only way out!"

And that was that. Even if we got Massha up and moving, all it meant was that we'd have to retrace our steps right back into the teeth of the mob. We had run our race...and were about to lose it rather spectacularly.

The others knew it, too.

"Well, it's been nice working with you, Guido," Aahz said with a sigh. "I know I've gotten on your case a couple of times, but you're a good man to have around in a pinch. You did some really nice crowd work getting us this far.

Sorry about that last turn call."

"No hard feelings," my bodyguard shrugged. "You gave it your best shot. This alley would have been my choice, too, if I'd been workin' alone. Boss, I warned you I was a jinx when it came to jailbreaks. I gotta admit, though, for a while there I really thought we were goin' to pull this one off."

"It was a long shot at best." I grinned. "At least you can't say that *this* one suffered from over-planning."

Aahz clapped a hand on my shoulder.

"Well, partner?" he said. "Any thoughts on how to play this one? Do we try to surrender peacefully, or go down swinging?"

I wasn't sure the crowd would give us a choice. They were almost at our alley, and they didn't sound like they cared much for talking.

"NOT THIS WAY! THEY'RE DOUBLING BACK TO-WARD THE JAIL!"

This unexpected cry came from the street near the mouth of our alley.

I couldn't believe it, but apparently the mob did. There were curses and shouted orders, but from their fast-fading manner it was plain that the crowd had turned and was now heading back the way they had come.

"What was that?" Massha managed, her voice returning at last.

I motioned her to be silent and cocked an eyebrow at Aahz, silently asking the same question.

He answered with an equally silent shake of the head.

Neither of us knew for sure what was going on, but we both sensed that the timely intervention was neither accidental nor a mistake. Someone had deliberately pulled the crowd off our backs. Before we celebrated our good fortune, we wanted to know who and why.

A pair of figures appeared at the mouth of the alley. "You can come out now," one of them called. "Sorry to interfere, but it looked like so much fun we just *had* to play, too."

I'd know that voice anywhere, even if I didn't recognize the figure as well as the unmistakable form of her brother.

"Tananda! Chumley!" I shouted, waving to pinpoint our position. "I was wondering when you'd show up."

The sister-brother team of Trollop and Troll hastened to join us. For all their lighthearted banter, I can think of few beings I'd rather have on or at my side when things get tight.

"Are you all right?" Tananda asked, stopping to help Massha to her feet.

"Really never had much dignity," my apprentice responded, "and what little I did have is shot to hell. Except for that I'm fine. I'm starting to see why you Big Leaguers are so down on mechanical magic."

Chumley seized my hand and pumped it vigorously.

"Now don't be too rough on your little gimmicks, ducks," he advised. "That little ring you left us was just the ticket we needed to get here in time for the latest in our unbroken string of last-minute rescues. Except for the typical hash you've made of your end-game, it looks like you've all done rather well without us. We've got all present and accounted for, including Aahz, who seems remarkably unscathed after yet one more near-brush with disaster. Seems like all that's left is a hasty retreat and a slow celebration…eh, what?"

"That's about the size of it," I agreed. "It's great having the two of you along to ride shotgun on our exit, though. Speaking of which, can you find the castle from here? I've gotten a little turned around…"

"Hold it right there!" Aahz broke in. "Before we get too wrapped up in congratulating each other, aren't there a few minor details being overlooked?"

The group looked at each other.

"Like what?" Tananda said at last.

"Like the fact that I'm still wanted for murder, for one," my partner glared. "Then again, there's the three fugitives we're supposed to be bringing back to Deva with us."

"Oh, come on, Aahz," the Trollop chided, poking him playfully in the ribs. "With the reputation you already have, what's a little thing like a murder warrant?"

"I didn't do it," Aahz insisted. "Not only didn't I kill this Vic character, nobody did. He's still around some-where laughing down his sleeve at all of us. Now while I'll admit my reputation isn't exactly spotless, it doesn't include standing still for a bum rap…or letting someone get away with making a fool of me!"

"Of course, saving the money for paying the swindlers' debts plus the fines involved has nothing to do with it, eh, Aahz?" Chumley said, winking his larger eye. "Well…that, too," my partner admitted. "Isn't it nice that we can take care of both unpleasant tasks at the same time?"

"Maybe we could settle for just catching Vic and let the others go," I murmured.

"How's that again, partner?"

"Nothing, Aahz," I said with a sigh. "It's just that…nothing. C'mon everybody. If we're going to go hunting, it's going to require a bit of planning, and I don't think we should do it out here in the open."

XIV.

"Relax, Julie. Everyone will understand."
ROMEO

FORTUNATELY, MASSHA'S ELEVATED position during our flight had given her an excellent view of our surroundings, and we were able to find our way back to the Dispatcher's without being discovered by the aroused populace. Now that our numbers had increased, however, Vilhelm's greeting was noticeably cooler.

"I'm starting to believe what everybody says," the little vampire complained. "Let one demon in, and the next thing you know the neighborhood's crawling with them. When I decided to talk to you folks instead of blowing the whistle on you, I didn't figure on turning my office into a meeting place for off-worlders."

"C'mon, Vilhelm," I said, trying to edge my foot into the doorway. "We don't have any place else to go in town. There aren't *that* many of us."

"We could always just wait out on the street until the authorities come by," Aahz suggested. "I don't imagine it would take much to convince them that this guy has been harboring fugitives."

"Can it, Green and Scaly," Massha ordered, puffing herself up to twice her normal size. "Vilhelm's been nice to us so far, and I won't listen to anyone threaten him, even you. Just remember that you'd still be cooling your heels in the slammer if it weren't for him. Either he helps of his own free will, or we look elsewhere."

Aahz gave ground before her righteous indignation. "Are you going to let your apprentice talk to me that way?" he demanded.

"Only when she's right." I shrugged.

"I say, Aahz," Chumley intervened. "Could you possibly curb your normally vile manners for a few moments? We don't really need one more enemy in this dimension, and I, for one, would appreciate the chance to extend my thanks to this gentleman before he throws us out."

When he's working, Chumley goes by the name of Big Crunch and does a Neanderthal that's the envy of half the barbarians at the Bazaar. On his own time, however, his polished charm has solved a lot of problems for us…almost as many as Aahz's bluster has gotten us into.

"Oh, come on in," the Dispatcher grumbled. "Enter freely and of your own accord and all that. I never could turn my back on somebody in trouble. Guess that's why I've never traveled the other dimensions myself. They'd eat me alive out there."

"Thanks, Vilhelm," I said, slipping past him into the office before he could change his mind. "You'll have to forgive my partner. He really isn't always like this. Being on death row hasn't done much for his sense of humor."

"I guess I'm a little edgy myself," the vampire admitted. "Strange as it sounds, I've been worried about you folks…and your motor-mouthed friend who's been keeping me company hasn't helped things much."

I did a quick nose count of our troop.

"Wait a minute," I frowned. "Who's been waiting for us?"

Now it was Vilhelm's turn to look surprised.

"Didn't one of you send out for a werewolf? He said he was with you."

"Aahh! But I am! My friends, they do not know me yet, but I shall be their salvation, no?"

With that, I was overwhelmed by a shaggy rug. Well, at least that's what I thought until it came off the floor and threw itself into my arms with the enthusiasm of a puppy…a very large puppy.

"What's *that?!*" Aahz said, his eyes narrowing dangerously. "Skeeve, can't I leave you alone for a few days without you picking up every stray in any given dimension?"

"That," in this case, was one of the scroffiest-looking werewolves I'd ever seen…realizing, of course, that until this moment I'd only seen two. He had dark bushy eye-brows (if you'll believe that on a werewolf) and wore a white stocking cap with a maple leaf on the side. His whiskers were carefully groomed into a handlebar mustache, and what might have been a goatee peered from beneath his chin. Actually, viewed piecemeal, he was very well-groomed. It's just when taken in its entirety that he looked scroffy. Maybe it was the leer…

"Honest, Aahz," I protested, trying to untangle myself. "I've never seen him before in my life!"

"Oh, but forgive me," the beast said, releasing me so suddenly I almost fell. "I am so stupeed, I forget to intro-duce. So! I am an artist extraordinaire, but also, I am ze finest track-air in ze land. My friends, the Woof Writers, they have told me of your pro-blem and I have flown like ze wind to aid you. No? I am Pepe Le Garou A. and I am at your service."

With that, he swept into a low bow with a flourish that if I hadn't been so flabbergasted I would have applauded. It occurred to me that now I knew why the Woof Writers had snickered when they told us they knew of someone who could help.

"Boss," Guido said, his voice muffled by his hand, which he was holding over his nose and mouth. "Shall I wait outside?"

Tananda cocked an eyebrow at him.

"Allergy problems? Here, try some of this. No dimension traveler should be without it."

She produced a small vial and tossed it to my body-guard. "Rub some onto your upper lip just below your nose.

"Gee, thanks," Guido said, following her instructions. "What is it?"

"It's a counter-allergenic paste." She shrugged. "I think it has a garlic base."

"WHAT?" my bodyguard exclaimed, dropping the vial.

Tananda favored him with one of her impish grins. "Just kidding. Nunzio was worried about you and told us about your allergies...all of them."

Her brother swatted her lightly on the rump.

"Shame on you, little sister," he said, smiling in spite of himself.

"After you get done apologizing to Guido, I suggest you do the same for our host. I think you nearly have him a heart attack with that last little joke."

This was, of course, just what I needed while stranded in a hostile dimension. A nervous vampire, a melodramatic werewolf, and now my teammates decide it's time to play practical jokes on each other.

"Ummm...tell me, Mr. A.," I said, ignoring my other problems and turning to the werewolf. "Do you think you can..."

"No, non," he interrupted. "Eet is simply Pepe, eh?"

"Pepe A.," I repeated dutifully.

"Zat's right," he beamed, apparently delighted with my ability to learn a simple phrase.

"Now, before we...how you say, get down to ze business, would you do me ze hon-air of introducing me to your colleagues?"

Pepe Le Garou R.

"Oh. Sorry. This is my partner, Aahz. He's…"

"But of course! Ze famous Aahz!

I have so long wished to meet you."

If there's anything that can coax Aahz out of a bad mood, it's flattery…and Pepe seemed to be an expert in that category.

"You've heard of me?" he blinked. "I mean…what exactly have you heard? There have been so many adventures over the years."

"Do you not remem-bair Piere? I was raised from a pup on his tales of your fight with Isstvan."

"Piere? You know Piere?"

"Do I know him? He is my uncle!"

"No kidding. Hey, Tananda! Did you hear that? Pepe here's Piere's nephew. Wait'll we tell Gus."

I retired from the conversation, apparently forgotten in the reunion.

"Say, Skeeve," Vilhelm said, appearing at my side. "It looks like this could take a while. Should I break out the wine?"

That got my attention.

"Wine? You've got wine?"

"Stocked up on it after your last visit," the vampire admitted with a grin. "Figured it might come in handy the next time you came through. I may gripe a bit, but talking to you and your friends is a lot more fun than watching the tubes."

"Well bring it out…but I get the first glass. Unless you've got lots there won't be much left after my partner there gets his claws on it."

I turned back to the proceedings just in time to see Pepe kissing my apprentice's hand.

"Do not be afraid, my little flow-air," he was saying. "Here is one who truly appreciates your beauty, as well as…how should I say it, its quantity?"

"You're kinda cute," Massha giggled. "But I never did go in much for inter-species dating, if you get my drift."

I caught Aahz's attention and drew him away from the group.

"Could you take over for a while here, partner?" I said. "I've been running nonstop since the start of this thing and could use a little time by myself to recharge my batteries before we fire up again."

"No problem," he nodded, laying a hand on my shoulder. "I figure we won't be moving before sunup...and Skeeve? I haven't had a chance to say it, but thanks for the bail-out."

"Don't mention it," I grinned weakly. "Tell me you wouldn't do the same for me."

"Don't know," he retorted. "You've never sucker-punched me at the beginning of a caper."

"Now *that* I still owe you for."

Just then, Vilhelm appeared with the wine, and Aahz hurried away to rejoin the group.

I managed to snag a goblet and retired to a secluded corner while the party went into high gear. Pepe seemed to be fitting in well with the rest of the team, if not functioning as a combination jester and spark plug, but somehow I felt a bit distant. Sipping my wine, I stared off into the distance at nothing in particular, letting my thoughts wander.

"What's the trouble, handsome?"

"Hmmm? Oh. Hi, Tananda. Nothing in particular. Just a little tired, that's all."

"Mind if I join you?" she said, dropping to the floor beside me before I could stop her. "So. Are you going to tell me about it? Who is she?"

I turned my head slowly to look at her directly. "I beg your pardon?"

She kept her eyes averted, idly running one finger around the rim of her goblet.

"Look," she said, "if you don't want to talk about it, just say so...it's really none of my business. Just don't try to kid me or yourself that there's nothing bothering you. I've known you a long time now, and I can usually tell when there's something eating you. My best guess right now, if I'm any judge of the phenomenon, is that it's a girl."

Ever since I'd met Tananda, I'd had a crush on her. With her words, though, I suddenly realized how badly I wanted someone to talk to. I mean, to Guido and Massha I was an authority figure, and I wasn't about to open up to Aahz until I was sure he'd take the problem seriously and not just laugh, and as for Chumley...how do you talk about woman problems with a troll?

"Okay. You got me," I said, looking back into my wine. "It's a girl."

"I thought so," Tananda smiled. "Where have you been keeping her? Tell me, is she beautiful and sensitive?"

"All that and more." I nodded, taking another drink from my goblet. "She's also on the wrong side."

"Woops," Tananda said, straightening up. "You'd better run that one past me again."

I filled her in on my encounters with Luanna. I tried to keep it unbiased and informative, but even I could tell that my tones were less controlled than I would have liked.

Tananda sat in silence for a few moments after I'd finished, hugging her legs and with her chin propped up on her knees.

"Well," she said at last, "from what you say, she's an accomplice at best. Maybe we can let her go after we get them all rounded up."

"Sure."

My voice was flat. Both Tananda and I knew that once Aahz got on his high horse there was no telling how merciful or vicious he would be at any given point.

"Well, there's always a chance," she insisted. "Aahz has always had a soft spot where you're concerned. If you intercede for her, and if she's willing to abandon her partners…"

"…and, if a table had wings, we could fly it back to the Bazaar." I frowned. "No, Tananda. First of all, she won't give up her partners just because they're in a crunch. That much I know. Besides, if I put that kind of pressure on her, to choose between me and them, I'd never know for sure if she really wanted me or if she was just trying to save her own skin."

Tananda got to her feet.

"Don't become so wise that you're stupid, Skeeve," she said softly before she left. "Remember, Luanna's already chosen you twice over her partners. Both times she's risked her life and their getaway to pass you a warning. Maybe all she needs is what you haven't yet given her—an invitation for a chance at a new life with a new partner. Don't be so proud or insecure that you'd throw a genuine admirer to the wolves rather than run the risk of making a mistake. If you did, I don't think I'd like you much…and I don't think you would either."

I pondered Tananda's advice after she'd gone. There was one additional complication I hadn't had the nerve to mention to her. Whatever Luanna's feelings for me were, how would they change when she found out I'd used her scarf…her token of affection, to guide a pack of hunters to their target?

XV.

"Everybody needs a career manager!"
LADY MACBETH

SO WHERE IS he?" Aahz grumbled for the hundredth time…in the last five minutes.

The sun had been up for hours, or at least as up as it seemed to get in this dimension. Since my arrival in Limbo, I had never seen what I am accustomed to think-ing of as full sunlight. Whether the constant heavy overcast condition which seemed to prevail during day-light hours was the result of magic or some strange meteoro-logic condition I was never sure, but it did nothing to alleviate the air of gloom that clung to the town of Blut like a shroud.

The whole team was impatient to get started, but Aahz was the only one who indulged himself in expressing his feelings as often…or as loudly. Of course, it might have been simply that he was making so much of a fuss that the others were willing to let him provide the noise for all of them rather than letting their own efforts get con-stantly upstaged.

"Just take it easy, partner," I said soothingly, struggling to keep from snapping at him in my own nervous impatience. "There aren't that many all-day stores in this dimension."

"What do you expect, dealing with a bunch of vampires," he snapped. "I still don't like this idea. Non-magical disguises seem unnatural somehow."

I heaved a quiet sigh inside and leaned back to wait, propping my feet up on a chair. This particular quarrel was old before Vilhelm had left on his shopping trip, and I was tired going over it again and again.

"Be reasonable, Aahz," Tananda said, taking up the slack for me. "You know we can't wander around town like this…especially you with half the city looking for you. We need disguises, and with-out a decent power source, Skeeve here can't handle disguises for all of us. Besides, it's not like we're using mechanical magic. We won't be using magic at all."

"That's what everybody keeps telling me," my partner growled. "We're just going to alter our appearances without using spells. That sounds like mechanical magic to me. Do you know what's going to happen to our reputations if word of this gets back to the Bazaar? Particularly with most of the competition looking for a chance to splash a little mud on the Great Skeeve's name? Remember, we're already getting complaints that our prices are too high, and if this gets out..."

The light dawned. I could finally see what was eating at Aahz. I should have known there was money at the bottom of this.

"But Aahz," I chimed in, "our fees *are* overpriced. I've been saying that for months. I mean, it's not like we need the money..."

"...and I've been telling you for months that it's the only way to keep the riffraff from draining away all your practice time," he shot back angrily. "Remember, your name's supposed to be the Great Skeeve, not the Red Cross. You don't do charity."

Now we were on familiar ground. Unlike the disguise thing, this was one argument I never tired of.

"I'm not talking about charity," I said. "I'm talking about a fair fee for services rendered."

"Fair fee?" my partner laughed, rolling his eyes. "You mean like that deal you cut with Watzisname? Did he ever tell you about that one, Tananda? We catch a silly bird for this Deveel, see, and my partner charges him a flat fee. Not a percentage, mind you, a flat fee. And how much of a flat fee? A hundred gold pieces? A thousand. No. TEN. Ten lousy gold pieces. And half an hour later the Deveel sells his 'poor little bird' for over a hundred thousand. Nice to know we don't do charity, isn't it?"

"C'mon, Aahz," I argued, writhing inside. "That was only five minutes' work. How was I supposed to know the silly bird was on the endangered species list? Even *you* thought it was a good deal until we heard what the final sale was. Besides, if I had held out for a percentage and the Deveel had been legit and never sold the thing, we wouldn't have even gotten ten gold pieces out of it."

"I never heard the details from your side," Tananda said, "but what I picked up on the streets that everybody at the Bazaar was really impressed. Most folks think that it's a master-stroke of PR for the hottest magician at the Bazaar to help bring a rarity to the public for a mere fraction of his normal fees. It shows he's something other than a cold-hearted businessman...that he really cares about people."

"So what's wrong with being a cold-hearted business-man?" Aahz snorted. "How about the other guy? Every-body thinks he's a villain, and he's crying all the way to the bank. He retired on the profit from that one sale alone."

"Unless Nanny misled me horribly when she taught me my num-bers," Chumley interrupted, "I figure your current bankroll could eat that fellow's profit and still have room for lunch. Any reason you're so big on squirreling away so much gold, Aahz? Are you planning on retiring?"

"No, I'm not planning on retiring," my partner snapped. "And you're missing the point completely. Money isn't the object."

"It isn't?"

I think everybody grabbed that line at the same time...even Pepe, who hadn't known Aahz all that long.

"Of course not. You can always get more gold. What can't be replaced is time. We all know Skeeve here has a long way to go in the magic department. What the rest of you keep forgetting is how short a life span he has to play with...maybe a hundred years if he's lucky. All I'm trying to do is get him the maximum learning time possible...and that means keeping him from using up most of his time on nickel-and-dime adventures. Let the small-time operators do those. My partner shouldn't have to budge away from his studies unless the assignment is something *really* spectacular. Something that will advance his reputation and his career."

There was a long silence while everybody digested that one, espe-cially me. Since Aahz had accepted me as a full partner instead of an apprentice, I tended to forget his role as my teacher and career man-ager. Thinking back now, I could see he had never really given up the work, just gotten sneakier. I wouldn't have believed that was possible.

"How about this particular nickel-and-dime adventure?" Tananda said, breaking the silence. "You know, pulling your tail out of a scrape? Isn't this a little low-brow for the kind of legend you're trying to build?"

The sarcasm in her voice was unmistakable, but it didn't phase Aahz in the least.

"If you'll ask around, you'll find out that I didn't want him along on this jaunt at all. In fact, I knocked him cold trying to keep him out. A top-flight magician shouldn't have to stoop to bill col-lecting, especially when the risk is disproportionately high."

"Well, it all sounds a little cold-blooded for my taste, Aahz," Chumley put in. "If you extend your logic, our young friend here is only going to work when the danger is astronomically high, and conversely if the advancement to his career is enough, no risk is too great. That sounds to me like a sure-fire way to lose a partner *and a* friend. Like the Geek says, if you keep bucking the odds, sooner or later they're going to catch up with you."

My partner spun to confront the troll nose-to-nose.

"Of course it's going to be dangerous," he snarled. "The magic profession isn't for the faint of heart, and to hit the top he's going to have to be hair-triggered and mean. There's no avoiding that, but I can try to be sure he's ready for it. Why do you think I've been so dead-set against him having bodyguards? If he starts relying on other people to watch out for him, he's going to lose the edge himself. *That's* when he's in danger of walking into a swinging door."

That brought Guido into the fray.

"Now let me see if I've got this right," my bodyguard said. "You don't want me and my cousin Nunzio around so that the Boss here can handle all the trouble himself? That's crazy talk, know what I mean? Now listen to me, 'cause this time I know what I'm sayin'. The higher someone gets on the ladder, the more folks come huntin' for his head. Even if they don't do nothin' they got people gunning for them, 'cause they got power and respect and there's always somebody who thinks they can steal it. Now I've seen some of the Big Guys who try to act just like you're sayin'…they're so scared all the time they don't trust nothin' or nobody. The only one they can count on is themselves, and everybody else is suspect. That includes total strangers, their own bodyguards, their friends, *and* their partners. Think about *that* for a minute."

He leaned back and surveyed the room, addressing his next comments to everyone.

"People like that don't last long. They don't trust nobody, so they got nobody. Ya can't do everything alone, and sooner or later they're lookin' the wrong way or asleep when they should be watchin' and it's all over. Now I've done a lot of jobs as a bodyguard, and they were just jobs, know what I mean? The Boss here is different, and I'm not just sayin' that. He's the best man I've met in my whole life because he likes people and ain't afraid to show it. More important, he ain't afraid to risk his neck to help somebody even if it *isn't* in his best interest. I work double hard for him because I don't want to see anything happen to him...and if that means comin' along on weird trips like this, then that's the way it is. Anybody that wants to hurt him is gonna have to come through me...and that includes fightin' any of you if you want to try to turn him into somethin' he isn't and doesn't want to be."

Massha broke in with a loud clapping of her hands.

"Bravo, Guido," she said. "I think your problem, Green and Scaly, is that your idea of success is out of step with everyone else's. We all want to see good things happen for Skeeve, here, but we also like him just the way he is. We've got enough faith in his good sense to back him in whatever move he makes in his development...without trying to frog-march or trick him up a specific path."

Aahz not only gave ground before this onslaught of protest, he seemed to shrink in a little on himself.

"I like him too," he mumbled. "I've known him longer than any of you, remember? He's doing fine, but he could be so much more. How can he choose a path if he can't see it? All I'm trying to do is set him up to be bigger than I...than *we* could ever think of being ourselves. What's wrong with that?"

Despite my irritation at having my life discussed as if I weren't in the room, I was quite touched, by my friends' loyal defense of me, and most of all by Aahz.

"You know, partner," I said softly, "for a minute there, you sounded just like my father. He wanted me to be the best...or more specifically, to be better than he was. My mom always tried to tell me that it was because he loved me, but at that time it just sounded like he was always being critical. Maybe she was right...I'm more inclined to believe it today than I was then, but then again, I'm older now. If nothing else, I've had to try to tell people I love them when the words just won't come...and gotten upset with myself when they couldn't see it when I tried to show them.

"Aahz, I appreciate your concern and I want your guidance. You're right, there are paths and options I can't even comprehend yet. But I also have to choose my own way. I want to be better eventually than I am today, but not necessarily the best. I think Guido's right, there's a big price tag attached to being at the top, and I'd want to think long and hard if I wanted to pay it...even if I was con-vinced I could, which I'm not. I *do* know that if it means giving up the trust

I have in you and everybody else in this room, I'll settle for being a nickel-and-dime operator. *That* price I'll never pay willingly."

Silence started to descend again as each of us re-treated into his or her own thoughts, then the werewolf bounded into the middle of the assemblage.

"But what is this, eh?" he demanded. "Surely this cannot be ze great team of Aahz and Skeeve, ze ones who can laugh at any dan-gair?"

"You know, Pepe," Aahz said warningly, "you've got a great future as a stuffed head."

"My head?" The werewolf blinked. "But she is not…oohh. I see now. You make ze joke, eh? Good. Zat is more like it."

"…and as far as laughing at danger goes," I joined in, determined to hold up my end of the legend, "the only danger I see here is dying of boredom. Where is Vilhelm anyway?"

"I know you and Aahz are fond of each other, Skeeve," Chumley yawned, "but you've *got* to spend more time with other people. You're starting to sound like him. Maybe you can tag along the next time I have an

assignment."

"Over my dead body," my partner said. "Besides, what could he learn from a troll that I couldn't teach him myself?"

"I could teach him not to catch birds for Deveels for ten gold pieces," the troll grinned, winking at his sister. "That seems to be a part of his education you've neglected."

"Izzat so!" my partner bristled. "You're going to teach him about price setting? How about the time you set your own sister up to steal an elephant without bothering to check…"

And they were off again. As I listened, I found myself reflecting on the fact that while it was nice to know the depths of my friends' feelings about me, it was far more comfortable when they managed to conceal it under a cloak of banter. For the most part, open sincerity is harder to take than friendly laughter.

XVI.

"Don't be fooled by appearances."
MALLOY

THINGS WERE PRETTY much back to normal by the time Vilhelm returned with our disguises…which was a good thing as the process of masking-up proved to be a test of everybody's sense of humor.

Until I had hooked up with Aahz, I had never had occasion to pretend I was anyone but myself. As such, I had no way of knowing how long it took to don a physical disguise without resorting to magic. By the time we were done, I had a new respect for the skills I had learned, not to mention a real longing for a dimension…any dimension with a strong force line to work with.

Tananda was a major help, her experiences with the assassin's guild came into play and she took the lead in trying to coach us into our new roles.

"Guido, straighten up!" she commanded, exasperation creeping into her voice. "You walk like a gangster."

"I am a gangster!" my bodyguard snarled back. "Besides, what's wrong with the way I walk? It got us to the jail, didn't it?"

"Half the town wasn't looking for you then," Tananda argued. "Besides, then you could pick your own route. We don't know where the opposition's holed up. We're going to have to walk through crowds on this hunt, and that walk just doesn't make it. Ninety percent of costuming is learning to move like the character you're trying to portray. Right now you move like you're looking for a fight."

"Try walking like Don Bruce," I suggested. "He's a gangster, too."

That earned me a black look, but my bodyguard tried to follow my instructions, rising up on the balls of his feet and mincing along.

"Better," Tananda said, leaving Guido prancing up and down the room with a scowl on his face.

"How are we doing?"

"Lousy," she confided in me. "This is taking a lot longer than it should. I wish there were more mirrors in this place…heck, any mirrors would be nice."

It hadn't been until we started gearing up that we realized the
Dispatcher had no mirrors at all. He claimed they weren't popular
or necessary among vampires. This left us with the unenviable job
of checking each others' make-up and costumes, a chore which
would have been Homeric even if less sensitive egos were involved.

"How're my teeth?" Massha demanded, sticking her head in
front of me and opening her mouth.

It was like staring into the depths of an underground cave.

"Umm...the left side is okay, but you're still missing a few on
the right. Hang on a second and I'll give you a hand."

Teeth were turning out to be a special problem. We had hoped
to find some of the rubber fangs so prevalent in the Bazaar novelty
stores to aid in our disguises. Unfortunately, none of the shops in
Blut had them. The closest thing they had in stock, according to
Vilhelm, were rubber sets of human teeth designed to fit over fangs.
The vampire assured us that locally they were considered quite

frightening. Faced by this unforeseen shortage, we were resorting to using tooth-black to blacken all our teeth except the canines
for a close approximation of the vampires we were trying to imitate. When we tried it out, it wasn't a bad effect, but the actual application was causing countless problems. When one tried to apply the
stuff on oneself without a mirror, it was difficult to get the right
teeth, and if one called on one's friends for assistance, one rapidly
found that said friend was soon possessed by an overpowering impulse to paint one's tongue black instead of the teeth.

"I don't like this cloak," Guido announced, grabbing my arm.
"I want to wear my trench coat."

"Vampires don't wear trench coats," I said firmly. "Besides, the
cloak really looks great on you. Makes you look...I don't know,
debonair but menacing."

"Yeah?" he retorted skeptically, craning his neck to try to see
himself.

"You think you've got problems?" Massha burst in. "Look at
what I'm supposed to wear! I'll trade your cloak for this rig any day."

As you might have noticed, the team was having more than a
little difficulty adapting to their disguises. Massha in particular was
rebelling against her costume.

After having been floated over our escape like a balloon over a
parade, we feared that she would be one of the most immediately

recognizable of our group. As such, we not only dyed her garish orange hair, we insisted that her new costume cover as much of her as possible. To this end, Vilhelm had found a dress he called a "moo-moo," a name which did nothing toward endearing the garment to my apprentice.

"I mean, *really*, High Roller," she said, backing me toward a corner. "Isn't it bad enough that half the town's seen me as a blimp? Tell me I don't have to be a *cow* now."

"Honest, Massha," Vilhelm put in. "The style is fairly popular here in Blut. A lot of the ladies wear it who are...that is, area bit..."

"Fat!?"

She loomed over the little vampire.

"Is that the word you're groping for, Short and About To Become Extinct?"

"Let's face it, dear," Tananda said, coming to the rescue. "You *are* carrying a little extra weight there. Believe me, if there's one time you can't kid yourself about your body, it's when you're donning costumes. If any-thing, that outfit makes you look a little slimmer."

"Don't try to kid a kidder, sweetie," Massha sighed. "But you're right about the costuming thing. This thing is *so drab*, though. First I'm a blimp, and now I'm an army tent."

"Now *that* I'll agree with," Tananda nodded. "Trust a man to find a drab mu-mu. Tell you what. There's a scarf I was going to use for a belt, but maybe you could wear it around your neck."

I was afraid that last crack would touch off another explosion, but Massha took it as a helpful suggestion and the two of them went off in search of other possible adornments.

"Got a minute, partner?"

From the tone of Aahz's voice, I knew the moment I had been dreading had arrived.

Chumley didn't have to worry about a disguise at all, as trolls were not uncommon in this dimension. Tananda also insisted that she looked enough like a vampire to pass with only minimal modifications. I hadn't seen any vam-pires with green hair, but she claimed that she had, so, as always, I yielded to her greater experience in these matters. I was also on the "minimal disguise" list, every-one agreeing that no one in Blut had gotten enough of a look at me to fix the image in their mind. While I wasn't wild about being so unmemorable, I went along with it...especially when I saw what Guido and Massha were going through. The problems with those two notables have already been mentioned: troublesome, but not insurmountable. Then there was Aahz…

"Is there something wrong?" I asked innocently.

"You bet your dragon there's something wrong!" my partner snarled. "And don't try to play innocent with me! It didn't work when you were my apprentice, and it sure isn't going to work now."

Aahz's disguise had presented us with some knotty problems. Not only was he the most wanted member of our party, he was also easily the most distinctive. After the trial and his time in jail, it was doubtful that there was a single citizen of Blut who wouldn't recognize him on sight. I mean, there just aren't that many scaly green demons wandering around any dimension…except pos-sibly his home dimension of Perv. It was therefore decided…almost unanimously…that not only would we change my partner's color with make-up, but that it would also be necessary to change his sex.

"Does this, perchance, have something to do with your dis-guise?" I inquired, trying to keep a straight face.

"Yes, it has something to do with my disguise," he mimicked, "and, so help me, partner or no, if you let that smile get away, I'll punch your lights out. Understand?"

With a great effort I sucked my cheeks in and bit my lower lip.

"Seriously, though," he said, almost pleading, "a joke's a joke, but you don't really expect me to go out in public looking like *this,* do you?"

In addition to the aforementioned make-up, Aahz's disguise re-quired a dress and a wig. Because of the size of his head (a problem Vilhelm had wisely down-played as much as possible) the selection of wigs available had been understandably small. In fact, the only avail-able in his size was a number called "Lady Go-GoDiva," which in-volved a high blonde beehive style offset by a long ponytail that hung down to his knees. Actually, the ponytail turned out to be a blessing in disguise, as the dark blue dress Vilhelm had selected for my partner turned out to have an exceptionally low neckline, and the hair draped over his shoulder helped hide the problem we had had finding ample or suitable material to stuff his bosom with. "As my wise old mentor once told me when I was faced with a similar dilemma," I said sagely, "what does it matter what people think of you? They aren't supposed to know it's you, anyway. That's the whole idea of a disguise."

"But this get-up is humiliating!"

"My words precisely when someone else I could name deemed it necessary for *me* to dress up as a girl, remember?"

"You're enjoying this, aren't you?" Aahz glowered, peering at me suspiciously.

"Well, there are a couple of other options," I admitted.

"That's more like it!" he grinned, reaching for his wig.

"You could stay behind…"

His hand stopped just short of its mission.

"…or we could forget the whole thing and pay the fine ourselves."

The hand retreated as my partner's shoulders sagged in defeat. I felt no joy at the victory. If anything, I had been half hoping he would be embarrassed enough to take me up on my suggestion of abandoning the project. I should have known better. When there's money involved, it takes more than embarrassment to throw Aahz off the scent…whether the embarrassment is his own or someone else's.

"All right, everybody," I called, hiding my disappointment. "Are we ready to go?"

"Remember your sunglasses!" Tananda added.

That was the final touch to our disguises. To hide our non-red eyes, each of us donned a pair of sunglasses. Surveying the final result, I had to admit that aside from Tananda and Chumley, we didn't look like us. Exactly what we *did* look like I wouldn't venture to say, but we sure didn't look like us!

"Okay," Aahz chimed in, his discomfort apparently behind him. "Does everyone have their marching orders? Vilhelm? Are you sure you can track us on that thing?"

"No problem," the little vampire nodded. "When things get slow around here I use this rig to do a little window peeking right here in town. Covering the streets is even easier.

"Remember," I told him, "watch for our signal. When we catch up with this Vic character, we're going to want you to get some responsible local witnesses there chop-chop."

"Well now," Aahz grinned evilly, "you don't have to be *too* quick about it. I wouldn't mind having a little time alone with him before we turn him over to the authorities."

My heart sank a little. Aahz sounded determined to exact a bit of vengeance out of this hunt, and I wasn't at all sure he would restrict himself to Vic when it came time to express his ire.

I think Tananda noticed my concern.

"Ease up a little, Aahz," she said casually. "I don't mind helping you out of a tight spot, but count me out when it comes to excessive force for the sake of vengeance. It lacks class."

"Since when did you worry about excessive violence?" Aahz growled, then shrugged his acceptance. "Okay. But maybe we'll get lucky. Maybe he'll resist arrest."

I was still worried, but realized that that was about the most restraint I would get out of my partner.

"Now that that's settled," I said, producing Luanna's scarf, "Pepe, take a whiff of this."

"Enchanting," he smiled, nuzzling the piece of cloth. "A young lady, no? Eef ze body is as good as ze aroma, I will follow her to the end of ze world whether you accompany me or not."

I resisted an impulse to wrap the scarf around his neck and pull.

"All right, everybody," I said, retrieving the scarf and tucking it back into my tunic in what I hoped was a casual manner. "Let's go catch us a renegade vampire."

XVII.

"The trail's got to be 'round here somewhere!"
D. BOONE

IT WAS ONLY a few hours short of sunset as we set out on our quest, a nagging reminder of exactly how long our efforts at physical disguise had taken. We had agreed to avoid following Pepe as a group so as not to attract attention. Instead, we moved singly or in groups of two, using both sides of the street and deliberately walking at different paces. The faster walkers averaged their progress with the slower by occasionally stopping to look into shop windows, thereby keeping our group together without actually appearing to. Tananda pointed out that not only would this procedure lessen our chances of being noticed, but also that it would maximize our chances for at least some of the group's escape if one of us should be discovered...a truly comforting thought.

Even though Luanna had claimed to have been watching for us at the Dispatcher's, it had been so long ago I fully expected her scent would have long since dissipated or at least been masked by the passage of numerous others. As such, I was moderately surprised when the werewolf signaled almost immediately that he had found the trail and headed off with a determined air. Either her scent was stronger than I had thought, or I had grossly underestimated Pepe's tracking ability.

The trail wound up and down the cobblestoned streets, and we followed as quickly as we could without abandoning our pretense of being casual strollers who did not know each other. For a while, our group made up the majority of the beings visible, causing me to doubt the effectiveness of our ruse, but soon the vampires began to emerge to indulge their taste for the nightlife and we became much less obvious.

I was paired up with Chumley, but the troll was strangely quiet as we made our way along. At first I thought he was simply concentrating on keeping the werewolf in sight, but as time wore on, I found the silence somehow unnerving. I had always respected Chumley as being one of the saner, leveler heads among our motley assemblage, and I was starting to have an uneasy impression that he was not wholeheartedly behind this venture.

"Is there something bothering you, Chumley?" I asked at last.

"Hmmm? Oh. Not really, Skeeve. I was just thinking."

"About what?"

The troll let out a small sigh.

"I was just contemplating our adversary, this Vic fellow. You know, from what's been said, he's quite resourceful in a devious sort of way."

That took me a little aback. So far I had considered our vampire foe to be everything from an annoyance to a nemesis. The idea of studying his methods had never entered my mind.

"What leads you to that conclusion?"

The troll pursed his lips as he organized his thoughts.

"Consider what he's accomplished so far. The entire time we've known of him, he's been on the run...first from the Deveels, and then from Aahz, who's no slouch at hunting people once he sets his mind to it. Now, assuming for the moment that Vic is actually the brains of the group, he was quick enough to take advantage of being left alone in your waiting room to escape out the back door. He couldn't have planned that in advance, even knowing about the door. He probably had some other plan in mind, and formulated this new course of action on the spot."

We paused for a moment to let a small group of vampires cross the intersection in front of us.

"Now, that would have sufficed for an escape in most instances, but they happened to pick an exit route that left you and Aahz responsible, which set your partner on their trail," Chumley continued. "With nothing to go on but your reputations, Vic not only correctly deduced that he would be followed, but he also managed to spot Aahz's weakness and exploit it to frame him and make it stick...again, not the easiest task, particularly realizing it involved convincing and coaching his two accomplices in their roles."

All of this was doing nothing for my peace of mind. I was having enough difficulty forcing myself to believe that we were really hunting a vampire, the sort of creature I normally avoid at all costs, without having to deal with the possibility that he was shrewd and resourceful as well. Still, I had learned that ignoring unpleasant elements of a caper was perhaps the worst way to prepare for them.

"Keep going," I urged.

"Well," the troll sighed, "when you stumbled on his hiding place at the Woof Writers, he didn't panic. He waited to hear as much of your plans as possible, all the while taking advantage of the opportunity to assess you first-hand, then timed his escape so as to catch you all flat-footed."

I digested this distasteful addition to the rapidly growing data file. "Do you really think he was sizing me up?" "There's no doubt in my mind. Not only was he gauging your skills and determination, he was successful enough at second-guessing you, based on the results of his studies, to be waiting to sound the alarm when you busted Aahz out of jail...a particularly bold move when one realizes that he was running the risk of being recognized, which would have blown his frame-up of your partner."

"Bold or desperate," I said thoughtfully. "That's probably why he waited until we had actually sprung Aahz and were on the way down before he blew the whistle. If we had gotten away unscathed, then the frame would be useless, so at that point he really wasn't risking anything."

"Have it your way," the troll shrugged. "The final analysis remains that we have one tough nut to crack. One can only wonder what he will do when we catch up with him this time."

"If he's performing up to par, it could be rough on us." Chumley shot me a sidelong glance.

"Actually, I was thinking it could be rough on your lady fair...if he has managed to observe the feelings you have for her."

I started to protest, then the impact of his theory hit me and my embarrassment gave way to concern.

"Is it really that apparent? Do you think he could spot it? If so, he might already have done something to Luanna for having contacted us."

"It stands out all over you to anyone who knows you," Chumley said, shaking his head. "As for someone watching you for the first time...I just don't know. He'd be more likely to deduce it from the information you had...such as his name. That kind of data had to come from somewhere, though there's an outside chance that with your current reputation he'll assume that you gleaned it by some magical source."

I barely heard him. My mind was focused on the possibility that Luanna might be-hurt, and that I might indirectly have been the cause. A black well of guilt was rising up to swallow me, when I felt a hand on my shoulder.

"Don't tune out now, Skeeve," Chumley was saying, shaking me slightly. "First of all, we're going to need you shortly. Secondly, even if Vic's figured out that you're in love with her, I don't think he'll have hurt her. If any-thing, he'll save her for a trump card to use against us."

I drew a deep ragged breath.

"...and he'll be just the bastard to do it, too," I said. "I don't know what I'll be able to do, for us or for her, but I'll be ready to try. Thanks, Chumley."

The troll was studying me closely.

"Actually, I wasn't thinking that he was such a blighter," he said. "More like a clever, resourceful person who's gotten in over his head and is trying his best to ad-lib his way out. Frankly, Skeeve old boy, in many ways he reminds me of you. You might think about that when attempting to appraise his likely courses of action and how to counter them."

I tried again to weigh what he was saying, but all I could think about was what the consequences of this hunt could mean to Luanna. It was difficult enough for me to accept that we would have to force Luanna and her cohorts to answer to the authorities for their indiscretions, but the thought of placing her in physical danger was unbearable.

I looked around for Aahz, fully intending to put an end to this hunt once and for all. To my surprise, the rest of the group was assembled on the corner ahead, and my partner was beckoning us to join them.

"What's going one?" I asked, almost to myself.

"Just off-hand," Chumley replied, "I'd say we've reached our destination."

A cold wave of fear washed over me, and I hurried to the rendezvous with Chumley close behind.

"We're in luck," Aahz announced as I arrived. "Guido here says he saw Vic entering the building just as we got here. It's my guess they're all inside right now."

"Aahz, I—I want us to quit right now," I blurted, painfully aware of how weak it sounded.

"Oh?" my partner said, cocking an eyebrow at me. "Any particular reason?"

I licked my lips, feeling the eyes of the whole group on me.

"Only one. I'm in love with one of the fugitives...the girl."

"Yeah. Now tell me something I didn't know," Aahz smirked, winking at me.

"You knew?"

"All of us knew. In fact, we were just discussing it. Remember, we all know you...and me probably best of all. It's already been pretty much decided to let your love-light go. Think of it as a present from us to you. The other two are ours."

Five minutes ago, that would have made me deliriously happy. Now, it only seemed to complicate things.

"But Chumley was just saying that there's a chance they might hurt her if they find out she helped us," I explained desperately. "Can't we just let them all go?"

"Not a chance, partner," Aahz said firmly. "In addition to our original reasons, you've just mentioned the new one. Your girlfriend could be in trouble, and the only way to be sure she's safe is to remove her partners...Fast."

"Believe him, Skeeve," Tananda urged. "It may not be nice, but it's the best way."

"Really, Boss," Guido said quietly. "Unless we finish this thing here and now, you're never goin' to know if she's safe, know what I mean?"

That almost made sense, but I was still worried. "I don't know, Aahz..."

"Well I do," my partner snapped. "And the longer we stand down here, the more chance there is that they'll either get away or set up a trap. If you're uncertain, stay down here...in fact, that's not a bad idea. Massha, you stay down here with him in case they try to bolt out this way. While you're waiting, watch for the witnesses that Vilhelm's supposed to be sending along. Tananda, you and Chumley and Guido come along with me. This is a job for experienced hard-cases. Pepe, we appreciate your help, but this isn't really your fight."

"But of course." The werewolf grinned. "Besides, I am a lo-var, not a figh-tar. I will wait here to see the finale, eh?"

"But Aahz..."

"Really, partner, you'll be more help down here. This isn't your kind of fight, and we need someone to deal with the witnesses. You're good at that kind of thing."

"I was going to ask if you had given the signal to Vilhelm."

"Signal?" Aahz blinked. "How's this for a signal?!" With that, he tore off his wig and threw it on the ground, followed closely by his dress.

"Think he'll get the message? Besides, no way am I going to try to fight in that get-up."

"Now you're talkin'!" Guido crowed.

In a flash he had discarded his cloak and was pulling on his now-familiar trench coat.

"Where did that come from?" I demanded.

"Had it with me all the time," the bodyguard said smugly. "It would have been like leaving an old friend behind."

"Well, if you and your old friend are ready," Tananda murmured, "we'd better get started."

"Itching for action?" Aahz grinned.

"No. More like eager to get off the street," she said. "Since you boys have shown your true colors, we're starting to draw a crowd."

Sure enough, the vampires on the street had ceased whatever they had been doing before and were gathering in knots, whispering together and pointing at our group.

"Umm...we'd better finish this fast," Aahz said, shooting a nervous glance around. "All right, gang. Let's go for the gusto!"

"Go for the what?" I asked, but they were already on their way into the building.

I noticed they were all moving faster than normal. I also noticed that Massha, Pepe, and I were the only ones

left on the street...and now the crowd was pointing at us!

XVIII.

"I didn't come all this way to sit out the fight!"
R. Balboa

WHAT'S GOING ON?"

I looked around to find that one of the vampires had detached himself from his group of friends and was addressing me directly.

"Beats me," Massha interceded. "A bunch of offworlder types just took off into that building with blood in their eyes. I'm waiting to see what happens next."

"Far out," the vampire breathed, peering toward the structure. "I haven't seen that many off-worlders in one place except in the flickers. Wasn't one of them that escaped murderer, Aahz?"

I really didn't want this character to join our little group. While our disguises seemed to be holding up under casual inspection, I was pretty sure that prolonged close scrutiny would reveal not only the non-local nature of Massha and myself, but also the fact that we were trying to hide it.

"You may be right," I said, playing a hunch. "If so, it's a good thing you happened along. We're going to need all the help we can get."

"Help? Help for what?"

"Why to catch the murderer, of course. We can't let him get away again. I figure it's our duty to stop him ourselves or at least slow him up until the authorities arrive.

"We? You mean the three of you? You're going to try to stop a murderer all by yourselves?"

"Four of us now that you're here."

The vampire started backing away.

"Ummm…actually I've got to get back to my friends. We're on our way to a party. Sorry I can't help, but I'll spread the word that you're looking for volunteers, okay?"

"Hey, thanks," I called as if I believed him. "We'll be right here."

By the time I had finished speaking, he had disappeared into the crowd. Mission accomplished.

"Nicely done, my friend," Pepe murmured. "He does not, how you say, want to get involved, no?"

"That's right," I said, my eyes on the building again. "And to tell you the truth, I'm not too wild about the idea either. What do you think, Massha? It's awfully quiet in there."

"I'll say," my apprentice agreed. "I'm just trying to figure out if that's a good or a bad sign. Another ten minutes and I'm heading in there to check it out myself."

I nodded my consent, even though I doubted she saw it. We both had our eyes glued to the building, memorizing its every detail.

It was a four-story structure...or it would be if it weren't for the curved peak that jutted out from the roof fully half-again as high as the main building. It looked as if the builder had suddenly added the adornment in a last-minute attempt to have his work stand as tall or taller than its neighbors. From the number of windows in the main structure, I guessed it was an apartment building or a hotel or something. In short, it looked like it had a lot of little rooms. I found myself wondering exactly how our strike force was supposed to locate their target without kicking in every door in the place...a possibility I wouldn't put past Aahz.

I was about to express this fear to Massha when a loud crash sounded from within.

"What was that?" I demanded of no one in particular. "Sounded like a loud crash," my apprentice supplied helpfully.

I forced myself to remember that no one out here knew any more about what was going on inside than I did.

After the crash, everything was quiet once more. I tried to tell myself that the noise might have nothing at all to do with the strike force, but I didn't believe it for a minute. The crowd was talking excitedly to each other and straining to see the various windows. They seemed quite confident that something else would happen soon, much more than I, but then again, maybe as city dwellers they were more accustomed to such vigils than I.

Suddenly, Tananda appeared in the doorway.

"Did they come out this way?" she called.

"No one's been in or out since you went in," I responded.

She swore and started to re-enter the building. "What happened?" I shouted desperately.

"We nailed one of them, but Vic got away. He's loose in the building somewhere, and he's got the girl with him."

With that, she disappeared before I could make any further inquiries.

Terrific.

"Exciting, eh?" Pepe said. "I tell you, I could watch such a chase for hours."

"Well, I can't," I snapped. "I've had it with sitting on the sidelines. Massha? I'm going in there. Want to come?"

"I dunno, Hot Stuff. I'd like to, but somebody should be here to plug this escape route."

"Fine. You wait here, and I'll..."

I turned to enter the building and bumped headlong into Vilhelm.

"What are you doing here?" I demanded, not really caring.

The Dispatcher shook his head slightly to clear it. Being smaller, he had gotten the worse of our collision.

"I'm here with the witnesses, remember? I was sup-posed to bring them."

"You were supposed to *send* them. Oh well, where are they?"

"Right here," he said, gesturing to a sullen group of vampires standing behind him. "This is Kirby, and Paul, and Richard, and Adele, and Scott...some of the most respected citizens in town. Convince them and you're home free."

Looking at the group, I suddenly realized how Aahz had ended up on death row. If the jury had been anything like these specimens, they would have hung their own mothers for jaywalking. While I didn't relish the thought of trying to convince them of anything, I found myself being very glad I didn't have to deal with them on a regular basis.

"Okay. So we're here," the one identified as Kirby growled. "Just what is it we're supposed to be witnessing? If this is one of your cockamamie deals, Vilhelm..."

I interrupted simply by taking my sunglasses off and opening my eyes wide, displaying their whites. The bad reputation of humans in this dimension was sufficient to capture their undivided attention.

"Perhaps you recall a certain murder trial that took place not too long ago?" I said, trying to work the tooth-black off with my tongue. "Well, the convicted murderer who escaped is my partner, and right now he's inside that building. He and a few of our friends are about to show you one surprisingly lively corpse...specifically the fellow that my partner is supposed to have killed. I trust that will be sufficient to convince you of his innocence?"

While the vampires were taken aback by my presence in their midst, they recovered quickly. Like I said, they were real hard cases and didn't stay impressed very long.

"So how much time is this going to take?" Kirby said impatiently. "I'm giving up my sleep for this, and I don't get much of it."

That was a good question, so, not having an answer, I stalled.

"You sleep nights? I thought..."

"I'm a day owl," the vampire waved. "It's easier to get my work done when the phone isn't ringing every five minutes...which usually means waiting until everyone else is asleep. But we're getting off the subject. The bottom line is that my time is valuable, and the same holds true for my colleagues. If you think we're going to just stand around here until..."

There was a sudden outcry from the crowd, and we all looked to find them talking excitedly and pointing up at the roof.

A figure had emerged, fighting to pick his way across the steeply sloped surface while dragging a struggling girl by one arm.

Vic!

This was the first time I had gotten a clear look at my foe, and I was moderately surprised. He was younger than I had expected, barely older than myself, and instead of a menacing cloak, he was sporting a white turtleneck and sunglasses. It suddenly occurred to me that if sunglasses enabled me to pass for a vampire, that they would also let a vampire pass undetected among humans.

The vampire suddenly stopped as his path was barred by Tananda, who appeared as if by magic over the edge of the roof. He turned to retrace his steps, only to find that the trio of Aahz, Guido, and Chumley had emerged behind him, cutting off his retreat.

"I believe, gentlemen and lady, that up there is the elusive body that started this whole thing," I heard myself saying. "If you can spare a few more moments, I think *my* colleagues will have him in custody so that you might interrogate him at your leisure."

"Don't be too sure of that, High Roller," Massha cautioned. "Look!"

His chosen routes of escape cut off, Vic was now scrabbling up the roof peak itself, Luanna hanging in his grip. While I had to admire his strength, I was at a loss to understand what he was trying to accomplish with the maneuver. It was obvious that he had been exposed, so why didn't he just give it up?

The answer became apparent in the next few moments. Reaching the apex of the roof, the vampire underwent a chilling metamorphosis. Before the strike force could reach him, he hunched forward and huge batwings began to grow and spread from his back. His plans gone awry, he was getting ready to escape.

In immediate response to his efforts, Tananda and Guido both produced projectile weapons and shouted something to him. Though the distance was too great to make out the words clearly, it was obvious to me that they were threatening to shoot him down if he tried to take to the air.

"We may have a murder case yet," Kirby murmured, squinting to watch the rooftop drama unfold.

"Murder?" I exclaimed, turning on him. "How can you call it murder if they're only trying to keep from escaping *your* justice?"

"That wasn't what I meant," the vampire said, never taking his eyes from the action. "Check it out."

I looked...and my heart stood still.

Aahz had been trying to ease up the roof peak closer to Vic and his hostage. Vic must have seen him, because he was now holding Luanna out over the drop as he pointed an angry finger at my partner. The threat was unmistakable.

"You know, eet is people like zat who give ze vampires a bad name, eh?" Pepe said, nudging me.

I ignored him, lost in my own anxiety and frustration at the stalemated situation.

A noticeably harder jab from Massha broke my reverie, however.

"Hey, Hot Stuff. Do you see what I see?"

I tore my gaze away from the confrontation and shot a glance her way.

She was standing motionless, her brow furrowed with concentration and her eyes closed.

It took me a few moments to realize what she was doing, then I followed suit, scarcely
daring to hope.

There it was! A force line! A big, strong, beautiful, glorious force line.

I had gotten so used to not having any magical energy at my disposal in this dimension that I hadn't even bothered to check!

I opened myself to the energy, relished it for a fleet moment, then rechanneled it.

"Excuse me," I said with a smile, handing my sunglasses to Kirby. "It's about time I took a hand in this directly."

With that, I reached out with my mind, pushed off against the ground, and soared upward, setting a course for the cornered vampire on the roof.

XIX.

"All right, pilgrim.
This is between you and me!"
A. HAMILTON

I HAD HOPED to make my approach unobserved, but as I flew upward, the crowd below let out a roar that drew the attention of the combatants on the roof. Terrific! When I wanted unobtrusive, I got notoriety.

Reaching a height level with that of the vampire, I hovered at a discreet distance.

"Put away the nasties," I called to Tananda and Guido. "He's not getting away by air."

They looked a bit rebellious, but followed the order.

"What's with the Peter Pan bit, partner?" Aahz shouted. "Are you feeling your Cheerioats, or did you finally find a force line?"

"Both." I waved back, then turned my attention to Vic.

Though his eyes were obscured by his sunglasses, I could feel his hateful glare burning into me to the bone.

"Why don't you just call it quits?" I said in what I hoped was a calm, soothing tone. "It's over. We've got you outflanked."

For a moment he seemed to waiver with indecision.

Then, without warning, he threw Luanna at Aahz. "Why can't you all just leave me alone!" he screamed, and dove off the roof.

Aahz somehow managed to snag the girl's hurtling form, though in the process he lost his balance and tumbled backward down the roof peak, cushioning the impact with his own body.

I hesitated, torn between the impulse to check on Luanna's welfare and the desire to pursue Vic.

"Go get him!" my partner called. "We're fine!"

That was all the encouragement I needed. Wheeling to my right, I plunged after the fleeing vampire.

What followed was one of the more interesting experiences of my limited magical career. As I mentioned before, my form of flying magically isn't really flying…it's controlled levitation of one-self. This made enthusiastic pursuit a real challenge to my abilities. To counterbalance the problem, however, Vic couldn't really fly either...at least he never seemed to flap his wings. Instead, he appeared content to soar and bank and catch an occasional updraft. This forced him to continually circle and double back through roughly the same area time and time again. This suited me fine, as I didn't want to wander too far away from my energizing force line now that I had found it. The idea of running out of power while suspended fifty feet in the air did not appeal to me at all.

Anyway, our aerial duel rapidly became a curious matching of styles with Vic's swooping and circling in his efforts to escape and my vertical and horizontal maneuverings to try to intercept him. Needless to say, the conflict was not resolved quickly. As soon as I would time a move that came close enough to an interception to justify attempting it again, Vic would realize his danger and alter his pattern, leaving me to try to puzzle out his new course.

The crowd loved it.

They whooped and hollered, their words of encouragement alternately loud and faint as we changed altitude.

It was impossible to tell which of us they were cheering for, though for a while I thought it was me, considering the approval they had expressed when I first took off to join the battle. Then I noticed that the crowd was considerably larger than it had been when I entered the fray, and I realized that many of them had not been around to witness the beginning of the conflict. To them, it probably appeared that a monster from another dimension was chasing one of their fellow beings through the sky.

That thought was disquieting enough that I spared some of my attention to scan the surrounding rooftops on the off-chance that a local sniper might be preparing to help his fellow countryman. It turned out to be the wisest decision I had made.

As I was looking over my shoulder, I plowed full force into Vic, who had doubled back on his own path. The feint would have probably worked if I had seen it, but as it was we collided at maximum speed, the impact momentarily stunning us both. I managed to grab a double handful of the vampire's turtleneck as we fell about ten feet before I adjusted my levitation strength to support us both.

"What's the matter with you!" I demanded, trying to shake him, which succeeded only in moving us both back and forth in the air. "Running away won't help."

Then I realized he was crying.

Somehow, this struck me as immensely unfair. I mean, how are you supposed to stay mad at a villain that cries? Okay. So I'm a soft tough. But the crying really did make a difference.

"I can't fight you all!" he sobbed, tears streaming down his cheeks. "Maybe if I knew some magic I could take one of you with me…but at least you're going to have to work for your kill!"

With that he tore loose from my grasp and swooped away.

His words stunned me so much I almost let him escape. Fortunately, I had the presence of mind to call out to him.

"Hey, dummy! Nobody's trying to kill you!"

"Yeah, sure," he shouted back. "You're up here just for the fun of it."

He was starting to bank toward the street, and I knew I'd only have time for one more try.

"Look! Will you stop running if I quit chasing you? I think there's a major misunderstanding here."

He glanced back over his shoulder and saw that I was still where I was when we collided. Altering his course slightly, he flared his wings and landed on a carved gargoyle ornament jutting out from the side of the building.

"Why should you want to talk?" he called, wiping his face with one hand. "I thought nothing I could say would change your mind."

"You'd be surprised," I shouted back. "Say, do you mind if I land on that ledge near you? I feel pretty silly just hanging here."

He glanced at the indicated ledge, and I could see his wings flex nervously.

"C'mon," I urged. "I'll be further away from you there than I was when we started this chase back on the roof. You'll still have a clean shot at getting away if I try anything."

He hesitated, then nodded his consent.

Moving slowly so as not to alarm him, I maneuvered my way to my new perch. Truth to tell, I was glad to get something solid under my feet again. Even using magic, flying can take a lot out of you, and I was relieved to get a chance to rest. Now that I was closer, I could see that Vic was breathing heavily himself. Apparently his form of flying was no picnic either.

"All right," I said in a much more conversational tone. "Let's take this thing from the top. Who says we're trying to kill you?"

"Matt does," the vampire responded. "He's the one who filled me in on you and your pet demon. To be honest with you, I had never even heard of you until Matt explained whose home we had stumbled into."

"Matt?" I frowned.

Then I remembered. Of course. The third member of the fugitive party. Luanna's old con artist partner who nobody had been paying attention to at all. A germ of an idea began to form in my head.

"And he says we're out to kill you?"

"That's right. According to him nobody crosses the Great Skeeve or makes a fool of him and lives...and using your house as an escape route definitely qualifies.

The reputation thing again. I was beginning to realize why so many magicians preferred to lead the lives of recluses.

"That's crazy, Vic." I said. "If I tried to kill everybody who's made a fool of me, I'd be armpit-deep in corpses."

"Oh yeah?" he shot back. "Well, if you aren't out to kill me, why did you send your pet demon after us?"

Despite my resolve to settle this thing amicably, I was starting to get annoyed.

"First of all, he's not my pet demon. He's my partner and his name is Aahz. Secondly, I didn't send him. He knocked me out cold and came himself. Third and final, he was never out to kill you. He was trying to bring you and your cohorts back to Deva so we wouldn't get stuck paying off the people you swindled plus a hefty fine. Are you getting all this, or am I going too fast for you?"

"But I didn't swindle anybody," the vampire pro-tested. "Those two offered me a job helping them sell magic charms. I didn't know they weren't genuine until Matt said the customers were mad and we had to run. I suggested we hide out here because it's the only place I know besides the Bazaar."

"Uh-huh," I said, studying the sky. "Next you'll be saying you didn't frame my partner or sound the alarm on us when we tried to spring him."

Vic's wings dropped as he hung his head.

"That much I can't deny...but I was scared! I framed the de-mon because it was the only way I could think of to get him off our trail for a while. I really thought he could get loose on his own, and when I saw you at the Woof Writers', I knew he was going to get away. I sounded the alarm hoping you would all get caught and be detained long enough to give us a head start. Looking back on it, they were pretty ratty things to do, but what would *you* do if you had a pack of killer demons on your trail?"

Now *that* I could identify with. Chumley's words about Vic and I being alike echoed in my ears. I had had to improvise in some pretty hairy situations myself.

"Wait a minute!" I growled. "Speaking of killer demons, what was that bit with you dangling Luanna over the edge of the building back there?"

"I was bluffing," the vampire shrugged. "Your friends were threatening to shoot me if I tried to fly away, and it was the only thing I could think of to try to get them to back off. I wouldn't deliberately hurt anyone…especially Luanna. She's sweet. That's why I was trying to help her escape with me after they caught Matt."

That brought me to the question that had been nagging at my mind since I started this wild chase.

"If you don't mind me asking, why didn't you just change into mist and drift away? We could never have caught you then."

Vic gave a short, bitter laugh.

"Do you know how rough it is to turn into mist? Well, you're a magician. Maybe you do know. Anyway, you might as well know the truth. I'm not much in the magic department…in fact, I'm pretty much a bust as a vampire. I can't even change all the way into a bat! These wings are the best I've been able to do. That's why I was looking for a new life in the Bazaar. I'd rather be a first-class anything than a third-rate vampire. I mean, I don't even like blood!"

"You should meet my bodyguard." I grinned despite myself. "He's a gangster who's allergic to garlic."

"Garlic? I love garlic."

I opened my mouth to offer him Guido's job, then shut it rapidly. If this character was half as desperate as he sounded, he'd probably take the offer seriously and accept, and then where would I be? All we needed to complete our menagerie was a magic-poor vampire.

"Well," I said instead, "I guess that answers all my questions except one. Now that you know we aren't trying to kill you, are you ready to quit running and face the music?"

The vampire gnawed his lower lip as he thought. "You're sure it will be all right?"

"I can't say for sure until I talk to my partner," I admitted, "but I'm pretty sure things will be amenable. The main problem is to get the murder charges against him dropped...which I think we've already accomplished. As for you, I think the only thing they could have against you is false arrest, and there's no way Aahz will press charges on that one."

"Why not?"

I gave him my best grin.

"Because if he did, we couldn't take you back to Deva to deal with the swindling charge. Believe me, if given a chance between revenge and saving money, you can trust Aahz to be forgiving every time."

Vic thought about it for a few more moments, then shrugged.

"Embarrassment I'm used to dealing with, and I think I can beat the swindling rap. C'mon, Skeeve. Let's get this thing over with."

Having finally reached a truce, however temporary, we descended together to face the waiting crowd.

XX.

"There's no accounting for taste!"
COLONEL SANDERS

"BUT SKEEVE..." BANG!

"...I told you before..."

BANG! BANG!

"...I could never abandon Matt..."

BANG!

"...he's my partner!"

BANG! BANG! "But Lu..." BANG!

"...excuse me. HEY, PARTNER! COULD YOU KNOCK OFF THE HAMMERING FOR A MINUTE? I'M TRYING TO HAVE A CONVERSATION HERE!"

"Not a chance," Aahz growled around his mouthful of nails. "I'm shutting this door permanently before anything else happens. But tell you what, I'll try to hammer quietly."

If you deduce from all this that we were back at our place on Deva, you're right. After some long, terse conversations with the citizens of Blut and fond farewells to Vilhelm and Pepe, our whole crew, including our three captives, had trooped back to the castle and through the door without incident.

I had hoped to have a few moments alone with Luanna, but, after several attempts, the best I had been able to manage was this conversation in the reception room under the watchful eyes of Aahz and Matt.

Matt, incidentally, turned out to be a thoroughly unpleasant individual with a twisted needle-nose, acne, a receding hairline, and the beginnings of a beer-belly. For the life of me, I couldn't figure out what Luanna saw in him.

"But that was when you thought he was in a jam," I said, resuming the argument. "Aahz and I have already promised to help defend him *and Vic* when they go before the Merchants Association. There's no need to stand by him yourself."

"I don't understand you, Skeeve," Luanna declared, shaking her head. "If I wouldn't leave Matt when he was in trouble, why should I leave him when things look like they're going to turn out okay? I

know you don't like him, but he's done all right by me so far...and
I still owe him for getting me away from the farm."

"But we're making you a good offer," I tried again desperately.
"You can stay here and work for Aahz and I, and if you're interested
we could even teach you some real magic so you don't have to..."

She stopped me by simply laying a hand on my arm.

"I know it's a good offer, Skeeve, and it's nice of you to make
it. But for the time being I'm content to stay with Matt. Maybe
sometime in the future, when I have a little more to offer you in
return, I'll take you up on it...if the deal's still open."

"Well," I sighed, "if that's really what you want..."

"Hey! Don't take it so hard, buddy," Matt laughed, clapping his
hand on my shoulder. "You win some, you lose some. This time you
lost. No hard feelings. Maybe you'll have better luck with the next
one. We're both men of the world, and we know one broad's just
like any other."

"Matt, *buddy*," I said through clenched teeth, "get that hand off
my shoulder before it loses a body."

As I said, even on our short trip back from Limbo I had been so
underwhelmed by Matt that I no longer even bothered trying to be
polite or mask my dislike for him. He could grate on my nerves faster
than anyone I had ever met. If he was a successful con artist, able to
inspire trust from total strangers, then I was the Queen of May.

"Matt's just kidding," Luanna soothed, stepping between us.

"Well I'm not," I snarled. "Just remember you're welcome here
any time you get fed up with this slug."

"Oh, I imagine we'll be together for quite some time," Matt
leered, patting Luanna lightly on her rump. "With you big shots vouch-
ing for us we should be able to beat this swindling rap...and even if
we lose, so what? All it means is I'll have to give them back their
crummy twenty gold pieces."

Aahz's hammering stopped abruptly...or maybe it was my heart.

I tried vainly to convince myself that I hadn't heard him right.

"Twenty gold pieces?" I said slowly.

"Yeah. They caught on to us a lot quicker here at the Bazaar than
I thought they would. It wasn't much of a haul even by my standards. I can't get over the fact that you big shots went through so
much trouble to drag us back here over a measly twenty gold pieces.
There must be more to this principle thing than I realized."

"Ummm…could I have a word with you, partner?" Aahz said, putting down his hammer.

"I was about to ask the same thing," I admitted, stepping to the far side of the room.

Once we were alone, we stared at each other, neither wanting to be the first to speak.

"You never did get around to asking Hay-ner how much was at stake, did you?" Aahz sighed absently.

"That's the money side of negotiations and I thought you covered it," I murmured.

"Funny, we both stood right there the whole time and heard every word that was said, and neither of us caught that omission."

"Funny. Right. I'm dying." My partner grimaced.

"Not as much as you will if word of this gets out," I warned. "I vote that we give them the money to pay it off. I don't want to , but it's the only way I can think of to keep this thing from becoming public knowledge."

"Done." Aahz nodded. "But let me handle it. If Matt the Rat there gets wind of the fact that the whole thing was a mistake on our part, he'd probably blackmail us for our eyeteeth."

"Right," I agreed.

With that, we, the two most sought-after, most highly-paid magicians at the Bazaar, turned to deal with our charges, reminded once more why humility lies at the core of greatness.

Little
Myth Marker

I.

*"The difference between an inside straight
and a blamed fool is callin' the last bet!"*
B. MAVERICK

"CALL!"

"Bump."

"Bump again."

"Who're you trying to kid? You got elf-high nothing!"

"Try me!"

"All right! Raise you limit."

"Call."

"Call."

"Elf-high nothing bumps you back limit."

"Fold."

"Call."

For those of you starting this book at the beginning (Bless you! I hate it when readers cheat by reading ahead!), this may be a little confusing. The above is the dialogue during a game of dragon poker. What is dragon poker, you ask? Well, it's reputed to be the most complicated card game ever invented…and here at the Bazaar at Deva, they should know.

The Bazaar is the biggest shopping maze and haggling spot in all the dimensions, and consequently gets a lot of dimension travelers (demons) passing through. In addition to the shops, stalls, and restaurants (which really doesn't do justice to the extent or variety of the Bazaar) there is a thriving gambling community in residence here. They are always on the lookout for a new game, particularly one that involves betting, and the more complicated the better. The basic philosophy is that a complicated game is more easily won by those who devote full time to its study than by the tourists who have dabbled in it or are trying to learn it as the game goes on. Anyway, when a Deveel bookie tells me that dragon poker is the most complicated card game ever, I tend to believe him.

"Fold."

"Call."

"Okay, Mr. Skeeve the Grater. Let's see you beat this! Dragons full!"

He exposed his hole cards with a flourish that bordered on a challenge. Actually, I had been hoping he would drop out of the hand. This particular individual (Grunk, I think his name was) was easily two heads taller than me and had bright red eyes, canines almost as long as my forearm, and a nasty disposition. He tended to speak in an angry shout, and the fact that he had been losing steadily had not mellowed him in the slightest.

"Well? C'mon! What have you got?"

I turned over my four hole cards, spread them next to the five already face up, then leaned back and smiled.

"That's it?" Grunk said, craning his neck and scowling at my cards. "But that's only..."

"Wait a minute," the player on his left chimed in. "It's Tuesday. That makes his unicorns wild."

"But it's a month with an `M' in it!" someone else piped up. "So his ogre is only half of face value!"

"But there's an even number of players..."

I told you it was a complicated game. Those of you who know me from my earlier adventures (blatant plug!) may wonder how it is I understand such a complex system. That's easy. I don't! I just bet, then spread the cards and let the other players sort out who won.

You may wonder what I was doing sitting in on a cutthroat game of dragon poker when I didn't even know the rules. Well, for once, I have an answer. I was enjoying myself on my own for a change.

You see, ever since Don Bruce, the Mob's fairy godfather, supposedly hired me to watch over the Mob's interests at the Bazaar and assigned me two body-guards, Guido and Nunzio, I've rarely had a moment to myself. This weekend, however, my two watchdogs were off making their yearly report to Mob Central, leaving me to fend for myself. Obviously, before they left, they made me give my solemn promise to be careful. Also obviously, as soon as they were gone, I set out to do just the opposite.

Even aside from our percentage of the Mob's take at the Bazaar, our magic business had been booming, so money was no problem. I filched a couple thousand in gold from petty cash and was all set to go on a spree when an invitation arrived to sit in on one of the Geek's dragon poker games at his club, the Even-Odds.

As I said before, I know absolutely nothing about dragon poker other than the fact that at the end of a hand you have five cards face up and four face down. Anytime I've tried to get my partner, Aahz, to teach me more about the game, I've been lectured about "only playing games you know" and "don't go looking for trouble." Since I was already looking for mischief, the chance to defy both my bodyguards *and* my partner was too much to resist. I mean, I figured the worst that could happen was that I'd lose a couple thousand in gold. Right?

"You're all overlooking something. This is the forty-third hand and Skeeve there is sitting in a chair facing north!"

I took my cue from the groans and better-censored expressions of disgust and raked in the pot.

"Say, Geek," Grunk said, his red eyes glittering at me through half-lowered eyelids. "Are you *sure* this Skeeve fellow isn't using magic?"

"Guaranteed," responded the Deveel who was gathering the cards and shuffling for the next hand. "Any game I host here at the Even-Odds is monitored against magic *and* telepathy."

"Weelll, I don't normally play cards with magicians, and I've heard that Skeeve here is supposed to be pretty good in that department. Maybe he's good enough that you just can't catch him at it."

I was starting to get a little nervous. I mean, I wasn't using magic...and even if I was going to, I wouldn't know how to use it to rig a card game. The trouble was that Grunk looked perfectly capable of tearing my arms off if he thought I was cheating. I began racking my brain for some way to convince him without admitting to everyone at the table just how little I knew about magic.

"Relax, Grunk. Mr. Skeeve's a good player, that's all. Just because he wins doesn't mean he's cheating."

That was Pidge, the only other human-type in the game. I shot him a grateful smile.

"I don't mind someone winning," Grunk muttered defensively, "But he's been winning all night."

"I've lost more than you have," Pidge said, "and you don't see me griping. I'm tellin' you Mr. Skeeve is *good*. I've sat in on games with the Kid, and I should know."

"The Kid? You've played against him?" Grunk was visibly impressed.

"And lost my socks doing it," Pidge admitted wryly. "I'd say that Mr. Skeeve here is good enough to give him a run for his money, though."

"Gentlemen? Are we here to talk or to play cards?" the Geek interrupted, tapping the deck meaningfully.

"I'm out," Pidge said, rising to his feet. "I know when I'm out-classed—even if I have to go in the hole before I'll admit it. My marker still good, Geek?"

"It's good with me if nobody else objects."

Grunk noisily slammed his fist down on the table, causing several of my stacks of chips to fall over.

"What's this about markers?" he demanded. "I thought this was a cash-only game! Nobody said any-thing about playing for IOUs."

"Pidge here's an exception," the Geek said. "He's always made good on his marker before. Besides, you don't have to worry about it, Grunk. You aren't even getting all of *your* money back."

"Yeah. But I lost it betting against somebody who's betting markers instead of cash. It seems to me…"

"I'll cover his marker," I said loftily. "That makes it personal between him and me, so it doesn't involve anyone else at the table. Right, Geek?"

"That's right. Now shut up and play, Grunk. Or do you want us to deal you out?"

The monster grumbled a bit under his breath but leaned back and tossed in another chip to ante for the next hand.

"Thanks, Mr. Skeeve," Pidge said. "And don't worry. Like the Geek says, I always reclaim my marker."

I winked at him and waved vaguely as he left, already intent on the next hand as I tried vainly to figure out the rules of the game.

If my grand gesture seemed a little impulsive, remember that I'd been watching him play all night, and I knew how much he had lost. Even if all of it was on IOUs, I could cover it out of my winnings and still show a profit.

You see, Grunk was right. I had been winning steadily all night…a fact made doubly surprising by my ignorance of the game. Early on, however, I had hit on a system which seemed to be working very well: Bet the players, not the cards. On the last hand, I hadn't been betting that I had a winning hand, I was betting that Grunk had a losing hand. Luck had been against him all night, and he was betting wild to try to make up for his losses.

Following my system, I folded the next two hands, then hit them hard on the third. Most of the other players folded rather than question my judgment. Grunk stayed until the bitter end, hoping I was bluffing. It turned out that I was (my hand wasn't all that strong), but that his hand was even weaker. Another stack of chips tumbled into my hoard.

"That does it for me," Grunk said, pushing his remaining chips toward the Geek. "Cash me in."

"Me too."

"I should have left an hour ago. Would have saved myself a couple hundred."

The Geek was suddenly busy converting chips back to cash as the game broke up.

Grunk loitered for a few minutes after receiving his share of the bank. Now that we were no longer facing each other over cards, he was surprisingly pleasant.

"You know, Skeeve," he said, clapping a massive hand on my shoulder, "it's been a long time since I've been whipped that bad at dragon poker. Maybe Pidge was right. You're slumming here. You should try for a game with the Kid."

"I was just lucky."

"No. I'm serious. If I knew how to get in touch with him, I'd set up the game myself."

"You won't have to," one of the other players put in as he started for the door. "Once word of this game gets around, the Kid will come looking for you."

"True enough," Grunk laughed over his shoulder. "Really, Skeeve. If that match-up happens, be sure to pass the word to me. That's a game I'd like to see."

"Sure, Grunk," I said. "You'll be one of the first to know. Catch you later."

Actually, my mind was racing as I made my goodbyes. This was getting out of hand. I had figured on one madcap night on my own, then calling it quits without anyone else the wiser. If the other players started shooting their mouths off all over the Bazaar, there would be no hope of keeping my evening's adventure a secret...particularly from Aahz! The only thing that would be worse would be if I ended up with some hot-shot gambler hunting me down for a challenge match.

"Say, Geek," I said, trying to make it sound casual. "Who is this 'Kid' they keep talking about?"

The Deveel almost lost his grip on the stack of chips he was counting. He gave me a long stare, then shrugged.

"You know, Skeeve, sometimes I don't know when you're kidding me and when you're serious. I keep forgetting that as successful as you are, you're still new to the Bazaar...and to gambling specifically."

"Terrific. Who's the 'Kid'?"

"The Kid's the current king of the dragon poker circuit. His trademark is that he always includes a breath mint with his opening bet for each hand...says that it brings him luck. That's why they call him the 'Sen-Sen Ante Kid.' I'd advise you to stay away from him, though. You had a good run tonight, but the Kid is the best there is. He'd eat you alive in a head-to-head game."

"I hear that." I laughed. "I was only curious. Really. Just cash me in and I'll be on my way."

The Geek gestured at the stacks of coins on the table.

"What's to cash?" he said. "I pulled mine out the same time I cashed the others' out. The rest is yours."

I looked at the money and swallowed hard. For the first time I could understand why some people found gambling so addictive. There was easily twenty thou-sand in gold weighing down the table. All mine. From one night of cards!

"Urn...Geek? Could you hold on to my winnings for me? I'm not wild about the idea of walking around with that much gold on me. I can drop back by later with my bodyguards to pick it up."

"Suit yourself," the Geek shrugged. "I can't think of anyone at the Bazaar who would have nerve enough to jump you, with your reputation. Still, you might run into a stranger..."

"Fine," I said, heading for the door. "Then I'll be..."

"Wait a minute! Aren't you forgetting something?"

"What's that?"

"Pidge's marker. Hang on and I'll get it."

He disappeared before I could protest, so I leaned against the wall to wait. I had forgotten about the marker, but the Geek was a gambler and adhered more religiously to the unwritten laws of gambling than most folks obeyed civil law. I'd just have to humor him and...

"Here's the marker, Skeeve," the Deveel announced. "Markie, this is Skeeve."

I just gaped at him, unable to speak. Actually, I gaped at the little blond-headed moppet he was leading by the hand. That's right. A girl. Nine or ten years old at the most.

I experienced an all-too-familiar sinking feeling in my stomach that meant I was in trouble...lots of it.

II.

"Kids? Who said anything about kids?"
CONAN

THE LITTLE GIRL looked at me through eyes that glowed with trust and love. She barely stood taller than my waist and had that wholesome, healthy glow that young girls are all supposed to have but so few actually do. With her little beret and matching jumper, she looked so much like an oversized doll that I wondered if she'd say "Mama" if you turned her upside down, then right-side up again.

She was so adorable that it was obvious that anyone with a drop of paternal instinct would fall in love with her on sight. Fortunately, my partner had trained me well; any instincts I had were of a more monetary nature.

"What's that?" I demanded.

"It's a little girl," the Geek responded. "Haven't you ever seen one before?"

For a minute, I thought I was being baited. Then I remembered some of my earliest conversations with Aahz and controlled my temper.

"I realize that it's a little girl, Geek," I said carefully. "What I was really trying to ask is a) who is she? b) what is she doing here? and c) what has this got to do with Pidge's marker? Do I make myself clear?"

The Deveel blinked his eyes in bewilderment.

"But I just told you. Her name is Markie. She's Pidge's marker... you know, the one you said you would cover personally?"

My stomach bottomed out.

"Geek, we were talking about a piece of paper. You know, 'IOU, etc.'? A marker! Who leaves a little girl for a marker?"

"Pidge does. Always has. C'mon, Skeeve. You know me. Would I give anyone credit for a piece of paper? I give Pidge credit on Markie here because I know he'll be back to reclaim her."

"Right. *You* give him credit. I don't deal in little girls, Geek."

"You do now," he smiled. "Everyone at the table heard you say so. I'll admit I was a little surprised at the time."

"...But not surprised enough to warn me about what I was buying into. Thanks a lot, Geek old pal. I'll try to remember to return the favor someday."

In case you didn't notice, that last part was an open threat. As has been noted, I've been getting quite a reputation around the Bazaar as a magician, and I didn't really think the Geek wanted to be on my bad side.

Okay. So it was a rotten trick. I was getting desperate.

"Whoa. Hold it," the Deveel said quickly. "No reason to get upset. If you don't want her, I'll give you cash to cover the marker and keep her myself..."

"...at the usual terms, of course."

I knew I was being suckered. *Knew* it, mind you. But I had to ask anyway.

"What terms?"

"If Pidge doesn't reclaim her in two weeks, I sell her into slavery for enough money to cover her father's losses."

Check and mate.

I looked at Markie. She was still holding the Geek's hand, listening solemnly while we argued out her fate. As our eyes met, she said her first words since she had entered the room.

"Are you going to be my new daddy?"

I swallowed hard.

"No, I'm not your daddy, Markie. I just..."

"Oh, I know. It's just that every time my *real* daddy leaves me with someone, he tells me that they're going to be my pretend daddy for a while. I'm supposed to mind them and do what they tell me just as if they were my real daddy until my real daddy comes to get me. I just wanted to know if you were going to be my new pretend daddy?"

"Ummm..."

"I hope so. You're nice. Not like some of the scumbags he's left me with. Will you be my new daddy?"

With that, she reached out and took hold of my hand. A small thrill ran through me like an autumn shiver. She was so vulnerable, so trusting. I had been on my own for a long time, first alone, then apprenticed to Garkin, and finally teamed with Aahz. In all that time, I had never really been responsible for another person. It was a funny feeling, scary and warming at the same time.

I tore my eyes away from her and glared at the Geek again.

"Slavery's outlawed here at the Bazaar."

The Deveel shrugged. "There are other dimensions. As a matter of fact, I've had a standing offer for her for several years. That's why I've been willing to accept her as collateral. I could make enough to cover the bet, the cost of the food she's eaten over the years, and still turn a tidy profit."

"That's about the lowest…"

"Hey! The name's `the Geek,' not `the Red Cross'! I don't do charity. Folks come to me to bet, not for handouts."

I haven't thrown a punch at anyone since I started practicing magic, but I was sorely tempted to break that record just this once. Instead, I turned to the little girl.

"Get your things, Markie. Daddy's taking you to your new home."

MY PARTNER AND I were currently basing our operations at the Bazaar at Deva, which is the home dimension of the Deveels. Deveels are reputed to be the sharpest merchants, traders, and hagglers in all the known dimensions. You may have heard of them in various folk tales in your own home dimension. Their fame lingers even in dimensions they have long since stopped trading in.

The Bazaar is the showcase of Deva…in fact, I've never seen a part of Deva that wasn't the Bazaar. Here the Deveels meet to trade with each other, buying and selling the choicest magics and miracles from all the dimensions. It's an around-the-clock, over-the-horizon sprawl of tents, shops, and barter blankets where you can acquire anything your imagination can conjure as well as a lot of things you never dreamed existed…for a price. Many inventors and religious figures have built their entire career from items purchased in one trip to the Bazaar. Needless to say, it is devastating to the average budget …even if the holder of the pursestrings has above-average sales resistance.

Normally I enjoy strolling through the booths, but tonight, with Markie beside me, I was too distracted to concentrate on the displays. It occurred to me that, fun as it is for adults, the Bazaar is no place to raise a child.

"Will we be living by ourselves, or do you have a girlfriend?"

Markie was clinging to my hand as we made our way through the Bazaar. The wonders of the stalls and shops dispensing magic reached out to us as they always do, but she was oblivious to them, choosing instead to ply me with questions and hanging on my every word.

" 'No' to both questions. Tananda lives with me, but she isn't my girlfriend. She's a free-lance assassin who helps me out on jobs from time to time. Then there's Chumley, her brother. He's a troll who works under the name of Crunch. You'll like them. They're nice...in a lot of ways they're nicer than I am."

Markie bit her lip and frowned. "I hope you're right. I've found that a lot of nice people don't like little kids."

"Don't worry," I said, with more confidence than I felt. "But I'm not done yet. There's also Guido and Nunzio, my bodyguards. They may seem a little gruff, but don't let them scare you. They just act tough because it's part of their job."

"Gee. I've never had a daddy who had bodyguards before."

"That's not all. We also have Buttercup, who's a war unicorn, and Gleep, who's my very own pet dragon."

"Oh, lots of people have dragons. I'm more impressed by the bodyguards."

That took me aback a little. I'd always thought that having a dragon was rather unique. I mean, nobody else I knew had a dragon. Then again, nobody else I knew had bodyguards, either.

"Let's see," Markie was saying. "There's Tananda, Chumley, Guido, Nunzio, Buttercup, and Gleep. Is that all?"

"Well, there's also Massha. She's my apprentice." "Massha. That's a pretty name."

Now, there are lots of words to describe my apprentice, but unfortunately 'pretty' isn't one of them. Massha is huge, both in height and breadth. There are large people who still manage to look attractive, but my apprentice isn't one of them. She tends toward loud, colorful clothes which invariably clash with her bright orange hair, and wears enough jewelry for three stores. In fact, the last time she got into a fight here at the Bazaar was when a nearsighted shopper mistook her for a display tent.

"Aahh...you'll just have to meet her. But you're right. Massha is a pretty name."

"Gee, you've got a lot of people living with you."

"Well...umm...there is one more."

"Who's that?"

"His name is Aahz. He's my partner."

"Is he nice, too?"

I was torn between loyalty and honesty."

"He…aah…takes getting used to. Remember how I told you not to be scared of the bodyguards even if they were a little gruff?"

"Yes."

"Well, it's all right to be scared of Aahz. He gets a little upset from time to time, and until he cools down it's best to give him a lot of room and not leave anything breakable—like your arm—within his reach."

"What gets him upset?"

"Oh, the weather, losing money, not making money…which to him is the same as losing money, any one of a hundred things that I say…and you! I'm afraid he's going to be a little upset when he meets you, so stay behind me until I get him calmed down. Okay?"

"Why would he be upset with me?"

"You're going to be a surprise to him, and he doesn't like surprises. You see, he's a very suspicious person and tends to think of a surprise as a part of an unknown plot against him…or me."

Markie lapsed into silence. Her brow furrowed as she stared off into nothingness, and it occurred to me that I was scaring her.

"Hey, don't worry," I said, squeezing her hand. "Aahz will be okay once he gets over being surprised. Now' tell me about yourself. Do you go to school?"

"Yes. I'm halfway through Elemental School. I'd be further if we didn't keep moving around."

"Don't you mean Elementary School?" I smiled. "No. I mean…"

"Whoops. Here we are. This is your new home, Markie."

I gestured grandly at the small tent that was our combination home and headquarters.

"Isn't it a little small for all those people?" she frowned, staring at the tent.

"It's bigger inside than it is outside," I explained. "C'mon. I'll show you."

I raised the flap for her and immediately wished I hadn't.

"Wait'll I get my hands on him!" came Aahz's booming voice from within. "After all the times I've told him to stay away from dragon poker!"

767

It occurred to me that maybe we should wait for a while before introducing Markie to my partner. I started to ease the flap down, but it was too late.

"Is that you, partner? I'd like to have a little chat, if you don't mind!"

"Remember. Stay behind me," I whispered to Markie, then proceeded to walk into the lion's den.

III.

"I'm doing this for your own good!"
ANY ESTABLISHMENT EXECUTIONER...OR ANY PARENT

AS I TOLD Markie, our place at the Bazaar was bigger on the inside than on the outside...lots bigger! I've been in smaller palaces...heck, I've lived and worked in smaller palaces than our current domicile. Back when I was court magician at Possletum, to be exact.

Here at the Bazaar, the Deveels think that any display of wealth will weaken their position when they haggle over prices, so they hide the size of their homes by tucking them into 'unlisted dimensions." Even though our home looked like just a humble tent from the street, the inside included multiple bedrooms, a stable area, a courtyard and garden, etc., etc. You get the picture.

Unfortunately for me, at the moment it also included my partner, Aahz.

"Well, if it isn't the Bazaar's own answer to War, Famine, Death, and Pestilence! Other dimensions have the Four Horsemen, but the Bazaar at Deva has the Great Skeeve!"

Remember my partner, Aahz? I mentioned him back in Chapter One and again in Chapter Two. Most of my efforts to describe him fail to prepare people for the real thing. What I usually forget to mention to folks is that he's from the dimension Perv. For those of you unfamiliar with dimension travel, that means he is green and scaly with a mouth big enough for any other three beings and teeth enough for a school of sharks...if shark's teeth got to be four inches long, that it. I don't deliberately omit things from my descriptions. It's just that after all these years I've gotten used to him.

"Have you got anything at all to say for yourself? Not that there's any acceptable excuse, mind you. It's just that tradition allows you a few last words."

Well...I've *almost* gotten used to him.

"Hi, Aahz. Have you heard about the card game?"

"About two hours ago," Massha supplied from a nearby chair where she was entrenched with a book and a huge box of chocolates. "He's been like this ever since."

"I see you've done your usual marvelous job of calming him down."

"I'm just an apprentice around here," she said with a shrug. "Getting between you two in a quarrel is not part of my game plan for a long and prosperous life."

"If you two are *quite* through," Aahz growled, "I'm still waiting to hear what you have to say for yourself."

"What's to say? I sat in on a game of dragon poker..."

"WHO'S BEEN TEACHING YOU TO PLAY DRAGON POKER? That's what there is to say! Was it Tananda? Chumley? How come you're going to other people for lessons all of a sudden? Aren't I good enough for the Great Skeeve any more?"

The truth of the situation suddenly dawned on me. Aahz was my teacher before he insisted that I be elevated to full partner status. Even though we were theoretically equals, old habits die hard and he still considered himself to be my exclusive teacher, mentor, coach, and all-around nudge. What the *real* problem was was that my partner was jealous of someone else horning in on what he felt was his private student! Perhaps this problem would be easier to deal with than I thought.

"No one else has been teaching me, Aahz. Everything I know about dragon poker, I learned from you."

"But I haven't taught you anything."

"Exactly."

That stopped him. At least, it halted his pacing as he turned to peer suspiciously at me with his yellow eyes.

"You mean you don't know anything at all about dragon poker?"

"Well, from listening to you talk, I know about how many cards are dealt out and stuff like that. I still haven't figured out what the various hands are, much less their order...you know, what beats what."

"I know," my partner said pointedly. "What I don't know is why you decided to sit in on a game you don't know the first thing about."

"The Geek sent me an invitation, and I thought it would be sociable to..."

"The Geek? You sat in at one of the Geek's games at the Even-Odds to be sociable?" He was off again. "Don't you know that those are some of the most cutthroat games at the Bazaar? They eat amateurs alive at those tables. And you went there to be sociable?"

"Sure. I figured the worse that could happen would be that I lost a little money. The way things have been going, we can afford it. Besides, who knows, I might get lucky."

"Lucky? Now I know you don't know anything about dragon poker. It's a game of skill, not luck. All you could do was throw your money away...money we've both risked our lives for, I might add."

"Yes, Aahz."

"And besides, one of the first things you learn playing any kind of poker is that the surest way to lose is to go in *expecting* to lose."

"Yes, Aahz."

Out of desperation, I was retreating behind my strongest defense. I was agreeing with everything he said. Even Aahz has trouble staying mad at someone who's agreeing with him.

"Well, what's done is done and all the shouting in the world won't change it. I just hope you've learned your lesson. How much did it cost you, anyway?"

"I won."

"Okay. Just to show you there're no hard feelings, we'll split it. In a way it's my fault. I should have taught you..."

There was a sudden stillness in the room. Even Massha had stopped with a bonbon halfway to her mouth. Very slowly, Aahz turned to face me.

"You know, Skeeve, for a minute there, I thought you said..."

"I won," I repeated, trying desperately not to smile. "You won. As in 'better than broke even' won?"

"As in 'twenty thousand in gold plus' won,"
I corrected.

"But if you didn't know how the game was played, how could you..."

"I just bet the people, not the cards. It seemed to work out pretty well."

I was in my glory now. It was a rare time indeed that I managed to impress my partner, and I was going to milk it for all it was worth.

"But that's crazy!" Aahz scowled. "I mean, it could work for a while, but in the long run..."

"He was great!" Markie announced, emerging from behind me. "You should have seen it. He beat everybody."

My "glory" came tumbling down around my ears. With one hand I shoved Markie back behind me and braced for the explosion. What

I really wanted to do was run for cover, but that would have left Markie alone in the open, so I settled for closing my eyes.

Nothing happened.

After a few moments, I couldn't stand the suspense any more and opened one eye to sneak a peek. The view I was treated to was an *extreme* close-up of one of Aahz's yellow eyes. He was standing nose to nose with me, apparently waiting until I was ready before launching into his tirade. It was obvious that *he* was ready. The gold flecks in his eyes were shimmering as if they were about to boil...and for all I knew, they were.

"Who...is...that?"

I decided against trying to play dumb and say "Who is what?" At the range he was standing, Aahz would have bitten my head off...literally!

"Umm...remember I said that I won twenty thousand plus? Well, she's the plus."

"YOU WON A KID IN A CARD GAME!?!!"

The force of my partner's voice actually knocked me back two steps. I probably would have gone farther if I hadn't bumped against Markie.

"ARE YOU OUT OF YOUR MIND?? DON'T YOU KNOW THE PENALTY FOR SLAVERY IS..."

He disappeared in mid-sentence behind a wall of flesh and tasteless color. Despite her earlier claims of valuing self-preservation, Massha had stepped between us.

"Just cool down a minute, Green and Scaly." Aahz tried to get around her.

"BUT HE JUST..."

She took a half step sideways and blocked him by leaning against the wall.

"Give him a chance to explain. He is your partner, isn't he?"

From the sound of his voice, Aahz reversed his field and tried for the other side.

"BUT HE..."

Massha took two steps and leaned against the other wall, all the while talking as if she wasn't being interrupted.

"Now either he's an idiot...which he isn't, or you're a lousy teacher...which you aren't, or there's more to this than meets the eye. Hmmm?"

There were several moments of silence, then Aahz spoke again in a voice much more subdued.

"All right, *partner.* Let's hear it."

Massha relinquished her spot and I could see Aahz again...though I almost wished I couldn't. He was breathing hard, but whether from anger or from the exertion of trying to get around Massha I couldn't tell. I could hear the scales on his fingers rasp as he clenched and unclenched his fists, and I knew that I'd better tell my story fast before he lost control again.

"I didn't win *her,*" I said hastily. "I won her father's marker. She's our guarantee that he'll come back and make his losses good."

Aahz stopped making with the fists, and a puzzled frown creased his features.

"A marker? I don't get it. The Geek's games are always on a cash-and-carry basis."

"Well, he seems to have made an exception in Pidge's case.

"Pidge?"

"That's my daddy," Markie announced, stepping from behind me again. It's short for Pigeon. He loses a lot...that's why everyone is always so happy to let him sit in on a game."

"Cute kid," Aahz said drily. "It also might explain why you did so well in the game tonight. One screwball can change the pace of an entire game. Still, when the Geek *does* take markers, he usually pays the winners in cash and handles the collecting himself."

"He was willing to do that."

"Then why..."

"...and if Markie's father didn't show up in two weeks, he was going to take her off-dimension and sell her into slavery himself to raise the money."

From her chair, Massha gave a low whistle. "Sweet guy, this Geek."

"He's a Deveel." Aahz waved absently, as if the statement explained everything. "Okay, okay. I can see where you felt you had to accept custody of the kid here instead of leaving her with the Geek. Just answer me one question."

"What's that?"

"What do *we* do with her if her father doesn't show up?" Sometimes I like it better when Aahz is ranting than when he's thinking.

"Aahh...I'm still working on that one."

"Terrific. Well, when you come up with an answer, let me know. I think I'll stay in my room until this whole thing blows over."

With that he strode out of the room, leaving Massha and me to deal with Markie.

"Cheer up, Hot Stuff," my apprentice said. "Kids aren't all that much of a problem. Hey, Markie. Would you like a piece of chocolate?"

"No, thank you. It might make me fat and ugly like you."

I winced. Up until now, Massha had been my ally on the subject of Markie, but this might change everything. She was very sensitive about her weight, so most of us tended to avoid any mention of it. In fact, I had gotten so used to her appearance that I tended to forget how she looked to anyone who didn't know her.

"Markie!" I said sternly. "That wasn't a very nice thing to say."

"But it's true!" she countered, turning her innocent eyes on me.

"That's why it's not nice," Massha laughed, though I noticed her smile was a little forced. "C'mon, Markie. Let's hit the pantry and try to find you something to eat...something low-calorie."

The two of them trooped out, leaving me alone with my thoughts. Aahz had raised a good question. What *were* we going to do if Markie's father didn't come back? I had never been around kids before. I knew that having her around would cause . problems, but how many problems? With everything else we had handled as a team, surely Aahz and I could handle a little girl. Of course, Aahz was...

"There you are, Boss! Good. I was hopin' you were still up."

I cleared my mind to find one of my bodyguards entering the room.

"Oh. Hi, Guido. How did the report go?"

"Couldn't be better. In fact, Don Bruce was so happy he sent you a little present."

In spite of my worries, I couldn't help smiling. At least *something* was going right.

"That's great," I said. "I could use a little cheering up just now."

"Then I've got just the thing. Hey, Nunzio! Bring her in here!"

My smile froze. I tried desperately not to panic. After all, I reasoned, people refer to a lot of things as "her." Boats, for example, or even...

"Boss, this is Bunny. Don Bruce sends her with his compliments on a job well done. She's going to be your moll."

The girl they were escorting into the room bore no resemblance at all to a boat.

IV.

"A doll is a doll is a doll."
F. SINATRA

BUNNY WAS A top-heavy little redhead with her hair in a pixie cut and a vacant stare a zombie would envy. She was vigorously chewing something as she rubbernecked, trying to take in the entire room at once.

"Gee. This is quite a place you guys's got here. It's a lot nicer than the last place I was at, ya know?"

"This is just the waitin' room," Nunzio said with pride. "Wait'll you see the rest of the layout. It's bigger'n any hangout I've ever worked, know what I mean?"

"What'sa matter with you two?" Guido barked. "Ain't ya got no manners? First things first. Bunny, this is the Boss. He's the one you're goin' to be workin' under."

Bunny advanced toward me holding out her hand. From the way her body moved under her tight-fitting clothes, there was little doubt what she was wearing under them...or not wearing, as the case may be. "Pleased ta meetcha, Boss. The pleasure's mutual," she said brightly.

For once, I knew exactly what to say.

"No."

She stopped, then turned toward Guido with a frown.

"He means not to call him `Boss' until you get to know him," my bodyguard assured her. "Around here he's just known as Skeeve."

"Gotcha," she winked. "Okay, *Skeeve...ya* know, that's kinda cute."

"No," I repeated.

"Okay. So it's not cute. Whatever you say. You're the Boss."

"NO!"

"But..."

I ignored her and turned directly to Guido.

"Have you lost your marbles? What are you doing bringing her in here like this?"

"Like I said, Boss, she's a present from Don Bruce."

"Guido, lots of people give each other presents. Presents like neckties and books...not girls!"

My bodyguard shrugged his shoulders helplessly. "So Don Bruce ain't lots of people. He's the one who assigned us to you in the first place, and he says that someone with your standin' in the Mob should have a moll."

"Guido...let's talk. Excuse us a minute, Bunny."

I slipped an arm around my bodyguard's shoulders and drew him off into a corner. That may sound easy until you realize I had to reach *up* to get to his shoulders. Both Guido and Nunzio are considerably larger than me.

"Now look, Guido," I said. "Remember when I explained our setup to you?"

"Sure, Boss."

"Well, let's walk through it again. Don Bruce hired Aahz and me on a non-exclusive basis to watch over the Mob's interests here at the Bazaar. Now, he did that because the ordinary methods he employs weren't working...Right?"

"Actually, he hired *you* and included your partner. Except for that...right."

"Whatever. We also explained to you that the reason the Mob's usual methods weren't working was that the Bazaar merchants had hired us to chase the Mob out. Remember?"

"Yea. That was really a surprise when you told us. You really had us goin', know what I mean?"

"Now that brings us to the present. The money we're collecting from the Bazaar merchants and passing on to Don Bruce, the money he thinks they're paying the Mob for protection, is actually being paid to us to keep the Mob away from the Bazaar. Get it?"

"Got it."

"Good. Then, understanding the situation as you do, you can see why I don't want a moll or anyone else from the Mob hanging around. If word gets back to Don Bruce that we're flim-flamming him, it'll reopen the whole kettle of worms. That's why you've got to get rid of her."

Guido nodded vigorously.

"No," he said.

"Then all you have to...what do you mean, 'no'? Do I have to explain it all to you again?"

My bodyguard heaved a great sigh.

"I understand the situation, Boss. But I don't think *you* do. Allow me to continue where you left off."

"But I..."

"Now, whatever you are, Don Bruce considers you to be a minor chieftain in the Mob running a profitable operation. Right?"

"Well..."

"As such, you are entitled to a nice house, which you have, a couple of bodyguards, which you have, and a moll, which you don't have. These things are necessary in Don Bruce's eyes if the Mob is to maintain its public image of rewarding successful members...just as it finds it necessary to express its displeasure at members who fail. Follow me?"

"Public image," I said weakly.

"So it is in the interests of the Mob that Don Bruce has provided you with what you have failed to provide yourself...namely: a moll. If you do not like this one, we can take her back and get another, but a moll you must have if we are to continue in our existing carefree manner. Otherwise..." He paused dramatically.

"Otherwise...?" I prompted.

"If you do not maintain the appearance of a successful Mob member, Don Bruce will be forced to deal with you as if you were unsuccessful...know what I mean?"

I suddenly felt the need to massage my forehead. "Terrific."

"My sentiments exactly. Under the circumstances, however, I thought it wisest to accept his gift in your name and hope that you could find an amicable solution to our dilemma at a later date."

"I suppose you're...Hey! Wait a minute. We already have Massha and Tananda in residence. Won't they do?"

Guido gave his sigh again. "This possibility did indeed occur to me as well. Then I said to myself: `Guido, do you really want to be the one to hang the label of moll on either Massha or Tananda, knowing those ladies as you do? Even if it will only be bantered around the Mob?" Viewed in that light, it was my decision to go along with Don Bruce's proposal and leave it to you to make the final decision...*Boss.*"

I shot a sharp glance at him for that last touch of sarcasm. Despite his affected speech patterns and pseudo-pompous explanations, I occasionally had the impression that Guido was far more intelligent than he let on. At the moment, however, his face was a study in innocence, so I let it ride.

"I see what you mean, Guido. If either Massha or Tananda are going to be known as 'molls,' I'd rather it was their choice, not mine. Until then, I guess we're stuck with...what's her name? Bunny? Does she wiggle her nose or something?"

Guido glanced across the room at the other two, then lowered his voice conspiratorily. "Just between you and me, Boss, I think you would be well advised to accept this particular moll that Don Bruce has personally selected to send. Know what I mean?"

"No, I don't." I grimaced. "Excuse me, Guido, but the mind's working a little slow just now. If you're trying to tell me something, you're going to have to spell it out."

"Well, I did a little checkin' around, and it seems that Bunny here is Don Bruce's niece, and..."

"HIS N...

"Ssshh. Keep it down, Boss. I don't think we're supposed to know that."

With a supreme effort, I suppressed my hysteria and lowered my voice again. "What are you trying to do to me? I'm trying to keep this operation under wraps and you bring me Don Bruce's niece?"

"Don't worry..."

"DON'T..."

"Sshh! Like I said, I've been checking around. It seems the two of them don't get along at all. Wouldn't give each other the time of day. The way I hear it, he doesn't want her to be a moll, and she won't go along with any other kind of work. They fight over it like cats and dogs. Anyway, if you can trust any moll to not feed Don Bruce the straight scoop, it's her. That's why I was sayin' that you should keep this one."

My headache had now spread to my stomach.

"Swell. Just swell. Well, at least..."

"The one thing I couldn't find out, though," Guido continued with a frown, "is why he wants her with you. I figure that it's either that he thinks that you'll treat her right, or that he expects you to scare her out of bein' a moll. I'm just not sure which way you should play it."

This was not turning out to be a good night for me. In fact, it had gone steadily downhill since I won that last hand of dragon poker.

"Guido," I said. "Please don't say anything more. Okay? Please? Every time I think that things might not be so bad, you drag out something else that makes them worse.

"Just tryin' to do my job," he shrugged, obviously hurt, "but if that's what you want...well, you're the Boss."

"And if you say that one more time, I'm liable to forget you're bigger than me and pop you one in the nose. Understand? Being the 'Boss' implies a certain degree of control, and if there's one thing I don't have right now, it's control."

"Right, B...Skeeve," my bodyguard grinned. "You know, for a minute there you sounded just like my old B...employer. He used to beat up on Nunzio and me when he got mad. Of course, we had to stand there and take it..."

"Don't give me any ideas," I snarled. "For now, let's just concentrate on Bunny."

I turned my attention once more to the problem at hand, which was to say Bunny. She was still staring vacantly around the room, jaws working methodically on whatever it was she was chewing, and apparently oblivious to whatever it was Nunzio was trying to tell her.

"Well, uh...Bunny," I said, "it looks like you're going to be staying with us for a while."

She reacted to my words as if I had hit her "on" switch.

"Eeoooh!" she squealed, as if I had just told her that she had won a beauty pageant. "Oh, I know I'm just goin' to *love* workin' under you, Skeevie."

My stomach did a slow roll to the left.

"Shall I get her things, Boss?" Nunzio said. "She's got about a mountain and a half of luggage outside."

"Oh, you can leave all that," Bunny cooed. "I just know my Skeevie is going to want to buy me a whole new wardrobe."

"Hold it! Time out!" I ordered. "House rules time. Bunny, some things are going to disappear from your vocabulary *right now*. First, forget 'Skeevie.' It's Skeeve...just Skeeve, or if you must, the Great Skeeve in front of company. Not Skeevie."

"Gotcha," she winked.

"Next, you do not work *under* me. You're...you're my personal secretary. Got it?"

"Why sure, sugar. That's what I'm always called." Again with the wink.

"Now then, Nunzio. I want you to get her luggage and move it into...I don't know, the pink bedroom."

"You want I should give him a hand, Boss?" Guido asked.

"*You* stay put." I smiled, baring all my teeth. "I've got a special job for you."

"Now just a darn minute!" Bunny interrupted, her cutie-pie accent noticeably lacking. "What's this with the `pink bedroom'? Somehow you don't strike me as the kind that sleeps in a pink bedroom. Aren't I moving into your bedroom?"

"*I'm* sleeping in my bedroom," I said. "Now isn't it easier for you to move into one of our spares than for me to relocate just so you can move into mine?"

As I said, it had been a long night, and I was more than a little slow. Lucky for me, Bunny was fast enough for both of us.

"I thought we was goin' to be sharin' a room, Mr. Skeeve. That's the whole idea of my bein' here, ya know? What's wrong? Ya think I got bad breath or sumpin'?" "Aahh...ummm..." I said intelligently.

"Hi, Guido...Nunzio. Who's...oh wow!"

That last witty line didn't come from me. Massha had just entered the room with Markie in tow and lurched to a halt at the sight of Bunny.

"Hey, Boss! What's with the kid?"

"Guido, Nunzio, this is Markie...our *other* house guest. Massha, Markie, this is Bunny. She's going to be staying with us for a while...in the *pink* bedroom."

"Now I get it!" Bunny exclaimed. "You want we should play it cool because of the kid! Well, you can count on me. Discretion is Bunny's middle name. The pink bedroom it is!"

I could cheerfully have throttled her. If her meaning was lost on Markie, it certainly hadn't gotten past Massha, who was staring out at me from under raised eyebrows.

"Whatever!" I said rather than take more drastic action. "Now, Nunzio, you get Bunny set up in the pink bedroom. Massha, I want you to get Markie settled in the blue bedroom next to mine...and knock it off with the eyebrows. I'll explain everything in the morning."

"*That* I want to hear," she snorted. "C'mon, kid."

"I'm not tired!" Markie protested.

"Tough!" I countered. "I am."

"Oh," she said meekly and followed Massha.

Whatever kind of a crumb her father might be, somewhere along the line she had learned when adults could be argued with and when it was best to go with the flow.

"What do you want me to do, Boss?" Guido asked eagerly.

I favored him with my evilest grin.

"Remember that special assignment I said I had for you?"

"Yea, Boss?"

"I'll warn you, it's dangerous."

That appealed to his professional pride, and he puffed out his chest. "The tougher the better. You know me!"

"Fine," I said. "All you have to do is go upstairs and explain Bunny to Aahz. It seems my partner isn't talking to me just now."

V.

"Such stuff dreams are made of."
S. BEAUTY

LUANNA WAS WITH me. I couldn't remember when she arrived or how long she had been here, but I didn't care. I hadn't seen her since we got back from the jailbreak on Limbo, and I had missed her terribly. She had left me to stay with her partner, Matt, and a little piece of me went with her. I won't be so cornball as to say it was my heart, but it was in that general vicinity.

There was so much I wanted to tell her...wanted to ask her, but it didn't really seem necessary. We just lay side by side on a grassy hill watching the clouds, enjoying each other's company in silence. I could have stayed like that forever, but she raised herself on one elbow and spoke softly to me.

"If you'll just skootch over a little, Skeevie, we can both get comfy."

This was somehow jarring to my serenity. She didn't sound like Luanna at all. Luanna's voice was musical and exciting. She sounded like...

"BUNNY!"

I was suddenly sitting bolt upright, not on a grassy knoll, but in my own bed.

"Ssshh! You'll wake up the kid!"

She was perched on the edge of my bed wearing something filmy that was even more revealing than the skin-tight outfit she had had on last night.

"What are you doing in my room!?"

I had distinct memories of stacking several pieces of furniture in front of the door before I retired, and a quick glance confirmed that they were still in place.

"Through the secret passageway," she said with one of her winks. "Nunzio showed it to me last night."

"Oh, he did, did he?" I snarled. "Remind me to express my thanks to him for that little service."

"Save your thanks, sugar. You're goin' to need them when I get done with you."

With that she raised the covers and slid in next to me. I slid out the other side of the bed as if a spider had just joined me. Not that I'm afraid of spiders, mind you, but Bunny scares me stiff.

"Now what's wrong?" she whined.

"Urn...ah...look, Bunny. Can we talk for a minute?"

"Sure," she said, sitting up in bed and bending forward to rest her elbows on her knees. "Anything you say."

Unfortunately, her current position also gave me an unrestricted view of her cleavage. I promptly forgot what I was going to say.

"Aaah...I...um..."

There was a knock at the door.

"Come in!" I said, grateful for the interruption. That is beyond a doubt the dumbest thing I have ever said.

The door opened, sweeping the stacked furniture back with amazing ease, and Chumley walked in.

"I say, Skeeve, Aahz has just been telling me the most remarkable...Hal-lo?"

I mentioned before that Chumley is a troll. What I didn't say was that he could blush...probably because I didn't know it myself until just now. Of all the sights I've seen in several dimensions, a blushing troll is in a category all its own.

"You must be Chumley!" Bunny chirped. "The boys told me about you."

"Umm...quite right. Pleased to make your acquaintance and all that," the troll said, trying to avert his eyes while still making polite conversation.

"Yeah. Sure, Chum. Don't you have somethin' else to do...like leavin'?"

I clutched at his arm in desperation.

"No! I mean...Chumley always comes by first thing in the morning."

"Ahh...Yes. Just wanted to see if Skeeve was ready for a spot of breakfast."

"Well, I got here first," Bunny bristled. "If Skeevie wants something to nibble on, he can..."

"Good morning, Daddy!"

Markie came bounding into the room and gave me a hug before any of us knew she was around.

"Well, well. You must be Skeeve's new ward, Markie," the troll beamed, obviously thankful to have something to focus on other than Bunny.

"And you're Chumley. Hi, Bunny!"

"Hiya, kid," Bunny responded with a noticeable lack of enthusiasm as she pulled the covers up around her neck.

"Are you up, Skeeve?"

The voice wafting in from the corridor was immediately identifiable as Tananda.

Chumley and I had rarely worked together as a team, but this time no planning or coordination was necessary. I scooped Markie up and carried her into the hall while Chumley followed, slamming the door behind him with enough force to crack the wood.

"Pip pip, little sister. Fine day, isn't it?"

"Hi, Tananda! What's new?"

Our cordial greetings, intended to disarm the situation, succeeded only in stopping our colleague in her tracks.

Tananda is quite attractive—if curvaceous, olive-skinned, green-haired women are your type. Of course, she looks a lot better when she isn't pursing her lips and narrowing her eyes suspiciously.

"Well, for openers, I'd say the little girl under your arm is new," she said firmly. "I may not be the most observant person, but I'm sure I would have noticed her if she had been around before."

"Oh. Well, there are a few things I've got to debrief you on," I smiled weakly. "This is one of them. Her name is Markie, and…"

"Later, Skeeve. Right now I'm more curious about what my big brother's up to. How 'bout it, Chumley? I've seen you slam doors on the way *into* bedrooms before, but never on the way out."

"Ummm…that is…" the troll mumbled awkwardly.

"Actually," I assisted, "it's more like…you see…"

"Exactly what I had in mind," Tananda declared, slipping past us and flinging the bedroom door open.

My room was mercifully empty of occupants. Apparently Bunny had retreated through whatever secret panel she had emerged from. Chumley and I exchanged unnoted glances of relief.

"I don't get it," Tananda frowned. "You two acted like you were trying to hide a body. There's nothing here to be so secretive about"

"I think they didn't want you to see the girl in my daddy's bed," Markie supplied brightly.

I wanted to express my thanks to Markie but decided that I had enough problems without adding murder to the list.

"Well, Skeeve?" Tananda said, her eyebrows almost reaching her hairline.

"Ummm...actually, I'm not really her daddy. That's one of the things I wanted to debrief you about."

"I meant about the girl in your room!"

"That's the other thing I wanted to..."

"Cut him some slack! Huh, Tananda? It's uncivilized to beat up on someone before breakfast."

That was Aahz, who for once had approached our gathering without being seen...or heard. He's usually not big on quiet entrances.

For that matter, I had never known him to be at all reluctant about beating up on someone—say, for example, me—before breakfast. Still, I was grateful for his intervention.

"Hi, Aahz. We were just..."

"Do you know what your partner is doing!?" Tananda said in a voice that could freeze wine. "He *seems* to be turning our home into a combination day-care center and..."

"I know all about it," Aahz interrupted, "and so will you if you'll just cool down. We'll explain everything over breakfast."

"Well..."

"Besides," Markie piped up, "it's not *your* home. It's my daddy's. He just lets you live here. He can do anything he wants in *his* house!"

I released my hold on her, hoping to dump her on her head. Instead, she twisted in midair and landed on her feet like a cat, all the while sneering smugly.

Tananda had stiffened as if someone had jabbed her with a pin.

"I suppose you're right, Markie," she said through tight lips. "If the 'Great Skeeve' wants to romp with some bit of fluff, it's none of my business. And if I don't like it, I should just go elsewhere."

She spun on her heel and started off down the hall. "What about breakfast?" Aahz called after her.

"I'll be eating out...permanently!"

We watched her departure in helpless silence.

"I'd better go after her," Chumley said at last. "In the mood she's in, she might hurt someone."

"Could you take Markie with you?" Aahz requested, still staring after Tananda.

"Are you kidding?" the troll gaped.

"Well, at least drop her off in the kitchen. I've got to have a few words with Skeeve in private."

"I want to stay here!" Markie protested.

"Go," I said quietly.

There must have been something in my voice, because both Markie and Chumley headed off without further argument.

"Partner, you've got a problem."

"Don't I know it. If there was any way I could ship her back to Don Bruce, I'd do it in a minute, but…"

"I'm not talking about Bunny!"

That stopped me.

"You aren't?"

"No. Markie's the problem, not Bunny."

"Markie? But she's just a little girl."

Aahz heaved a small sigh and put one hand on my shoulder… gently, for a change.

"Skeeve, I've given you a lot of advice in the past, some of it better than others. For the most part, you've done pretty well at winging it in unfamiliar situations, but this time you're in over your head. Believe me, you don't have the vaguest idea of the kind of havoc a kid can cause in your life…especially a little girl."

I didn't know what to say. My partner was obviously sincere in his concern, and for a change was expressing it in a very calm, low-key manner. Still, I couldn't go along with what he was saying.

"C'mon, Aahz. How much trouble can she be? This thing with Tananda happened because of Bunny…"

"…after Markie started mouthing off at the wrong time. I already had Tananda cooling off when Markie put her two cents in."

It also occurred to me that Markie was the one who had spilled the beans to Tananda in the first place. I shoved that thought to the back of my mind.

"So she doesn't have enough sense to keep her mouth shut. She's just a kid. We can't expect her to…"

"That's my point. Think about our operation for a minute, partner. How many times in one day can things go sour if someone says the wrong thing at the right moment? It's taken us a year to get Guido and Nunzio on board…and they're adults. Bringing a kid into the place is like waving a torch around a fireworks factory."

As much as I appreciated his efforts to explain a problem to me, I was starting to weary a bit of Aahz's single-minded pursuit of his point.

"Okay. So I haven't had much experience around kids. I may be underestimating the situation, but aren't you being a bit of an alarmist? What experience are you basing *your* worries on?"

"Are you kidding?" my partner said, laughing for the first time in our conversation. "Anyone who's been around as many centuries as I have has had more than their share of experience with kids. You met my nephew Rupert? You think he was born an adult? And he's only one of more nieces, nephews, and grandchildren than I can count without being reduced to a nervous wreck by the memories."

And I thought I couldn't be surprised by Aahz any more.

"Really? Grandchildren? I never even knew you had kids."

"I don't like to talk about it. That in itself should be a clue. When someone who likes to talk as much as I do totally avoids a subject, the memories have got to be less than pleasant!"

I was starting to get a bit worried. Realizing that Aahz usually tends to minimize danger, his warnings were starting to set my overactive imagination in gear.

"I hear what you're saying, Aahz. But we're only talking about one kid here. How much trouble can one little girl be?"

My partner's face suddenly split into one of his infamous evil grins. "Remember that quote," he said. "I'm going to be tossing it back at you from time to time."

"But..."

"Hey, Boss! There's someone here to see you!"

Just what I needed! I had already pretty much resolved not to take on any more clients until after Markie's father had reclaimed her. Of course, I didn't want to say that in front of Aahz, especially considering our current conversation.

"I'm in the middle of a conference, Guido!" I called . "Tell them to come back later."

"Suit yourself, Boss!" came the reply. "I just thought you'd want to know, seein' as how it's Luanna..."

I was off like a shot, not even bothering to excuse myself. Aahz would understand. He knew I'd had a thing for Luanna since our expedition into Limbo.

On my way to the waiting room, I had time to speculate as to whether or not this was one of my bodyguard's little pranks. I decided that if it was, I would study hard until I knew enough magic to turn him into a toad.

My suspicions were groundless. She was there. My beautiful blond goddess. What really made my heart leap, though, was that she had her luggage with her.

"Hi, Luanna. What are you doing here? Where's Matt? How have things been? Would you like something to drink? Could I…"

I suddenly realized that I was babbling and forced myself to pause.

"Aahh…what I'm trying to say is that it's good to see you."

That got me the slow smile that had haunted my dreams. "I'm glad, Skeeve. I was afraid you'd forgotten about me."

"Not a chance," I said, then realized I was leering. "That is, no, I haven't forgotten a thing about you."

Her deep blue eyes locked with mine, and I felt myself sinking helplessly into their depths.

"That's good," she said in that musical voice of hers. "I was worried about taking you up on your offer after all this time."

That got through the fog that was threatening to envelop my mind. "Offer? What offer?"

"Oh, you don't remember! I thought…oh, this is embarrassing."

"Wait a minute!" I cried. "I haven't forgotten! It's just that…let me think…it's just…"

Like a beam of sunlight in a swamp the memory came to me. "You mean when I said that you could come to work for Aahz and me? That's it? Right?"

"That's what I was talking about!" The sun came from behind the clouds as she smiled again. "You see, Matt and I have split, and I thought…"

"Do you want any breakfast, Daddy? You said…oh! Hello."

"DADDY!!??"

Markie and Luanna stared at each other.

I revised my plans rapidly. I would study hard and turn *myself* into a toad.

"I can explain, Luanna…" I began.

"I think you should keep this one, Daddy," Markie said, never taking her eyes off Luanna. "She's a lot prettier than the other one."

"THE OTHER…Oh! You mean Tananda."

"No, I mean…"

"MARKIE!" I interrupted desperately. "Why don't you wait for me in the kitchen. I'll be along in a minute after I finish talking to…"

"Skeevie, are we going to go shopping?" Bunny slithered into the room. "I need…who's that!?"

"Me? I'm nobody." Luanna responded grimly. "I never realized until just now how much of a nobody I am!"

"Well, the job's already taken, if that's what you're here for," Bunny smirked.

"Wait a minute! It's a different job! Really! Luanna, I can… Luanna??"

Sometime during my hysteria, the love of my life had gathered up her bags and left. I was talking to empty air.

"Gee, Skeevie. What're you talkin' to her for when you got me? Aren't I…"

"Daddy. Can I…"

"SHUT UP! BOTH OF YOU! Let me think!"

Try as I might, the only thought that kept coming to me was that maybe Aahz was right. Maybe kids were more trouble than I thought.

VI.

"Bring the whole family…but leave the kids at home!"
R. MCDONALD

REALLY, HOT STUFF. Do you think this is such a great idea?"

"Massha, please! I'm trying to think things out. I couldn't get my thoughts together back at Chaos Central with Aahz nattering at me, and I won't be able to do it now if you start up. Now, are you going to help or not?"

My apprentice shrugged her massive shoulders. "Okay. What do you want me to do?"

"Just keep an eye on those two and see that they don't get into any trouble while I think."

"Keep them out of trouble? At the Bazaar at Deva? Aren't Guido and Nunzio supposed to…"

"Massha!"

"All right. All right. I want it noted, though, that I'm taking this assignment under protest."

I'm *sure* I didn't give Aahz this much back talk when I was apprenticed to him. Every time I say that out loud, however, my partner bursts into such gales of laughter that now I tend to keep the thought to myself, even when he isn't around.

After some resistance, I had agreed to take Bunny and Markie on a stroll through the Bazaar. As I said to Massha, this was more to get a bit of time away from Aahz than it was giving in to Bunny's whining, though that voice was not easy to ignore.

In acknowledgment of Aahz's repeated warnings of trouble, I had recruited my apprentice to accompany us so I'd have a backup if things went awry. Guido and Nunzio were along, of course, but they were more concerned with things coming at me than with anything anyone in our party might do to the immediate environment.

All in all, we made quite a procession. Two Mob bodyguards, a woman-mountain disguised as a jewelry display, a moll, a kid, and me! For a change, I wasn't the "kid" of the party. There was something to be said for having an honest-to-goodness child traveling with you. It automatically made one look older and somehow more responsible.

We had been in residence at the Bazaar for some time now, and the neighborhood merchants were pretty much used to us. That is, they knew that if I was interested, I'd come to them. If I wasn't, no amount of wheedling or cajoling would tempt me into buying. That might seem a little strange to you, after all my glowing accounts of the wonders for sale at the Bazaar, but I had fallen into the pattern quite naturally. You see, if you just visit the Bazaar once in a while, it's all quite impressive, and you feel compelled to buy just to keep from losing out on some really nifty bargains. If you live there, on the other hand, there's no real compulsion to buy anything right now. I mean, if I need a plant that grows ten feet in a minute, I'll buy it…when I need it. Until then, the plant can stay in its shop three doors from our tent, and my money can stay in my pocket.

That's how things were, normally. Of course, my situation to-day was anything but normal. I had known this all along, of course, but I hadn't really stopped to think through all the ramifications of my current state of affairs.

Okay. So I was dumb. Remember, I was taking this stroll to try to get a chance to think. Remember?

Maybe I hadn't zeroed in on what my party looked like, but the Deveels spotted the difference before we had gone half a block.

Suddenly, every Deveel who hadn't been able to foist off some trinket on me for the last two years was out to give it one more try.

"Love potions! Results guaranteed!"

"Snake necklaces! Poisonous and non!"

"Special discounts for the Great Skeeve!"

"Special discounts for any *friend* of the Great Skeeve!"

"Try our…"

"Buy my…"

"Taste these…"

Most of this was not aimed at me, but at Bunny and Markie. The Deveels swarmed around them like…well, like Deveels smelling an easy profit. This is not to say that Guido and Nunzio weren't doing their jobs. If they hadn't been clearing a path for us, we wouldn't have been able to move at all. As it was, our progress was simply slowed to a crawl.

"Still think this was a good idea, High Roller?"

"Massha! If you…"

"Just asking. If you can think in this racket, though, you've got better concentration than I do."

She was right, but I wasn't about to admit it. I just kept staring forward as we walked, tracking the activity around me out of the corners of my eyes without turning my head.

"Skeevie! Can I have…"

"No."

"Look at…"

"No."

"Couldn't we…"

"No!"

Bunny was getting to be a pain. She seemed to want everything in sight. Fortunately, I had developed the perfect defense. All I had to do was say "No!" to everything.

"Why did we go shopping if we aren't going to buy anything?"

"Well…"

So much for my perfect defense. Not to be stymied, I switched immediately to Plan B, which was simply to keep our purchases at a minimum. I didn't seem to be too successful at that, either, but I consoled myself by trying to imagine how much junk we would have gotten loaded down with if I hadn't been riding the brake.

Surprisingly enough, despite all of Aahz's dire predictions, Markie wasn't much trouble at all. I found her to be remarkably well mannered and obedient, and she never asked me to buy her anything. Instead, she contented herself with pointing out to Bunny the few booths that individual overlooked.

There weren't many.

My only salvation was that Bunny did not seem interested in the usual collection of whiz-bangs and wowers that most visitors to the Bazaar find irresistible. She was remarkably loyal to her prime passion apparel. Hats, dresses, shoes, and accessories all had to pass her close scrutiny.

I'll admit that Bunny did not indulge in random purchases. She had a shrewd eye for fabric and construction, and better color sense than anyone I have ever known. Aahz always said that Imps were flashy dressers, and I had secretly tried to pattern my own wardrobe after their example. However, one afternoon of shopping with Bunny was an education in itself. Imps have nothing on molls when it comes to clothes sense.

The more I watched Bunny peruse the fashions available at the Bazaar, the more self-conscious I became about my own appearance. Eventually, I found myself looking over a few items for myself, and from there it was a short step to buying.

In no time flat, we had a small mountain of packages to cart along with us. Bunny had stocked upon a couple of outfits that changed color with her mood, and was now wearing an intriguing blouse which had a transparent patch that migrated randomly around her torso. If the latter sounds distracting, it was. My own indulgences were few, but sufficient to add to the overall bulk of merchandise we had to transport.

Guido and Nunzio were exempt from package-carrying duties, and Massha flatly refused on the basis that being a large woman trying to maneuver through the Bazaar was difficult enough without trying to juggle packages at the same time. Realizing the "you break it, you bought it" policies of the Bazaar, I could scarcely argue with her cautious position.

The final resolution to our baggage problem was really quite simple. I flexed my magic powers a bit and levitated the whole kit and kaboodle. I don't normally like to flaunt my powers publicly, but I figured that this was a necessary exception to the rule. Of course, having our purchases floating along behind us was like having a lighthouse in tow; it drew the Deveels out of their stalls in droves.

To my surprise, I started to enjoy the situation. Humility and anonymity is well and good, but sometimes its nice to be made a fuss over. Bunny hung on my arm and shoulder like a boneless falcon, cooing little endearments of appreciation...though the fact that I was willing to finance her purchases seemed to be making as much as or more of an impression on her than my minor display of magic.

"Can't say I think much of her taste in clothes," Massha murmured to me as we paused once more while Bunny darted into a nearby booth.

To say the least, I was not eager to get drawn into a discussion comparing the respective tastes in clothes of Bunny and my apprentice.

"Different body types look better in different styles," I said, as tactfully as I could.

"Yeah? And what style looks best on *my* body type?" "In all honesty, Massha, I can't picture you dressing any differently than you do."

"Really? Say, thanks, Skeeve. A girl always likes to hear a few appreciative noises about how she looks."

I had narrowly sidestepped that booby-trap and cast about frantically for a new subject before the other interpretation of my statement occurred to her.

"Umm...hasn't Markie been well-behaved?"

"I'll say. I'll admit I was a little worried when you first brought her in, but she's been an angel. I don't think I've ever known a kid this patient and obedient."

"Undemanding, too," I said. "I've been thinking of getting her something while we're out, but I'm having trouble coming up with anything appropriate. The Bazaar isn't big on toy shops."

"Are you kidding? It's one big toy shop!"

"Massha..."

"Okay, okay. So they're mostly toys for adults. Let me think. How old is she, anyway?"

"I'm not really sure. She said she was in the third grade at Elementary School...even though she calls it Elemental School...so that would make her..."

I realized that Massha was staring at me in wideeyed horror.

"Elemental School!?"

"That's what she called it. Cute, huh? Why, what does..."

My apprentice interrupted me by grabbing my arm so hard that it hurt. "Skeeve. We've got to get her back home...QUICK!!"

"But I don't see..."

"I'll explain later! Just get her and go! I'll round up Bunny and get her back, but you've got to get moving!" To say the least, I found her manner puzzling. I had never seen Massha so upset. This was obviously not the time for questions, though, so I looked around for Markie.

She was standing, fists clenched, glaring at a tent with a closed flap.

All of a sudden everyone was getting uptight. First Massha, and now Markie.

"What's with the kid?" I said, tapping Guido on the shoulder.

"Bunny's in trying on some peek-a-boo nighties, and the owner chased Markie out," my bodyguard explained. "She don't like it much, but she'll get over it.

It's part of bein' a kid, I guess."

"I see. Well, I was just going to take her back home anyway. Could one of you stay with…"

"SKEEVE! STOP HER!!"

Massha was shouting at me. I was turning toward her to see what she was talking about when it happened, so I didn't see all the details.

There was a sudden WHOOSH followed by the sounds of ripping canvas, wood splintering, and assorted screams and curses.

I whipped my head back around, and my jaw dropped in astonishment.

The booth that Bunny was in was in tatters. The entire stock of the place was sailing off over the Bazaar, as was what was left of the tent. Bunny was trying to cover herself with her hands and screaming her head off. The proprietor, a particularly greasy-looking Deveel, was also screaming his head off, but his emotions were being vented in our general direction instead of at the world in general.

I would say it was a major dilemma except for one thing. The displays on either side of Bunny's tent and for two rows behind it were in a similar state. *That* is a major dilemma, making the destruction of a single booth pale in comparison.

A voice sprang into my head, drowning out the clamor of the enraged merchants. "If you break it, you bought it!" the voice said, and it spoke with a Devan accent.

"What happened?" I gasped, though whether to myself or to the gods, I wasn't sure.

Massha answered.

"What happened was Markie!" she said grimly. "She blew her cork and summoned up an air elemental…you know, like you learn to do at *Elemental* School? It appears that when the kid throws a tantrum, she's going to do it with magic!"

My mind grasped the meaning of her words instantly, just as fast as it leaped on to the next plateau. Aahz! I wasn't sure which was going to be worse: breaking the news to Aahz, or telling him how much it had cost us to learn about it!

VII.

"There's a time to fight, and a time to hide out!"
B. CASSIDY

I'VE HEARD THAT when some people get depressed, they retire to their neighborhood bar and tell their troubles to a sympathetic bartender. The problem with the Bazaar at Deva (a problem I had never noticed before) is that there are no sympathetic bartenders!

Consequently, I had to settle for the next best thing and holed up in the Yellow Crescent Inn.

Now, a fast-food joint may seem to you to be a poor substitute for a bar. It is. This particular fast-food joint, however, is owned and managed by my only friend at the Bazaar who isn't living with me. This last part was especially important at the moment, since I didn't think I was apt to get much sympathy in my own home.

Gus is a gargoyle, but despite his fierce appearance he's one of the friendliest beings I've ever met. He's helped Aahz and me out on some of our more dubious assignments, so he's less inclined to ask "How did you get yourself into this?" than most. Usually, he's more interested in "How do you get out of it?"

"How did you get yourself into this one?" he said, shaking his head.

Well, nobody's perfect...especially friends.

"I *told* you, Gus. One lousy card game where I expected to lose. If I had known it was going to backfire like this, so help me I would have folded every hand!"

"You see, there's your problem," the gargoyle said, flashing a grin toothier than normal. "Instead of sitting in and losing, you'd be better off not sitting in at all!"

I rewarded his sound advice by rolling my eyes.

"It's all hypothetical anyway. What's done is done. The question is, 'What do I do now?'"

"Not so fast. Let's stick with the card game for a minute. Why did you sit in if you were expecting to lose?"

"Look. Can we drop the card game? I was wrong. Okay? Is that what you want to hear?"

"No-o-o," Gus said slowly. "I still want to hear why you went in the first place. Humor me."

I stared at him for a moment, but he seemed perfectly serious.

I shrugged. "The Geek sent me an invitation. Frankly, it was quite flattering to get one. I just thought it would be sociable to…"

"Stop!" the gargoyle interrupted, raising his hand. "There's your problem."

"What is?"

"Trying to be sociable. What's the matter? Aren't your current round of friends good enough for you?"

That made me a little bit nervous. I was having enough problems without having Gus get his nose out of joint.

"It isn't that, Gus. Really. The whole crew—yourself included—is closer to me than my family ever was. It's just…I don't know…"

"…you want to be liked. Right?"

"Yeah. I guess that's it."

"And that's your problem!"

That one threw me.

"I don't get it," I admitted.

The gargoyle sighed, then ducked behind the counter. "Have another milkshake," he said, shoving one toward me. "This might take a while, but I'll try to explain."

I like to think it's a sign of my growing savoir-faire that I now enjoy strawberry milkshakes. When I first visited the Bazaar, I rejected them out of hand because they looked like pink swamp muck. I was now moderately addicted to them, though I still wouldn't eat the food here. Then again, maybe it was a sign of something else completely if I thought a taste for strawberry milkshakes was a sign of savoir-faire!

"Look, Skeeve," Gus began, sipping at a milkshake of his own, "you're a nice guy…one of the nicest I've ever known. You go out of your way to 'do the right thing'…to be nice to people. The key phrase there is 'go out of your way.' You're in a 'trouble-heavy' profession anyway. Nobody hires a magician because things are going well. Then you add to that your chosen lifestyle. Because you want to be liked, you place yourself in situations you wouldn't go near if it was for your own personal satisfaction. Case in point: the card game. If you had been out for personal gain, i.e., wealth, you wouldn't have gone near it, since you don't know the game. But you wanted to be friendly, so you went expecting to lose. That's not normal, and it resulted in a not-normal outcome, to wit, Markie. That's why you get into trouble."

I chewed my lip slightly as I thought over what he was saying.

"So if I want to stay out of trouble, I've got to stop being a nice guy? I'm not sure I can do that, Gus."

"Neither am I," the gargoyle agreed cheerfully. "What's more, if you could, I don't think I or any of your other friends would like you any more. I don't even think you'd like yourself."

"Then why are you recommending that I change?"

"I'm not! I'm just pointing out that it's the way you are, not any outside circumstances, that keeps getting you into trouble. In short, since you aren't going to change, get used to being in trouble. It's going to be your constant state for a long while."

I found myself massaging my forehead again.

"Thanks, Gus," I said. "I knew I could count on you to cheer me up."

"Don't knock it. Now you can focus on solving your current problem instead of wasting time wondering why it exists."

"Funny. I thought I was doing just that. Someone *else* wanted to talk about what was causing my problems."

My sarcasm didn't faze the gargoyle in the least.

"Right," he nodded. "That brings us to your current problem."

Now you're talking. What do you think I should do, Gus?"

"Beats me. I'd say you've got a real dilemma on your hands."

I closed my eyes as my headache hammered anew. "I don't know what I'd do without you, Gus."

"Hey. Don't mention it. What are friends for? Whoops! Here comes Tananda!"

The other disadvantage to holing up at the Yellow Crescent Inn, besides the fact that it isn't a bar, is that it's located right across the street from my home. This is not good for someone who's trying to avoid his house-mates.

Fortunately, this was one situation I could handle with relative ease.

"Don't tell her I'm here, Gus," I instructed.

"But…"

Not waiting to hear the rest of his protest, I grabbed my milkshake, slipped into a chair at a nearby table, and set to work with a fast disguise spell. By the time Tananda hit the door, the only one she could see in the place besides Gus was a potbellied Deveel sipping on a strawberry milkshake.

"Hi, Gus!" she sang. "Have you seen Skeeve around?"

"He…aahh…was in earlier." The gargoyle carefully avoided the lie.

"Oh, well. I guess I'll just have to leave without saying goodbye to him, then. Too bad. We weren't on particularly good terms the last time I saw him."

"You're leaving?"

Gus said it before the words burst out of my own mouth, saving me from blowing my disguise.

"Yea. I figure it's about time I moved on."

"I…umm…have been hearing some strange things about my neighbors, but I've never been sure how much to believe," the gargoyle said thoughtfully. "This sudden departure wouldn't have anything to do with the new moll that's been foisted off on Skeeve, would it?"

"Bunny? Naw. I'll admit I was a bit out of sorts when I first heard about it, but Chumley explained the whole thing to me."

"Then what's the problem?"

Gus was doing a terrific job of beating me to my lines. As long as he kept it up, I'd be able to get all my questions answered without revealing myself. It had occurred to me to confront Tananda directly as soon as I heard what she was up to, but then I realized that this was a rare chance to hear her thoughts when she didn't think I was around.

"Well, it's something Markie said…"

Markie again. I definitely owed Aahz an apology

…She made some crack about her daddy, that's Skeeve, letting me live there, and it got me to thinking. Things have been nice these last couple years…almost too nice. Since we haven't had to worry about overhead, Chumley and I haven't been working much. More important, we haven't been working at working. It's too easy to hang around the place and wait for something to come to us."

"Getting fat and lazy, huh?" Gus grinned.

"Something like that. Now, you know me, Gus. I've always been footloose and fancy free. Ready to follow a job or a whim at the drop of a hat. If anyone had suggested to me that I should settle down, I would have punched their lights out. Now all of a sudden, I've got a permanent address and family…family beyond

Chumley, I mean. I hadn't realized how domestic I was getting until Skeeve showed up with Markie. A kid, even. When I first saw her, my first thought was that it would be nice to have a kid around the place! Now I ask you, Gus, does that sound like me?"

"No, it doesn't."

The gargoyle's voice was so quiet I scarcely recognized it as his.

"Right then I saw the handwriting on the wall. If I don't start moving again, I'm going to take root...permanently. You know, the worst thing is that I don't really want to go. That's the scariest part of all."

"I don't think Aahz or Skeeve want you to go either."

"Now don't you start on me, Gus. This is hard enough for me as it is. Like I said, they're family, but they're stifling me. I've got to get away, even if it's only for a little while, or I'm going to lose a part of me...forever."

"Well, if you've made up your mind...good luck."

"Thanks, Gus. I'll be in touch from time to time. Keep an eye on the boys in case they buy more trouble than they can sell."

"I don't think you have to worry about Chumley. He's pretty levelheaded."

"Chumley's not the one I'm worried about."

I thought that was going to be her parting shot, but she paused with one hand on the door.

"You know, it's probably just as well that I couldn't find Skeeve. I'm not sure I could have stuck to my guns in a face-to-face...but then again, maybe that's why I was looking for him."

I could feel Gus's eyes on me as she slipped out.

"I suppose it's pointless to ask why you didn't say something, *Mister* Skeeve."

Even though I had worried earlier about getting Gus angry with me, somehow it didn't matter anymore.

"At first it was curiosity," I said, letting my disguise slip away. "Then, I didn't want to embarrass her."

"And at the end there? When she flat-out said that you could talk her out of going? Why didn't you speak up then? Do you *want* her to disappear?"

I couldn't even manage a spark of anger. "You know better than that, Gus," I said quietly. "You're hurting and lashing out at whoever's handy, which happens to be me. I didn't try to get her to stay for the same reason you didn't try harder. She feels we're stifling her, and if she wants out, it'd be pretty small of us to try to keep her for our own sakes, wouldn't it?"

There was prolonged silence, which was fine by me. I didn't feel much like talking anymore.

Rising, I started for the door.

"You were looking the other way when she left," the gargoyle said. "You might like to know there were tears in her eyes."

"Mine too," I replied without turning. "That's why I was looking the other way."

VIII.

"What did I do wrong?"
LEAR, REX

WITH A HEAVY heart, I headed back home. I was no longer worried about Aahz yelling at me. If anything, I was rather hoping he would. If he did, I decided that for a change I wouldn't even argue back. In short, I felt terrible and was in the mood to do a little penance.

Sliding through the tent flap, I cocked an ear and listened for Aahz. Actually, I was a little surprised that I couldn't hear him from the street, but I was sure I would be able to locate his position in the house with no difficulty. As I've said before, my partner has no problem expressing his moods, particularly anger.

The house was silent.

From the lack of reverberations and/or falling plaster, I assumed that Aahz was out...probably looking for me with blood in his eye. I debated going out to look for him, but decided that it would be better to wait right here. He'd be back eventually, so I headed for the garden to make myself comfortable until he showed up.

What I call the garden is actually our courtyard. It has a fountain and an abundance of plants, so I tend to think of it as a piece of the outdoors rather than as an enclosed area. I had been spending more and more time there lately, especially when I wanted time to think. It reminded me of some of the quieter spots I would find from time to time back when I was living on my own in the woods...back before I met Garkin, and, through him, Aahz.

That memory led me to ponder a curious point: Were there other successful beings, like myself, who used their new prosperity to recreate the setting or atmosphere of their pre-success days? If so, it made for a curious cycle.

I was so preoccupied with this thought as I entered the garden that I almost missed the fact that I wasn't alone. Someone else was using my retreat...specifically, Aahz.

He was sitting on one of the stone benches, chin in his hands and elbows on his knees, staring blankly into the water as it flowed through the fountain.

To say the least, I was surprised. Aahz has never been the meditative type, particularly in times of crisis. He's more the "beat on someone or something until the problem goes away" type. Still, here he was, not agitated, not pacing, just sitting and staring. It was enough out of character for him to unnerve me completely.

"Umm…Hi, Aahz," I said hesitantly.

"Hello, Skeeve," he replied without looking around.

I waited for a few moments for him to say something else. He didn't. Finally I sat down on the bench next to him and stared at the water myself a bit.

We sat that way for a while, neither of us saying anything. The trickling water began to have a tranquilizing, hypnotic effect on me, and I found my mind starting to relax and drift.

"It's been quite a day, hasn't it, partner?"

My mind reflexively recoiled into a full defensive posture before it dawned on me that Aahz was still speaking quietly.

"Y…Yes."

I waited, but he seemed off in his own thoughts again. My nerves shot, I decided to take the initiative. "Look, Aahz. About Markie…"

"Yes?"

"I knew about the Elemental School thing. She told me on the way back from the Geek's. I just didn't know enough to realize it was important."

"I know," Aahz sighed, not looking at me. "I hadn't bothered to teach you about elemental magic…just like I hadn't taught you about dragon poker."

No explosion! I was starting to get a little worried about my partner.

"Aren't you upset?"

"Of course I'm upset," he said, favoring me with a fleeting glimpse of bared teeth, a barely recognizable smile. "Do you think I'm always this jovial?"

"I mean, aren't you mad?"

"Oh, I'm past 'mad.' I'm all the way to 'thoughtful.'"

I arrived at the startling conclusion that I liked it better when Aahz was shouting and unreasonable. *That* I knew how to deal with. This latest mood of his was a total unknown.

"What are you thinking about?"

"Parenthood."

"Parenthood?"

"Yeah. You know, that state of total responsibility for another being? Well, at least, that's the theory." I wasn't sure I was following this at all.

"Aahz? Are you trying to say you feel responsible for what happened with Markie because you hadn't taught me more about magic and poker?"

"Yes. No. I don't know."

"But that's silly!"

"I know," he replied, with his first honest grin since I had entered the garden. "That's what got me thinking about parenthood."

I abandoned any hope of following his logic.

"You'll have to explain it to me, Aahz. I'm a little slow today."

He straightened up a bit, draping one arm around my shoulders.

"I'll try, but it isn't easy," he said in a tone that was almost conversational. "You see, regardless of what I said when I was ranting at you about how much of a problem Markie was going to be, it's been a long time since I was a parent. I've been sitting here, trying to remember what it was like. What's so surprising to me is the realization that I've never really stopped. Nobody does."

I started to shift uncomfortably.

"Hear me out. For once I'm trying to share some of my hard-won lessons with you without shouting. Forget the theories of parenthood! What it's really all about is taking pride in things you can never be sure you had a hand in, and accepting the responsibility and guilt for things you either didn't know or had no control over. Actually, it's a lot more complicated than that, but that's the bare bones of the matter."

"You don't make it sound particularly attractive," I observed.

"In a lot of ways, it isn't. Your kid expects you to know everything…to be able to answer any question he asks and, more important, to provide a logical explanation of what is essentially an illogical world. Society, on the other hand, expects you to train your kid in everything necessary for them to become a successful, responsible member of the community…even if you aren't yourself. The problem is that you aren't the only source of input for the kid. Friends, schools, and other adults are all supplying other opinions, many of which you don't agree with. That means that if your kid succeeds, you don't really know if it was because of or in spite of your influence. On the other hand, if the kid goes bad, you always wonder if there was something else you could have said or done or done differently that could have salvaged things before they hit the wall."

His hand tightened slightly on my shoulder, but I don't think he did it consciously.

"Now, I wasn't a particularly good parent...which I like to think places me in the majority. I didn't interact much with my kids. Business was always a good excuse, but the truth was that I was glad to let someone else handle their upbringing as much as possible. I can see now that it was because I was afraid that if I tried to do it myself, that in my ignorance and uncertainty I would make some terrible mistake. The end result was that some of the kids turned out okay, some of them...let's say less than okay. What I was left with was a nagging feeling that I could have done better. That I could have—should have—made more of a difference."

He released his hold on my shoulders and stood up. "Which brings us to you."

I wasn't sure if I should feel uncomfortable because he was focusing on me, or glad because he was pacing again.

"I've never consciously thought of you as a son, but in hindsight I realize that a lot of how I've treated you has been driven by my lingering guilt from parenthood. In you, I had another chance to mold someone...to give all the advice I felt I should have given my own kids. If at times I've seemed to overreact when things didn't go well, it's because deep inside I saw it as a personal failure. I mean, this was my second chance. A time to show how much I had learned from my earlier perceived failures, and you know what? Now I'm giving it my full attention and my best shot, and things are *still* going wrong!"

This was doing nothing to brighten my mood. On top of everything else, now I had the distinct feeling I had somehow let Aahz down.

"I don't think you can say it's your fault, Aahz. I mean, you've tried hard and been more patient with me than anyone I've ever known. Nobody can teach someone else everything, even if they could remember what should be taught. I've got a certain saturation point. After that, I'm not going to learn anything new until I've digested what I've got. Even then, I've got to be honest and say there are some things I don't believe no matter how often you tell me. I've just got to find out for myself. A craftsman can't blame his skill if he has defective material."

"That's just what I've been thinking," Aahz nodded. "I can't keep blaming myself for everything. It's very astute of you to have figured this out at your age...without going through what I have."

"It's no big thing to figure out that I'm a dummy," I said bitterly. "I've known it all along."

Suddenly, I felt myself being lifted into the air. I looked past Aahz's hand, which was gripping my shirt by the collar, down the length of his arm, and into his yellow eyes.

"Wrong lesson!" he snarled, sounding much like his old self. "What you're supposed to be learning isn't that you're dumb. You're not, and if you were listening, I just complimented you on that fact."

"Then what..." I managed, with what little air I had left.

"The point is that what's happened in the past isn't *my* fault, just like what's happening now isn't *your* fault!"

"Aaggh...urk..." was my swift rebuttal.

"Oh! Sorry."

My feet hit the floor and air flooded back into my lungs.

"All a parent, *any* parent, can do is give it their best shot, right or wrong." Aahz continued as if there had been no interruption. "The actual outcome rests on so many variables, no single person can assume responsibility, blame, or praise for whatever happens. That's important for me to remember in my dealings with you...and for you to remember in your dealings with Markie. It's not your fault!"

"It isn't?"

"That's right. We both have strong paternal streaks in us, though I don't know where you got yours from, but all we can do is our best. We've got to remember not to try to shoulder the blame for what other people do...like Tananda."

That sobered me up again. "You know about that, huh?"

"Yeah. She told me to tell you goodbye if she didn't see you, but I guess you already know."

I simply nodded, unable to speak.

"I was already worried about how you were going to react to the problems with Markie, and when Tananda left I knew you were going to take it hard. I've been trying to find a way to show you that you aren't alone. Right or wrong, what you're feeling has been around for a long time."

"Thanks, Aahz."

"Has it helped at all?"

I thought for a moment.

"A bit."

My partner heaved another sigh.

"Well," he said, "I tried. That's what's important...I think."

"Cheerio, chaps. How's every little thing?"

I glanced up to find Chumley striding toward us, beaming merrily. "Oh. Hi, Chumley."

"I thought you'd like to know," the troll announced, "I think I've figured out a way to charge the damage Markie caused this afternoon back to the Mob as a business expense!"

"That's swell, Chumley," Aahz said dully.

"Yeah. Terrific."

"'Allo, 'allo?" he said, cocking his head at us. "Any time the two biggest hustlers at the Bazaar fail to get excited over money, there's got to be something wrong. Out with it now. What's troubling you?"

"Do you want to tell him, Aahz?"

"Well..."

"I say, this wouldn't be about little sister leaving the nest, would it? Oh, there's a giggle."

"You know?" I blinked.

"I can see you're all broken up over it," Aahz said in a dangerous tone.

"Tish tosh!" the troll exclaimed. "I don't see where it's anything to get upset about. Tananda's just settling things in her mind, is all. She's found that she likes something that goes against her self-image. It might take a few days, but eventually she'll figure out that it's not the end of the world. Everybody goes through it. It's called 'growing up.' If anything, I think it's bloody marvelous that she's finally having to learn that things don't stay the same forever."

"You do?" I was suddenly starting to feel better.

"Certainly. Why, in just the time we've been chumming around together, Aahz has changed, you've changed, so have I, though I don't tend to show it as dramatically as you two or little sister. You blokes have just got a bad case of the guilts. Poppycock! You can't take the blame for everything, you know."

"That's good advice," I said, standing up and stretching. "Why can't you ever give me good advice like that, partner?"

"Cause any fool can see it without being told," Aahz snarled, but there was a twinkle in his eye. "The problem is that Pervects aren't just any fool."

"Quite right," Chumley grinned. "Now how about joining me in a little Happy Hour spot of wine while I tell you how clever I am at saving you money."

"I'd rather you impressed us with a solution to our baby-sitting problems," my partner said grimly, heading for the lounge.

I followed in their wake, strangely happy. Things were back to normal...or as normal as they ever get around here. Between us, I was sure we could find a positive course of action. I mean, after all, how much trouble could one little girl...

That thought crumbled in front of an image of elemental-blown tents.

I resolved to do more listening than talking in the upcoming war council.

IX.

"They never let you live it down. One little mistake!"
NERO

RELAXING OVER DRINKS with Aahz and Chum-ley, I felt the tensions and depressions of the day slipping away. It was nice to know that when things really got tough, I had friends to help me solve my problems, however complex or apparently hopeless.

"Well, guys," I said, pouring another round of wine for everyone. "Any ideas as to what we should do?"

"Beats me," Chumley said, toying with his goblet.

"I still think it's *your* problem," Aahz announced, leaning back in his chair and grinning evilly. "I mean, after all, you got into it without our help."

Like I said, it's great to have friends.

"I can't say I go along with that, Aahz old boy," the troll said with a wave. "Although I'll admit it's tempting.

The unfortunate reality is that as long as we're living and working as closely as we are, his problems are our problems, don't you know?"

As much as I appreciated the fact that Chumley's logic was moving them closer to lending me assistance, I felt the need to defend myself a little.

"I'd like to think it's a two-way street, Aahz. I've gotten dragged into a few of *your* problems as well."

He started to snap back, then pursed his lips and returned his attention to his wine. "I'll avoid comparing lists of how often which of us has gotten us in how much trouble and simply concede the point. I guess that's part of what a partnership is all about. Sorry if I seem a little snorky from time to time, but I've never had a partner before. It takes getting used to."

"I say! Well said, Aahz!" Chumley applauded. "You know, you're getting more civilized every day."

"Let's not get too carried away just yet. How about you, Chumley? You and your sister have helped us out often enough, but I don't recall either of *you* bringing your problems home with you. Isn't that a little lopsided?"

"I've always figured it's our way of kicking in on the rent," the troll said casually. "If our problems ever start interfering with your work, then I'll figure we've overstayed our welcome."

This came as a total surprise to me. I realized with a start that I was usually so busy with my own life and problems that I never got around to asking much about the work Chumley and Tananda were doing.

"Whoa up a minute here," I said. "Are you two having problems I don't know about?"

"Well, it isn't all beer and skittles," the troll grimaced briefly. "The subject at hand, however, is *your* problems. There's nothing on my plate that has a higher priority just now, so let's get to work on the latest crisis, shall we? I suggest we all put on our thinking caps and brainstorm a little. Let's just stare at the ceiling and each toss out ideas as they occur to us."

I made myself a little promise to return to the subject of Tananda and Chumley's problems at a later date, then joined the others in staring thoughtfully at the ceiling.

Time crawled along, and no one said anything.

"Well, so much for brainstorming," Aahz said, reaching for the wine again. "I'll admit I'm coming up blank."

"Perhaps it would help if we started by defining the problem," Chumley urged. "Now, as I see it, we have two problems: Markie and Bunny. We're going to have trouble figuring out what to do about Bunny until we find out what Don Bruce has up his sleeve, and we've got to come up with a way to keep Markie from totally disrupting our lives until her father comes to pick her up."

"*If* he picks her up," my partner corrected helpfully.

"I'll admit, I still don't know how you did so well in that game to end up with Markie in the first place," the troll said, cocking one outsized eye at me and ignoring Aahz.

"Dumb luck...with the emphasis on *dumb*."

"That's not the way I heard it," Chumley smirked. "Whatever your method was, it was successful enough to make you the talk of the Bazaar."

"What!?" Aahz said, sitting up in his chair again.

"You would hear it yourself if you weren't spending all your time sulking in your room," the troll winked. "When I went out after little sister today, it seemed that all I was hearing about was the new dragon poker champion of Deva. Everybody's talking about the game, or what they've heard about the game. I suspect they're embellishing upon the facts, from some of the descrip-tions of the hands, but there are those who are taking it all as gospel."

I remembered then that when the game broke up, the other players had been very enthusiastic about my playing. At the time, I had been worried about the secret of my night out reaching Aahz (which, you'll recall, it did before I got home). The troubles with Markie and Bunny had occupied my mind and time ever since, so I hadn't stopped to think of other potential repercussions of the game gossip. Now, however...

Aahz was out of his seat, pacing back and forth. "Chumley, if what you're saying is true...are you following this, partner?"

"Too bloody well," I growled.

That got my partner to pause momentarily to roll his eyes.

"Watch yourself," he warned. "You're starting to talk like Chumley now."

"You want I should talk like Guido instead, know what I mean?"

"I don't understand," the troll interrupted. "Is something amiss?"

"We don't have two problems," Aahz announced. "We've got *three!* Markie, Bunny, *and* the rumor mill!"

"Gossip? How can that be a problem?"

"Think it through, Chumley," I said. "All I need right now is to have a bunch of hotshot dragon poker players hunting me up to see if I'm as good as every-body says."

"That's only part of it, partner," Aahz added. "This could hurt our business and public images as well." I closed my eyes and sighed.

"Spell it out for me, Aahz. I'm still learning, remember?"

"Well, we already know your reputation at magic has been grow-ing fast...almost too fast. The competition hates you because you're taking all the prime assignments. No big deal! Professional jealousy is the price of success in any field. There comes a time, however, when you can get too big too fast. Then it isn't just your rivals you worry about. Everybody wants you taken down a peg or two if for no other reason than to convince themselves that your success is abnormal...that they don't have to feel bad for not measuring up."

He paused to stare at me hard.

"I'm afraid this dragon poker thing just might push you into the second category. A lot of beings excel here at the Bazaar, but they're only noted in one field. The Geek, for example, is a recognized figure among the gamblers, but he doesn't have any reputation to speak of as a magician or merchant. People can accept that...work hard and you rise toward the top of your group. You, on the other hand, have just made a strong showing in a second profession. I'm afraid there's going to be some backlash."

"Backlash?" I echoed weakly.

"It's like I've been trying to tell you: people aren't going to want you to get too much above them. At the very least they might start boycotting our business. At most...well, there are ways of sabotaging other people's success."

"You mean they're going to..."

"That's enough!" Chumley declared, slapping his palm down on the table loudly.

It suddenly occurred to me that I had never seen Chumley mad. It also occurred to me that I was glad our furniture was strong enough to withstand even Aahz's tirades. If not, the troll would have destroyed the table just stopping the conversation.

"Now listen up, both of you!" he ordered, leveling a gnarled finger at us. "I think the current crisis has gone to your heads. You two are overreacting...snapping at shadows! I'll admit we've got some problems, but we've handled worse. This is no time to get panicky."

"But..."

"Hear me out, Aahz. I've listened to you bellow often enough."

I opened my mouth to make a witty comment, then, for once, thought better of it.

"Markie is a potential disaster, but the key word there is *potential.* She's a good kid who will do what we say...*if* we learn to watch what we say to her. The same goes for Bunny. She's smart as a whip and..."

"Bunny?" I blurted, forgetting myself for a moment.

"Yes, Bunny. It's been a long time since there's been anyone around here I could discuss literature and theater with. She's really quite intelligent if you bother to talk to her."

"We *are* talking about the same Bunny, aren't we?" Aahz murmured.

"The one who comes across dumb as a stone," Chumley confirmed grimly. "Just remember how I come across when I'm putting on my Big Crunch act...but we're wandering. The subject is problems, and I maintain with a little coaching Bunny won't be one."

He paused to glare at us.

"As to the rumor of Skeeve's abilities at dragon poker, I've never in my life heard anyone get as alarmed as you, Aahz. Sure, there are negative sides to any rumor, but you have to get pretty extreme to do the projections that have been voiced just now."

"Hey, Boss!" Guido called, sticking his head in the door. "The Geek's here to see you."

"I'll handle this," Aahz said, heading for the reception area. "You stay here and listen to what Chumley has to say. He's probably right. I have been edgy lately...for some unknown reason."

"If I am right, then you should hear it, too," the troll called after him.

"Talk to me, Chumley," I said. "That's probably the closest you'll ever hear to an apology from Aahz, anyway."

"Quite right. Where was I? Oh, yes. Even if Aahz's appraisal of the reaction to your success is correct, it shouldn't have too much impact on your work. The small fry may go to other magicians, but you've been trying to cut down on unimportant jobs anyway. When someone is *really* in trouble, they're going to want the best available magician working on it...and right now, that means you."

I thought about what he was saying, weighing it carefully in my mind.

"Even if Aahz is just a little right," I said, "I'm not wild about having any ill feeling generated about me at the Bazaar. Admiration I don't mind, but envy makes me uneasy."

"Now that you'll just have to get used to," the troll laughed, clapping a hand lightly on my shoulder. "Whether you know it or not, that's been building for some time...long before this dragon poker thing came up. You've got a lot going for you, Skeeve, and as long as you do, there will be blokes who envy it."

"So you really think the dragon poker rumors are harmless?"

"Quite right. Really, what harm can come from idle gossip?"

"You know, Chumley, you aren't wrong very often. But when you miss, you really miss."

We looked up to find Aahz leaning in the doorway.

"What's wrong, Aahz? You look like someone just served you water when you were expecting wine."

My partner didn't even smile at my attempted humor.

"Worse than that," he said. "That was the Geek downstairs."

"We know. What did he want?"

"I was hoping he had come to pick up Markie for her father..." Aahz's voice trailed off to nothing.

"I take it he didn't?" I prompted.

"No, he didn't. In fact, the subject never came up."

Almost without thinking, my partner's hand groped for his over-sized goblet of wine.

"He had an invitation...no, make that a challenge. The Sen-Sen Ante Kid has heard about Skeeve here. He wants a showdown match of head-to-head dragon poker. The Geek is making the arrangements."

X.

"A spoonful of sugar helps the medicine go down!"
L. BORGIA

JUST LET THE energy flow."

"That's easy for you to say!"

"Did I stutter?"

"You know, Hot Stuff, maybe it would be better if I..."

"Quit talking and concentrate, Massha."

"You started it."

"And I'm finishing it. Focus on the candle!"

If some of that sounds vaguely familiar, it should. It's the old 'light the candle' game. Theoretically, it builds a student's confidence. In actuality, it's a pain in the butt. Apprentices hate the candle drill. I did when I was an apprentice. It's a lot more fun when you're on the teaching end.

"Come on, Skeeve. I'm getting too old to learn this stuff."

"And you're getting older the longer you stall, *apprentice*. Remember, you came to me to learn magic. Just because we've gotten distracted from time to time doesn't mean I've forgotten completely. Now light the candle."

She turned her attention to the exercise again with a mutter I chose to ignore.

I had been thinking hard about my conversations with Aahz and Chumley. The whole question of what to do about the challenge from the Kid was touchy enough that for once I decided to seek the counsel of my advisors before making a commitment I might later regret. Wiser heads than mine were addressing the dilemma at this very moment. Unfortunately, aforesaid wiser heads were in total disagreement as to what course of action to follow.

Aahz was in favor of refusing the match, while Chumley insisted that a refusal would only inflame the situation. He maintained that the only sane way out would be to face the Kid and lose (no one seriously thought I would have a chance in such a game), thereby getting me off the hot seat once and for all. The main problem with that solution was that it involved voluntarily giving up a substantial amount of money...and Aahz wouldn't hear of it.

As the battle raged on, I thought about the earlier portions of our conversations. I thought about parenthood and responsibility. Then I went looking for Massha. When we first met, Massha was holding down a job as court magician for one of the city-states in the dimension of Jahk…that's right. Where they hold the Big Game every year. The problem was that she didn't really know any magic. She was what is known in the field as a mechanic, and all her powers were purchased across the counter in the form of rings, pendants, and other magical devices. After she saw us strut our stuff in the Big Game, she decided to try to learn some of the non-mechanical variety of magic…and for some unknown reason picked or picked on me to provide her with lessons.

Now, to say the least, I had never thought of Massha as a daughter, but she was my apprentice and therefore a responsibility I had accepted. Unfortunately, I had dodged that responsibility more often than not for the very reasons Aahz had listed: I was unsure of my own abilities and therefore afraid of making a mistake. What I hadn't done was give it my best shot, win or lose. That realization sparked me into a new resolve that if anything happened to Massha in the future, it wouldn't be because I hadn't at least tried to teach her what she asked.

I was also aware that I wanted to learn more about any problems Chumley and Tananda were having, as well as getting a better fix on just who or what Bunny was. At this moment, however, Tananda was absent and Chumley was arguing with Aahz, putting that objective on hold. Bunny was around somewhere, but given a choice between her and Massha, I opted for addressing old obligations before plunging into new ones. Ergo, I rousted out Massha for a long-overdue magic lesson.

"It's just not working, Skeeve. I told you I can't do it."

She sank back in her chair dejected and scowled at the floor. Curious, I reached over and felt the candle wick. It wasn't even warm.

"Not bad," I lied. "You're showing some improvement."

"Don't kid a kidder." Massha grimaced. "I'm not getting anywhere."

"Could you light it with one of your rings?"

She spread her fingers and made a quick inventory.

"Sure. This little trinket right here could do the job, but that's not the point."

"Bear with me. How does it work? Or, more important, how does it feel when it works?"

She gave a quick shrug.

"There's nothing to it. You see, this circle around the stone here moves, and I rotate it according to how tight a beam I want. Pressing the back of the ring activates it, so all I have to do is aim it and relax. The ring does all the work."

"That's it!" I exclaimed, snapping my fingers. "What's it?"

"Never mind. Keep going. How does it feel?"

"Well," she frowned thoughtfully, "It sort of tingles. It's like I was a hose and there was water rushing through me and out the ring."

"Bingo!"

"What's that supposed to mean?"

"Listen, Massha. Listen closely."

I was speaking carefully now, trying hard to contain my excitement over what I hoped was a major breakthrough.

"Our problem with teaching you non-mechanical magic is that you don't believe in it! I mean, you know that it exists and all, but you don't believe that you can do it. You're working hard at overcoming that every time you try to cast a spell, and that's the problem: You try...You work hard. You know you've got to believe, so you work hard at overcoming your disbelief every time you..."

"Yeah. So?"

"It means you tense up instead of relaxing the way you do when you're working your rings. Tensing blocks the flow of the energies, so you end up with less power at your disposal than you have when you're just walking around. The idea of casting a spell isn't to tense up, it's to relax...if anything, it's an exercise in forced relaxation."

My apprentice bit at her lower lip. "I don't know. That sounds too easy."

"On the one hand it's easy. Viewed a different way, one of the hardest things to do is relax on cue, especially if there's a crisis raging around you at the time."

"So all I have to do is relax?" she asked skeptically.

"Remember that 'hose' feeling you get when you use the ring? That's the energies being channeled through you and focused on your objective. If you pinch off a hose, how much water gets through?"

"I guess that makes sense."

"Try it...now. Reach out your hand and focus on the candle wick as if you were going to use your ring, only don't activate it. Just tell yourself that the ring is working and relax."

She started to say something, then changed her mind. Instead, she drew a deep breath, blew it out, then pointed a finger at the candle.

"Just relax," I urged softly. "Let the energies flow."

"But..."

"Don't talk. Keep your mind on the candle and hear me like I'm talking from a long way off."

Obediently, she focused on the candle.

"Feel the flow of the energies...just like when you're using the ring. Relax some more. Feel how the flow increases? Now, without tensing up, tighten that flow down to a narrow beam and aim it at the wick."

I was concentrating on Massha so much I almost missed it. A small glow of light started to form on the candle wick.

"That's it," I said, fighting to keep my voice calm. "Now..."

"Daddy! Guido says..."

"Ssshh!!!" I hissed. "Not now, Markie! We're trying to light the candle."

She paused in the doorway and cocked her head quizzically.

"Oh, that's easy!" she beamed suddenly and raised her head.

"MARKIE!! DON'T..."

But I was too late.

There was a sudden flash of light in the room, and the candle lit. Well, it didn't exactly light, it melted like a bag of water when you take away the bag. So did the candle holder. The table lit, though... briefly. At least one corner of it did. It flared for a moment, then the fire died as abruptly as it had appeared. What was left was a charred quarter-circle of tabletop where the corner used to be. That and a table leg standing alone like a burnt-out torch. The fire had hit so fast and smooth the leg didn't even topple over.

I don't remember reaching for Markie, but somehow I had her by the shoulders shaking her.

"WHAT DID YOU DO THAT FOR??" I said in my best paternal tones.

"You...you said...you wanted the...candle lit."

"That's lighting a candle?!?"

"I still have a little trouble with control…but my teacher says I'm doing better."

I realized I was having a little trouble with control, too. I stopped shaking her and tried to calm myself. This effort was aided by the fact that I noticed that Markie's lip was quivering and she was blinking her eyes rapidly. It suddenly dawned on me that she was about to cry. I decided that, not knowing what would happen when she cried, I would do my best to stay ignorant by heading her off at the pass.

"Umm…that was a Fire Elemental, right? Did you learn that at Elemental School?"

Getting someone to talk often serves to stave off tears…at least, it had always worked on me.

"Y…Yes," she said meekly. "At Elemental School, we learn Fire for starters."

"It's…ummm…very impressive. Look, I'm sorry if I barked at you, Markie, but you see, I didn't just want the candle lit. I wanted Massha to light it. It was part of her magic lesson."

"I didn't know that."

"I know. I didn't think to tell you. That's why I'm apologizing. What happened here was my fault. Okay?"

She nodded her head, exaggerating the motion until it looked like she had a broken neck. It was an interesting illusion, one that I vastly preferred to the idea of her crying…especially in the mood I was in. The thought of Markie with a broken neck…

"Aahh…you *did* interrupt Massha's lesson, though," I said, forcing the other concept from my mind. "Don't you think it would be nice if you apologized to her?"

"That's a great idea, Daddy," she beamed. "I'll do that the next time I see her. Okay?"

That's when I realized my apprentice had slipped out of the room.

"What do you think you're doing, Massha?"

Leaning casually in the doorway of Massha's bedroom, I realized my voice lacked the intimidating power of Aahz's, but it's the only voice I've got.

"What does it look like I'm doing?" she snarled, carrying a massive armload of clothes from her closet to dump on the bed.

"I'd say, offhand, that it looks like you're packing. The question is, why?"

"People usually pack because it's the easiest way to carry their things when they travel. Less wear and tear on the wardrobe."

Suddenly, I was weary of the banter. Heaving a sigh, I moved in front of her, blocking her path. "No more games, Massha. Okay? Tell me straight out, why are you leaving? Don't you owe your teacher that much at least?"

She turned away, busying herself with something on her dresser.

"C'mon, Skeeve," she said in a tone so low I could barely hear it. "You saw what happened downstairs."

"I saw you on the verge of making a major breakthrough in your lessons, if that's what you mean. If Markie hadn't come in, you would have had the candle lit in another few seconds."

"Big deal!"

She spun to face me, and I could see that she was trying not to cry. There seemed to be a lot of that going around.

"Excuse me, Skeeve, but big fat hairy deal. So I can light a candle. So what?! After years of study, Massha can light a candle...and a little girl can blow the end off the table without even trying! What does that make me?

A magician? Ha ha! What a joke."

"Massha, I can't do what Markie did downstairs...or what she did in the Bazaar either, for that matter. I told you when you first approached me to be my apprentice exactly how little magic I knew. I'm still learning, though...and in the meantime we're still holding our own in the magic business...and that's here at the Bazaar. The Magic Capital of the dimensions."

That seemed to settle her a bit, but not much.

"Tell me honestly, Hot Stuff," she said, pursing her lips. "How good do you think I could ever be with magic...really?"

"I don't know. I'd like to think that with work and practice you could be better than you are now, though.

That's really all any of us can hope for."

"You may be right Skeeve, and it's a good thought.

The fact still remains that in the meantime, I'll always be small potatoes around here...magically, of course. The way things are going, I'm destined to be a hanger on. A leech. You and Aahz are nice guys, and you'd never throw me out, but I can't think of one good reason why I should stay."

"I can."

My head came around so fast I was in momentary danger of whiplash. Framed in the doorway was..."TANANDA!"

"In the flesh," she said with a wink. "But that's not the subject here. Massha, I can't speak for long-term conditions, but I've got one good reason why you shouldn't leave just now. It's the same reason I'm back."

"What's that?"

"It involves the Great Skeeve here. C'mon down-stairs. I'm going to brief everybody at once at a war council. We've got a full-blown crisis on our hands."

XI.

"I believe we're under attack."
COL. TRAVIS

ONE OF THE rooms in our extra-dimensional palace had a large oval table in it surrounded by chairs. When we moved in, we dubbed it the Conference Room, since there didn't seem to be any other practical use for it. We never used it for conferences, mind you, but it's always nice to have a conference room.

Tonight, however, it was packed to capacity. Apparently Tananda had rounded up the whole household, including Markie and Bunny, before locating Massha and me, and everyone was already seated as we walked in.

"Can we get started now?" Aahz asked caustically. "I *do* have other things to do, you know."

"Really?" Chumley sneered. "Like what?"

"Like talking to the Geek about that invitation," my partner shot back.

"Without talking to your partner first?"

"I didn't say I was going to refuse or accept. I just want to talk to him about..."

"Can we table the argument for the moment?" I interrupted. "I want to hear what Tananda has to say."

"Thanks, Skeeve," she said, flashing me a quick smile before dropping back into her solemn manner. "I guess you all know I was moving out of here. Well, poking around the Bazaar, I heard a rumor that's changed my mind. If it's true, we're all going to have our hands full dealing with it."

She paused, but no one else said anything. For a change, we were all giving her our undivided attention.

"I guess I should drop the shoe first, then we can all go on from there. The talk on the street is that someone's hired the Ax to do a number on Skeeve."

There was a few heartbeats of silence; then the room exploded.

"Why should anyone..."

"Who's hired the Ax?"

"Where did you hear..."

"Hold it! HOLD IT!" Tananda shouted, holding up her hands for silence. "I can only answer one question at a time...but I'll warn you in advance, I don't have that many answers to start with."

"Who's hired him?" Aahz demanded, seizing first position.

"The way I heard it, a group of magicians here at the Bazaar is none too happy with Skeeve's success. They feel he's taking all the choice assignments these days...getting all the glory work. What they've done is pool their money so they can hire the Ax to do what they're all afraid to do themselves...namely, deal with Skeeve."

"Do you hear that, Chumley? Still think I'm being melodramatic?"

"Shut up, Aahz. Where'd you hear this, little sister?"

"Remember Vic? The little vampire that relocated here from Limbo? Well, he's opened his own magic practice here at the Bazaar. It seems that he was approached to contribute to the fund. He's new enough here that he didn't know any of them by name, but they claim to have the support of nearly a dozen of the smalltime magicians."

"Why didn't he warn us as soon as he heard?"

"He's trying to stay neutral. He didn't contribute, but he also didn't want to be the one to blow the whistle to Skeeve. The only reason he said anything to me was that he was afraid that anyone close to Skeeve might get caught in the crossfire. I must admit, he seems to have a rather exaggerated idea of how much Skeeve here can handle on his own."

"Can I ask a question?" I said grimly. "As the intended victim?"

"Sure, Skeeve. Ask away."

"Who's the Ax?"

At least half the heads at the table swiveled toward me while the faces attached to them dropped their jaws. "You're kidding!"

"Don't you know who..."

"Aahz, didn't you teach him any..."

"Whoa! Hold it! I shouted over the clamor. "I can only take so much of this informative babbling at one time. Aahz! As my friend, partner, and sometimes mentor, could you deign to tell me in simple terms who the Ax is?"

"Nobody knows."

I closed my eyes and gave my head a small shake in an effort to clear my ears. After all this "Gee, why don't you know that?" brouhaha, I could swear he said...

"He's right, handsome," Tananda chimed in. "The Ax's real identity is one of the most closely guarded secrets in all the dimensions. That's why he's so effective at what he does."

"That may be true," I nodded. "But from the reaction in this room when you dropped the name, I'd guess that somebody knows *something about* him. Now, let me rephrase the question. If you don't know *who* the Ax is, could someone enlighten me as to *what* he is?"

"The Ax is the greatest Character Assassin in all the dimensions," Aahz said with a snarl. "He works freelance and charges fees that make ours look like pocket change. Once the Ax is on your tail, though, you might as well kiss it goodbye. He's ruined more careers than five stock-market crashes. Haven't you ever heard the expression 'take the ax to someone'? Well, that's where it comes from."

I felt that all-too-familiar "down elevator" sensation in my stomach. "How does he do it?"

"It varies," my partner shrugged. "He tailor-makes his attack depending on the assignment. The only constant is that whatever you were when he started, you're not when he's done."

"I wish you'd quit saying 'you' all the time. I'm not dead yet."

"Sorry, partner. Figure of speech."

"Well, that's just swell!" Guido exploded. "How're Nunzio n' me supposed to guard the Boss when we don't know what's comin' at him?"

"You don't," Aahz shot back. "This is out of your category, Guido. We're talking about character assassination, not a physical attack. It's not in your job description."

"Izzat so!" Nunzio said in his squeaky voice. "Don Bruce says we should guard him. I don't remember him sayin' anything about physical or non-physical attacks. Right, Guido?"

"That's right! If the Boss has got someone after his scalp, guardin' him is our job...if that's all right with you, MISTER Aahz!"

"I wouldn't trust you two to guard a fish head, much less my partner!" Aahz roared, surging to his feet.

"Stop it, Aahz!" Tananda ordered, kicking my partner's chair so that it cut his legs out from under him and plopped him back into his seat. "If we're up against the Ax, we're going to need all the help we can get. Let's stop bickering about the 'who' and concentrate on the `how." Okay? We're all scared, but that doesn't mean we should turn on each other when it's the Ax that's our target."

That cooled everybody down for the moment. There were a few glares and mutters exchanged, but at least the volume level dropped to where I could be heard.

"I think you're all overlooking something," I said quietly.

"What's that?" Tananda blinked.

"Aahz came close a minute ago. This is my problem...and it's not really in any of your job descriptions. We're all friends, and there are business ties between Aahz and me, as well as Guido and Nunzio, but we're talking about reputations here. If I get hit, and everyone seems to be betting against me right now, anyone standing close to me is going to get mud splashed on them, too. It seems to me that the best course of action is for the rest of you to pull back, or, better still, for me to move out and present a solo target. That way, we're only running the risk of having one career ruined...mine. I got where I am by standing on your shoulders. If I can't maintain it on my own, well, maybe it wasn't much of a career to start with."

The whole room was staring at me as I lurched to a halt.

"You know, Skeeve old boy," Chumley said, clearing his throat, "As much as I like you, some times it's difficult to remember just how intelligent you are."

"I'll say," Tananda snarled. "That's about the dumbest...Wait a minute! Does this have anything to do with my leaving?"

"A bit," I admitted. "And Massha leaving and Aahz's talking about responsibility, and..."

"Stop right there!" Aahz ordered, holding up his hand. "Let's talk about responsibility, *partner*. It's funny that *I* should have to lecture *you* about this, but there are all sorts of responsibilities. One of the ones that I've learned about from you is the responsibility to one's friends: helping them out when they're in trouble, *and* letting them help you in return. I haven't forgotten how you came into a strange dimension to bust me out of prison after I'd refused your help in the first place; or how you signed us on to play in the Big Game to bail Tananda out after she was caught thieving; or how you insisted that Don Bruce assign Guido and Nunzio here to you when they were in line for disciplinary action after botching their assignment for the Mob. I haven't forgotten it, and I'll bet they haven't either, even if you have. Now, I suggest you shut up about job descriptions and let your friends help you...*partner*."

"A-bloody-men." Chumley nodded.

"You could have left me with the Geek for the slavers," Markie said thoughtfully, in a surprisingly adult voice.

"So, now that that's settled," my partner said, rubbing his hands together, "let's get to work. My buddy Guido here has raised a good point. How do we defend Skeeve when we don't know how or when the Ax will strike?"

We hadn't really settled it, and Aahz wasn't about to give me a chance to point it out. I was just as glad, though, since I really didn't know what to say.

"All we can do is be on the lookout for anyone or anything strange showing up." Tananda shrugged.

"Like a showdown match of dragon poker with the Sen-Sen Ante Kid," Chumley said, staring into the distance.

"What's that?"

"You missed it, little sister. It seems that our boy Skeeve has drawn the attention of the king of dragon poker. He wants a head-to-head showdown match, and he wants it soon."

"Don't look at me like that, Chumley." Aahz grimaced. "I'm changing my vote. If we want to preserve Skeeve's reputation, there's no way he can refuse the challenge. *Now* I'm willing to admit it'll be money well spent."

"My daddy can beat anybody at dragon poker," Markie declared loyally.

"Your daddy can get his brains beaten out royally," my partner corrected gently. "I just hope we can teach him enough between now and game time that he can lose gracefully."

"I don't like it," Tananda growled. "It's too convenient. Somehow this game has the Ax's fingerprints all over it."

"You're probably right," Aahz sighed. "But there's not much else we can do except accept the challenge and try to make the best of a bad situation."

"Bite the bullet and play the cards we're dealt. Eh, Aahz?" I murmured.

I thought I had spoken quietly, but everyone around the table winced, including Markie. They might be loyal enough to risk their lives and careers defending me, but they weren't going to laugh at my jokes.

"Wait a minute!" Nunzio squeaked. "Do you think there's a chance that the Kid is actually the Ax?"

"Low probability," Bunny said, speaking for the first time in the meeting. "Someone like the Ax has to work a low profile. The Sen-Sen Ante Kid is too noticeable. If he were a character assassin, people would notice in no time flat. Besides, when he wins, nobody thinks it's because his opponents are disreputable...it's because the Kid is good. No, I figure the Ax has got to be like the purloined letter...he can hide in plain sight. Figure the last person you'd suspect, and you'll be getting close to his real identity."

The conversation swirled on around me, but I didn't listen very closely. For some reason, a thought had occurred to me while Bunny was talking. We had all been referring to the Ax as a "he," but if no one knew his real identity, he could just as easily be a "she." If anything, men were much less defensive and more inclined to brag about the details of their careers when they were with a woman.

Bunny was a woman. She had also appeared suddenly on our doorstep right around the time the Ax was supposed to be getting his assignment. We already knew that she was smarter than she let on...words like "purloined" didn't go with the vacant stare she so carefully cultivated. What better place for the Ax to strike from than the inside?

I decided that I should have a little chat with my moll as soon as the opportunity presented itself.

XII.

"No one should hide their true self behind a false face."
L. CHANEY

IT WAS WITH a certain amount of trepidation that I approached Bunny's bedroom. In case you haven't noticed, my experience with women is rather limited…like to the fingers of one hand limited.

Tananda, Massha, Luanna, Queen Hemlock, and now Bunny were the only adult females I had ever had to deal with, and thus far my track record was less than glowing. I had had a crush on Tananda for a while, but now she was more of a big sister to me. Massha was…well, Massha. I guess if anything I saw her as a kid sister, someone to be protected and sometimes cuddled. I've never really understood her open admiration of me, but it had stood firm through some of my most embarrassing mishaps and made it easy for me to confide in her. Even though I still thought of Luanna as my one true love, I had only spoken to her on four occasions, and after our last exchange I wasn't sure there would ever be a fifth meeting. The only relation-ship I had had with a woman which was more disastrous than my attempt at love was the one I had had with Queen Hemlock. She might not shoot me on sight, but there was no doubt in anyone's mind that she would like to…and she's the one who wanted to marry me!

Of course, none of the women I had dealt with so far was anything like Bunny, though whether this was good or bad I wasn't entirely sure. The fact still remained, however, that I was going to have to learn more about her, for two reasons: first, if she was going to be a resident of our household, I wanted to get a better fix on where she was coming from so I could treat her as something other than a mad aunt in the cellar; and second, if she was the Ax, the sooner I found out, the better. Unfortunately, the only way I could think of to obtain the necessary information was to talk to her.

I raised my hand, hesitated for a moment, then rapped on her door. It occurred to me that, even though I had never been in front of a firing squad, now I knew how it felt.

"Who is it?"

"It's Skeeve, Bunny. Have you got a minute?"

The door flew open and Bunny was there, grabbing my arm and pulling me inside. She was dressed in a slinky jumpsuit with the neck unlaced past her navel, which was a great relief to me. When I called on Queen Hemlock in her bedroom, she had received me in the altogether.

"Geez! It's good to see you. I was startin' to think you weren't ever comin' by!"

With a double-jointed shift of her hips she bumped the door shut, while her hands flew to the lacings in her outfit. So much for being relieved.

"If you just give me a second, hon, I'll be all set to go. You kinda caught me unprepared, and…"

"Bunny, could you just knock it off for a while? Huh?"

For some reason the events of the last few days suddenly rested heavy on my shoulders, and I just wasn't in the mood for games.

She stared at me with eyes as big as a Pervect's bar bill, but her hands ceased their activity. "What's the matter, Skeevie? Don't you like me?"

"I really don't know, Bunny," I said heavily. "You've never really given me a chance, have you?"

She drew in a sharp breath and started to retort angrily. Then she hesitated and looked away suddenly, licking her lips nervously.

"I…I don't know what you mean. Didn't I come to your room and try to be friendly?"

"I think you *do* know what I mean," I pressed, sensing a weakening in her defenses. "Every time we see each other, you're hitting me in the face with your 'sex-kitten' routine. I never know whether to run or applaud, but neither action is particularly conducive to getting to know you."

"Don't knock it," she said. "It's a great little bit. It's gotten me this far, hasn't it? Besides, isn't that what men want from a girl?"

"I don't."

"Really?"

There was a none-too-gentle mockery in her voice. She took a deep breath and pulled her shoulders back. "So tell me, what *does* cross your mind when I do this?"

Regardless of what impression I may have left on you from my earlier exploits, I do think fast. Fast enough to censor my first three thoughts before answering.

"Mostly discomfort," I said truthfully. "It's impressive, all right, but I get the feeling I should do something about it and I'm not sure I'm up to it."

She smiled triumphantly and let her breath out, easing the tension across her chest and my mind. Of the two, I think my mind needed it more.

"You have just hit on the secret of the sex kittens. It's not that you don't like it. There's just too much of it for you to be sure you can handle it.

"I'm not sure I follow you."

"Men like to brag and strut a lot, but they've got egos as brittle as spun glass. If a girl calls their bluff, comes at them like a seething volcano that can't be put out, men get scared. Instead of fanning a gentle feminine ember, they're faced with a forest fire, so they take their wind elsewhere. Oh, they keep us around to impress people. 'Look at the tigress I've tamed,' and all that. But when we're alone they usually keep their distance. I'll bet a moll sees less actual action than your average coed…except our pay scale is a lot better."

That made me think. On the one hand, she had called my reaction pretty close. Her roaring come-on *had* scared me a bit…well, a lot. Still, there was the other hand.

"It sounds like you don't think very much of men," I observed.

"Hey! Don't get me wrong. They're a lot better than the alternatives. I just got a little sick of listening to the same old lines over and over and decided to turn the tables on 'em. That's all."

"That wasn't what I meant. A second ago you said 'That's what men want from a girl.'" It may be true, and I won't try to argue the point. It's uncomfortably close to 'That's *all* men want from a girl,' though, and that I *will* argue."

She scowled thoughtfully and chewed her lower lip. "I guess that is over-generalizing a bit," she admitted. "Good."

"It's more accurate to say 'That's all men want from a *beautiful* girl.'"

"Bunny…"

"No, you listen to me, Skeeve. This is one subject I've had a lot more experience at than you have. It's fine to talk about minds when you look like Massha. But when you grow up looking good like I did—no brag, just a statement of fact—it's one long string of men hitting on you. If they're interested in your mind, I'd say they need a crash course in anatomy!"

In the course of our friendship, I had had many long chats with Massha about what it meant to a woman to be less than attractive. However, this was the first time I had ever been made to realize that beauty might be something less than an asset.

"I don't recall 'hitting on you,' Bunny."

"Okay, okay. Maybe I *have* taken to counter-punching before someone else starts. There's been enough of a pattern that I think I'm justified in jumping to conclusions. As I recall, you were a little preoccupied when we met. How would you have reacted if we ran into each other casually in a bar?"

That wasn't difficult at all to imagine...unfortunately.

"Touche!" I acknowledged. "Let me just toss one thought at you, Bunny. Then I'll yield to your experience. The question of sex is going to hang in the air over *any* male-female encounter until it's resolved. I think it lingers from pre-civilization days when survival of the species hinged on propagation. It's strongest when encountering a member of the opposite sex one finds attractive...such as a beautiful woman, or, I believe the phrase is, a 'hunk.' Part of civilization, though I don't know how many other people think of it this way, is setting rules and laws to help settle that question quickly: siblings, parents, and people under age or married to someone else are off limits...well, usually, but you get my point. Theoretically, this allows people to spend less time sniffing at each other and more time getting on with other endeavors...like art or business. I'm not sure it's an improvement, mind you, but it has brought us a long way."

"That's an interesting theory, Skeeve," Bunny said thoughtfully. "Where'd you hear it?"

"I made it up," I admitted.

"I'll have to mull that one over for a while. Even if you're right, though, what does it prove?"

"Well, I guess I'm trying to say that I think you're focusing too much on the existence of the question. Each time it comes up, resolve it and move on to other things. Specifically, I think we can resolve the question between us right now. As far as I'm concerned, the answer is no, or at least not for a long time. If we can agree on that, I'd like to move on to other things...like getting to know you better."

"I'd say that sounds like a pass, if you weren't saying 'no' in the same breath. Maybe I have been a little hypersensitive on the subject. Okay. Agreed. Let's try it as friends."

She stuck out her hand, and I shook it solemnly. In the back of my mind was a twinge of guilt. Now that I had gotten her to relax her guard, I was going to try to pump her for information.

"What would you like to know?"

"Well, except for the fact that you're smarter than you let on and that you're Don Bruce's niece, I really don't know much about you at all!"

"Whoops," she giggled, "You weren't even supposed to know about the niece part."

It was a much nicer giggle than her usual brain-jarring squeal.

"Let's start there, then. I understand your uncle doesn't approve of your career choice."

"You can say that again. He had a profession all picked out for me, put me through school and everything. The trouble was that he didn't bother to check with me.

Frankly, I'd rather do anything else than what he had in mind."

"What was that?"

"He wanted me to be an accountant."

My mind flashed back to my old nemesis J. R.

Grimble back at Possletum. Trying to picture Bunny in his place was more than my imagination could manage. "Umm...I suppose accounting is okay work. I can see why Don Bruce didn't want you to follow his footsteps into a life of crime."

Bunny cocked a skeptical eyebrow at me. "If you believe that, you don't know much about accounting."

"Whatever. It does occur to me that there are more choices for one's livelihood than being an accountant or being a moll."

"I don't want to set you off again," she smirked, "but my looks were working against me. Most legitimate businessmen were afraid that if they hired me their wives, or partners, or board of directors, or staff would think they were putting a mistress on the payroll. After a while I decided to go with the flow and go into a field where being attractive was a requirement instead of a handicap. If I'm guilty of anything, it's laziness."

"I don't know," I said, shaking my head. "I'll admit I don't think much of your career choice."

"Oh, yeah? Well, before you start sitting in moral judgment, let me tell you..."

"Whoa! Time out!" I interrupted. "What I meant was there isn't much of a future in it. Nothing personal, but nobody stays young and good-looking forever. From what I hear, your job doesn't have much of a retirement plan."

"None of the Mob jobs do," she shrugged. "It pays the bills while I'm looking for something better." Now we were getting somewhere.

"Speaking of the Mob, Bunny, I'll admit this Ax thing has me worried. Do you know offhand if the Mob ever handles character assassination? Maybe I could talk to someone and get some advice."

"I don't think they do. It's a little subtle for them. Still, I've never known Uncle Bruce to turn down any kind of work if the profit was high enough."

It occurred to me that that was a fairly evasive no-answer. I decided to try again.

"Speaking of your uncle, do you have any idea why he picked you for this assignment?"

There was the barest pause before she answered. "No. I don't."

I had survived the Geek's dragon poker game watching other people, and I'm fairly good at it. To me, that hesitation was a dead giveaway. Bunny knew why she was here, she just wasn't telling.

As if she had read my thoughts, a startled look came over her face.

"Hey! It just dawned on me. Do you think I'm the Ax? Believe me, Skeeve, I'm not. Really!"

She was very sincere and very believable. Of course, if I were the Ax, that's exactly what I would say and how I would say it.

XIII.

"Your Majesty should pay attention to his appearance."
H. C. ANDERSON

THERE ARE MANY words to describe the next day's outing into the Bazaar. Unfortunately, none of them are "calm," "quiet," or "relaxing." Words like "zoo," "circus," and "chaos" spring much more readily to mind.

It started before we even left our base...specifically, over whether or not we should go out at all.

Aahz and Massha maintained that we should go to ground until things blew over, on the theory that it would provide the fewest opportunities for the Ax to attack. Guido and Nunzio sided with them, adding their own colorful phrases to the proceedings. "Going to the mattresses" was one of their favorites, an expression which never ceased to conjure intriguing images to my mind. Like I told Bunny, I'm not *totally* pure.

Tananda and Chumley took the other side, arguing that the best defense is a solid offense. Staying inside, they argued, would only make us sitting ducks. The only sane thing to do would be to get out and try to determine just what the Ax was going to try. Markie and Bunny chimed in supporting the brother-sister team, though I suspect it was more from a desire to see more of the Bazaar.

After staying neutral and listening for over an hour while the two sides went at each other, I finally cast my vote...in favor of going out. Strangely enough, my reasons aligned most closely with those of Bunny and Markie: while I was more than a little afraid of going out and being a moving target, I was even more afraid of being cooped up inside with my own team while they got progressively more nervous and short-tempered with each other.

No sooner was that resolved than a new argument erupted, this time over who was going along. Obviously, everyone wanted to go. Just as obviously, if everybody did, we would look like exactly what we were: a strike force looking for trouble. I somehow didn't think this would assist our efforts to preserve my reputation.

After another hour of name-calling, we came up with a compromise. We would all go. For discretion as well as strategic advantage, however, it was decided that part of the team would go in disguise. That is, in addition to making our party look smaller than it really was, it would also allow our teammates to watch from a short distance and, more important, listen to what was being said around us in the Bazaar. Aahz, Tananda, Chumley, Massha, and Nunzio would serve as our scouts and reserve, while Markie, Bunny, Guido, and I would act as the bait...a role I liked less the more I thought about it.

Thus it was that we finally set out on our morning stroll...early in the afternoon.

On the surface the Bazaar was unchanged, but it didn't take long before I began to notice some subtle differences. I had gotten so used to maintaining disguise spells that I could keep our five colleagues incognito without it eating into my concentration...which was just as well, because there was a lot to concentrate on.

Apparently word of our last shopping venture had spread, and the reaction among the Deveel merchants to our appearance in the stalls was mixed and extreme. Some of the displays closed abruptly as we approached, while others rushed to meet us. There were, of course, those who took a neutral stance, neither closing nor meeting us halfway, but rather watching us carefully as we looked over their wares. Wherever we went, however, I noticed a distinct lack of enthusiasm for the favorite Bazaar pastime of haggling. Prices were either declared firm or counteroffers stacked up with minimum verbiage. It seems that, while they still wanted our money, the Deveels weren't eager to prolong contact with us.

I wasn't sure exactly how to handle the situation. I could take advantage of their nervousness and drive some shameless bargains, or grit my teeth and pay more than I thought the items were worth. The trouble was that neither course would do much to improve my image in the eyes of the merchants or erase the memory of our last outing.

Of course, my life being what it is, there were distractions.

After our talk, Bunny had decided that we were friends and attacked her new role with the same enthusiasm she brought to playing a vamp. She still clung to my arm, mind you, and from a distance probably still looked like a moll. Her attention, however, was now centered on me instead of on herself.

Today she had decided to voice her opinion of my wardrobe. "Really, Skeeve. We've *got* to get you some decent clothes."

She had somehow managed to get rid of her nasal voice as well as whatever it was she had always been chewing on. Maybe there was a connection there.

"What's wrong with what I'm wearing?"

I had on what I considered to be one of my spiffier outfits. The stripes on the pants were two inches wide and alternated yellow and light green, while the tunic was a brilliant red and purple paisley number.

"I wouldn't know where to start," she said, wrinkling her nose. "Let's just say it's a bit on the garish side."

"You didn't say anything about my clothes before."

"Right. Before. As in `before we decided to be friends." Molls don't stay employed by telling their men how tacky they dress. Sometimes I think one of the qualifications for having a decorative lady on your arm is to have no or negative clothes sense."

"Of course, I don't have much firsthand knowledge, but aren't there a few molls who dress a little flamboyantly themselves?" I said archly.

"True. But I'll bet if you checked into it, they're wearing outfits their men bought for them to dress up in. When we went shopping, you let me do the selecting and just picked up the bill. A lot of men figure if they're paying the fare, they should have the final say as to what their baby-doll wears. Let's face it, molls have to pay attention to how they look because their jobs depend on it. A girl who dresses like a sack of potatoes doesn't find work as a moll."

"So you're saying I dress like a sack of potatoes?" "If a sack looked like you, it would knock the eyes out of the potatoes."

I groaned my appreciation. Heck, if no one was going to laugh at my jokes, why should I laugh at theirs? Of course, I filed her comment away for future use if the occasion should arise.

"Seriously though, Skeeve, your problem is that you dress like a kid. You've got some nice pieces in your wardrobe, but nobody's bothered to show you how to wear them. Bright outfits ate nice, but you've got to balance them. Wearing a pattern with a muted solid accents the pattern. Wearing a pattern with a pattern is trouble, unless you really know what you're doing. More often than not, the patterns end up fighting each other…and if they're in two different colors you've got an all-out war. Your clothes should call attention to you, not to themselves."

Despite my indignation, I found myself being drawn into what she was saying. If there's one thing I've learned in my various adventures, it's that you take information where you find it.

"Let's see if I'm following you, Bunny. What you're saying is that just buying nice items, especially ones that catch my eye, isn't enough. I've got to watch how they go together...try to build a coordinated total. Right?"

"That's part of it," she nodded. "But I think we'd better go back to step one for a moment if we're going to educate you right. First, you've got to decide on the image you want to project. Your clothes make a statement about you, but you've got to know what that statement should be. Now, bankers depend on people trusting them with their money, so they dress conserva-tively to give the impression of dependability. No one will give their money to a banker who looks like he spends his afternoons playing the ponies. At the other end of the scale, you have the professional entertainers. They make their money getting people to look at them, so their outfits are usually flashy and flamboyant."

This was fascinating. Bunny wasn't telling me a thing I hadn't seen for myself, but she was defining patterns that hadn't registered on me before. Suddenly the whole clothes thing was starting to make sense. "So what kind of image do I project?"

"Well, since you ask, right now you look like one of two things: either someone who's so rich and successful that he doesn't have to care what other people think, or like a kid who doesn't know how to dress. Here at the Bazaar, they know you're successful, so the merchants jump to the first conclusion and drag out every gaudy item they haven't been able to unload on anyone else and figure if they price it high enough, you'll go for it."

"A sucker or a fool," I murmured. "I don't really know what image I want, but it isn't either of those."

"Try this one on for size. You're a magician for hire, right? You want to look well off so your clients know you're good at what you do, but not so rich that they'll think you're overcharging them. You don't want to go too conservative, because in part they're buying into the mystique of magic, but if you go too flashy you'll look like a sideshow charlatan. In short, I think your best bet is to try for 'quiet power.' Someone who is apart from the workaday crowd, but who is so sure of himself that he doesn't have to openly try for attention."

"How do I look like that?"

"That's where Bunny comes in," she said with a wink. "If we're agreed on the end, I'll find the means. Follow me."

With that, she led me off into one of the most incredible shopping sprees I've ever taken part in. She insisted that I change into the first outfit we bought: a light blue open-necked shirt with cream-colored slacks and a matching neck scarf. Markie protested that she had liked the pretty clothes better, but as we made our way from stall to stall, I noticed a change in the manner of the proprietors. They still seemed a little nervous about our presence, but they were bringing out a completely different array of clothes for our examination, and several of them complimented me on what I was wearing...something that had never happened before.

I must admit I was a little surprised at how much some of these "simple and quiet" items cost, but Bunny assured me that the fabric and the workmanship justified the price.

"I don't understand it," I quipped at one point. "I thought that accountants were all tightfisted, and here you are: the ultimate consumer."

"You don't see me reaching for *my* bankroll, do you?" she purred back. "Accountants can deal with necessary expenses, as long as it's someone else's money. Our main job is to get you maximum purchase power for your hard-earned cash."

And so it went. When I had time to think, it occurred to me that if Bunny *was* the Ax, she was working awfully hard to make me look good. I was still trying to figure out how this could fit into a diabolical plan when I felt a nudge at my elbow. Glancing around, I found Aahz standing next to me.

Now, when I throw my disguise spell, I still see the person as they normally are. That's why I started nervously before I remembered that to anyone else at the Bazaar he looked like a fellow shopper exchanging a few words.

"Nice outfit, partner," he said. "It looks like your little playmate is doing some serious work on your wardrobe."

"Thanks, Aahz. Do you really like it?"

"Sure. There is one little item you might add to your list before we head for home."

"What's that?"

"About five decks of cards. While he might be impressed by your new image, I think it'll make a bigger impact on the Kid if you spend a little time learning how to play dragon poker before you square off with him."

That popped my bubble in a hurry. Aahz was right.

Clothes and the Ax aside, there was one thing I was going to have to face up to soon, and that was a showdown with the best dragon poker player in all the dimensions.

XIV.

"Sometimes luck isn't enough."
L. LUCIANO

"OGRE'S HIGH, SKEEVE. Your bet."

"Oh! Umm…I'll go ten."

"Bump you ten."

"Out."

"Twenty to me? I'll go twenty on top of that."

"Call."

By now, you should know that sound. That's right. Dragon poker in full gallop. This time, however, it was a friendly game between Aahz, Tananda, Chumley, and me. Of course, I'm using the phrase "friendly" rather loosely here.

Aside from occasional shouting matches, I had never been in a fight with these three before. That is, when there had been trouble, we formed our circle with the horns out, not in. For the first time I found myself on the opposite side of a conflict from my colleagues, and I wasn't enjoying it at all. Realizing this was just a game, and a practice game at that, I was suddenly very glad I didn't have to face any one of them in a real life-and-death situation.

The banter was still there, but there was an edge on it. There was a cloud of tension over the table as the players focused on each other like circling predators. It had been there at the game at the Even-Odds, but then I was expecting it. One doesn't expect support or sym-pathy from total strangers in a card game. The trouble was that these three who were my closest friends were turning out to be total strangers when the chips were down…if you'll pardon the expression.

"I think you're bluffing, big brother. Up another forty."

I gulped and pushed another stack of my diminishing pile of chips into the pot.

"Call."

"You got me," the troll shrugged. "Out."

"Well, Skeeve. That leaves you and me. I've got an elf-high flush."

She displayed her hand and looked at me expectantly. I turned my hole cards over with what I hoped was a confident flourish.

Silence reigned as everyone bent forward to stare at my hand.

"Skeeve, this is garbage," Tananda said at last. "Aahz folded a better hand than this without his hole cards. I had you beat on the board."

"What she's trying to say, partner," Aahz smirked, "is that you should have either folded or raised. Calling the bet when the cards she has showing beat your hand is just tossing away money."

"Okay, okay! I get the point."

"Do you? You've still got about fifty chips there. Are you sure you don't want to wait until you've lost those, too? Or maybe we should redivide the chips and start over...*again*."

"Lighten up, Aahz," Tananda ordered. "Skeeve had a system that had worked for him before. Why shouldn't he want to try it out before being force-fed something new?"

What they were referring to was my original resistance to taking lessons in dragon poker. I had pretty much decided to handle the upcoming game the same way I had played the game at the Even-Odds rather than try to crash-learn the rules. After some discussion (read: argument) it was agreed that we should play a demonstration game so that I could show my coaches how well my system worked.

Well, I showed them.

I could read Aahz pretty well, possibly because I knew him so intimately. Chumley and Tananda, though, threw me for a loop. I was unable to pick up any sort of giveaway clues in their speech or manner, nor could I manage to detect any apparent relationship between their betting and what they were holding. In a depressingly short period of time I had been cleaned out of my starting allotment of chips. Then we divvied the stacks up again and started over...with the same results. We were now closing in on the end of the third round, and I was ready to throw in the towel.

As much as I would have liked to tell myself that I was having a bad run of cards or that we had played too few hands to set the patterns, the horrible truth was that I was simply outclassed. I mean, usually I could spot if a player had a good hand. Then the question was "how good," or more specifically, if his was better than mine. Of course, the same went for weak hands. I depended on being able to detect a player who was betting a hand that needed development or if he was simply betting that the other hand in the round would develop worse than his. In this "demonstration game," however, I was caught flatfooted again and again. Too many times a hand that I had figured for guts-nothing turned out to be a powerhouse.

To say the least, it was depressing. These were players who wouldn't dream of challenging the Sen-Sen Ante Kid themselves, and they were cleaning my clock without half trying.

"I know when I'm licked, Aahz," I said. "Even if it does take me a little longer than most. I'm ready to take those lessons you offered...if you still think it will do any good."

"Sure it will, partner. At the very least, I don't think it can hurt your game, if tonight's been an accurate sample."

Trust a Pervect to know just what to say to cheer you up.

"Come on, Aahz old boy," Chumley interrupted. "Skeeve here is doing the best he can. He's just trying to hang on in a bad situation...like we all do. Let's not make it any rougher for him. Hmmm?"

"I suppose you're right."

"And watch comments like that when Markie's around," Tananda put in. "She's got a bad case of hero-worship for her new daddy, and we need him as an authority figure to keep her in line."

"Speaking of Markie," my partner grimaced, peering around, "where is our portable disaster area?"

The tail end of our shopping expedition had not gone well. Markie's mood seemed to deteriorate as the day wore on. Twice we were saved from total disaster only by timely intervention by our spotters when she started to get particularly upset. Not wishing to push our luck, I called a halt to the excursion, which almost triggered another tantrum from my young ward. I wondered if other parents had ever had shopping trips cut short by a cranky child.

"She's off somewhere with Bunny and the body-guards. I thought this session would be rough enough without the added distraction of Markie cheering for her daddy."

"Good call," Chumley said. "Well, enough chitchat. Shall we have at it?"

"Right!" Aahz declared, rubbing his hands together as he leaned forward. "Now, the first thing we have to do is tighten up your betting strategy. If you keep..."

"Umm...Aren't you getting a little ahead of your-self, Aahz?" Tananda interrupted.

"How so?"

"Don't you think it would be nice if we taught him the sequence of hands first? It's a lot easier to bet when you know whether or not your hand is any good."

"Oh. Yeah. Of course."

"Let me handle this part, Aahz," the troll volunteered. "Now then, Skeeve. The ascending sequence of hands is as follows:

High Card
One Pair
Two Pair
Three Of A Kind
Three Pair
Full House (Three Of A Kind plus a Pair)
Four Of A Kind
Flush
Straight (those last two are ranked higher and reversed because of the sixth card)
Full Belly (two sets of Three Of A Kind)
Full Dragon (Four Of a Kind plus a Pair)
Straight Flush
Have you got that?"

Half an hour later, I could almost get through the list without referring to my crib sheet. By that time, my teachers' enthusiasm was noticeably dimmed. I decided to push on to the next lesson before I lost them completely.

"Close enough," I declared. "I can bone up on these on my own time. Where do we go from here? How much should I bet on which hands?"

"Not so fast," Aahz said. "First, you've got to finish learning about the hands."

"You mean there are more? I thought..."

"No. You've got all the hands...or will have, with a little practice. Now you've got to learn about *conditional modifiers*."

"Conditional modifiers?" I echoed weakly.

"Sure. Without 'em, dragon poker would be just another straightforward game. Are you starting to see why I didn't want to take the time before to teach you?"

I nodded silently, staring at my list of card hands that I somehow had a feeling was about to become more complex.

"Cheer up, Skeeve," Chumley said gaily, clapping me on the shoulder. "This is going to be easier than if we were trying to teach you the whole game."

"It is?" I blinked, perking up slightly.

"Sure. You see, the conditional modifiers depend on certain variables, like the day of the week, the number of players, chair position, things like that. Now since this match is prearranged, we know what most of those variables will be. For example, there will only be the two of you playing, and as the challenged party you have your choice of chairs...pick the one facing south, incidentally."

"What my big brother is trying to say in his own clumsy way," Tananda interrupted by squeezing my arm softly, "is that you don't have to learn *all* the conditional modifiers. Just the ones that will be in effect for your game with the Kid."

"Oh. I get it. Thanks, Chumley. That makes me feel a lot better."

"Right-o. There can't be more than a dozen or two that will be pertinent."

The relief I had been feeling turned cold inside me. "Two dozen conditional modifiers?"

"C'mon, big brother. There aren't that many."

"I was going to say I thought he was underestimating," Aahz grinned.

"Well, let's bloody well count them off and see." "Red dragons will be wild on even-numbered hands..."

"...But unicorns will be wild all evening..."

"...The corps-a-corps hand will be invalid all night, that's why we didn't bother to list it, partner..."

"...Once a night, a player can change the suit of one of his up cards..."

"...Every five hands, the sequence of cards is reversed, so the low cards are high and vice versa..."

"...Threes will be dead all night and treated as blank cards..."

"...And once a four-of-a-kind is played, that card value is also dead..."

"...Unless it's a wild card, then it simply ceases to be wild and can be played normally..."

"...If there's a ten showing in the first two face-up cards in each hand, then sevens will be dead..."

"...Unless there is a second ten showing, then it cancels the first..."

"...Of course, if the first card turned face up in a round is an Ogre, the round will be played with an extra hole card, four face up and five face down..."

"...A natural hand beats a hand of equal value built with wild cards..."

"Hey—that's not a conditional modifier. That's a regular rule."

"It will still be in effect, won't it? Some of the conditional modifiers nullify standing rules, so I thought we should..."

"ARE YOU PUTTING ME ON?!!"

The conversation stopped on a dime as my coaches turned to stare at me.

"I mean, this is a joke. Right?"

"No, partner," Aahz said carefully. "This is what dragon poker is all about. Like Chumley said, just be thankful you're only playing one night and get to learn the abbreviated list."

"But how am I supposed to stand a chance in this game? I'm not even going to be able to remember all the rules."

An awkward silence came over the table.

"I...uhh...think you've missed the point, Skeeve," Tananda said at last. "You don't stand a chance. The Kid is the best there is. There's no way you can learn enough in a few days or a few years to even give him a run for his money. All we're trying to do is teach you enough so that you won't embarrass yourself—as in ruin the reputation of the Great Skeeve—while he whittles away at your stake. You've got to at least *look* like you know what you're doing. Otherwise you come across as a fool who doesn't know enough to know how little he knows."

I thought about that for a few.

"Doesn't that description actually fit me to a 'T'?"

"If so, let's keep it in the family. Okay?" my partner winked, punching me playfully on the shoulder. "Cheer up, Skeeve. In some ways it should be fun. There's nothing like competing in a game without the pressure to win to let you role-play to the hilt."

"Sure, Aahz."

"Okay, so let's get back to it. Just listen this time around. We'll go over it again slower later so you can write it all down."

With that, they launched into it again.

I listened with half an ear, all the while examining my feelings. I had gone into the first game at the Even-Odds expecting to lose, but I had been viewing that as a social evening. It was beyond my abilities to kid myself into believing this match with the Kid was going to be social. As much as I respected the views of my advisors, I was having a lot of trouble accepting the idea that I would help my reputation by losing. They were right, though, that I couldn't gracefully refuse the challenge. If I didn't stand a chance of winning, then the only option left was to lose gracefully. Right?

Try as I might, though, I couldn't still a little voice in the back of my mind that kept telling me that the ideal solution would be to take the Kid to the cleaners. Of course, that was impossible. Right? Right?

XV.

"I need all the friends I can get."
QUASIMODO

WHILE MY LIFE may seem convoluted and depressing at times, at least there is one being who never turns from me in my hours of need.

"Gleep!"

I've never understood how a dragon's tongue can be slimy and sandpapery at the same time, but it is. Well, at least the one belonging to *my* dragon is.

"Down, fella...dow...hey! C'mon, Gleep. Stop it!"

"Gleep!" my pet declared as he deftly dodged my hands and left one more slimy trail across my face.

Obedient to a fault. They say you can judge a man's leadership ability by how well he handles animals.

"Darn it, Gleep! This is serious!"

I've often tried to convince Aahz that my dragon actually understands what I say. Whether that was the case here or if he was just sensitive to my tone, Gleep sank back on his haunches and cocked his head attentively.

"That's better," I sighed, daring to breathe through my nose again. Dragons have notoriously bad breath (hence the expression "dragon mouth"), and my pet's displays of affection had the unfortunate side effect of making me feel more than slightly faint. Of course, even breathing through my mouth, I could still taste it.

"You see, I've got a problem...well, several problems, and I thought maybe talking them out without being interrupted might..."

"Gleep!"

The tongue flicked out again, this time catching me with my mouth open. While I love my pet, there are times I wish he were...smaller. Times like this...and when I have to clean out his litter box.

"You want I should lean on the dragon for you, Boss?"

I looked around and discovered Nunzio sitting on one of the garden benches.

"Oh. Hi, Nunzio. What are you doing here? I thought you and Guido usually made yourself scarce when I was exercising Gleep."

"That's usually," the bodyguard shrugged. "My cousin and me, we talked it over and decided with this Ax fella on the loose that one of us should stick with you all the time, know what I mean? Right now it's my shift, and I'll be hangin' tight...no matter what you're doin'."

"I appreciate that, but I don't think there's any danger of getting hit here. I already decided not to take Gleep outside until the coast is clear. No sense tempting fate."

That was at least partially true. What I had really decided was that I didn't want to give the Ax a chance to strike at me through my pet. Aahz already complained enough about having a dragon in residence without adding fuel to the fire. Of course, if my suspicions were correct and Bunny *was* the Ax...

"Better safe than sorry...and you didn't answer my question. You want I should lean on the dragon?"

Sometimes the logic of my bodyguards eluded me completely.

"No. I mean, why should you lean on Gleep? You look comfortable where you are."

Nunzio rolled his eyes. "I don't mean 'lean on him' like really lean on him. I mean, do you want me to bend him a little? You know, rough him up some. I stay outta things between you and your partner, but you shouldn't have to put up with that kind of guff from a dragon."

"He's just being friendly."

"Friendly, schmendly. From what I've seen, you're in more danger from getting knocked off by your own pet than by anyone else I've seen at the Bazaar. A11 I've ever asked is that you let me do my job...I *am* supposed to be guardin' your body, ya' know. That's how my position got its lofty title."

Not for the first time, I was impressed by Nunzio's total devotion to his work. For a moment I was tempted to let him do what he wanted. At the last minute, though, an image flashed through my mind of my outsized bodyguard and my dragon going at it hammer and tongs in the middle of the garden.

"Umm...thanks, but I think I'll pass, Nunzio. Gleep can be a pain sometimes, but I kind of like him jumping all over me once in a while. It makes me feel loved. Besides, I wouldn't want to see him get hurt...or you either, for that matter."

"Jumpin' up on you is one thing. Doin' it when you don't want him to is sompin' else. Besides, I wouldn't hurt him. I'd just...here, let me show you!"

Before I could stop him, he was on his feet, taking a straddle-legged stance facing my dragon.

"C'mere, Gleep. C'mon, fella."

My pet's head snapped around, then he went bounding toward what he thought was a new playmate. "Nunzio. I…"

Just as the dragon reached him, my bodyguard held out a hand, palm outward.

"Stop, Gleep! Sit! I said SIT!!"

What happened next I had to reconstruct later from replaying my memory, it happened so fast.

Nunzio's hand snaked out and closed over Gleep's snout. With a jerk he pulled the nose down until it was under my pet's head, then pushed up sharply.

In mid-stride the dragon's haunches dropped into a sitting position and he stopped, all the while batting his eyelashes in bewilderment.

"Now stay. Stay!!"

My bodyguard carefully opened his hand and stepped back, holding his palm flat in front of my pet's face.

Gleep quivered slightly but didn't budge from his sitting position.

"See, Boss? He'll mind," Nunzio called over his shoulder. "Ya just gotta be firm with him."

I suddenly realized my jaw was dangling somewhere around my knees. "What…that's incredible, Nunzio! How did you…what did you…"

"I guess you never knew," he grinned. "I used ta be an animal trainer…mostly the nasty ones for shows, know what I mean?"

"An animal trainer?"

"Yeah. It seemed like a logical extension of bein' a schoolteacher…only without the parents to worry about."

I had to sit down. Between the demonstration with Gleep and the sudden insight to his background, Nunzio had my brain on overload.

"An animal trainer *and a* schoolteacher."

"That's right. Say, you want I should work with your dragon some more now that he's quieted down?"

"No. Let him run for a while. This is supposed to be his exercise time."

"You're the Boss."

He turned toward Gleep and clapped his hands sharply. The dragon bounded backwards, then crouched close to the ground, ready to play.

"Get it, boy!"

Moving with surprising believability, the bodyguard scooped an imaginary ball from the ground and pre-tended to throw it to the far end of the garden.

Gleep spun around and sprinted off in the direction of the "throw," flattening a bench and two shrubs as he went.

"Simply amazing," I murmured.

"I didn't mean to butt in," Nunzio said, sinking into the seat beside me. "It just looked like you wanted to talk and your dragon wanted to frolic."

"It's all right. I'd rather talk to you, anyway."

I was moderately astounded to discover this was true. I'd always been a bit of a loner, but lately it seemed I not only was able to talk to people, I enjoyed it. I hoped it wouldn't seriously change my friendship with Gleep.

"Me? Sure, Boss. What did you want to talk about?"

"Oh, nothing special. I guess I just realized we've never really talked, just the two of us. Tell me, how do you like our operation here?"

"It's okay, I guess. Never really thought about it much. It's not your run-of-the-mill Mob operation, that much is for sure. You got some strange people hangin' around you...but they're nice. I'd give my right arm for any one of them, they're so nice. That's different right there. Most outfits, everybody's tryin' to get ahead...so they spend more time watchin' each other than they do scopin' the opposition. Here, everybody covers for each other instead of nudging the other guy out."

"Do you want to get ahead, Nunzio?"

"Yes and no, know what I mean? I don't want to be doin' the same thing the rest of my life, but I'm not pushy to get to the top. Actually, I kinda like workin' for someone else. I let them make the big decisions, then all I gotta do is figure out how to make my part happen."

"You certainly do your part around here," I nodded. "I never knew before how hard a bodyguard works."

"Really? Gee, it's good to hear you say that, Boss. Sometimes Guido and me, we feel like dead weight around here. Maybe that's why we work so hard to do our jobs. I never thought much about whether I do or don't like it here. I mean, I go where I'm assigned and do what I'm told, so it doesn't matter what I think. Right? What

I do know, though, is that I'd be real sorry if I had to leave. Nobody's ever treated me like you and your crew do."

Nunzio might not be an intellectual giant or the swiftest wit I've known, but I found his simple honesty touching...not to mention the loyalty it implied.

"Well, you've got a job here as long as I've got anything to say about it." I assured him.

"Thanks, Boss. I was startin' to get a little tired of how the Mob operates, know what I mean?" That rang a bell in my mind.

"Speaking of that, Nunzio, do you think the Mob would ever get involved with something like this character assassination thing?"

The bodyguard's brow furrowed with the effort of thinking.

"Naw!" he said at last. "Mostly people pay us *not* to do things. If we do have to do a number on someone, it's usually to make an example of them and we do something flashy like burn down their house or break their legs. Who would know it if we wrecked their career? What Tananda was sayin' about the Ax was interesting, but it's just not our style."

"Not even for the right price?" I urged. "How much do you think it would take to get Don Bruce to send someone in here after us?"

"I dunno. I'd have to say at least...wait a minute! Are you askin' if Bunny's the Ax?"

"Well, she did..."

"Forget it, Boss. Even if she could handle the job, which I'm not too sure she could, Don Bruce would never send her after you. Heck, you're one of his favorite chieftains right now. You should hear him..."

Nunzio suddenly pressed his palms against his cheeks to make exaggerated jowls as he spoke. "...Dat Skeeve, he's really got it on the ball, know what I mean? Mercy! If I had a hundred like him I could take over dis whole organization."

His imitation of Don Bruce was so perfect I had to laugh.

"That's great, Nunzio. Has he ever seen you do that?"

"I'm still employed and breathin', aren't I?" he winked. "Seriously, though. You're barkin' up the wrong tree with Bunny. Believe me, you're the apple of her uncle's eye right now."

"I suppose you're right," I sighed. "If you are, though, it leaves me right back where I started. Who is the Ax and what can..."

"Hi guys! Is that a private conversation, or can anyone join?"

We glanced up to find Bunny and Markie entering the garden.

"C'mon over, Bunny!" I waved, nudging Nunzio slightly in the ribs. "We were just going to…"

"GLEEP!!!"

Suddenly my dragon was in front of me. Crouching and tense, he didn't look playful at all. I had only seen him like this a couple of times before, and then…

"STOP IT, GLEEP! GLEEP!!!" I screamed, realizing too late what was about to happen.

Fortunately, Nunzio was quicker than I was. From his sitting position he threw himself forward in a body check against my pet's neck, just as the dragon let loose with a stream of fire. The flames leapt forward to harmlessly scorch a wall.

Bunny swept Markie behind her with one arm. "Geez! What was…"

"I'll get him!" Markie cried, balling up her fists. "MARKIE!! STOP!!"

"But Daddy…"

"Just hold it. Okay? Nunzio?"

"I've got him, Boss," he called, both hands wrapped securely around Gleep's snout as the dragon struggled to get free.

"Bunny! You and Markie get inside! Now!!!"

The two of them hurried from sight, and I turned my attention to my pet.

Gleep seemed to have calmed down as fast as he had exploded, now that Bunny and Markie were gone. Nunzio was stroking his neck soothingly while staring at me in wide-eyed amazement.

"I dunno what happened there, Boss, but he seems okay now."

"What happened," I said grimly, "was Gleep trying to protect me from something or someone he saw as a threat."

"But Boss…"

"Look Nunzio, I know you mean well, but Gleep and I go back a long way. I trust his instincts more than I do my own judgment."

"But…"

"I want you to do two things right away. First, put Gleep back in his stable…I think he's had enough exercise for one day. Then get word to Don Bruce. I want to have a little talk with him about his 'present'!"

XVI.

"I thought we were friends!"
BANQUO

I TELL YOU, partner, this is crazy!"

"Like heck it is!"

"Bunny can't be the Ax! She's a space cadet." "That's what she'd like us to think. I found out different!"

"Really? How?"

"By...well, by talking to her."

I spotted the flaw in my logic as soon as I said it, and Aahz wasn't far behind.

"Skeeve," he said solemnly, "has it occurred to you that if she's the Ax and you're her target, that you would probably be the last person she would relax around? Do you really think you could trick her into giving away her I.Q. in a simple conversation?"

"Well...maybe she was being clever. It could be that it was her way of trying to throw us off the track."

My partner didn't say anything to that. He just cocked his head and raised one eyebrow *very* high.

"It *could* be," I repeated lamely.

"C'mon, Skeeve. Give."

"What?"

"Even you need more evidence than that before you go off half-cocked. What are you holding back?"

He had me. I was just afraid that he was going to find my real reason even less believable than the one I had already stated.

"Okay," I said with a sigh. "If you really want to know, what finally convinced me was that Gleep doesn't like her."

"Gleep? You mean that stupid dragon of yours? That Gleep?"

"Gleep isn't st..."

"Partner, your dragon doesn't like *me!* That doesn't make me the Ax!!"

"He's never tried to fry you, either!"

That one stopped him for a moment. "He did that? He really let fly at Bunny?"

"That's right. If Nunzio hadn't been there..."

As if summoned by the mention of his name, the bodyguard stuck his head into the room.

"Hey, Boss! Don Bruce is here."

"Show him in."

"I still think you're making a mistake," Aahz warned, leaning against a wall.

"Maybe," I said grimly. "With luck I'll get Don Bruce to confirm my suspicions before I show my cards."

"This I've got to see."

"There you are, Skeeve. The boys said you wanted to see me."

Don Bruce is the Mob's fairy godfather. I've never seen him dressed in anything that wasn't lavender, and today was no exception. His ensemble included shorts, sandals, a floppy brimmed hat, and a sports shirt with large dark purple flowers printed all over it. Maybe my wardrobe sessions with Bunny were making me overly sensitive on the subject of clothes, but his attire hardly seemed appropriate for one of the most powerful men in the Mob.

Even his dark glasses had violet lenses.

"You know, this is quite a place you got here. Never been here before, but I heard a lot about it in the yearly report. It doesn't look this big from the outside."

"We like to keep a low profile," I said.

"Yeah, I know. It's like I keep tellin' 'em back at Mob Central, you run a class operation. I like that. Makes us all look good."

I was starting to feel a little uncomfortable. The last thing I wanted to discuss with Don Bruce was our current operation.

"Like some wine?" Aahz chimed in, coming to my rescue.

"It's a little early, but why not? So! What is it you wanted to see me about?"

"It's about Bunny."

"Bunny? Oh yeah. How's she workin' out?"

Even if I hadn't already been suspicious, Don Bruce's response would have seemed overly casual. Aahz caught it too, raising his eyebrow again as he poured the wine.

"I thought we should have a little chat about why you sent her here."

"What's to chat about? You needed a moll, and I figured..."

"I mean the *real* reason."

Our guest paused, glanced back and forth between Aahz and me a couple of times, then shrugged his shoulders. "She told you, huh? Funny, I would have thought that was one secret she would have kept."

"Actually, I figured it out all by myself. In fact, when the subject came up, she denied it."

"Always said you were smart, Skeeve. Now I see you're smart enough to get me to admit to what you couldn't trick out of Bunny. Pretty good."

I shot a triumphant glance at Aahz, who was suddenly very busy with the wine. Despite my feeling of victory over having puzzled out the identity of the Ax, I was still more than a little annoyed.

"What I can't figure out," I said, "is why you tried it in the first place. I've always played it pretty straight with you."

At least Don Bruce had the grace to look embarrassed. "I know, I know. It seemed like a good idea at the time, is all. I was in a bit of a spot, and it seemed like a harmless way out."

"Harmless? Harmless! That's my whole life and career we're talking about."

"Hey! C'mon, Skeeve. Aren't you exaggerating a little bit there! I don't think…"

"Exaggerating??"

"Well, I still think you'd make a good husband for her…"

"Exaggerating? Aahz, are you listening to…"

As I turned to appeal to my partner, I noticed he was laughing so hard he was spilling the wine. Of all the reactions I might have expected from him, laughing wasn't…

Then it hit me.

"Husband?!?!?"

"Of course. Isn't that what we've been talkin' about?"

"Skeeve here thinks that your niece is the Ax and that you turned her loose on him to destroy his career," my partner managed between gasps.

"The Ax???"

"HUSBAND????"

"Are you crazy??"

"One of us is!!"

"How about both?" Aahz grinned, stepping between us. "Wine, anyone?"

"But he said…"

"What about…"

"Gentlemen, gentlemen. It's clear that communications have gotten a little fouled up between the two of you. I suggest you each take some wine and we'll start all over again from the top."

Almost mechanically, we both reached for the wine, eyeing each other all the while like angry cats.

"Very good," my partner nodded. "Now then, Don Bruce, as the visiting team I believe you have first serve."

"What's this about the Ax!?!" the mobster demanded, leaning forward so suddenly half the wine sloshed out of his glass.

"You know who the Ax is??"

"I know *what* he is! The question is, what does he have to do with you and Bunny?"

"We've heard recently that someone's hired the Ax to do a number on Skeeve," Aahz supplied.

"…Right about the same time Bunny showed up," I added.

"And that's supposed to make her the Ax?"

"Well, there *has* been some trouble since she arrived."

"Like what?"

"Weill…Tananda left because of things that were said when she found out that Bunny was in my bedroom one morning."

"Tananda? The same Tananda that said 'Hi' to me when I walked in here today?"

"She…ummm…came back."

"I see. What else?"

"She scared off my girlfriend."

"Girlfriend? You got a girlfriend?"

"Well, not exactly…but I might have had one if Bunny wasn't here."

"Uh-huh. Aahz, haven't you ever told him the 'bird in the hand' story?"

"I try, but he isn't big on listening."

I can always count on my partner to rally to my defense in times of crisis.

"What else?"

"Ummm…"

"Tell him!" Aahz smiled.

"Tell me what?"

"My dragon doesn't like her."

"I'm not surprised. She's never gotten along with animals...at least the four-footed kind. I don't see where that makes her the Ax, though."

"It's...it's just that on top of the other evidence..." My voice trailed off in front of Don Bruce's stony stare.

"You know, Skeeve," he said at last. "As much as I like you, there are times, like now, I wish you was on the other side of the law. If the D.A.s put together a case like you do, we could cut our bribe budget by ninety percent, and our attorney's fees by a hundred percent!"

"But..."

"Now listen close, 'cause I'm only goin' to go over this once. You're the representative for the Mob, and *me*, here at the Bazaar. If you look bad, then we look bad. Got it? What possible sense would it make for us to .hire someone to make you, and us, look bad?"

On the ropes, I glanced at Aahz for support.

"That was going to be the next question *I* was going to ask, partner."

Terrific.

"Well," Don Bruce announced, standing up. "If that's settled, I guess I can go now."

"Not so fast," my partner smiled, holding up a hand. "There's still the matter of the question that Skeeve asked: if Bunny isn't the Ax, what's she doing here? What was that you were saying about a husband?"

The mobster sank back into his chair and reached for his wine, all the while avoiding my eyes.

"I'm not gettin' any younger," he said. "Some day I'm goin' to retire, and I thought I should maybe start lookin' around for a replacement. It's always nice to have 'em in the family...the real family, I mean, and since I got an unmarried niece..."

"Whoa! Wait a minute," Aahz interrupted. "Are you saying that you're considering Skeeve as your eventual replacement in the Mob?"

"It's a possibility. Why not? Like I said, he runs a class operation and he's smart...at least I used to think so."

"Don Bruce I...I don't know what to say," I said honestly.

"Then don't say nothin'!" he responded grimly. "Whatever's goin' to happen is a long way off. That's why I didn't say anything to you direct. I'm not ready to retire yet."

"Oh." I didn't know whether to feel disappointment or relief.

"About Bunny?" my partner prompted.

The mobster shrugged. "What's to say that hasn't already been said? She's my niece, he's one of my favorite chieftains. I thought it would be a good idea to put 'em close to each other and see if anything happened."

"I...I don't know," I said thoughtfully. "I mean, Bunny's nice enough...especially now that I know she isn't the Ax. I just don't think I'm ready to get married yet."

"Didn't say you were," Don Bruce shrugged. "Don't get me wrong, Skeeve. I'm not tryin' to push you into this. I know it'll take time. Like I said, I just fixed it so you two could meet and see if anything develops...that's

all. If it works out, fine. If it doesn't, also fine. I'm not about to try to force things or kid myself that you two will make a pair if you won't. If nothing else, you've got a pretty good accountant while you find out...and from lookin' over your financial figures you could use one."

"Izzat so?"

He had finally tweaked Aahz close to home...or his wallet, which in his case is the same thing.

"What's wrong with our finances? We're doing okay."

"Okay isn't soarin'. You boys got no plan. The way I see it, you've spent so much time livin' hand-to-mouth you've never learned what to do with money except stack it and spend it. Bunny can show you how to make your money work for you."

Aahz rubbed his chin thoughtfully. It was interesting to see my partner caught between pride and greed.

"I dunno," he said at last. "It sounds good, and we'll probably look into it eventually, but we're a little tight right now."

"The way I hear it, you're tight all the time," Don Bruce commented drily.

"No. I mean right now we're *really* tight for finances. We've got a lot of capital tied up in the big game tonight."

"Big game? What big game?"

"Skeeve is going head to head with the Sen-Sen Ante Kid at dragon poker tonight. It's a challenge match."

"That's why I wanted to talk to you about Bunny," I said. "Since I thought she was the Ax, I didn't want her around to cause trouble at the game."

"Why didn't anybody tell me about this game?" Don Bruce demanded. "It wasn't in your report!" "It's come up since then."

"What are the stakes?"

I looked at Aahz. I had been so busy trying to learn how dragon poker was played that I had never gotten around to asking about the stakes.

For some reason, my partner suddenly looked uncomfortable. "Table stakes," he said.

"Table stakes?" I frowned. "What's that?"

I half-expected him to tell me he'd explain later, but instead he addressed the subject with surprising enthusiasm.

"In a table stakes game, each of you starts with a certain amount of money. Then you play until one of you is out of chips, or..."

"I know what table stakes are," Don Bruce interrupted. "What I want to know is how much you're playing for."

Aahz hesitated, then shrugged. "A quarter of a million each."

"A QUARTER OF A MILLION???"

I hadn't hit that note since my voice changed. "Didn't you know?" the mobster scowled.

"We hadn't told him," my partner sighed. "I was afraid that if he knew what the stakes were, he'd clutch. We were just going to give him the stack of chips to play without telling him how much they were worth."

"A quarter of a million?" I repeated, a little hoarser this time.

"See?" Aahz grinned. "You're clutching."

"But, Aahz, do we *have a* quarter of a million to spare?"

My partner's grin faded and he started avoiding my eyes.

"I can answer that one, Skeeve," Don Bruce said. *"No one* has a quarter of a million to spare. Even if you've got it, you don't have it to spare, know what I mean?"

"It's not going to take *all* our money," Aahz said slowly. "The others have chipped in out of their savings, too: Tananda, Chumley, Massha, even Guido and Nunzio. We've all got a piece of the action."

"Us too," the mobster declared. "Put the Mob down for half."

I'm not sure who was more surprised, Aahz or me. But Aahz recovered first.

"That's nice of you, Don Bruce, but you don't understand what's really happening here. Skeeve here is a rank beginner at the game. He had one lucky night, and by the time the rumor mill got through with it, he had drawn a challenge from the Kid. He can't refuse without looking foolish, and with the Ax on the loose we can't afford any bad press we can avoid. That's why we're pooling our money, so Skeeve can go in there and lose gracefully. The actual outcome is preordained. The Kid's going to eat him alive."

"...And maybe you weren't listening earlier," the mobster shot back. "If Skeeve looks bad, we look bad. The Mob backs its people, especially when it comes to public image. Win or lose, we're in for half, okay?"

"If you say so," Aahz shrugged.

"...And try to save me a couple seats. I'm gonna want to see my boy in action—firsthand."

"It'll cost!"

"Did I ask? Just..."

I wasn't really listening to the conversation any more. I hadn't realized before just how solidly my friends were behind me.

A quarter of a million...

Right then something solidified in my mind that had been hovering there for several days now. Whatever the others thought, I was going to try my best to win this game!

XVII.

"Shut up and deal!"
F.D.R.

THERE WAS AN aura of expectation over the Bazaar that night as we set out for the Even-Odds. At first I thought I was just seeing things differently because of my anticipation and nervousness. As we walked, however, it became more and more apparent that it was not simply my imagination.

Not a single vendor or shop shill approached us, not a Deveel hailed us with a proposed bargain. On the contrary, as we proceeded along the aisles, conversation and business ground to a halt as everyone turned to watch us pass. A few called out their wishes of "good luck" or friendly gibes about seeing me after the game, but for the most part they simply stared in silent fascination.

If I had ever had any doubts as to the existence or extent of the rumor mill and grapevine at the Bazaar, that night put them to rest forever. Everybody and I mean *everybody* knew who I was, where I was going, and what was waiting for me.

In some ways it was fun. I've noted earlier that I generally kept a low profile in the immediate neighbor-hood and have gotten used to walking around unnoticed. My recent shopping trips had gained me a certain notoriety, but it was nothing compared to this. Tonight, I was a full-blown celebrity! Realizing the uncertainty of the game's outcome, I decided to seize the moment and play my part to the hilt.

To a certain degree it was easy. We already made quite a procession. Guido and Nunzio were decked out in their working clothes of trenchcoats and weapons and preceded us, clearing a path through the gawkers. Tananda and Chumley brought up the rear looking positively grim as they eyeballed anyone who seemed to be edging too close. Aahz was walking just ahead of me, carrying our stake money in two large bags. If anyone entertained the thought of intercepting us for the money, all they had to do was look at Aahz's swagger and the gleam in his yellow eyes, and they would suddenly decide there were easier ways to get rich…like wrestling dragons or panning for gold in a swamp.

We had left Markie back at our place over her loud and indignant protests. I had stood firm, though. This game was going to be rough enough without having her around as a distraction. Massha had volunteered to stay with her, claiming she was far too nervous about the game to enjoy watching it anyway.

Bunny was decked out in a clinging outfit in brilliant white and hung on my arm like I was the most important thing in her life. More than a few envious eyes darted from her to me and back again.

No one was kidding anyone, though, as to who the center of attention was. You guessed it. Me! After all, I was the one on my way to lock horns with the legendary Sen-Sen Ante Kid on his own terrain...a card table. Bunny had chosen my clothes for me, and I was resplendent in a dark maroon open-necked shirt with light charcoal gray slacks and vest. I felt and looked like a million...well, make that a quarter of a million. If I was going to have my head handed to me tonight, I was at least going to be able to accept it in style...which was the whole point of this exercise, anyway.

I didn't even try to match Aahz's strut, knowing I would only suffer by comparison. Instead, I contented myself with maintaining a slow, measured, dignified pace as I nodded and waved at the well-wishers. The idea was to exude unhurried confidence. In actuality, it made me feel like I was on the way to the gallows, but I did my best to hide it and keep smiling.

The crowds got progressively thicker as we neared the Even-Odds, and I realized with some astonishment that this was because of the game. Those without the clout or the money to get space inside were loitering around the area in hopes of being one of the first to hear about the game's outcome. I had known that gambling was big at the Bazaar, but I never thought it was *this* popular.

The assemblage melted away before us, clearing a path to the door. I began to recognize faces in the crowd, people I knew. There was Gus waving enthusiastically at me, and over there...

"Vic!"

I veered from our straight line and the whole procession ground to a halt.

"Hi, Skeeve!" the vampire smiled, clapping me on the shoulder. "Good luck tonight!"

"I'm going to need it!" I confided. "Seriously, though, I've been meaning to stop by and thank you for your warning about the Ax "

Vic's face fell. "You might have trouble finding me. I'm about to lose my office."

"Really? Is business that bad?"

"Worse. There's an awful lot of competition here."

"Well, tell you what. Why don't you stop by my place tomorrow and we'll talk. Maybe we can work out a small loan or maybe even subcontract some assignments until you're established."

"Gee. Thanks, Skeeve!"

A sudden inspiration hit me. "Come by around noon. We'll do lunch!"

It seemed like a really good idea to me. I wondered why businessmen hadn't thought of talking out ideas over lunch before! For some reason, Vic winced before returning my smile.

"Lunch it is," he said.

"Umm...I hate to interrupt, partner, but you *do* have an appointment you're supposed to be at."

"Right, Aahz. Vic! Tomorrow!"

With that, I allowed myself to be ushered into the Even-Odds.

A ripple of applause broke out as I entered the main bar and gaming room, and I barely caught myself from turning to look behind me. For me or against me, the people were here to watch the game and if nothing else were grateful to me for providing the evening's entertainment.

Terrific. I was about to risk a quarter of a million in gold so that folks wouldn't have to watch summer reruns.

The club had been rearranged since the last time I was there. One card table stood alone in the center of the room, while scores of people lined the walls. While the crowd outside might have been larger, the group inside the club made up with clout what they lacked in numbers. While I didn't begin to recognize everyone, the ones I did spot led me to believe that the 'Who's Who' of Deva was assembled to watch the game. Hay-ner, my landlord and leader of the Devan Chamber of Commerce was there along with his usual clutch of cronies. He nodded politely when our eyes met, but I suspected he was really hoping to see me lose.

Don Bruce was there as promised, and raised his hands over his head, clenched them together, and gave them a brief shake, smiling all the while. I guessed it was some sign of encouragement. At the very least, I hoped I wasn't being hailed with some secret

Mob death sign. Of course, that didn't occur to me until after I had waved back.

"Skeeve. SKEEVE! Have you got a moment?"

I glanced around to find the Geek standing at my elbow.

"Sure, Geek," I shrugged. "What can I do for you?"

The Deveel seemed extremely nervous, his complexion several shades off its normal hue. "I...you can promise not to hold a grudge. I promise you that tonight was none of my doing. All I did was make the arrangements after the Kid issued the challenge. I didn't give him your name...honest."

To say the least, I found his attitude surprising. "Sure, Geek. I never thought you..."

"If I had known it would lead to this, I never would have invited you to my game in the first place, much less..."

I was suddenly very alert.

"Wait a minute, Geek! What are you talking about?"

"You're outclassed!" the Deveel explained, glancing around fearfully. "You don't stand a chance against the Kid. I just want you to understand, if you lose all your money tonight, that I didn't mean to set you up. I don't want you or your crew looking for me with blood in your respective eyes."

Now, as you know, I knew that I was outclassed. What intrigued me was that the Geek knew it, too.

"Geek, I think we'd better..."

A loud burst of applause and cheers interrupted me. By the time I got through craning my neck to see what was going on, the Geek had disappeared into the crowd. With that discussion closed, I turned my attention again to the subject at hand.

"Who's that?" I said, nodding toward the figure that had just entered the club.

Aahz slid a comforting arm around my shoulders. "That's him. That's the Sen-Sen Ante Kid."

"THAT'S the Kid???!!"

The man in the door was enormous, he was huge...that is to say, he was Massha's size. For some reason, I had been expecting someone closer to my own age. This character, though, was something else.

He was totally hairless, no beard, no eyebrows, and completely bald. His skin was light blue in color, and that combined with his fat

The Kid

UNICYCLE
A♠

PAN·DIMENSION CARD CO.,
CYNOSURE

and and wrinkles gave the overall impression of a half-deflated blue bowling ball. His eyes were extremely dark, however, and glittered slightly as they fixed on me.

"That's the Kid?" I repeated.

Aahz shrugged. "He's had the title for a long time."

The man-mountain had two bags with him which looked very similar to the ones Aahz had carried for us. He handed them casually to one of the onlookers.

"Cash me in!" he ordered in a booming voice. "I hear there's a game here tonight."

For some reason, this brought a loud round of laughter and applause from the audience. I didn't think it was all that funny, but I smiled politely. The Kid's eyes noted my lack of enthusiasm and glittered with increased ferocity.

"You must be the Great Skeeve."

His voice was a dangerous purr, but it still reverberated off the walls. He moved toward me with a surprisingly light tread, holding out his hand in welcome.

The crowd seemed to hold its breath.

"...And you must be the one they call the Sen-Sen Ante Kid." I responded, abandoning my hand into his grip.

Again I was surprised...this time by the gentleness of his handshake.

"I just hope your magic isn't as good as your reputation."

"That's funny, I was just hoping your luck is as bad as your jokes."

I didn't mean to be offensive. The words just kind of slipped out before I could stop them.

The Kid's face froze.

I wished someone else would say something to change the subject, but the room echoed with deathly quiet.

Suddenly, my opponent threw his head back and laughed heartily. "I like that!" he declared. "You know, no one else has ever had the nerve to tell me my jokes stink. I'm starting to see where you had the guts to accept my little challenge."

The room came to life, everybody talking or laughing at the same time. I felt like I had just passed some kind of initiation ritual. A wave of relief broke over me...but it was tinged with something else. I found myself liking the Kid. Young or not, he was definitely not the boogey-man I had been expecting.

"Thanks, Kid," I said quietly, taking advantage of the cover noise. "I must admit, I appreciate someone else who can laugh at themselves. I have to do it so often myself."

"Ain't that the truth," he murmured back, glancing around to be sure no one else was listening in. "If you let it, all this stuff can go to your head. Say, would you like a drink or something before we get started?"

"That confident I'm not," I laughed. "I want to have a clear head when we square off."

"Suit yourself," he shrugged.

Before I could say anything else, he turned to the crowd and raised his voice again. "Can you keep it down?" he roared. "We're ready to play cards up here!"

Like magic, the noise stopped and all eyes turned to the two of us again.

I found myself wishing I had accepted the drink.

XVIII.

"Cast your fate to the winds."
L. BERNSTEIN

THE TABLE WAS waiting for us. There were only two chairs with chips stacked neatly in front of them.

I had a sudden moment of panic when I realized I didn't know which chair was facing south, but Aahz came to my rescue. Darting out of the crowd, he pulled out one chair and held it for me to sit in. To the crowd it looked like a polite gesture, but my friends knew I had come dangerously close to changing the rules I had labored so hard to memorize.

"Cards!" the Kid ordered, holding out one hand as he eased into the chair facing me.

A new deck materialized in his hand. He examined it like a glass of fine wine, holding it up to the light to be sure the wrapping was intact and even sniffing the seal to be sure the factory glue was the same.

Satisfied, he offered the deck to me. I smiled and spread my hands to show I was satisfied. I mean, heck! If he hadn't found anything wrong, it was a cinch that I wouldn't be able to detect any foul play.

The gesture seemed to impress him though, and he gave me a small bow before opening the deck. Once the cards were out of the box, his pudgy fingers seemed to take on a life of their own. Moving swiftly, they removed the jokers and cast them aside, then began peeling cards off the deck two at a time, one from the top and one from the bottom.

Watching the process, I began to realize why his handshake had been so gentle. Large as they were, his fingers were graceful, delicate, and sensitive as they went about their task. These were not the hands of a rough laborer, or even a fighter. They existed to do one thing: to handle a deck of cards.

By now the deck had been rough mixed. The Kid scooped up the pile, squared it, then gave it several quick shuffles. His moves were so precise he didn't even have to re-square the deck when he was done…just set it on the center of the table.

"Cut for deal?" he asked.

I repeated my earlier gesture. "Be my guest."

Even this seemed to impress the Kid...and the crowd. A low murmur rippled around the room as the pluses and minuses of my move were discussed. The truth of the matter was that after watching the Kid handle the deck, I was embarrassed to show my own lack of skill.

He reached for the deck, and the cards sprang to life again. With a hypnotic rhythm he began cutting the deck and riffing the cards together, all the while staring at me with unblinking eyes. I knew I was being psyched out, but was powerless to fight the effect.

"For the ante, shall we say one thousand?" "Let's say five thousand." I returned.

The rhythm faltered. The Kid realized he had slipped and moved swiftly to cover it. Setting the cards aside for a moment, he reached for his chips.

"Five thousand it is," he said, tossing a handful into the center of the table. "And...my trademark."

A small white breath mint followed the chips into the pot.

I was counting out my own chips when something occurred to me.

"How much is that worth?" I said, pointing at the mint.

That surprised my opponent.

"What? The mint? One copper a roll. But you don't have to..."

Before he had finished speaking I added a small coin to my chips, pushed them into the center of the table, grabbed his mint, and popped it into my mouth.

This time the audience actually gasped before lapsing into silence. For several heartbeats there was no sound in the room except the mint crunching between my teeth. I almost regretted my bold move. The mint was incredibly strong.

Finally the Kid grinned.

"I see. You eat my luck, eh? Good. Very good. You'll find, though, that it takes more than that to disturb my game."

His tone was jovial, but his eyes darkened even more than they had been and his shuffling took on a sharper, more vengeful tone. I knew I had scored a hit.

I stole a glance at Aahz, who winked at me broadly.

"Cut!"

The deck was in front of me. Moving with forced nonchalance, I cut the deck roughly in half, then leaned back in my chair. While I tried to appear casual, inside I was crossing my fingers and toes and everything else crossable. I had devised my strategy on my own and hadn't discussed it with anyone...not even Aahz. Now we got to see how it worked.

One card...two cards...three cards came gliding across the table to me, face down. They slid to a stop neatly aligned, another tribute to the Kid's skill, and lay there like land mines.

I ignored them, waiting for the next card.

It came, coasting to a stop face up next to its brethren. It was the seven of diamonds and the Kid dealt himself...

The ten of diamonds. A ten!

The rules came back to me like a song I didn't want to remember. A ten face up meant my seven was dead...valueless.

"So much for eating my luck, eh?" the Kid chuckled, taking a quick glance at his hole cards. "My ten will go...five thousand."

"...And up five."

The gasp from the crowd was louder this time...possibly because my coaches had joined in. I heard Aahz clear his throat noisily, but wouldn't look in his direction. The Kid was staring at me in undisguised surprise. Apparently he had either expected me to fold or call...possibly because that would have been the sane thing to do.

"You're awfully proud of that dead card," he said thoughtfully. "All right. I'll call. Pot's right."

Two more cards floated onto the table face up. I got a ten! The ten of clubs, to be specific. That canceled his ten and made my seven live again.

The Kid got the unicorn of hearts. Wild card! Now I had ten-seven high against his pair of tens showing. Terrific.

"I won't try to kid you." my opponent smiled. "A pair of tens is worth...twenty thousand."

"...And up twenty."

The Kid's smile faded. His eyes flicked quickly to my cards, then he nodded. "Call."

No comment. No witty banter. I had him thinking.

The next cards were en route. The three of hearts slid into my lineup. A dead card. Opposing it, the Kid got...

The ten of hearts!

I was now looking at three tens against my ten-seven high! For a moment my resolve wavered, but I shored it up again. I was in too far to change now.

The Kid was eyeing me thoughtfully. "I don't suppose you'd go thirty on that?" he said.

"I'll not only go it, I'll raise you thirty."

There were muffled exclamations of disbelief in the room...and some not so muffled. I recognized the voices of some of the latter.

The Kid just shook his head and pushed the appropriate number of chips into the pot without a word. The crowd lapsed into silence and craned their necks to see the next cards.

The dragon of spades to me, and the ogre of hearts to the Kid.

No apparent help for either hand...except that now the Kid had three hearts face up.

We both studied each other's cards for a few moments.

"I'll admit I can't figure out what you're betting, Skeeve," my opponent sighed. "But this hand's worth fifty."

"...And up fifty."

Instead of responding, the Kid leaned back in his chair and stared at me.

"Check me on this," he said. "Either I've missed it completely, or you haven't looked at your hole cards yet."

"That's right."

The crowd started muttering again. At least some of them had missed that point.

"So you're betting blind?"

"Right."

"...And raising into me to boot."

I nodded.

"I don't get it. How do you expect to win?"

I regarded him for a moment before I answered. To say the least, I had the room's undivided attention.

"Kid, you're the best there is at dragon poker. You've spent years honing your skills to be the best, and nothing that happens here tonight is going to change that. Me, I'm lucky...if you can call it that. I got lucky one night, and that somehow earned me the chance to play this game with you tonight. That's why I'm betting the way I am."

The Kid shook his head. "Maybe I'm slow, but I still don't get it."

"In the long run, your skill would beat my luck. It always does. I figure the only chance I've got is to juice the betting on this one hand...go for broke. All the skill in the dimensions can't change the outcome of one hand. That's luck...which puts us on an equal footing."

My opponent digested this for a few moments, then threw back his head and gave a bark of laughter.

"I love it!" he crowed. "A half million pot riding on one hand. Skeeve, I like your style. Win or lose, it's been a pleasure matching wits with you."

"Thank you, Kid. I feel the same way."

"In the meantime, there's this hand to play. I hate to keep all these people hanging in suspense when we already know how the betting's going to go."

He swept the rest of his chips into the pot. "I'll call your raise and raise you back...thirty-five. That's the whole stake."

"Agreed," I said, pushing my chips out.

"Now let's see what we got," he winked, reaching for the deck.

The two of diamonds to me...the eight of clubs to the Kid... then one more card each face down.

The crowd pressed forward as my opponent peered at his last card.

"Skeeve," he said almost regretfully. "You had an interesting strategy there, but my hand's good...real good."

He flipped two of his down cards over.

"Full Dragon...four Ogres and a pair of tens."

"Nice hand." I acknowledged.

"Yeah. Right. Now let's see what you've got."

With as much poise as I could muster, I turned over my hole cards.

XIX.

"Can't you take a joke?"
T. EULENSPIEGEL

MASSHA LOOKED UP from her book and bon-bons as we trooped through the door.

"That was quick," she said. "How did it go?"

"Hi, Massha. Where's Markie?"

"Upstairs in her room. After the second time she tried to sneak out, I sent her to bed and took up sentry duty here by the door. What happened at the game?"

"Well, I still say you were wrong," Aahz growled. "Of all the dumb stunts you've pulled…"

"C'mon, partner. What's done is done. Okay? You're just mad because I didn't check with you first."

"That's the least of…"

"WILL SOMEBODY TELL ME WHAT HAPPENED?"

"What? Oh. Sorry, Massha. I won. Aahz here is upset because…"

I was suddenly swept up in a gargantuan hug and kiss as my apprentice expressed her delight at the news.

"I'll say he won. In one hand he won," Tananda grinned. "Never seen anything like it."

"Three unicorns and the six of clubs in the hole," Aahz raged. "Three wild cards, which, when used with the once-a-night suit shift rule on the seven of diamonds, yields…"

"A straight-bloody-flush!" Chumley sang. "Which took the Kid's Full Dragon and the largest pot that's ever been seen at the Bazaar."

"I knew you could do it, Daddy!" Markie shrieked, emerging from her hiding spot on the stairs.

So much for sending her to bed early.

"I wish you could have seen the Kid's face, Massha," the troll continued merrily. "I'll bet he wishes now that he carries antacids instead of breath mints."

"You should have seen the crowd. They're going to be talking about this one for years!"

Massha finally let me down and held up a hand.

"Hold it! Wait a minute! I get the feeling I've missed a lap here somewhere. Hot Stuff here won. Right? As in walked away with all the marbles?"

The brother and sister team nodded vigorously. I just tried to get my breath back.

"So how come Green and Scaly is breathing smoke? I should think he'd be leading the cheering."

"BECAUSE HE GAVE THE MONEY AWAY! THAT'S WHY!!!"

"Yes. That would explain it." Massha nodded thoughtfully.

"C'mon, Aahz! I didn't *give* it away."

As I've discovered before, it's a lot easier to find your breath when you're under attack.

"Whoa! Wait!" my apprentice said, stepping between us. "Before you two get started again, talk to Massha."

"Remember, I'm the one who wasn't there."

"Well, the Kid and I got to talking after the game. He's really a nice guy, and I found out that he had pretty much been betting everything he had…"

"That's what he *claimed*," Aahz snorted. "I think he was making a play for our sympathies."

"…and I got to thinking. I had worked hard to be sure that both the Kid's and my reputations would be intact, no matter how the game came out. What I really wanted to do was to retire from the dragon poker circuit and let *him* take on all the hotshot challengers…"

"That much I'll agree with."

"Aahz! Just let him tell it. Okay?"

"…But he couldn't keep playing if he was broke, which would leave me as the logical target for the up-and-comings, so I let him keep the quarter of a million he had lost…"

"See! SEE!!! What did I tell you?"

"…as a LOAN so he could use it as a stake in future games…"

"That's when I knew he had…a loan??"

I grinned at my partner.

"Uh-huh. As in 'put your money to work for you instead of stacking it,' a concept I believe you found very interesting when it was first broached. Of course, you had already gone off half-cocked and stomped away before we got to that part."

Any sarcasm I had managed to load into my voice was lost on Aahz, which is not surprising when you realize we were talking about money.

"A loan, eh?" he said thoughtfully. "What were the terms?"

"Tell him, Bunny."

"BUNNY??"

"Hey! You weren't there, remember? I decided to see what our accountant could do. Bunny?"

"Well, I've never dealt with stake money before, no pun intended, so I had to kind of feel my way along. I think I got us a pretty good arrangement, though."

"Which was…"

"Until the Kid pays us back…and it's got to be paid back in full, no partial payments, we get half his winnings."

"Hmmm," my partner murmured. "Not bad."

"If you can think of anything else I should have asked for, I'm open to…"

"If he could think of anything else," I said, winking at her, "you can believe he would have roared it out by now. You did great, Bunny."

"Gee. Thanks, Skeeve."

"Now then, if someone would be so kind as to break out the wine, I feel like celebrating."

"Of course, Boss, you realize that now a lot of people know that you've got a lot of cash on hand," Guido pointed out, edging close to me. "As soon as Nunzio gets back, I think we'd better take a look at beefin' up security on the place, know what I mean?"

"Where is Nunzio, anyway?" Massha said, peering around.

"He'll be along in a bit," I smiled. "I had a little errand for him after the game."

"Well, here's to you, Skeeve!" Chumley called, lifting his goblet aloft. "After all our worrying about whether your reputation could survive a match with the Kid, I dare say you came out of it well ahead of where you were before."

"That's right," his sister giggled. "I wonder what the Ax thinks about what happened."

That was the cue I had been waiting for. I took a deep breath and a deeper drink of wine, then assumed my most casual manner.

"Why bother speculating, Tananda? Why not ask direct?"

"What's that, Skeeve?"

"I said, why not ask the Ax directly? After all, she's in the room right now."

The gaiety of the mood vanished in an eyeblink as everybody stared at me.

"Partner," Aahz murmured, "I thought we settled this when we talked to Don Bruce."

I cut him off with the wave of a hand.

"As a matter of fact, I'm a little curious about what the Ax is thinking myself. Why don't you tell us...Markie?"

My young ward squirmed under the room's combined gaze.

"But, Daddy...I don't...you...oh, heck! You figured it out, huh?"

"Uh-huh." I nodded, not feeling at all triumphant.

She heaved a great sigh. "Oh, well. I was about to throw in the towel anyway. I had just hoped I could beat a retreat before my cover was blown. If you don't mind, I'd like to join you in some of that wine now."

"Help yourself."

"MARKIE?!?"

Aahz had finally recovered enough to make noise. Of course, it comes reflexively to him. The others were still working on it.

"Don't let the little-girl looks fool you, Aahz," she winked. "Folks are small and soft on my dimension. In the right clothes, it's easy to pass yourself off as being younger than you really are. Lots younger."

"But...but..."

"Think about it for a minute, Aahz," I said. "You had all the pieces the first day. Kids, particularly little girls, are embarrassing at best, trouble at worst. The trick is that you *expect* them to be trouble, so you don't even consider the possibility that what they're doing could be premeditated and planned."

I paused to take a sip of wine, and for once no one interrupted me with questions.

"If you look back on it, most of the problems we've been having have originated directly or indirectly from Markie. She mouthed off about Bunny being in my bed to get Tananda upset, and when that didn't work she made a few digs about her living here free that got her thinking about leaving...just like she deliberately made Massha look bad in the middle of her magic lesson for the same reason, to get her to leave."

"Almost worked, too," my apprentice observed thoughtfully.

"The business in the Bazaar was no accident, either," I continued. "All she had to do was wait for the right opportunity to pretend to get mad so we wouldn't suspect she was blasting things deliberately. If you recall, she even tried to convince me that I didn't need to take dragon poker lessons."

"Of course," Markie put in, "that's not easy to do when people think you're a kid."

"The biggest clue was Gleep. I thought he was trying to protect me from Bunny, but it was Markie he was really after. I keep telling you that he's smarter than you think."

"Remind me to apologize to your dragon," Aahz said, still staring at Markie.

"It was a good plan," she sighed. "Ninety-nine percent of the time it would have worked. The problem was that everyone underestimated you, Skeeve…you and your friends. I didn't think you'd have enough money to pay off the irate merchants after I did a number on their displays, and your friends…"

She shook her head slowly.

"Usually if word gets out that I'm on assignment, it makes my work easier. The target's associates bail out to keep from getting hit in the crossfire, and trying to get them to stay or come back only makes things worse. Part of sinking someone's career is cutting them off from their support network."

She raised her wine in a mock toast to me.

"Your friends wouldn't run…or if they did, they wouldn't stay gone once they heard you were in trouble. That's when I started to have second thoughts about this assignment. I mean, there are some careers that shouldn't be scuttled, and I think yours is one of them. You can take that as a compliment…it's meant as one. That's why I was about to call it quits anyway. I realized my heart just wasn't in my work this time around."

She set down her wine and stood up.

"Well, I guess that's that. I'll go upstairs and pack now. Make you a deal. If you all promise not to tell anyone who the famous Ax is, I'll spread the word that you're so invincible that even the Ax couldn't trip you up. Okay?"

Watching her leave the room, I realized with some surprise that I would miss her. Despite what Aahz had said, it had been kind of nice having a kid around the place.

"That's it?" my partner frowned. "You're just going to let her walk?"

"I was the target. I figure it was my call. Besides, she didn't do any real damage. As Chumley pointed out a second ago, we're further ahead than we were when she arrived."

"Of course, there's the matter of the damages we had to pay for her little magic display at the Bazaar."

For once, I was ahead of my partner when it came to money.

"I haven't forgotten that, Aahz. I just figure to recoup the loss from another source. You see, what finally tipped me off was…wait. Here they are now."

Nunzio was just coming into the room, dragging the Geek with him.

"Hello, Skeeve," the Deveel said, squirming in my bodyguard's grasp. "Your…ah, associate here says you wanted to see me?"

"He tried to sneak out after I told him, Boss," Nunzio squeaked. "That's what took me so long."

"Hello, Geek," I purred. "Have a seat. I want to have a little chat with you about a card game."

"C'mon, Skeeve. I already told you…"

"Sit!"

The Geek dropped into the indicated chair like gravity had suddenly trebled. I had borrowed the tone of voice from Nunzio's dragon-training demonstration. It worked.

"What the Geek was starting to say," I explained, turning to Aahz, "is that before the game tonight he warned me that I was overmatched and asked me not to have any hard feelings…that the game with the Kid wasn't his idea."

"That's right," the Deveel interjected. "Word just got out and…"

"What I'm curious about, however, is how he knew I was outclassed."

I smiled at the Geek, trying to show my teeth the way Aahz does. "You see, I don't want to talk about tonight's game. I was hoping you could give us a little more information about the *other game*…you know, the one where I won Markie?"

The Deveel glanced nervously around the group of assembled scowls.

"I…I don't know what you mean."

"Let me make it easy for you. At this point I figure the game had to be rigged. That's the only way you would know in advance what a weak dragon poker player I am. Somehow you were throwing hands my way to be sure I won big, big enough to include Markie. I'm just curious how you did it without triggering the magic or telepathy monitors."

The Geek seemed to shrink a little in his chair. When he spoke, his voice was so low we could barely hear him.

"Marked cards," he said.

The room exploded.

"MARKED CARDS??"

"But how..."

"Wouldn't that..."

I waved them back to silence.

"It makes sense. Think about it," I instructed. "Specifically, think back to our trip to Limbo. Remember how hard it was to disguise ourselves without using magic? Everybody at the Bazaar gets so used to things being done magically, they forget there are non-magical ways to do the same things...like false beards, or marked cards."

The Geek was on his feet now.

"You can't hold that against me! So someone else paid me to throw the game your way. Heck, I should think you'd be happy. You came out ahead, didn't you? What's to be mad about?"

"I'll bet if I try real hard I could think of something."

"Look, if it's revenge you want, you already got it. I lost a bundle tonight betting against you. You want blood, I'm bleeding!"

The Deveel was sweating visibly now. Then again, he's always been a little nervous around me for some reason.

"Relax, Geek. I'm not going to hurt you. If anything, I'm going to help you...just like you helped me."

"Yeah?" he said suspiciously.

"You say you're short of cash, we'll fix it."

"What!!??" Aahz roared, but Tananda poked him in the ribs and he subsided into sullen silence.

"Bunny?"

"Yeah, Skeeve?"

"First thing tomorrow I want you to run over to the Even-Odds. Go over the books, take inventory, and come up with a fair price for the place."

The Geek blinked.

"My club? But I…"

"…Then draw up an agreement for us to take it off the Geek's hands…at half the price you arrive at."

"WHAT!!??" the Deveel screeched, forgetting his fear. "Why should I sell my club for…"

"…More than it will be worth if the word gets out that you're running rigged games?" I finished for him. "Because you're a shrewd businessman, Geek. Besides, you need the money. Right?"

The Geek swallowed hard, then licked his lips before he spoke. "Right."

"How was that, Geek?" Aahz frowned. "I didn't quite hear you."

"I did," I said firmly. "Well, we won't keep you any longer, Geek. I know you'll want to get back to your club and clean up a bit. Otherwise we'll have to reduce the amount of our appraisal."

The Deveel started to snarl something, then thought better of it and slunk out into the night.

"Do you think that will make up for what we had to pay in damages, partner?" I said innocently.

"Skeeve, sometimes you amaze me," Aahz said, lifting his wine in a salute. "Now if there are no more surprises, I'm ready to party."

It was tempting, but I was on a roll and didn't want to let the moment slip away.

"There is one more thing," I announced. "Now that we've taken care of the Ax and the Kid, I think we should address the major problem that's come up…while everyone is here."

"Major problem?" my partner scowled. "What's that?"

Taking a deep breath, I went for it.

XX.

"So what else is new?"
W. CRONKITE

THE WHOLE CREW was staring at me as I rolled my goblet of wine back and forth in my hand, trying to decide where to start.

"If I've seemed a little distracted during this latest crisis," I said at last, "it's because I've been wrestling with another problem that's come to my attention…a big one. So big that, in my mind, the other stuff took a lower priority."

"Whatever you're talking about, partner," Aahz frowned, "I've missed it."

"You just said it, Aahz. The magic word is 'partner.' Things have been going real well for you and me, but we aren't the only ones in this household. When we were talking to Chumley and he said that his life wasn't all beer and skittles, it took me a while to puzzle out what he was talking about, but it finally came clear."

I looked at the troll.

"Business is off for you, isn't it, Chumley?"

"Well, I don't like to complain…"

"I know, but maybe you should once in a while. I had never stopped to think about it before, but you've been getting fewer and fewer assignments since you moved in with us, haven't you?"

"Is that true, Chumley?" Aahz said. "I never noticed…"

"No one's noticed because the attention has always been on us, Aahz. The Aahz and Skeeve team has been taking priority over everything and everyone else. We've been so busy living up to our big-name image that we've missed what it's doing to our colleagues, the ones who have to a large extent been responsible for our success."

"Oh, come now, Skeeve old boy," Chumley laughed uneasily. "I think you're exaggerating a bit there."

"Am I? Your business is off, and so is Tananda's. I hate to say it, but she was right when she left, we are stifling her with our current setup. Guido and Nunzio knock themselves out trying to be super-bodyguards because they're afraid we'll decide we don't really need them and send them packing. Even Massha thinks of herself as a non-contributing team member. Bunny's our newest arrival, and she tried to tell me that the only way she could help us is as an ornament!"

"I feel better about that after tonight, Skeeve," Bunny corrected. "Between negotiating with the Kid and getting the assignment to price out the Even-Odds, I think I can do something for you besides breathe heavy."

"Exactly!" I nodded. "That's what's giving me the courage to propose the plan I've cooked up."

"Plan? What plan?"

"That's what I wanted to talk to you about, Aahz. Actually, what I wanted to talk to all of you about. What we're dealing with in this household isn't really a partnership...it's a company. Everybody in this room contributes to the success of our group as a whole, and I think it's about time we restructured our setup to reflect that. What we really need is a system where all of us have a say as to what's going on. Then clients will be able to approach us as a group, and we quote prices, hand out assignments or subcontract, and share the profits as a group. That's my proposal, for what it's worth. What do the rest of you think?"

The silence stretched on until I started to wonder if they were trying to think of a tactful way to tell me I belonged in a rubber room.

"I don't know, Skeeve," Aahz said at last.

"What aren't you sure of?" I urged.

"I don't know if we should call ourselves Magic, Inc., or Chaos, Ltd."

"Magic, Inc., has already been used," Tananda argued. "Besides, I think the name should be a little more dignified and formal."

"You do that, then the clients are goin' to be surprised when they actually see us, know what I mean?" Guido put in. "We ain't exactly dignified and formal ourselves."

I leaned back in my chair and took a deep breath. If that was their only concern, my idea was at least deemed worthy of consideration.

Massha caught my eye and winked.

I toasted her back, feeling justifiably smug.

"Does this company accept new applicants?"

We all turned to find Markie in the door, suitcase in her hand.

Markie picked up her suitcase and started for the door. At the last
moment, though, she turned back to me and I could see tears in her eyes.

"I don't think I have to tell you all about my qualifications," she
continued, "but I admire this group and would be proud to be a
part of it."

The crew exchanged glances.

"Well, Markie…"

"It's still nebulous…"

"You've got the Elemental stuff down cold…"

"What do you think, Skeeve?" Aahz said. "You're the one who's
usually big on recruiting old enemies."

"No," I said firmly.

They were all looking at me again.

"Sorry to sound so overbearing right after claiming I wanted
everybody to have a say in things," I continued, "but if Markie's in,
I'm out."

"What's the problem, Skeeve?" Markie frowned. "I thought we
were still on pretty good terms."

"We are," I nodded. "I'm not mad at you. I won't work against
your career or hit you or hold a grudge. You were just doing your job."

I raised my head and our eyes met.

"I just can't go along with how you work, is all. You say you
admire our group—well, the glue that holds us together is trust. The
way you operate is to get people to trust you, then betray it. Even if
you stayed loyal to our group, I don't think I want to be associated
in business with someone who thinks that's the way to turn a profit."

I stopped there, and no one else raised a voice to contradict me.

Markie picked up her suitcase and started for the door. At the last
moment, though, she turned back to me and I could see tears in her eyes.

"I can't argue with what you're saying, Skeeve," she said, "but I
can't help wishing you had settled for hitting me and let me join."

There was total silence as she made her departure.

"The young lady has raised a valid point," Chumley said at last.
"What is our position on new members?"

"If we're open, I'd like to put Vic's name up for consideration,"
Massha chimed in.

"First we've got to decide if we need anyone else," Tananda
corrected.

"That raises the whole question of free-lance vs. exclusive contracts," Nunzio said. "I don't think that it's realistic to have all our
shares equal."

"I've been doodling up a plan on just that point, Nunzio," Bunny called, waving the napkin she had been scribbling on. "If you can hold on for a few minutes, I'll have something to propose officially."

As interested as I was in the proceedings, I had trouble concentrating on what was being said. For some reason, Markie's face kept crowding into my mind.

Sure, what I said was rough, but it was necessary. If you're going to run a business or a team, you've got to set a standard and adhere to it. There's no room for sentimentality. I had done the right thing, hadn't I? Hadn't I?